TEA WITH TERRORISTS

TEA
WITH
TERRORISTS

Who They Are

Why They Kill

What Will Stop Them

Craig Winn & Ken Power

Published by

CRICKETSONG BOOKS

A division of Virginia Publishers,
a wholly owned subsidiary of The Winn Company, LLC

TeaWithTerrorists.com

Cricketsong Books and its Cricket image are trademarks of
Virginia Publishers, a wholly owned subsidiary of The Winn Company, LLC.

Book, cover design, and illustration by Ken Power

With the exception of internationally known public figures, all characters are purely
fictional. Any resemblance to real persons, dead or alive, is strictly coincidental.

Winn, Craig.
Tea with terrorists : Who they are, why they kill, what will stop
them / Craig Winn, Ken Power. — 2nd ed.

p. cm.
Includes bibliographical references.
ISBN 0-9714481-1-6

1. Terrorism—Religious aspects—Islam—Fiction. 2. Terrorists—
Fiction. 3. Islamic Fundamentalism—Fiction. 4. Muhammad,
Prophet, d. 632.—Fiction. 5. September 11 Terrorist Attacks, 2001—
Fiction. 6. God (Islam)—Koranic teaching—Fiction.
I. Power, Ken. II. Title.

PS3623.I66T43 2002   831'.6
QBI33-608

2 3 4 5 6 7 8 9 10

To

Megan

whose love inspired us to seek the truth

TO THE READER

On September 11th America spoke of the New York and Washington bombings as if they were synonymous with the surprise attack on Pearl Harbor. Yet our response was entirely different. Rather than defending ourselves by identifying the enemy, declaring war, and galvanizing America's resolve by disseminating truth, we enriched our enemy, lamely attacked a symptom, and told our people a lie—one that will lead to global war if we don't come to understand the root cause of terror.

We met with the enemy—actually sat down and had tea with them: al-Qaeda, Hamas, Islamic Jihad, Fatah, Force 17, and Aqsa Martyrs' Brigade. We dug into the deepest caves of a doctrine that drives them to madness and murder. We know who they are, why they kill, and what can be done to stop them. Soon, you will too.

Our political leaders and many in the media have been involved in a cover-up. Whether reckless or purposeful, their errant portrayal of the deadliest story of our time has already led to the deaths of thousands—and soon terrorist weapons of mass destruction, ignited by a warmongering doctrine, may kill millions. *Tea with Terrorists* leaves no stone unturned (or unthrown) in the most controversial issue of our day: terrorism. We shine a bright light on Islam, Judaism, Christianity, Communism, Fascism, political correctness, profiling, intelligence gathering, American, Israeli, and Islamic politics, the so-called Palestinians, martyrdom, and the peace process, as well as the media's coverage of these issues.

Though a novel, much of this book is nonfiction. For example, the chapter entitled *Tea with Terrorists* actually occurred just as it is written. The scene is meticulously recreated, as are our questions and their answers. Our meetings with Israeli and Palestinian ministers have been woven into our tale. The press accounts within the story depict actual events and are presented as they were reported. Intelligence briefings from Israel's IDF, Mossad, and Shin Bet and America's military, CIA, and FBI are faithfully portrayed. Much of the drama, set three years in the future, was derived from Biblical and Qur'anic sources. The geopolitical, economic, and societal conditions depicted are accurate, as well.

The world is in a precarious place, standing on the edge of a horrible abyss, not unlike the one that awaited us in the 1930s. We compare the similarities between Muhammad and Hitler, the rise of Islam and Nazism, and the "peace process" in Palestine as it relates to the abandonment of Czechoslovakia—the catalyst for the last world war.

Hopefully, we will not miss the signs once again.

Today's terrorists have but one thing in common: Islam. And Islam itself is based entirely upon the Judeo-Christian scriptures. The Qur'an can't be understood apart from the Bible any more than terror can be understood apart from Islam. Our journey of discovery tours these ancient scriptures with a sometimes critical, always discerning, and uniquely revealing eye. They show, as nothing else can, the heart, purpose, and soul of terror.

We are indebted to the scholars who preceded us. We found Sir John Glubb's work *The Life and Times of Muhammad* to be a well-researched portrayal of Islam. When comparing the similarities between Muhammad and Hitler and the rise of Islam and Nazism, we relied on a scholarly work entitled *The Hitler Cult,* by Ian Kershaw. While its author draws no connection between the two leaders or their doctrines, we have incorporated a number of his historical insights into the dialog. Thoughts on the holocaust's prophetic significance were inspired by David Dolan's *Israel in Crisis.* The anthology, *Israel and a Palestinian State: Zero Sum Game,* contributed to our ability to provide factual evidence.

When quoting from the scriptures of the Jewish, Christian, and Islamic faiths, we combined existing versions, concordance analysis, and our own translations to communicate the meaning of what was written in as clear, contemporary, and accurate a manner possible. Although meanings were never altered, we took the liberty of abridging narratives and making the English more intelligible for modern readers.

Our story's "Yasman Alafat" is a composite character, fictional, yet modeled on the Chairman of the PLO, founder of Fatah, and President of the Palestinian Authority, Yasser Arafat. His actions prior to the publishing of our story are based upon his actual words and deeds. After that time the characterization is fictional. We can only speculate how a man with his past might conclude his life. With the exception of internationally known public figures, all other characters are purely fictional.

Our strategy was to prove our case through an abundance of factual evidence. The impact *Tea With Terrorists* will have on you will differ depending upon your personal perspectives, beliefs, biases, and political views. If you share some of ours, we hope you'll be inspired to be part of the solution. If your beliefs, biases, and politics are diametrically opposed to what we've discovered, we suspect you will be troubled by what we have to say. For those in the middle—the swing vote politically, agnostics spiritually—you will find truth. No one, however, will be bored.

Craig Winn, Ken Power
Charlottesville, Virginia
July 2002

CONTENTS

1

BEST LAID PLANS

"Men are useless." A shortish blonde woman, in roughly the same shape as the office she occupied, leaned back in her chair. She plopped her size tens on what otherwise was an elegant mahogany desk. Madam President wasn't happy this morning. She squinted up at the eagle carved in the ceiling and continued to rant. "I've had it with the lot of you."

That was true in more ways than one. The first woman to hold the office, she had arrived on the backswing of the political pendulum. The previous occupant of this noble house had been devoted to family and faith, a simple man of simple ideas. But this President had divorced her husband, albeit after the election, and within days of her inauguration had shocked the nation by announcing that she was a lesbian. Tough as steel and just as cold, this new breed of president seemed to have faith in nothing but her own invincibility, and to fear nothing but anonymity.

The man she had narrowly defeated the previous November had been something of a hawk, forced by fate and circumstances to focus his attention upon military matters. Terrorists, most of them sons of Ishmael, all of them Islamic, had consumed his presidency. He would be remembered for little else than this seemingly unwinnable war into which he had been plunged. His ninety percent approval ratings in the early years had eroded over time as America grew weary of it all. Even with a clearly defined protagonist, an irresistible show of arms, and the "unwavering" support of the American people, the battle had not gone well. The country had sent cruise missiles after phantoms, bombed boulders until they were no bigger than pebbles, and pummeled its share of two-bit terrorists. But in the process, America had managed to manufacture far more of them than it had killed.

Ever fickle, the American people had elected a dove, a peacemaker, or so her campaign had promised. She was schooled in political correctness and all manner of new-world-order solutions. Everything she said sounded so reasoned, so civilized. Well, in front of the cameras, anyway....

"This is your last shot," the President hissed.

The assembled uniforms and suits cringed.

"Screw this up and I'm going to solve this sorry mess once and for all—*my* way."

"We'll get 'em this time, Madam President," the newly minted Chairman of the Joint Chiefs oozed. The uniform was as hollow as his promise. General William Hasler was as unpopular among the troops as he was in the halls of the Pentagon. He had "earned" this position with his outspoken support of the President during her campaign. It had been a reward, not a promotion.

Knowing something of the General's past, the President knew she could browbeat him. "Yeah, right. I've heard *that* before," she said, glaring out the windows toward the ellipse. "I'll believe it when I see it on FOX News. They've got better intel than you have."

That last remark made the Secretary of Defense sit up a little straighter. Susan Ditroe had been thrilled by her cabinet appointment, but while she agreed with the President on every conceivable issue, she now felt a twinge of guilt: shouldn't she be defending the once proud institution she had sworn to serve?

Secretary Ditroe's turmoil was not only moral; it was visual as well. A slender brunette wearing a powder blue pantsuit, she looked ridiculous on the blood-red overstuffed couch that now dominated the Oval Office. The furnishings the previous administration had commissioned had been too small, too traditional, too *white*, for the new occupant. The new furnishings—and the new president—were far more colorful.

The woman in charge had made it clear that the military was no longer a priority. Her campaign had promised a new paradigm in which political solutions, not guns or bombs, would shape America's future.

"Fail this time, General, and your funding will go down with your mission." It was going to anyway, but the decline would be more precipitous if she had a good excuse.

This attitude was nothing new. When nations shortchanged their supply of bullets, their adversaries often sensed this vulnerability and attacked, causing them to expend an inordinate amount of their children's blood. 9/11 had been a wake-up call, as yet unanswered.

"If I may speak freely, Madam President." Chairman Hasler's back was straight, his chin was up, but his pride was on the ropes. "Our readiness is already at an all-time low." Trying to muster a little backbone, he recounted America's alarming reality. He was fighting for whatever little sustenance she was willing to give the military. "We have gone from an active fleet of six hundred ships to less than half that. Our merchant marine flotilla is mothballed. It took us five months to ready ourselves to fight Iraq in '90 and even longer in 2003. To move an equivalent amount of men and material today, we would need a very patient enemy."

The room grew cold. Hasler was treading on thin ice.

"To keep our planes in the sky, we've had to scavenge parts from other birds. If it weren't for duct tape, our B-52s would have disintegrated. We'd struggle to field five Army divisions. We've even shortchanged our technology."

With a divided Congress, a fluctuating economy, and the constant smokescreen of political maneuverings, America no longer knew if it was coming or going. Military readiness programs were started, cut off, reinstated, diminished, and then convoluted to the point the nation was equipping its soldiers with million-dollar coffins.

"That's just it," the President snapped. "It's all boys and their toys. You can't protect the American people, General; you can't even find the enemy. Invading Iraq again was senseless, a bloody disaster."

All one had to do was peer out the window, as the President was doing, to confirm the harsh reality. The Washington Monument stood wounded, half toppled, the victim of yet another terrorist event. The once proud obelisk was now an unmistakable symbol of America's impotence.

Airplanes had come down, offices had been bombed, fuel depots attacked, power grids sabotaged, and anthrax was sent through the mail. Sites both strategic and symbolic had been pummeled. Predictably, metropolitan water supplies had been contaminated. Suicide bombers and murderous snipers, common for years in Israel, were now blasting the nation. There was no denying it: the United States was vulnerable. Paralyzed by the confusion between racial profiling and common sense, America allowed the death merchants to operate with impunity.

"Bill," the President continued, "I don't want to hear your tale of woe. With this economy we inherited, you're lucky to have a job!"

Business, the engine of the nation's industrial might, had shriveled under the onslaught. The markets were deflated. Travel was hit hard and consumer spending was anemic. Threats of an oil embargo had caused gas prices to rise. The terrorists had won the first round.

The American public had no clue why they were being attacked. And this was the biggest problem of all.

Slumped in the overstuffed sofa, Secretary Ditroe tried to defend the boss. "Bush's war on terrorism was a bust. There was no end in sight. Every time he killed one terrorist, ten more scurried in behind."

Curiously, America had, in a way, *created* its assailants. Every time the United States had bombed a village suspected of harboring al-Qaeda members or Saddam loyalists, it had made more of them. It was like Vietnam in the '60s. There, the Viet Cong had only needed to point to the insignias on the B-52s to convert those caught in the crossfire.

By sending smart bombs and cruise missiles, the nation looked cowardly to young men willing to die for the honor of representing their god. But that wasn't the worst of it. America had managed to kill its share of religious clerics, plenty of gun-toting Muslim militants, thousands of innocent bystanders, and a few United Nations workers—*anyone* but a meaningful number of actual terrorists.

Hasler tried to deflect criticism away from the military's prior failures. "This is a tough battle, ma'am. Our would-be targets don't wear uniforms or name badges. With the exception of a few dozen leaders, nobody even knows what they look like. Well, that's not completely true. They look like everybody else in that part of the world."

The President swept a stray blond hair behind an ear. "Bush spent five billion dollars a month, yet captured only a fraction of the militants al-Qaeda trained. Regime change in Iraq cost two hundred billion, and we got nothing for it but a black eye. Even if you knew who our enemy was, General, the economics are unforgivable. Our aim was good enough, but it took five million-dollar cruise missiles to take out four thousand-dollar sheds."

What the President did not know, or at least was unwilling to accept, was that neither Saddam nor al-Qaeda were the real enemy. One was a common tyrant, the other just one of a hundred terrorist clubs operating around the world. She, like so many, refused to recognize that they were merely symptoms of a much larger problem.

Failure had become predictable, almost inevitable. Bush II had announced his attacks months before he made them. W, like his father before him, was great with people, so he did what came naturally. He formed international alliances. Initially, it appeared that he had even gotten some of the "moderate" Arab nations to go along. It was a triumph of political correctness.

But that in itself merely exacerbated the problem. By the time the alliances had been formed and all the permissions properly requested and duly received, the majority of terrorists were long gone. Islamic warriors were particularly good at hiding among their children and under the dresses of their women. So in the first round, when America bombed the "terrorist training camps," they splintered some wood, blasted some rocks, stirred up some dust, and no doubt scared some camels to death, but that was about it—except for congratulating themselves on the fine job they had done removing the Taliban, the Pakistani-backed Islamic warlords, from power. In reality, that had only paved the way for Iranian-backed warlords to take over. It was the terrorists' version of musical chairs. More concerning still, by forcing al-Qaeda into Pakistan, America had destabilized the only Muslim nation with nuclear weapons. Best-laid plans....

Round two in Iraq had been more futile still. Changing regimes without first dealing with the underlying problem of Islam was like replacing Lenin with Stalin in the old USSR without first neutering Communism. Saddam's hero was Hitler. He simply followed his *fuhrer's* lead. Hiding in a Baghdad bunker he equipped Muslim youth with his most lethal weapons. Inspired by promises of direct admission into the lustful Islamic paradise, such boys willingly sacrificed themselves, becoming martyrs. While they did not fight for Saddam, they were zealous crusaders for Islam and Muhammad. And their bullets and pestilence didn't much care why they were fired.

Unlike Desert Storm, this war, predictably, had been fought in the cities. Hussein was a tyrant, not a fool. By not allowing his troops to play in the open desert, Saddam had given America two equally horrendous options: bomb civilian centers into submission—and in the process kill tens of thousands of innocent women and children—or send in troops with guns like America did in Mogadishu and have them die instead. The world was not tolerant the first option and America didn't much like the second. As a consequence, America's spirit, conscience, and prestige became the war's greatest casualty. Islamic terrorism had scored yet another victory.

Reagan, unlike either Bush, had isolated his target. He had hit first and asked questions later. When he suspected Libya of foul play, he promptly pulverized the place. The Arab world squawked, the Communist regimes griped, and the French whined, but Kadafi kept his head down for decades.

"Intelligence. That's where we need to invest our money," Ditroe asserted, not recognizing how futile this was. Listening to the prevailing wisdom, America had already tried doubling its $30 billion intelligence budget. But the results hadn't matched the promise. Consistent with the international outcry for more "human" intelligence, the CIA had tried to recruit Arabs to serve the cause. Not surprisingly, those crazy enough to take Uncle Sam's money were too crazy to be of any value.

Suitable candidates were few and far between. The bad guys typically recruited overly religious sixteen-year-old boys from troubled Arab neighborhoods. Americans obviously didn't have the stomach for enlisting children to do their dirty work, and even if they had, it's unlikely that the GI

Bill and a little spending money would have been enough to persuade someone ready to die for "Allah's Cause" to turn against the home team.

Besides, Uncle Sam was a cheapskate. The Islamic states paid the families of suicide bombers more than America paid its president.

Secretary Ditroe tried again. "We know we must do more with less militarily, but the Chairman is confident he has a good plan." Susan Ditroe, a five-foot-six ex-IBM exec, had just celebrated her thirty-sixth birthday. The brunette crossed her skinny legs and waited for the President's response.

"You've missed the point, Ms Ditroe. Militarily, we will do *less* with less. I want to rein in the military. You haven't been listening."

"Yes, ma'am," the Secretary squirmed. She knew that the President's rise to power had been the result of a carefully crafted strategy of investing the peace dividend—one funded by a policy of peaceful coexistence. The plan took money earmarked for the national defense and reallocated it to the President's constituents, rewarding them for their support.

The populace, accustomed to being coddled, may have been gullible, but they weren't stupid. They had learned that they could vote themselves a raise, and they had. America had begun a decline into an abyss littered with the carcasses of decaying civilizations.

Madam President's plan, her party's plan, had been ingenious. Over the course of the last couple of decades, the left side of the aisle had virtually eliminated federal taxation on the preponderance of their supporters. At the same time, they had increased the burden on the most successful Americans, recognizing that they represented a smaller, and thus less significant, voting bloc. The party called it "paying their fair share." It sounded reasonable at first blush, but in reality it was just a modern-day version of Robin Hood: stealing from those they deemed rich and giving the plunder to those more numerous voters they deemed poor.

"Ma'am," Hasler interrupted, trying to refocus the conversation, "we have Captain Thurston Adams waiting in your conference room. He has a PowerPoint presentation we'd like you to see, a combination intelligence briefing and game plan." The general was a tall, handsome man in his early fifties, with short grey hair and a neatly trimmed moustache.

"A *captain?*" the President asked, putting her feet back down on the floor. "I thought you had a gaggle of generals over there."

"Yes ma'am, we do. Captain Adams is a Naval officer, so his rank is equivalent to an Army colonel, just below rear admiral." General Hasler, who had only recently acquired his fourth star, was familiar with the President's contradictory attitude toward titles. She hated the military but was nevertheless impressed by rank. "He's the leader of our best anti-terrorism team, Task Force 11."

The President let out a groan as she stood, letting her minions know she was not eager to endure a thirty-minute briefing. It was ironic, she thought, that as the world's most powerful person, she had less control of her time than anyone. Every moment of her day was scheduled by others. Resigned, she walked past the elegant domed bookcases, behind the seating area across from her desk, and out into the hallway.

The president's conference room has two doors. The main entrance adjoins a reception area commonly used by members of Congress. The attendees waiting to address the President had arrived through this door. Diagonally across the room is the president's entrance, only a few strides from the Oval Office.

Inside, portraits of the Roosevelts, Teddy and Franklin, adorned flanking walls. Battle ribbons from each service hung from flags near the common entrance. From Yorktown to Gettysburg, Midway to the Persian Gulf, they quietly proclaimed that our freedom was anything but free. Today they were just collecting dust.

The President made no attempt to greet the sea of strangers already ensconced as she made her way into the room. She plopped herself down in a chair at the end of the long table. The Chairman and Secretary, after shaking hands with their colleagues, sat next to her. Captain Adams stood at attention at the far end of the room. He had a remote control clicker in his left hand. A laser pointer sat on the table in front of him. He was flanked by an Admiral, the Director of the CIA, and a member of his staff. A portable screen had been erected in the corner.

"Madam President," General Hasler began, "This is Captain Thurston Adams, Navy Special Forces. He will be presenting his plan for the capture of Halam Ghumani, leader of the al-Qaeda terrorist network. You know Mr. Barnes from the CIA. He will be providing the intelligence briefing. Standing next to him is Ms. Nottingly, Middle East Bureau Chief, who will be assisting him. Admiral Gustoff, Atlantic Fleet CINC, will explain the logistical components of the mission. Director Barnes, you may begin."

"Good morning, Madam President. May I have the lights dimmed, please. Captain, the first slide. As you can see from this satellite photo, we have reason to believe that the al-Qaeda network is rebuilding a training camp in the Hindu Kush region of northeastern Afghanistan."

That in itself was remarkable. America had bombed the fundamentalist Islamic Taliban into submission only a few years back. And while they had promised that Allah would make America's missiles go astray, Allah had never been in the miracle business. The Taliban had been summarily pounded. Like most bullies, they had cowered when confronted.

Unfortunately, the bully pulpit was all the Afghanis knew. In the vacuum of leadership America had created, Taliban rule had been temporarily replaced by another, more "moderate" group of thugs. This drove the "extremists" into hiding up north, where the moderate rebels had once been confined. Al-Qaeda, evidently having an affinity for caves, had retreated to this hostile, remote land, moving across the porous border with Pakistan. In the mountains they were once again harbored by sympathetic Muslims.

"Next slide, please." The CIA Director continued his presentation. "This picture was taken yesterday, 21:30 our time. Notice the framework for an obstacle course of some sort. We've become accustomed to seeing these things on the recruiting videos we've intercepted."

James Barnes had been on the job only a few weeks. His confirmation had not gone smoothly. Embarrassing questions about his personal life, his indiscretions, had been raised. The conservatives had tried to use his past to compromise him, to blackmail him into bowing out. But the furor had mysteriously died down when it became apparent that the Chairman of the Senate Committee, a Republican, had been no less indiscreet. As a result of his ordeal, Barnes was eager to prove himself.

"Next slide, please, Captain. As you can see, there has been some digging—here and here," Barnes said as he pointed out the two locations. 'We assume the holes are for protection against our bombs."

"What is it you think they're building, Mr. Barnes?" the President asked, raising an eyebrow.

Sarah Nottingly, noticing the "help-me" look on her boss's face, answered. "They've erected camouflage netting above these areas, Madam President, so we aren't certain. We've seen a track hoe, a dozer, and several dump trucks in the area. As they move equipment around, they've been careful to sweep up their tracks. We've seen them hauling dirt away and returning with a variety of materials, construction goods: wood beams, plywood, concrete, some industrial canisters, HVAC equipment, even a generator. The barracks they're building are ramshackle affairs, poorly constructed. The obstacle training course makes little sense to any of our analysts. For some reason they've built everything at right angles, which is quite unusual. And they've done all of this out in the open, in a high mountain ravine, not hidden in caves like before." At twenty-nine, Sarah was the youngest person in the room. She was arguably the most intelligent. She was easily the most attractive.

Chairman Hasler turned to face the President. "These are the first real targets we've had in some time, ma'am—at least in a country we're willing to attack. We caught them rebuilding. They must have thought that since we'd pulled our forces away from Afghanistan and focused them on Iraq, they'd regained some measure of anonymity. But we're on to them."

The President acknowledged the intelligence coup with a begrudging grunt. Al-Qaeda had been her predecessor's enemy. "Ms....what did you say your name was?" she asked, eyeing the CIA Bureau Chief. The agent had legs Michelangelo couldn't have improved upon. Both the President and the Captain seemed to be enjoying the artistry.

"Agent Nottingly," Sarah answered.

"Yes, Ms. Nottingly. What can you tell me about al-Qaeda?"

Sarah stepped closer. "The network emerged out of the Russian invasion of Afghanistan back in 1979. A Palestinian academic, Abdallah Azzam, established the 'religious organization'," she said, using her fingers to form quotation marks, "to provide Islamic instruction to the *Mujahadin*— 'Allah's warriors'. It was funded by Osama bin Laden. Al-Qaeda grew even stronger when an Egyptian physician, Ayman al-Zawahiri, merged his anti-everything-he-didn't-like organization, al-Jihad, or 'holy war', into Azzam's. Shortly thereafter, the Palestinian founder, the Saudi financier, and Egyptian logistician were joined by *another* Palestinian, Abu Zubaydah, who became responsible for their international operations. He's now a Guantanamo Bay detainee, ma'am."

The others were all dead, or at least really quiet. Eliminating them had cost the United States a scant ten billion *each*. But in a world rife with bitterness, inflamed by religious zeal, and fanned by insatiable hatreds, replacements had been a dime a dozen. That was the new math.

The President dragged her eyes away from Sarah's legs and focused them reluctantly on General Hasler. "So you want me to approve spending...what? Another thirty million bucks for a couple dozen cruise missiles to eradicate an exercise course, some plywood barracks, and a few holes in the ground? You must be crazier than I think you are." With that, the President pushed her chair back. She was ready to leave.

Secretary Ditroe placed a hand on the President's arm. With her other hand she motioned for her to stay a moment longer. They shared a glance. More than a glance. "Madam President," she said. "We've managed to plant an operative inside al-Qaeda. He's reporting that Halam Ghumani and his lieutenants Omen Quagmer and Kahn Haqqani are overseeing this camp. *Personally*."

"Really?" That tidbit was tasty indeed. Even a dove would gain kudos acing three of the baddest boys on the planet. The President sat back down. "Go on."

Susan Ditroe motioned to Admiral Gustoff.

Dwight Gustoff filled the uniform. Fit and muscular at fifty-six, he was all man, having served his country admirably in the Gulf War. He was now Commander-in-Chief of the Atlantic Fleet. "No cruise missiles this time, ma'am. The plan Captain Adams and Agent Nottingly have developed calls for a small incursion force.

"Logistically, we are prepared to stage their operation here, on the Island of Diego Garcia." Admiral Gustoff used the laser pointer to highlight the spot on the satellite photo. "From there they will fly three S-3 Vikings to the *Ronald Reagan*, stationed near Bombay. They'll refuel and fly northeast over India, landing at a remote airbase near Pakistan."

Shifting his weight, standing more erect now, the Admiral asked for the next slide. "Three Sea Hawk helicopters, each loaded with four combatants, two crewmen, and added fuel bladders, will fly through the deep valleys of the Himalayan Range." He traced the laser pointer along the route that had been projected on the screen. "They'll enter the Hindu Kush and go on into the high mountain country of northeastern Afghanistan." He turned and looked at the President. "It would be prudent militarily, ma'am, to have some Warthogs, Sea Cobras, and a Spectre Gunship fly cover during this portion of the mission."

"Forget it!" the President bellowed. "You know better than that. I'm not going to let you boys send in an invasion force. You're not going to blast us back into some insane war."

"Yes, ma'am, we thought you might see it that way." Admiral Gustoff was saddened by the President's reaction, embarrassed really. She had no business being Commander-in-Chief. "I understand your position," he lied. "So we've worked out a second scenario that's less risky politically. Would you consider allowing us to fly a simultaneous mission from the *Ronald Reagan* as a decoy?"

She waited for more information.

"When the Special Forces team departs, we could launch a diversion—a strike force of Sea Cobras and F-18s. They would fly over the task force, high enough to be picked up by Pakistani radar, and then divert to a fake bombing run, perhaps over the no-fly zone in Iraq."

"Why not? A fake bombing run doesn't sound any different than a training mission."

The Admiral cleared his throat. "Yes, ma'am." It had been a small victory. "Now, Madam President, Captain Adams will brief you on the plan to capture Halam Ghumani and the core of al-Qaeda's leadership."

Captain Thurston Adams was all of six foot two. His dark brown hair was curly, even wiry, trimmed short. A barrel chest, thick neck, and protruding movie-star chin were his most prominent features. He was thirty-nine years old but looked younger. As a result of his SEAL training, called BUD/S, he was in the best shape of his life. He was bright by any measure, having attended the Naval Academy in Annapolis, graduating second in his class, a history major.

Adams began, "We're proposing a multinational force composed of British, Israeli, and American Special Forces personnel. The team will be using the latest technology: Special Forces Gear—SFGs. If I could have the lights back up for a moment."

Thurston, known to his friends as "Thor," stepped toward the door, less than two strides from where he had stood under Teddy Roosevelt's picture. Turning the brass handle, he motioned for an oddly attired Lieutenant to enter the room.

Kyle Stanley had graduated from BUD/S with Thor. They had grown close. Stanley was a twenty-eight-year-old African American, handsome, six foot one, bright, and athletic. He wasn't only a soldier; he was Thor's best friend.

"This is Lieutenant Stanley," Adams said as he closed the door. "The suit he is wearing has been designed for special forces covert operations. Of particular interest is the video mini-cam mounted on his helmet. It transmits images on a private frequency to a PC/satellite uplink, like those you've seen on the network news. The difference is we'll be wearing them, and the pictures will be transmitted to the White House via one of the NSA's satellites in real time. In a sense, you'll be able to go on the mission with us, Madam President."

"Your communications team can edit the footage as soon as the mission has been declassified," Agent Nottingly interjected. "You can control the release of information, rather than merely reacting to it."

"The pictures from the network satellite cams are awful. Are these going to be any better?" the President asked.

Unhappy being ignored, Secretary Ditroe interrupted, challenging the CIA Bureau Chief. "The video won't do the President any good if the images themselves are bad."

"The helmet cams run at twenty-five frames a second, Secretary Ditroe. Near-broadcast quality," Sarah replied. She picked up on the tension: the Secretary was jealous. Uncomfortable, Sarah cast Thor a glance.

His reassuring smile refocused her. "Madam Secretary, Madam President, it must be disconcerting for the White House when news agencies like CNN and FOX broadcast mission results even before the CIA and the Pentagon have been briefed." Scooping the media, she knew, would go a long way toward selling their mission. "This technology will solve that problem."

The President relaxed. Visions of political capital danced in her head. Edited by her own staff, video clips of the capture of Halam Ghumani would be the ultimate P.R. plum, the very grease she needed to lubricate the wheels of her personal agenda. *For this reason alone it might be worth the risk,* she thought, silently if not secretly. Everyone could see it in her eyes.

"The suit is made of woven Kevlar and titanium threads," Thor continued. "As you can see, it covers everything—from boot to head. Lieutenant, could you remove your helmet?" Jet black, it looked like one a motorcyclist might wear, wrapping around the entire head. It even had a visor that locked down into place, covering Kyle's face.

"The suit is limber enough for Army Rangers to move freely on land, and both waterproof and insulated, so it works for Navy SEALs. It's supposed to provide some protection against normal military ammunition."

Holding the helmet, Thor explained, "The H.U.D. is state of the art."

"The what?" the President asked.

"Heads Up Display. It's integrated here, in the helmet's visor. May I show you, ma'am?" The Captain and Lieutenant walked to the other side of the room and invited the President to put on the specially designed helmet. So as not to flop around on her head like an oversized bowl, Thor placed a piece of foam rubber Sarah had provided inside. POTUS's head was big only in the figurative sense.

Curious but cautious, the President reached for the high-tech gear. It was tethered electronically to the pack Stanley was wearing, so Kyle moved alongside.

"Are there any photographers in the room?" she asked. "I don't want to look like a fool, like Dukakis riding around in a tank. The world doesn't need to see me wearing this thing."

Assured by her staff that the coast was clear, President and helmet became one. It definitely looked better on Stanley.

Captain Adams had taken the liberty of removing the video cam, placing it on the table facing her. Knowing that the President was more interested in her image than anything else, he moved it so that she could see herself in the Heads Up Display. Smiling, she adjusted her hair, what little fell below the bottom of the high-tech headwear. "What's all this I'm looking at, besides myself, that is?"

"Data displays. The image you're seeing of yourself is from the helmet cam. The video can be switched from normal to enhanced light…could I have the lights dimmed, please."

"Whoa—what's happening?"

"This is the infrared mode," Adams said as Lieutenant Stanley pressed another button on his control unit. "It's reading heat signatures."

"You all look freaky. Pretty neat toy, boys," she said as she removed it.

Thor used the laser wand to point to the image he had projected on the screen. "You noticed the built-in data display. We've got a GPS moving map, transponder, compass, ground speed, and bearing to target, as well as other essential functions."

"Even though the helmet covered my ears, I could have sworn my hearing was enhanced. Was it, Captain?"

"Yes, ma'am. We can amplify sound or even cancel it if the situation calls for it. It's all controlled from the CPU here on the Lieutenant's back." He motioned for Stanley to turn around. "Onboard computer, cooling unit, enhanced imagery, GPS, audio gear, even the chameleon mechanism."

"Chamele...."

"Yes indeed. Watch." He nodded to Stanley. The suit changed from jungle camouflage to shades of the desert, to snow white, and then to midnight black. "The outer fabric reacts to an electrical current. One uniform can serve more than one purpose. We actually have a couple of these that will change coloration to mimic the surrounding environment. They're covered with a micro-thin layer of fiber optics. The wearer completely disappears."

"You don't say. I'd like to have one of those," the President joked. "There are times when being invisible would come in handy."

"Yes, ma'am. The system was developed by the Israelis. The leader of their team will have one, as will I. The full chameleon function is still experimental, you understand."

"Did I hear you say 'as will I?' Are you planning on leading this mission yourself, Captain?"

Standing more erect and smiling, Adams nodded imperceptibly.

"My, my. A modern-day Colonel Doolittle. If I have my history right, he led the B-something raid, what was it...?"

"Twenty-five, ma'am."

"Yes, a testosterone-fueled B-25 bombing run on Tokyo a few months after Pearl Harbor—off an *aircraft carrier*. Made our boy a genuine American hero."

"Made him a General," Chairman Hasler noted.

"Got any political ambitions, Captain?" the President asked.

"No, ma'am. I just want to lead my men, get the job done. We haven't fared real well on these missions, as I'm sure you know. We're operating in their back yard, and we stick out like a sore thumb," he said, motioning to the map of Afghanistan. "Over there it's hard for us to tell the good guys from the bad guys. It's like Vietnam in a way—little boys shoot at us while their moms lob hand grenades."

"You said Israelis are going on this mission with you? Why? Don't they know we're going to vote against them at the United Nations?" The President was determined to exit the Middle East controversy. The United States would just walk away, giving the Palestinians what they wanted, their own independent state. It seemed the only prudent thing to do. During the previous decade, Egypt, Syria, Iran, and Iraq had accounted for a staggering forty percent of the world's total arms purchases. There was clearly too much testosterone in that corner of the globe.

Besides, America's staunchest allies were in lock step. For their part, they had little choice. Europe was under water, inundated with sympathetic Arabs. Young Muslim militants had found Great Britain, Germany, and France to be safe havens. These nations had turned a blind eye to fanaticism in return for having a source of cheap foreign labor.

America was losing control in the least likely place, her prisons. The Islamic Prison Ministry had quietly "recruited" some five percent of the nation's 2,000,000 incarcerated felons, mostly African Americans and Hispanics, to do their dirty work. Disgruntled and angry, convicts had found Islam appealing.

"I'm a soldier, ma'am. I'm not privy to the Administration's policy in the Middle East." Actually, Thor knew more than he was willing to admit, but he didn't think it would be appropriate to share his opinion with his Commander-in-Chief.

Hasler spoke up. "Much of the human intelligence for this mission came from the Mossad, Madam President. They were a full partner in establishing the strategy we'd like to deploy. And they, with the Brits, helped us develop the SFGs. Fact is, ma'am, they volunteered."

It was a good thing they had. America's intelligence was handicapped. Congressional leaders from the President's party had seen to that. They had berated senior FBI and CIA leaders, threatening to curtail funding if they "profiled." The intelligence community had to promise not to single out and investigate Arabs or Muslims, even though they were the only ones attacking America.

The Captain and the Agent went on to brief the President, the Secretary of Defense, the Joint Chiefs, and the other assembled suits on their plan. Many already supported the mission. Others were seeing their bold strategy for the first time. And for reasons as varied as their private agendas, they all came to the same conclusion: this might actually work.

✡ ☦ ☾

AFTER RECEIVING a begrudging thumbs up from the President, Sarah Nottingly and Thor Adams, with Kyle Stanley a step behind, darted out the door and into the reception area. Making their way east through a maze of intersecting halls, they turned right and entered Sarah's favorite room. She glanced to her left, above the fireplace, at the painting of George Washington. She admired the two hundred-year-old French wallpaper that adorned the room. It was so old that the artist had portrayed Native Americans as Indians, from India, turbans and all, not knowing any better.

Thor looked straight ahead through the French doors that were aligned with Washington's other symbol, the first President's wounded obelisk. He would soon be facing the same enemy who had been willing to die to bring it down. He hoped he and his team would fare better.

Bolting out the south-facing door, walking under the colonnade and across some of the most photographed gardens in the world, they reached the olive-green helicopter. Kyle climbed aboard, saluting the Marine Color Guard and crew. That left the Captain and the agent alone on the South Lawn.

"Are you going to wish me luck?"

She took a step forward and kissed him instead.

✡   ✝   ☾

"HOW ARE YOU COMING, Anwar?" The Middle Eastern voice was a bit crackly over the satellite phone. The English was stiff, but good enough.

"We are within days of having a working prototype. But we need the next installment to build all the machines you requested."

"Yes. I will inform Charlie Three. They should have sold their candy by now. It will be more than enough to build thirty-six units."

"And when should I expect the ingredients?"

"Bravo Three will bring them in due time. Allah is great."

"Yes. Death to the infidels."

2

JOURNEY INTO NIGHT

The Israelis arrived first. With Major Isaac Newcomb in command, Yacob Seraph, Moshe Keceph, and Joshua Abrams piled out of the troop transport onto the tarmac and yawned. Yacob and Joshua belonged to the Israeli version of America's Delta Force, *Shu'alei Shimshon*. Moshe and Isaac had left the IDF, the Israeli Defense Force, to join the Mossad, the Israeli equivalent of America's CIA. That meant they were assassins, committed to retribution, an eye for an eye. No one killed a Jew without paying a price. These men made certain of it.

The Brits came screeching in an hour or so later. They were led by another Major, a veteran of Desert Storm and Enduring Freedom, Blake Huston. Accompanying him were Lad Childress, Ryan Sullivan, and Cliff Powers. They were all members of the elite SAS. Tough as they come, they were the ultimate combatants."

Covert Operation "Bag 'Em and Tag 'Em" was underway. As soon as the President had approved the mission, Adams and Stanley had flown from the White House to Andrews Air Force Base. Now aboard a C-17, they were winging their way to the rendezvous point, flying the great circle route over Europe, across the eastern Mediterranean, then down above portions of Saudi Arabia. Diego Garcia was south of the equator in the middle of the Indian Ocean. Even at just under the speed of sound, the voyage from Washington would consume nearly eighteen hours.

The plan was to fly carrier-based S-3 Vikings into northern India, transferring to specially-rigged Sea Hawks, SH-60Hs. By hugging the rugged terrain of the Western Himalayas and Hindu Kush, they would be able to sneak through disputed territories and enter the northern and most mountainous region of Afghanistan. They would have preferred sufficient force to sneaking, but the pacifist President had nixed the big guns.

The team of twelve planned to rappel from the helicopters and make their way up to the enemy camp. Climbing through a high mountain pass, they would arrive at the encampment just before first light. There they would seize Halam Ghumani, Omen Quagmer, and the infamous Kahn Haqqani. As captives, the world's most notorious terrorists would be escorted out along a ridgeline near a partially frozen lake. The Sea Hawks would meet the team at a predetermined set of GPS coordinates. All the while, the mission would be broadcast to the folks back home.

Lieutenant Stanley and Captain Adams both donned their SFG suits, complete with gloves, coordinated boots, and wrap-around helmets. They wanted to double-check their systems, all of which were complex and prone to malfunction—a fact Adams had not mentioned to the President. The Lieutenant pulled out a laminated checklist from one of his Velcro pockets. "Battery?" he said into his integrated mike. The high-tech helmets included an intercom system.

"Check; ninety-seven percent life remaining." The Captain, like Lieutenant Stanley, was looking at the H.U.D. projected on his helmet's transparent front shield.

"Cooling systems?"

"Check. System is showing a four-degree delta." Inside the waterproof suit, it was possible for temperatures to rise several degrees while the soldier was at rest, and as much as ten degrees—effectively cooking the wearer—when exerting himself in combat. Without the cooling systems, the suits were little more than expensive coffins in all but the coldest climes. The four-degree delta Thor was reporting reduced the inside temperature from thirty-four degrees Celsius down to thirty degrees, or about eighty-six Fahrenheit.

"Chameleon function?" Both men switched their setting from midnight to desert and then to jungle camouflage. They laughed as they watched each other change coloration.

Adams switched his SFG to the invisible mode. He knew it was operational because Kyle immediately reached out to touch him. The system worked by converting the imagery that small cameras captured around the wearer. An image of whatever was opposite the side being seen by the camera was projected through the fiber optics. It was as if the soldier simply disappeared.

"Noise canceling?" The incessant roar of the airplane's engines evaporated, vanishing electronically. Had it not been for the remainder of the checklist, they would have retained this position and nodded off to sleep. It would be some time before they got a night's rest.

"Check." Having memorized the list, Thor carried on. "I'm good with NES." That stood for Noise Enhancement System. As the name implied, it amplified surrounding sounds by as much as one hundred times.

"*Yaaah!*" Kyle shouted as he struggled to disable the feature. "Mine's calibrated way too high. Nearly blew out my eardrums." He found and punched the disarm button.

The Captain motioned for Stanley to move on with the test. "How do you read me on intercom one?"

"Five by five," he reported, recovering. "Man, that hurt." He shook his head. "How do you read com two?"

"Loud and clear."

"Data display?"

"Speed: six hundred and two. Tracking: one two seven degrees. Bearing to target: zero nine eight. ETA: forty-two minutes. The GPS thinks we're going to fly directly there—tonight, aboard this overstuffed bird. Surprise. Surprise."

"My data checks with yours. How's your moving map? Try a three twenty-mile scale." Adams was focused.

"Pretty cool. Not much chance of getting lost."

"How 'bout terrain?"

"I'm showing a malfunction. Crap. I'm going to need that to navigate when the valley tightens." It was Kyle's second equipment glitch.

"Mine's working fine," Adams said into his mike. "My IRF is functional, but my ELV's intermittent."

IRF was an acronym for Infra-Red Functionality. ELV stood for Enhanced Light Vision.

"Just great. We're gonna be like the zebra and the wildebeest. One can't hear well enough to stay out of trouble, and the other can't see a lion at a hundred paces. I've got ears and you've got eyes. We're going to need to stick together."

Kyle Stanley nodded. It was what they did best. "Most everything works, Cap. Better than the last time."

"Let's check out the video feeds before we take the gear off."

"I'm able to switch from my cam to the view from yours."

"Not me," Adams groaned. "I'm not picking up your remote at all. What do you say we shut down before anything else fails."

"Have I ever told you how much I hate these flippin' things?" Stanley griped as he removed the jet-black helmet. "They weigh a ton, and they're guaranteed to break just when we need 'em. Even with all the data, I seem to lose touch."

"But we wouldn't be here without the gear. The President would have axed the mission if we didn't have video. If we want to bag some bad guys, it's the price of admission."

✡ ✝ ☾

"HOW CLOSE ARE WE to being ready?" Halam Ghumani asked his lieutenant.

"It'll be loaded before dawn. The boys want to give you a tour before anything's activated." Omen Quagmer was proud of his achievement. "The 'sleeping sentry' positions have been installed as you ordered. They're down the canyon from the bunker on the valley walls."

"When are we expecting our guests?"

"It could be as early as tonight." Omen laughed. "They think one of the Afghani boys, Amad, is an infiltrator. The infidels are paying him. Of course he passes their money on to us—along with everything they say."

"The infidels are funding *Jihad*."

"Oh, that's not the half of it. The American candy business brought in more than fifty million U.S. last quarter." Quagmer was in charge of accounting. Under his stewardship, al-Qaeda had become a substantial exporter of illegal drugs. It had started with heroin, though the "religious" network was now branching out. They euphemistically called it "candy" because their largest market segment was children.

"How do we keep Amad looking like a mole?"

"We tell him what to pass on. Some of what he gives the CIA is even truthful. We sacrifice a few of our own—mostly boys we're uncertain of. The infidels trust him."

"And what has he told us?"

"That he was asked to lay low tonight."

Halam smiled. "Good. I want out of this godforsaken place. There's nothing here but dirt, rocks, and ugly women."

"We'll be gone soon enough, sir. Our chartered plane is ready take us to Baghdad. Our insurance business paid for it."

✡ ✝ ☾

"HAVE WE HEARD ANYTHING from our boys?" the President asked.

"No, ma'am. Not a peep. It'll be a good while longer, I suppose, before it gets interesting," Secretary Ditroe told her boss over a private dinner in the White House. They often ate together, but usually alone, seldom in the White House Mess with the other officers.

"How about our Arab informant? Do we have anything more from him? Is he still with Ghumani?"

"Yes. We encouraged him to keep his head down. We've got a bundle invested in that boy."

The President lifted the linen napkin from her lap and placed it near her plate. She pushed her chair back and turned to her friend. "Do you want dessert, Susan, or are you ready for bed?"

"I thought they were one and the same," the Secretary answered as she placed her hand on the President's. Their fingers interlaced.

✡   ✝   ☾

THE C-17 TOUCHED DOWN heavily on the uneven British airstrip. The island provided the closest friendly airport long enough to accommodate an intercontinental transport. It was approaching noon. They weren't far from the equator, and the air that greeted the two Navy SEALs was heavy. Had it not been for the light breeze, they would have melted.

Thor and Kyle would have a few hours to get acquainted with their team, pull their gear together, and review the harrowing plan. They weren't calling it a suicide mission, but fewer than one in ten Special Forces incursions had prevailed as planned over the last two years. The bad guys had always managed to elude the good ones.

"Captain Adams!" a stocky fellow called out. He was wearing the Israeli equivalent of Special Forces fatigues. In his early thirties, he had dark eyes, brown curly hair, and olive skin. He hadn't shaved in days and had grown the start of a good beard.

"Yes. You must be Major Newcomb." Adams saluted and then held out his hand. "Call me Thor."

"Yitsak," he said as he returned the salute. The Israeli military doesn't salute, but Newcomb understood the difference between tradition and good manners. "Call me Isaac." He reached out his hand and enveloped the Captain's. The two men stood for a moment, sizing one another up. Each was aware of the other's career, having all but memorized his counterpart's dossier.

Most Israelis had taken Hebrew last names, but not Isaac. He had grown up in America. His father had been a successful American Jew, a retail merchant. Isaac loved him, but he loved adventure more.

Stanley, still at the top of the gangway, tossed the Captain's gear down to him. Isaac quickly scooped it up, proud to carry the seventy-pound duffel for the man he had come to admire, if only through his reputation.

It was Newcomb's way of letting the Captain know that all nationalistic posturing aside, he was ready to serve.

"The briefing room is this way, sir," he said, motioning to the left with his free hand. "The tower gave us a heads up on your arrival, so I took the liberty of assembling the men. They're waiting."

The accommodations on Diego Garcia were anything but posh. The palm trees added to the ambience, but this was hardly a resort destination. The briefing room was reminiscent of the War in the Pacific against the Japanese. As the Americans had advanced, they'd built Quonset huts, like these on Diego Garcia, throughout the South Pacific. To call them functional was too kind.

Entering the second largest hut in a cluster of buildings, Adams greeted his team for the first time. There were four Brits, the best of the best—all SAS. The Captain loved working with them. Isaac was about to learn why. They rose and snapped to attention, as did the others.

In addition to Isaac there were three more Israelis, all strong and dedicated. Two other Americans were already on the island: Major Cole Sumner and Lieutenant Bentley McCaile, both Delta Force, Rangers by training. They looked dapper in their black berets.

Introductions were made as the team settled into briefing mode. The Captain unveiled the same PowerPoint presentation he had shown in the President's conference room. As he made his way through the various elements, he asked each man if he had checked his SFG. The replies revealed the same sorts of problems he and Kyle had discovered aboard the C-17. Some things worked, some didn't.

Each nation's suit had essentially the same features. The only prominent differences were the flags and insignias of the respective countries and military units.

"Alright, men, we've got one hour before we board the S-3s. Make sure your batteries are charged. We won't have the luxury of using the solar cells, and it's an eighteen-hour mission. Go back to the barracks and get some shut-eye if you can. It's going to be a long night."

✡   ✝   ☾

AS THE SUN began to sink in the west, the twelve combatants boarded three carrier jets. At nineteen hundred hours local time, they began a journey that would change their lives.

Sitting aboard the Viking S-3s, the men watched as their F-14 Tomcat escorts took to the sky before them. The scene brought to mind images of the apocalypse; the red swirl of gasses from the afterburners looked like six setting suns. Moments after lifting off, the task force turned right and headed due north toward the pride of America, her newest carrier, the *USS Ronald Reagan.*

Screaming along the seventy-degree latitude line, they paralleled the Maldives as the darkness of the moonless night engulfed them. The Carrier Battle Group had positioned itself a hundred miles northwest of Bombay in the Arabian Sea. This leg of the journey was seventeen hundred nautical miles. It was scheduled to take three and a half hours.

Nature was uncooperative. Headwinds caused Team Uniform to arrive fifteen minutes behind schedule. "Uniform" was the military code for the letter "U." While it stood for a "united" multinational team of combatants, Thor liked the double entendre. "Uniform" also represented the high-tech Special Forces Gear they were wearing, the gear that had earned the mission the required presidential approval.

The space provided for each team aboard the carrier jets was constrained. The birds were fast but not particularly comfortable. Extra inboard and outboard fuel tanks had been added to accommodate a flight whose duration was beyond their normal operating limits.

Viking S-3s had been first flown in 1975. Their mission was anti-sub warfare. An attractive yet aging design, they were powered to speeds of 450 knots by twin turbo-jet engines. Designed to be flown off carriers, the S-3s were equipped with tail hooks but had neither spoilers nor thrust reversers. Therefore, on the second leg of this trip, the Vikings would chew up a considerable amount of runway in the thin air of the Himalayas.

A flight crew of two normally commanded the aircraft, with two enlisted men operating the sophisticated electronic gear behind them. Tonight, the technicians' seats had been pulled and the bomb bay doors locked, creating enough room for four men and their equipment—barely. Team Uniform stretched out on the deck of the small cabin, leaning up against their duffels.

As is the Navy custom, the pilots had pegged their ejection seats for this flight. Because the men behind them would be unable to eject if trouble arose, the pilots were now tradition-bound to share a similar fate. One dies, all die. Honor was alive and well among America's finest.

Unfortunately, this elaborate rendezvous off the Indian coast was not an optional part of the plan. Pakistan was no longer much of an ally. Its support during the first phase of the War on Terrorism had precipitated a series of terrorist events and assassinations, eventually crippling the pro-

West government. The support America had bought by canceling billions in debt went for naught. Radical Islamic clerics were now calling the shots. The team would not have permission to overfly their airspace.

Iran was more hostile than ever, and thus entry from the west was impossible. While they were Persians, not Arabs, they viewed any assault against their Muslim brothers as a serious affront. Although they had wooed many in the West with talk of reform and support, when it came nut-cutting time, they were nowhere to be found.

Adams had considered using staging facilities in Uzbekistan, the southernmost area under the control of the Russian Federation, but there was no way to keep such an operation covert. Between the Kremlin, Washington, and European bureaucracies, too many approvals needed to be sought and received to keep anything under wraps. There was also the little problem of the population of Uzbekistan; they were Muslims.

But with the House of Islam rising up against the United States, a new ally had emerged. India welcomed U.S. efforts to thwart Islamic extremism. She had been doing so for over fifty years. Thus Thor and his team of commandos not only had permission to fly through Indian airspace but also had a green light to commandeer her northernmost base.

The carrier landings were a thrill for everyone but Adams. He had made hundreds of them before losing his wings. For his men it was another story. Without seats or restraining systems, his fellow passengers were launched forward, along with their duffels. Thor had warned them, suggesting one hand for themselves and another for their gear. But reality exceeded expectations as the tail hook caught the arrestor cable, abruptly stopping their subsonic jet.

Less than a minute separated the harrowing jolts. Each machine was quickly moved aside and unloaded. Three new aircraft were already fueled and waiting to go when they arrived.

The carrier touch and go was scheduled for thirty minutes, kind of like an elaborate NASCAR pit stop. Everything was handled with trained precision. With five minutes to spare, the men grabbed some chow, discharged their bladders, and boarded their new rides. While the mission was still ten minutes behind schedule, a thirty-minute buffer had been built into the plan.

Catapulted off the carrier deck, Team Uniform was thrown to the back of their plane. The rapid acceleration was stunning. Moments after their harrowing departure, a diversionary force climbed above them, turned northwest, and skirted the Pakistani coastline. They flew up the Persian Gulf and on into Iraq.

Returning to level flight, the commandos were more comfortable than they had been en route to the carrier. This run was shorter and fuel was no longer an issue. As a result, the teams were more relaxed and talkative. Major Newcomb and Captain Adams elected to ride together.

"Tell me, Captain," Isaac asked, "aren't you a little old and decorated for this sort of thing?"

"I came up with the harebrained scheme. The least I could do was help carry it out," he answered, leaning back against his duffel bag.

The long answer was far more interesting. Adams, after being disowned by his parents, had enlisted right out of high school. Bright and motivated, he had found his way into Naval Intelligence. Six years of working hard and keeping his nose clean had earned him the rank of Petty Officer First Class, an E6. A prolific reader and solid citizen, he had been awarded a Fleet Appointment to the U.S. Naval Academy in Annapolis at twenty-three. Following his lifelong fascination with flight, Thor had become a naval aviator, flying F-18 Hornets after graduation. But sadly, five years after he had earned his wings, they were clipped. A problem had arisen with his peripheral vision, something that disqualified him, NPQ'd him, in Navy parlance, from flying jets on and off carriers.

A flightless Lieutenant at thirty-two, Adams had elected to do the unthinkable. He qualified for BUD/S, the Navy SEAL School, even though he was four years older than the next oldest man. Nearly a year later, he was one of only sixty in his class to survive the rigorous ordeal, not ringing the bell. Over the next five years, Thor Adams had demonstrated what a finely tuned mind could achieve in a body of steel. As both an Intelligence Officer and a SEAL, he had planned and led some of the most daring covert operations in history.

The incursion into northwestern India was just over twelve hundred nautical miles. If all went well, the team would cover the distance in two and a half hours. With the prevailing jet stream raging at altitude, they might even make up some time.

Their bearing was north by northeast, zero four zero degrees magnetic. They would meet the Indian coast near Vadodara, cross the Tropic of Cancer, and then fly west of Jaipur. The plan was to continue north about fifty miles east of Lahore on the Pakistan border and into the Punjab. From there, the expedition would enter Jammu and the disputed Kashmir State, just prior to reaching the southern edge of the Himalayas. Descending against the backdrop of the world's most massive mountain range, Team Uniform would then turn north and fly low through a river valley, landing at an Indian airbase near Srinagar.

"Tell me, Captain," Major Newcomb queried, "how did you manage to get a green light? We all thought your gal was going to shut down the

American military. She's the last one we thought would approve a new covert op."

"The SFGs."

"No way. There's got to be more to it."

"Sad but true. She's coming along with us. We arranged for a live audio and video feed into the White House. As soon as we're out, she gets to edit the film, stifle her critics, and bask in the glory."

"Well, that answers my other two questions."

"What?"

"Why we're wearing these camo-coffins, and why we're attacking at first light."

"No 'coffins,' would mean no satellite cams. And though we'd have a much better chance in the dark, without daylight the video's a bust. For Madam Prez, the video's the whole deal."

"The fact that we have no cover, is that political as well?"

"Yeah, no Spectre or Cobra Gunships. She was vehement—not interested in shouldering the political risk."

"But she's a-okay with us risking our necks?" Isaac questioned.

"No problem, so long as we do it quietly and make her look good."

Isaac shook his head. "Captain, have you calculated our odds on this thing?" The Major laid back on his duffel, closing his eyes.

"They're not good."

With his fingers laced behind his head and his eyes shut, Newcomb recounted the challenges, "If we don't get a SAM shot up our butts flying over the disputed territories, don't catch a mountain wave rolling off the Himalayas, don't get detected entering Afghanistan, and don't have one of our birds crash and burn like they did in Carter's Iranian raid, we've got a decent chance of getting through the pass. Don't we?"

"Sure. But the open area around the lake worries me, even at night."

"The narrows between the lake and the high country is what scares me," the Israeli reported. "The whole valley can't be more than twenty paces wide. You just know it's littered with anti-personnel mines."

"Two of the SFGs have been retrofitted with detection gear. So long as they're not using composite materials, we should find most of them."

"That's comforting," Newcomb said, propping himself up on an elbow and staring at Adams. "So what do you think? What are the odds that we fly in undetected, that the gear works like it's supposed to, that we find the mines before they find us? That we sneak into the camp and nab the bad guys just as they're taking their morning dump? Fifty-fifty?"

Adams rubbed his protruding chin. He didn't want to answer. The odds weren't nearly that good. He looked away. Thor recognized that trying to overcome a superior-sized force, in their encampment, in the light of a new day, was plenty risky. Then there was the problem of a daylight extraction, this time in a box canyon.

"I'm a historian, not a math major, Major. I can't say I've calculated the odds. But I'll tell you what, if we pull this off, we'll make a little history."

"That bad, huh?"

Lulled by the ambient noise and vibration, each man finally heard the roar of the turbines diminish as the flight crew pulled the throttles back. One journey was ending; another was about to begin.

They slid forward as the jet began an abrupt descent, losing over thirty-five hundred feet a minute. The altimeter was spinning wildly counter-clockwise. Standard procedure calls for descents between a thousand and fifteen hundred feet a minute, but Thor wanted the team above hand-held missile range while they were near the Pakistani border, and then low, below the peaks, as they entered the Indian valley.

While Adams, a pilot himself, would have preferred to be in the left seat, he had plenty on his mind, although none of his distractions were personal. He was a bachelor. No kids, and no parents to speak of. He and his father were estranged. His dad's insecurity had ripped them apart. Mom, afraid of his father's wrath, had faded into a distant memory. Their rejection had made Thor perfect for this mission. He felt he had something to prove, and nothing to lose.

Well, almost nothing. There was Sarah, the Agent who had co-authored this elaborate mission. She was a stunning brunette, tall and lean, with legs that drove him crazy. He drifted off as he thought of her smile, thought about the first time he had touched her hair, their kiss on the White House lawn—their *only* kiss. They just knew each other professionally, he had to admit. They hadn't been on a single date. But there had been a spark. And down deep inside Thor Adams, it had kindled a fire.

Adams had never given women a second thought. They were always there: on every base, in every town, around every assignment. They had managed to connect, have some fun, then separate just as quickly as they had met. But Sarah Nottingly was different. She was a goddess, at least in his eyes, easily the smartest women he'd ever met. When she spoke, he melted. Yet it completely escaped him that she didn't seem to have this strange effect on anyone else. Only him.

Sarah was a graduate of Jefferson's *alma mater*, William and Mary. She had earned a master's degree in economics from Jefferson's other school, the one he'd founded in his hometown, the University of Virginia in Charlottesville. The CIA had discovered Ms. Nottingly at NGIC, the National Ground Intelligence Center, located on the road connecting

Charlottesville to its powerful neighbor, Washington, D.C. The talented young agent was now Middle East Bureau Chief.

Sarah and the Captain had worked together for months as covert operations to disrupt al-Qaeda were planned and then rejected. Standing near her as they peered over reconnaissance photos, sitting next to her at intelligence briefings, just being in the same room had given Thor goose bumps. The Captain, feeling like a teenager, had made it a game to see how close he could get before she would feel his presence and move away.

The kiss shouldn't have "counted." It was just for good luck as they said their goodbyes. It lasted but a second or two, and though it was just a peck, it was on the lips, not the cheek. They had separated slowly, gazing into one another's eyes. The gaze lasted a short eternity before he flinched and had to look away. Sarah *never* flinched.

These pleasant thoughts swirling in Adams' mind evaporated as he heard air rushing beneath him. The landing-gear doors were open, and the heavy sounds meant the hydraulics were doing their job. He smiled as he felt the gear lock into place. The small actuator motors driving the flaps from approach to landing configuration continued while the plane pitched down. Sixty seconds later, there was a chirp as rubber kissed tarmac. There were no spoilers to deploy, no thrust reversers, so the deceleration felt alarmingly slow. Adams missed the sudden jerk of the tail hook catching the cross deck pendant, something only a navy fighter jock would enjoy.

Within three minutes, all three planes were down and had rolled to a stop. They taxied back to the northeast corner of the ramp and cut their engines. As they spooled down, the crews disembarked. A strong wind came off the mountains, cutting right through their fatigues. They had yet to don their SFGs, and the thin cotton they were wearing was no match for these frigid conditions. Each man grabbed his weapons and duffel bag, running to the Quonset hut some fifty yards away. As they jogged, they caught sight of others, off to their left, pulling camouflage nets off a trio of helicopters. All was going according to plan.

Fifteen feet wide by thirty feet long, the metal Quonset hut was none too big for a dozen men and their equipment. Everybody was in motion. It was zero thirty hours, local. They had made up the time they'd lost battling headwinds off Diego Garcia. Adams had allotted thirty minutes for the men to put on their gear and ready their weapons.

The SFG skin itself was like a heavy jumpsuit. It went on over a pair of standard military briefs and blister-free Teflon socks. An integrated vest and equipment pack was next. It carried everything from an onboard computer to an integrated canteen, battery packs and ammunition pouches on either side. Each man strapped a communications device to his left wrist and an integrated smart weapon to his right forearm. They had no qualms about putting on the gloves, since it was freezing, even inside the metal shed. At least they were out of the wind.

A heavy web belt held a pistol, in most cases a Berretta 9mm or Glock, extra ammunition clips, a special-forces knife, and several grenades. The principal weapon varied from country to country, from man to man. Thor, Kyle, and Isaac each had an OIWC, a new high-tech computer-aided rifle and grenade launcher. The Brits, on the other hand, were more tradition-al, carrying Lee-Enfields. The other Israelis were using M-16s with stan-dard NATO rounds.

With their duffel bags now empty, the men spread them out on the gravel floor and sat cross-legged as the Captain addressed them. "We come from five services: the Israeli Mossad and *Shu'alei Shimshon*, U.S. Army Rangers and Navy SEALs, and the British SAS. But none of that matters here. We are now Team Uniform."

Every man was a decorated hero. Nine of the twelve had wives, seven of them kids. The lowest rank among them was lieutenant. With high-tech helmets in their laps, weapons at their sides, backs straight and eyes forward, they were the very picture of confidence. The Captain began to think they might actually pull this off.

"It's zero one hundred hours. In thirty minutes, we're going to fly those specially configured Sea Hawks you saw out there on the ramp through the highest passes in the Himalayas. Like you, they are the best of the best. They cannot be heard: acoustic-canceling systems suppress both rotor and engine noise. They work by broadcasting sound waves identical in length and frequency to those made by the blades, turbines, and exhaust, but their peaks and troughs are opposite. They cancel each other out. At night we can't be seen or heard. Unless someone is under the wash of our rotors, he won't even know we're there."

"If that's the case, sir," one of the Israelis spoke up, "why are we being extracted in broad daylight?"

"Political reasons, son." The young man asking the question was twenty-three, sixteen years younger than the man answering him, a life-time in the military. It was a good question, but not a very good answer. It didn't satisfy anyone, especially the six officers now standing behind the Captain, the Sea Hawk flight crews.

"These men are going to fly us to within seven clicks of the training camp. A journey of about three hundred nautical. We should arrive at the drop zone slightly ahead of schedule at zero four hundred. We'll need to cover this terrain at a pace of a mile every fifteen to eighteen minutes, even in the dark and carrying a hundred pounds of gear uphill. Satellite reconnaissance shows a narrow trail from our rappel site to the camp. I expect us to arrive at the enemy's perimeter between oh five thirty and oh six hundred. It's going to be tough—the air's real thin up there. And we're not acclimated; they are."

Thor scanned the room. Every man sat motionless, staring directly at him. "We'll observe them, gather intel, and then strike at first light, zero six hundred. The operation should take sixty minutes. We shoot the culls and use our spray cans of N^2, Nighty-Night, on our prime targets. They fall into dreamland and we use these snap ties," the Captain said, pulling several out of a side pocket, "to secure the victims' wrists and ankles before we cart them out on our shoulders."

"Nighty-Night" was the term the Delta Forces had coined to describe the effect the aerosol spray had on its recipient. Part anesthesia, part chloroform, it put the victim down in a hurry. The politicos wanted the perpetrators to stand trial rather than be killed outright. America wanted to show the world it was compassionate and civilized. Never mind the little fish. Team Uniform would just help them on their way to Allah.

"Our mission is to bag the top three terrorists: Halam, Omen, and Kahn. You've seen their mugs in your briefing materials. *Ugly*. We kill those we have to. Bag and tag."

"We'll be expecting you at the extraction point at eleven hundred hours," said one of the chopper pilots, Lieutenant Commander Dave Smith. "If you're late, we'll be gone. We won't be able to hang around. We don't like flying in daylight any more than you men do."

The pick-up zone was in the box end of a narrow canyon. The choppers would fly in over the deserted side of a lake, setting down in the tip of the ravine. The team would be under radio contact only when the distances were close. The radios, unlike the video communications gear, weren't satellite based. Their signal would simply bounce off the twenty-thousand-foot mountains.

"Once we get close, we should be able to follow your progress on our scanners," added Smith's copilot, Steve Wesson. "You're all wearing transponders, squawking discreet codes, complete with GPS coordinates."

"How about the movies, sir?" one of the younger Israelis asked.

"No movies," the Commander responded. "Just GPS transponder blips. They'll be encoded with bearing, range, and speed in addition to lat-long, but that's pretty much it."

Thor interrupted, "The audio and video feed is being scrambled, sent to an NSA satellite, and then directly to the Pentagon. From there they are going to provide a live show for the President. It's of no use to us."

Adams looked over his right shoulder toward the flight crews. "Did you guys bring the MREs?" Several pilots stepped outside and grabbed the twenty-four meals. They handed two to each man. One was for now, the other for when they returned. Silently, almost reverently, the twelve removed the covers, leaned against the leeward wall, and began eating what they knew might be their last supper.

It didn't take long for the timer on Thor's watch to remind him that the witching hour had arrived. It was zero one thirty. He told the men to leave their duffels, second meal, and fatigues. As each headed outside into the blistering cold, he turned downwind and relieved himself one last time.

With black Kevlar helmets in one hand and weapons in the other, twelve brave souls boarded the charcoal-gray birds. The engines slowly came to life, whirling the giant blades. Gradually gaining momentum, the turbines began to scream as the secondary fuel nozzles dumped Jet A into the hot sections of each engine. Moments later they leaned forward, lifted off, and began the final leg of their long day's journey into night.

The three Sea Hawks turned to a bearing of 320 degrees. Heading northwest, they attempted to climb to an altitude of twenty thousand feet. This was their service ceiling and, more to the point, less than a thousand feet above the floor of the pass they would be following between Rakaposhi and Disteghil. At 25,555 feet, Disteghil was just four feet taller than its twin brother. Soon they would turn and skirt the base of K2, the world's second-highest mountain.

Oxygen masks had been provided for Team Uniform. The helicopters were not pressurized since they were seldom flown much above ground-hugging elevations. Special oxygen canisters had been installed to give all onboard two hours of the vital gas. The flight crew had doubled their supply, enough for the return trip.

The passengers were instructed to don their masks as the choppers made their way through ten thousand feet. There were no complaints. Breathing pure oxygen was like drinking a whole pot of coffee. The brain seemed to love it. If anyone was weary after his long journey, he was now wide awake, sucking Os.

The Sea Hawk series of helicopters was the Navy's equivalent of the Army Black Hawk. Most were equipped with anti-submarine technology, but a special version had been configured to carry SEALs on special ops. They were designated SH-60Hs and flew with a crew of two pilots, both officers, and two enlisted men on machine guns. The gunners and their armaments had been jettisoned for this mission. The space and weight they normally displaced was replaced by fourteen hundred pounds of additional jet fuel for the turbines. This additional two hundred gallons extended the range of the birds by two hours, or three hundred nautical miles. It was just enough, they'd calculated, to make the return trip. There were no gas pumps between here and hell.

Isaac put on his helmet, curious as to where he was. He set the H.U.D. to the moving map mode on the GPS. They were still in the Himalayas, not far from the Hindu Kush, headed northwest. His display read: Track 292, Speed 132, Bearing to Target 045, Range 115, ETA 53 minutes.

They had just passed the village of Gupis and were approaching Brep. Mt. Nowshak, a towering giant at nearly twenty-five thousand feet, loomed ahead, slightly left of their present track. Then he saw it: Karl Marx. "Hey Thor, you're not gonna believe the name of the mountain just ahead, at two o'clock."

"Karl Marx, father of Communism."

"How'd you know, Captain?"

"Our target is only sixty clicks from Marx. We're going to veer right and fly less than a mile from the peak, through a valley in Tajikistan. Fortunately, the Tajiks love us for beating up on the Taliban. From there, we turn back to the left and descend into Afghanistan just above the village of Arakht, population ten—three goats, two camels, a pair of yaks, and three really crazy people."

Laughing, Isaac checked the landmarks before turning his system off and removing his helmet. "You're a history major, right?"

"Yeah, at Annapolis. The Academy," he returned with justifiable pride.

"Okay, Mr. History Major, where was the first Communist society?"

"A Kibbutz in Israel, not far from the Sea of Galilee. 1909, eight years before the Bolshevik revolution in the Motherland, comrade."

"Remind me not to bet against you," Isaac muttered.

"Tell me, comrade. Where in the Torah does it say Jews have to be liberal? In the States they're all Democrats. Heck, even Lenin was a Jew."

"It began with Abraham. When he ran into his nephew, Lot, near the Jordan River a few thousand years ago, the story is that Lot went right, so Abe went left. We Jews have been going left ever since," he laughed.

Even with a moonless night, the snowcapped peak of Karl Marx was starting to glow off the right side. The more impressive Nowshak, still dominated the view out the left windows. Now, at the extreme western end of the Himalayan Range, the winds had gained considerable force. The turbulence buffeting the three Sea Hawks instantly went from nauseating to unbearable, from concerning to terrifying.

Lenticular and rotor clouds could be seen blocking the starlight along the jagged ridges on both sides of the helicopters. Worse than thunderheads, these were the airmen's ominous sign that tumbling winds of wicked proportions awaited them.

The pilots pressed on, displaying more courage than discretion. As they made their way through the ridges, the high-tech birds became little more than corks. Swirling winds were having their way with them. Everything worked against man and machine as they traversed the world's tallest and most massive mountain range. It was here, along their western extremity, that the jet stream first caught the high ridges. The valleys were breathtakingly narrow, and the ridges on either side were steep and undulating.

To make matters worse, the air was unbearably thin. Hugging the terrain, they were a mere five hundred feet above the ground but a lung-pounding eighteen to twenty thousand feet above sea level. The turbines loved to perform in the thin, cold air, but the rotor blades struggled to gain sufficient bite.

Unpredictable and violent wind shear exacerbated the problem. As the jet stream made its way past the granite monoliths, it was forced to change direction. The choppers strained as they shifted from headwind to tailwind, from updraft to downdraft.

"Cap'n Adams," Commander Smith said into his headset microphone.

Thor was wearing his oxygen mask, complete with intercom. Straining to speak as he was tossed by the turbulence, he answered. "Y-yeah."

"We'd li-like to disable the noise-suppression systems. As you ca-can tell, we're fighting to keep the birds aloft. Wind sh-shear is awful. Need to he-hear the engines so...."

"I know. Go ahead. I'm a pilot, t-too. Keep us alive, Commander."

As Adams grabbed hold to keep from bouncing in the cramped interior, he heard the turbine engines roar back to life. Just then Team Uniform began to rise from the floor, almost weightless. That was a bad sign. "Commander, what's ha-happening?"

"I need full up collective," he shouted, lifting the stick in his left hand. "Redline it!" Smith screamed to Wesson as he pulled the stick back into his lap with his right. "We're fa-falling like a rock! Must be caught in a downdraft off that r-ridge."

The Captain moved between the pilots' seats, kneeling just behind them. "Push it right, next to the f-far wall. We need to catch an updraft be-before we strike a rotor."

"I'm t-trying, but we're g-gonna lose lift as we bank, sir."

"Just *do* it!" Adams commanded. "*Now!*"

As the words left his mouth, the chopper slammed into a rocky pinnacle so hard it drove the landing gear up through the floor. Each man attempted to brace himself, trying to keep from banging against the machine. Frigid air rushed in as the commandos scrambled to find their oxygen masks, all of which were tethered to the side of the craft and had been ripped off by the impact. Without them, they had only minutes of useful consciousness.

The Sea Hawk bounced to the right, placing its blades dangerously close to the valley floor. A fatal impact was only seconds away. But as the chopper struggled toward the eastern wall, it caught an updraft, just as the Captain had predicted. The gust was every bit as strong as the downdraft that had slammed them into the rocks. Now every man was pinned against the jagged floor of the debilitated bird. They were climbing faster than they had fallen.

The Captain found his oxygen mask, took three quick, deep breaths and threw it off. He grabbed a flashlight he'd seen stashed between the two pilots. Shining it toward the back of the craft, he could see that Isaac and Kyle had both lost their masks. Newcomb was turning a ghastly shade of blue. Stanley was turning white.

Isaac was closest. Pushing him upright and leaning him against the side door, Thor reached out for the mask dangling to his right. Although he was being pressed against the floor as the helicopter bounded skyward, he managed to lift his arms and wrap the device around the Major's head.

The aircraft careened wildly in the turbulent air. As he shined the light further back, the beam bounced erratically, as did Kyle's mask, still dangling above him. Adams pushed himself over the jagged floor and around what was left of the landing assembly, cutting his left hand in the process. He could see that Kyle had been knocked unconscious. Blood dripped down the right side of his face. As he had with his own, Adams took three quick, deep breaths from Stanley's mask. Then, lifting his head, he placed the life-giving oxygen against his best friend's nose and mouth. With his other hand, he pulled the strap behind Kyle's head.

Isaac had regained consciousness, at least enough to help. The Captain returned to his mask so he wouldn't pass out. The Sea Hawk had to be above twenty thousand feet now, well above its operating ceiling. With his mask on he could feel warmth begin to move down his body and into his extremities. Without oxygen, the cold was unbearable. The SFG was the only thing keeping him from freezing to death in the thin and frigid air.

Cole Sumner's mask was still on, but he didn't look good. He was on his side, obviously in pain. When the Captain shined the light in his direction, Cole motioned for him to lower it. As he did, the reason became clear. Sumner's left leg was twisted up in the landing gear apparatus. Air rushing through the opening in the bottom of the chopper made conversation, even with the masks and headsets, nearly impossible. Movement within the jagged confines of the Sea Hawk was as difficult.

As Kyle came back to life, Isaac was able to help Thor with Cole. Both men braced themselves and tugged at the displaced gear with gloved hands, hoping to free their comrade, but to no avail. After several such attempts, the Captain saw that a jagged shard from the undercarriage had pierced the Major's leg. Before they could lift him free, the knife-like wedge of aluminum would have to be cut.

Adams reached to his left and released the Velcro covering on his vest pocket. He handed the flashlight to Isaac and removed a tool that looked like James Bond meets Elmer Fudd, part high-tech apparatus, part all-in-one carpenter set. It was just what the doctor ordered. Adams found the right combination of tabs and levers. A three-inch hacksaw blade extended from the handle. He handed the tool to Isaac, grabbing the flashlight back. Both were now covered with the Captain's blood.

The Israeli Major had a better angle. He went to work, struggling to keep pressure on the shard as the chopper bounced violently. None too quickly, he cut through the metal wedge that bound Cole to the aircraft. With Adams' help, he was then able to slide the Major's leg free.

While it seemed like an eternity, the whole ordeal had taken less than ten minutes. The Sea Hawk was back under control and descending to a manageable altitude. Kyle appeared to be good to go, having wiped the blood from the gash on his forehead. Cole was not so fortunate. The damage to his leg would heal, but not quickly enough for him to carry out his role in the mission. Unfortunately, he was wearing one of only two mine-detection suits. The men would have to stay even closer together, as one group, not two as they had intended. That multiplied the risk.

As Thor moved back up to his position between Smith and Wesson, the copilot handed him a note. It read, "Other birds OK. No damage."

Team Uniform was now in Afghanistan, barely. In three minutes they would be in the most remote portion of Tajikistan, not that it mattered. Much of the territory they had covered was disputed. Drawing a map of this part of the world was a fool's folly. This tiny sliver of Afghanistan, no more than ten miles wide, protruded northeast, actually touching China. It was thought to be uninhabited, too high in the Himalayas to support intelligent life.

✡   ✞   ☾

"MR. HAQQANI!" The al-Qaeda sentry spoke excitedly into his hand-held radio. "I hear them coming. Can I shoot?"

"No. We're expecting them." Kahn Haqqani was third in command after Omen Quagmer. Even at this ungodly hour, the terrorists were too nervous to sleep. "What you have told us is important. If you hear or see them again, you may shoot, but not this time. Allah is great. Haqqani out."

Kahn turned to Omen. "You were right. Those fools are flying right through the Himalayas. They'd rather tempt nature than the Russians."

"How far out?" the pudgy Quagmer asked.

"Less than fifty kilometers."

"Are we ready, Kahn?"

"As you have asked, it has been done."

✡   ☦   ☾

IT WAS NEARING DINNERTIME at the White House. The Secretary was pensive. This was the first mission on her watch. Even though it was covert and could easily be denied if it failed, she was worried all the same. This night there would be no dessert.

"I've taken the liberty to set up multiple screens in the press room for the show tonight. I like it better than the situation room down in the basement."

The President nodded in agreement.

"I figured that since the audio-visual equipment was already there, as were the satellite feeds and projection equipment, why not?"

"The seating is theater style, too. It's kind of funny in a way. We'll be sitting in the seats the press corps normally uses to interrogate us." The two women were alone in the Oval Office. The President was slumped in an overstuffed chair while Secretary Ditroe sat on the blood-red sofa facing her employer/lover/Commander-in-Chief. A small coffee table separated them, littered with a nasty stack of briefing documents. The news from every corner of the world was black, as black as the moonless night just starting to envelop Washington.

"Susan," the President continued, "have you sealed off the room, sent the pool reporter home?"

"Yes. It was FOX News' turn tonight. He wasn't happy, but what could he say? The only folks left are our equipment operators. They're the two geeky-looking guys you always see sitting back in the corner, inside the glassed enclosure with all those cables."

"Do you think the American people have any idea how ugly the press room actually is?" the President grinned.

"No, and it's a good thing they don't. All they ever see is the rostrum with the Presidential Seal and the blue curtain with the White House insignia. The trimmings of power."

"Yeah, but the room is ugly as sin. Those threadbare orange chairs are hideous. They're even screwed down. The place must have been decorated during the Nixon era."

"Have you checked out the name plaques on 'em? They've got these little brass plates. One says ABC, another CBS. There's one for AP, *The Post*. Everybody has assigned seating." Ditroe eyed the President.

"Did you know the press room is over the old White House swimming pool? Rumor has it Jack Kennedy used to skinny-dip in it with Marilyn Monroe. It's still there, under the floor."

"Are you yanking my chain?" Susan asked. "The pool reporters are actually over the *pool?*"

"Would I lie to you?"

"Yeah."

"Hey, watch it," the President chuckled. "So, Susan, besides you and me, who else have you invited?"

"No one. The NSA, the Pentagon and the CIA all have their own feeds. They've each got at least six flat screens. They'll watch the party from their own situation rooms. Here, it's just you and me."

"Are you bringing popcorn?"

3

SURPRISING ENEMIES

Before encasing his head in the helmet, Captain Adams snapped a salute to his injured comrade. Major Sumner returned the gesture, reaching out his gloved hand to wish him luck. Truth is, they'd both need it.

Though still airborne, the helicopter was in rough shape. The left gear mechanism was a twisted wreck. It had been pushed up through the floor panels, making the Sea Hawk's undercarriage uneven. Landing without a rotor strike would be difficult even if they could find a safe landing zone. Leaking hydraulic fluid was starting to pool on the jagged floor, and its loss was making the machine much harder to control. With airframe damage, the helicopter would have to fly closer to the ground, making the wounded bird an easy target on its return flight. Adding insult to injury, Cole's oxygen canister was nearly empty. No one had counted on the combatants making a round trip.

Kyle Stanley opened the door and threw out the rappel line. He was the first to descend. Isaac Newcomb was next, followed by Thor Adams. Looking back up, they saw their injured friend pull the rope back into the chopper. Frustrated and ashamed, Cole Sumner felt like he had somehow failed his comrades, believing it was cowardly to go back without having faced the enemy.

The extent of the damage was all too evident from outside the crippled machine. The port side was so severely crumpled, it had actually pushed the starboard gear mechanism down and out, wedging it into an awkward position. Landing wouldn't be difficult; it would be impossible.

"Commander, how do you read?" Thor said into his radio intercom.

"How do we look, sir?" the pilot, Lieutenant Commander Dave Smith, asked.

"Not good. Landing's a no go. You're gonna have to ditch when you get back over India. Do you have parachutes?"

"For the crew. We'll have to get down low so your man can rappel, then go back up high enough for our chutes to work. We've got a couple of hours, God willing, to come up with a plan. Over."

"Commander, if the jet stream is still kicking up, the extraction team is gonna have to fly west of the peaks. They'll be more exposed to weapons fire, but I think Mother Nature is more dangerous than the terrorists."

"Roger that. Good luck, guys. Sea Hawk out."

The troops were on the ground. It was three-thirty in the morning, local time. The wind was howling, yet the frigid air was of little concern. The SFGs were doing their job. The men were down on one knee as Thor stood in the downdraft of the departing choppers. He attempted to count helmets, but it wasn't easy. The dust stirred up by the rotors covered the front of his visor. Although it had been coated with a discharge material, the static electricity created by the rotating blades in the dry mountain air had overwhelmed its capability.

The men instinctively tried to wipe the granular dust off their visors with gloved hands. But the abrasive Afghan soil merely scratched them, further impeding visibility. At least until sunup, they would have to rely on the electronic images projected inside their visors' Heads Up Displays.

"Alright, men. Yacob Seraph's up front. He's got our only mine-detection system. I want teams of two behind him. Brits, followed by Americans, then Israelis. Newcomb and I will bring up the rear. As we planned, the man on the right and his partner on the left will use opposing settings. Right's got NES to amplify sound, left on Noise Canceling so his intercom can be heard more clearly. I want right on IRF, left on ELV. Seraph, I want you to use Terrain mode up front. It's buddies, except with Sumner gone, we're all in one group, not two."

Adams paused as he looked at his display. "Set your GPS moving map to a five-mile ring. I show a bearing of two five zero and a range of nine point eight. Time to move out. Let's get this job done."

Team Uniform began jogging toward the terrorists. "Seraph, if you detect some'n, shout it out," Captain Adams huffed into his mike. "If you stop without warning, you're gonna have ten guys crawling up your butt. We'll knock you right into the mine."

"Yes, sir," Yacob answered.

As if mocking the fear lurking within each man, the stars were shining, forming a canopy above the blackened shapes. All each man could see was the reflection of the sky on the glossy black helmet of the man before him. The headgear should have been matte black like the rest of the SFGs on this setting, but some bozo must have thought they looked better shiny. As Adams peered through the only portion of his visor that wasn't covered in displays, he saw ten star-spattered helmets bouncing up and down.

Courage was one thing. Realistically assessing the situation was another. These men knew how far they were from safety, from support of any kind. For all practical purposes, those stars were no farther away.

All of the combatants were in superlative condition. Just carrying a hundred pounds of gear would be enough to stop most men. But these guys could run twenty miles with that load and still be ready to fight. At least they could on the bases where they'd trained. The surface of the lake they were now circumnavigating was at a lung-robbing 10,900 feet. Their lungs screamed for the oxygen they'd left behind in the choppers.

Adams began to feel lightheaded after about forty minutes. Out of breath, he ordered the team to rest. There were no dissenting voices. Doubled over, the guys hacked and wheezed. Breathing inside the enclosed helmets was none too easy at sea level. It was far worse in the thin mountain air. They lifted their visors; it seemed to help.

The surface of the lake, Kowl Shiveh—or Cold Shivers, in Kyle Stanley's parlance—was rippled by the steady northeast wind. Yet it was aglow with the fuzzy reflection of a billion stars. Looking up, Adams found the sight breathtaking. The jagged mountain ridges were jet black, like a serrated knife slicing through an ocean of light. The Milky Way was as bright as a new moon. There were no grays here. Everything was either black or white.

Five minutes was all it took. The visors were lowered, leaving a small opening for air this time. Captain Adams reported what they all knew, though the corroboration was somehow reassuring. They had covered 2.6 miles, with 7.2 to go. They had lost ten minutes trying to recover from their battle with nature, and another five catching their breath, but they were still ahead of schedule.

Although he knew they were transmitting video feeds to the satellite, Adams thought it was probably too early for an audience. The view wouldn't get interesting until sunrise. And audio? Oxygen was in short supply up here; nobody was expending it on conversation.

✡   ✝   ☾

ALL ELEVEN IMAGES were shown on the large flat screens in the Pentagon situation room. The audio was being broadcast on headsets, eight of them, for now just lying on the table. None of the brass had arrived, not even Admiral Gustoff, the man responsible for briefing the President.

The show so far was simply for the benefit of the operators, three officers who were relieved to see that everything was working. They, like their counterparts in the White House, sat in the corner, just opposite of the door. Behind them, out of sight, was a maze of computers and electronic surveillance and encoding equipment. The situation, or "war" room, as it's called, is smaller than the White House press room, only twenty by thirty feet, but is considerably more comfortable. It's buried in the basement of the Pentagon at the end of a long, painted concrete hall.

For those beneath the status of Joint Chiefs and Secretaries, the Pentagon's viewing room had been made available. Down the hall from the situation room, it was used for wartime briefings. Set up like a movie-theater balcony, the area seated thirty or forty people. Each row raised above the one in front of it. A glass panel separated the presenters and presentation equipment from viewers. One by one, staffers and aides on the short list of people who knew about the operation began to straggle in.

✡   ✝   ☾

AT LANGLEY, Sarah Nottingly was at her post, taking in the action. Her boss, James Barnes, the new CIA Director, was expected momentarily. For now, she sat alone, antsy and apprehensive.

The atmosphere in the main briefing room of CIA headquarters, known as "the firm" to insiders, bristled with excitement. Just being there, witnessing the drama of a covert operation, was arguably one of the most spine-tingling experiences a patriot could have.

Sarah often had butterflies before a mission, she reminded herself. Devoted, she often felt a sense of destiny just walking over the agency seal and past the Wall of Stars on her way to work each day. But this feeling was different. She was on the edge of her seat, palms clammy, heart pounding.

✡   ✝   ☾

IN THE WHITE HOUSE, the press room media managers had the images projected onto all but one of their twelve screens. They had elected to broadcast the sound over a pair of speakers they had installed up front so that the President wouldn't have to use a headset.

The action wasn't particularly interesting, and they found themselves peering out the north-facing windows at the traffic whizzing by on the recently reopened Pennsylvania Avenue. They could see the streetlights around Lafayette Park and some room lights in the upper-floor suites of the Hay Adams, a luxurious hotel across the way. In this town, one never knew what one might see.

It was now seven fifteen in Washington, a blustery late March evening. The President and her Secretary of Defense had good reason to be together tonight, obfuscating some of the usual gossip twisting through the White House grapevine. The two grabbed a quick meal in the President's private dining room, conveniently located near the west door of the Oval Office. Finished, they walked down the hall, past the Cabinet Room and toward the makeshift theater.

✡   ✝   ☾

SECRETARY DITROE had been right. The pool reporter from FOX News had been more than a little irritated at being sent home. His reporter's nose told him something was up. FOX was more conservative than the other networks, and he found plenty of sympathetic ears when he returned to the station. If there was an opportunity to embarrass the new administration, Blaine Edwards wanted in on it.

"Isn't there some way we can tap in?" Edwards asked his team.

"We get a live feed from the press room twenty-four seven," one of the associate producers said.

"Something's going down—we need to find out what it is."

"Why?" the station manager asked. "All they did was ask you to take the night off."

"Never happens. Especially coming from the Secretary of Defense."

"Well you know what they say about Sec-zy Suzzi. They say she likes working *under* the Prez. Maybe they just wanted the place to themselves."

"C'mon, Bob. I don't care if they want to run butt naked through the West Wing. They don't need us gone to do their thing. I'm telling you, something's up. I can smell it."

"Alright, Blaine," the station manager replied. "Tell ya what. I'll put a couple of guys on it. We'll see. I just hope you're right. If they catch us poking around, this could get nasty."

✡   ✝   ☾

IT WAS TIME for another rest. The last two 2.2-mile segments had been a struggle. The gear wasn't holding up any better than the men. Their visors were fogging, and visibility was nil. Scratches and dust stubbornly clung to the outside of the supposedly clear screens. Worse, functionality was becoming hit and miss. On Lieutenant Sullivan's suit the GPS worked great but not the infrared imaging. On Powers' and Keceph's, the enhanced light systems had failed. On Lad Childress' it was the data display that had gone awry. Blake Huston's suit had reverted to jungle camouflage; Bentley McCaile's was locked in desert motif. Thankfully, the invisible mode projected on both Adams' and Newcomb's suits was operational.

The cooling system on two SFGs was *kaput*, a glitch you'd think the men could live with in the thin, frigid, predawn air of the Hindu Kush. But jogging with a hundred pounds of gear mile after mile up a mountain grade was enough to turn a man into a furnace.

An hour and ten minutes had passed since their first stop. They had covered 7.3 grueling miles. The terrorist camp lay just 2.5 miles ahead. They were now five minutes behind schedule, but it was worse than it sounded. The next segment was steeper. There was no way they were going to traverse the distance without taking a break, not in the allotted eighteen-minutes-to-a-mile pace they had planned. By the time they arrived on the outskirts of the enemy's camp, they would be twenty minutes behind schedule, leaving them just forty minutes in which to complete an hour's mission. It was possible, but....

There wasn't much conversation. The troops were winded. Even if they had been of a mind to chat, very little would have come out. There wasn't a lot to see, either. The show back home didn't have much of a plot thus far. When they were stopped, catching their breath, they were all bent over, hands on knees, looking at the ground. And when they were running, the cameras bounced to the point that, even with image stabilization, the picture was impossible to follow without a handful of Dramamine. The only sounds were wheezes and heavy breathing. Cecil B. DeMille this was not.

"Alright, men," the Captain said, looking up. "Let's get out of here. Two clicks this time, stopping a thousand meters from the target. The valley's the narrowest there, giving us the best cover. We'll break outside the camp, and then attack."

Once again, Yacob Seraph led the way, swinging his mine detector to the right and left, back and forth, until his forearm burned so badly he could no longer bear the pain. He'd shift hands and repeat the torture until his other arm rebelled, tightening up into knots, quivering. There was nothing glamorous about his job.

The Brits, Major Blake Huston and Lieutenant Lad Childress, kept pace behind Seraph. Commanders Ryan Sullivan and Cliff Powers were on their heels. The Israelis, Moshe Keceph and Joshua Abrams, followed. Less than two paces behind, Kyle Stanley and Bentley McCaile jogged along stride for stride. Bringing up the rear were Adams and Newcomb, although to anyone looking on, they were not there. The only evidence that they were even part of the team was their footprints, which vanished among those of the nine men in front of them.

"Cap'n," Isaac said, huffing, "if we live through this…who are you going to celebrate with? You got a girl…back home?"

"No. Well, yeah, maybe. Don't know…."

"You don't know if you've got a girlfriend?" Newcomb came back.

The Captain wasn't particularly interested in talking about his love life, such as it was, on an open mike. It was bad enough that the other guys were listening, but there was also the Pentagon, the White House, *the CIA*. It probably wasn't the best way to let Agent Nottingly know how he felt. It was sort of like asking someone out on a date by putting a message up in Time Square, or on the big monitor at a ball game. Yet with his brain starved for oxygen, discretion was more than he could muster.

"We'll, she's definitely a girl, *and* a friend…back in D.C.," he wheezed. "Girlfriend? I dunno. She's amazing though…beautiful," he labored, panting as he spoke. "Something inside her…irresistible. I darn near lose it…every time…."

The breath needed to communicate was more than Adams could produce and still keep his legs pounding forward. Like films he had seen of weary men painfully placing one foot in front of another as they attempted to scale Everest, he had to concentrate in order to keep moving, to force his body to throw one leg in front of the other. Yet somehow, thinking of Sarah seemed to ease the pain. She lifted his spirits, even here, on the other side of the world.

Male-bonding protocol demanded that the Captain ask Isaac if *he* had a girl back home. Usually when guys ask their friends such questions, they're just fishing, hoping their pals will respond in kind so they can gloat about some hot babe, some wild and woolly exploit, to prove they've been awarded their full complement of testosterone. In Isaac's case, the "hottie" would have turned out to be his loving wife of eight years, the mother of his two sons. But the fact that Adams had read it in Newcomb's dossier didn't mean he actually comprehended any of it right now. He simply drifted away into his own private world.

That was a problem. For all of them. With their lungs burning for oxygen, their brains were on idle. They had the reaction time of a drunk driver. Everything was in slow motion, fuzzy, unclear, delayed. As a pilot, Adams knew what he was experiencing—the onset of hypoxia. In the thin mountain air, his body had undergone considerable stress. He could feel his respiration rate increase. He was unable to catch his breath. In short, the conversation with Isaac had nearly done him in.

"Mine!" Seraph shouted, bracing himself. Never had eleven men stopped so quickly or stood so quietly. It was as if they thought words might set it off. Yacob Seraph took three steps to his left as he kept swinging his detector. "Clear left," he said, allowing the team to breathe again. He marked the spot in the soft sand so the rest of the team could walk around it.

Although he was pleased they had adverted disaster, Captain Adams knew he was more confused, more disoriented, than he should have been. The vision problem with the SFG was a contributor, but it was more than that. As he plodded forward, he was having difficulty adjusting to the uneven ground. His coordination, normally as good as any athlete's, was now impaired. The fatigue was nearly unbearable. His head pounded. Intensely painful, his headache was similar to one he had experienced during an emergency descent. The canopy seal of his jet had ruptured, causing the cockpit to suddenly lose pressurization.

Thor began to feel dizzy, but this time he was not alone. Every man was with him, step for step, stride for debilitating stride. In their planning, they had presumed the onslaught of hypoxia would be manageable. Their highest point would *only* be 12,500 feet above sea level. They had all flown that high without oxygen and managed to function reasonably well. But then again, they hadn't attempted to do it for hours on end at a full gallop with a hundred pounds of gear strapped to their backs.

"Isaac," the Captain called out. "Is your vision starting to blur...or is it just me? Visor's a mess...seems to...getting worse."

"Me too. Starting to lose...color vision. H.U.D.'s not good...not same as when...started...altitude...no Os."

They heard Cliff Powers grumbling over their intercom. "Childress, stop flopping...around.... Stay behind...mine sweep...you'll get us all... killed."

Belligerence was another sign that hypoxia was beginning to set in. So was tunnel vision, the very thing that was causing Lad Childress to lose track of the terrain around him and sway from side to side. The team was in trouble, but they still had another mile to go and five hundred more feet to climb into the rarified air.

"Lay off. Let's break. Less than...one to go." They didn't have time to spare, but Adams knew he had no other option. If the men didn't start get-ting more oxygen to their brains, they would be at each other's throats long before they found the bad guys.

Had he been thinking more clearly, he would have turned the team around and headed to the extraction point. In their present condition, they just might make it before it was too late. Unfortunately, Adams' brain wasn't working. Not unlike the poor soul who had invested a year and a hundred grand trying to reach the summit of Everest or K2, he was mentally unable to turn back when the clock struck two—the turnaround time in any language. Few who had tried to storm the summit after the early afternoon had lived to tell the tale.

✡   ✝   ☪

"EDWARDS!" THE VOICE CAME screaming out of nowhere. "You were right. Something's goin' down." One of the assistant station man-agers had found Blaine sipping a cup of coffee in the studio cafeteria.

"What? *What!*" he asked as the young man nearly bowled him over try-ing to stop on the slippery tile floor.

"We're getting GPS coordinates, things like range and bearing. There are some video feeds too. Terrible quality. But there's a bunch of 'em. Some look like...what do you call it, the red stuff that detects heat?"

"Infrared."

"Yeah. Some looks like that. Some of the feeds are similar to night-vision binoculars. Have you ever used those?"

"No. They're for peeping toms, not journalists."

The kid remained focused. "You've gotta see this. They're on a mis-sion. There's a lot of heavy breathing, some bickering, stuff like that. Come on!"

The two jogged down the hall, turned a sharp left, and ran into the control room. Eleven of the twelve studio monitors were streaming video and electronic data from somewhere. The imagery was horrible. The qual-ity might have been better if it hadn't been so dark and if the cameras weren't being bounced up and down. The infrared was useless. There were no heat signatures other than those coming from the men them-selves. The enhanced light was better, but there was no color, only stars, helmets, rocks, and what looked like a high ridgeline. The terrain view was more interesting, colorful at least. Even an untrained eye could tell they were running through an alpine valley.

"Where are they? What country? Who are they? Where're they going?" Edwards asked, too impatient to let anyone answer.

"Don't know. We've got somebody looking up the GPS coordinates. He's a pilot and thinks he can figure it out."

"Have they said anything, or has it just been this huffing and puffing like we're hearing now?" Blaine asked, hoping for a little more insight.

"When the feeds first came up, we heard a guy—a Captain, I think—say he was hot for some babe here in D.C. Got it all on tape. A few minutes later the same fellow asked a man named Isaac if his vision was blurred. He answered in English, but with an accent. Sounded Middle Eastern."

"With a name like Isaac, could be Israeli." Edwards tried to sip his coffee, but it had spilled out in the hallway as he had sprinted to the control room. In frustration, he stared into the empty cup. "What are we gonna do?"

"Nothing. We don't even know what we've got. I called New York, but the big shots have gone home. It's what, nine o'clock?"

Blaine eyed the monitors expectantly. His adrenaline was pumping.

The station manager had no trouble reading the reporter's mind. "Edwards, nothing leaves this room unless we get approval. Clear?"

✡   ✝   ☾

SARAH WAS PETRIFIED. Pacing back and forth, she was driving Director Barnes and the rest of the senior staff up the wall. She didn't care. Nottingly knew the mission wasn't going according to plan. Her friend was in trouble. She, too, was a pilot, and knew hypoxia when she saw it.

"Director Barnes," she said. "Can we call our men, or are their antennas only for transmitting?"

"Just transmitting," he said. "You *know* that." His tone was more compassionate than demeaning. He, too, was worried. "If I had the power to call this thing off, I'd do it in a heartbeat. Those boys couldn't beat a little league team in their condition. How are they going to face a band of terrorists three times their number?"

One of her cohorts, a young analyst known as JT, piped up trying to brighten the mood. "Hey, Sarah. Who was Adams talking about?"

"Yeah," Barnes winked. "Has Captain Hunk taken a shine to you?"

"Not likely," Sarah said, trying not to blush. "Not by the way he described her. Besides, the scoop on the good Captain is that he has a river

of tears flowing behind him, an ocean of broken hearts in his wake."
Agent Nottingly hoped she was wrong.

✡   ✝   ☾

THE THREE SEA HAWKS flew in a formation of sorts. The structurally
sound machines flew behind and ahead of their wounded comrade.

"Bravo One to Bravo Two. Over," the pilot of the damaged bird said to
the crew of the Sea Hawk above and forward of his position.

"Bravo Two. Go ahead."

Engaging his push-to-talk button on the yoke again, Lieutenant Commander Dave Smith reported, "We're still running through fuel faster
than the engines should be able to burn it. We must have punctured the
bladder. At the present rate we'll be toast in twenty, maybe less. Over."

"Roger that, Commander. That puts us well short of destination.
There's no safe haven within forty nautical."

"We're aware. Suggest pulling away from the mountains. The terrain's
too steep for a pickup."

Smith selected the Ground Proximity feature on his multifunction
glass display. It was covered with dark brown, orange, and red lines, indicating that the ground below them was undulating and rugged. He and
his co-pilot switched back and forth from this setting to natural light so
they could read the cockpit display, then to their night-vision goggles as
they attempted to make the most direct course to base.

"Bravo One, our GPS shows an open area without any villages at a
heading of one nine five degrees. Over."

"Roger. Heading one nine five. Descending out of eleven thousand for
seven thousand two hundred MSL. That should be one hundred AGL."
Their actual elevation above mean sea level was just a guess. There
weren't any reporting stations within miles, thus their altimeter setting
was old and unreliable. But the helicopter was equipped with a radar
altimeter so that the crew would know exactly how high they were above
the ground, which was all that counted now. It engaged as they descended out of 9,900 feet MSL—2,500 feet AGL.

Lieutenant Commander Smith sat in the right seat, unlike the arrangement in a fixed-wing airplane. His copilot, Lieutenant Wesson, managed
the avionics. Working together, they determined that the closest city was
Mansehra. They had passed it fifty miles back. Within minutes they
would be entering the disputed territory between India and Pakistan.

That was a mixed blessing. Their odds were fifty-fifty of encountering a friend rather than a foe. In the all-Islamic state of Pakistan, downed American pilots would be as good as dead. Among the Hindus of India, they would be welcomed as heroes. This spot, however, had been selected because there wasn't supposed to be *anybody* there.

In the disputed territories, everyone was a combatant. Most carried assault rifles. They were vigilant and itching to pounce on an unsuspecting enemy. While SAMs, surface to air missiles, were rare, AK-47s were ubiquitous.

The chopper had given all she had. Bravo One was beyond salvation, though her crew was not. Wesson unfastened his four-point restraint system and extracted himself from the tight confines of the left seat. He stumbled across what had once been the floor. It was now covered with hydraulic fluid. Bracing himself, the copilot hastily informed Cole Sumner of their plan. Shouting above the hundred-mile-per hour wind rushing into the open deck, he yelled, "Can you use the rappel line?"

"Yeah." Wounded leg or not, Cole was ready for action.

"Good." Motioning with his right hand, he showed Sumner the hand signal he would use to tell the wounded Ranger when it was time to open the door and drop the rope. It was a clockwise rotation of the wrist. "The signal for you to rappel is thumbs down," he shouted, unnecessarily demonstrating the gesture.

Cole showed that he had understood by giving Steve a thumbs-up. For this he received a broad smile and a hearty pat on the shoulder.

Major Sumner scooted himself toward the door as the airman moved cautiously back to the cockpit. Cole checked the rope to make sure it wasn't snagged and could be tossed cleanly. He lifted his impaled leg into position. It was bleeding badly. The sawed-off shard that had once pinned him to the landing gear was still embedded and clearly visible. He couldn't feel anything from his knee down. He didn't know if that was good or bad.

Sumner planned to take the brunt of the fall on his good leg and then roll quickly onto his bottom to absorb the remainder of the impact. He put his helmet on and re-engaged the suit. He had a full eighteen hours of battery life remaining. He prayed he wouldn't need it. In preparation, he punched in the desired settings on the SFG. Done, Cole grabbed the door's release lever.

Steve Wesson reached behind the seats and got their emergency parachutes. He donned his first, as procedure dictated. Once it was secure, he handed Lieutenant Commander Smith his chute and took the controls.

As he flew farther from the base of the massive mountains, the sky took on a slightly lighter hue. All but the highest of the rising sun's rays were blocked by the most westerly peaks of the Himalayas. What terrain he could see through his goggles had settled down from rough to rolling. This was as good a spot as any.

Lieutenant Wesson wouldn't know if they had company until he switched to infrared mode. Even in the gray predawn light, infrared vision would show a heat signature for any man or beast within harm's way. He said a quick prayer.

Focused on the radar altimeter and holding the yoke in his left hand, the copilot, without looking around, held out his right arm and rotated his wrist. Normally, opening the door was a jolting experience, increasing the noise and wind inside the cabin, but not this time. Wesson had to look around to see if Sumner had managed to get it open.

At sixty feet AGL, the thumbs-down signal was given. The bird twisted to the left as Cole jumped out and hung on the pivot point above the gangway. A second later the aircraft became more buoyant, signifying that Sumner was on the ground.

"My chute's secure, Lieutenant," The pilot said into his mike. "I want you back at the door. When we get to four thousand AGL, I'll give you the thumbs down. You jump. Then I'll set the autopilot on a heading back into the mountains and follow you down."

"Yes, sir." Steve Wesson did as he was ordered.

"Bravo Two, this is Bravo One. Come in."

The pilot of Bravo Two didn't hesitate. "We saw your drop and have marked the coordinates. As soon as you're down, we'll swing back and pick you up. Over."

"I'm setting the autopilot to fly a course of zero one zero degrees, into the mountains. When it goes down for lack of fuel, the explosion should be less noticeable."

"Good call, Commander. We'll stay clear."

"We've activated our handheld radios. Are you picking up the GPS locator beacons?"

"Roger. Unfortunately, we're also picking up some heat signatures on infrared. A dozen men, maybe more."

"No time to deal with that now. Wish us luck. Out."

With that, Lieutenant Commander David Smith gave his copilot the thumbs-down sign. They exchanged a glance, hoping it wouldn't be their last. The Lieutenant jumped, pulling his ripcord a second into his freefall.

Autopilot set, Smith awkwardly turned to exit the cockpit. As he did, the pack containing his chute caught on one of the protruding levers. Directly behind his back, it wasn't in a place he could reach. He tried standing and leaning, but his movements were too restricted in both directions. Desperately, he attempted to sit back down, hoping that returning to the same position would undo the damage. It didn't help.

As David Smith reached for the release snaps on the front of the pack, his predicament worsened. The Sea Hawk ran out of fuel. He could hear the turbines beginning to spool down. At four thousand feet, it wouldn't take long before he was below a safe altitude to jump. It was decision time.

The chute was now off his shoulders and untangled from the lever. Instinctively he knew he had less than a second to make the call. He could crawl over the damaged floor and leap out of the falling machine while attempting to fasten his chute into place as he fell, or he could autogyro the rapidly decelerating blades and try to survive a controlled crash. The odds weren't good either way.

With one foot still in front of the right seat and the other in the cabin, either move looked suicidal. The pilot in him screamed to turn around, to let go of the chute and land—crash—the now-silent bird. The athlete in him begged him to jump.

He lifted his right leg above the seat, clenched his left hand around one of the shoulder straps of his chute, and lunged toward the door. But losing his footing on the slippery floor, he fell against the jagged metal that had once been the landing gear. To avoid plunging face first into the rubble, he instinctively thrust out his right hand. Unable to see in the dark cabin, his wrist was pierced by a serrated piece of metal, part of what had once been the armor that protected him. Sliced to the bone, bleeding in spurts from a severed artery, he didn't have the time to feel the pain. He lunged toward the door and jumped, falling headfirst and backwards.

Holding the chute in his good hand, the ghastly pulp of oozing flesh that had once been his right was useless. With no time to panic, he did the only sensible thing. He muscled the left side of the pack toward his face and bit down on the ripcord. As it engaged, it tore at his teeth, but that hardly mattered. It was all he could do to hang on.

He pulled his forearm inward, toward his body, hoping he could use the larger muscles to dampen the shock as the chute opened. He clamped his bleeding jaw shut, concentrating grimly on his dire reality.

At that moment, a serene vision of his beautiful wife and their baby boy flashed into his mind. He wished he was holding them instead.

Time seemed to stand still. Within a single moment, he felt the jerk as the chute unfurled, and heard the staccato sounds of automatic rifle fire. He mustered everything he had, fighting for his life, fighting to keep from letting go. The chute seemed to be yanking him skyward, though he knew it was merely decelerating his fall. In his mind, David Smith saw his wife smile again. Then with his eyes, he saw his nearly severed right hand being beaten by the rushing air. Oblivious to the pain, he fought desperately to hang on. He just wanted to feel the ground again, hear the approach of the rescue chopper, return to hold his son.

The sounds were unmistakable, terrifying. A hail of bullets whizzed by on his right, then left. Then, as quickly as it had begun, it was over. A single bullet pierced his heart. Two hundred feet from the relative safety of the earth, his lifeless hand released the parachute that could no longer save him. He fell to earth, dead before he hit the ground.

Cole Sumner had witnessed it all. Hunkering down behind a ridge, he had seen the first parachute open, the copilot's. He had seen men in white robes, their heads wrapped in turbans, throw themselves against whatever outcropping they could find. They had steadied their rifles, unloading their clips as the American flier hung from his open chute. He had heard the gunfire, in semiautomatic bursts, then the morbid shouts of crazed men. With his enhanced light vision and amplified sound, it had all been too real.

Well over a dozen warriors, cackling like demons, had begun to fire as soon as the first chute had opened. Although it was still dark, both man and parachute had been clearly visible, silhouetted against the bright swath of the Milky Way. Cole had watched as one shot, then a second and third, found their mark. They pushed and twisted the copilot as the bullets pierced his body. With the first impact, he had heard an anguished moan. With the second, the sound was muffled. With the third, there was no sound at all.

Sumner would have given his life to engage the enemy, even after the copilot had died. But the bastards were too far away. At over a thousand yards, they were out of range. Helpless to do anything, he watched the pilot lunge out of the falling chopper, his chute held aloft in his hand. He had come so close.

The broken bird, as if in sympathy, plunged into a ridge a few hundred yards from where its pilot had fallen. The amplified crunch was horrific, but there was no explosion. There was nothing left to burn.

Within minutes of the crash, the images of turbaned men scouring the site could be seen on Cole's H.U.D. They were shouting, *"Allahu-akbar,"* celebrating death, brandishing their guns and firing them into the air. *What kind of men*, he wondered, *love to kill?* Sumner, overcome with pain, vomited as quietly as he could.

Rolling onto his back and facing skyward, Cole Sumner collected himself enough to speak. "Bravo Two, this is Team Uniform. Come in."

"Bravo Two. Go ahead."

"We've got a bad situation here," the Army Ranger reported. "Both pilots are dead."

"No! Can't be!" The Sea Hawk crews were close. "We saw two ejections, two good chutes. We've got a beacon signal marking each location."

"Sorry, Cap…" Sumner was consumed with emotion. "They're dead."

"We still need to pick them up. We're heading back now."

"Negative," Cole said. "They'll kill you if you come back this way. You're a stripped-down Sea Hawk, not a Cobra Gunship. You've got no guns. There are at least twenty of them, maybe more, all armed. They don't know I'm here, but they're all over the pilots. The scene is…" he wanted to say "right out of hell," but even that wasn't sufficient. They don't sing and dance in hell.

"We can't leave you. We can't leave them. We're coming back."

"If you do, I'll shoot you myself! You've got a job to do. We can't risk losing another bird. If you go down, the men you dropped at the target are as good as dead. Get your butts out of here! That's an order." He didn't have rank, but he was right.

The frustrated pilot swore under his breath. Truth be known, he wanted to lean his chopper forward and run his blades through the crowd of celebrating hoodlums.

Sumner didn't respond. There was nothing more he could say. Two good men were dead.

All any of them could think of was the news footage from Somalia, ancient history now but still fresh in their minds. The images of the Black Hawk crewmen being stripped naked and paraded through the streets of Mogadishu by what looked to be sub-human thugs haunted them. The more zealously Rangers like Cole had tried to rescue their fallen comrades, the worse the situation had become. It was the Devil's own version of lose-lose.

"Keep your head down, Major. God willing, we'll pick you up on our way back. Your GPS signal is five by five. Bravo Two, Out."

✡   ☦   ☾

MAJOR SUMNER had not been the only one to witness the horrific deaths of the American pilots. His helmet cam had beamed the NSA's video feed to the situation room in the Pentagon, to the CIA, to the White House—and to FOX News.

"Perfect! They've screwed up another mission," the President seethed. "Thankfully, it's covert. Can you imagine the fallout if the press found out?"

"Madam President!" Susan protested in tears. "Those men! That was the most awful thing I've ever seen."

"Well, I'm not going to watch any more of this. I've *had it* with the lot of 'em. You shouldn't have talked me into this, Susan."

Ditroe was shocked; the wind had been knocked out of her. She stared in dismay and started to cry.

"I'm going to go to bed. Let me know how it turns out in the morning. And Suzzi," the President spun around as she reached the door, "call your pals at the Pentagon and make sure they keep a tight lid on this. I'd lay odds the rest of the mission is just as doomed. Captain Doolittle's done. The rest of those guys aren't even there yet, and they're about to puke their brains out." With that she walked through the eastern door of the press room and retreated upstairs.

✡   ✝   ☾

"I'VE GOT THE GPS coordinates, sir." The young studio exec steamed back into the control room. "Sorry it took so long, but I didn't have charts for that part of the world." He looked around. No one was listening. They were all staring blankly into the upper right monitor. It hadn't even been on when he'd left the room. "What did I miss?"

The station manager smiled grimly. "Only the most wonderfully horrible war video ever shot. One guy parachutes out of a helicopter that's all torn up. He gets shot a bunch of times. Then a second guy jumps, holding his parachute *in his hand!* Then they nail him, too. He lets go and smacks into the ground just before the chopper crashes. A minute later they're surrounded by all these diaper-headed crazies."

"It was all there, the shots, the moans, the crash, the idiots celebrating."

"Where are these guys?" Edwards asked.

"Those guys, I don't know. The others—the ones with the GPS numbers—are in the Hindu Kush just inside the border of northeastern Afghanistan. High country."

"We've got to release this, Bob," Blaine pleaded.

The station manager turned and told one of his subordinates to call New York again. "This time use their home and cell numbers. Dial anyone with a VP or better after their name."

Edwards was out of control, bouncing up and down.

"No, Blaine. You need to calm down. This isn't going anywhere until we get the green light."

"Come on, Bob! This is the story of a lifetime. It'll make our careers." Edwards, too, was on a mission.

✡   ✝   ☾

"GET ME ADMIRAL KERRINGTON with the *Ronald Reagan* Battle Group," Chairman Hasler ordered. "Now!"

Not even fifteen seconds passed. "Admiral Kerrington here."

"Chuck, this is Bill Hasler. We've got a problem. One of the Sea Hawks you stationed in northern India has crashed. We need another one delivered to Srinagar yesterday. In fact, send two."

"We're already on it, sir. One left here two hours ago. We got a call from the Sea Hawk pilots saying that one of our birds was damaged. They said they needed another for a successful extraction of your Special Forces team. I'm guessing they're working with the same twelve guys that came through here yesterday from Diego Garcia."

"That's right, Admiral. How many Cobra Gunships you have?"

"Four assigned to the *Ronald Reagan*. There're more on...."

"I want them sent to Srinagar," Hasler interrupted.

"Yes sir," the Admiral returned. "The unit that carried your boys in has already requested them. But without authorization, they haven't flown. We sent a request to the Pentagon some time ago, but no joy."

In the background, they could hear the Admiral talking to the Captain of the *Ronald Reagan*. A moment later he was back on the speaker. "They'll be en route in under ten, along with the second Sea Hawk. It'll take 'em a while to catch up with the other bird. Do you want air cover, sir?"

"Yes, but not F-18s. At least not as part of the extraction team. The threat is from the ground, not the air. The enemy is unsophisticated. We need something slower. Guns, not missiles or bombs."

"How about Spectre Gunships?" The AC-130Us are slow but deadly: howitzers and cannons.

The Chairman thought for a moment. "The nearest Air Force Base is Prince Sultan in Saudi, right?"

"Yes sir. Most everything has been pulled out, but between Riyadh and Qatar there may still be something left. I don't know what. Do you want me to call General Smithe and coordinate?"

"Yeah. But I'm afraid the AC-130s may be too slow. By the time they get there, this thing might be over. What about A-10s? Do we have any WartHogs in the region?" Hasler asked.

A-10 WartHogs were Air Force weapons, not Navy. Ugly (they earned the nickname) and relatively slow for a jet, they were designed as tank killers. A derivative was modified for close-in troop support. They were more than nasty enough to keep any enemy's head down—or failing that, take it off.

"If he's got 'em, send four A-10s as cover for the extraction team, and two AC-130s. Use your F-18s to provide air protection for the mission over India, but not over the disputed territories, and not over Afghanistan."

"Aye, aye, sir." There was a short pause. "General," Admiral Kerrington said, "we have General Smithe on line now."

"You tell him to make sure the A-10s have their full complement of cannons and small rockets, mostly anti-personnel ordnance."

"The General says he can have all six birds readied and up per your orders in less than twenty."

"Get 'em airborne. And Chuck, make sure there's enough fuel in Srinagar to complete the mission. If not, fly a tanker in there. I'm going to turn you over to Admiral Gustoff. He'll provide your team with the coordinates and briefing you'll need to get this done."

"Yes, sir. But tell me, sir, what happened to our men?"

"No time for that now, Admiral. Do this right, Chuck. We've got men in trouble."

A momentary silence descended upon the situation room as Admiral Gustoff went into the back office to complete the briefing. The assembled brass wondered if the Chairman had asked for too little or too much.

"You can't do that." Unfamiliar with military operations, the Secretary of the Air Force jumped into the fray. He was a civilian, as is customary, a political appointee. Reflecting the attitudes of the Administration, this Secretary, like the other suits around him, was actually hostile to the uniforms surrounding him.

While backward, that was nothing new. Most of the career officers, especially those who had served during the Clinton Administration, had come to expect such upside-down thinking. Horror stories of under-qualified youngsters swaggering into Pentagon briefings were commonplace. Time after time, a disciplined and devoted cadre of spit-and-polish officers would go into a meeting prepared, only to find that their politically appointed civilian overseers weren't. To their horror, and to the shame of their Commander-in-Chief, they were often disheveled in appearance, lackadaisical in attitude, and short in attention span. But somehow such news never seemed to make the papers. The Washington press corps must have had more important issues to cover than the readiness of America's national defense.

The Secretary of the Air Force slouched in his chair. He cleared his throat and spoke the words Hasler was dreading. "On whose authority are you doing this, General?"

"My own," he barked in the most condescending voice he could muster. "Nobody else dies on my watch. We're going to protect our men." He stared holes through the political weasel. "If I'm ordered to withdraw them, I'll resign." It was practically a dare.

"I understand you don't want a repeat of the Mogadishu Black Hawk thing on your hands, General, but this was supposed to be a limited covert operation."

That was the core of the issue. As in Mogadishu, disaster was assured because a politically motivated President had prohibited the military from using sufficient force. Clinton had been more concerned about the military presence not offending the Muslims than he had been about protecting the lives of the men he'd sent into harm's way. Without sufficient cover or an adequate show of force, Americans had been butchered by the very people he was trying not to offend.

"I've been instructed by the White House, by the Secretary of Defense herself, to keep this thing under wraps. We must consider the political fallout. The President doesn't want us to start World War III."

Hasler glared at the young man. "In case you didn't notice, Mr. Secretary, World War III began on September 11th, 2001."

✡   ✟   ☾

"SAY YOUR PRAYERS, MEN, if you're into that sort of thing. It's time to rumble." Adams wasn't much into prayers; he believed in guns. He had always thought "say your prayers" was a good luck wish, sort of like saying "*gesundheit*" after a good sneeze. He'd heard Sarah say she was praying for him, but the implications never registered.

"We're half a mile from the bunker—less than a mile from the barracks."

The briefing was redundant. Even in their current state, they were up to speed. They had memorized the briefing papers and the satellite images. Their enemy would be well armed and eager to fight. With bullets guaranteed to fly, the men knew every inch of the rebuilt training camp. It was etched in their minds.

"The valley reaches its narrowest point just before the first bunker. So stay focused. As we approach, bunch up behind Seraph's mine sweep. Keep your head down and stay together. Let's do our job and get out of here."

With their fourth five-minute break now history, the men's legs, if not their minds, seemed to spring back to life, at least temporarily.

"Yacob, lead us in," Thor ordered, speaking into his intercom. "Same pairings. Keep it tight. We didn't come this far to get blown up now."

The hypoxia-induced bickering they had experienced during the last leg had subsided. They were too exhausted to squabble. Yet somehow, as they moved in to surprise their enemy, each man actually began to feel a surge of energy. Their bodies were supplying ample doses of adrenaline.

If all went well, they would arrive at their target in less than fifteen minutes. The incline was steep but only slightly worse than what lay behind them.

Unfortunately, by this time Team Uniform was really starting to hate their uniforms. The SFGs had begun to chafe. There were too many straps, buckles, and belts. The Kevlar and titanium fabric was rough, and the weight of the batteries, fuel cells, integrated canteen, computer, electronics, and ammunition had shifted from side to side as the men had jogged up the final ridge. In places, their skin had been rubbed raw. Had they not been numbed by the shortage of oxygen, the constant irritation might have stopped them in their tracks.

The problem of shifting weight was grating on the systems as well. Not one soldier had a fully operational suit. There was only one properly functioning terrain system. Although most still had infrared and enhanced light capability, as the sunrise approached, these functions would become largely redundant. The projected camera images were useless in the dim light. Jogging rendered them nauseating, even with image stabilization.

The system glitches were aggravated by the harshness of the mountain environment, the cold, the dust, and the uneven terrain. With every passing hour, functionality deteriorated. With the exception of Isaac and Thor, they were now an Army of many colors. The chameleon feature had more bugs than a fat frog.

"Halt!" Seraph whispered as loudly as he dared. The briefing worked. No one ran over him, wisely respecting the mine he'd detected. But this time it wasn't a mine. Seraph spoke softly, "Left, right."

He didn't need to say anything more. No matter what form of visual enhancement they were using, the image was the same. On each side of the troop, on both ridges, less than fifteen yards away, they spied a guard asleep at his post. Each wore a white robe and turban, making them all too easy to spot. Their guns were tossed off to the side. Whatever respect the international team had held in reserve for these al-Qaeda fighters evaporated. *Anybody that lazy deserves to get shot!* they thought. *I can't wait to send them to Allah.*

In a voice not much louder than a whisper, the Captain said, "Move out, quietly. Heel-toe. Tighten up. Isaac, you stay with me."

With impaired peripheral vision, the Captain stared directly at the terrorist on his right. He knew that if either of these guys woke up while the team had their backs to them, they would be slaughtered. A few automatic bursts from an assault rifle and it would be all over. "Once you're clear, we'll take out the guards," he told his troops.

With eyes still fixed on the man closest to him, Adams whispered, "Left is yours. Shoot when the men are a hundred meters out."

The SFGs had their advantages. As difficult as it was to feel one's surroundings, and as irritating as they were to wear, delivering these instructions would have been impossible without the intercoms. Their voices would have awakened the sentries.

As Adams eyed the guard on his side of the canyon ridge, he heard him groan, and saw him squirm, trying to get comfortable on the rocks. Thor held his breath, drawing his gun. Isaac did the same.

Newcomb carried a Glock 9mm with silencer and subsonic rounds. With its ceramic components and tight tolerances, it was arguably the world's finest sidearm. The Captain used a heavier Berretta 9mm semi-automatic pistol. Elegant and reliable, it too was equipped with a silencer. Even its muzzle blast was subdued. Unless the fired projectile struck a rock or careened off a metallic object, the whole affair would go unnoticed—except, of course, by the unfortunate sentries.

The Captain and the Major crouched down, steadying themselves. Their first shots would find their marks as soon as Team Uniform was a safe distance away.

Bunched together as ordered, continuing to march, the men were now nearly a hundred yards ahead. Thor maneuvered for the perfect shot. But then he saw it. The sleeping sentry nearest him was grinning.

"It's a trap! Shoot! *Now!*" He was no longer whispering. Adams instantly wiped the grin off the guard's face. A split second later Isaac finished Mr. Left. Both sentries keeled over without a sound, shot through the heart. Allah had claimed two more martyrs.

"Trap!" Adams repeated, screaming. "Fall back!"

But it was too late. Yacob Seraph had already felt the tug of a wire yanking his right foot. "Mine!" he barked out instinctively, drowning out the Captain's order.

In an instant, horrific explosions engulfed the team. Multiple flashes of brilliant white light lit up the mountainous terrain like paparazzi around a movie star. There were at least four enormous percussions, but it was hard to tell with everything echoing off the valley walls, reverberating.

Team Uniform was instantly blinded. With their H.U.D.s set on either the light enhancement mode or heat-detecting infrared, the blasts overwhelmed them. Their hearing was shot too, especially those with operational noise-enhancement systems. The sudden sensory overload was completely disorienting.

Adams and Newcomb watched, frozen in the moment. They were pummeled with rocks and debris. The coating of dust that had made their visors so ineffective went from annoying to intolerable. Their eardrums were throbbing. Half a dozen white spots seemed to circle in front of them. Gasping for air following the impact in the narrow confines of the steep ravine, they rubbed their sides to determine where they had been hit. But they could find no injuries. Their men hadn't tripped a mine. There was no shrapnel. *So what was it?*

All Isaac and Thor knew was that there had been multiple explosions, some in front of the column, some behind. They appeared to have been underground, to the left and right of their team. But it was so hard to tell. A giant plume of dust was now all that was left of Team Uniform.

By the time the air had cleared, their men had vanished. They had simply disappeared.

Running forward, Adams instinctively called out, "Kyle, what's happening? Where are you?"

"Can't see, sir."

The only reason he could hear was that his noise-amplification system was inoperative.

"The ground just gave way," he coughed. "We've fallen into a pit!" he said, choking out the words. "I can feel," his voice slowed, "the ot.h..e..r..s a...r...o...u...n...d...." And then he was gone. Stanley's mike went dead.

"Kyle!" the Captain cried out to his best friend. There was no reply. "Bentley! Blake!" Nothing. "Lad, Ryan, Cliff, anyone!" The Captain beseeched his troops to respond.

"Moshe?" the Major pleaded. "Yacob? Joshua?" he shouted.

Still cautiously moving forward, Thor suddenly felt a tug on his left shoulder. Newcomb was holding him back. If it was a trap, they would soon have company.

"Sir, listen," the Mossad agent said.

They saw dozens of armed combatants storming toward the pit from the opposite direction, screaming at the top of their lungs like savages intent on butchering their foe. Waving their weapons in the air, they rushed in. *"Allahu-akbar!"* they cried.

Neither the Captain nor the Major knew if they should charge or retreat. The odds looked hopeless. Their hearts urged them to rush into the marauding mass and rescue their fallen comrades. Their heads, their training, told them that to do so would help no one but the terrorists.

Isaac, his right hand still firmly ensconced on the Captain's left shoulder, pulled him back. "We must retreat."

"No!" Adams felt both impotent and responsible.

"Yes, and *now!*" Isaac was thinking more clearly. "We need to assess the damage—come up with a plan. We can't fire into that plume of dust."

Thor was still trying to pull forward.

"They haven't seen us, Cap'n. We've gotta go—for our men's sake."

He was right. They didn't know if they were fighting twenty or two hundred and twenty.

"It's the suits. We're invisible," Adams realized. He could tell from the way the approaching mob was acting. Thor looked toward Isaac. Had it not been for the infrared image in his H.U.D., his comrade would have been impossible to see, though he was right at his side.

"You're right," the American agreed. "If we don't fall back, they'll kill us, too."

"Walk backwards, sir."

Looking down, they recognized that the only evidence of their presence was their boot prints in the soft Afghan soil. If they moved backwards, the terrorists wouldn't know anyone had escaped. It might buy them the time they needed to figure out what had happened—and more important, what to do about it.

Jogging backwards and looking over their shoulders, the two men retreated to a small cave they had spotted a quarter mile back. As they moved off the center of the trail, they brushed out their footprints until they reached rocky ground. Climbing up the canyon wall, they were careful not to dislodge any of the rocks along their way.

The cave was no more than thirty-five yards off the narrow path, east of the trail and up some forty feet. There were enough boulders near the entrance to close off much of the opening.

Thor and Isaac felt like cowards, as if they'd deserted their men. But the sickening emotion evolved not into depression, but determination—a resolve to resurrect a rapidly deteriorating situation.

Adams knelt down close to the mouth of the small cave and peered outside. He could no longer see the place where his men had vanished, but he could still hear the shouts of their captors. *"Allahu-akbar! Allahu-akbar! Allahu-akbar!"* The chant went on and on. "Allah is Most Great!"

Frustrated, he turned so that his antenna was facing southwest, out the cave, and over the next ridge. "This is Team Uniform. We have a bad situation here. Nine of our eleven men have vanished into what appears to be a large pit. Thirty or more al-Qaeda troops, all well armed, are now hovering over the area. We do not know if our men are dead or alive."

For the moment, it was all Thor could do to provide the grim play by play. He was in denial. His mind told him this couldn't be happening. Was it playing tricks on him? Was it the fatigue, oxygen starvation, a lack of situational awareness caused by his SFG? No. He'd seen what he'd seen.

He continued his account. "Do not launch rescue at this time. Clouds are building and ceilings are well below the peaks. We don't know if the enemy has SAMs. They appear to be well equipped." Then he lowered his voice, almost as if embarrassed. "They were expecting us. I repeat: They knew we were coming!"

4

NAILED

"How'd you know it was a trap?"

"I saw the guard grinning."

"It saved our lives." Isaac leaned back against the cave wall.

"Maybe, but it was too late to save our men."

"We're not beat yet." Newcomb sounded heroic.

"That's only because you were thinking. I'd have charged in and gotten everybody killed." Adams bowed his head in shame. He was torn between prudence and gallantry.

"You don't think they're dead, do you?" The Mossad Major grimaced.

"No, they're alive. If they wanted 'em dead, they would've shot 'em like fish in a barrel." Adams put his helmet on and punched up the amplified listening mode. There was only silence. He peeked outside, trying every function. Nothing.

The sun's early rays were making their first tenuous efforts to brighten the sky, much of which was obscured by an ominous buildup of towering clouds. They were perfectly white on their eastern edge and black as night on the west. The winds were warmer now, but blustery. If these clouds were to let loose, the snow would be heavy and wet. As Thor looked up with foreboding, he knew they were in trouble. There would be no flights, no rescue, not in these conditions.

Hiding from an enemy that seemed to have disappeared, the warriors agonized. Their retreat had cost them nearly ten minutes, they had spent at least that long in the cave, and it would be another ten minutes before they reached the pit. Thor leaned back in, "We need to go."

"Right behind you, pal," Isaac said as they began their descent.

Although their helmet cameras were now fully functional in the light of a new day, they were not eager to have their signal broadcast back home. Despite the encouraging words, despite all their renewed courage, Team Uniform had failed. If they'd had their druthers, they would have preferred to be as invisible to the folks in Washington as they hoped they were to those here in hell. If anyone was watching back home, Thor knew, they would feel the same way.

Step by careful step, the Captain and the Major inched their way down the steep incline. If they stumbled, loose rocks and debris would bounce and crash noisily until everyone knew they were here.

With being cloaked more critical than being combat ready, the men moved forward with their guns sheathed. The hunted were now hunters. Their SFGs included rifle and pistol holsters made of the same material as the suits. Each component plugged into the symbol generator. As long as their weapons were in their cases, they too faded into their surroundings.

Safely on the valley floor, Isaac and Thor marched to the place where they had seen their comrades disappear. The bogus sentry posts were unmanned. There was no one in sight, no sound, nothing. The terrorist mob had vanished into the hills from which they had come.

"Look," Isaac said into his mike.

Up to a point, the footprints swirled in all directions, but those going south stopped just after they had passed the sentry posts. Having found no retreating prints, they had turned and joined the rest of the celebrants.

"Good call. I owe you one." Had they turned and run, the villains would have pursued and captured them.

Nearing the depression, Thor moved right and Isaac left. As they reached its southern edge, the first snowflakes began to fall.

The pit was crude, just a hole in the ground eight or nine feet deep. It had a dirty, uneven floor made of wood, and earthen walls. It was empty. Team Uniform was gone. There wasn't even any blood.

"Look at the craters," Isaac said. He pointed to the indentations, forgetting that Adams couldn't see his hand. "Al-Qaeda set their explosives a foot or so below ground." There were eight impact craters, not four, as they had expected. The longer stretches of the wall, running parallel to the trail, had been divided into three sections.

"The floor panels are the same length as the distance between the impact craters," Thor pointed out.

"Yeah. I'm sure that's not a coincidence."

Shattered and splintered wood was strewn all about. In the middle of each of the four earthen walls, gas canisters, six of them all together, had been strategically placed at about knee level, along with some rough ductwork. While the setup gave the appearance of crude HVAC equipment, it clearly wasn't intended to heat or cool the pit.

"What do you suppose the canisters and ducts are for, Isaac?"

Newcomb had no answers, only questions. Looking up, he spotted a pair of crude ladders at the far end of the depression. "I'm going down."

As Thor walked toward the second ladder, he noticed a glistening reflection. Moving closer and dropping to one knee, he examined the source. "What do you make of this?" he asked, lifting a wire with his gloved hand.

"It's a tiger trap! Remember the last thing Kyle said? 'The ground gave way.'"

Adams could feel the wind rush out of him. He'd been played for a fool.

"It's like the Trojan Horse in reverse." Isaac descended the ladder.

"Then this must have been the trigger."

"Yeah. That's why Seraph yelled 'mine' just before the explosions. He snagged it with his boot."

The Captain yanked the broken strand. The business end pulled the remnants of makeshift explosive devices out of the cratered walls. They clattered innocently on the floor.

"The explosions blew out the floor supports." Isaac tossed one of them off to the side, out of his way. "The deck used to be up at ground level. It was covered with dirt so it looked like part of the trail."

"Yeah, and the timbers are heavy. That would have kept them from bouncing, especially since I'd just ordered the men to walk quietly, heel-toe. Our guys never knew what hit 'em."

"Wearing these 'coffins' didn't help." The Major adjusted his. The suit was chafing. The places that had been rubbed raw during the ascent were oozing, gluing his skin to the fabric.

"The blasts we saw were under the support posts." Now the Captain caught himself pointing. He sheepishly lowered his arm.

Newcomb traversed the length of the crude bunker amid an ever-increasing flurry of large snowflakes. "When the beams let go, the platform fell into the pit with our men on it."

"They were trapped."

"But they weren't killed, Captain. There's no blood or shrapnel." Isaac was relieved and apprehensive, all at the same time. Down on his knees, his partner stood behind him on the undulating wooden deck. "Whatever happened has something to do with these canisters. The valves," the Major said, "must have been attached to the trigger." Isaac reached in to pull one out. He was careful, as if he thought it might spring to life and bite him.

Adams pushed the ductwork aside and grabbed a tank, reopening the gash on his left hand. Ignoring the pain, he read the label, finding their first clue, their first real indication that their men were alive.

The canisters were marked in English. The labels proudly boasted their maker's logos and the industry trade name for a nauseous mixture of gases. There was no mistaking the recipe. "N^2, Nighty-Night," Thor said into his mike. "Those disgusting thieves."

"How'd they get it?" Isaac asked. "It's supposed to be secret. Doesn't your government keep stuff like this locked up, like it was…?" *Like it was a biochemical weapon* was what he was thinking, but he didn't want to insult Thor—or contemplate what else the terrorists might have stolen.

"They used the same thing on us that we planned to use on them." Their knees buckled. *Who was this enemy, anyway?*

"They put our guys to sleep, Cap. Why would they do that?"

✡   ✞   ☾

WITH OSAMA BIN LADEN'S promotion from exalted leader to worshiped martyr, the ranks of terrorist militias like al-Qaeda had swelled. And working together they had confounded the infidels once again.

So it was with extreme pride that al-Qaeda's newly minted leadership began to celebrate their latest achievement. And they were not alone. They were joined this day by Aymen Halaweh, a handsome young Palestinian engineer, who was also relishing the moment. This is what he had dreamed of doing ever since his tormented boyhood in Gaza.

Aymen was barely twenty-five. His dark olive skin was as smooth as his new beard. Al-Qaeda's latest prize was a smallish man, just five foot nine and a scant one hundred and fifty pounds. Today was to be his initiation, his "swearing in" ceremony.

Ironically, Halaweh had been educated by the infidels, at America's most prestigious engineering school, MIT. The nation had a long history of equipping her enemies. Aymen was but the latest example of this myopia. But America was not alone. Islamic terrorist excursions into colleges in Germany, France, and Great Britain were commonplace.

A technology maven himself, Halam Ghumani was delighted to have an engineer at his side. And the timing couldn't have been better. They had just captured nine infidel soldiers wearing the latest in high-tech uniforms. Who better than Aymen Halaweh to evaluate their fortuitous catch?

Besides, the leadership wanted to test young Aymen's mettle. He was not yet a "made" man. They needed to be sure he was properly devoted, sufficiently enraged. If he became squeamish, they would be worried.

Lying on the dirt floor inside the *faux* barracks, the four men from

Great Britain and two from America were joined in their imposed slumber by three from the "occupied Palestinian territories"—Jews. In less than ten minutes' time, the terrorists had lifted them out of the bunker that had ensnared them and carried them to this, the largest of the crude enclosures in their "rebuilt training camp."

With thirty-six men and boys under their control, the three al-Qaeda leaders and their neophyte prodigy were having the time of their lives. The ratio was perfect, precisely one militant Muslim available to grab every infidel arm and leg, four to a man.

Under the direction of Aymen Halaweh, the unconscious men were stripped down to their skivvies. The watchful eyes of Halam, Omen, and Kahn followed the proceedings. They were as interested in the high-tech gear as was their protégé.

The labor had been divided among the leaders. Kahn was responsible for the party they had planned for their guests. Omen had raised the money that had made this and other celebrations possible. He had also arranged for the team's imminent departure. If all continued according to plan, they would be bound for Baghdad in less than an hour.

Aymen gathered the SFGs, helmets, and weapons and began evaluating them. He was enthralled by their complexity. An impish grin crept across his face as he beheld the technology that had been intended to thwart him and his new friends. It had obviously cost millions, and yet they had defeated it with a simple snare, like you'd use to catch a dumb animal.

Halam was in charge of gloating. For this he was perfectly suited. "What are the fishhooks for, Kahn?" He was hoping for a ghoulish answer.

"A bit of history. Thousands of years ago, the Jews were conquered by the Assyrians, from what is now Iraq. When they led them off into captivity, they fish-hooked their noses, as we are doing." He inserted one, twisting it.

"Besides the pain and humiliation, why go to the trouble?"

"To make a point. The elitist infidels think we're barbarians. They joke that we're wearing our turbans too tight, wearing 'diapers on our heads.'" Kahn adjusted his. "I want to confound them with a historic twist." Then he stooped down and savagely yanked another large barbed hook into one of the Jewish men's noses. He winked, looking up at Halam.

"Boys, grab 'em before they wake up. Let's carry them out to our 'obstacle course'." Kahn was having entirely too much fun.

"What did Muhammad say we are to do with Jews and Christians who fall under our control?" Halam Ghumani knew the answer, but he wanted to hear it again. It was one of his favorite sayings.

"Allah's Messenger, peace be unto him, told us to kill them."

"And what else did he say?"

"That we are to lay in wait for the infidels and inflict such pain upon them as will be a lesson for others," Aymen recited appropriate admonitions from the Qur'an.

With Halam joyfully leading the procession, the entourage carried Team Uniform outside. Four to a man, white-robed Afghanis tugged at each combatant's arm or leg. Across the open clearing they shuffled, their victims swinging helplessly between them.

Just a few yards from the massive, rough wooden structures that had been arranged to confuse the Americans, the Afghanis dropped their sleeping cargo. The convoluted maze of timbers were all set at right angles. It didn't make much sense as an obstacle course. But in reality, mastering an obstacle course had little value in preparing suicide bombers or anthrax mailers anyway. It was merely part of the show.

Kahn Haqqani turned to face the assembled. Blowing snow now danced at his feet. The speed at which it accumulated reminded him of how swiftly his team had capitalized on their successes.

The visual contrast was beginning to suggest foreboding echoes of past evils, if only one were there to notice. The ten-inch-square rough-hewn beams were a deep darkish brown, nearly black. As the ground turned white, the image was reminiscent of the early black-and-white Nazi propaganda film, *The Triumph of the Will*. There, as here, was order, an overwhelming sense of purpose, and zealous pride—all emanating out of a demented doctrine. And like the Nazi films of old, outside of the leadership, no one knew what was coming.

"Stop," Kahn hollered. "We need Omen to finish setting up the satellite cam. Boy, you over there," Haqqani pointed. "Get the flags. There should be twenty-three of them—one for each of the Islamic nations supporting our cause."

Jihad had consumed the Muslim world. It had spread from a series of isolated brushfires, burning only within the most unbalanced of Islamic minds, to a raging inferno, threatening to sweep the globe.

As the flags were hoisted, Aymen Halaweh darted out of the barracks carrying one of the infidel helmets and a backpack. He was excited, waving them in the air. "Mr. Haqqani, look what I've found."

"What?" Kahn didn't like being interrupted.

"They were wearing satellite cameras. Look at this," he said thrusting the confiscated gear toward his new boss.

Kahn looked directly into the camera. "Is it on?" he asked, vainly stroking a long beard that masked the angularity of his face. Haqqani was a short, skinny man in his late forties. A touch of gray dusted his hair.

"Yes. The battery is built into the pack. It powers the camera and the satellite PC. There is a display inside each visor, an H.U.D."

"A what?" Haqqani queried.

"A Heads Up Display. State-of-the-art stuff."

"If this is a satellite cam, where's the antenna?" Kahn was more familiar with the type Omen had just erected, the kind the media used.

"Built into the soldiers' packs, sir," the new recruit answered. He turned the unit over so the boss could get a better look.

"How do you know it's on?"

"When you talk into one, you can hear it in another. You can also switch camera views." Halaweh turned around and shouted, "Brother, bring me another helmet and pack." One of the young Afghanis, standing guard just outside an open doorway, did as he was instructed. With two sets of SFGs, Aymen demonstrated what he had learned. "Here, see for yourself, sir."

Kahn and Halam each grabbed a helmet and tried to put it on. But they were not designed to be worn over turbans. They considered unwrapping them but thought better of it. If they were being filmed, they didn't want to look foolish. Uncovering their heads, revealing their long, matted hair, wouldn't impress anyone.

"As far as I can tell, these are broadcasting what we're doing right now. They came to life the moment I reconnected them to the backpacks."

With that, Halam readjusted his turban. Kahn smiled. And the pudgy, clean-shaven Omen ducked for cover. Scurrying away, Quagmer glanced at the sky's low, dark, and foreboding clouds. He relaxed a little. The forty-year-old terrorist knew there would be no men coming to the infidels' rescue, not in these conditions. And yes, with the fate of their commandos still uncertain, there would be no cowardly cruise missiles either. They were safe, at least for now. Refocused, Omen hastened to his duties, completing the preparations for their departure to Iraq.

"They want a show, do they?" Haqqani said, still fixated on the helmet cams. He arched his back and shouted, "Then let's give them a show!" The charismatic Kahn Haqqani raised his arms above his head. Swinging them wildly, he incited the men around him into a frenzied dance. "Let the show begin!" The ringmaster was ready.

"You two, over there," Halam Ghumani pointed. "Pick up two large rocks from the ridge." There was a sharp boulder-encrusted rise on each side of the clearing. "Bring them here."

As the men stumbled back, Haqqani ordered the grunting would-be terrorists to drop their heavy loads beside Omen's satellite cam. Without complaint, they complied.

Kahn turned to his young Palestinian engineer. "Place the helmet cams on the rocks and face them this way. They want a performance. They shall have one."

With the SFG cameras in position and reconnected to their packs, Kahn focused on his job. There was much to be done before the anesthesia wore off and his guests awoke. Having choreographed the entire affair, he now found himself slightly behind schedule. Fifteen minutes had passed since the trap had been sprung.

"The four of you," he bellowed to a group of white-robed men standing next to Yacob Seraph. "Bring him to me. Yes. Bring my favorite Jew boy over here. Isn't he the ugly one!" Kahn added, revealing his inbred animosity. Actually, apart from being a bit on the short side at five feet eight, the same height as Kahn, Yacob was a magnificent specimen. Barrel chested and strong as an ox, his upper arms were the circumference of the average man's legs. Conscious, he would have been capable of breaking Haqqani's pencil neck with one hand.

"Set him face up on this beam." Haqqani patted the crude wooden structure in front of him. "Everyone needs to pay attention. I'm going to show you what I want done. Aymen and Halam, you too."

As they moved in closer, surrounding him, Kahn reached beneath his elegant robe and into a pocket of the rumpled trousers beneath. Haqqani pulled out three long plastic ties, holding them up. "These were confiscated from the infidels. They were going to use them to bind us." Haqqani loved the irony. He had plenty of rope available, but he relished the idea of turning the tables on his tormentors.

"Position each man so his legs rest on the long beam like I have done," he said, making sure the alignment was perfect. "Spread his arms out on the shorter one like this," he said, as he moved them. "It's called the *patibulum*." Kahn loved words. They were the tools of his trade.

"Hold the Jew in place," he sneered. "We wouldn't want our guest to fall and hurt himself." The beams were set on pilings, about three feet above the ground. Kahn held his audience in the palm of his hand. "Now, take a plastic tie and secure each arm. When you thread the lock tie correctly, and yank on the end, it tightens and can't be loosened." Kahn pulled the strap so hard it dug into Yacob's wrist.

"It doesn't look like any of our guests have knives on them," he joked, looking over their nearly naked bodies, "so I guess they won't be going anywhere." Kahn humored the crowd, but he was playing to the camera.

"In a moment," he continued, gazing out over the assembled robes and turbans, "you will repeat what I have done." Kahn turned his attention back to Yacob, though, of course, he didn't know his name. Embroidered fabric labels bearing the wearer's identity, common on most uniforms, were omitted from these. They were designed for stealthiness, not recognition.

Haqqani handed a lock tie to Halam, who secured the other arm. "We must also tie the infidel's legs. Place the straps above his ankles."

Ghumani looked disappointed. This didn't look as painful as he had imagined. He loved watching others suffer. "You led me to believe...."

"Yes, I haven't forgotten." Kahn motioned for one of the boys to bring him a short-handled sledge. He reached into his pocket, extracting a spike, a rather large, crude nail. He held it up for all to see. It was enormous, a quarter inch across near the tip and better part of a half an inch thick at the head. The wrought-iron spike was rectangular, not round. A deep brownish black, it nearly matched the dark wood beams. The menacing implement was over eight inches long.

The nails, like so much in the Muslim world, had been scavenged. Just as their Prophet's clan had risen to power on the wealth they had plundered from caravans, these spikes had come courtesy of the British. They were intended for a railroad they had planned to build across Afghanistan nearly a century ago. Now they would be used to inflict revenge on the very nation that had brought them here—the nation that had brought the detested Jews back to Palestine, their former oppressor, and now staunch ally of their sworn enemy, the Great Satan. Revenge was a dish best served cold. And so it would be on this frosty Friday.

A crooked grin swept across Kahn's sadistic face as he placed the first nail near Yacob's left hand. He lifted the sledge into the snow-laden air. Then he stopped. Melodramatically, he brought the heavy tool back down to his side.

"No, my brothers, I want the Jew to feel the full impact of the treatment I have in store for him. I'll demonstrate the proper technique on one of our fine English lads. It's only fair."

Kahn had a flair for historical irony, although it was totally lost on his audience, both here and at the other end of the satellite link. He mulled it over in his mind. It had been the English, along with the French, who had volunteered so readily, and in such great numbers, to attack the holy city of Jerusalem, to slaughter the innocent children of Muhammad during their bloodthirsty Crusades. It had been the English who had colonized their revered lands, defiling Mecca and Medina with their arrogance and unbelief, subjecting the Islamic people to their suffocating imperialism. Yes. It was only fair that a British soldier should go first.

Haqqani gazed over to his right. "That one there," he said. "Lay that one, with the reddish hair, on the far set of wood beams just as I have done with his Jew friend. Secure his unbelieving body with the ties."

Kahn joined them at the far side of the clearing. He supervised every detail, correcting their mistakes, condemning the Afghanis openly and arrogantly for their errors, real and imagined. He had a low regard for those who had harbored him. Afghans, he knew, occupied a much lower branch of the family tree than Arabs like himself, Quagmer, and Halaweh. In fact, he, like Omen and Aymen, were Palestinians—the most elite of Arabs. His kin had founded al-Qaeda, and now they were back in charge, doing what came naturally.

Kahn asked Halam to step closer. "I'll do this one. You do the next." With that he placed the nail in the recess between the two bones in Ryan Sullivan's right wrist. "I have been careful to avoid the large veins that flow through this area. If you hit one, the infidel will bleed to death, and that's not what we want." He pressed the long spike into the *destot*, checking the position to ensure he would inflict the most pain.

"I thought we were going to nail their hands, like in the pictures." Halam was surprised by the placement of the nail.

"No. I have studied this. They didn't do it that way. The infidels drew their paintings wrong. They weren't smart enough to know that when this was the execution mode of choice, the wrist was considered part of the hand. If we nail the palm, it will rip. The flesh will support only forty kilos. Trust me on this."

Kahn double-checked the position of the crude spike. He raised his hammer. But once again he stopped, glaring at the crowd he had gathered around him. "Move back, you imbeciles. You're blocking the cameras!"

They scrambled to get out of the way. Kahn Haqqani turned his head ever so slightly toward the helmet cams. On stage, it's called "cheating out." Satisfied with the image he was projecting, he raised the sledge slowly, dramatically, as giant snowflakes swirled around him. Then he brought it down, driving the spike through Sullivan's wrist. But he wasn't done. He raised the heavy mallet twice more, pounding the spike deep into the heavy wooden beam.

Ryan's hand contracted. His thumb shot inward. The nail, as planned, had pierced Sullivan's median nerve. But he was as yet unable to feel the full effect. He was just beginning to awake.

The black head of the hammer driving down through the snow created a dramatic contrast for the cameras. Haqqani was always aware that it was a show. He was pleased by the shocking visual effect he had created, and thrilled with his role. He was now a player on the world's stage, larger than life. He was a man to be reckoned with.

Sullivan's hand contorted into a knot. "See that?" Kahn boasted. "That's exactly how it's supposed to work. When he wakes up, the pain will be excruciating." The anesthesia would last less than thirty minutes.

Now Kahn moved quickly, nailing the Brit's other hand. He improved with practice, achieving minimal blood loss and maximum nerve contraction. With no wasted motion, Haqqani, the great performer, acted out his part in the drama he himself had choreographed.

"Ever bang your elbow hard on the funny bone?" Kahn asked Halam. "Multiply that pain a hundred times; then imagine taking a pair of pliers and squeezing that nerve, twisting it side to side," he said in a sadistic tone, as he mimicked the deed. "Pulling and pushing it. That's what these boys are going to feel."

Moving to the bottom of the longer beam, near Sullivan's feet, he said, "Here you have a choice. You can affix both to the beam with a single nail just above the heel. Or, if you like carpentry, you can do them separately, with two nails. I prefer two, myself." It was as if he did this sort of thing every day.

Actually, he was no neophyte to brutality. During the good old days of the Taliban, Kahn Haqqani had tortured noncompliant Muslims, along with their wives and children. When he had grown bored with tormenting them, he took his victims to Kabul's soccer stadium where he'd had them flogged and hanged. He considered himself a professional.

Setting an example for the others, the great Kahn forced Sullivan's bare feet apart and positioned them against a wedge of wood that had been tacked to the beam. They were perfectly aligned. If he erred, the elaborate reenactment he was directing would fail, killing the infidel before he had suffered sufficiently.

Upon placing the spike, he raised his hammer and pounded the long nail through Ryan's right foot. He put another through the left. Each sliced between the metatarsal bones before boring into the wood block. With two more blows, the job was done, the tip of the spike coming to rest deep within the weathered wooden beam.

The sharp riveting sound of hammer striking nail drowned out the softer sounds of scraped bones, ripping cartilage, tearing tendons, and skewered flesh. But the semiconscious Sullivan was no longer silent. As the nails were driven into his feet, they agitated raw nerves, causing him to let out a haunting, inhuman scream. Even under the lingering effects of the anesthesia, the horrid spikes were having their desired effect.

"Boys. You and you," he said, pointing at two young Afghanis standing near Sullivan's hands. "Grab the beam below his arms."

They did as he commanded.

"Now, lift it up." Kahn instructed others to guide the bottom of the angular wooden structure into the concrete recess that had been designed to hold it. "Now that our first guest has been nailed, take your knives and cut the ties before he is raised any farther."

Lieutenant Sullivan was awake. Pain permeated his body. "If you want, you can rip the infidel's underwear off, too. Humiliation is part of the treatment."

The beam onto which Ryan was affixed was raised. Higher and higher it went into the snow-laden air. When it was nearly upright, Kahn's excitement grew beyond reason. Higher, higher still, until the long beam was vertical. Sullivan cried out. The agony became unbearable as the upright slammed down into the hole. Haqqani's first victim screamed as the nails ripped his flesh.

Ryan Sullivan was being crucified.

He was the first to relive the most brutal form of execution ever conceived, a form of death so inhuman it had been banished for nearly two thousand years. Yet it was one advocated by Allah and preached by his Messenger, Muhammad. This was their legacy.

Haqqani turned to face the cameras. "'The retribution for those who fight Allah and His Messenger, for those who commit such horrendous crimes, is to be killed or crucified, or to have their hands and feet cut off on alternate sides.'" Kahn had memorized his favorite verse, Qur'an 5:33.

Ryan's mind told him to scream, told him that it would somehow release him from the agony. But as he tried, no sound emerged. The air had rushed out of his lungs as his arms bore the full weight of his fall.

Thus began the terror of crucifixion. Ryan Sullivan would suffocate within minutes, drown in his own bodily fluids, if he just hung from his nailed wrists. It was only by pushing up against his spiked feet, a torturous exercise, that he could breathe. The only thing more painful than putting weight on his pierced feet was starving for air. Over and over again he repeated the drill, three times every minute. It was excruciating, but that was the idea. The Romans had seen their victims endure for days, refusing to yield to the mercy of death.

While Sullivan's bones held, his sockets did not. His shoulders ripped out, first one, then the other. As they did, his arms began to stretch, inch by inch, adding to the anguish.

From his perch above the snow-covered earth, Ryan gazed upon his comrades. They were freezing and nearly naked. He watched helplessly as they too were carried and tied to crosses identical to his. Mental anguish compounded the physical torment as these animals in flowing robes lashed their victims and drove their spikes.

A shrill voice pierced the air. "I want more cameras!" Kahn bellowed. "Bring them all to me."

Their job done, the men responsible for Sullivan scurried inside the ramshackle hut and retrieved the seven remaining helmets and backpacks. Stumbling to a halt in the newly fallen snow, they looked quizzically at Kahn as if to say, "Now what?"

"You, the ones who carried the Jew, get more stones for the new cameras." Soon the scene was captured from every conceivable angle.

With Ryan nailed and Yacob secured, seven four-man teams gathered the remaining plastic lock ties and affixed the squirming solders, rendering their extremities immobile. It had all taken less than ten minutes.

All nine members of Team Uniform were coming out of their chemically induced comas. Thirty minutes had passed since they had been captured. As they lay bare, spread-eagled on the beams, they shivered. The wet snow blanketed their bodies, covered their faces, and blurred their vision. Unable to look behind them, they didn't know what was coming. Although they could hear their comrade moaning, they did not know why.

Unable to suck enough air into his lungs, Ryan was nearly mute. As badly as he had wanted to shout out a warning, he couldn't, not that it would have done any good.

Kahn had arranged for four mallets, but he would use only three. Preparations had been made for twelve crosses, laid out in four groups of three. With just nine guests, one section would be abandoned. Kahn had expected twelve infidel soldiers, knowing that a dozen was considered the optimal number to conduct a raid of this nature. Yet in this, his moment of glory, he was hardly disappointed.

The great Kahn gave one mallet to Halam and one to Aymen. He held the third. Had there been a fourth group, the hammer would have been swung, reluctantly, by Omen. Quagmer was devoted to the cause, but the sight of blood made him squeamish.

With time of the essence, Omen was content to finish loading one of their two Russian personnel carriers. An aircraft was waiting at a makeshift airstrip just thirty minutes' drive from the north end of the valley. The relative affluence of Baghdad was calling. He glanced up at the glowering sky, thanking Allah the plane had flown in the day before.

Kahn ordered the Afghanis to take up their positions. Scrambling into place, they stood at attention behind each cross, in nine groups of four. All ten cameras, the one al-Qaeda had brought and the nine that had been provided courtesy of the Allied Forces, captured the moment.

Halam pulled rank, choosing to nail the Jews. He decided to torment

Yacob Seraph first. "It is said you led this expedition into battle, so you shall lead them into death." With that he struck the first blow. The nail pierced Yacob's left wrist. Seraph tried in vain to suppress a scream.

"How does it feel, Jew?" Ghumani sneered, staring into his immobile victim's eyes. He smiled as he showed Yacob the second nail. He tapped it on Seraph's forehead, dragged it over his nose, across his upper lip, and then forced it down his throat, gagging him. Halam laughed as he swirled it around. Pulling the spike out, he drew a line on Yacob Seraph's neck, pressing so hard it sliced through his skin, drawing blood, separating his flesh. Then he ripped it across Yacob's chest and along his outstretched arm. Moving so that he was facing the cameras, Halam placed the spike in the recess of Yacob's right wrist. Lifting the sledge high into the frosty air, he drove the second nail. As Seraph let out an ungodly cry, Ghumani howled, like a wolf to the moon.

For Ryan Sullivan, the pain of watching what was happening was nearly as excruciating as his own physical torment. He struggled to release himself from his ordeal, to pull his feet and hands free of the nails. But the heads were far too large. He twisted his extremities, convulsing in spasms of torment, desperate to save his comrades. All the while, the Afghanis pointed, cackled, and danced—shouting praises to Allah.

Incredibly, the intolerable scourge of mass crucifixion unfolding before Ryan was being reprised for the first time in nearly two millennia. Not since the days of pagan Rome had mankind felt the need to satiate their hopeless spirits like this, to assuage their vengeful souls with this most demented means of execution. But thanks to Muhammad, cruelty was making a comeback.

Enjoying himself, terrorist chief Halam Ghumani elected to nail Yacob's feet one by one. Less schooled in the procedure than his sadistic partner, he caused considerably more blood loss than had Khan.

As his feet were being pierced, Yacob's thoughts raced back to the city of his birth, the world's holiest place. It seemed a million miles away, although it's God, his God, was not. Seraph had rediscovered Yahweh, the God of Abraham, Moses, David, and the prophets. He had been on a spiritual journey that had led him right up to the cross of another Jew, a long time ago—and to his haunting question, as yet unanswered: "Who do you say that I am?"

Being crucified himself, the question no longer seemed academic. As these thoughts, these questions, raced through Yacob's mind, his body convulsed. Almost uncontrollably, he swung himself side to side. It did no good. The combination of lock ties and nails held fast. Ghumani was able to torment him at will, and he did so with glee, mocking his every move.

Yacob's blood-curdling scream pierced the mountain air, but no one came to his aid. His God, like his homeland, now seemed so very far away.

The victim's inability to fight back is an essential ingredient in the terrorist recipe. Therefore, it was with great pleasure that Halam Ghumani sauntered up to his next prize, Moshe Keceph. He sized up his enemy. This was all going too quickly.

Just by looking at his face, Halam Ghumani could tell that the Mossad Captain hated him as much as he hated Jews. The four thousand-year-old family feud between the sons of Isaac and Ishmael was still burning within both men. Had the hammer been in the other's hand, Moshe would not have hesitated.

No matter how much pain he inflicted, Halam Ghumani would get no pleasure from nailing this Jew. The Israeli warrior would see to that. With each blow Keceph gritted his teeth, tightening his stomach so as not to utter a sound. This simply enraged Halam, whose ego fed on the suffering of others. He was furious. No Jew would deprive him of this treat.

Incensed, the terrorist leader did what came naturally. He lifted the heavy mallet and slammed it into Moshe's clinched fingers, not once, but twice. It brought him as much pleasure as it brought his prey pain. With each blow, Moshe Keceph vowed revenge.

Halam would have continued pulverizing his hand had it not been for Kahn's bloody schedule. "It's his turn, my leader." Haqqani gently escorted his enraged comrade to the cross bearing the third and final Jew.

Halam let his heavy hammer drop onto Joshua Abrams' bare chest, knocking the wind out of him. He liked the sound it made as it forced the air out of Abrams' lungs. He did it again, and again, until his victim had nothing left to give.

Joshua, like his namesake Yeshua two thousand years before, knew what was coming. He was about to be sacrificed. And Joshua, like Moshe, did all he could to remain stoic, accepting his fate. He thought of his wife, his two young boys. He remembered his *bar mitzvah* and the great celebration that had followed his wedding, then the joy they had shared when their sons were born. He reflected on his nation. While it did nothing to dull the pain, it gave him a sense of pride, of purpose, a reason for suffering. He was proud of his heritage, his people. He managed to hold his response to a muffled moan. Ghumani was disgusted, but he was too tired to pummel Joshua Abrams' bones as he had done to Moshe Keceph's.

Halam had punished the Jews: gagging one, smashing the hand of another, and pounding the chest of the third. His brutality had been symbolic. The words, deeds, and spirit, the essence of Israeli pride, had all been wounded.

Kahn had a thing for Brits. After demonstrating the proper technique on Ryan Sullivan, he focused his devilish attention on Blake Huston, their leader. The Major was as tough as the nails piercing his flesh. He was a tribute to all who are called Royal Marines. While he was unclear on the exact nature of the torture that awaited him, he knew his men were being nailed to wooden beams like the one upon which he had been sprawled.

Haqqani would have preferred a more vocal victim, but smashing fingers was beneath him. Kahn was not a barbarian, at least not in his own mind. He was simply a player, committed to acting out his role. If all continued to go according to plan, the whole world would soon know his name. He was about to be famous, a celebrity of sorts, the next bin Laden.

The sadistic Kahn Haqqani was a student of history. He had studied torture, the most effective and humiliating techniques from the Assyrians and Babylonians to the Chinese and Japanese—including the Catholic Church in the Dark Ages. Their methods had been particularly gruesome. He had even visited with Saddam Hussein, the king of present-day terrorists.

But for his money, nothing beat crucifixion. If the recipient was strong, and not beaten in advance, he could extend his life by torturing himself, prolonging the pain. In a way, it's a participatory form of death. Once affixed, the victim gets to choose how and when he dies.

White men on black crosses set against a carpet of silvery snowflakes—for dramatic effect, it was near perfection. Only the color of the united Arab flags waving triumphantly in the background, and a trickle of blood here and there, betrayed Kahn's hideously colorful imagination.

Lad Childress lay silently, face up, shivering under a two-inch blanket of snow. He would have given anything to be buried, out of sight, but it wasn't to be. The coarse plastic lock ties tore into his skin. As he struggled to break free, the Afghanis taunted him, spitting in his face. Then they took turns hitting him before jumping away, as if it were a children's game. When they were ordered to stand guard behind him, one grabbed his briefs, ripping them off. Another pounded his groin with the butt of a rifle. Childress did his best to ignore the assault. His fate was sealed.

They called him "infidel," "idolater," "unbeliever." "Taste Allah's punishment," they cried. "You are the ally of the Great Satan." Muhammad may have died, but his legacy lived on.

Lad Childress' mental anguish had been punctuated by the sounds of hammering, haunting screams, and demonic celebration. It soon got worse. The Great Kahn began driving the rusty spikes into his body.

His imminent death caused him to reflect on his life and relationships. He thought of his little girls, giggling and squirming in his lap as his wife looked on. They were dependent on one another. She wouldn't be able to go on without him. He feared for her. He prayed to a God he hardly knew, pleading with him to protect and comfort her.

Haqqani moved to Lad's feet, using the point of the ten-inch spike to probe for the right depression, the best spot between the bones. Childress grimaced, knowing what was to come. He dreamed of his childhood in the lush rolling hills of Ireland, the rock walls, the green grass, the indomitable spirit of his people. These images were so vivid, he hardly noticed as Kahn pounded the last nail. Or perhaps it was just that the pain from the other intrusions violating his body had overwhelmed his senses.

Kahn continued to improve with practice. The nailing of Cliff Powers was nearly perfect: minimum blood and maximum pain. Haqqani was pleased with his performance. He turned and bowed to the camera.

Aymen Halaweh was the most deliberate. The engineer in him demanded perfection: the perfect position, the perfect strike, the ideal result. Deeply religious, he was here to serve Allah. His Messenger had called him to *Jihad*—to fight a Holy War against the Christians and Jews. He had been told the same thing by Allah in His Holy Book, the Qur'an. Aymen had read Muhammad's speeches and knew he was performing exactly as he had been instructed. Halaweh had submitted to the will of Allah, or at least to that of his Prophet.

Aymen was happy to have been assigned the Americans. He resented them, even though they had treated him to the best they had to offer. It only embittered him. Americans had what he coveted: prosperity, self-confidence, a sense of purpose. They flaunted their wealth. Their extravagance and wastefulness angered him. Their decadence was, in his eyes, unforgivable. America was the Great Satan. The Jews used their guns to kill his fellow Palestinians. This day he would avenge their deaths.

Captain Bentley McCaile, the Ranger from sunny California, was his first victim. Bentley had it all: Hollywood good looks, wavy blonde hair, twinkling blue eyes. He had gone to college on a baseball scholarship, graduating *magna cum laude* from the University of Southern California. A patriot, he had enlisted in the Army. He'd wanted to become a Ranger, to serve God and country, to make his parents proud.

In McCaile's presence Aymen Halaweh was timid. Even with his victim shackled, the disparity in their relative stature was extreme. As Aymen nervously struck the first nail, he failed, not generating enough force. It bounced away, tumbling into the snow. Embarrassed, the MIT engineer squatted, probing the fresh powder around his feet.

The snow reminded him of Boston, of fat, happy, brainwashed Americans. It rekindled his rage. On his hands and knees, Aymen found the elusive spike. He grasped both it and his hammer with renewed vigor. This time he managed to drive the crude blackened wedge through McCaile's muscular wrist. The diminutive Palestinian was becoming a man. This was his rite of passage.

He drove the second nail with more force than he could control. The heavy mallet glanced off the nail's head and broke McCaile's left wrist. Miffed at his blunder, he sheepishly glanced toward Haqqani, relieved that he hadn't seen his mistake. With his wrist shattered, Bentley's torment would be more intense, although it would not last as long.

Halaweh wanted above all else to avoid Kahn's wrath. Haqqani intimidated him. For that matter, almost everyone intimidated him. Shy and bookish, Aymen had never been able to form a meaningful relationship with anyone, not even in his own family. His dad had beaten him while his mother cowered. He had been forced to hold his sisters down as his father mercilessly circumcised—mutilated—them. The experience still haunted his soul. His oldest brother had died a martyr killing a busload of Jews. With nineteen dead and forty-two injured, he was a hero. Aymen had never measured up.

Aymen, thankful that his leader was focused on other things, quickly scurried to Bentley's feet. Shaking, he managed to drive both spikes with relative precision. His confidence returned.

Only one man remained unpierced. Kyle Stanley lay silent and still. He knew exactly what to expect. He expected that his faith would grow—in direct proportion to the pain. It had been one thing to read about what Christ had endured; it would be another to experience it first hand.

Kyle was willing, though not particularly eager, to lay down his life. He would have preferred that the terrorists were laying down theirs, but Stanley had no qualms about suffering for his comrades, for God and country. He was every bit a hero.

As Muhammad's followers ruthlessly performed their ghastly spectacle, Stanley prayed for strength, for deliverance from the pain. He wasn't afraid of death, but he wasn't in a hurry. He would soon be in a better place.

His mind drifted back to his intended mission. Had he not come here to do the same as was being done to him? No torture or gloating, of course, no pleasure in killing. But he was trained to kill; he was *here* to kill. Killing murderers saved lives, he knew. Kyle shook his head, trying to banish the thought. Unable, he felt the burning pain of the first nail skewering him under the force of Aymen's hammer.

No, he thought. *That's not right. I was here to bring terrorists to justice, to trial. I had no quarrel with the Afghanis. They would only die if they protected the terrorists, if they harbored the scourge of humanity.*

With their men nailed, Kahn and Halam made their way over to Stanley's cross. "Hey, nigger boy," Halam said as he grasped Kyle's chin, forcing him to look in his direction. "Did you know that Muhammad's first convert was a black boy, just like you?"

It wasn't true, but Kyle didn't know that. The Prophet's first wife, a rich businesswoman nearly twice his age, had been his first "believer." Or, Muhammad was *her* first convert, depending on your point of view.

"Confess that Allah is God and Muhammad is his Messenger, and I will spare your life. Our war isn't with your kind." The racist Kahn had offered Kyle the Devil's own bargain.

Lieutenant Stanley gritted his teeth and quoted the same scripture that Jesus had recited when tempted by the Devil: "You shall worship the Lord your God, and him only shall you serve." If we all worshiped the same God, as Muhammad and the Islamic clergy had claimed, that should have been sufficient. It wasn't.

"Sorry, wrong answer, nigger," Kahn said in his most condescending voice. Bored, the al-Qaeda leaders turned away. Halaweh grabbed another spike and prepared to pound it into Kyle's left wrist.

I must not hate these men, Stanley thought. As his mind turned from revenge, the pain seemed to ease. His Lord's words comforted him.

The serene expression on Kyle's face distracted Halaweh. Aymen scratched his head. Muhammad's message evoked rage. This man's God brought him peace. It unnerved him. Something was wrong.

Shaking, Halaweh struggled to raise his hammer. At this moment he was more afraid of Kahn's wrath than he was of Kyle's spirit. Focusing on steadying himself, Aymen conceived a solution to his sudden case of jitters. He carefully tapped the nail he was holding into Stanley's wrist, just enough that it stood erect on its own. This allowed him to use both hands to raise his sledge. Lifting it, the Palestinian engineer let go, bringing the mallet down with considerable force, sufficient to affix Stanley's dark brown arm to the matching wood beam.

Halaweh moved to Kyle's left foot. Overwhelmed with all manner of questions, he was still nervous. *Why is he acting this way?* Aymen tried not to look, turning his back to his tormentor's face. He held his second-to-last spike firmly in his left hand, the heavy mallet in his right. Now squeamish, he did his best to serve Allah as he had been instructed. None too quickly or well, nail, foot, and beam became inseparable.

Unable to resist, Aymen glanced back up at Kyle Stanley. He was sure that his last act, as ghoulish as it was, would have wiped the tranquil expression from his victim's face. But what he witnessed instead was serenity. Halaweh stumbled, falling into the snow.

Reminding himself of the Prophet's promises of booty and paradise for service such as this, Aymen slowly regained his composure. Standing, he looked sideways at the American soldier's almost-radiant face.

His victim spoke. "Forgive him, Lord, for he knows not what he does."

Panic set in. Aymen Halaweh dropped his hammer. It vanished in the white powder. The last nail fell from his hand as he ran away.

Once Halam Ghumani had tired of tormenting his Jewish guests, he accepted the job of removing the plastic restraints. He was eager, wanting the final ceremony to begin. Nails were fine, a good start, but nothing says terror like a good old-fashioned hanging. That, for him, was familiar territory.

He had nearly completed his rounds when he turned to Stanley. He took a careless whack at the tie that bound his foot, slicing deeply into Kyle's ankle. It began to bleed profusely. Halam swore under his breath. Just because he was a terrorist, living in a cave in Nowhere-istan, unshaven, unbathed, and wearing a robe that hadn't been washed in months, it didn't mean he was sloppy.

Ghumani placed his left hand on Kyle's other ankle, holding it securely while he cut the plastic restraint. With blood everywhere, he didn't notice the young engineer's carelessness. As he turned to cut Stanley's arms free of the ties, he also was taken aback by his victim's countenance. But while surprised, Halam was too hardened to be bothered. His conscience, unlike Aymen's, had died decades ago.

"I want every man to go back to his guest," Kahn announced. "The men that carried the legs shall position the base of the cross. Those who were assigned arms shall lift the patibulum. When I raise my hands to Allah, you shall raise the crosses."

His stooges shuffled into position. The great Kahn stood in front of them, his back to the camera. His hands were at his sides, palms forward. He looked to his right and then to his left. Every eye was glued to his hands. Melodramatically, he began to shake them as if stirring an orchestra. Staring ahead, a smile beamed from his face. His eyes danced. He began to lift his arms.

The Afghanis were mesmerized. Hypnotically, they followed his lead. Emulating their leader, they raised the crosses. They were angled at forty-five degrees by the time Haqqani's arms were in the same position. His flowing robe billowed in the gusting wind as snow flurries caressed his angular face, flakes sticking in his beard. As the Muslim militants lifted the crucified men heavenward, their own souls descended one step closer to hell.

Haqqani raised his arms, hands still open, palms facing the clouded sky. They received a dusting of virgin snow as he held them there, quivering for effect. He was the conductor, the Afghanis were his orchestra, and the suffocating men were his instruments.

Every inch the crucified men were lifted stretched their flesh. The spikes tore at their feet and hands. The higher they rose, the more they began to cry out. It was an ungodly chorus. Then there was silence. The air was forced out of their lungs, and they began to die. Kahn Haqqani was stirred to passion.

"Higher," he shouted as he raised his hands, as if to touch the heavens. "Higher." This was his moment of glory, the moment he had dreamt about for three long years. "Higher!" Retribution, revenge. Blood for blood. It had been worth the wait. *"Higher!"*

As he raised his face, he felt the chill of the fresh, falling snow. He yelled, "O, great Allah. I have brought you these infidels. May they witness your wrath. Let those we hate *burn!"* His tirade reached a crescendo. "Cast them into the Hell Fire!"

He lowered his arms, clenched his fists, and heard the sound he had lusted for—the heavy thud of the last eight crosses falling in quick succession into the depressions he had crafted. The shock ripped the men's extremities and jerked violently at their bones. Their arms stretched in excruciating pain; then one by one their shoulders dislocated.

Kahn fell to his knees in the swirling snow, his arms outstretched, pretending to pray. This, like everything in his life, was an act, a charade. But the performance, he knew, endeared him to his followers.

The deed done, he stood, turned, and smiled, facing the cameras. He bowed, like an actor, at the waist, as if he were accepting applause at the end of a play.

The whole performance had taken only forty minutes—right on schedule. As Haqqani bowed, the men's shouts became thunderous. They pounded their hands together in jubilation. *"Allahu-Akbar!*—Allah is the Greatest," they screamed. Then, seeing their leader's pleasure, they began to dance in the snow.

5

HELL FROZEN OVER

Blaine Edwards had seen more than he could handle. With all the composure he could muster, he scooted down the hall and into the men's room. He slid down onto his knees, hugging the nearest toilet. Wrapping his arms around it, he puked his brains out.

Others were not as composed. They vomited on their shoes, on their tables, their chairs. The crucifixions were the most horrible thing they had ever witnessed. They had no idea what to do. So they just stood there, sat there, lay there, some sobbing, some too stunned to move, most swimming in their own vomit.

✡   ✟   ☾

SUSAN DITROE WAS PARALYZED. *This isn't possible,* she thought. *Not in a civilized world, not in my world, not on my watch!*

"Secretary Ditroe?" the technician exclaimed.

Startled, she turned and stared at him, wild eyed.

"Ms. Ditroe, you need to *do* something."

Speechless, but now at least mobile, she stood carefully, as if to test her legs. She looked around the room. It didn't look so shabby anymore. The Secretary of Defense moved toward the door, still without saying a word. She started to run. Climbing the stairs she passed a guard, who nodded politely, wisely keeping his opinions to himself. Without knocking, she burst into the President's bedroom.

POTUS was sitting in bed poring over the day's risk assessment. Wearing a sexy black negligee, she patted the sheets beside her.

"No. *No!*" Susan cried out. "I...I...can't."

"What's wrong, Suzzi?" the President asked. She wanted to comfort her Secretary.

Not knowing what else to do, Ditroe collapsed in her arms, sobbing.

"Now, now, tell me all about it." The President stroked Susan's back. "What could be all that bad?"

✡ ✝ ☾

BILL HASLER pounded his fist on the table. He turned to the men in the operating station. "Get me Admiral Kerrington!"

"What are you going to do?" asked one of the gilded elite.

"I'm going to send in every plane, every man, everything we've got. I won't let our men hang on those crosses!" The General was enraged. "The second they're out, we ought to unleash hell's fury. It's about time we teach those camel jockeys a lesson!"

"General Hasler, this is Captain Derron on the *Ronald Reagan*. Admiral Kerrington is being patched through."

There was a five-second pause. Hasler stewed.

"Kerrington here. What can I do for you, Bill?"

"Chuck, I want an update," the Chairman barked. "Where are those Cobras, the WartHogs? And where are my Spectre Gunships?"

"All en route, sir."

"How about HALO jumpers?"

"Can do. I've got three SEALs ready. They jury-rigged an S-3, just in case."

"Equip 'em and rip 'em."

✡ ✝ ☾

DIRECTOR BARNES was beside himself. It had been his agency's intelligence that had sprung—in the negative sense—the trap. Heads would roll, he swore. In the end, his might be one of them. He was pacing, ranting.

By contrast, Sarah Nottingly was silent and still. She was in agony, tortured inside. Sarah knew that she had made the mistake of her life. The bunker, the HVAC equipment, the ramshackle barracks, even the obstacle course, all made sense now. She and her staff had been suckered.

Sitting in the CIA's briefing room, she knew Thor was still alive. The images from his and Major Newcomb's cameras had been projected the whole time. But with the other cameras capturing the crucifixion, she had been the only one to notice. She prayed, "Please bring him back. Help him save his men...."

She touched her lips and wondered if their first kiss would be their last.

✡   ✟   ☾

THE ONLY TWO PEOPLE in a position to do anything about the torturous events unfolding before them, Thor and Isaac had no idea what was happening in the clearing just a half mile ahead. They had tried to use their alternative camera views, but that function had become inoperative.

"Pentagon, this is Team Uniform. We are heading to target. We do not know what we're going to find." Thor searched his mind for what to say next. "The pit was a trap. Our men were anesthetized. We don't know why. We believe they are still alive. We're going to find them now."

He looked back up at the sky. Large, moist flakes covered his visor. The storm was getting worse. "Do not send rescue at this time. Ceiling is low, below the peaks, too low even for choppers. Visibility is less than one hundred meters." It was not a message he wanted to send. On the other hand, he didn't even know if it had been received.

Adams reached into his holster and removed his Beretta. With it out, some of his camouflage was gone. Still, it was worth the risk. Newcomb unsheathed his Glock.

Side by side they moved deliberately up the trail toward the unknown. Climbing the slippery snow-laden slope was nearly impossible with the added weight of the SFGs. For every three steps they took forward, they lost one to gravity.

Isaac was the first to view the terrorist training camp. The buildings appeared to be abandoned. He moved out past a large rock outcropping as Thor knelt next to him.

Though the blowing flurries obscured their view, they could see what looked like dancing men. Then trees, bare and stripped, ugly trees, as if they had been tormented by nature. They seemed to be writhing. No, they were too angular, too rigid to be natural. This wasn't making sense.

Thor switched his audio to the amplified mode. He heard celebratory chants—praises to Allah. It sounded crazed, as unearthly as the scene. Then Adams spied a lone man wielding an ax, hacking at the repulsive trees. The Captain thought he must be hallucinating. Nothing had prepared him for this. "Isaac. What are we looking at?"

"Too weird for words. Unlike anything I've ever seen."

"Let's move in behind the barracks. We need get closer."

The back of the first building was nothing more than a brown drape. It was a façade, like a movie set. The Captain lifted a corner, finding the building empty. They cautiously slipped inside, crossed the room, and peered out the doorway. What they saw was beyond imagination.

Their prime target, Halam Ghumani, was nearest them. At the far side of the clearing, on the other side of the hideous trees, were three dozen robed men brandishing automatic weapons. They danced all about, cheering, laughing. Between them were crosses, not trees. Their men were hanging on them.

Frozen, they watched Halam raise the hooked side of what looked to be a bush ax, catching and then cutting the men's underwear, one after another. When he had finished stripping each of whatever dignity clothing could have provided, he raised the ax again, turning it so that the flat side faced the men he was tormenting. He cackled as he whacked at their genitals. To the men hanging in agony, it was a mosquito bite. They paid it no heed, so the game quickly lost its appeal.

Team Uniform was still alive, rising and falling, gasping for air. Some were cursing their plight. Others cursed their adversaries. Some appeared to be praying. They were all too weak to scream. And even if their cries had been audible, they would have been drowned out by the celebratory songs of Islamic glory.

The rescuers were in a quandary. There appeared to be no way to win. By firing upon the celebrants, their comrades would be killed in the crossfire. But if they didn't shoot, none of them would leave this place alive.

Halam moved from man to man, poking at them with his ax. He used the hook to pull them down as they tried to rise, and then used the curved top to hold them up as they began to fall.

"What kind of religion causes men to do this?" Adams growled under his breath. He was a student of history, but this was an epiphany. Yet it was no less sick, he recognized, than slicing stewardesses' throats, killing pilots, and then flying fuel-laden planes into buildings populated with innocents. Whatever he had been conditioned to believe about the sanctity of religion and the fundamental goodness of man crumbled before his eyes. As the terrorists shouted their praises to Allah, any respect he might have held in reserve for Islam died as well.

Isaac and Thor surveyed their men. Some were in worse shape than others. Kyle Stanley looked nearly dead. With one foot dangling, he was having trouble pushing himself up for air. Two Jews, Moshe Keceph and Joshua Abrams, looked even worse. Their heads were bent over. They were not rising and falling like the others. Their chests were moving, but barely. Their legs, it would transpire, had been broken. Bentley McCaile was also in serious shape. Unable to carry any weight on his broken wrist, his breathing was impaired.

Crucifixion is an agonizingly slow form of death by asphyxiation. The victims' diaphragms are stretched, forcing their lungs and chest cavities into the inhale position. To exhale, the tormented must push up on their feet to relieve the tension. But by so doing, the nails tear at their nerves and grate against their tarsal bones. After exhaling, they must release the pressure on their feet. This aggravates the damaged nerves in their wrists and stresses already dislocated shoulders. All this must be endured just to survive another twenty to thirty seconds. The cycle is repeated until exhaustion and pain overwhelm the will to live.

Breathing is slowed, increasing the buildup of carbon dioxide in the blood, forming carbonic acid. This leads to an irregular heartbeat, an accumulation of fluid, profound weakness, and ultimately death if the victims don't die of asphyxiation first. Some actually drown while dying of thirst. Fluids drain into their lungs, leaving them craving drink.

Dancing and shouting, dozens of Islamic warriors fired their weapons into the air, waving their arms in jubilation. The situation looked dire. Somehow Thor and Isaac had to devise a plan to even the odds. Thirty-seven to two was pushing it—even for an American and a Jew.

Halam Ghumani turned his attention to Yacob Seraph. After poking him, he lifted the curved, two-sided ax over his right shoulder. Halam wanted to make certain the Jews died, now—in his presence. He lunged forward, swinging the hellish tool violently. His goal was to break Seraph's left leg just above the ankle. Slipping in the snow, he missed. The blade sliced the outside of Yacob's calf instead. Winded, he paused before raising the ax for another try.

That was enough for Adams. There was no more time for assessing the battlefield. He focused his 9mm laser site on Ghumani's left leg, just above the knee—an eye for an eye. The sub-sonic round was silent. Halam spun around and collapsed in the snow, too shocked to scream. Using the bush ax as a crutch, he pushed himself up. Newcomb fired the next shot, hitting his right arm. The terrorist spun around again, falling face down in a newly formed drift of white powder. In his turban and robe, he nearly disappeared.

The shouting dancers behind the crosses were too crazed to notice the silent assault or Halam Ghumani's moaning pleas for help. The Muslim marauders were clearly out of their minds, whipped into a demonic fervor.

Thor and Isaac knew that they couldn't unload on the bad guys from their present position. Their own men were in the line of fire. They would have to separate. The Navy Captain ordered the Mossad Major to the left, the enemy's right flank. He headed south.

There were well-defined ridges and protective rock outcroppings for cover on both sides of the amphitheater-like clearing. More importantly, both Isaac and Thor would be above their foes, shooting down into them, hence not at each other. Even with their clumsy gear and the slippery conditions, they were properly positioned within minutes, ready to start their own *Jihad*.

In addition to a pistol, rifle, knife, and grenades, each man had a high-tech weapons pod strapped to his right wrist. This would be the first time they were deployed in combat. The wrist pods contained four 15mm high-explosive air-bursting fragmentation rounds, slightly lighter than the 20mm versions they dispensed from their Objective Individual Combat Weapons. Both versions were significantly more advanced than the M203 grenade launchers normally attached to M16s. The ordnance contained in each was automatically programmed to burst at a calculated range. The distance was determined by an onboard fire-control computer and laser rangefinder. The boys were about to find out if the stuff was worth its weight.

Now high up on the surrounding ridges and above their enemy, they pulled their high-tech firearms out of their concealed sleeves. As Isaac lifted his, one of the Afghanis saw the sinister black weapon float in the snow-laden air. Dumfounded, he screamed, "The angel Gabriel. He is fighting with us."

Instinctively the others turned toward their observant comrade, who was now pointing to a spot behind them. With the terrorists in disarray, the odds looked better.

"Fire grenades," the Captain ordered into his microphone. Using the scope on his OICW, he focused his range finder on the back of the man who had spotted Isaac and was now running to greet him. Thor held his breath, steadied his body, and squeezed the trigger. The 20mm round left the titanium barrel with considerable force, an unmistakable muzzle flash, and a roaring boom. The Afghanis who were in the process of turning to see what their compatriot had spotted swung back toward the noise.

Before they could spin around, there was a second explosion. Isaac fired his initial salvo. Both shots were followed by multiple echoes as the roar bounced between the opposing ridgelines, making it sound as if the place was surrounded by an army. Traveling at the speed of sound, it didn't take either fragmentation round long to cover the hundred yards to its target. Within less than a second, both shots pierced the lower backs of the enemy, emerging from their stomachs and exploding a few feet away.

As the men on the flanks began to fall, the Captain and the Major sent their second and third 20mm projectiles toward the marauding mob. The snow was instantly splattered with blood and torn flesh. Targets that had once been difficult to see in their white robes were now either silhouetted against a deep red backdrop or spattered with the blood of their fallen brothers.

The scene quickly grew chaotic. Some al-Qaeda members ran for their lives. Many convulsed in pain, as their victims had been doing for some time. Others lifted their assault rifles and began sending return fire at the mysterious levitating guns. The eerie vision of rifles floating in mid-air was confusing for faithful Muslims. After all, Allah was on *their* side.

Wounded in one leg yet able to crawl, a badly injured Halam Ghumani used his one good arm to drag himself toward the Russian troop carrier he was to have used for his retreat. Inside, he found his AK-47 assault rifle. Halam, having seen the floating guns on the left and right ridges, had no illusions. Having supervised the removal of the SFGs, he knew who and what was behind them. Propping himself up against the back bumper and lifting his Kalashnikov, he unloaded in Isaac's direction.

The second three-shot burst pounded Newcomb's chest, throwing the Major back against the rocks. The impact disabled Isaac's chameleon function. No longer able to project the image of snow, the suit turned black, the worst possible scenario. Winded and wounded but with his wits about him, the Israeli tried to switch to arctic mode, but the suit wouldn't comply. Halam fired again. This time he hammered the Major's helmet, leaving him stunned and disoriented.

Clearly visible now and nearly incapacitated, Isaac collapsed as the bewildered Afghanis unleashed hell's fury. With the Major disabled and only a dozen or so white robes down, the odds were worse than ever.

Visibility deteriorated in the ever-increasing snow. Thor switched to infrared mode, which seemed to help. He sent fragmentation rounds four, five, and six into the middle of the Afghani horde. As they reached their targets, the projectiles splintered into jagged pieces of shrapnel. Some shards hit their mark, incapacitating the robed men. Others disappeared benignly into the powdery white drifts. A few fragments hit the backs of crosses holding members of Team Uniform.

Thor's 20mm clip was now empty. But rather than take the time to reload, he used his right thumb to switch his OICW to discharge standard NATO 5.56mm kinetic rounds from the upper barrel. Although he was still invisible, his rifle was not. The Captain took heavy fire from three Afghans who managed to get off murderous bursts. They were attempting a retreat, using the cratered bodies of their fallen comrades as shields.

The SFG performed its magic. The rounds that made contact stung but didn't penetrate the Kevlar and titanium fabric. One bullet glanced off his helmet, ringing his bell but doing no real harm. Ignoring the onslaught as best he could, Thor swung left, steadied himself, and focused on Halam Ghumani. He was barely visible between the crosses. If the terrorist leader continued to fire, an errant shot could mortally wound one of his men. While a bullet in the side might have provided blessed release from the torture, Adams was as yet unwilling to admit defeat, for himself or for the men under his command.

With composure a lesser man couldn't have summoned, the Captain slowed his breathing. He discharged a three-round burst. As if in slow motion, he traced the projectiles' path to the rifle being held by the world's most despised terrorist. The impact of the kinetic rounds on the Kalashnikov's barrel sent a celebratory explosion of sparks into the air as the gun cartwheeled into the snow well out of Ghumani's reach. "Die, scum."

His triumph was short lived. Within seconds, two more al-Qaeda bullets found their mark. The first scored a direct hit on Thor's right bicep, and while it didn't penetrate the high-tech fabric, the impact fractured his humerus. The other ripped its way through a seam and into his right thigh, tearing into muscle tissue but missing the bone.

The Muslim assault was akin to shooting a grizzly bear with a twenty-two. Thor was angry. He slid behind a boulder as he turned right to face his tormentors. With his left hand, he lifted his right forearm, aggravating the fracture. Enduring the pain, he pointed the laser finder on his wrist-mounted weapon pod into the mass of convulsing humanity below. Adams released the first two of his four 15mm fragmentation rounds. There were two more explosions, a great splattering of blood and flesh. He fired his final mini grenades into those still standing. Stillness followed.

Thor looked down on his men. Most were still moving, gasping for air. He looked across the clearing toward where Newcomb had been hit. All he saw was a black lump partially covered by snow.

Returning his attention to the bloody ground behind the crosses, Thor grasped his rifle. With his good hand, he pressed a release button, freeing the assault rifle from the 20mm barrel, laser rangefinder, and fire-control computer. Lighter, it would be easier to handle on his weaker left side. He tossed the grenade launcher toward the base of the nearest cross—Kyle Stanley's.

Limping down off the ridge and into the clearing, Adams found himself firing single rounds into several of the bodies he found quivering. With his men hanging above them, he had no alternative. As the Captain stumbled

toward where he had last seen Newcomb, he did two counts in his head—
how many robed protagonists had been dancing when they had arrived,
and how many rounds he had discharged from his 30-shot clip. He had a
second clip for each of his four weapons, but there might not be time to
unleash and install them if things turned ugly again.

There were thirty dead Afghanis in addition to Halam Ghumani. That
was fewer than the three dozen they had counted earlier. It wasn't over,
he reflected, wondering what had made some turn to fight, others turn
tail to run, and more still to walk toward the barrage as if they wanted to
die. And then there was the look in their eyes—evil, ungodly, hateful.

Thor was somehow unwilling to pass on the other side of the crosses
and stare into his men's faces. He knew that alone there was nothing he
could do to provide relief, to get them down. Gazing up at them and then
leaving to find Isaac was more than either victims or savior could have
endured.

Adams called out to his friend over the intercom, but there was no
response. With the assault rifle in his left hand and his right arm dangling
at his side, he made his way to the north ridge. As he began to climb, his
right leg became a liability. He couldn't lift it high enough to step over or
around the boulders in his path. The puncture wound in his thigh was
bleeding profusely, and the pain nearly immobilized him.

"Great," he said to no one in particular. He couldn't decide if he
should open his first-aid kit and diminish the bleeding or press on to find
his fallen comrade. Acquiescing to his training, he sat down on the rock
he was trying to scale, put the rifle down, and reached into his vest pocket.
Removing its contents, he attend to his wounds. If he bled to death, they
would all die.

Tying a tourniquet-style bandage loosely in place, Adams scaled the
incline without his rifle. The ascent was slower than he would have liked,
and certainly more painful, but he knew he was within moments of finding Isaac. And he knew he was still alive; he *had* to be. There was no other
way to get their men off the infernal crosses.

About thirty feet up the northern ridge, Thor found Newcomb lying
face down. He was still breathing but unconscious. Adams picked up
Isaac's rifle and placed it to one side. With his left arm he reached for the
Israeli's uphill side, turning him over. Isaac's wraparound helmet was riddled with dents. Removing it with one hand was harder than he expected.

Reaching into his open first-aid pouch, Thor found the smelling salts.
He placed the vial under the Major's nose. Startled and a little surprised
to be alive, Isaac looked up groggily at Thor. "What'd I miss?"

The scene was hell frozen over. Nine nearly naked men were hanging on crosses, dying. Thirty crimson-spattered robes were piled in heaps throughout the clearing. Ghumani had mostly disappeared beneath a reddened blanket of powder.

Isaac tried to stand but immediately slumped back down. "Ahhhrgh. I think my ribs are busted," he groaned.

"Can you move?"

"Yeah. Help me up, Cap'n," Isaac coughed. "Let's get our guys down." Seeing double, there were more of them than he had remembered.

✡   ✞   ☾

OMEN QUAGMER, Kahn Haqqani, and Aymen Halaweh made their way to the crude landing strip in the first of the two Russian personnel carriers. Their plane, having flown in the previous afternoon, was waiting for them under the same camouflage tenting that had once hidden the training camp bunker from satellite view. Halam Ghumani was supposed to join them as soon as he was finished gloating.

With the starry-eyed Aymen Halaweh at his side, Omen Quagmer worked with the pilots, uncovering the plane and loading their gear. First on board was their new high-tech treasure. They stashed it safely inside the baggage compartment. They had nine SFG suits, four British, three Israeli, and two American. All had a matching helmet and support pack. Their prize included a collection of state-of-the-art weapons all begging to be re-tasked.

During the rough twenty-minute ride out of the mountainous camp, Omen had wondered why the distribution of uniforms was so odd. Why nine? Why twice as many Royal Marines as American Special Forces? Why three Israelis? Had they missed something? A stickler for detail, the inconsistencies troubled him. He had heard a rumor about a downed American helicopter in Kashmir. Maybe that explained it.

Kahn couldn't be bothered with such trivia. He was as proud as a peacock in the elegantly embroidered robe he had donned for the occasion. He couldn't wait to reach Baghdad, meet with the press, strut. He was far too important to get his hands dirty helping the others.

Ready to go, Omen Quagmer looked up in pride. The plane was as perfect as his plan, proof positive he was one of the world's great logisticians. He had chosen a Pilatus, the only aircraft with the unique combination of performance criteria needed to make their rapid escape into Iraq. It came equipped with the avionics to fly in and out of these horrid conditions, land in less than a thousand feet on gravel, and take off again without refueling. Flying high and swiftly to their destination fifteen hundred miles away, this was a magic carpet for the new world order.

The insatiable Halam Ghumani had predictably announced that he wanted to stay with his guests a little while longer. As the party's host, he didn't want to be rude. Besides, he had grown fond of crucifixions. "By the time you have the plane readied, I'll be there," he had promised the unbelieving Omen.

Not surprisingly, Halam was late. Quagmer dialed Ghumani's satellite phone. There was no answer. "Mohammed," he shouted to the pilot, "did you bring a satellite cam as I instructed?"

"Yes, sir. It's in the cabin, behind the right rear seat," he responded. "I'll get it for you."

Omen scrambled to set up the satellite cam's computer and antenna. Kahn, still pacing, looked on. He had been rehearsing his responses to the questions he thought the adoring Muslim media might ask, especially his supporters at al-Jazeera.

Quagmer reached for his Palm XIV, looked up the number of Sky Cam One, and dialed. In accordance with their plan, they had left a satellite camera in the clearing intending to broadcast the culmination of the crucifixions. Befuddling the infidels had been a great victory. The gruesome scene was sure to stir wild celebrations among Muslims and wailing cries for retreat and peace in the West.

The connection made, the picture Omen had been expecting burst onto the screen—nine men hanging on crosses, fighting for their lives. He breathed a sigh of relief. *At least Halam's gone*, he thought.

Any moment now, Omen knew, they would be winging their way out of Afghanistan, over Iran, and into Iraq. It would be first class. The ride had been catered. The aircraft came complete with two mini-galleys stuffed with rich foods and fine wines. Abstinence was for the masses.

Not wanting to delay their departure, Omen reached out and hit the shut-off switch. But as he pressed the button, the image of two men dressed in suits like those he had just loaded onto the plane came into view. The picture faded to black.

Suddenly queasy, Quagmer hit the power switch again. As soon as the lights flickered, he hit redial. "Kahn, Aymen, come here!" he shouted.

As the three terrorists gathered around the screen, their eyes widened. They watched as two men dragged something, somebody, into view. The trio looked on in horror as they raised the bloodied head of their fallen leader.

Omen switched the power off again. He folded up the computer as

Kahn took care of the antenna. The three ran toward the gangway. "We depart *now!*" Omen ordered, clearly distressed.

"I thought we were expecting a fourth passenger," the pilot protested.

"There won't be a fourth passenger. He's dead. Let's get out of here before they kill us too!" Quagmer quickly took his seat, across the aisle from Aymen. He fastened his seatbelt, shaking violently.

Kahn sat directly behind them. There was more room in the rear seats for his bloated ego. The loss of Halam Ghumani, he reflected, was not an altogether bad thing. He smelled opportunity. With Halam gone, it would be his turn to shine, his turn to do Allah proud—or at least that's what the faithful would be led to believe. They lost one in battle, so Kahn Haqqani was about to go to war.

Omen was paranoid, as nervous as an overweight lamb at a wolf's convention. Without Halam's charisma, would money still flow into al-Qaeda's coffers? Without Halam's prestige, would anyone be able to control Kahn's insanity, his insatiable ego? They had won the battle, but had they lost the war?

The copilot raised and locked the gangway door. The pilot reached up to hit the battery switch and checked as the engine instruments came alive. Sensing the panic in Omen's voice, he dispensed with the normal checklist and fired the ignition.

The pilot taxied to the downwind end of the two thousand-foot-long mountain airstrip. He lowered the flaps to thirty degrees. At an altitude of nine thousand feet, they would need all the lift the wings could provide.

The flight crew was grateful for a reduced fuel load and for the weight saved by one fewer passenger. They would have preferred to have another thousand feet of runway and a few more minutes of flight prep, but Omen was frantically motioning for them to go. It was like he expected an attack to suddenly roar out of the clouded sky. The pilots knew only fools would fly in these conditions.

The makeshift runway had been created by partially straightening and widening a dirt road between neighboring villages. There had once been telephone poles along the side, but they had been brought down long before the strip was built, victims of a war that never seemed to end.

The pilot taxied the expensive bird to the last place wide enough for him to swing the fifty foot wingspan around without scraping rocks. They were now covered with a heavy dusting of snow. That wasn't going to help. Generating sufficient lift was challenge enough at this altitude.

Facing down the "runway," the pilot moved the plane back by lifting two control levers on the throttle, reversing the prop's pitch. The five-ton aircraft rolled backwards, giving the plane the maximum opportunity to get airborne. Then, with the brakes locked, he moved the throttles full forward. The machine skidded on the loose gravel no matter how hard the crew pushed on the pedals. The brakes were no match for a twelve hundred horsepower turbine at full gallop.

Released, the turboprop lunged forward as if out of a slingshot. Within fifteen hundred feet the nose wheel left the bumpy strip. In ground effect, the pilot accelerated, following the curvature of the road before finally pulling back on the yoke and pointing the craft skyward. The miracle of climbing at over two thousand feet per minute in the thin air was both good and bad. Within seconds they would be IMC, in the clouds, blind as a bat.

Encircled by "cumulo-granite," the pilots' dark euphemism for the stone "clouds" that surrounded them, they would be entirely reliant on their instruments to "see" their way out of the narrow canyon. Their very lives depended on the technology.

Technology. Kahn appreciated the irony and laughed out loud. He had counted on the enemy's technology to get his trap noticed. It had been the latest military technology that had brought them to his doorstep in the middle of a moonless night. Yet he had defeated the infidels' wizardry with a simple trap. Even his crosses were decidedly low-tech.

On outstretched wings their magic carpet rose, veered to miss the peaks, then turned west out of the high valley. At 25,000 feet they broke through the tops of the clouds and chased the sun.

6

RESURRECTION

Relative calm had descended upon the clearing. Halam Ghumani's wrists and ankles were now shackled with the same kind of lock ties that had secured Team Uniform. He was wounded but alive, bleeding badly from the face, leg, and arm. Adams kicked Halam's shattered gun away. Isaac kicked its owner's crotch. It was small consolation.

Friday night's long journey into hell now seemed like ancient history. The outcome of their battle with nature had been a bad omen. Adams wished he could turn back the clock, rewind the tape, and start all over.

Isaac noted the severity of Thor's wounds. "You okay?"

"I'll live," he said, hobbling to the nearest cross. Both men had removed their helmets. Thor had slithered out of his pack as well, keeping it attached to the helmet cam. It was his only link to salvation.

Adams looked up at the dark body of his best friend. He screamed inside. With only one foot attached to the upright, Kyle Stanley had been unable to push himself up and breathe. He was nearly dead. "We're going to get you off that thing, pal. Hold on."

Using his good arm and leg, the Captain leaned his shoulder against his friend's cross and lifted as the Major, broken ribs and all, mustered what strength he could. They strained and grunted but to no avail. The base of the wooden beam had swollen within its snow-filled recess. The men repositioned themselves. "On the count of three," Thor panted.

"One, two, *lift!*" they grunted in unison. They gave it all they had. It began to break free, but as it did the top-heavy cross tilted backwards. Isaac threw his body underneath it to deaden the blow. The heavy beam caught him squarely in the back, pounding him into the snow.

The wind rushed into Kyle's lungs and out of Isaac's. Stanley tried to speak, but his tongue was stuck to the roof of his mouth. The fluids had drained from his body and pooled in his lungs. He managed to croak out a word fragment, "thirs...."

Hoping he had understood, the Captain pulled his canteen tube from his side and leaned over, giving his friend a drink.

"Thought I was gonna die," he coughed, involuntarily trying to remove the fluid from his lungs. "Get...others," he panted.

With Thor's help, Newcomb was able to crawl out from under the cross. But the impact had forced one of his broken ribs into a lung, puncturing it. Gasping for air, it took all the strength he could muster just to climb to his feet. Bent over, hands on his knees for support, he staggered toward McCaile's cross.

Adams looked on in amazement. "You gonna be able to do this?"

Isaac swung his head, motioning Thor over. "No choice."

The Captain limped into position. "One, two, *lift!*" They both groaned in pain as they struggled with the rough timber. Adams thought about the logs he'd had to lift to prove himself at BUD/S. He thought about Kyle, still nailed to one. Reaching deep down, he summoned more strength. The cross slowly began to rise. Unlike the one before it, Bentley's cross tumbled forward, out of control.

The two men did all they could to arrest the fall, but the farther it leaned the faster it plunged. If it had not been for the eight inches of powdery snow, Bentley would have been crushed. Thor used his left arm to raise and twist the crossbar. As the beam settled back, facing the sky, Adams apologized, "Sorry, McCaile. We're not very good at this."

Being dumped face down in the snow hadn't been all bad. Melted ice crystals had moistened McCaile's parched tongue enough to release it. "Cut...hand free. Fix...shoulder. I'll do...the rest."

"Your hacksaw," Newcomb choked out. "Still have it?"

"Yeah. Right front pocket...but, um, can you give me a hand? I can't get to it," Thor said, trying to reach around with his left hand. If the situation hadn't been so dismal, they would have laughed at their predicament.

Isaac removed the all-purpose tool and unleashed the hacksaw as he had seen the Captain do earlier. He leaned over Bentley's upper torso, placing his hands on his knees. Looking at McCaile, he wheezed, "Right or left handed?"

"Right." There was no need to tell him that his left wrist had been crushed by Aymen's errant hammering.

The Major moved into position and began sawing. It took less than a minute to sever the spike where it was the thinnest, just below Bentley's right wrist. The metal was old, brittle, and corroded. He carefully lifted his hand and jerked the nail free.

"Now this is gonna hurt," Thor said as he worked McCaile's rotator cup, forcing the ball back into its socket.

Bentley hardly grimaced, chewing on a mouthful of snow. "You do good work, sir. I'll take it from here. Get the Israelis down 'fore they die. Ghumani axed their legs."

With his feet still affixed and a hole in his wrist, Bentley awkwardly sawed his other hand free. He wondered where his strength had gone. It felt as if his heart had melted within him.

Yacob Seraph was next. The two men assumed the same positions they had used to free Stanley and McCaile. At first they failed. Moving down lower on Yacob's cross and trying to use the larger muscles in their legs to lift, they threw themselves so aggressively into the second attempt, the cross broke loose and went airborne. Somehow Isaac was able to pull the base toward him, causing man and tree to settle a bit more gently, this time facing up.

Yacob made an ungodly sound as he gasped for air. The pain was overwhelming. His cry was long overdue. He was surprised his vocal cords still worked after having been rearranged by Ghumani's jab.

"We'll cut you...." Isaac was unable to complete his sentence. He looked down at the ground. His punctured lung was killing him.

"Let me." With his "good" hand McCaile sat Isaac down near his comrade. "I'll take over as soon as you reset my left shoulder."

"Where's...saw?" Isaac's voice was barely audible.

"With Kyle. I cut a hand free and set his shoulder. He'll bring it to you when he's done with the other nails."

With hammered feet, two strong legs, and one functional hand, Bentley helped the Captain lift the next cross, the one tormenting Moshe Keceph. He had been the third up and would be the fourth down. As Moshe's cross fell softly into the snow, Adams stared at his crushed hand.

"What kind of animal would do this?"

"*That* kind," Bentley said, pointing toward Halam Ghumani. "Evil."

They gave Moshe water, but he didn't speak. Rage consumed his words. He craved revenge. Nothing short of the deaths of Kahn and Halam would satiate his blood lust.

Nearly nude, Kyle Stanley crawled to Joshua's cross. He had managed to yank what was left of his underwear up to cover himself. With one good leg and lots of heart, he tried to lift the cross himself, but he'd lost too much blood. The knife wound he had suffered at Ghumani's hands had taken its toll. Hanging on a cross hadn't helped much either.

Seeing Stanley struggle, McCaile and Adams moved in. With the strength of three, they were able to control Joshua's cross as it came down. Unfortunately, he wasn't breathing. Like Moshe before him, his legs had been broken. The pounding mallet blows Halam Ghumani had given his heart had nearly killed him.

Adams responded immediately. He knelt beside Joshua and gave him mouth to mouth, filling his lungs with air. It did no good.

Knowing his own experience, McCaile coughed, "We need to drain his lungs."

Stanley feverishly went to work cutting Abrams' wrists free. It took several minutes. All the while, Adams continued breathing for him. Once he was released, they bent Josh over the best they could. His feet were still nailed. Lifting him at the waist, Stanley was able to eliminate some of the bodily fluids that had pooled in his lungs. Then, in a frantic rush to save his life, Thor resumed mouth-to-mouth resuscitation. The contusions on Joshua's chest precluded shifting to CPR. Over time, success came—slowly, but it came. Joshua coughed, smiled weakly, and tried to give his friends a thumbs-up. His thumbs worked no better than his lungs.

As Thor worked on Joshua, Kyle and Bentley tended to the first of the Brits. They looked up at Blake Huston. There was no rank anymore, no national favoritism. The nearest cross was brought down first. The freed simply made their way down the line.

The Americans lifted the Major's cross with relative ease. They had developed a system, and it appeared to be working. As they laid Huston back into the snow, he quickly filled his lungs with a deep breath. Adams gave him a drink. "I'm probably in the best shape." He wasn't bragging. "If you can get me off this thing, I can help."

"Major Newcomb, do you still have the saw?" McCaile asked.

"Yeah," he wheezed. He had just finished freeing Yacob. Isaac tossed the tool to Bentley, who went to work freeing Huston's right wrist. When he had finished, he and Kyle set his shoulder and moved on.

There were only three crosses remaining—all bearing Brits: Childress, Powers, and Sullivan. Bentley and Kyle stared up at them for a brief moment. The image was unmistakable: Golgotha, Calvary, the place of crucifixion in Jerusalem. There, two thousand years ago, there had been three crosses like these, also erected on a Friday afternoon in April.

In position, Stanley, the Navy SEAL, and McCaile, the Army Ranger, began to lift. But as they did, a hellish barrage of gunfire whistled past them. The only men standing, they were the best targets. The second burst found them. Stanley was creased in the side; McCaile was hit in the thigh. Both men fell.

Adams had left his rifle on the north ridge. Cursing his carelessness, he reached around his body with his left hand and grabbed his Beretta. Lying in the snow, gun pointed in the direction of the incoming fire, he searched for the enemy.

Isaac had brought his rifle with him off the ridge. It was now leaning against the base of Kyle's cross. Having just finished cutting Moshe loose, he wheezed, "Cap'n, my gun…first cross." It was all he could do to get the words out.

They were in trouble. The situation had gone from bad to worse. Two had broken legs. Joshua was breathing, but barely. Moshe was still affixed to his cross. Isaac's concussion, broken ribs, and punctured lung had rendered him more liability than asset. The three Americans had but three fully functional legs between them, if you didn't count nail holes. Two of them had but one arm that still worked; the other had a bullet wound in his side. Huston was feverishly trying to extricate himself. He had been nailed to a cross for what seemed like hours.

"They're on the south ridge," Bentley coughed out. That was the farthest from the three remaining crosses. As they began to fire again, Isaac remembered that his 15mm fragmentation weapon was still strapped to his wrist. *Perfect.* The Afghanis were hiding behind rocks high up on the ridge and would be tough to hit any other way. Both the Captain and the Major still had standard grenades strapped to their belts, but there was no way to throw them, not that far, not in their condition.

Propping himself up on a fallen cross, Isaac aligned his right wrist with his right eye. He set the laser rangefinder for the rocks just beyond the gunman, but his vision was badly blurred. There were two of everything. Except terrorists—there were six of them. Firing the first fragmentation round, he watched as it splintered on a rock outcropping.

Sitting up so he could saw his feet free, Huston was now an ideal target. The Afghanis nicked him twice—in the left arm and shoulder.

McCaile dragged himself toward the nearest pile of dead Afghanis and searched their remains for a suitable weapon. He had heard automatic rifle fire as they'd cavorted in ecstasy over the plight of their captives; he hoped the Afghanis hadn't wasted all their ammo in celebration. Crawling through the bloody snow, the Lieutenant was almost as disappointed as he was cold. The first three guns were little better than clubs, their clips empty. Bentley began pushing dead bodies around in hopes of finding something that would shoot back. Having been rendered one-handed didn't make the task any easier.

Adams hadn't discharged a shot. Unless the robed men charged, his pistol would be of little value. Rolling on his side, then his back, side, and stomach again, Thor negotiated his way toward Newcomb's rifle.

Isaac picked a different focal point. He sent the second fragmentation round on its way. It was no more effective than the first. The assailants had found a perfect position, surrounded by boulders on all sides. They were free to rain fire upon those below without being targets themselves.

McCaile found an AK-47 with a nearly full clip and began to fire up into the rocky fortress. It did no damage, but at least it kept the Afghanis from shooting back as freely. Within moments, Yacob joined him.

Taking advantage of the distraction, Adams pulled Isaac's rifle to his chest and continued rolling toward the south ridge. As he did, he compounded his agony, separating the bones in his broken right arm. Newcomb, McCaile, and Seraph followed his progress and provided cover.

Now on the backside of the ridge, Adams was in familiar territory. This is where he had first seen the living trees and their hideous silhouettes. With his good leg and arm, he pulled himself up as his comrades kept the Afghanis pinned down. There was still plenty of return fire, but it was less focused now that their foe was distracted.

Thor reached a vantage point on the knoll. He unstrapped the first of his three grenades. Quickly glancing over a protective rock, he located his target and lobbed it with his left hand. It bounced off an outcropping and exploded harmlessly in front of the makeshift bunker, cascading rocks everywhere. While causing an ear-piercing barrage of echoes, it did little more than frighten the gunmen. He tossed the second as the Afghanis turned to shoot him. It fared no better. With two grenades gone, the good guys were in trouble.

Adams, now visible with his SFG pack down in the clearing, dragged himself higher while the ambulatory members of Team Un-uniformed provided covering fire. He knew he would have to find a spot closer to the enemy. With just one grenade left, his last toss would have to be perfect. As time ticked relentlessly by, his men began to take more hits. Between nails and bullets, they averaged nearly five holes per man.

Isaac fired his last two fragmentation rounds. They were ineffective. Bentley was now on his second rifle, having shot the first clip dry. Freed at last, Huston joined him, providing additional cover.

Growing more brazen, almost as if they wanted to die, the robed men sprayed a concentrated volley. They hit Newcomb and Stanley. Then for good measure they raised their sights and began to shoot at the three Brits still hanging on crosses. Now bleeding profusely, they would die if not brought down.

Adams continued to struggle with rocks and snow as he crawled up the back side of the ridge. He redoubled his efforts, summoning strength from deep inside. He even offered a prayer to a God he didn't know. Ignoring the pain, the debilitated Captain succeeded in reaching the summit of the imposing crest. From this spot, directly above the Islamic warriors, Thor prepared to drop his last grenade. He pulled the pin, released the handle, and counted, "Muslim one, Muslim two...." With that, he dropped his surprise package into their rocky sanctuary. It exploded a second later, killing the robed riflemen, the last of the enemy, he hoped.

Once again able to move, Isaac finished cutting Joshua's feet free. It was slow going—his right arm had been hit in the last attack. After releasing him, he directed his attention to damage control. Everyone was still alive, but barely. He had no idea how they were going to get the Brits down. "Who can still walk?" the Major choked out.

"I can," Huston said, setting down his borrowed rifle.

"So can I," McCaile and Seraph coughed in unison. In reality, they could barely limp.

Stanley was in bad shape. So were the Israelis. That left the walking wounded to do the impossible. Grabbing the base of Lad Childress' cross, they gave it all they had, but it didn't budge. Figuring it had swollen in the wet snow, they moved on to Cliff Powers. They failed again.

At the base of Captain Ryan Sullivan's tree, they prayed silently. His cross at least moved. They redoubled their efforts, moved lower, and lifted it. But as before, they lost control of the heavy beam as it worked free. It crashed back into the snow. Sullivan was so dazed he didn't seem to care. The first to be crucified, he had hung there longer than anyone. Isaac gave him water from his canteen, then worked to cut him free.

By the time McCaile, Seraph, and Huston returned to Powers, they were joined by Adams. Now, with four good legs and four strong arms, they managed to extract Cliff's cross before he bled to death. As each man was lowered, the others cut him loose and set his shoulders. They used the material in Newcomb's first-aid kit to treat the worst of the injuries.

And then there was one. Childress alone hung from his cross. Rising and falling, he fought for his life. But try as they might, the combined strength of Adams, McCaile, Seraph, and Huston was insufficient. The base had swollen too large for the men to remove.

"Isaac, give me my saw." Thor limped over to his friend. "Huston, I need you down on your hands and knees in front of Lad's cross. I'm going to climb on your back, step on the spikes sticking out of his feet, and then cut his arms free. Lad, are you listening?" the Captain asked.

He nodded.

"Good. When I cut the heads off the nails, don't slide your wrists forward until I free your feet. Otherwise, who knows what'll happen."

Thor managed to climb up on Huston's back, stepping on his hips to avoid aggravating his dislocated shoulders. He lifted his injured leg, balancing himself with his left arm. In position, he wrapped it around the cross so he could raise his left foot and hang it precariously over both nails. He hoped they'd be sturdy enough to hold his weight.

Ignoring his own pain, Adams did the impossible. He used his fractured right arm to brace himself and cut with his left. As he did, Lad continued forcing his body up to exhale, letting it down to breathe in.

"Hang in there, pal." *Probably not the most sensitive thing I ever said.* "I'm halfway through the second nail."

Childress tried to smile. Blessed relief was but a five convulsive rises away. Even with the Captain draped over him, he knew he could endure the additional pain.

With the second spike headless, Huston resumed his position. The Captain stepped off the nails onto Blake's back. Once down, he handed his saw to McCaile. Bentley did the honors, slicing both spikes above Lad's feet. Thor and Bentley held his ankles. Blake and Yacob reached up to catch Childress.

"Okay, Lad. Pull your wrists off the nails and lean forward. We'll catch you." Thor couldn't even imagine how much pain he was asking his comrade to bear.

Lad took in one final breath, gritted his teeth, pushed up on his feet, released his hands, and threw his body forward, hoping his friends would lift his feet from the spikes as others caught him. It worked exactly as Thor had hoped. They were all down, all alive. He nearly cried.

"Oww!" Bentley yelled, stepping away from Lad's cross.

"What?" His companions turned to look.

He held up his index finger. "I got a splinter!"

Somehow, at that moment, they all knew there was hope.

Although they were down, they were nowhere near out. It wouldn't be long before the sun would descend beneath the towering peaks to the west, casting long chilling shadows over the clearing. The men now had a new enemy. They prayed they had not endured all this pain only to freeze to death in the end. It would still take a miracle to survive. Just two of the eleven were wearing clothes.

The four semi-ambulatory men worked together, dragging the others to the relative comfort of the barracks. They pulled Joshua and Moshe in first, trying to figure out how they were going to splint their broken legs. The Brits were hauled in next. The wounds they'd sustained in the final gun battle were as life-threatening as the crucifixions had been. They wouldn't survive long without rescue.

Isaac and Kyle were the last of the non-ambulatory men to be pulled into the shelter of the faux barracks. Thor Adams, Bentley McCaile, Yacob Seraph, and Blake Huston headed back outside. It was still snowing as late afternoon segued into early evening. The temperature had dropped from its balmy high of 34 degrees Fahrenheit, to a damp 26.

"McCaile, Huston," Adams said. "See what you can take from the Afghanis. Clothes first. We need to get you and the others covered. Then guns, ammo, water, whatever. Even if a rifle is old, we can use the stock as a splint. Yacob, let's go see what we can find in the other barracks."

It was sort of like Valley Forge. Washington's Colonials had only tattered clothing, worn boots, and precious little ammunition. They didn't have the sustenance to fight off the cold, much less the Hessians. But the German mercenaries who had been hired to fight on behalf of the British had the best of all these things. So the audacious Washington crossed the nearly frozen river and took them. It was his first victory in what had already been a long war of retreat and attrition. And so it was for Thor Adams. The Captain needed a victory this cold day, no matter how small.

Thor and Yacob learned that every building was constructed in a similar fashion. They were amazed they hadn't blown away. The winds were howling through the mountain passes as the men ripped down the brown drapes that had comprised the back "walls" of the barracks. Adams and Seraph figured they could be used to cover the floor—and the wounded. They would provide insulation until McCaile and Huston could retrieve enough of the slain Afghanis' robes.

Back with his men, the Captain said, "Guys, we're gonna pull you aside for a minute. We found some large sheets. We'll spread one out as a carpet; the other will serve as a blanket." Those that could, moved; others were helped. Thor handed a corner to Yacob.

As they spread the first sheet, the Israeli spoke softly to himself, just loud enough that others could hear. It was scripture, eerie and appropriate: "Like the whirlwinds sweeping through the southland, an invader comes from the desert, from a land of terror. A dire vision has been shown to me. The traitor betrays; the looter loots. I will bring an end to all the groaning they have caused."

The Captain was mesmerized by the poignancy of Seraph's words. But he wasn't done. As they moved the wounded back into position and spread the second brown sheet-like blanket over them, he continued from memory. "My body is racked with pain. I am staggered by what I hear. I am bewildered by what I see. My heart falters; fear makes me tremble. The twilight I longed for has become a horror to me."

"Is that from the Torah, Yacob?" the Captain asked, staring at the gash Halam Ghumani had carved in the Israeli's throat.

"The Prophet Isaiah. Appropriate, isn't it?" Yacob coughed.

"Sounds like it was written for us, right down to being staggered and bewildered by what I've seen and heard."

"It goes on, Captain. It talks about spreading rugs, like we're doing now. That's what brought it to mind. Then it says the officers are to get up, prepare their shields, and go and be on the lookout."

"Yeah. Good idea," Adams answered. "That Isaiah guy's right. Who can go with me?"

Before anyone could volunteer, Bentley McCaile and Blake Huston hobbled through the door carrying their first load of Afghani clothing. "It ain't much, men, but it's gotta beat bare skin," McCaile said.

Seeing that the purloined clothing was frozen stiff, the Captain headed back to the far barracks where he had noticed a small stash of firewood. He would ready his shield and post a lookout when he returned. Right now, they needed a little heat to keep the twilight from becoming a horror.

The draped side of the "infirmary" was downwind. Thor built his fire a few feet beyond using a flint implement that was part of his collapsible 'toolbox'. He raised and parted the drape as the blaze grew large enough to provide warmth.

Bentley and Blake continued to "requisition" all they could from the dead Muslim warriors. They found thirty-one rifles, some of which were antiques—World War II vintage. Many, however, looked reliable enough to keep the bad guys at bay should there be another attack.

Adams delivered more firewood as Huston and McCaile attempted to thaw and dry clothing for their comrades. Yacob Seraph tore some of the robes into bandages. But he knew his efforts would be in vain if they were not rescued soon. Most every man needed a transfusion, and in these filthy conditions their wounds would soon become infected.

The Israelis still had fishhooks hanging from their noses. The barbs had made them difficult to dislodge. As McCaile made tasteless jokes about Jewish punk rock musicians, he used the needle-nose apparatus on Adams' tool to cut off Yacob's hook. Then Yacob removed the others' Assyrian facial jewelry.

The Captain dragged himself back to the north rim of the clearing. He wanted to retrieve his assault rifle before it was dark. He had picked up his helmet and pack on the way, tossing Isaac's helmet toward the barracks. Climbing the lower part of the ridge was more difficult than he remembered. He had lost a great deal of blood, and the bullet wound in his leg was now debilitating. With a God-given ability to tolerate pain, Adams, still running on adrenaline, made his way to the top of the ridge, picking up his rifle along the way.

From his perch he scanned the horizon. Remembering for the first time in hours that there was a world beyond this place, he began to broadcast their dilemma. "Captain Thor Adams to Pentagon. I sure hope you can hear me. All eleven members of Team Uniform are alive. I repeat, all men are alive. Every man has been shot, at least once, some multiple times. We have busted legs and shattered arms. Nine were being crucified when we found them. Yeah," he said, collecting himself, "you heard me right. They *crucified* nine of my men. Whatever we've come to believe about these people is *wrong*. If we don't make it out of here, learn that from our sacrifice."

The Captain caught his breath and started in again. "It is early evening, snowing, ceilings are still low, maybe fifty feet AGL in the valley. The wind is strong and variable, swirling in all directions. Extraction at this time is impossible."

Impossible or not, Thor needed to get his men out. He hated the idea of asking others to risk their lives, but he couldn't just watch good men die. "HALO jumpers would help, but the terrain, low viz, and flukie winds are a problem. Hopefully, conditions will improve. I'm going down to the clearing now. The open area between ridges is two hundred meters wide. I will broadcast my GPS coordinates from its center. Even with poor visibility tomorrow, choppers, one at a time, should be able to hover above the debris and extract our team. Adams out."

Before he descended, the Captain put his SFG through all of its functions. He looked over the back side of the ridge. Using the infrared mode, he saw several small red blobs moving in the distance. They would soon have visitors.

In half the time it took him to ascend the craggy incline, Adams made it back to the valley floor. He limped to the center and picked up the grenade launcher he had tossed near the cross that had once held his best friend. "Captain Adams to Pentagon. GPS coordinates are...." He read them off carefully, down to the fraction of a second. "There is but one cross still standing. It is set along the northern ridge." He didn't want a chopper blade clipping it.

"On infrared I spotted what looked like three men at a range of two miles headed in this direction. They are currently zero five zero degrees from my present position. We will try to hold them off." Before he turned and headed inside the barracks, he added, "Their behavior seems irrational. When we attacked, some stood and walked toward us like they wanted to die. Others ran. Now they're returning. Doesn't make sense."

Inside, the scene looked like the aftermath of Gettysburg. Broken and bloodied bodies littered the ground. Silhouetted by a raging fire, Adams began a roll call. "Kyle?"

There was no answer. "He's unconscious, sir," Bentley said. "He was shot in the side and in the buttocks. His left leg's got a nasty wound. He's not gonna live if we don't get him out of here."

Adams would have given his life to save any man under his command. But in Kyle's case he would have done so without regret. "How are you holding together, McCaile?"

The Army Ranger did an inventory. "My left wrist is shattered. Bullet wounds in my right thigh and left shoulder. Superficial. My feet are pretty busted up and...well, you know about the rest." McCaile was as tough as the nails that had pierced him.

"Can you shoot a gun?"

"Yeah. Who do you want me to kill?" The bravado was endearing but unrealistic. Had it not been for Bentley's relative strength, Adams would have looked for another volunteer.

"We're expecting company. Three men at less than two miles. Who else can shoot?" the Captain asked.

"I can," Major Blake Huston answered.

"What kind of shape are you in?"

"Just the regular stuff. You know, nail holes in my wrists and feet. Bullet holes in my left side and arm. Can't breathe real well. Other than that, I'm good to go. Got a gun?"

"Use mine. I've got Newcomb's. How you making out, Isaac?"

"Bad. The lung..." he hacked. "No more gun fights for me. Things'll kill ya."

"You still seeing double?"

"Yeah, unless you got a twin."

"Okay. Just stay put, pal. I figure we've got enough enemies as it is."

"Captain," Yacob Seraph hacked. "I can shoot. Got a busted foot, but my eyes are good. My thumb's screwed, but nothing's wrong with my trigger finger." His voice sounded peculiar. The wound to his throat had damaged his vocal cords.

"Mine's fine too, sir." Powers, had a hacking cough as well. Fluid had gathered in everyone's lungs. "But I'm the last of it. Sullivan's unconscious. So is Childress. They lost too much blood. I know they've got to be thirsty, but I can't get any water in 'em. Moshe and Joshua are in worse shape. We're all weak. Something about hanging there wiped us out."

Thor just shook his head. Cliff Powers, like the others, wasn't going to be much good in a fight. "*Man,* I'm proud of you guys." Regaining his composure, he added, "Here, use my knife to cut some holes to shoot through down low in the front wall. These thin boards aren't going to provide much protection."

"Captain, we could use the crosses as barricades." Huston volunteered. "Let's drag a few over."

"Sure," Thor answered as the two limped out into the snow. They were quite a sight. The Captain was wearing the best of the best, high-tech all the way. The Major was modeling a filthy Afghani robe at least three sizes too small. He was even sporting a turban. Forget about the lice; it kept his head warm. Most of the Afghanis had feet smaller than his sister's, so he had wrapped his in strips of cloth cut from their robes.

"What do you make of these guys?" the Major asked.

Turning to answer, the Captain did a double take. Blake Huston, in his blood-spattered robe and turban, looked a whole lot like one of them. "Different species, aren't they?"

"Got a clue what makes 'em tick? I mean, screaming out Allah's name while they're torturing us—that's just too bloody bizarre."

"They believe they've got a mandate from Allah to kill."

"A bloodthirsty god? That's bull." The Major was dumfounded.

"You ever read the Qur'an? Know anything about Muhammad?"

"'Fraid not. I haven't even read the Bible," Blake confessed. "You?"

"The Bible? Yeah. The history's interesting. But the Islamic scriptures, they're something else altogether."

"Why'd you bother?" Huston helped Adams heft the second cross.

"Every time I was sent out, I found myself fighting Muslims. I wanted to understand them, that's all. Suicide bombings didn't make any sense. Nor did targeting civilians."

"Blood-thirsty killers."

"Yeah, but the most bizarre thing is what we saw here. Muslims *celebrate* death."

After lowering the cross into place, they leaned against each other, trying to catch their breath. A moment later they went off to get another. "What'ja find in the Qur'an?"

"Enough to know we're in trouble. It's mostly hateful rantings, like hearing one side of an argument. No chronological order, no historical context—at least none that I could discern. But Allah—he's got it in for Christians and Jews. He not only wants 'em dead, he can't wait to see them roast in hell. Eye-opening garbage. And Allah's pal Muhammad...," he just shook his head.

"So he's a real guy, not a god or anything."

"Just a regular guy—born, worked for a living, married money, lived well, then died. But along the way he claimed to have wrestled with a spirit in some cave."

"A cave?" Blake laughed. "Some things never change. These blokes still have a thing for caves."

"Yeah, and they're acting a lot like the Muhammad I read about. But that's another story."

Picking up the next cross, they noticed that Halam Ghumani was still alive, whimpering in the snow. "Think we ought to drag the bugger inside?" Huston asked, pushing his tormentor with his swollen foot.

"Naah. Let him freeze. If we pull him inside, the men'll kill him." As they walked away, something unnatural caught Thor's eye. It was partially hidden under the snow. "Hey, what's that, next to the rock?"

Blake leaned down to pick it up. "It's one of those satellite cams. Do you think the guys can get it to work?"

After positioning the last of the barricades, Adams carried the high-priced gear and the antenna that had collapsed next to it inside. He handed them to Yacob. "See what you can do with this thing."

Thor and Blake went back outside to inspect their fortifications. "So what'd you mean when you said 'they were acting like Muhammad'?"

"Their Prophet was a killer."

"*No bloody way.*" They repositioned the top cross on the pile, making the barricade about three feet tall.

"Yeah. I'm no expert but from what I read, he was one brutal son of a gun—like these guys we saw here today."

"It goes back that far?"

"'Fraid so," Adams said.

Just then, Seraph hollered out, "Cap'n, it works! I've got the Mossad on the line. Do you want 'em to patch in the Pentagon?"

"Heck, yeah!"

Moments later Chairman Hasler's voice entered the barracks in Nowhere, Afghanistan. "Captain Adams, are you there?"

"Yes, sir, General. It's good to hear your voice."

"Captain, we received your transmissions. I'm proud of you, son. Glad to see you got your men down. That was an ugly battle."

"Yes sir."

"Adams, we've got four Sea Hawks scheduled to extract you at first light. They've got your coordinates."

"My men are in rough shape. It'll be none too soon."

"The Sea Hawks are being accompanied by four Cobra Gun Ships, four Wart Hogs, and two Spectre Gunships. Shoot, Captain, after what we've seen, I'll send in the Marines, too, if you want 'em. *All* of 'em."

"Sir, what we need is a medic. If we don't get my men stabilized, your rescue team is going to be extracting corpses. Do you have anybody crazy enough to jump in here tonight?"

"As a matter of fact, three HALO jumpers left a couple of hours ago. Every SEAL on the *Ronald Reagan* volunteered, son. And they haven't seen the film. If the crew had seen what we saw, you'd already have the whole Navy in there, medics included."

"We could use 'em. The men need transfusions bad. We've all lost a lot of blood. We need plasma, IVs, antibiotics, bandages, clean blankets, and warm clothing. We're all dehydrated. I don't know what they did with our SFGs. Those who are conscious could use somethin' to eat, and we need weapons. Looks like it's gonna be a rough night."

"Like I said, we've got men airborne now. I'm told they're well supplied. You'll have HALO jumpers within...." the Chairman turned to his team. "They tell me less than two hours. They've got all they can carry. Should get you through till morning."

"Tell the jumpers we'll keep a fire going. The clearing is thirty meters east of that. We'll clear it of obstacles before they arrive."

"Hang in there. We're gonna get you out."

"Yes, sir...."

Hasler thought he heard gunfire as the Captain spoke.

"General, I'm gonna have to go. We've got company."

✡ ☦ ☾

SECRETARY DITROE had fallen asleep in the President's arms. By morning she had managed to compose herself. Over breakfast she explained what she'd seen in blood-curdling detail.

The President and her Defense Secretary walked back downstairs to the Press Room. The technicians had prepared a "highlights" videotape. Ditroe, unfortunately, had not been exaggerating.

The President sat silently as the tape ran. Her fingers and Susan's were interlaced. She squeezed the Secretary's hand each time a nail found its mark. It was all she could do to watch.

"Who else knows about this?" the President asked after the first man had been nailed.

"NSA, CIA, the Pentagon—the support team, that's all."

"What are they going to do with the tape, Susan?"

"Nothing. At least, not until you release it, ma'am."

"*Release it?* I want it *erased!* Where are Richard Nixon and Rosemary Woods when you need 'em?"

"Erased?" Susan repeated in disbelief.

Just then a phone rang in the AV cubicle. A man's voice could be heard over the speaker. "I'm looking for Secretary Ditroe. Is she there?"

"One moment," the technician replied.

"Ask who it is," the Secretary said just loud enough to be heard. She wasn't in a very good mood.

"Tell the Secretary it's Blaine Edwards from FOX News."

Susan stood up. Her legs were wobbly. Cautiously, she walked to the back of the room. "This is Secretary Ditroe. What can I do for you?"

"I'm the guy you kicked out of the White House Press Room yesterday, remember?"

"Yes."

"I was just wondering if you'd like to make a statement."

"A statement regarding what, Mr. Edwards?" She was trembling.

"The video. We're not going to release it until you get our men out, but when *they're* out, *it's* out.

"No, please, no, no...."

"Secretary Ditroe, would the President care to issue a statement?"

"No...no," she stammered, afraid. She stared blankly at the President who was shaking her head. The technician disconnected the call.

"How much time do we have, Susan?"

"Madam President," the techie spoke, knowing the Secretary was unable.

"Yes, son?"

"A few minutes ago, there was a satellite phone call between Chairman Hasler and Captain Adams, in Afghanistan. We weren't connected on the call, but we got it through the Captain's video cam system...."

"And...?" The President was impatient, motioning him on.

"Well, they're planning on picking them up at dawn."

"Nine this evening, ma'am," the other tech replied.

"Susan, let's get Hasler on the line."

The President hurried into the Oval Office. A few steps behind, Ditroe paused long enough to have a secretary dial the Pentagon. By the time she entered the room, they were already yelling.

"What do you mean you're sending in more men? *On whose authority?*"

"Mine."

"You *have* no authority! *I'm* the Commander-in-Chief."

"Yes, ma'am."

"Your mission was supposed to be covert, General. Now the whole world is going to see just how lame you boys are. Makes me want to puke."

"At least we agree on one thing, ma'am."

"You and your testosterone make me sick," the President added unnecessarily. "You've got one shot at getting them out, Bill. You better not escalate this thing," she threatened. "They chose to go. It was their plan. They screwed up. You send in more than the minimum needed to extract those boys, and we're gonna have a billion Muslims climbing up our butt. You can't start your own war, Bill!"

"I'm just doing my job."

"Well you can *stop* doing your job. You're *fired!*"

Hasler was calm. "After what's happened, ma'am, you're not going to find anyone willing to call off the rescue. So we're going to have to work this thing through. I'm going to get our men out. *Then* you can fire me. Ma'am."

✡   ✝   ☾

WITH THE FIRE behind them, they felt like ducks in a shooting gallery. Ironically, the crosses that had once been their damnation were now their only salvation.

"Captain, this is no good," Yacob Seraph said between bursts of automatic gunfire. "They can see us, but we can't see them."

Adams knew they were in trouble. "We've got two SFGs. Chameleon function only works on one of 'em, but since Newcomb's failed in night mode, it should be okay."

"Major, will you trade with me? Your suit for my robe?" Yacob Seraph volunteered. "I'm shorter, so it'll fit." Isaac's helmet had been hammered by Ghumani's barrage, but it was still quasi-functional.

With their gear switched on, Yacob and Thor slipped out through the draped back of the barracks. The Captain took the south ridge, leaving the enemy's right flank to the Israeli. Adams carried two of Isaac's grenades. Seraph took the other. Both men had fresh clips in their OICWs, NATO and 20mm fragmentation rounds. Their pistols, Glock and Beretta, were readied as well, clips inserted, safeties off, rounds chambered. With guns in hand, they went hunting.

The Afghanis were not easy to find. The children's game of hit and run they had played earlier when tormenting their victims was revisited. The three assailants peeked their heads over the ridgeline just long enough to fire into the barracks. Then, as quickly as they appeared, they retreated.

Cranky, sore, and shot up, the Captain was in no mood for games. With each attack he pressed on, determined to find his foe before the HALO team arrived—and before he lost any of his men. Relentlessly dragging himself over rocks and ridges, he moved ever closer, following his assailants' heat signatures and muzzle flashes.

With two punctured feet, Yacob wasn't quite as nimble as the limping Captain. He tried to climb to a higher vantage point, but couldn't. Using his infrared setting, he could trace Adams' progress. On occasion, he even spotted the Afghanis as they popped their heads over the ridge. If they got careless, he would own them.

Thor climbed down the south hill and moved in alongside the terrorists. The next time they returned to take a shot, they would pay.

Seconds turned slowly into minutes, and minutes became half an hour, but his persistence was rewarded. Three gunmen in robes, a man and two boys, slowly, quietly, made their way up the snow-covered incline. Still a quarter of a mile away, the Captain switched his H.U.D. to standard vision and then to enhanced light. He wanted to see what they might be seeing from their perspective. He was pleased. It was a total whiteout.

Switching back to infrared, the Captain knew he could be patient, wait for his best shot. Without the light of the moon, the Afghani men would never see him, no matter how close they came. Minutes continued to pass like hours as the small troop picked their way up the incline. Adams switched his rifle from fragmentation to standard ordnance. Closer they came, now within a hundred yards.

They looked like a father and his sons. But this was no ordinary family. All three were carrying Russian-made assault rifles. They weren't out on a family camping trip, a boys' weekend. They were here to kill—or be killed. There was no other choice.

Fifty yards, then twenty-five. Thor set his rifle down and unsheathed his pistol. He could hear the snow crunching beneath their feet. At ten yards he pulled the trigger, squeezing off three rounds in rapid succession. Kush, kush, kush. There was hardly a sound. Even the normal clink of expended cartridges hitting the ground was muted in the wet snow. The man and his boys simply fell in their tracks. It was all so anticlimactic.

Adams felt for pulses, grabbed their rifles, and headed back home. *Home*, he thought. What he wouldn't give to be home. The Devil himself would be embarrassed to live here.

✡ ✝ ☪

APPROACHING THE TARGET, the Viking flight crew donned oxygen masks and depressurized their craft. They slowed to a crawl, just above a 100 knots. They had finished their descent out of 35,000 feet for 21,000.

It would be the first HALO jump from a jet aircraft. The fastest turboprop aboard the *Ronald Reagan* would have taken too long to reach them.

The copilot turned to face the jumpers, telling them he was opening the bomb-bay doors. "Sixty seconds to drop."

HALO stood for High Altitude Low Opening. Today, however, it would be HAHO. Conceived during the Vietnam Conflict, the technique was designed to insert men clandestinely behind enemy lines.

"We're overloaded," the Commander warned. "We're gonna stress our chutes. Jumping lower's gonna help, but to survive, you'll need to pull your cord much sooner—nineteen thousand feet MSL—sixty-five hundred feet above the valley floor. That's a thousand feet below the highest peaks. Altimeter is thirty point one two."

Each man checked the Coleman window on his wrist-mounted altimeter. They would freefall the first 1,000 feet in eight seconds. The second thousand would evaporate in the count of three.

"Ten seconds to drop," the copilot said. "On my mark." He held up five fingers, counting down inaudibly until there was nothing but a closed fist. Just that quickly, the HALO jumpers stepped out of the bomb-bay doors and were gone.

To Thor's surprise, the SEALs beat him to the barracks. They had used the beacon fire and GPS coordinates to zero in on the clouded clearing. And they had come bearing gifts. The barracks was positively jubilant.

As Thor entered, the SEALs stood and saluted. Adams, however, dispensed with formalities and gave each a one-armed hug. Tonight they looked like angels. "Where's Yacob?" he asked.

"He hasn't returned yet, Captain," Blake answered.

Adams did an about face in hopes of finding his man. Just then the returning Israeli shouted, "Don't shoot! It's me. I am one of us!" The SEAL on sentry duty had heard Seraph's footsteps in the now-crusty snow and had come within a heartbeat of firing at him. Yacob's English wasn't the greatest, but it was good enough to save his life.

Seraph sat down, exhausted. One of the SEALs tended to his wounds. He even shared some of his unspent oxygen.

The rescue mission was carried out with flawless precision. Fresh bedding was spread, IVs inserted, wounds dressed, bandages applied. Soon every man was wearing military fatigues. They burned the robes. Team Uniform once again looked like a team, sort of. You had to overlook the busted limbs and a myriad of body piercings. Cleaned, splinted, and fed, most were even conscious. The plasma, combined with the HALO jumpers' bottled oxygen, had done wonders.

Surveying it all, Thor Adams came as close to tears as he could remember. As horrible as the sight was, it was far better than it had once been, a world better than what it might have been.

"We were as good as dead," Bentley reported to one of the SEALs. "Looking at us, it's hard to believe we won."

"I think even Stanley's gonna make it, sir," Huston said.

"Thank God." The Captain surprised himself. "How'd you guys get here so fast, anyway?"

"S3 Viking. We stepped out of the bomb-bay door."

"No way." He stared in disbelief.

"Just another day at the office, sir" the SEAL Commander replied calmly. They had brought good news. Major Cole Sumner was alive. But this wasn't the time or place for the bad news. They had been sworn to secrecy on the fate of the pilots who had brought them to this foreboding place. A man can only handle so much torment.

As his men were nursed back to life, the Captain allowed himself to relax. Soon the SEALs were focusing their attention on him, no matter how vociferously he protested. They fussed all over him, patching his wounds and setting his broken right arm. They pumped in a pint of fresh plasma and prepared a Ready-to-Eat.

The bullet in his leg had passed cleanly through the muscle and out the other side. The medic found the spent cartridge in the pant leg of the SFG and handed it to him. "A souvenir from hell, sir."

"Captain, they showed us the video before we took off. They wanted us to know what we were up against." The Commander was moved. "The most incredible thing I ever seen. I'm proud to be here, sir."

"*You're* the heroes," Yacob told the SEAL HALO jumpers. "We didn't know what we were getting into—you did. It takes balls of bronze to jump in here like Jack Wayne. We wouldn't have made it without you."

No one even bothered to correct him. Shoot, John Wayne would have changed his name for the privilege of serving with these guys.

"Now, tell me the truth. How'd you guys get here, *really?*" The Captain was having a hard time buying their Viking story.

"Bombs away, sir," one of the SEALs grinned. "I did a triple tuck, jack-knife, with a twist on the way down."

"It had to be done, sir," another answered somberly.

So it was with thankfulness in their eyes and visions of homecoming dancing in their heads, the men settled down for some much-needed shut-eye. Dead to the world, they knew nothing of the skirmishes continued throughout the night. The SEAL HALO jumpers were not only superb with their medical care, not only was their culinary prowess with an MRE a thing of legend, but they were also warriors. The odds could have been fifty to one. It didn't matter. As dawn broke over the Hindu Kush, the allied force was alive. All of them. A considerable number of Islamic militants, however, were not.

The Sea Hawks arrived at dawn, looking more like limousines than military hardware. The men could hear the sounds of rockets being launched and cannons fired. The Cobras, WartHogs, and Spectre Gunships were doing their thing, and they were close by, from the sound of it. The good guys were winning this round.

"Welcome aboard," the Sea Hawk pilot said as each man was loaded. Ryan Sullivan, Moshe Keceph, Joshua Abrams, and Lad Childress were carried onto the first chopper. Cliff Powers, Kyle Stanley, and Isaac Newcomb were placed on the second, a minute or two later. Under their own power, Yacob Seraph, Blake Huston, Bentley McCaile, and Captain Thurston Adams hobbled aboard the third bird.

The SEAL HALO jumpers boarded the last ride out. They had a guest, a shackled and sullen Halam Ghumani. They had given him just enough care to keep him alive.

The clouds had lifted during the night. It had finally stopped snowing. Thor looked down over what had been the most horrific place he had ever been. Their fire was still smoldering. The fallen crosses were clearly visible as was the one that remained erect. So were the naked and bloodied bodies of thirty-five Islamic terrorists. The hills around the ravine were littered with others.

As the helicopter rose, Adams took in the scene, observing every detail. He closed his eyes for a moment to verify how accurate his mental etching had been. Opening them again, he compared reality to the vision he had recorded in his brain. He wanted to retain it all. He knew that the scourge of Muslim madness was something few understood. He had just been on the front lines of a battle that was reshaping the world.

"What do you make of it, sir?" Yacob asked, trying to get comfortable. Filled with fluids, food, and pain medication, he was rarin' to go.

"Scary. Like kamikazes— the 'Divine Wind'—in World War II. They're dying to die. Hard to fight that," the Captain said through the pain.

"But the Japanese Emperor was no more God than I am," Yacob Seraph moaned. "Dying for him was just dying. What about those boys down there? What's their excuse?"

"If I had to guess, I'd say it was Muhammad's fault," Adams shifted to his good side. The pain of his injuries slowed his speech. "I've got a lot to learn, but from what I've read, Muhammad was a terrorist."

"That would explain it," Bentley said. "But it still doesn't make any sense. How's a guy like that start a religion? Why so many followers?"

Blake knew. "Look at Hitler, Mao, Lenin. They weren't exactly choir boys, but look at how many followers they had."

"Follow or die," Yacob coughed. "It's the same with these guys, only worse. They think dying is *good*. They're promised virgins in paradise." Like most Israelis, Seraph knew what drove the Islamic faithful to madness. Living in the shadow of the Palestinians, it was hard to miss.

McCaile was also drugged enough to be chatty. Compared to a few hours ago, he felt great. "Captain, I heard you and the Major talking about the Qur'an and the Bible last night. Everybody says they're similar, that we worship the same God. What do you think?"

"I'm no Christian, Bentley. I wouldn't know God if I saw him." Had they not just left hell, speaking of heaven would have seemed odd. But it's times like these that give rise to wisdom. It's why there are no atheists in foxholes. "I've read the Old Testament, though, you know, for the history."

"And..."

"And..." the Captain drew a deep, painful breath, "the only similarity between the Bible and the Qur'an, from what I can tell, is that one is based loosely on the other. But the stories are different. If one got 'em right, the other got 'em wrong. If one's inspired by a real God, the other one ain't."

He shifted, trying to get comfortable. "All I know for sure is that the jerks who nailed you to that cross were singing Allah's praises. You don't have to be a religious nut to know that Allah's no friend of ours."

Adams was quiet for a while, thinking. "If I were to guess, I'd say Muhammad's a fraud. The Bible was written before the Qur'an, and it's full of stories he obviously lifted. But he got 'em all fouled up. At least that's what it sounds like to me."

"How's that possible if he got it from God?" Yacob questioned.

"Guys, at this point I don't know enough to be dangerous. But there's a skunk in the woodpile someplace."

"Then follow the stench," Bentley suggested, holding his nose.

"Yeah. I think Prophet-boy's full of it," Yacob voted.

McCaile pushed it. "Where does that leave Jews and Christians, Cap?"

Adams didn't answer right away. He was comfortable being an agnostic, happy not having to deal with anybody's religious mumbo-jumbo. "Like I said, I'm not the religious type. So you're asking the wrong guy." Thor swallowed hard. "But, *somebody* was watching out for us down there."

The four Sea Hawks finally rose above the high mountains of the Hindu Kush. The sun rose in a cloud-dappled sky to the East. It was Easter Sunday. Resurrection day.

✡   ✝   ☾

"WE INTERRUPT our regular programming to bring you this Fox News Alert." Viewers saw headlines screaming, "MEN CRUCIFIED."

Blaine Edwards began at precisely nine o'clock. He had prevailed. FOX's management had decided it was in the public's interest (or at least in *their* interest) to release the tape they had bootlegged from the White House Press Room.

"Good evening." Edwards was a proud as a peacock. "The most recent battle in the war against terrorism has been won, but at what cost? International terrorist leader Halam Ghumani is in custody, currently aboard an American helicopter flying over India. Yet in the mission to apprehend him, nine men under the command of Navy Captain Thor Adams were captured and crucified. Yes, *crucified*. Ironic, considering we're reporting this on, of all days, Easter Sunday. In a moment we will show the most incredible war film ever recorded. But first, a warning: the footage is graphic. It is not suitable for children." That remark was calculated to superglue every viewer over the age of seven to the set.

Edwards sat up a little straighter and turned to the camera on his right, suppressing a grin. "Our story begins with the death of two American pilots over the disputed territories between India and Pakistan. This unbelievable video was shot by an American serviceman, Major Cole Sumner. I will let it speak for itself."

FOX News broadcast the sights and sounds captured by Sumner's SFG satellite cam. The world saw two men, one jumping, the other diving, out of a crippled military helicopter. The undercarriage was ravaged and the blades were barely turning, as if in slow motion. As the first pilot jumped, the audience heard the unmistakable sound of gunfire. They saw his body swing backward and spin as the assailants' bullets pierced him. Then they saw the second pilot's desperate leap, saw him pulling the ripcord with his teeth as he hung by one arm. Finally, they saw him fall to his death after another volley of automatic weapons fire.

There was no need for commentary. The whole world held its collective breath, terrified, mesmerized.

"What you are going to hear next are the words of Army Ranger Cole Sumner." FOX ran the audio of Cole telling the pilots of Sea Hawk Two that their comrades were down, that they were dead. They played a slow-motion sequence of the doomed Sea Hawk's final moments as the audience heard the heroic Ranger tell his would-be rescuers to leave the area, to abandon him. It was the stuff of legend.

Edwards had arranged for the editors to stop the tape when the Islamic militants began storming the downed chopper. Showing the post-attack festivities wasn't worth the risk of upsetting the Muslims upon whom FOX relied to grant their news crews access. They had learned what happened to film crews who captured and broadcast such celebratory images.

Following the opening salvo of Islam's war on America, September 11th, Muslim men, women, and children had been ecstatic. Spontaneous parties had burst out around the globe. But the media had decided that it wasn't in anyone's interest to broadcast their celebrations. The executives chose to protect their access to Islamic sources instead. It was a case of economic self-preservation. Besides, they knew these boys played rough.

"We are pleased to report that Cole Sumner, the Army Ranger whose voice you just heard, is safe. The men you saw jump out of the helicopter are both dead. Their names have not been released."

Edwards was cued to face the center camera again. Holding his typed script, he read from the teleprompter, "Normally, the capture of the world's most celebrated terrorist leader, Halam Ghumani, would be our top headline, but not tonight. The film you are about to see is more gruesome, more violent, than anything this reporter has ever witnessed."

With that, FOX News ran an edited tape of Team Uniform's excursion. They compressed the timeline of the hike toward the terrorist base, choosing video from whatever helmet cam provided the most interesting perspective. Blaine Edwards provided a running commentary.

"This team is comprised of three Americans plus the injured Major Sumner, all Navy SEALs and Army Rangers. There are four British Royal Marines—SAS—and four Israelis, Mossad and IDF Special Forces. What you are looking at are enhanced light, infrared, and terrain modes, broadcast by the latest high-tech military gear. These images and sounds were sent via satellite to the White House earlier today.

"As you will see in a moment, all but two of the eleven soldiers were trapped in a large pit. The explosions overwhelmed the men and their gear. The images we are showing you now came from the camera of the mission's leader."

Thor Adams, Edwards explained, wasn't your average Naval officer. The quick bio the news staff had prepared revealed that he was highly decorated, had received a Fleet Appointment to the Naval Academy as an enlisted man, had become a Naval Aviator, and had achieved celebrity of sorts when he had become a SEAL at thirty-two, a good four years older than any previous survivor of the grueling BUD/S training. As the leader of a dozen Task Force 11 operations, he had been interviewed so often that America had become familiar with his rugged, no-nonsense style, his courage, and candor. Thor was a Navy recruiter's dream.

"What you are seeing now is incredible footage. The satellite cameras worn by the captured incursion force were set up to broadcast this elaborate plan, allegedly designed to punish us for waging war on al-Qaeda." Blaine concluded his opening remarks and fell quiet again. The sights and sounds being sent around the world needed no explanation. The film was edited only in choosing the best camera angle as the terrorists moved from cross to cross, finally raising them. The video ran for the better part of fifteen minutes before Edwards interrupted with commentary.

"The rescue was orchestrated by Captain Adams and an Israeli Mossad officer, Major Isaac Newcomb. Roll tape."

For the next fifteen minutes, the world was at war. Christians and Jews were praying for Thor and Isaac. Muslims were rooting even more passionately for Halam Ghumani and his Afghani Freedom Fighters.

Those espousing the "peace process" were simply critical of the whole mess, though they, too, were glued to their televisions. Sanctimonious, they knew better: violence would only beget more violence. This was all so childish, they thought. Negotiation was the answer. We just needed to understand these people, appreciate their problems, see them as victims, and everything would work out fine. Appeasement was so much more enlightened, so much more civilized than all this testosterone-soaked barbarism on the screen.

With divided interests, polarized perspectives, and separate agendas, the world watched in morbid fascination. The most appalling sights and sounds ever captured on film made Blaine Edwards an instant star, a media celebrity—and a traitor, willing to imperil the lives of men far more courageous than he for his fifteen minutes of fame.

Men like Blake Houston, Isaac Newcomb, and Cole Sumner became heroes this night. But Captain Thurston Adams had become the most celebrated, most newsworthy, most *interesting* man in the world.

7

A HERO'S WELCOME

Friday's failure had become Sunday's celebration. The transfer from rotary to fixed-wing aircraft took place as scripted. Battered and bruised, Team Uniform was racing toward the *Ronald Reagan*.

"What now, Cap?" Kyle Stanley asked. "Going to Disney World?"

"Naah," he sighed through the pain.

"We'll avenge the death of the Sea Hawk pilots, yes?" Yacob's eyes betrayed a grim determination. The flight crews had tried valiantly to conceal the bad news, but they were lousy liars.

"No, revenge isn't the answer. We've gotta make sense of this somehow." It didn't sound much like a guy who had just kicked serious terrorist butt.

"Good grief, Cap!" Stanley shot back, feeling almost alive. "That's what I'd expect the witch to say." Kyle was in way too much pain to feign respect for his Pacifist-in-Chief.

"That's *Madam* Witch to you, Lieutenant," Yacob Seraph quipped, though he too was surprised. "You going soft on us?"

"No, not hardly. But if all we know is revenge—an eye for an eye, a tooth for a tooth—we'll end up blind and livin' on oatmeal."

Moshe was in no mood for philosophy. After a lifetime of looking over his shoulder for suicide bombers and signs of impending Arab invasion, revenge sounded just fine. "So the ch-chopper pilots get m-murdered hanging from their p-parachutes, and we're just going to l-let it g-go?"

Yacob looked at Moshe, alarmed. He knew he had battled stuttering all his life, finally conquering it—temporarily, it now appeared. Why had the torment returned? Were old hatreds forcing their way to the surface? Yacob had heard the stories of how Moshe's parents had been horribly disfigured by a terrorist's car bomb. Only his father's mangled body had saved him from the brunt of the blast. Unlike his parents, Moshe's scars were on the inside. For Captain Keceph, the pain was personal.

"They didn't die in vain, Moshe." Kyle struggled to get the words out.

He understood the Mossad's mission of making sure no crime against Jews went unpunished; it meshed nicely with his own military code of honor. "They got Sumner out. We got the world's number-one bad guy and sent forty terrorists to Allah. I'd say they're avenged."

"No! N-not until Kahn Haqqani dies." Despite the outburst, Moshe appeared a little calmer. "W-what would have happened if the C-captain hadn't saved our b-butts?"

The question stung Adams. "I led us right into a trap."

"Don't be blamin' yourself, Cap'n." Kyle understood his friend's torment. "Whatever trips those boys' triggers is way beyond any of us."

"I'm gonna figure it out," Thor said. "I swear. That's better than revenge. It'll make the suffering count for something. We'll never stop 'em until we know what makes 'em crazy."

"It started as a family feud." Yacob was a student of history, *his* history. "This has been going on four thousand years. You know the story?"

"You mean about Arabs and Jews tracing their heritage back to Abraham? I thought that was just symbolic, you know, folklore."

"It's history, Cap."

Bloody and broken warriors discussing ancient scriptures was hardly an everyday occurrence. But this wasn't an average postmortem. Something about a crucifixion shuffles one's priorities.

"Maybe. The historical accuracy of your scriptures is really some'n. Makes you wonder if the Bible might be...."

Adams was having trouble completing his sentence. He was a historian, a soldier, not a philosopher—definitely not a believer. Outside of chapel at the Academy, he had never seen the inside of a church. His world was historical documents. He had only just started to grapple with this uncomfortable conundrum.

"Inspired. That's the word you were searching for," the Israeli warrior said. "It isn't possible to explain any other way."

Thor tried to roll to his other side, but it screamed out in pain.

"Its prophecies are freaky stuff," Yacob reported. He and Kyle both knew that the Old Testament was a treasure trove of predictions.

Kyle stared at his bandaged wrists. "The rise and fall of nations were foretold long before they happened, Cap'n. When it was predicted that Egypt would quake at the sight of the Jews, the idea was absurd."

"But it happened in '67. The Six Day War." Thor knew his history, especially military history. Moshe and Yacob knew it too. Every Israeli reveled in the scope of that victory. A tiny nation had turned away the combined wrath of the Arab world. Their stunning victory over the Muslims was a miracle by any standard.

"In Psalm 102," Yacob reflected, "God even predicted the Holocaust; then he said we'd return to Israel. That's what happened."

"Three thousand-year-old intel. Is that crazy or what?"

"No k-kidding. But if you w-want to find out what happened b-back there, you're going to have to s-study *Islam's* scriptures."

"He's right," Yacob agreed. "If you want to find your way around hell, you can't use a roadmap to heaven."

Stanley turned to Yacob. "So tell me about Psalm 102. That's a new one on me. It actually *predicted* the Holocaust?"

As the words left his lips, the Viking pitched down. The flaps were extended and the throttles retarded. The gear doors opened to the sound of rushing air and whining hydraulic pumps. The tail hook was released moments before the controlled crash onto the deck of the *Ronald Reagan*, catching the center pendant. This time the men were prepared. Already bruised, no one wanted to keep flying after the airplane had stopped.

Safely on deck, they were happy to be one step closer to home, nearer to getting some relief. But to a man, they were more curious than they had ever been.

✡   ✝   ☾

"ANWAR, HAVE YOU gotten a blower to work?"

"I thought you'd be calling, sir. I cannot believe they captured Halam."

"We will make them pay," Omen Quagmer said with grim resolve. "Now, how are you coming?"

"The prototype works fine. We received the funds you promised from Charlie 3. The first machines will be ready within a week." Abu was good at his job.

"Charlie" was code for "candy." Charlie 3 represented the drug money from the sales of narcotics to American college students. The "3" was code for the third initiative deployed during the current year. The leaders of al-Qaeda figured that by using American-style nomenclature they would be less noticeable. It was the hide-in-plain-sight mentality.

"When will you be ready to receive Bravo 3?" "Bravo" stood for the biochemical ingredients to be used in Plan 3.

"Whenever. We've built the containment facility. Allah is great."

"I want to send Echo 3 out just as soon as you're ready," Omen told his American agent.

"Your execution team can pick up the first six blowers in two or three days. Where are they going to go, sir?" Anwar Abu shouldn't have asked, and he knew it. Only Omen knew the full extent of every plan.

"That's of no concern to you," Quagmer answered coldly.

"Death to the infidels," Anwar replied, not knowing what else to say.

✡ ✝ ☾

"THAT WAS QUITE a performance, Captain Adams," the President choked out. This was the last call she wanted to make. The video of Thor's bravery and of his men's ordeal was now being broadcast around the world by every network, translated into every language. There would be no erasing the tape, no turning back the clock. Adams had become a living legend.

"Thank you, Madam President, but I'm no hero. My plan failed." The Captain was still angry at himself for having stumbled into a trap, for underestimating his enemy. And while miffed at the President, he was unwilling to blame her publicly for failing to provide proper air support.

"Well, Captain," the President continued from the Oval Office, "now that you're a modern-day Colonel Doolittle, what's next?" To her chagrin, it had turned out just as she'd predicted.

"I want to understand this enemy, ma'am." He wasn't seeking glory. Thor dreaded the limelight he knew awaited him.

"Who?" They were evidently fighting different foes.

"Madam President," Adams replied, "the enemy we encountered is unlike any other. We've got a serious problem. I'd like to come back to the White House and brief you on what we experienced."

"No, Captain, that won't be necessary. I'm already better briefed on this than I'd like to be."

The President hung up and turned to her advisors. "Now what?"

"The nation is crying for a retaliatory strike, Madam President." Hasler was standing behind the blood-red sofa, his arms behind his back.

"More killing? Is that what they want? Does everyone have a death wish?"

"Yes, ma'am, apparently." Secretary Ditroe was in her usual position, swallowed by the overstuffed upholstery. "This morning's poll numbers aren't terribly ambiguous. Ninety percent are in favor of killing terrorists, *any* terrorists. They don't care where we bomb. They just want us to blow something up."

"That's insane."

"The outcry to punish them is universal," Hasler reported. The

General wanted to send what was left of Afghanistan back to the Stone Age and then return to bloody Iraq some more. The behavior of the Islamic faithful had frustrated him.

On the way to the briefing, he had read one of the many leaflets Muslims had spread around Afghanistan. Although they were "impoverished" and begging for aid, they were offering hundred-thousand-dollar rewards for the capture of American soldiers. And if that wasn't incentive enough, they threatened to kill anyone aiding the West, calling them un-Islamic. It irked him.

These pamphlets were designed to fan the flames of racial hatred. The one he had read this morning claimed that American soldiers had used biological weapons on hundreds of thousands of Muslim women and children. And while the bogus claims angered him, what scared him most was that Muslims believed them to be true.

Susan sat up a little straighter. "If the American people had their way, Madam President, they'd dispense with the trial. They want Halam Ghumani *crucified*." No longer a pacifist, the Defense Secretary agreed.

"This is a nightmare." The President was deeply troubled. Securing Halam Ghumani was supposed to be the highlight of her resume. Bringing him to America for trial should have been proof that her policies were superior. But it had all backfired.

✡   ✞   ☾

SEATED IN A WHEELCHAIR, Captain Adams was mobile enough to make the rounds. With an antibiotic drip dangling from one steel IV pole and pain meds hanging from another, he rolled from bed to bed in the *Ronald Reagan's* onboard hospital. It did him good.

Kyle was asleep and Isaac was in surgery, so his first visit was with Cole Sumner. The Major explained how the pilots had jumped for their lives, only to lose them in midair to an enemy they never even saw. It was cathartic. The two men quietly cursed the lack of air support that made the tragedy possible, then praised the heroism of the Cobra crews who had risked death to bring their fallen comrades home. With some prodding, Sumner related his story of personal agony as he dragged himself to safety, hiding from the pursuing Muslim militants.

Down the hall, Adams knocked on Major Seraph's door, rolling in next to the Israeli's bed. They compared broken bones and body piercings. Yacob won.

"In a couple weeks, after you've had a chance to heal," the optimistic one said, "can I come visit?"

Yacob grinned broadly. "My home is your home, sir."

"I need to learn more about this 'family feud,' as you call it, and figure out what the deal is with Islam."

"Sure, Cap. We all need to bone out on this."

Yacob's errant Americanisms were becoming legendary. Thor was having a hard time keeping a straight face. "You mean 'bone *up?*'"

"Yes. Study. Punch the books."

"Right," Adams laughed. "Last time I read the Qur'an, I was amazed at how often Allah slimed the 'People of the Book,' *your* book. It's like Allah—or maybe Muhammad—had an inferiority complex."

"Nothing's changed, sir."

✡   ✞   ☾

THE RIDE HOME was considerably more comfortable than had been their cramped journey into hell. The Air Force had arranged for G-5s, as they're called by civilians, to fly each country's team home from an airbase in Bombay. These Gulfstream jets were second only to the Global Express in providing first class international travel to politicos, corporate bigwigs, and top military brass. At forty million dollars a copy and an operating cost of over five thousand dollars per hour, they weren't normally used to ferry lieutenants, majors, and captains. But these men were no longer ordinary. This was a flight of heroes.

The four Americans seemed unimpressed with their cushy in-flight surroundings. After a hot meal, a cold beer, and a few minutes of curiously pushing buttons, they fell asleep. The flight attendant, a pretty Air Force Private, fussed all over the bruised gladiators. But the men were oblivious.

The sleek powder-blue mini Air Force One set down in Great Britain for fuel. It was nearing two o'clock in the afternoon. They were halfway home. As they taxied to the ramp, the Americans were surprised to see a great crowd. The British contingent of Team Uniform was enjoying a warm welcome.

Their British friends wanted the Americans to take a bow, give a speech, accept their gratitude. All Thor and team wanted to do was take a pee. Forget adulation. As great as the beer had tasted, it was now a liability.

There was a head on the luxurious jet, of course, but it was too small for men in casts to successfully navigate. With shattered feet, shot up and broken limbs, pierced wrists, and more bandages than King Tut, they were unable to stand up on their own, much less negotiate the narrow passage. Back in Afghanistan, desperation and adrenaline had enabled them to carry on, to do their duty. Now there was only pain.

In a way, their frustration was indicative of how their lives would be for the foreseeable future. The men had so little left to give. They wanted to pull the sheets up over their heads and sleep for a month. Yet an adoring public wanted to put them on a pedestal.

The captain of the G-5 solved the first problem in a practical but somewhat less than elegant manner. He loaned Thor his "Range Extender," an emergency device he, like many pilots, carried under his seat. The red plastic container with a two-inch opening, white screw-on lid, and handle would hold about a quart of fluid waste. With an embarrassed smile, Thor capped it and handed the golden fluid to the hostess, who flushed it down the onboard head. Without comment she handed the life-saving device to the next man in line.

"You're gonna have to pass on Stanley," Thor told the Private. "It's not big enough. Why don't you give it to Sumner."

"Hey, I represent that statement," Kyle pretended to be indignant.

"You shouldn't. I didn't say *what* wasn't big enough."

"Somebody's had a little too much morphine," Kyle chided his pal.

After a good laugh, the less-than-ambulatory men relieved themselves, one after another. Now if they could only figure out how to get down the stairs and wave to the assembled throng....

✡   ☩   ☾

"They're on their way, Sarah. Took off from England an hour ago."

"Thanks, JT," she said, putting down her coffee. "How'd it go?"

Her assistant grinned. "Just like you said it would. Heathrow was a zoo. Four hundred thousand Brits waving the Union Jack and tying up traffic for miles around. Your counterpart at MI-6 told me that Team Uniform was, I think he phrased it, 'warmly received'. You've gotta love British reserve. 'Course, he said the crowd went stark-raving *nuts* when your Captain Hunk peeked his head out of the airplane."

"I'd say he earned it, wouldn't you?" Sarah ignored the innuendo.

"C'mon Sarah, face reality."

"What reality?"

"He was talking about *you*. You're his heartthrob."

"Please, JT. No way. You've read his file, remember? Thurston 'Hunk' Adams belongs to no woman. He doesn't even phone his mother."

"You're in denial, boss. Admit it. Look me in the eye and tell me you're not going out to Reagan National like everybody else east of the Appalachians. You know you're the one."

She grinned sheepishly, blushing ever so slightly. "Y'really think so?"

"Sarah, for an intelligence officer, you can be really dense. Didn't you see the way he looked at you, the way he'd move his chair a couple of inches closer to yours at those pre-op briefings? I don't know how *you* feel, but he's got it bad."

She was really blushing now, but being too much of a lady to stammer, she said nothing.

"Look," JT carried on, "Barnes already said you could go. Heck, half the office has already left. So go. I'll watch the store."

"Thanks. You're the best." Sarah turned to leave, but her pal stood in her path, arms crossed, rubbing his chin.

"What?"

"You're not wearing *that*, are you?"

She looked down at herself. Tailored navy suit. The skirt reached her knees. Off-white blouse. Sensible shoes. In other words, invisible. "Okay. I may be dense, but I'm teachable. I'll stop by my apartment and change. I'm sure I can find something that'll make me stand out in a crowd of a million crazed hero worshipers."

✡   ✝   ☾

IT SEEMED LIKE the perfect place. Partially crippled since 9-11-01, Reagan National was being readied to receive the most famous men in the world. Two of the three runways had been closed to make room for the enormous crowd. There were thousands of flags, large and small. Most every high school and college marching band within driving distance of Washington had piled into their buses and made the trek.

Americans in greater numbers than could be imagined were making a pilgrimage. Nothing had stirred the collective national spirit more than the images of sacrifice and heroism they had seen on their televisions.

Over the past three years, the airport had been throttled back. Each of its three runways intersected some place of national prominence. The approach to one-five was directly above the Pentagon. Less than a minute from the threshold of runway one-nine, directly under its extended centerline, was the White House. Not to be outdone, a straight-in approach to runway two-two was over the Capitol. To keep planes from violating the prohibited airspace above these national shrines, they were required to make unnervingly steep turns down low and on short final. But today, the powder-blue G-5 with United States of America painted on its fuselage could do loops and rolls over any of the three buildings and no one would care.

As Team Uniform approached, the bands played and the dignitaries found their places. As they had for the post-9/11 memorial at the National Cathedral, Members of Congress and White House staffers had boarded busses to attend the gala event. A giant grandstand had been erected for them. A special stage, draped with red, white, and blue bunting, was constructed with a ramp to accommodate the wounded men.

One would have expected to see a few uniforms since the airport was only a minute or two from the Pentagon. But every military contingent within three hundred miles of the nation's capital had arrived in force. They were there in the tens of thousands: Navy, Marines, Army, Air Force, Coast Guard, and National Guard troops with their bands and color guards. It was an awesome spectacle.

And then there was the media. A quick scan of the surrounding area revealed more cameras, cables, spotlights, and satellite trucks than had ever been gathered for any event. It was like the Super Bowl, a Presidential Inauguration, and Lindbergh landing in Paris, all rolled into one.

As they crossed the Chesapeake Bay, the hostess offered Thor, Kyle, Bentley, and Cole an assortment of toiletries so they could freshen up—attempt to awaken from their drug-induced slumber. The G-5's captain explained that they were headed for Reagan National, not Andrews, and that there might be a greeting committee.

Thor looked down out of the left side of the aircraft. While the crippled Washington Monument looked like he felt, the Capitol, the White House, and the Lincoln and Jefferson Memorials looked beautiful with their gleaming white stone washed in the golden light of the late-day sun. As they turned toward the final approach to runway one-five, Thor began to wonder why the pilot hadn't lowered the gear, extended the flaps, and finished his descent.

Peering out the window, it became obvious. The airport was covered with a sea of people. Millions of Americans appeared to be waving as the Gulfstream circled overhead, making the tarmac, from Thor's vantage point, seem to writhe and shimmer.

✡ ✝ ☪

"THIS IS BLAINE EDWARDS reporting from Reagan National Airport in the nation's capitol. Flying overhead in the light-blue Air Force jet is the world's most famous man, Captain Thor Adams. With him are the three American members of Team Uniform, Kyle Stanley, Bentley McCaile, and Cole Sumner. As you all know, Lieutenants Stanley and McCaile survived crucifixion at the hands of al-Qaeda terrorists in Afghanistan while Major Sumner heroically eluded near-certain death in the disputed territories between India and Pakistan. Gentlemen," Edwards said standing in front of the camera, "welcome home."

The fighter escorts peeled off, and Blaine Edwards turned to look over his right shoulder as the roar of the G-5's jet engines began to overwhelm the sounds of the battling bands. With the Lincoln Memorial gleaming in the background, the Air Force jet began its flair over the threshold. The giant turbines were brought back to idle, and the craft settled down gently, slowing to taxi speed.

A tug attached a boom to the front gear of the Gulfstream, and it was towed into position. The door was opened while the crowd held its collective breath. A lift, decked out in red, white, and blue, was brought up into position. With the help of the flight crew, Cole Sumner, the most ambulatory, emerged first. The crowd went wild.

"First out is Major Sumner," Blaine broadcast. "The images from his helmet cam thrust this story onto center stage. The nation, I dare say the whole world, will never forget his words as he told the pilots of the Sea Hawk helicopters to fly away and leave him there, surrounded by enemy troops." They weren't troops, but it was more politically correct than calling them Muslim murderers.

Edwards looked back over his shoulder. "That's Kyle Stanley, and yes, Bentley McCaile is right behind him. To look at them brings it all back. See how their feet are in casts; their wrists are bandaged." The camera zoomed in on the two Americans, showing the pain on their faces as they were placed in the wheelchairs.

"There he is...Captain Thurston Adams." No one heard what the FOX commentator said next. A million voices were raised in celebration.

The four overwhelmed heroes were carried to the stage on the aviation lift. The bands played the National Anthem and millions sang along. Even nature appeared to be celebrating. The sun seemed to salute as it sank below the western horizon. The high clouds gradually morphed from white to yellow, through pinkish orange to an intense patriotic red.

Under the lights, the guests of honor were rolled off the lift and onto the stage. The men were surprised to see the President, the Secretary of Defense, the Speaker of the House, and the Senate Majority and Minority leaders. The nation's most popular vocalists were there, too. One after another they sang America's treasured songs, culminating, as they had in the National Cathedral following the bombing of the Twin Towers, with "The Battle Hymn of the Republic." Once again, it was a call to war.

This time, however, unlike the 9/11 gala event at the National Cathedral, when the Islamic imam got up to read a prayer and passages from the Qur'an, someone had the good sense to shut off his mike. They recognized that asking an imam to say a prayer here was like asking Hitler to give the benediction for Auschwitz. Average citizens were coming to realize what their politicians missed: Allah was America's enemy. Had Thor been able, he would have choked him.

Following the last eloquent prayer for peace, the President moved toward the rostrum. Someone scrambled to attach the Presidential Seal as one act finished and another began.

"My fellow Americans," the President bellowed. A chorus of boos drowned her out. "Thank you," she said, thinking she was being cheered.

The boos grew louder. The crowd waved their arms, signifying that they wanted her off the stage—out of their lives. Pacifists, it seemed, had gone out of style.

Undaunted, the President turned to her prepared speech. She stared directly into the teleprompter. "Join me in welcoming our men home." The audience nearly shouted her down. At this moment she would have given anything for an SFG suit, one that would make her invisible.

"I approved this mission because I wanted to show the world that we could solve our problems peaceably. My administration promised to bring the terrorists to trial and let justice take its course. I am proud to...." She had to pause. The audience was angry.

"I am proud to inform you tonight that...." Their boos stopped her again, drowning out her amplified voice. "...that we have Halam Ghumani in custody and will force him to stand trial for his crimes."

She wasn't finished, but no one was interested in listening to her. Flustered, she turned in disgust and sat down. That created a problem, for the President was scheduled to introduce Team Uniform.

Recognizing the dilemma, General Hasler walked up the inclined ramp and onto the stage. He shook the men's hands as he walked by. Reaching the rostrum, he began: "We are here to honor four brave Americans."

The crowd went berserk. It was hard to tell if the audience was celebrating the fact they had forced the unpopular President to sit down, or if they just wanted to let their wounded know they were appreciated.

One at a time, the four warriors were wheeled up front. They were given a mike and asked to say a few words.

Bentley began. "I thank God we are back home. Back with you. This is so much more than we...." The celebrants cheered, drowning out McCaile's words. Unable to compete, he concluded by saying, "There's a terrible evil lurking in the world. America, we have a problem."

The enormous crowd burst into another ovation. They wanted their voice heard, their will understood. They didn't want to deliberate; the verdict had already been rendered. They craved revenge.

Kyle Stanley was next. "It's great to be an American—great to have all of us united against this enemy. It helps to make what we endured somehow worth the pain." Even in his wheelchair, Stanley was an imposing figure. He thrilled the crowd. "Our pilots died serving you, serving a nation that now must serve the world by cleansing it of a horrible disease. Neither terrorists, nor the regimes that encourage them, should be allowed to live. For if they live, we die."

The audience applauded wildly. America's mood had come full circle.

Cole Sumner shared similar insights. The multitude was equally gracious. But as he concluded, a giant swell of energy swept through the audience. The applause became rhythmic as the drums played percussion.

"Thor. Thor. Thor," they chanted.

Adams swung his injured leg off the wheelchair and struggled to his feet, leaning against the armrest and using his left arm to prop himself up. He stood on his strong leg and limped with the help of General Hasler to the rostrum. It was shades of Roosevelt though the Captain looked more like Kennedy. Everyone was mesmerized. Even the White House staffer responsible for removing the Presidential Seal from the rostrum was frozen in the moment. "If I get out of line and say more than I should, General, blame it on the pain medication, okay?"

Hasler looked Thor in the eyes. "Give 'em both barrels, son."

With that endorsement, Captain Thurston Adams turned to address the crowd. "It is good that we honor our fighting men," he began. "The world is full of evil, and our enemies would like nothing more than to break our spirit, crush our economy, and steal our freedoms. But we must not let them. To protect these things, to endure as a great nation, we must not flinch. I realize that there will be a cost—and that the price is high. But freedom is worth any sacrifice. The pilots of the downed Sea Hawk, Steve Wesson and David Smith, paid the ultimate price."

The crowd hung on every word.

"You have seen the spirit and courage of the men who comprised

Team Uniform: the Americans—Kyle Stanley, Cole Sumner, Bentley McCaile; the Brits—Blake Huston, Lad Childress, Ryan Sullivan, and Cliff Powers; and the Israelis—Isaac Newcomb, Yacob Seraph, Moshe Keceph, and Joshua Abrams. In honoring them, we honor America, Great Britain, and Israel—the world's proudest democracies."

The ovations that followed the mention of these now-legendary names were genuine and heartfelt. Aside from the President, who felt more slighted than proud, there wasn't a dry eye among the million in attendance, nor among the hundreds of millions glued to their televisions.

Adams had purposely presented his men without rank. There had been no real hierarchy on the mission, and there would be none now that they were home. Courage knew no rank.

"Do not forget the men who brought us into and out of harm's way. They risked everything in service to you, to all Americans. I especially want to thank the HALO jumpers. Without their bravery and skill, none of us would have made it through the night." The ovations were so great that Adams found himself bracing his wounded frame against the incessant roar. The waves of adoration seemed like they might blow him off the stage.

"America, we have a terrible enemy, one who has us directly in their sights. This enemy is, by any definition, evil. We must come to understand them, for they are a clear and present danger." Adams scanned the crowd, looking for a familiar face. "We will not, we cannot, prevail against this foe by attacking the wrong enemy or by fighting a limited war, for they recognize no limits. There is no end to the terror they are willing to inflict. From what I can tell, we have not fought them wisely or well. All we have done, I'm afraid, is create martyrs, increase their numbers, and strengthen their resolve."

Having unloaded one barrel, the Captain discharged the other. "We have witnessed the utter failure of homeland security. All we have done is handicap our citizens and burden our economy. I believe this battle must be taken to the enemy, not fought here at home." The crowd was overjoyed. "We have witnessed the failure of a politically correct war built upon international alliances and hopeful compromises. There was no cessation of terror. I have learned...."

The roar of millions literally took his breath away. He wanted to raise his hand as he had seen others do to quiet the assembly, but he didn't have one to give. His right was strapped to his side. His left was holding him up as he leaned against the rostrum.

He tried again. "I have learned that this enemy knows no honor. Based upon the lies they promulgate, their pledges are worthless. We must save our breath and our noble ideals for reasonable people, for those who are capable of living peaceably in a civilized world. In my judgment, nothing will dissuade Muslim militancy other than a fierce determination and a steely resolve. Harsh words will not cause them to repudiate terror. They will cower only at the point of a sword."

Thor knew he had grossly overstepped his bounds, but thought that this might be his only chance to speak his mind. Even if he were relieved from duty, it was worth the risk. The sacrifice others had made to bring him to this place deserved no less.

However, the world interpreted these words as a one-man declaration of war. They knew that Thurston Adams was just a captain, unable to set American policy. Yet at this moment, it was the President who was incapacitated; the Captain was standing tall.

"I pledge to learn about this enemy, to discover what vile doctrine drives them crazy, and somehow I will find a way to end their reign of terror. Give me time..." the Captain said, swept along by the exuberance of the multitude, "and I will...."

Suddenly, he saw her. Thor's repeated scan of the crowd had found the one face, the one smile, that had carried him through it all, to hell and back. A million faces, but there she was.

"Sarah!" he shouted out. "*Sarah!*"

Nottingly raised her hand, signaling the Captain to forget about her for the moment and finish his speech. Then she smiled and winked, telling him without words that she would be at his side when he was done.

Adams turned back to the crowd. "Please excuse my lapse; it's just so good to be home." They went wild.

"Give me time, and I will learn about this enemy, understand their history, their beliefs, and their motives, and their means. And I promise, I will find a strategy to thwart them. For the sake of those who have died, for the sake of the families who have suffered, I *will* find an answer!"

These were not the words of a mere captain. They sounded altogether presidential, or at least like the words of a serious candidate. But no one resented him for saying them. America knew he had earned the right. They wanted him to succeed. They needed to know *why*. These challenges were as important as any in human history. The world's fate literally hung in the balance.

Then, in words that surprised even him, Thor Adams lifted his good arm, waved to the crowd, and shouted, "God bless America!"

With that the bands struck up an uncoordinated but somehow beautiful medley of patriotic songs. Millions stood proudly, placed their hands over their hearts and sang along. But Adams didn't hear them. He was again searching for Sarah. She was no longer standing where he had last seen her. His heart sank.

Nottingly, however, was on her way. After telling the military guards around the stage that she was Sarah, *the* Sarah, they let her through. The fact that she had a top security clearance and a badge that proclaimed her status as a CIA bureau chief didn't matter. She was *Sarah*.

Wearing an electric-blue dress with a red and white scarf, she was more than beautiful. As she leaped toward the center of the stage, the Captain let go of the rostrum. He would have fallen had she not caught him, wrapping her arms around him. As he leaned against her, as she held him, time stood still. It was as if they were alone, just the two of them. Sure, the whole world was watching. So what?

Captain Thor Adams, Academy grad, fighter pilot, and Navy SEAL, had never felt better. He knew it now. He was falling in love.

General Hasler moved back to the rostrum, smiling broadly. More had been done to strengthen America's military during the last five minutes than had been accomplished in all the years since Ronald Reagan had led the nation back from its malaise. The military the President wanted so desperately to dismantle now had a gargantuan advocate.

"My fellow Americans, it gives me great pleasure to introduce our newest, bravest, and most famous *Admiral*. The Chairman's voice boomed. "Rear Admiral Thurston Adams." Congress, eager to align themselves with the hero, had quickly approved his appointment.

The Captain heard his name, but being in Sarah's arms was making his head swim. It was all a blur.

"Captain, I mean Admiral," Sarah whispered in Thor's ear. "You've just been promoted." She helped him turn around.

The General reached out and handed Thor Adams his Admiral's stripes. Nothing could have pleased the crowd more.

To an inspiring medley of patriotic songs, a grateful nation celebrated by launching more fireworks than anyone could remember. Sarah stood at Thor's side and looked skyward. Their arms were touching as they pondered their fate.

"Would you consider having dinner with me tonight, Sarah?" The newly minted Admiral asked.

She smiled. "Are you asking me out on a date, or is this a debriefing?"

"Would you come if it were a date?" He was more nervous now than he had been stalking terrorists.

"Do you always answer a question with a question?" she teased. "I suppose you'll have to muster the courage to ask, Admiral."

"You're not making this easy."

"Good. You've probably filled your quota of women who fit that description." Her expression was flirtatious enough to encourage him on.

Just then a spectacular series of fireworks exploded overhead. Thor felt the percussions permeate his body. "Beautiful," he said. He let Sarah think he was talking about the fireworks. "It's a date. I'm asking you out on a date. Will you join me for dinner this evening?"

"Yes." She reached for his hand and squeezed it.

As if coordinated by heaven above, the grand finale burst into the night sky. Washington was all aglow. So was Thor.

☆   ✟   ☾

OMEN QUAGMER and Kahn Haqqani were not amused. They watched the proceedings in Washington with disdain.

"The infidels must pay for this travesty." Kahn's fist was clenched.

Their surprise party had backfired. Terror had driven the Americans to the brink of capitulation, but al-Qaeda's cruelty had now precipitated an about face. The terrorists had won so much of what they had sought, only to see their gains evaporate. Allah's advice on crucifixion hadn't worked out as they had expected.

Of course, what the President had wanted to give them wouldn't have been good enough. It never is with people this insecure. A concession is only as good as a drug addict's latest fix. If there were no infidels in Arabia, if all of Palestine were conceded, even if every Jew were slaughtered, they wouldn't be satisfied. If every foe on earth were conquered and every coveted treasure plundered, it still wouldn't be enough.

Omen turned and spoke to Aymen Halaweh. "I want you to go to America, Aymen. The blowers I have told you about are too small. Operating inside the air-conditioning systems of buildings is good but not nearly good enough. Not now."

"What would you like, sir?" the Palestinian engineer asked.

"I want blowers large enough to infect entire cities."

Kahn's eyes lit up. "We could carry them on helicopters or fly them strapped to the bellies of airplanes. We could spray millions of people."

"I don't think it's possible. Something that large would destroy the aerodynamics," Aymen explained. "And it would be entirely too heavy for a helicopter."

"We did not bring you here to tell us what we cannot do, Halaweh." Kahn spoke as if *he* had paid for his education.

"Yes, sir. If Allah wills it, I will find a way."

"It *is* Allah's will; of that I'm certain," Kahn replied.

Omen nodded. "Now, before you leave, lets get Anwar Abu on the line." It took less than a minute.

"I want you to stop making the small blowers, Abu. You have six complete, right?"

"Yes. I have components to build thirty more," Anwar answered.

"Has Bravo 3 delivered the ingredients?"

"We have more than enough for the first six blowers. The powder is of excellent quality."

"Then you can expect Echo 3 within two days. Give them the blowers and the spores, excuse me, *ingredients*."

Omen seldom slipped like that. There was no way of knowing when a phone call would be intercepted by the NSA. He was angry at himself. So much was at stake.

Their hosts, the Iraqis, hated America as much as they hated Jews. And they were all too eager to reward those who killed them. But they also hated being embarrassed. With the aftermath of the crucifixions, al-Qaeda had done just that.

"I will arrange for another visit, Anwar. This one from Charlie 4. The contribution will be considerable. I want twelve, no, *thirty-six* giant blowers, big enough to condition great cities."

"That may take some time, sir. Just how big do you want these?"

"I want them so big that two or three will be large enough to condition places the size of Los Angeles and Chicago...America's greatest cities, *that's* how big, Abu. I am sending you a helper, an MIT-trained engineer. Make it happen."

"I will pray to Allah for understanding."

✡   ✝   ☾

"SUSAN, I HAVE NEVER been so embarrassed. We've got to stop this."

"The country's smitten with Admiral Adams, ma'am. I don't know how to stop the rising tide. People want war."

"We must regain control, get our agenda back on track.

The President and her Secretary of Defense were in the White House. They were eating in the Officer's Mess, downstairs in the basement near the OEOB. The Old Executive Office Building is the ugly five-story structure just west of the White House, the one that looks so out of character with the rest of the city.

The dining room was deserted. Most feared the President's legendary temper, and they knew she would be on the warpath. Ironically, the two were eating in the Officers' Mess because misery loves company.

"We need to schedule a news conference." Susan Ditroe was Secretary of Defense, not Chief of Staff, but at the moment she appeared to be the President's only ally, the only one whose personal agenda still meshed with the boss'. "America needs to know that you're in control. Even if the people aren't supportive, you know the press will be."

"Who can we count on to help us?" the President asked between bites of her Greek salad.

"How 'bout Katie Couric on the *Today Show?* She loves you."

"Sure. We could start off the day shaping the news. 'Course, what if they've already asked Adams to be on their program? Y'know they will."

"Couric is one of us. She'll bump Adams even if it impacts ratings. I'll call her when we're finished."

"What am I going to say, Susan?"

"Stick to your guns. Tell them we can put an end to this whole sorry mess by placing Jerusalem under the auspices of the United Nations. It should be a peaceful and holy city, safe for the entire world. Who could be against that?" the Secretary asked.

"I suppose I can give lip service to Team...what did they call it?"

"Team Uniform, ma'am."

"Yes. I'll tell everybody how grateful we are that they screwed up their mission and became a thorn in our sides. Then we'll talk of investing in a more peaceful world, like we did on the campaign. Maybe it'll still work."

Susan put down her fork, turned to the waiter, and ordered dessert. Crafting the President's message wasn't going to be easy.

✡   ✝   ☪

"HOW ABOUT the Capitol Grill?"

Sarah was driving. The restaurant wasn't her favorite, but she figured Thor would like it. They served red meat in every cut, size, and description. Actually, she didn't have a clue what he liked, other than her. She was just guessing.

"Considering my condition, I'm going wherever you're going."

Sarah pulled her car up front. A valet opened her door. "You're that *girl*. You're *Sarah!*" he said loud enough to draw a small crowd.

"'Fraid so," she smiled, as she handed the valet the keys. "I could use a hand." She gestured toward her passenger.

"Admiral Adams! It's such an honor, sir." He helped the disabled warrior extract himself from the confines of Sarah's car. It wasn't easy. She had a hot set of wheels, a Jaguar convertible, an XK-8 roadster. The seats were low and snug, barely big enough for the muscular SEAL. Light blue, it matched her eyes.

The Maitre 'd stepped outside. "Admiral!" he exclaimed as he rushed to Thor's side. "It's such a privilege to have you here." Sarah was all but brushed out of the way. She hoped this wasn't the beginning of a trend.

"Thank you," he answered, a little embarrassed. Adams looked over at his date, who was now following a couple of steps behind. He liked leaning on her better.

"We don't have a reservation, but...."

"My restaurant is your restaurant. Please, just one moment. I will prepare my best table. Your dinner will be on the house, sir." He scurried off to the back corner of his elegant establishment.

A party of four was enjoying prime rib and New York strip when the Maitre'd arrived at their table all excited. "Excuse me, Mr. LaTourrette. Admiral Thurston Adams is here tonight, unexpectedly. You could do me a great favor, I mean, I'd like to give him...."

"Yes, your best table. Absolutely!" the gracious patron said as he stood, placing his napkin on the tablecloth. "Where would you like us to move, Jacques?"

Just that quickly, the back corner booth was reset, and the Admiral and the Agent were escorted to the restaurant's most intimate setting. Along the route, they were heralded with a chorus of greetings: "We love you," "Thank you, sir," and "God bless you."

For Adams this was quite a change. He had gone from being shot at to being a national treasure over the last three days. While he would have liked a little more privacy, he was grateful in a way for his new celebrity. In all the commotion, he had forgotten his wallet.

"You sure know how to impress a girl, Admiral," Sarah said.

"Oh, don't be too impressed. Soon enough they'll forget all about me. I'll be the same old guy you gave your briefs to."

"Not likely. I don't wear briefs," she teased.

Oh dear god, what have I gotten myself into? he thought, but said, "Sarah, I'm glad you said yes. I thought a lot about you. The blacker things got, the more I remembered your smile, your kind words." He wanted to say "your kiss," but he didn't have the courage. Sarah was different from every woman he'd ever met—or least his reaction to her was. Sometime during the countless hours they had worked together preparing the mission, he had been ambushed by Cupid.

So had she.

"I've been praying for you ever since you left." It wasn't the most romantic response. "If you didn't get back soon, I was going to have calluses on my knees."

"So you're a Christian?" Thor asked. "I thought you might be."

"Yes, are you?" Sarah's voice must have raised two octaves. She was encouraged by the question. She had prayed for his safety *and* his soul.

"No. I'll bet that saddens you. I'm an agnostic."

She tried to hide her disappointment.

"But I'm curious," he added with a disarming grin.

"Fair enough, Admiral. I'll take that as a challenge."

Adams nodded. "Well, if that's what makes you so…well, *you,* then I'd like to know more. After what I've seen in the last few days, I'm as open minded as I'll ever be." He smiled at her. "But only if you promise to call me Thor, not 'Admiral'."

"Okay, Thor." She reached her hand out across the table.

Adams looked down, then back into Sarah's vibrant blue eyes. His left arm felt like it weighed a thousand pounds. He was petrified. She was so beautiful, so inviting, he almost melted into the booth as he gathered the courage to touch her fingers. *Some hero.* She slid her hand closer, placing it on top of his. He parted his fingers and she let her glossy red nails fall between the gaps. There was enough electricity to light the room.

Thor had known scores of women, but falling in love was new territory. He felt like a teenager on his first date, and like an adult who'd been around the block, all the same time. This wasn't a game. Sarah wasn't a conquest. Thor didn't quite know what to do. His skin tingled. His face was flushed. He was short of breath. Nothing hurt anymore.

"Are you feeling what I'm feeling, Sarah?" he asked, a bit bewildered.

"It *is* kind of warm in here."

She owned him. Thor just stared. "You are so beautiful." *There must be a God,* Thor thought. *I'm in heaven.*

"Thanks sailor, but I've read your file. It says your eyesight isn't very good." Sarah was smitten, but cool.

"There's nothing wrong with my sense of touch," he responded, caressing the inside of her palm with his thumb.

Sarah wasn't crazy about the line. She cleared her throat, pulled her hand back, and shot him a look. This left Adams' hand alone on the table. "Sorry, Admiral. That ain't gonna happen. Not with this girl."

"Do you have a boyfriend?" he asked, wanting to change the subject.

"No, do you?" she smiled.

Thor relaxed. He had recovered. "*I'll* never tell."

The Clinton Administration's ridiculous "don't ask, don't tell" policy had been a running gag for years. Sarah played along. "I'm told you have a girl in every port."

"That was in another life," Thor answered. "I was young and foolish when I was young enough to be foolish."

"Oh, so you're a changed man?" she inquired.

"Yeah. There's nothing like watching your buddies get crucified to shift your priorities."

Sarah reached out for his hand again. She felt like a fool. He *was* a different man. Nothing would ever be the same. Once again her fingers interlaced his. This time she rubbed *his* palm with her thumb.

"My comment was insensitive. I'm sorry. I just don't want to be this week's conquest, that's all. You're going to have women throwing themselves at you. I can't compete against that."

Thor knew she was right. If he wanted to, he could bed a new girl every night. They would be standing in line. But he didn't want them, not now.

"I've been with my share of women. There's no denying that. But it's overrated, really."

"You just haven't been with the right girl." She placed her left hand on top of his. "I may not be an expert like you, but...." *I'm plenty flirtatious,* she finished the sentence with her eyes.

Thor's whole world disappeared into her shimmering crystal blues. He studied her face. He looked at her hair, her lips, her neck. There was more woman looking back at him than he could hope to explore in a lifetime. *God, if you're there, please don't let me screw this up.*

"You didn't answer either of my questions," she said, breaking the silence. "That's not fair. I answered yours."

"No girlfriends, certainly no boyfriends." He laughed.

Adams sat up a little straighter. "But this week's conquest? I like the sound of that, and hopefully next week's, and the week after that...."

"Wow. A three week stand with the most admired man in the world. That's quite an honor."

"Okay, I deserved that. But I can do better."

She lifted her left hand and used the polished red nail of her index finger to draw circles on the back of his. "I'm listening," she said with a smile that would have melted all the snow in Afghanistan.

He wasn't very good at this sort of thing. If he said too little now, he feared, she would view him as shallow and insincere and walk out of his life. If he inferred too much, if he came on too strong, she might get scared and run.

He took a deep breath. Sarah looked like a goddess in the soft light. Thor knew he was in trouble. His stomach was full of butterflies.

"I surrender," he said.

She looked quizzically at him. *Surrender to what, to whom?* Why was the toughest, most heroic man in the world surrendering? "I don't understand. What do you mean, surrender?"

"I...I like you. You're different. I want to get to know you. With other women it's been a game, a contest. Not with you." He paused for a moment and summoned some courage. "I want to figure out what makes you, well, *you*. So between now and the time you've had your fill of me, I'm yours." He looked up, hopeful.

Sarah shifted in her seat, flustered and a little confused. She didn't really know him, although she wanted to. Sure, there was a spark, but that was only natural. He was movie-star handsome. He was a naval officer— an admiral no less, strong, intelligent, and famous. But there was more, she sensed. Any woman on the planet would have loved to be in her shoes.

"Sarah, I'm sorry. Did I offend you? You seem to have gone away."

"No! I...ah...I've never had a man, you know, *surrender* before." It was Sarah who was blushing now. "I don't quite know what to say." She lifted her hand and covered her cheek. *Yes, it's definitely warm in here.*

8

DISCOVERY

Echo 3 had come and gone. The plan was perfect, right down to the last detail. It had to be. Omen Quagmer was in charge. The blowers had been loaded into two panel vans that said Smith's Heating and Air Conditioning on the sides. The drivers even wore matching coveralls with company logos.

Omen had taken the initiative of picking names for the technicians that would deflect suspicion. The fact that all the terrorist bombers on September 11th had been Muslim, with names like Abdul, Atta, and Muhammad, had caused some Americans to be more discerning. So the name patches stitched onto these jumpsuits read "Carlos" and "Manuel." No one would suspect that they were on a mission for Allah.

The blowers looked like air-processing devices. They had been designed to be inserted into the ductwork of commercial buildings. They even bore nameplates with serial numbers, a model designation, the UL logo, and "ILM Manufacturing" proudly at the top. That was Omen's idea of a joke: *ilm* was Arabic for "knowing what's right."

The "Hispanic" delivery boys were instructed to tell building security officers, if they were asked, that they were installing air-quality monitoring systems to help insure the workers' safety. Omen loved trickery. This was like counterfeiting, a plausible solution designed to fool the gullible. It was a lot like Islam.

A brilliant man, Omen was under no illusions. He knew the truth about Muhammad and Allah. But he wasn't in this business for the eternal blessings. He craved power and money in the here and now. Fortunately, Islam had something for everyone.

His blowers were ingenious. They had been built to collect the dust inside the ductwork of a building's HVAC system. His "air quality" devices were designed to mix this duct dust with anthrax spores, introducing them into office environments. This material was less than ideal— it was both oversized and electrostatically charged. But it was plentiful.

Anthrax spores are microscopic. Billions fit nicely into a small canister. A one-gallon pail would hold enough bacteria to kill every man, woman, and child on the planet. But the pathogen must be mated to a particulate to be effective—to stay airborne long enough to infect the intended victims. Dust particles would help get the job done. But dust is bulky compared to the insidious spores. A device designed to *collect* it could be smaller, less conspicuous, than one that had to carry a full supply.

Research Triangle Park in North Carolina was the perfect place to build such devices. Small warehouses harboring aspiring new companies dotted the horizon. The industrial area outside Raleigh-Durham was always bustling with the comings and goings of people. Strangers were the norm. Better yet, the high-tech firms that congregated here hired people from around the world. No one looked out of place.

There was even a fairly high concentration of Muslims. A tremendous number of Pakistani developers had been hired to write cheap code for many of the nation's largest technology firms. Anwar Abu and his new associate, the Palestinian engineer Aymen Halaweh, blended right in.

So it was from this base of operation that "Carlos" and "Manuel" made their way north. With three blowers inside their van, they would stop at assigned sites in Washington and Baltimore. A similar van had left a few hours earlier. It was being driven to Philadelphia, New York, and Boston by "Jose" and "Fernando."

As each team arrived, they would gain access by appearing like they belonged. They carried the right credentials, right down to having plausible-looking purchase orders from the firm that managed each building. They knew the brand of equipment being used and had blueprints of the HVAC systems.

Much of this information was public, available in Building Department files. Anwar had been pleased to discover that a discreet fifty bucks would buy everything he needed at the county recorder's office.

Each crew was prepared to do their duty quickly and quietly. Without drawing attention to themselves, they would slip in, then out, moving on to the next building. No one would even remember that they had been there. That is, until the unlucky occupants started dying.

✡   ✠   ☾

EVERYTHING RELATED to Admiral Thurston Adams was now big news. And no one had benefited more from the tragedy-turned-spectacle than Blaine Edwards. Now, backed by a photograph of Sarah Nottingly, he was telling the world what he had learned about the beautiful agent. "She manages the Middle East Bureau at the CIA, is unmarried, and lives near the Capitol. Ms. Nottingly is twenty-nine years old and has a Masters in economics." The news had evolved. This mutation was called tabloid journalism. Blaine didn't care. Ratings were soaring.

FOX and other networks had arranged for cars to tail the hot couple like *paparazzi* following a prince and princess. Adams' personal life was now no less public than his mission.

✡   ✟   ☾

SURRENDERED OR NOT, the newly minted Admiral felt less than virile being driven around by his new flame. The car was stylish enough, and plenty muscular, but it wasn't the same having a woman at the controls. It was a guy thing, or maybe a pilot thing. He wasn't sure.

"I suppose you'd like me to take you home, Thor."

"I thought you weren't that easy." Before she could protest, he placed his hand on hers. "Just kidding."

Sarah accelerated as she turned right onto Constitution Avenue along the north side of the mall. The tires chirped, throwing Thor in her direction. His head fell on her shoulder. "*Your* home, silly, not mine."

Adams sighed. "Alright, but not yet. Let's check out the memorials. We could sit and talk for a while."

"And what army of guys is going to help me carry you up the steps?"

"I just want to *talk*."

"Are all you admiral types so chatty?"

"We're good at giving orders."

"I thought you said I was in charge."

"You are. Turn right at the next light. I live in Georgetown."

With that, sweet Sarah shoved the Jag down into second gear, thrust her right foot against the pedal, and threw the roadster into another sharp right turn. She kind of enjoyed right turns, she decided.

Within minutes she had pulled into his lot and shut down the engine. Miraculously, they had survived the drive without accident or ticket. But now they would need another miracle. It was all Sarah could do to help her wounded friend out of his seat. With that hurdle overcome, they had to negotiate a short flight of steps before even reaching the building.

Laughing, Sarah tried to position herself under Thor's good arm. As he leaned against her, she buckled. She was athletic, but supporting a six-foot-two SEAL was more than her slender frame could manage.

They had a problem. For this to work, Nottingly really needed to be under Adams' right arm. That way she could take the weight off his injured right leg. Unfortunately, he couldn't separate his broken right arm from his body, much less transfer any weight onto it. Focused, they could have mastered the stairs in a matter of minutes, but they were having way too much fun; it had become a game, a contact sport.

Once inside the building they simply rode the elevator to Adams' third-floor apartment. Stairs were fun, but.... All too quickly, they reached his floor in the small, traditional-looking apartment complex. This time, with the benefit of experience, Sarah positioned herself in front of Thor. This let him lean against her, bracing himself by placing his left hand on her right shoulder. They both knew that with an injury to both his right arm and leg, crutches were useless, as was a cane. A wheelchair was what the doctor had ordered, but where was the fun in that?

Not only had Thor left his wallet back at the base, he had left his keys there as well. Fortunately, he had hidden a key atop the door frame back when he had been a mere captain. As he opened the door, he could tell Sarah was impressed. The décor was tasteful, not "bachelor," decorated in blues and beiges. The furniture was traditional and things coordinated, more or less.

"Can I show you around?"

"Are you kidding? You're going down. It was all I could do to get you here." She led him to the nearest couch, one facing a brick fireplace. It was flanked on either side with shelves—filled with books, not a family photo on the lot of them. She didn't see a TV. She presumed he owned one.

A few steps away, Sarah stood, eyeing him, crumpled up in the sofa. *Now what?* she asked herself. *Just look at him. He's a mess.*

"Yeah, I know. I'm pretty pathetic," Thor said, reading her mind. "They wanted me to hang at the hospital, but I was dying to get home."

"Now that you're home, fly-boy, how are you going to take care of yourself? You can't drive. You can hardly walk."

He looked up at her with the sorriest eyes he could muster.

"No. No way. I like you and all, but I'm *not* spending the night here. I don't want to see my smiling mug on the front page of *The Washington Post,*" she said, waving her arms in the air. "The last thing this city needs is another bimbo."

"I'm not suggesting that you sleep with me. Just help me get to bed—after we talk awhile...and maybe come back in the morning. We'll figure something out from there."

"All right," she sighed. "I must be a sucker for a man in uniform. I'll help you out tonight and come back in the morning. Where's that key you used?"

Thor handed it to her, holding onto her hand. "Thank you."

"So, what's a girl got to do to get a drink in this joint? Do you have any wine?"

"Over there," Thor pointed to a rack near the kitchen. "The opener is in the first drawer. The white wines are in the fridge." Thor stared as she walked toward his decidedly un-bachelor-like kitchen. She looked as good going as she did coming.

"A *Gervertstramiener* from *Clos Du Bois*. Very nice," Sarah said, holding the bottle against her like it was a long-lost friend. "Do you like them?"

"Sweet, like you," he smiled. "My wine glasses are in the cupboard," he added before it dawned on him. "Hey, aren't you Christian types supposed to be teetotalers?"

"You'll never see me tipsy, Thurston. But abstinence is a man-made rule. Jesus not only drank wine, he made it—an excellent vintage, by all accounts."

Although she wouldn't have admitted it, Sarah was having a great time exploring. With every door she opened, every drawer she pulled, every question she asked, she was getting to know Adams better. And she liked what she was learning. For one thing it was obvious he could cook, that he liked to cook. She reached for the glasses and headed to the couch.

"Now, I suppose you'd like me to open it."

Thor tried to lift his broken right arm as if to say that there wasn't much choice if they wanted to drink it any time soon. "Yes, and while you're at it, could you light the fire, too?"

Rather than smack him, Sarah simply placed the wine bottle, opener, and crystal glasses on the coffee table in front of the couch. She had noticed that the fireplace had already been prepared. The wood was stacked neatly on the grate, ready to go. It looked like he had been a Boy Scout. She bent down, opened the mesh screen, lit a match, and started the fire. Taking a moment to appreciate her handiwork and enjoy its warmth, Sarah reflected on all that had happened to bring her to this place.

"If I promise not to bite, will you come back over here?"

Just then the phone rang. With the Admiral pointing in its direction, Sarah raced to a corner of the kitchen. She knew from experience that Thor had an answering machine and that it picked up after the third ring. In her official duties she had called him at his apartment many times.

"Hello, this is Cap... I mean *Admiral* Adams' residence." She wondered how often she would get to say that. "May I help you?"

"Yes. This is NBC calling from New York. The *Today Show*. Katie Couric and Matt Lauer would like to have Admiral Adams on the show tomorrow morning. Is he available?"

"I don't know. Let me ask." She covered the mouthpiece.

"It's the *Today Show*. They want to interview you tomorrow morning. What would you like me to tell them, your majesty?" Sarah giggled.

"Well, let's see. It's ten thirty now. To be on the show, we'd have to be in the New York area by six o'clock. In anything less than an F-18, that'd mean we'd have to leave Washington at five—at least if we hoped to be in the city by seven. No, I don't think so."

She removed her hand from the phone. "He says thank you, but no. It's too late, he's tired, and the arrangements would be too difficult."

"What if we arranged for a limousine to take him to the airport and had our corporate jet fly him to New York?"

She placed her hand back on the phone. "They're begging. Offering the corporate jet, limousine, dancing girls. What say you, O exalted one, and what did you mean by 'we'?"

"I'm not going unless you're going."

"You forget, I'm a workin' girl. What makes you think I can get time off?"

"The last thing the CIA wants is for a fully briefed Admiral going on national television and revealing something that's classified, right? You're my expert. You can brief me on what I can and cannot say."

"Not bad," she confessed, still covering the mouthpiece. "Barnes will probably buy that. But what makes you think I'm going to run off to New York City with a notorious bachelor?"

"'Cause you like me?" he grinned hopefully.

"You *are* pretty adorable in your present condition. And not terribly threatening." She returned his smile. "Okay, I'll go, but separate rooms." So much for not being easy. "I suppose you'd like me to make the arrangements."

"Please."

"Admiral Adams says he would be willing to be interviewed the day after tomorrow, Thursday."

"That's great."

"He will be traveling with Sarah Nottingly, the CIA agent that briefed him prior to the incursion."

"*The* Sarah Nottingly?" the *Today Show* representative asked.

"Yes." *How many Sarah Nottinglies are there in this town?*

"Would she be willing to be on the show too?"

"I don't think so. Now, the Admiral would like the jet to pick him up at National Airport tomorrow at...just one moment, please."

She looked over at Thor. "What time would you like to leave tomorrow? I'll get them to arrange rooms at the Plaza."

"How about ten. We could have lunch in the park."

"He'd like to be picked up at ten. And please, the jet needs to be big enough, a Gulfstream, a Falcon, or maybe a Challenger. He's pretty banged up. He'll need a wheelchair too, one that can be collapsed and put in the trunk of a car."

"NBC has a Falcon 900 here in New York. But how are we going to fly into Reagan National? It's been closed to general aviation, even charters, since 9/11."

"The Admiral has friends in high places. Your pilots will have no trouble. Now, the Admiral and Miss Nottingly would like rooms at the Plaza, overlooking the Park."

"Certainly. Would you like them adjoining? Is Miss Nottingly going to be providing protection for the Admiral? A lot of our guests have their security details stay in adjoining rooms."

Protection? Yeah right. She paused for a short eternity. *What am I getting myself into?* "Yes, that'd be fine."

"Okay. We'll have a limousine and collapsible wheelchair ready when he arrives. Normally our charters fly into Teterboro, but with his connections he might want to fly into La Guardia. Normally, it's a nightmare to get in and out of, but..."

"Yes, make it La Guardia." Sarah was feeling her oats.

"And how about dinner reservations and a show? We often arrange for such things when an important guest agrees to be on the program."

"Let me ask."

"Would you like to go to dinner and see a show?"

"Are you asking me out on a date, Sarah?"

"Why, yes, I believe I am, Admiral." She winked at him.

"Yes, he would like to see a show, and would enjoy a good dinner. How about Tavern on the Green?" It wasn't one of New York's snootiest restaurants, but it was romantic enough, and it would give them the opportunity to ride a carriage around Central Park.

"As you may know, the hottest ticket in town is the restaging of Rodgers and Hammerstein's *The Sound of Music*. Would that please the Admiral?"

"Yes, I'm sure it would." She didn't bother asking. She wanted to see it, and it was her date, after all. "Two tickets, please. He may want to bring Miss Nottingly." Sarah almost doubled over laughing.

"Normally, I'd have to say I'll try, but seeing that it's Admiral Adams,

I'm sure they'll find seats—probably in the front row."

The *Today Show* executive paused as he wrote a note to himself. "The show starts at nine o'clock. I'll arrange dinner for seven. Is there anything else I can do for the Admiral?"

"No. I think we...he'll be fine." *Oops.*

"Okay then. We'll have a car waiting at the Plaza at six thirty Thursday morning to take Ms. Nottingly and the Admiral to the studio."

"Wheee!" Sarah jumped up and down and squealed as she placed the phone back on the hook. "New York City, dinner at Tavern on the Green, *The Sound of Music*, the Plaza Hotel. Am I good or *what?*"

Excitedly she made her way across the room and sat down in one of the living room chairs facing Thor. *All Julie Andrews had was a Navy Captain. I'm flirting with an Admiral.*

Adams patted the section of the sofa closest to him.

Sarah shot him a look but complied. She sat down and leaned against him, placing her head on his shoulder. For the longest time they just sat there gazing into the fire.

"I suppose I should open the wine," she finally said, leaning forward and reaching for the bottle. In a move right out of high school, Adams lifted his arm and placed it on her back. She smiled. It made her tingle as she unscrewed the cork from the chilled bottle. He rubbed the back of her neck, under her hair. She pretended to ignore what he was doing.

Making a clinking sound on top of the glass as she filled them, Sarah handed one to Thor. He was forced to remove his arm from around her shoulders. What he would have done for a second good hand.

"I'd like to propose a toast." Adams lifted his glass. "Here's to getting to know you."

"And you," she smiled, lifting the goblet to her lips. "So what would you like to know?"

The fire was crackling in front of them. "What are some of your favorite things?"

"Oh, 'silver white winters that melt into springs, wild geese that fly with the moon on their wings'," she said, stealing a line from *The Sound of Music.*

"Okay, you got me, but *really*...."

"Well, I like to sing. I like to read, mostly non-fiction. I play golf, ski, scuba dive when I get a chance. I'm a pilot. Generally, I like to have fun. How 'bout you Admiral? Are you a fun guy?"

Thor smiled. "I can't sing a note, but other than that, your list sounds like mine." He took another sip of his wine. "Would you sing for me?"

"Sure. Come to church with me. I'm in the choir."

"I'd like that. How about next Sunday?" Adams asked.

"It's a date." She couldn't have been happier. "It's getting late. I need to go home and pack for tomorrow. Come to think of it, I probably need to pack for you, too. When would you like me back in the morning?"

"Twelve-oh-one?"

She didn't bite.

"Okay, I'll settle for zero eight hundred."

Sarah gave him a big smile. "You're pretty cute all busted up."

With that Thor set down his glass. He stared into Sarah's eyes, then down at her lips. They both knew what was coming. She put her glass down next to his. The fire's reflection danced within them. They closed their eyes and leaned forward.

✡   ✝   ☾

"MAY I HELP YOU?" the guard asked.

"We're here to install an air cleaner. Here's the work order."

"Nobody told me." He inspected the documents. "But, um, your papers look okay," the security officer replied, handing the file back to the driver. "Sign here."

"*Gracias.*" After thanking the guard, "Carlos" and "Manuel" drove their van into the basement parking level of the Prosperity Building in Washington.

"The map says we need to find the southwest corner." The Pakistani crewman pointed past the driver. "Over that way."

It was eleven-thirty. The basement was well lit, evidently as a deterrent to crime, but no one was around. Tonight, the lights would only serve the perpetrators.

The men parked their van, got out, and removed the first of their three blowers. It was heavy, but had it not been so awkward, one man could have carried it alone.

Setting the diabolical system on the floor, they retrieved box cutters from their toolboxes and began slicing the tape securing the largest of the ducts. With the tape removed, a series of screws was exposed. It took less than five minutes to remove them all.

Allah's helpers picked up a small container of anthrax spores and installed the deadly pestilence as they had been instructed. Satisfied with their handiwork, they lifted the now-armed blower into position and set the timer to go off at nine o'clock.

Returning to the van, they lifted a large box out of the cargo area. The carton was marked "Commercial Filters." The box was actually filled with a powdery dust, an extra supply just in case the blower was unable to find enough particulate inside the air-conditioning system to satisfy the requirements. Omen left little to chance.

The Pakistani Muslims set about attaching the feeder hose from the base of the carton to the side of the blower unit. To do so, they first had to drill a small hole into the side of the ductwork. With the hose in place, it looked like a humidifier attachment.

Moving around to the back of the large HVAC unit, they reached for the electrical wiring they had taped to blower. One located the closest splice and connected his wires. The other watched for the light on the unit to flash, indicating that the connection was live.

With the blower secured inside the duct and the wiring and tubing all in place, it was time to reattach the panel they had removed. Armed with electric screwdrivers and self-tapping metal screws, the section went back up even faster than it had been removed.

Using commercial-grade duct tape, the Islamic technicians hid all traces of their tampering. Stepping back they surveyed their work.

"Manuel" closed their toolboxes and checked the floor for any clues they might have left. "Carlos" grabbed a spray bottle of industrial-strength cleaner and a rag. He returned to the HVAC unit and proceeded to obliterate any fingerprints that could inadvertently point investigators in their direction. The job was done. It had taken just twenty-three minutes.

All that was required now was to wave to the guard as they drove out of the basement and motor on to their next site, the FOX News Headquarters Building in downtown Washington. It was that easy. Within less than nine hours, three to five thousand men, women, and children in each of six different buildings in five cities would be dying. And with any luck, one of them would be their least-favorite newscaster, Blaine Edwards.

✡   ✝   ☪

"I DON'T NEED an MIT graduate to tell me it's hard," Omen Quagmer spat into the phone. He and Kahn Haqqani were livid. Even with one mission under way, the terrorists were insatiable. They craved a bigger fix.

The Islamic clerics were climbing down their throats, angered by the setbacks they had suffered as a result of a newly unified America. Their Iraqi hosts were equally perturbed. They wanted *more* killing, not *less*.

The Iraqis knew that the only reason America had been brought to the brink of capitulation had been the overwhelming amount of terror al-Qaeda and others had inflicted. That's what terror was all about, wearing an adversary down to the point they were willing to capitulate, to acquiesce to the terrorist's agenda. There was no other way to explain America's about-face, her willingness to relinquish her longstanding support for Israel or her willingness to exit the Middle East. But now the nation's resolve had been rekindled.

Sure, we've suffered a setback. But it's nothing a little more chaos and killing can't fix, Kahn reflected. Islam thrived on chaos, terror, and war.

"Like I thought, blowers big enough to cover a city are too heavy to be carried aloft. At least with enough particulate to do any good," Aymen Halaweh explained patiently.

"There *must* be a way," Haqqani raged. "Think harder!"

"I want to help. That's why I'm here. But I'm not a magician. The numbers don't add up." The young engineer was becoming frustrated. "Only Allah can break the laws of physics."

"We don't need you preaching to us, boy," Omen jumped back in.

Young Halaweh placed one hand over the receiver and turned to his host. "What now?"

"Don't make them mad, whatever you do. Say you'll keep trying," Anwar Abu advised. "Don't think for a minute they won't kill us."

"We'll keep worki...." Aymen stopped abruptly, staring out the warehouse window.

"You'll what?" Omen asked over the phone from Baghdad. But all he could hear was beep, beep, beep. "*Hello?*"

"I'm sorry, sir. I have an idea." The Research Triangle Park Recycling Authority, better known as the trash man, was doing his duty just outside the window.

"Do we know anybody in the refuse business?" Halaweh asked.

"The what?"

"Trash. Garbage."

"Sure, we must. Why?"

"Can you get us one of those big trucks, a ten wheeler?" the young Palestinian asked his boss. "Commercial grade?"

"I suppose so. What for?" Omen inquired.

"You like the idea of hiding in plain sight, don't you, sir?"

"Yes, he does. Why ask? Stop the games, kid." Kahn was growing impatient. He wanted revenge, not dialog. "Why trash trucks?"

"I could build a blower large enough to condition a whole city inside a garbage truck. No one would suspect a thing."

"Okay. I'll check my Palm Pilot and figure something out."

Omen and Kahn were pleased. They had found the right boy. He was a little religious for their taste, but they could work with that.

The call finished, Kahn turned to Omen and asked, "Who's running the insurance scam in America?"

"Our American coordinator is...let's see." He played with his Palm XIV. "Abdul Halliz. I'm sure he's protecting somebody's garbage."

The "insurance business" had become a lucrative affair, offering life, casualty, and fire protection. If the insureds paid their premiums and kept their mouths shut, they got to go on living, their businesses didn't become casualties, and their homes and offices didn't burn to the ground. It was a deal no one could refuse. And as the insureds learned that Muslims were crazy enough to do most anything, the extortion flourished.

✡   ✝   ☾

"WE ARE HONORED to have the President of the United States as our guest," Katie Couric beamed. "Good morning, Madam President."

The image of the smiling POTUS filled the screen. She was sitting in front of an elegant fireplace. The setting was familiar to most Americans. The room was used to welcome foreign leaders and as a dramatic backdrop for the requisite photo op. Sitting in front of Gilbert Stuart's famous portrait of Washington, the one saved by Dolly Madison as the British were burning the White House during the war of 1812, she looked positively Presidential.

"Good morning, Katie, and good morning, America."

Couric wanted to say, "No, that's the other show." She bit her lip instead. "You must be pleased that your men captured Halam Ghumani."

"Yes, I am. During the campaign, I promised that we could put an end to the bloodshed by capturing terrorist leaders and bringing them to justice. I have done just that."

"So Halam Ghumani is now in custody in the United States?"

"Yes," she fibbed. "He will pay the price for the pain he has inflicted. It's time we close the books on this nightmare. This terrorist is finished."

"Do you think this is a fatal blow for al-Qaeda?"

"Yes. I believe so. We can all go back to living our lives. And, more importantly, we can start investing in our people rather than war."

If there had been a live audience, they might have booed her off the stage as they had done the previous evening at Reagan National. But

Couric appeared sympathetic, or at least respectful.

"Does that mean you'll be pressing ahead with your Middle East initiative, Madam President?" Katie asked.

The short blond Chief Executive sat taller in her chair. She was pleased with the question. "Yes, Katie. Just as soon as we encourage the Israelis to leave the Occupied Territories and give the Palestinian people their freedom, this terrorist mess will be behind us. After all, what right do they have to tell the Palestinians how to live? Equally important, Jerusalem should be an international city, a peaceful city, a city where everyone can go and pray. I support the peace process."

She had returned to her campaign patter. "You know, we all worship the same god, Jews, Christians, and Muslims alike. Why shouldn't we worship in the same city?" It sounded good, anyway.

"Are you still planning on addressing the United Nations next week?"

"We're considering every option. When the time is right, I'll recommend a UN-sponsored international peace-keeping force for Jerusalem."

Couric didn't want to embarrass the President, but she knew she had to ask. "What do you think of Admiral Adams and his men?"

"It was *my* operation, Katie. And while the crucifixion scene was horrible, I'm pleased with the end result. I have fulfilled my promise to capture Ghumani. With him out of commission, terrorism will diminish. By working smarter, we have made the world safer."

"And Admiral Adams?" Katie gently prodded.

"He's really something, isn't he?"

"You know," Couric concluded, "he's agreed to be on our show."

"Really." The President forced a smile. "I'm sure he will make an entertaining guest." *At least he's leaving town.*

✡   ✝   ☾

SARAH AWOKE EARLY. This was going to be a great day. She agonized over what to pack—travel clothes for the jet, stroll-in-the-park clothes for the afternoon, a sexy cocktail dress for dinner and the play, and evening attire appropriate for adjoining rooms, conservative enough not to give the wrong impression. And then there was tomorrow. What would tomorrow bring?

"Oh drat," she said out loud. "Just pick something, girl." *What's he gonna do, say I look ugly and send me home? He can't even walk on his own.*

At issue was the flirt factor. In a weak moment Sarah had purchased a cocktail dress, some lingerie, and a variety of "date outfits" that were a good deal more provocative than she had ever been comfortable wearing. Yet if she was ever going to gallivant in them, this was the time.

Ultimately, she threw caution to the wind. What she chose was on the skimpy side, but it was tasteful enough, she convinced herself. Surprised that she could still get her bag closed, she threw in a pair of jeans, an old sweat shirt, and a couple of books, just in case. Now in a hurry, Sarah slipped into her favorite spring dress, zipping it up as she reached for her roller bag, and headed out the door.

Nottingly pressed the remote trunk release on her Jag, smiling as it popped open and greeted her with a friendly chirp. She sped off with the top up so she wouldn't muss her hair. Minutes later, Sarah pulled into the crowded parking lot of Thor's Georgetown digs.

At first she was taken aback by all the commotion. *Was there an accident?* Then the ugly reality dawned on her. Men carrying large video cameras started rushing in her direction.

"Sarah. *Sarah Nottingly!* Can we have a word with you?" they shouted.

Trucks sporting satellite dishes were everywhere. NBC, ABC, CBS, CNN, and, of course, FOX. She thought she even recognized Blaine Edwards, but it couldn't be. Surely someone with his ego wouldn't make house calls.

"No thank you," she said respectfully, waving her hands. It didn't matter. They rushed in like a pack of hyenas, pinning her inside the car, frightening her, angering her.

"Please, back away. I have nothing to tell you. I'm asking you nicely." That didn't work, so she summoned her most commanding CIA voice. "Get your cameras out of my face and *back off,*" she said firmly. "*Now! Please!*" She unlatched the door and tried to open it. "You should be ashamed." *Thank God I didn't spend the night here.*

They finally parted just enough to let her wiggle her way between them. As quickly as her long legs would carry her, Sarah walked up the front steps and made a beeline to the elevator. She wasn't happy with the way she'd addressed the unruly mob, but at least she'd made it through the gauntlet.

Upstairs, she looked all around before pulling Thor's key out of her purse. Confident she was alone in the narrow hallway, she knocked first, then opened his door. Closing it quickly behind her, she turned the latch and hollered, "Thor, I'm back. Are you awake?"

"In here," Adams' voice boomed from his bedroom.

"Are you decent?"

"Better than that. Come on in, Sarah."

"How did you manage all this?" she asked incredulously, looking at a man who had obviously showered, shaved, and almost finished dressing.

"It wasn't easy. I've been going at it for a couple of hours."

"Poor baby," she replied in her most nurturing voice. She sat down beside him on the bed, reaching out her hand and caressing his recently shaved face. He leaned over and gave her a kiss.

Jumping to her feet, she asked, "Okay! What do you need me to do?"

"Pack. My suitcase is on the shelf inside my closet."

Sarah walked over and stood on her tiptoes. As she raised her arms, her dress, already short, showed way more leg than the Admiral had yet seen. Realizing what she'd done, Nottingly quickly grabbed the small case and turned around. "Enjoy the show?" she asked.

He was too embarrassed to answer.

"It's okay. I'm glad you like 'em. Now what?"

Thor smiled. "What do you think, a suit or a uniform for the show?"

"Hmm. Can I sew your new admiral stripes on one of your captain's uniforms?"

Adams was dumfounded.

"Don't look at me that way," she laughed. "Yes, I can sew."

"Can you cook?"

"Don't push your luck."

Thor grinned. "Actually, I don't have anything to sew with."

"I do. I always carry a needle and thread, just in case." Peering into the closet, she asked, "Is it too early for dress whites?"

"Yes. I'll need one of the dark ones."

She removed a dress uniform, along with all the trappings. Now how about a suit for tonight? I'm wearing a cute little pink number. Do you have something that would look good with a pink tie? You do *have* a pink tie?

"Yeah. Never worn it. Try the khaki suit or maybe the gray one."

She looked at them both on the hanger and removed the gray suit. Thumbing through his ties, she found what she was looking for, grabbed a shirt, and laid them on the bed. "Mind if I pick out something casual for tomorrow?"

"Be my guest. You're doing great."

Sarah finished packing her friend's gear, everything from socks to belts, ditty bag to shoes. Boxers, she noted, not briefs. Zipping up her second bag of the morning, she glanced back at the Admiral. He was sitting on the bed, unsuccessfully trying to button his shirt with one hand.

"Let me," she said as he looked up into her eyes. He was like a puppy. Sarah was thoroughly enjoying this. She was now confident she had picked the right outfits. This was definitely going to be more date than assignment.

"Now all we have to do is get you off this bed, out the door, and past the marauding horde."

"The what?"

"Your parking lot is crawling with *paparazzi*. I had to fight my way in. They're really obnoxious. I'm afraid I wasn't very nice to them."

The Admiral bristled.

"Down, boy," she said, feeling his muscles tense. "You can fight for me some other time. We're going to have to talk our way out today."

✡   ✝   ☾

EVERYTHING WAS WORKING according to plan. The timers had gone off on schedule. Six skyscrapers were being surreptitiously infected with insidious spores.

The perpetrators were back in Research Triangle Park. Planning was proceeding apace on their next endeavor. They knew it would be several days before the first victims contracted the disease and reported their condition to the authorities. So between now and what they hoped would be a glorious celebration of Allah's victory, they focused on the task at hand.

The administrators of al-Qaeda's lucrative insurance business had managed to commandeer a trash truck, so the boys had plenty to do. The vehicle was well worn and more than authentic. Although its contents had been dumped before delivery, it arrived with a rich aroma.

Suffering in North Carolina, rather than Afghanistan, they were without a handy horde of crazed Muslim Militants. Aymen and Anwar were forced to do the dastardly deed themselves. With flashlight, hose, brush, and cleanser in hand, Halaweh climbed into the fragrant interior of the vintage refuse hauler. As soon as he could see the steel interior through the grime, Aymen hollered for Anwar to turn off the hose. Even inside the small drive-in warehouse, it was uncomfortably cold.

Anwar Abu had already bought components based upon Omen's impractical demand for a flying city conditioner. Much of what they required was commercially available. Since they had been through the drill with the smaller HVAC blowers, they knew exactly where to find what they needed. This time the components were just bigger and more powerful.

"How are we going to build the machine inside the truck?" Anwar asked the engineer.

"Kinda like they build a ship in a bottle. We'll build the mixer outside first, to the exact dimensions of the interior. Then we'll separate the components, carry them inside, and bolt 'em together. The existing trash compaction unit will be replaced with the blower. Can you see if someone makes one that runs hydraulically rather than on electrical current?"

"Sure," Anwar shrugged. "I think the company I bought these from has one."

"Good. It'll outperform the electric unit and be easier to integrate into the existing hydraulics of the truck."

"I see."

"We'll need to leave a reservoir for the particulate powder," Halaweh said, rubbing his sparse whiskers. He hadn't shaved in weeks, but it was hard to tell. "I'd also like a dehumidifier. The pathogen loses its killing power when it absorbs moisture."

The warehouse they were working in was well equipped. The boys had at least two of most everything Craftsman made, from pneumatic tools to the best contractor-grade electric saws, drills, and grinders. Standing back, the Muslim brothers proudly surveyed a series of giant red boxes, their drawers stuffed with a full complement of hand tools. While they were short on men, they were long on manly paraphernalia.

✡ ✝ ☾

SARAH FELT LIKE a movie star as she pulled her Jaguar beneath the wing of the three-engine Falcon jet. *A girl could get used to this,* she thought. She removed the key and waited for the steering wheel to automatically lift up and move out of her way. Then she pushed another button and the trunk popped open. The XK-8 was quite a ride, but nothing compared to what loomed above her.

"Let me help you, sir," the pilot said to Admiral Adams. The co-pilot assisted Sarah with the door. The crew looked professional, dressed in their official corporate flight-crew regalia. They formed their arms into a sling and carried the Admiral up the stairs, walking sideways. Once inside, he was good to go on his own. He braced himself on the backs of the custom leather executive chairs as he hobbled to the first starboard seat facing forward. He would rather have gone to the couch in the rear and reprised last night's kiss, but with the pilots up front, he was reasonably certain Sarah wouldn't oblige.

Nottingly didn't like the idea of parking her prized possession outside in what had once been a busy lot. Signature had been a vibrant FBO, the only Fixed Base Operator on the field at Reagan National. With a monopoly, their lobby had witnessed the comings and goings of Washington's big shots. Corporate types coming to beg the government for contracts and politicos scamming rides home from their access-hungry constituents had kept the place buzzing.

But that was all gone now. America was a nation at war, living in fear. Although there had never been a terrorist incident originating at Reagan National, nor one in which general aviation had even been a factor, the place had been shut down by some brilliant committee of bungling bureaucrats. It was deserted. Yet Sarah was convinced that while the FBO was shut down, the criminals were not. America's most liberal city was also its most crime-ridden. She didn't want to return to find her car in pieces, or missing.

Recognizing her dilemma, a lineman suggested she park inside one of the giant white hangers that lined the ramp. They had once held the sleekest corporate jets. Now there was plenty of room for a sexy convertible.

Prancing back to the plane, she scampered up the stairs. Peeking inside, Sarah saw Thor sitting in the right seat, sipping a cup of orange juice. She sat down beside him.

The copilot briefed the pair about the weather and the expected duration of the flight. He encouraged them to fasten their lap belts. As they complied, he offered Miss Nottingly a cup of coffee and a pillow. This was tall cotton for a simple southern girl.

"Clearance, this is Admiral One at Signature. We have the numbers and would like to pick up our IFR routing to LaGuardia," the copilot said into his mike. They had dubbed their craft "Admiral One" for the occasion. The flight crew knew they would get the red-carpet treatment.

"You are cleared direct to LaGuardia, Captain. You may disregard all normal departure instructions and prohibited airspaces. Climb to thirty-five thousand feet as requested. Squawk 1001. Frequency upon departure will be 118.95. Taxi to runway one. Contact ground on 121.9. Have a great flight."

That was hardly a normal clearance. It was tantamount to being told, "Do whatever you please." The flight crew was as excited as the passengers. Entering the new frequency, the copilot pressed the push-to-talk button on his yoke. "National Ground, this is Falcon 2 November, Bravo, Charlie... I mean, this is Admiral One, ready to taxi."

"Yes, Admiral One, you are cleared past the firehouse to runway one. It's good to have you with us. That celebration last night was one for the ages. It's great to see the country smiling again."

"That's a tally ho," the pilot replied.

Reaching the departure end of runway one, the copilot switched the radio to the tower frequency. Before he could even speak, a voice boomed in his headset. "Admiral One, you are cleared for departure. God Bless." Yes, indeed. This was a different place and time.

"Admiral One, rolling." With that, the pilot accelerated, pressed on the left rudder pedal, and positioned his craft in the center of the runway, heading zero one zero degrees, ever so slightly east of north. The flight crew scanned the instruments one last time before advancing the throttles. Within moments, everyone onboard was pressed back in their seats as the corporate jet became airborne—flying directly over the Pentagon. They were headed back to the city where it had all begun—where the Twin Towers had once proudly stood guard, Ground Zero.

Sarah took a sip of her coffee. Reaching down, she pulled a book out of her purse. She didn't want the Admiral to think she would be smothering him with attention. She flipped on the overhead light.

"What are you reading?" he asked.

"Oh, it's a book on Israel. It might shed some light on what happened back there on our mission." Although she hadn't gone on the incursion, Nottingly had played a major role in selecting the target and crafting the strategy the Captain had deployed. She never shirked responsibility.

The book's cover pictured a trio of fighter jets—F-14 Tomcats, she thought—over a barren stretch of mountainous terrain somewhere in Israel. As Sarah picked up where she had left off the day before, Thor asked, "Would you mind reading out loud? That way we can both learn something."

"Okay, but just so you know, it's not about the jets pictured on the cover. It's full of Biblical references."

"Please. That's all right. In fact, it's better. I already know about Navy jets." He smiled.

"I suppose you're right." She turned back to the beginning.

"No, that's okay," he said, watching her. "You can pick up from wherever you were."

"Alright, if you don't mind." Turning back, she took another sip of her coffee and began to read. "The author says, 'The Bible links the Jews' return to Israel with the Nazi Holocaust and with the end of this age.'"

"What does he mean, 'end of this age'?" Thor was an active listener. If he didn't understand something, he'd jump right in with a question. Drove most people nuts.

"The Bible prophets tell of the events that the last generation will witness before Christ returns," she said, not knowing if her explanation would help or just confuse things.

"He's coming back? Did he forget something?"

"No, silly. Didn't you ever go to Sunday School when you were a boy?"

"No, but that's a long story." Adams didn't want to share the pain he still carried with him from his youth. It wouldn't endear him to Sarah.

"Well, Jesus told his disciples that he would return. See, the first time he came, it was to show us what God was like and what he expected of us. Then he allowed himself to be crucified, just like your friends were."

"If he died, then how's he coming back?"

"He beat death, kinda like your friends...well, no. Not exactly. He died, but then he rose from the dead three days later. It was also on a Sunday morning. The first Easter."

"Oh, yeah. Yours is the only religion where the founder beats the rap."

"Beats the rap?"

"Yeah. Escapes death—which is the only real guarantee we have in life." It was spoken like a true soldier.

"He didn't *escape* death, Thor. He *conquered* it. He didn't have to hang on that cross outside Jerusalem. He could have torched the place, like he did Sodom and Gomorrah. But instead, Christ sacrificed himself for us."

Thor looked puzzled. "I don't get it. How does getting nailed to a cross and dying help us? How does it help anybody?"

"The Bible says, 'We have all sinned and have fallen short of God's glory.' A just God can't allow sin to go unpunished any more than just society can allow a criminal to go free without sacrificing something. Without consequences there'd be instant anarchy. Justice means getting what you deserve—whether that's good or bad. With me so far?"

"That makes sense."

"Okay. Look at sin and crime the same way. If you commit a crime somebody has to pay the price for what you've done to make you right with society or God." She looked directly into Thor's eyes. "That's what Jesus did on the cross. He made the sacrifice, paid the price, if you will, for our sins—our crimes—so we don't have to."

She could see that he wasn't getting this. Sarah tried a different tack. "You ever get a reckless driving ticket?"

"Speeding," he smiled, "but not reckless. I must be more conservative than you are."

"Not likely, but just pretend. You show up in court and you're found guilty, 'cause you are. You know it, the cop knows it, so does the judge."

"Okay."

"So the judge passes sentence. He says the ticket is going to cost you more than you can pay, and they're gonna lock you up. What do you do?"

"Umm, go to jail?"

"Right. That's the whole concept of crime and punishment. When you do something wrong, society requires a sacrifice: your money, your freedom, or your life. Only now, suppose that the judge comes down from the bench, takes off his robe, pulls out his checkbook, and pays your fine—even goes to jail for you."

"Nice guy."

"Yeah. He is. But pay attention. At this point you've got two choices. You can either accept his gift, or you can decline and go to jail."

"I think I'll opt for the charity."

"Smart move. The Bible calls it grace. That's what happened on the cross. The judge, the *ultimate* Judge, paid your fine for you."

"Why would he do that?"

"You ever heard of John 3:16?"

"The thing plastered all over every sporting event?"

"Yes. The verse says that God loved us so much, he personally paid our fine."

Thor stared straight ahead. His head was swimming. "Look, Sarah, I'm gonna need some time to think about all this."

"Sure. I understand. Want me to keep reading?"

"Please. The guy was talking about the Holocaust...."

Sarah brought the cup back up to her lips and drank the last of her coffee. "The author says that this prophecy comes from an anonymous Psalm."

"That wouldn't be Psalm 102, would it? One of the guys, Yacob Seraph, said something...."

"I don't know. Let me look." She flipped ahead. "Yeah, it *is* Psalm 102." Her interest now piqued, she started to read. "'The Jews' return did not occur in a vacuum but in the wake of the worst event in human history: the Holocaust.'"

Sarah set the book down. "It wasn't our proudest moment."

"What do you mean? You're not German."

"No, I'm not. I'm human. When I was in college, I visited one of the concentration camps. It was horrible—as bad as watching your guys hang. The Nazis created a man-made hell."

He nodded, encouraging her to carry on.

"The author suggests that Psalm 102 speaks of that hellish event. I brought my Bible with me. Let's see what the Psalm actually says." Sarah pulled a thin leather-bound book from her purse. She opened it to Psalm 102. "Before I begin, Thor, you need to understand something about

Biblical prophecies. They're written in a poetic style, and in a three thousand-year-old vocabulary. God may predict the Holocaust, but he's not going to call it that, because the word hasn't been coined yet. Neither has 'German', 'Hitler', 'Nazi', 'cremation', or 'cyanide'. He's not going to tell you it will happen in 1935, because that calendar hasn't been invented. That's why you can sometimes read a passage, as I have this one, and not catch the significance until someone points it out to you."

"Okay. I understand."

Sarah read, "'Do not hide your face from me in my time of anguish, for my days perish in smoke, and my body is scorched like glowing embers in a hearth.' That sounds a lot like cremation, like what I saw in Auschwitz."

Thor winced. "In my opinion, the systematic cremation of Jews was the most gruesome act in all of history."

She returned to the passage. "He says, 'My heart is striken; I am so beaten, I am oblivious, forgetting to eat.'"

"Could be someone in pain, preferring starvation to facing another day in the Nazis' tender care. Or am I reading too much into this?"

"No, you may be right. Listen to what comes next. It says, 'I am reduced to skin and bones; my flesh clings to them.' For me, one of the most haunting memories of the concentration camp was the walls of black and white pictures showing starving people, with legs and arms so emaciated they looked more like birds than humans. I looked at their faces, and then turned and stared at the mountain of human ash that still remains—a reminder, lest we forget what happened there."

"Who wrote this Psalm, Sarah? How old is it?"

She checked. "Well, 101 and 103 were written by King David. He reigned about 1000 BC. I don't know if he wrote 102, but it's got to be several thousand years old."

"Is there more?"

"'I am like a vomiting bird in desolation. My eyes are sunken within their cavities. I am sleepless, always on the lookout. All day long, those who hate me taunt me; they strip and exposed me. Those who are enraged against me, celebrating and boasting, use *my name* as a curse.' Thor, do you remember the pictures of Jews during the Nazi reign of terror?"

"Yes. They were forced to wear yellow stars on their clothing, over their hearts."

"The star of David, the six-pointed star, the symbol for the Jews. They had 'Jude' written on them, *Jew*. They were cursed because of *their name*."

"Is all prophesy like this? I mean, predicting that a people would be singled out and cursed by name, then be starved to the point their flesh clung to their bones, only to have those bones burned *en masse*—that's amazing. The combination of these things happened only once in all of recorded history. You know that, don't you, Sarah?"

"Yes. The day I visited Auschwitz changed my life, changed my view of what we're like apart from God."

Thor shook his head. "So Psalm 102 is what you Christians call prophecy. Are there a lot of these things?"

"More than you can imagine. The Jews are God's chosen people—the people he chose to reveal himself through. He tells us everything that's going to happen to them, right up to the end of time."

Sarah lifted the book again to see how the Psalm ended. "'For I eat ashes, and mingle my drink with tears.' Did you know that..." she paused to wipe a tear away, "...that the Jews in the concentration camps were forced to breathe in the ashes of those who'd been cremated before them? The smoke that came out of the crematorium chimneys rained right back down on the camps, on the Jews themselves."

Thor didn't know what to say.

"'The Lord gazed upon the earth to hear the groaning of the prisoners and to set free those who were doomed to death.'" She continued to read, "'Because of your displeasure, you have taken me up and cast me aside.' Much of the Old Testament speaks about God's covenant with the Jews, Thor. He tells them what wonderful things he'll do for them if they hold up their end of the bargain, and what wrath they'll endure if they don't. When they *don't*, God tells them that they're going to be expelled from the land he gave them—dispersed among the nations. He's just saying it a thousand years before it happens."

Sarah reached out for Adams' hand. "If you're still open to this, I'll share some more prophecies with you later."

"I'd like that. But..." he paused, "that doesn't mean *all* I want to do is wrestle with this stuff. If it's all right with you, I'd like to sneak in a kiss or two along the way."

"Is that how they got you to learn your lessons at Annapolis?" She liked yanking his chain. "Okay, Thor. If you're a good boy, you'll earn a kiss or two." She was happy to oblige.

A little embarrassed, Sarah returned to her Bible. The Psalmist wasn't through. "The story has a happy ending. 'But you, O Lord, endure through all generations.' Loosely translated, that means God is going to be around to pick up the pieces. The Psalmist goes on to say, 'You will arise and have compassion on Jerusalem, your capital, 'for it is time to be gracious to her; the appointed time has come. For her stones are dear to your servants; even her dust moves them to emotion.'"

"Is he talking about returning the Jews to Jerusalem?"

"Could be. The Bible says that in the last days, God, in spite of everything the Jews have done, will bring them back into the Promised Land."

"So even though the world thinks the United Nations gave the Jews their land back in 1948, it was prophesied ages ago? They were exiled for two thousand years, yet they remained intact as a people. In fact, they're probably the only people to have been conquered and dispersed, yet still remain a distinct nation today. But if what you're saying is true, man had nothing to do with their getting Judea back."

"You're a good student, sailor. That deserves a kiss." Sarah leaned over, hoping the pilots wouldn't turn around, and gave the Admiral his reward. "Do you know why the British and the United Nations even *considered* giving the Jews a homeland, why they passed the resolution?"

"Do I get another kiss if I get it right?"

"I'll give you another even if you get it wrong; it just won't happen as quickly."

Thor was motivated. "1917. Synthetic acetone. Used in explosives. A British Jew, Chaim Weizmann, invented it. Turned the course of World War One. Lloyd George asked him what he wanted in return for saving the nation. He could have asked for anything. Weizmann told him he wanted his ancestral homeland, but the Brits dragged their feet, even though they now owned it, having taken Judea from the Turks. Then, as a direct result of the Holocaust, the United Nations voted overwhelmingly to give the Jews their land back. *Quid pro quo.* These things are all related."

With his good arm, Adams made like he was pulling the handle of a slot machine. "Ka-ching." It was childish but cute.

Nottingly glanced toward the cockpit again. The flight crew was busy doing their job. She wasn't crazy about public displays of affection (PDAs, in her vernacular), but a promise was a promise. She leaned over again and gave Thor a kiss. A little moan sort of slipped out, an excited, let-your-guard-down kind of sound that said, ever so eloquently, "It was my pleasure."

"I could get used to this. Is that the end of the Psalm, or is there more?"

Sarah couldn't remember. Her mind had packed its bags and left for the Bahamas. "What? I'm sorry. I don't.... What did you ask me?" she said, blushing so red her cheeks matched her painted nails.

Showing good form, Thor elected not to embarrass her. He merely repeated his question.

"Yes. It goes on to say, 'The Lord will rebuild Israel and appear in his glory.' And then, 'Let this be written for a future generation, that a people not yet created may clearly see Yahweh'—that's God's personal name."

When she had finished the Psalm, Sarah picked up the other book she'd been reading, the one with the F-14s on the cover. She read, "'The Hebrew does not say "future generation" but *final* generation. The phrase in the original Hebrew is written *l'dor acharon*. Hebrew dictionaries say *acharon* means "last" or "final."' Oh, my."

"What did the writer mean by 'last generation?'" Getting no response, he asked her again.

But the answer was more than Thor was ready to hear. The Psalmist had said that God would return to Earth, restore Israel to greatness and faith, and that the world would worship him in Jerusalem. The Holocaust—the darkest chapter of the history of man—would begin it all; yesterday's moral eclipse would be the event heralding this most radiant of tomorrows. And all of this was to be a sign to the *last* generation.

As the Falcon touched down in New York, Sarah was still dazed, wondering whether this chapter in her life was beginning or ending.

9

PRETTY IN PINK

New York's Plaza Hotel is something special. Its location on the southeast corner of Central Park, its gleaming white exterior, traditional lines, and French windows all contribute to its ambiance. Marble floors and crystal chandeliers greet the well heeled as they enter.

"Thank you, kind sir," Sarah said as a bellman opened the door and offered to help her out of the seat. "But what I really need is someone to assist my crotchety ol' friend here. He's pretty feeble." Sarah winked at the Plaza's attendant and whispered, "It's Admiral Adams."

"Yes, we've been expecting him," he said in hushed tones.

Another attendant joined in. "I know you," he beamed. "You're Sarah, the CIA agent, the *girlfriend*."

"I'm pretty sure about that first part, but not the girlfriend thing."

The bellman just gave her a puzzled look. She wasn't fooling anybody.

"Hey, remember me? What's a guy hafta do to get out of here?" Being an invalid made the Admiral cranky.

Sarah and the driver scurried to the trunk. They removed the collapsible wheelchair but didn't have a clue what to do next. They searched for a lever to unfold it. *Oh, I see. You just pull these two handles apart, and voila!*

"Hello? I could sure use a hand."

"Keep your pants on, big boy," Sarah chided. It probably wasn't the best comeback she could have chosen.

As others figured out who was in the car, a small crowd surrounded the white stretch limo. "Thor, Thor, Thor," they chanted.

With nothing else to do, Adams lowered the window and waved to his fans, thankful his nickname had stuck. *Thurston, Thurston, Thurston* wouldn't have had quite the same ring. Celebrity was a new experience for him, though at the moment he would gladly have exchanged it all for a pair of working legs.

"Sarah? Could you come here for a moment?"

Nottingly sat down backwards in the car, her legs dangling outside.

Leaning back against Thor, she said, "Yes, dear."

No one had ever called him "dear." "Say that again and you're gonna have a shadow."

"What do you say we go for a carriage ride through the park—*dear?*"

He smiled. "Don't we have to check in?"

"Nope. I can't even give 'em a tip. The manager says they're going to take our stuff to our room, and that everything's comped."

"What do you mean 'our room'?"

"Yeah! She's giving us the Presidential Suite. Two bedrooms. I asked."

"My, my. Haven't we been busy. But the carriage thing? I don't know. So far you haven't even been able to get me out of the *car.*"

Looking around, she said, "I think we might find a volunteer."

With the help of two grinning passers-by (who beat out twenty others for the privilege), the Admiral was lifted into an elegantly appointed carriage. Sarah jumped in beside him, held his hand and laid her head on his shoulder. Her wavy brunette hair cascaded softly down Thor's chest and tickled his neck. This felt a lot better than getting shot in Afghanistan.

The stately horse-drawn carriage pulled away from the Park Avenue curb, veered left, and descended into Central Park. All along the way, strollers and joggers turned, stared, smiled, and then expressed their gratitude to America's new prince and princess. The image was like Prince Charles and Lady Di, except these two actually *were* falling in love.

Springtime in Central Park is a wonderful experience. Spindly redbuds scream in their passionate purple garb, while stately dogwoods stand majestically alongside dressed in their elegant whites. Beneath them, islands of azaleas blush in purple, red, and pink as if falling in love with the scene above. The towering hardwoods are just beginning to sprout in their vibrant greens. The clicking of the large steel-rimmed wooden wheels on the narrow and winding roads somehow added to the romance. The chill of the spring air felt refreshing on their cheeks. Sarah pointed toward a large pond with a profusion of azaleas on the embankment beyond, reflecting their splendor in the still water. The Admiral looked and smiled. Neither said much of anything.

After some time, Sarah spotted a hotdog vendor and asked the carriage driver to stop. It was past lunchtime and this looked like the perfect place. After dressing their dogs, Sarah helped Thor hobble over to a wooden park bench. A family of mallards caught their eye. They watched as mom led the way, her ducklings all in a row behind her. The proud papa, splendid in his iridescent green and blue plumage, waddled alongside.

They both silently wondered, hoped perhaps, that this might someday be them, married, with family in tow. Thor reflected, however, that unlike the ducks, she would wear the prettiest feathers in the family.

"Sarah. This Christian stuff is important to you, isn't it? I mean, your religion means a lot to you, right?" He knew the answer. The question was a doorway to something else.

"Yes and no. Why do you ask?"

"You know I don't share your faith."

"Yes."

"Does that bother you?"

"Yes."

"We obviously like each other. I mean, I like you, and...."

"And I like you." She knew where he was going now.

"Our relationship: is it dependent upon me agreeing with you?"

"Believing yes, agreeing no. We can disagree on many things without it being a problem. See, my faith is a relationship, not a religion. Actually, I don't like religion very much. As a matter of fact, neither did Jesus. He wasn't the least bit religious."

Adams cocked his head. He was puzzled.

"For me it all boils down to one thing. Is Jesus God? If he is, my life has meaning. If he isn't, I'm a fool, and I don't have a clue how we got here or where we're going."

"I don't believe in miracles, and I've never been able to stomach anybody's religious mumbo jumbo. But you're nobody's fool, of that I'm certain. And there's something good going on inside you."

"Thank you, Thurston." She smiled, wrapping her arms around him. "You say the sweetest things."

"So how do I get from where I am to where you are?"

"Faith." Sarah could see that her answer deflated him. "Don't worry. Ultimately it takes more faith to believe there's *no* God than to acknowledge that he lives. It's not a leap in the dark, just a step into the light."

His smile returned. He was embarking on a grand adventure. "So how are you gonna convince me?"

"Oh, I'm not. God is."

Sarah jumped up off the bench and reached for his hand. She'd seen another carriage out of the corner of her eye. "I've got a date tonight with this really cute sailor, so if you don't mind, I'd like to get ready."

They found themselves being escorted to the Presidential Suite. The bellman opened the door, and Sarah wheeled Adams inside. The room, actually a suite of them, was as opulent as anything she had ever seen, and she had seen a lot. Thor, on the other hand, had absolutely no frame of reference. The barracks at Diego Garcia it was not.

Nottingly leaned down and gave Thor a peck on the cheek. The bellman coughed to remind the amorous couple that he was standing right behind them. "Where would you like these things?"

"Oh, I'm sorry," Sarah blushed.

"It appears there's a room upstairs," Thor said. "Put her things—that would be the *big* bag—up there if you would."

Sarah followed the bellman up the elegantly curved staircase as Thor wheeled himself around the lower floor, but with only one arm, moving straight was a challenge. Unaccustomed to being a left winger, he found himself going in circles. He noticed that the suite's living room was strategically placed in the corner overlooking Fifth Avenue and the Park. It came complete with a wood-burning fireplace and a baby grand piano. There was a full dining room, a small but elegant kitchen, and even a library. Around the corner, he found his room. A beautifully cushioned king-sized bed stood beneath a stunning crystal chandelier.

Rolling toward his bathroom, he was taken aback by its extravagance. It looked nearly as big as his living room back in Georgetown. There were a couple of vanities and a separate shower and roman tub, all constructed of a gorgeous black granite shot through with rich burgundy veining.

The bellman turned and asked, "May I hang your clothes, sir?"

"Sure, thanks. As you can see, I'm not very mobile."

"My pleasure, sir." He placed Thor's bag on a tapestry stand and hung its contents in the walk-in closet, and placed the remainder of the things Sarah had packed for him in the dresser.

The Admiral struggled to get his wallet. He wasn't used to the tight confines of the wheelchair.

"No sir, please. That won't be necessary. It is our privilege to host you. Stay as long as you'd like—as our guests. The manager has asked me to give you this note. It confirms our hospitality."

Thor reached out for the letter and opened it. It said that he and Sarah were welcome but that their money wasn't.

"If you'd like, I can arrange breakfast here in your dining room tomorrow morning, before or after you do the *Today Show*. Oh, and sir, Ms. Nottingly asked me to inform you that she would like an hour to prepare for this evening. She'll be ready by six o'clock."

The Admiral chuckled. "She will, will she? The question is, will I be ready for her? Easy on the eyes, that one."

"Yes, sir," the bellman replied. "If I may say so, sir, she's what my daddy would call a 'keeper'."

"Yeah, smart too, but more than that, she's a saint."

Adams had a way of putting people at ease, and the bellman was no exception. He found himself chatting with the famous Admiral as if he were an old friend.

"The whole country's smitten with her. You're perfect together."

"Let's hope I can get her to agree," Thor laughed.

The bellman just smiled. "I've placed your theater tickets next to the menus on the dining-room table, but I doubt you'll need them. The theater has already called us. They're as excited as we are. You're a hero, Admiral, especially here in New York."

Thor expressed his personal gratitude for the courage so many New Yorkers displayed during those dark days.

The bellman turned to leave. "Oh. Your car: I'm told it will be waiting for you at the Fifth Avenue entrance at six thirty. You'll want to be ready to go by six forty-five. The Tavern on the Green is just around the corner. Later, the driver will take you to the theater. Tomorrow morning, the same driver will be back at six. He'll take you to Rockefeller Center. It's only about thirty blocks from here. Should take you less than ten minutes."

"You guys are great," Thor told his newest fan.

"I've placed a couple of keys on the table next to your tickets, Admiral," the bellman smiled, "but you won't need them, either. We'll have security at your door, and the NYPD has a detail of plain-clothes officers stationed throughout the hotel. We want to keep you safe."

"Thank you."

Before leaving, he held out his hand. The Admiral made another effort to find his wallet, but the bellman didn't want a tip. He was reaching out in friendship. The reluctant hero returned the gesture.

Now alone, Adams rolled his chair to the door and checked the room rate. It was almost two months' salary. He pushed back, turned and looked up the curved stairs. The door at the top was open just a crack.

With some effort, he made his way back to his room and guided his chair into the walk-in closet. Locking the left wheel, he pushed up on the armrest, retrieving the suit Sarah had chosen. Adams positioned his chair so that he could lift himself onto his bed. Awkwardly, he undressed himself and wiggled into his gray suit. He managed most everything single-handedly except for the buttons on his shirt and, of course, his tie. Hopefully, Sarah wouldn't mind.

Adams rolled into the bathroom, washed his face, and combed his hair. He was forced to use his teeth to open the bottle of cologne he had brought. Setting it down on the counter, he spit the lid into his hand, grimacing at the bitter taste it left in his mouth. Now he'd have to brush his teeth again, reprising this morning's challenge of placing the toothpaste on the brush with one hand. He was quickly gaining respect for handicapped folks, who put up with worse problems every day of their lives without complaint.

He tipped the cologne bottle back into his hand, spilling much more than he had intended. With the bottle back on the counter, he shook the excess into the sink and rubbed what remained on his neck and chest. *Some hero,* he thought. *Now I smell like a three-dollar floozy.*

Mission accomplished, the good Admiral pushed his chair back into the bedroom, this time without himself in it. He wanted to wait for Sarah on the elegant couch at the bottom of the stairs so she could sit next to him. He hobbled from door jamb to bed, to the nearest leather chair, and onward to the door of the library. This proved easier to navigate, for it was small and filled with furnishings. His leg had been healing faster than his arm, he observed. No broken bones there. Without even breaking a sweat, he traversed the remaining distance and plopped himself triumphantly on the sofa where he awaited his date/shirt-buttoner.

✡   ✝   ☾

THEY WERE PLEASED with their progress. Everything was falling together. The new components had arrived overnight as requested. They were just what the doctor ordered, or the engineer, in this case. The doctor would come later.

As they worked, Anwar had arranged to have a TV nearby. He and Aymen had come to love hating Blaine Edwards as he waxed poetic about his role in bringing *the* story to the American people. FOX news had long since passed CNN in the ratings game, but there was nothing like scooping their rivals on something as gruesome as a crucifixion to widen the Nielsen gap. Of course, it wasn't beneath Edwards to rub it in. He was a bottom feeder; there was very little beneath him.

Both Arabs turned around as the familiar and hated voice intoned, "We interrupt this program to bring you the following News Alert. FOX News has just learned that the Prosperity Building in Washington may have been infected with anthrax." Edwards had no hard evidence of contamination, but hey, a scare was as good as the real thing.

Abu and Halaweh dropped their socket wrenches and stared at each other. How had they found out so soon? It should have taken days before the symptoms started showing up.

"You suppose one of our delivery boys got careless?" Aymen asked.

Before Anwar could answer, Blaine explained. "We have an exclusive interview with Robert Mosley, President of EnviroCare, a Washington area heating and air-conditioning firm. Mr. Mosley, what did you discover?"

Mosley, conducting his end of the conversation outside his D.C. office, cleared his throat. "Well, Blaine, as part of our service here at EnviroCare, we provide our best customers with a regular monthly inspection package, just to make sure everything is operating at peak performance."

Edwards wasn't interested in the commercial but he allowed the overzealous businessman his fifteen seconds of fame. "One of our men, about two hours ago, found something suspicious at the Prosperity Building. He called his supervisor, who immediately raced to the scene. He notified me, and I in turn called the police."

"And what did they find?" the arrogant newscaster probed.

"Well, Blaine, my men found a commercial filter box sitting on the floor next to the main system."

"Isn't that normal?"

"No. Our guys bring their replacement filters with them. We don't leave cases on site. But they also noticed that this case had a tube running down into it. Come to find out, the box is filled with a white, powdery dust. Rather than removing particles from the air like a filter is supposed to do, this contraption was actually *adding* contaminants."

Edwards' face immediately turned ashen. "Mr. Mosley, did you say this device was *adding* a white powder to the office environment?"

"Yes. That's exactly what it was doing."

Blaine coughed, obviously struggling to regain his composure. "Does the dust look something like this?" Edwards motioned for the operator on his right to lower his camera so that it could pick up the thin layer of fine white powder that had collected on the news anchor's desk. He drew his finger across the surface. Edwards was no stranger to white powder, but this wasn't the same stuff he normally put up his nose.

Back on location, one of the FOX technicians showed Mr. Mosley a monitor. The particulate on Edwards' anchor desk was clearly visible.

"Yep, it looks just like that." The President of EnviroCare had just changed young Edwards' life.

"Does your firm service our building?"

"Why, yes, we do. Do you think *you* might have a problem?"

At this point the audience had no idea what was going on. Why was their favorite program being interrupted for a smattering of dust so fine it could hardly be seen? Sure, Edwards was full of himself; that was part of the mystique. But this was pushing it.

Uncharacteristically, Blaine turned away from the center camera and looked behind him. That move alone sent the studio's executives, all of whom were monitoring the breaking story from their offices, scurrying.

"We have a problem," Edwards growled, although only the back of his head could be seen. Removing his mike from his jacket lapel, and his ear-piece, Blaine dropped them on the floor, stood abruptly, and marched out of camera's view, presumably out of the room. Not knowing what else to do, FOX News cut to black, leaving America in the dark.

Anwar Abu and Aymen Halaweh looked at each other as if to ask, *"Now what?"* Their window of opportunity had been slammed shut. They hadn't expected anyone to discover their blowers for several more days, giving them enough time to receive the remaining components for the new, bigger systems before any suspicion was raised. A sizable order had been placed, but would it ship?

"You think the Feds will find us, Aymen?"

"How common are the components you used on the small blowers?"

"Very, I think." Anwar was starting to sweat, despite his reassuring response. "They can be used for a lot of things. The distributor didn't think twice about it. And yesterday I divided up our new order between four different outfits so they wouldn't be suspicious. I've already wired them the money."

"Then we may be okay, at least for now," Halaweh concluded, his voice rattling. "None of the large components are even made by the same factories. I checked that yesterday. They're a different scale, too, and they're hydraulic, not electric. And you know the Feds are never going to find ILM. I'd say we've still got time before the FBI figures anything out."

"But we need to call the boss, let him know what's up."

"And we need to hurry. We've gotta find out when the rest of the trucks are coming—and then find some fools to clean them for us."

✡   ☦   ☾

SARAH PEEKED around the door. She hoped Thor was dressed and waiting, so she could make a grand entrance. "Are you ready?"

The grin on Adams face spoke volumes. Pleased, she sauntered down the stairs with a flirtatious walk that was somehow both sultry and demure. Whatever it was, it was having the desired effect. Thor's prodigious jaw dropped. He had seen her walk many times—always an enjoyable experience—but never with the express purpose of pleasing him.

"Well?" she asked. "What do you think?" *Yes, Count Dracula, what do you think of O positive blood?*

"Miss Nottingly, you are too beautiful for words, and that *dress....*"

It was evidently a good answer. She navigated the final steps and gave her reviewer a kiss. Standing back up, she lifted her arms and twirled around. Her shoulder-length brown hair was perfectly curled and full of body. It floated outward, bouncing softly against her neck.

The pink cocktail dress was tight above the waist, revealing her slim figure, but loose around what little leg it covered. Sarah wasn't dumb; she knew her legs were her best feature. But before tonight, she had never had the nerve to show them off quite like this.

"You look positively…" he searched for a word. "Perfect."

"Thank you. And you, my dear Admiral, look smashing. I think this is the first time I've seen you out of uniform. In a suit, I mean." She smiled. "And just as I hoped, my dress matches your tie."

Yeah, and they're about the same size, too, he thought. But he said, "Would you do the honors? I managed everything but the buttons and tie."

"I know what to do with buttons. The tie…I've never done one. How do you make 'em work?"

"You're going to have to stand behind me so I can guide your hands as if they were my own."

After finishing the buttons she did as instructed, adjusting the large and small ends of his tie. Somehow, with more laughter, fumbling, and starting overs than were probably necessary, they tied a decent single Windsor around Thor's muscular neck.

Stepping back to admire her handiwork, Sarah bumped into the piano. Smiling, she rolled off an *arpeggio*.

"You can play that thing?"

"Eight years of lessons with Cassie Summers. You can learn a lot from a lady who earns her living playing piano in smoky dives. But I haven't touched a keyboard for months. Been a little busy."

"Play something for me. Sing something. Anything."

"We have enough time?" Sarah was kind of hoping they didn't.

Thor looked at his watch. It was just past six. "We have a lifetime."

Fighting off stage fright, she pulled out the piano bench and swished her hands under her bottom so she wouldn't wrinkle her dress as she sat down. It wasn't the piano she was worried about. She knew that well enough. It was the audience. *What if he's into Garth Brooks? What if all he listens to is Barenaked Ladies? He's going to run away, screaming. Oh, what the heck. You wore the dress; let it all hang out.*

"Okay. In honor of tonight's play, Admiral, how about something from *The Sound of Music?*"

"Great."

So far, so good. Looking back down at the keyboard, she placed her hands gracefully on the ivories. With some difficulty, she managed to get through the instrumental introduction. She hadn't expected a piano, and she was rusty. But she'd been trained as a jazz pianist. The songs were in her head, and that was all she really needed. Her first few bars sounded more like Thelonius Monk than Bill Evans, but she smoothed out as she warmed up.

The piano was turned so that her right side was exposed to him, not hidden by the instrument. And quite a view it was. Her dress featured a plunging neckline that revealed just enough to avoid being risqué. The whole affair was precariously held up with tantalizingly thin spaghetti straps nestled in the hollow between the rise of her shoulder blades and the base of her neck. Even the back was cut low.

Normally Sarah had a voice that would make a robin blush, not strong, certainly not operatic, but light and sweet, a good match for her delicate piano style. But at the moment, she was struggling a bit. She hadn't soloed in a while, was unsure of the words, and was trying far too hard to please her audience. For his part, Thor was enthralled.

"'My day in the hills has come to an end, I know.'" She stopped, lifted her hands, and took a deep breath. "I'm afraid I'm a little rusty."

"You sound as good as you look," he smiled.

As the words came back to her, she started again. Thor seemed pleased, so she pressed on, singing "Climb Every Mountain," "I Am Sixteen, Going on Seventeen," and an upbeat rendition of "My Favorite Things." With each song Sarah gained confidence. She found herself slipping into the role of Maria, embarking on a crusade to soften a captain's heart. Okay, an admiral.

Their thirty minutes passed all too quickly. "'It's time...to go. I cannot tell a lie-ie,'" the Admiral croaked, betraying his familiarity with the play. "Listen. Can we forget the wheelchair? I think I can make it, if we don't move too fast."

"Sure. Your leg, your call."

Arm in arm, they made their way out of the room, past the guards, down the elevator, and to their waiting car. Before they had settled into their seats, they arrived. The Tavern looked inviting as its thousands of crystal window panes illuminated the twilight. It was like something out of a fairy tale.

Seated, they placed their orders and looked at each other awkwardly for a moment, wondering what to say.

Sarah jumped into the deep end. "I want to apologize."

"For what?"

"I was responsible for sending you in there. It was my job to interpret the intelligence data and I...I muffed it. I nearly lost you because of my ignorance—arrogance, really."

There was something slightly incongruous about hearing that kind of admission from someone in a pink dress, especially *that* dress. But she was serious. As much as Thor wanted to laugh, he knew better.

"A lot of us looked at the film, Sarah. We all saw what we wanted to see. I was the one they played for a fool. You want the truth? You saved *me*. Every time I had to muster a little more resolve, I thought of you. I needed to come back and find out if our first kiss was anything more than, 'Good luck, sailor.' Was it?"

"Yes. So you forgive me?"

"Well…" Thor sensed an opportunity. "I'm not so sure. I might need a little convincing."

"Now flyboy, don't be pressin' your luck," she said, batting her lashes.

"How guilty do you feel?" he replied, pushing it.

"A hundred on a one-to-ten scale. I'd do pretty much anything to know you'd really forgiven me." She liked the idea of becoming vulnerable. This could be interesting. "What would you like?"

"You," he said. "*You* are what I want."

"What do you mean? I'm right here." A touch of concern crept into her voice. She closed her eyes and bit her lip. It was time, she thought, to get something off her chest. Not that there was much there. "Thor, you need to know that I…." She paused. "I'm a virgin. What's more, I plan to stay that way until my wedding night."

He regained his balance nicely. "Well, there you go. You've gone and wrecked a perfectly good illusion. All this time I thought a virgin was an ugly girl in the third grade."

Sarah shook her head in mock disgust, but she had trouble suppressing a grin. "So now I'm ugly *and* retarded, am I?" she laughed. You're digging yourself a pretty deep hole there, mister." She waited a moment. "Now that you know you're not gettin' any, do you still want…*me?*"

"Yep. I want the virgin Nottingly."

"Okay. You've got yourself a girlfriend. Now what?" Now that the relationship had been taken to the next level, turnabout was fair play.

"Then I think it's time you let me check under the hood." It was probably not the best choice of words, and Sarah wasn't sure what he meant. Worse, the dress was clearly having its intended effect. Thor was a man of discipline, a gentleman, but he was only human, and male to boot. No longer able to help himself, his eyes fell, an inch at a time, gazing first at her lipsticked mouth, down to her gracefully pearled neck, and then to the small yet perfect curves below.

"Under the hood? What hood?" she asked, raising her eyebrows. She had dared herself to be flirtatious, but now she was afraid she'd gone too far. She felt exposed, self-conscious, and drastically under-dressed. *God, I wish he'd stop staring at me like that.*

Thor lifted his eyes. They met hers. "Under the bonnet, silly. I want to know what you think. Being an agnostic doesn't make me a pagan."

"I could have sworn your eyes were looking elsewhere."

He smiled sheepishly. "Can you blame me? I mean, you'd look great in a burlap sack, but in *that* dress...."

"You're right. I've got no one to blame but myself. I've never had the courage to wear it before." She relaxed. "So what do you want to know?"

Thor did his best not to look down. There would be no retreat, no giving back the ground he'd gained. He simply lost himself in her eyes.

"Umm, Earth to Thor. Do you read me? Come in, please," she said, tapping her nails on the table. "What do you want to know?"

He came to. "Just enjoying the view."

"I'm glad you like what you see. But...."

"The staircase is grand, but it's what's upstairs that counts."

"Why, Prince Charming, the things that fall from your lips."

Thor sat up and cleared his throat. "Sarah, you're the CIA Bureau Chief for the Middle East. You should know more than anyone. So tell me: what causes Muslims to kill. Islam is obviously the only common denominator in all of this. You're an intelligence analyst—analyze that."

Nothing like a simple question to get a date off on the right foot.

"That's only the world's most important conundrum." His question had taken her by surprise, coming out of the blue like that, yet somehow she was pleased. She relished the idea of being appreciated for her mind, not just her looks. This was a refreshing change for Nottingly. Sarah had become accustomed to boys, and later men, pursuing her because of her appearance, only to run away when they discovered she could think. She usually intimidated those who'd courted her, but not this time.

"You mean *them*, as in our pals Ghumani, Haqqani, and Quagmer?"

"No. I've already figured out that they're just a symptom, one of many Islamic clubs. I was speaking more generally, as in Muslim militants."

"It's so odd using a religious term to describe a violent group, isn't it? *Muslim militants,*" she repeated. "*Islamic Jihad, Holy War.* Even the names *al-Qaeda, Hamas,* and *Jemaah Islamia* have religious roots. *Hezbollah* means Allah's party, for cryin' out loud. I don't like being judgmental, but...."

"There's something wrong with murdering for Allah," Thor said. "Even more with the way they turn their murderers into martyrs. Sarah, I don't know much about this either, but I'll bet we're going to find our answers buried in the words of Muhammad."

"In Muhammad's Hadith," she said, "not Allah's Qur'an, right?"

"I'm the one checking under the hood, remember? You're the intelligence officer, so I get to ask the questions."

"Sir, yes, sir!" she replied, snapping a passable salute. "Ask away." She adjusted one of her straps.

"Tell me, Sarah. Since these people are your business, what does the CIA know about them?"

She sighed. "The CIA doesn't know enough to be dangerous. We're focused on everything but the *one* thing they all have in common. But, like you, I've read the Qur'an." She dove right in. "I've also read Tabari and Hisham's edits of Ibn Ishaq's biography of Muhammad. It's the earliest source, edited a couple of centuries after the Prophet died. Sadly, from a historical standpoint, it's about as useful as Homer's *Odyssey*. You know, you catch bits and pieces that help you put things in context, but it doesn't exactly ooze credibility, especially since he admitted leaving out anything he thought might discredit Muhammad. But the problem is, without it and Tabari's History, the Qur'an doesn't make any sense."

Thor just looked at her in amazement. *Homer? Yes, indeed. I do believe Helen of Troy here has something upstairs.* "So you don't think the answer's in the Qur'an."

"Apart from Muhammad, not really. Tied to him, certainly. It's easily the worst book I've ever read. There's no rhyme or reason to it. No chronological order, no grouping things by subject. It's just random rantings. Heavily plagiarized. And Allah's completely out of character—not only hateful, but he speaks in first, second, and third person, singular and plural, all in the same surah. And repetitive—good grief! The same butchered Biblical accounts are repeated dozens of times. If God wrote the Qur'an, as Muslims claim, he needs an editor."

"The real goldmine is the Hadith. If you're interested in Muhammad's words, that's where you'll find them. And I think you're right; all the terrorist types seem plenty interested in what their Prophet had to say."

Adams found his eyes drifting. Fortunately, his mind wasn't. "It's so odd. Here you are, a CIA Intelligence Officer, and me, I'm a soldier, yet here talking about a religion—one that no one wants to talk about. Did you notice how fast the media started calling them 'radical groups' and 'extremists' rather than Muslims, or even Muslim militants?"

"They think we're fighting terrorists, not Islam. But that's like saying we fought *Kamikazes*—not Japanese—in World War II," Sarah observed. "Al Qaeda is to Islam as the S.S. was to Nazism."

"How can we understand what causes them to kill if we don't understand who they are and what they believe?" he asked.

She nodded, earrings dangling. "Ultimately, Islam *is* Muhammad, just as Buddhism's appeal is in the life of Buddha. Confucianism rises no higher than the mind of Confucius, and Judaism stands or falls on the truth of Moses' words."

"Is this all your opinion, or did you learn this stuff on duty?"

"Are you kidding?" She tossed her hair. "At the firm, religion is off limits. It's considered profiling." The waiter topped off her champagne, though she had only had a sip. It looked inviting in its crystal flute.

"Handicapped intelligence." Adams shook his head. "They want you to find the answer but don't allow you to look in the most logical place. The terrorists are from many nations, men and women, young and old. They have but one thing in common—Islam. How could you *not* look there? No wonder we're so clueless."

Sarah and Thor took time out between bites to fill their minds as well as their stomachs. They found life's mysteries more interesting than good food or idle chatter. Sarah, for one, was happy to have Thor focused on the place between her ears instead of the space between her breasts. Occasionally, though, she let a strap fall and linger on her arm.

"Considering their present animosity for Jews, Islam's beginnings are particularly intriguing," Sarah shared. "Muhammad—well, it's supposed to be Allah speaking—tells stories in the Qur'an about Abraham, Adam, Noah, even Moses, the guy who wrote the Torah. Yet Moses was a *Jewish* leader, a *Jewish* prophet. Fact is, Muhammad says the Torah was from Allah, as were Jesus and his Gospel."

"The stories are all messed up, aren't they?" he asked rhetorically. "From what I can tell," he said, hoping to impress his date, "Muhammad's struggle was complicated by the fact that he was illiterate. He didn't understand the Jewish scriptures, so he got them all twisted around."

"Yes, but the question is, was it incompetence, or were Muhammad's errors purposeful?" Sarah observed, taking a bite of her appetizer. "I believe there's an agenda behind the way the Bible stories were altered. Anyone with their eyes open can see right through the Prophet's act. But either way, in the seventh century there were plenty of Jews in Arabia. They knew their scriptures. When Muhammad butchered their history, they called him on it."

Thor connected the dots. "So the Messenger gets steamed. He doesn't like being contradicted. To get back at the Jews for embarrassing him, he claims Allah wants them *dead*. Backed by the Big Guy, he goes from pretending to be one of them to being their worst enemy."

"That's the Qur'an in a nutshell. In a duet with Allah, Muhammad tells his followers to kill any Jew or Christian under their control—*crucify* them." Sarah had shared something few in the West knew.

"Crucify?"

"Yep. Literally. It's worse than you realize, Thor. Everything they did to you and your men came right out of the Qur'an. Lying in wait came from Qur'an 9:5. Inflicting a punishment sufficiently grievous to be a warning for others is from 8:57. And crucifixion? Surah 5:33."

"We spent fifty billion on intelligence gathering and we would have learned more reading a five-dollar book?"

Sarah nodded. After what you've been through, you should reread surahs four, five, eight, nine, thirty-three, forty-seven, and forty-eight. They're a manifesto for war against Christians and Jews—more racist and vengeful than *Mein Kampf.*"

"That was my take the first time through. Allah clearly wants us dead. And that sure seems to explain Muslim behavior, doesn't it?"

"Yes, but we need to learn more about this stuff." She took her second sip of Champagne. "I'll tell you something, though; every rock I turn over has a snake under it."

"Same for me," Thor confessed. "But I'm a long way from figuring this out. I'd like to learn more about the relationship between Muhammad and Allah and find the connection between Islam and terror. I believe there is one. Otherwise, why would they celebrate killing? Driving nails into men while singing *Allahu-akbar* is about as sane as honoring a suicide bomber in a parade after he's murdered a slew of innocent people."

Sarah pushed her dinner around on her plate. "I can tell you this much: Allah commands Muslims to fight—surah 4:77. In at least four places, he tells them to terrorize. And in dozens more he promises paradise to anyone who's martyred killing infidels."

"Nothing's changed in fourteen hundred years. It all started with Muhammad."

"True," Sarah agreed. "Take the History of Tabari. Page after page it's the same story. Muhammad led a terrorist cell in Medina. He and his followers routinely butchered civilians, terrorizing them for financial gain."

The historian in Thor began to emerge. "Islam's first two caliphs were no better. Abu Bekr started the War of Compulsion—forcing every Arab to surrender to Islam or die. Then Umar savaged civilians from Persia to Egypt. They led the second and third Islamic terrorist cells."

"Yes. The fourth Islamic terrorist network was called *el-Kharij.* They assassinated Muhammad's cousin—then-caliph Ali—because he wasn't a 'good enough' Muslim. Bin Laden is a *Kharij*, Thor. They specifically target 'bad' Muslims and kill anyone who impedes Islamic rule."

"What do you mean 'bad' Muslims?"

"Well, 'good' Muslims are like good devotees of any doctrine. They study their leader's writings, emulate his deeds, and try to follow his commands. Since Muhammad was a terrorist, ordering his faithful to murder infidels, that makes all 'good' Muslims bad people. But 'bad' Muslims simply pick and choose the parts they like and ignore the rest."

"So what happened after *Kharij?*"

"In the eleventh century the *el-Hashashen*—the marijuana terrorists—began killing Sunni Muslims. Then Ibn Taymiyah terrorized people around thirteen hundred. His no-tolerance tactics foiled the Mongolian Muslim invasion into Syria."

"Muhammad ibn Abd al-Wahhab and his *Wahhabis* came next, right?"

"Very good, Thor. They were seventh on the Muslim militant hit parade. Their goals were identical to those of Muhammad, Bekr, Umar, *el-Kharij, el Hashashen,* and Taymiyah—death to all who stood in the way of global Islamic rule. The *Wahhabis* fought the Muslim Turks around 1750. Today's Saudi dictators, by the way, are *Wahhabis.*"

"Okay, Sarah. Fast forward to the 1920s, and you'll find the Egyptian, Sheik, Hassan al-Banna, right? He started the Muslim Brotherhood to combat the non-Islamic governments in Egypt and Turkey."

"Yes. Al-Banna was a student of *el-Kharij* and deployed the same methods. In '48, Sayyid Qutub went from managing Egyptian public education to writing books on behalf of the Muslim Brotherhood. His book, *Signposts Along the Road,* made him the Martin Luther of Islamic terror. Up to this point most of the victims had been 'bad' Muslims. But Qutub was more generous with his hate, expanding it to include Jews and Americans. He saw us as impediments to a one-world Islamic government. His most famous line: 'Demolish all nations established by man and destroy whatever conflicts with true Islam.' His followers were the first to preach that nuclear bombs could be used to destroy the West."

Thor nodded. "And this all brings us to a name most Americans know, or ought to: Sheik Abdel Rahman."

"Right. He was the senior professor of Qur'anic studies at Al-Azhar, Islam's preeminent university. But he's in prison today in America. As you know, he's the blind sheik who was convicted of masterminding the '93 bombing of the World Trade Center. He was also the one who plotted the assassination of Anwar Sadat. As the most respected authority on the Qur'an, Rahman is the spiritual leader of today's Islamic terrorists."

"Wait a minute! The media keeps saying that the terrorists have corrupted Islam. But how's that possible if the leading Qur'anic scholar for the leading Islamic university is a convicted terrorist?"

The waiter refilled her coffee cup. He had been listening too. "May I interest you in dessert?" He offered her a menu.

"No, not for me. I won't be able to wear things like this if I eat anything on that."

"Nothing for me, either. But I'd like the check. We're off to see a play."

"*The Sound of Music.* I know. The theater asked us to call them as soon as you were on your way. I think they may have something special planned. Oh, and as for the bill, there won't be one. You're our guests."

"That's kind, but please," Thor protested. "At least let me leave a tip,"

"No, sir. We all drew straws for the honor of serving you. I won. All I want is what every American wants. Answers. How do we stop the killing? He filled Adams' cup. "I voted for the President, I'm embarrassed to say. A lot of us did. But now I've changed my mind."

"And why is that?" Sarah was at the edge of her seat.

"We need to elect Admiral Adams President. One more promotion."

"*What?*" Nottingly almost slid out of her chair. She hadn't figured on being first in line for the First Lady's spot.

"We've gotta put an end to this. I mean, who do you think is responsible for today's terrorist attacks? I'll bet their names aren't Flanagan, Fortunado, or François." From the expressions on their faces, the waiter could tell they hadn't heard. "You don't know, do you?"

"What? What happened?" the nation's most famous intelligence officer queried the waiter.

"About an hour ago they reported on TV that two office buildings in Washington were poisoned with anthrax. Looks like they may have even gotten that loudmouth Blaine Edwards."

Thor was no fan of Edwards, but the battle was bigger than one fool's lack of restraint. "You said they poisoned *buildings?*"

"Yeah, from what they reported the crazies built a contraption that fit inside air-conditioning systems. Real ingenious."

"What buildings did they attack? Has anyone claimed credit?" Sarah was particularly upset by all of this. The likely perpetrators were her beat and she was AWOL, hundreds of miles away, on a date no less. To make matters worse, she suddenly felt naked, wearing an outfit she wouldn't be caught dead in at Langley.

"The Prosperity Building and FOX News. But they're pretty sure there were others," the waiter replied.

Nottingly looked down and reached for her tiny purse. She moved her diminutive 38 caliber aside and pulled out a cell phone, CIA issue like the pistol. In the digital mode the phone was reasonably secure. She quickly transitioned back from date to agent.

She pushed the call button with a perfectly manicured nail. The blush color had been chosen, like Thor's tie, to match her dress. Even with a gun in her purse, she looked a lot more like a Bond girl than a secret agent. On the other hand, there was no longer anything secret about Miss Nottingly.

"Hello, Sarah. It's JT." A sophisticated version of caller ID had identified her.

"Hi, pal. What's this I hear about HVAC systems?" Jonathan, JT to his coworkers, was Nottingly's most senior agent. Their unit was focused exclusively on Islamic militants, but to avoid being accused of religious bigotry or racial profiling, they used the moniker Middle East Bureau. Geography didn't have lobbyists. Their focus was also the reason for her gun. Muslims weren't shy when it came to eliminating perceived threats.

"Real clever this time. The plan was so well orchestrated, all roads point to your pal Omen Quagmer. Although it hasn't been announced, we've found two more infected buildings. One is in Boston, the other in Baltimore. They're set on crippling our economy. A lot of people are gonna die this time, Sarah."

"They won't be happy until we're all dead," she growled, swept up in the anguish of the moment. It was an observation she should have kept to herself, especially in this place, with so many ears. Her view wasn't public policy. And in truth, she didn't even know who "they" were.

"Be careful," JT admonished. "Look for a dusting of white powder on dark horizontal surfaces. That'll be your best clue if you're in one of the poisoned buildings."

She listened intently. The only sign of what was being said, beside her momentary lapse, was her expression. And even that didn't help. Sarah, on duty, was as coy as they came. She could play poker with the best.

"How long since the install?" she asked, knowing that the answer would have a substantial impact on the number of casualties.

"Twenty-four hours. The FBI is rounding up everyone who was in the first two buildings. We've begun testing them, and started giving everybody a full cycle of Cipro. We're fingerprinting them, too, just as a precaution, in case it was an inside job. Actually, we're doing it to prove it *wasn't* an inside job. This has become so politicized the media is insinuating that the anthrax is being spread by radical right-wing extremists."

"Has Director Barnes informed the White House?"

"Yes. That's the reason we're late in releasing the info on the other two buildings. The President's concerned this will agitate her opponents and push us toward war again, or some such rot....Sorry, Sarah," Jonathan caught himself. "We work for Madam President. I shouldn't have added the editorial comment."

"Should I return? Does the Director want me back on duty?"

"No. I already asked him," JT replied. Then he whispered, "He's loyal to the President, but secretly I think he likes your Admiral. Stay with him. I'll call if something changes. Enjoy the play. And the presidential suite."

Sarah smiled. "Can't a girl have any secrets?" she asked her friend and coworker.

"No," JT laughed. It was true. Sarah was a hot commodity, prime time the world over. Secrets for this CIA agent were now few and far between. Her every hiccup was in the unforgiving glare of the media spotlight, something she could have done without. "Admit it, Sarah. I was right about the Admiral, wasn't I?"

Sheepishly, Nottingly replied, "Yes. Thanks, JT. I owe you one."

Hanging up, Sarah turned to Thor, "Sorry. I had to call the office. But there's good news: I get to stay."

Thanking the waiter, America's couple made their way across the crowded room. The restaurant's patrons applauded as they passed. They even managed a cheerful rendition of "God Bless America." It was a far cry from waiters singing "Happy Birthday" to an embarrassed patron.

Once outside, they were surprised again. There were three motorcycle units and three police cars on either end of their white stretch limo. This was getting a bit overwhelming. With a great deal of commotion and fanfare, they climbed into the back seat. The procession pulled away from the Tavern, weaved its way out of the park, and then headed down New York City's fabled Fifth Avenue.

Each intersection along the way was replete with additional police directing traffic away from the procession. Word had reached the good folks of Manhattan. Thousands were now lining what looked like a parade route. Both sides of Fifth Avenue were two or three deep with waving spectators. Some held signs aloft. "Adams for President," read one. Another said "Promote Admiral Adams." A third: "NY-heart-TA." Sarah even saw one that read, "Princess Sarah for First Lady."

It was like Beatlemania in the sixties, but the crowd was more diverse. Those who wanted Adams to run for public office didn't even know what party he belonged to. In truth, they didn't care, nor did Thor. As career military he'd avoided politics with a passion. Yet overnight, America had all but dragged him into the gilded arena of egos. *Thanks, but no thanks,* he thought quietly to himself.

Sarah, sitting on Adams' bad side, squeezed his right hand. She didn't know if she was supporting him or if it was the other way around. Perplexed by it all, They instinctively rolled down their windows to wave to the adoring crowd. While they didn't understand all the fuss, they couldn't help but feel appreciated.

Silently they pondered how fate had brought them to this peculiar place. Grappling with their destiny, they felt inadequate and ill prepared. Uncharacteristically, neither said a word. Normally gregarious, and now more at ease with each other, they didn't know what to say.

The crowd grew consistently larger and more vocal as the motorcade approached 42nd Street. Acknowledging those who had gathered to wish them well, the Admiral and the Agent entered the theater to more applause. Thor and Sarah thanked everyone, waved, and blushed. Uncomfortable with the attention, they gestured for the audience to sit down. No one did. Instead, the announcer proclaimed, "Ladies and Gentlemen, tonight we have the honor of sharing our theater with a genuine hero, Admiral Thurston Adams and CIA Agent Sarah Nottingly. Thanks for all you've done to bring us together."

With that the curtain was raised but not to begin the play. The cast all gathered around: Maria, the Nuns, the Captain, even the children. Borrowing a scene from the real-life drama that had inspired *The Sound of Music*, the orchestra began to play "America the Beautiful." As the cast lifted their voices, the audience joined in. It was like singing "Edelweiss," the national song of Austria, in the face of the sulking Nazis. This time America was thumbing its collective nose at a different breed of terrorist. The nation was announcing, ever so eloquently, that it was united again.

After a short eternity, the ovation finally subsided. The curtains were drawn closed, then opened again. Maria rushed back onto center stage twirling, arms and face raised to the mountains. As she began singing her opening number, Thor's mind drifted back to their hotel room where a lifetime ago his own Maria had sung the same song. The parallels were lost on no one. But only Sarah and Thor knew just how similarly their lives mirrored the play. There were no children, covetous uncles, or greedy baronesses, but the rest of the story fit like a glove.

As dates go, this was shaping up to be a good one. But all too soon it was over. Adams and Nottingly were invited backstage to meet the cast. They met the theater's owners, powerful businessmen and women, celebrities, even the mayors, Bloomberg and Giuliani.

Finally, America's couple made it back to their suite. Sarah sat on the hearth, lighting the fire. The Admiral had a bottle of Merlot wedged between his legs. Corkscrew in hand, he made a valiant effort to remove the cork. The wine, like the room, had been a gift.

Sarah seemed mesmerized by the fire. Its soft, warm light flooded the room as it danced off the walls and furnishings. The crystal chandelier had been turned down low so they could enjoy the panoramic views of the still-vibrant city. They would have given anything to be able to stop time at this very moment.

Love can be an irresistible force all on its own, but surroundings like these couldn't help but kindle the flame. The wine glasses were half filled with the libation of lovers.

Even with his arm in a sling, the Admiral was dashing, yet there was still a playful, boyish look about him. Though confident, he could be shy at times. He wore his emotions openly. All of that combined to drive women crazy, and this woman had clearly gone round the bend.

Sarah turned to face her companion. He returned her smile. Reassured, she no longer cared where he looked. She knew that she pleased him, all the way from her flowing hair down to the pink shoes matching her dress—high heels, nothing sensible about them. Still sitting ten feet apart, they just looked at each other. The recipe was one part discovery, one part admiration, and ten parts anticipation. As eternity's moment marched on to the drumbeat of a crackling fire, Sarah was sure Thor could hear her heartbeat. Her body warmed, but not from the flame, from the fire raging within. None of this felt like anything she had ever experienced.

He felt the same melody of emotions. There would be no conquering. They had both surrendered to the most powerful force in the world.

Suddenly words, *the* words, began to rise in the Admiral's chest. His heart longed to say them. But he longed to speak them with her heart pounding next to his. Thor was certain he would be able to feel it beating through the thin fabric of her dress.

But his head said no. The argument between his head and heart wasn't about what to say, only when to say it. As he sat there admiring her, his head and heart engaged in a spirited debate.

Then Sarah kicked off a shoe. Thor's heart jumped. She looked so desirable. His body screamed to hold her. Any moment now she would stand and cross the room, long legs, graceful hips, slender waist, flowing hair, and a face so radiant its image was burned into his very soul.

Now! If he didn't speak now, his heart would overwhelm his head and the words he was hungering to say would be lost. The moment, this moment, could never be repeated. The other shoe fell to the floor. His head and his heart now cried out in unison, commanding him to say, "Sarah, I love you."

10

PLAYING THE ODDS

Morning came early, especially for Sarah. She had set her alarm for five o'clock. While depriving her of sleep, it gave her time to scribble some notes in anticipation of discussing prophecy with Thor. And then there was the promise she had made to sew his Admiral's stripes on his dress uniform.

In the morning's shower she sang her favorite *Sound of Music* song, "I Have Confidence." It seemed to fit the occasion and her mood. She relived the last twenty-four hours in her mind: chartered jets, mind-numbing prophecies, carriage rides in the park, a thoughtful dinner, their reception at the theater, the play, and then...*the moment.* The words she had dreamed of hearing since she was a little girl had been spoken.

Moving on to humbler things, she strolled downstairs with needle and thread. Her knees nearly buckled as she walked past the couch. The image of him sitting there saying "I love you" stirred her all over again. It had been a night to remember.

Entering the small kitchen, she found coffee, filters, and a couple of mugs. With the pot dripping away, she tiptoed through the library toward Thor's slightly open door, knocking softly as she peeked inside. It wasn't yet six. He was still asleep.

Sarah found his dress uniform in the closet. Turning to leave, she stopped. He looked so peaceful. Before Thor awoke, Sarah hurried out of the room. Sitting at a table in the adjoining library, she began sewing, pondering how she was going to deal with all of this. She was putty in his hands, and she was sure he knew it. While Sarah was a virgin, she wasn't a prude. What had been easy, or at least easier, to avoid in the past was now problematic. She no longer wanted to say no.

Last night his hands had never strayed lower than her neck. No clothing had been loosened. Yet it had been an hour of seductive indulgence. She smiled when she remembered that it had been Thor who'd sent *her* off to bed.

Finished, Nottingly rose from the library table and made her way to the kitchen where she poured a cup of coffee. She remembered that he liked it black. Tapping on his door, coffee in hand, she said, "Thor, time to get up."

Sarah walked over to his bed and sat down beside him, shaking him gently. "Thor," she touched his bare arm.

He smiled and began to stir. Eyes closed, he reached over and wrapped his arm around her waist.

"Come on," she said. "We've gotta get your lazy bones out of bed."

He opened his eyes, giving her a look that suggested other possibilities.

"Sorry, sailor. It's already six o'clock."

Thor sat up, rubbed his face, and made an effort to pat down his hair, not wanting to scare Sarah away.

"You look fine," she said. "In fact, you look better than fine, but you've got a show to do. I made some coffee." She offered him the mug. "I've also made you an admiral; I sewed your stripes on your jacket. Now, what else can I do?"

"Good morning," he said. "I was hoping last night wasn't a dream. You're prettier than I remember."

"Thank you. And thank you for last night." The words seemed so inadequate. She simply smiled, stood, and walked out of the room.

Thor took a giant gulp of coffee and moved to the edge of the bed. To his surprise, he felt stronger. Some of the pain had subsided. He was able to place more weight on his injured right leg. The caffeine would soon kick in and he would be as good as new, excuse the broken arm. It was going to be a marvelous day.

Twenty minutes later, Adams was scrubbed and clothed. Once again he asked Sarah to do the honors with his tie. He liked feeling her standing behind him, breathing in his ear, both arms wrapped around his neck.

They found their limousine waiting downstairs. Pulling away, they began the short drive back down Fifth Avenue.

"Have you decided what you're going to say?" Sarah asked. After all, it had been her job to brief him.

"Yes. It's important to be honest with folks. I'm going to tell them the truth about what happened. But don't worry. I'll be discreet when it comes to our intelligence."

"What if they ask you about your promise?"

"Figuring out why they're so crazy?"

"Yeah, that one," she said. "I don't want to lose you to a pack of zealots off on some *fatwa*." She knew what Muslims did to those with the courage to reveal the truth about Islam.

"I need to learn more before I start sharing things like that publicly. Our dinner discussion was just between the two of us."

"Good," Sarah replied. "Now, you know they're going to ask you about the President and her strategies."

"I'm prepared. I'll respect the office while disagreeing with her policies if I have to. What's she gonna do—demote me?"

"Not likely. It wouldn't be in her interest." Then she paused, batting her lashes. "What if they ask about us?"

He rubbed his chin. "What would you like me to say?"

"Oh, the three words you used last night would be fine with me, but are you ready for a public announcement?"

"As much as I'd like our relationship to be private, that isn't going to happen. So why not share how we met, how thinking of you gave me the courage to press on, even how I've fallen head over heels, drooling-dog-out-of-control, totally and completely in *like* with you." He winked as she punched him teasingly in the side.

✡   ✝   ☾

ANWAR ABU AND AYMEN HALAWEH were back at it. They had completed their first "city conditioner," and a half-dozen additional trucks were scheduled to arrive this morning. They had even managed to find a number of young volunteers at a nearby mosque to clean the ugly beasts. Although they were eager to serve Allah, they quickly found that trash was a dirty business.

At the appointed time, Abu and his pal entered a private office and closed the door. Omen was notorious for his anal desire to stay on schedule. It was four o'clock in the afternoon in Baghdad when the phone rang, precisely seven A.M. eastern.

Anwar pushed the button. "Hello."

"How are things progressing?"

"On schedule, sir," Aymen responded. "The first of the large systems is operational. My calculations show that without refilling the particulate bins, we can disperse enough confetti to dust ten square blocks."

Just in case there were others listening, they'd agreed to call it confetti. That sounded somewhat less threatening than "anthrax spores."

"No. That's not enough," an angry voice shot back. Kahn Haqqani's words sent shudders down Aymen's spine. "We need ten times that much, boy. Not buildings, not blocks. We want to infect whole cities. I thought that was why you trashed our crop duster idea and turned to garbage."

"It was, sir." Aymen beseeched Allah for the courage to respond. "Each truck can carry enough confetti to do fifty square blocks, and I've designed it so that we can refill the powder storage bin."

"Well, now you're talking, boy. All we need is to find some brothers to refill your trucks, right?" Haqqani asked, demanded, and ordered, all in the same breath.

"Yes," Abu jumped into the fray. "We think we have an answer for that too, at least with your help and approval."

"Go ahead," Omen said.

"The average city block is about a hundred meters long. I've measured them. The trucks will be going around 40 kilometers per hour. With stop lights and stop signs, they should be able to cover a ten-block section in around thirty minutes."

Worrying about traffic signs and lights seemed hilarious to Kahn. They intended to kill a million people, and the kid was concerned about getting a traffic ticket.

"At the end of each ten-block section, we will need to have ten trash cans waiting to be picked up, each filled with the particulate." It had been Aymen's calculation, but it was Anwar speaking. He wanted to share in the glory. "Lowe's sells thirty-gallon plastic trash cans. We'll need one hundred of 'em for each city."

"Actually, we'll only need eighty per city," Aymen corrected him, "because the first batch for each truck will already be in the bin. These thirty-gallon cans, filled to the brim, are still light enough for two men to lift. Anwar and I have done it."

"More importantly, properly washed they are static free."

"And they come with lids to keep the powder dry, sir."

"Good, gentlemen." Omen knew that eliminating the static charge from the powder was as important as it's being dry and the proper size. "I will get the particulate delivered in the quantities you need. A volunteer in each city will fax a grid recommending how he proposes handling each section. Review it, Aymen, and see if the places they designate for replenishment fit within your calculations. We'll handle the rest."

"Yes, sir. Now, if I may ask, when will we get more trucks?"

"You should have six delivered before noon, your time. Six more will arrive in the late afternoon. I have arranged for a third set for midnight. The final five will be at the warehouse before daybreak. I assume you have found additional space to store them, out of sight?"

Anwar Abu was all too eager to answer. "The Americans will do anything for money. I rented the whole building, all four warehouses. With the damage we've done to their economy, they were vacant."

Kahn deflated him. "You're good—at spending our money, that is." Actually, it wasn't his money. Even with their "business" interests, most al-Qaeda funding came from the Saudis. The Iranians and the Iraqis were benevolent, too, but they endowed other clubs.

"Son," Omen Quagmer took over, "I can do the calculations on particulate requirements. Fifteen hundred gallons per truck means thirty-six thousand gallons all together."

"That's right, and we'll want one liter of confetti for each truck. That's more than enough to cover the area required, but I'm not exactly sure what kind of yield we're going to get, especially if it gets humid. I know that's a lot. Is it too much?" the Palestinian engineer asked sheepishly.

Omen knew that making anthrax was easy. It's called an "oldie-moldy" in the trade because, like the bubonic plague, it's particularly easy to grow. Everything needed to cultivate the little buggers is readily accessible from mail-order catalogs. And a plant sufficient to produce the required amounts fits quite nicely in a standard garage.

"We are very, shall I say, motivated these days, young man. Nothing is impossible now. You convert the trucks. We will arrange for the supplies." Omen was clearly feeling the heat, and it wasn't just the desert sun. Quality might suffer, but he would deliver the goods.

✡   ✝   ☾

THIS MORNING they had awakened in each other's arms. The President craved the reassurance and wanted the attention. Like all insecure people, she *needed* to feel loved.

The nation's Chief Executive was dressed in her favorite black nightie, sitting up and smoking a cigar. The Secretary of Defense was nude. Lying face down, only her bottom was covered by the satin sheets. For variety, they had spent the night on the traditional four-poster in the Lincoln bedroom.

"How can you smoke that rope in the morning?" Susan asked in a muffled voice. To keep from suffocating, her head was buried in a pillow.

"It's my victory stogie, Suzzi."

Ditroe hated being called Suzzi, but what was she to do? Complain to her boss? "And what are we celebrating?"

"I think I was good yesterday. The Couric interview went just like we planned. We've regained the momentum. Even the day's little setbacks can't stop us now."

"*Little?*" Ditroe said, turning on her side and bringing the covers to her chest. There wasn't much to hide, but she suddenly felt underdressed, exposed, in the presence of a woman who would call the poisoning of thousands "a little setback."

"Oh, in the big scheme of things, Suzzi, it was nothing." She took another big puff from her cigar. "So, what do you say we go another round? You were pretty good last night, too."

"No. I don't think so. I'm not feeling very good at the moment." Ditroe coughed. "I'm going to shower and then head to the office." Susan walked around to the President's side of the bed, taking the covers with her. She found her teddy and robe on the floor.

"If you're still here sucking on that thing in fifteen minutes, don't forget to turn on the *Today Show*," the Secretary said, covering herself the best she could. "Your pal, 'Colonel Doolittle' is scheduled. You may want to hear what he has to say."

"Why?" the President asked as she watched Susan climb back into her teal robe, slipping her teddy into its pocket. "That boy will be yesterday's news soon enough. He's got no staying power, no political instincts. The media will chew him up and spit him out. You watch."

"I hope so, for your sake, for *our* sake," Ditroe corrected herself. "But I've got a bad feeling. I had an analyst study his National speech. That boy's got an agenda," she added, fastening her robe. "And his poll numbers are sky high. Last night they showed him and his girl-toy gallivanting down Fifth Avenue. The crowd went nuts. He looked like JFK riding down the streets of Dallas, although I'll admit, the end result was a little different."

"Yeah, he got shot *before* he went on the drive." The President took another deep drag on her long cigar, rolling it between her fingers as she removed it from her mouth.

"You know, out of uniform he actually looks like JFK, only bigger. Even she, the little tramp, looks a lot like Jackie. Doesn't dress as well. She shows way too much leg for my taste."

"If I had legs like hers, I'd flaunt 'em too. So would you, my dear." Madam President smiled as she checked out Ditroe's, at least what she could see of them through the crack in her robe.

Susan pretended to ignore the President's comment. She didn't appreciate having her legs dismissed. "If we want to push your peace initiative, we're going to have to deal with those two."

"Listen, the sheeple want peace. They don't want war. Not really. And as soon as we abandon Israel, we'll *have* peace. The Muslims will have no reason to come after us anymore, especially once we complete our Saudi pullout. They've even promised to lower oil prices." She looked up at Susan. "How's that going, anyway?"

Forgetting for a moment that she was still in lingerie, the Secretary of Defense tried to answer professionally. "Oil prices have gone up, not down. But our troops are mostly out. We have a few hundred advisors left. We'll have the tanks and personnel carriers gone by the end of the month. And if you'll recall, the remainder of our A-10s and C-130s left a week ago to rescue Adams. So we're ahead of schedule."

"Good. We're golden just as soon as we're out of the Middle East."

"There's nothing but crazies there anyway, Madam President."

"We had no business being the world's policeman. Let 'em settle their own scores. That's what I say."

"You know I'm loyal. No matter what, I'll stay by your side."

"Good, then hop back into bed."

Susan turned on the TV instead.

✡   ✟   ☾

BLAINE EDWARDS was in the hospital, positive he was going to die. He had IVs in every flavor imaginable pouring their life-saving juices into each arm. But he was all alone this morning.

Having tried to finagle a double dose of antibiotics from every doctor in town, he had developed a reputation. The nurses were avoiding him like the plague. They disdained complainers and found him both rude and chauvinistic. Without the attention, he was miserable. The world was a happening place, and he was missing it. Blaine was in limbo. The network took a dim view of anchors who walked off sets during the airing of special reports. It made them look bad.

Sitting alone, Edwards had darn near worn out the nurse call button. He couldn't understand why they weren't swarming all over him. He was a celebrity. He didn't know that they'd disconnected his ringer during the night. The light still blinked; they just ignored it.

In agony, Blaine was forced to watch a rival, a woman well beneath his stature, sit in *his* seat and deliver the morning news. *She's such a tramp. I'm sure she's doing the boss. Why else would she have been considered for the job, much less my equal.*

With sparkling green eyes, glistening lips, perfectly coiffed blonde hair, and a polished delivery, Trixi Lightheart read the news. For Blaine, this was a fate worse than death.

"FOX News has just learned that four more buildings have been hit with deadly doses of anthrax. In addition to the Prosperity Building and our own headquarters here in Washington, spores have been discovered in office buildings in Philadelphia, Baltimore, Boston, and New York."

She was speaking from their facilities in neighboring Baltimore. It would be months before their Washington studios would be habitable again, if ever. There were millions of spores suspended in the air and billions more clinging to every surface—floors, furnishings, equipment, walls, and ceilings.

In fact, depending on how well the metabolic process of the living bacteria had been suspended following the breeding process, the buildings might never be habitable again. They had become festering petri dishes. Worse, they couldn't even be torn down. The very act of dismantling them would spread the lethal pathogen.

"Between the six business centers, an estimated twenty-five thousand people have been exposed. Experts fear that the final number could be many times that amount." The recently promoted anchorwoman concentrated on maintaining a stern, professional demeanor. Although she was thrilled to be sitting in Edwards' anchor seat, she knew that any hint of a smile would hamper her career. And she had a lot invested in it. Plastic surgery didn't come cheap.

"Healthcare professionals are concerned because the people working in these buildings have now gone home to their families carrying millions of spores on their clothing. Some have gone out to dinner, to the theater, or shopping, dispersing anthrax with each step."

Trixi Lightheart turned right and began to read off of the teleprompter screen that covered the lens of camera two. "A spokesperson for the Centers for Disease Control predicted this morning that the situation may deteriorate. Preliminary reports indicate that this particular airborne strain of anthrax is more effective in its killing power and less receptive to antibiotics. Considerable expertise was displayed in weaponizing these spores, the CDC said. At two to three microns across," she explained, "less than the width of a human hair, the spores are small enough to embed themselves into their victims' lungs."

Blaine Edwards squeezed his call switch with such force the red button popped out and fell to the floor. Angered, he flung the remaining portion toward the doorway, forgetting that it was secured to the ceiling by a cable. It swung back as fast as it had been thrown, bruising his lip. In agony, the enraged former anchor began to scream. He was dying and no one cared.

✡ ✝ ☾

LESS THAN FIFTEEN MINUTES after they'd left the Plaza Hotel, Adams and Nottingly arrived at Rockefeller Center. It was mobbed. Thousands had gathered to see America's hero and his princess. They were waving and hoisting signs suggesting all manner of things. The flags around the ice rink fluttered joyfully in the background, adding to the spectacle.

Sarah had called JT and asked for an update. He had told her that Omen Quagmer and Kahn Haqqani had already claimed credit for the contamination. She had passed on the grim news to Thor.

"Any warnings about pestilence in the Qur'an, Miss Intelligence Officer?"

"No, but I'm pretty sure there's one in the Psalms," she reported as the driver opened the door.

The Admiral felt compelled to shake a few hands and thank the folks for their support. Someone handed him a bullhorn he had been using to address the crowd.

"We love New York," he told those gathered around him. "Sarah and I appreciate your courage." At the mention of her name they cheered. Placing his left arm on the shoulder of a police officer, Thor continued, "You have suffered more than any other city, and this morning's news on the anthrax infestation is another bitter pill. It's about time we shut this pharmacy down!"

Thousands of people burst into a spontaneous roar. He spoke confidently into the megaphone. "We will not stand for this. We have made a promise. We are going to learn why they kill—why they celebrate killing. Within a month's time, I will report back to you what we've learned, and we will put them out of business."

While the first half of that was certainly within Adams' prerogative, his last statement was not. He had no authority to commit America to anything, especially war, but he had grown angry when Sarah shared that it had been Haqqani's and Quagmer's doing. The thought of thousands more dying at the hands of those he'd tried to capture tormented him.

Having said more than he should have, Adams returned the megaphone and with Sarah's help walked inside. They were promptly escorted into the make-up room where a staffer greeted the guests.

Sarah recognized the man's voice. He had been the one who had called Thor's apartment. "I trust you enjoyed the flight, dinner, and show?"

"Yes," she smiled. "We've had a lovely time. Thank you."

Her voice sounded familiar to him as well. "When would you like to fly back home?"

Sarah answered again. "Tomorrow, sometime in the late afternoon. Does that work for you?"

"We're at your disposal. The Admiral is the most sought-after guest we've had in quite some time." He hadn't forgotten the President's appearance the day before. "We're pleased that you've honored us with your first interview, sir. We're expecting one of the largest audiences in our history."

"We couldn't help but notice the crowd. It seemed bigger than usual." Sarah had watched the *Today Show* and knew that they made a habit of mingling with the folks that gathered outside.

Thor had been quiet until now. He had never been made up before and wasn't sure he liked it very much. He motioned the make-up artist away and turned in his chair. "I may have overstepped my bounds," he confessed. "I was angered that Haqqani and Quagmer took credit for the anthrax contamination. I'm only an Admiral. I don't have the right to promise resolution," he said, wishing he did.

"Yes, I know. You were on camera. It was *great*," the exec smiled. "We always have one outside when the crowd is part of the story. We had no idea you were going to say anything, but you were live on national television. And I must say, you were very well received."

Sarah didn't know how to counsel him. She knew General Hasler had called him aside warning him about such outbursts following his speech at Reagan National. But she agreed with what he had said. So did the country. By saying it, however, he had put himself squarely in opposition to the President of the United States. That's an unforgiving place for an admiral to be. It was likely he would lose his job, as would she. The only question was who would be dismissed first.

Thor looked over at Sarah as if to say, *now what?*

She didn't respond.

"Sarah. I need your advice."

"I know, sweethear...Admiral. I think you did the right thing. It may have cost you your job, and mine, but...."

"I'm sorry."

"I'm not."

"You're not mad, not even disappointed?"

"No. I'm proud of you. Let's figure this thing out, like you promised. We'll do it together. Being unemployed will just give us more time."

The exec turned to Sarah. "Agent Nottingly, with what you've just said, would you reconsider? Will you join the Admiral on the show?"

She looked over at Thor, who nodded. "Yes, I believe I will."

"Make-up!" he shouted. "We need another make-up." He darted out of the room. He couldn't wait to share the good news.

✡   ✝   ☾

CHAIRMAN HASLER ARRIVED at the Pentagon early. He had wanted to see the show with his staff so they would be prepared for any questions that might arise as the day progressed. He knew that Adams had the potential to be controversial. But he had no inkling it would be this bad— or good, depending upon your perspective.

"Mr. Chairman," his administrative assistant interrupted the gathering. "The Secretary of Defense is on the line."

"Put the call through, Judy." The entourage of generals, admirals, captains, and colonels got up to leave, knowing that the Chairman was in hot water. But he motioned for them to stay.

"Good morning, Secretary Ditroe. How may I help you?" General Hasler said into his speakerphone.

"Are you watching the *Today Show?*" she asked.

"Yes."

"Then you know why I'm calling."

"Yes."

"The President wants you to relieve Admiral Adams."

"I do not think that would be wise, Madam Secretary." Rather than simply refusing the order, the Chairman elected to counsel his boss. "He's the most popular man in the country, maybe in the world, right now. Firing him isn't a very good idea, especially for a politician."

"Do you have a better solution, General?" she asked. Ditroe was barely dressed, and her hair was still wet. "The President's livid."

"Yes, ma'am. I propose commissioning him. Invite him and Agent Nottingly to the White House. Play nice. Ask him to chair a blue ribbon panel to look into all this radical terrorist stuff."

Ditroe wanted to say no. She cringed at the very idea of having *that* woman's legs in the President's presence again. But it was too shallow an excuse, so she searched for a better one.

Uncomfortable with her silence, Hasler shared his rationale. "If the commission fails, you can blame it on him, saying he just wasn't cut out for such a thing. Even if it succeeds, it'll take years, and it's sure to get mired in partisan bickering. His report will be so rife with compromise it'll be ignorable. You and the President can give it lip service and go on your way. But at least she'll still be President and you'll still be Secretary of Defense."

It was a compelling argument. In their arena, Adams would surely prove to be mortal. The power of politics was ultimately corrupting. Given time, they would find his Achilles heel. Ditroe remembered the President's advice: stay close to your friends and closer to your enemies. "All right, Mr. Chairman. I'll propose it to the President and call you back with her decision."

In truth, the General had no use for blue ribbon commissions or any other political masturbation. He merely wanted to buy time. If forced to fire the Admiral, he would resign instead, and so would hundreds, maybe thousands, of senior officers. That wouldn't be good for the nation. For once in his life, Hasler had his priorities straight.

✡ ☩ ☾

KATIE COURIC AND MATT LAUER decided to do the interview together. It was one of the biggest of their careers. They had their staff hastily arrange for a fourth chair in as casual a setting as possible. They wanted America to see them as sympathetic to, even supportive of, the world's most popular couple. This morning they would be tossing softballs—nothing controversial.

Sarah was almost disappointed when the make-up artist stopped fussing. She loved the experience. Thor, on the other hand, couldn't wait to leave. He thought he looked ridiculous, not knowing that everyone endures the same treatment. The glaring studio lights are murder on unprepped skin.

Matt Lauer was gracious as he shook hands and welcomed Sarah and Thor to NBC's Studio 1A. Katie Couric was responsible for announcing their arrival. She scurried over the moment she was done, sitting down without comment. A professional, she was saving her personality for the show. The lights were raised, and crews dashed back to their positions. Thor could see an assistant director holding up a hand, mouthing five, four, three, two, one as he eliminated fingers. He pointed to Lauer, who introduced his guests. He told the audience the long and short of Adams' career: enlistment in the US Navy, intelligence training, fleet appointment to the Naval Academy, F-18 Hornet pilot, oldest man to survive SEAL training. Then he recounted his most famous missions, ending with his heroics in Afghanistan.

Couric described Sarah's past: graduation from William and Mary, a graduate degree in economics from UVA, her work for the National Ground Intelligence Center, and her role at the CIA. The camera showed her holding hands with Thor.

"Well, thank you very much," Adams said, standing up. "It's been a pleasure being on your show."

The hosts' faces went ashen.

"Just kidding." He sat back down as everyone smiled, including the crew. "That introduction was so long, I thought it was the interview. My mistake," Thor said with an impish grin. Then he added. "Matt, I was wondering if you'd be available for my eulogy? The way I've been living, I may need one soon."

This time even the hosts burst into laughter.

"I thought you were bulletproof." Matt played along.

"Well, I *am* against death, especially mine. But as you can see," he added, raising his slinged arm, "I'm not bulletproof."

"A hero with a sense of humor," Katie exclaimed. "Maybe that's why so many are saying you two have brought a smile back to our nation."

Sarah beamed.

Matt and Katie traded questions about the trap, the crucifixions, and the rescue. Thor answered each with disarming humility and heartfelt sympathy for those who had suffered.

The heavy lifting over, Lauer inquired, "How did you meet?"

"I was responsible for briefing the Admiral—Captain at the time—on the intelligence we'd collected on the whereabouts of al-Qaeda's leadership. I thought he was cute, very sweet. But being in intelligence, I knew he had a girl in every port. So I pretty much just did my job."

"But..." Thor interrupted, "she *did* give me a good-luck kiss on the White House lawn before the mission. I don't think that's required by the CIA."

Sarah blushed.

Katie was next. "We heard you talk about the girl back home on the videos from Afghanistan, and we watched your embrace the day you returned. America feels like we're part of your romance. You've become our prince and princess."

"Katie, I'm no prince. Frog, maybe; I've got my share of warts. But I agree with the princess part." He winked at Sarah.

That was enough small talk for Thor. He was on a mission, and it was time to move out. "Katie, Matt, we're here because the world needs answers. It's time we understand our enemy and stop deluding ourselves. The terrorist problem is much bigger, and it runs far deeper, than we realize." He had just unloaded both barrels.

"That's right," Sarah agreed. "We're going to get to the bottom of this. No matter how unpopular or politically incorrect the answer may be, we're going to expose the enemy, find what makes the madmen mad, and then figure out what can be done to stop them."

"Admiral Adams, outside this morning, you went one step further," Couric challenged.

Matt leaned forward in his chair. "That was quite a speech you made. It sounded presidential. Do you have any political aspirations?"

"No. I'm not a fan of politics, Matt. I'm no good at compromise. I respect people with character," he said, turning his focus to Couric. "I prefer progress to positioning, Katie, reality to perceptions. I respect people who are willing to intelligently debate an issue. In short, I'm the antithesis or what makes a good politician."

"Sounds perfect. *I'd* vote for you," Katie exclaimed.

"So would I," Matt volunteered, sounding genuine. "Tough times require tough leaders."

"The most recent polls show you beating every candidate in both parties, including the President. Why not run?" Katie asked the question that was on everybody's mind.

"Katie, Matt, you don't know if I'm a liberal or a conservative, a Republican or a Democrat. Nor does America."

"It doesn't matter. America needs to feel whole again, safe. We need to smile. You've brought laughter back. We've seen you under fire, Admiral, and I think I speak for all of us when I say I liked what I saw."

"That's kind of you, but right now Sarah and I are on a mission. With good intel we have a fighting chance of winning this war."

Matt remarked, "Some are comparing you to a modern-day JFK. Actually, you and Ms Nottingly even look a little like Jack and Jackie."

"In a way, the comparison is interesting. I've listened to John Kennedy's speeches. And while he's considered a liberal, his convictions were *right* of today's conservatives. He was a proponent of supply-side economics. He was right about Communism being evil, right about the need for a strong defense. He recognized that we pay for our freedom with either coin or blood. More than anything, he was right when he said, 'Ask not what your country can do for you; ask what you can do for your country.' Think about that," Thor implored. "Nothing good happens without sacrifice."

Katie, like most in the media, loved the Kennedy quote, but she had never considered its implications. Nor would she today. Instead of discussing the profound nature of what Thor had just shared, she changed the subject. "Yesterday we had the President on our show. What do you think about her plan to solve these problems peaceably by getting out of the affairs of other nations, by no longer trying to be the world's policeman?"

"I've never met a bully who was impressed with capitulation, or one who was satiated when he got his way. Giving the terrorists what they want will backfire, Katie. Israel is our only real friend in the Middle East, the only democracy and, from what I can tell, the only voice of reason. Abandoning Israel will only serve to inspire the bullies. Historically, the 'peace process' has invariably led to war. If we capitulate *there*, we will simply move the battlefield *here*."

"Some would say it's already here. Yesterday was a prime example."

"Thank you, Katie, for saying that. It gives Sarah and me the opportunity to apologize. We failed, and we're sorry. Our plan was to capture the terrorists, but they got away, and more people will die as a result."

Sarah tugged on Thor's hand, indicating she wanted to say something. "Yesterday morning the President boasted that it was all over, now that the Admiral's international force had captured Halam Ghumani. But based on this morning's news, that just isn't so. There are hundreds of Ghumanis, and they have millions of followers. America spent countless billions trying to find and kill Osama bin Laden. Yet the madness marched on without missing a beat. *If I'm going to get fired, I might as well get my licks in.*

Trying to lighten the mood, Matt changed the subject. "So, Sarah, is America's most eligible bachelor accounted for? What do you have to say to the millions of women out there who'd like to be in your shoes?"

Sarah, comfortable on any stage, stood up and pretended to throw punches in the direction of the camera. "I say, put 'em up, girls." Laughing, she ended her pretend sparring session and turned to Thor. "Maybe your question should be directed to the Admiral, Matt. Mr. Bachelor, are you still available?" She put up her dukes again, threatening to KO Adams if he answered poorly.

Instead of speaking, the Admiral stood, grasped Sarah's clenched hands, and pulled them toward his chest. Then, in a move that melted the cameras, he kissed her on the lips.

"No, I don't suppose he is," Katie guessed as they cut to a commercial break.

✡   ✝   ☾

"HALAM, MY GOOD FRIEND, they want you crucified."

That wasn't the most pleasant of greetings. Yet its recipient was unfazed. "They'll not have the pleasure," Ghumani told his attorney.

"I'm good, but I can't get you out of this place. No one can."

They were whispering so as not to be overheard. The lawyer had arranged to hold the meeting outside. They walked slowly through an open area in the center of a military prison not far from Washington, D.C.

"I believe I can get you life instead of death," the attorney added brightly. "My firm holds sway over a great many politicians here in town as well as many of the most prominent people in the media. They're beholden to us. We can use them to help shape public opinion, make you look like a victim, and justify your actions. We've done that sort of thing before."

"Do what you can to promote our cause. That's what we pay you for. But listen well." Halam looked his advocate in the eye. "They will not have the pleasure of seeing me tried, because you will help me kill them."

"Kill who?" the lawyer asked nonchalantly.

"All of them. You will help me rewrite history. I've had some free time," Ghumani said, stating the obvious while hobbling along. "I've been reading the only book in this godforsaken place. I have decided to bring Armageddon to the Infidels."

The attorney was being paid by the Brethren, a group of religious power brokers in Washington. He knew that Armageddon was prophesied to be the last battle fought on planet earth. It was apparent that, with time on his hands, Halam had been reading the Bible. "I thought that battle is supposed to be fought in Israel, Halam, not America."

"That's why I said we would be *rewriting* history. You don't listen very well for a lawyer."

"I'm sorry, sir. What, precisely, would you like me to do?"

✡   ✝   ☾

FOLLOWING THE *TODAY SHOW*, Sarah and Thor made the short pilgrimage from Rockefeller Center to Ground Zero. A massive depression was all that was left of the mighty towers, of the businesses, of the people. A fading memory for most, it moved the agent to tears.

Adams was on his knees, facing the other direction. On the back wall of the viewing platform, erected so families could mourn their loved ones, he saw a note, now faded and yellowed. "My daddy is Mike Wholey. I love him." The child had glued a picture of her papa to the middle of the page. She'd signed her name in crayon at the bottom: "Megan."

Thor stood and turned to Sarah. "If for no other reason than for Megan, I will learn why those bastards killed her father."

The ride back to their suite at the Plaza was quiet. One little girl had said enough. Upstairs, they settled into the cozy library. Sarah lit the fire, though one was already raging within both of them. Its crackling sounds had become their song.

"Are you ready to go to work?" she asked as she sat down in the chair next to his.

"Give me your best shot." He took a deep breath, distracted. Mike Wholey's soul was haunting him—as were Megan's tears.

Somber, Sarah knew she had to press on, to get her man to reengage. Exposing what had killed NYPD's Mike Wholey and three thousand other colleagues and friends, husbands and wives, dads and moms, sons and daughters, would take more than Adams had to give. He would need help.

"Sweetheart, the reason Megan no longer has a father is explained in this book." She opened her Bible to the beginning and placed her hand over the pages. "It tells who the murderers are, why they kill, and even how we can stop them."

"How?" Adams was eager.

"No. You're not ready to hear the answer. If I were to give it to you now, you'd either misinterpret the message or rush off half-cocked and make things even worse. You're a warrior—and an agnostic. To appreciate what this book has to say, you first have to come to grips with its inspiration. And only then will you grasp the causal link between these words and Islamic terror."

Thor looked puzzled. *Why is she withholding information.* He wanted resolution, now. "If the answer to why terrorists killed Megan's father is in that book, I want to know. I *need* to know."

"Yes, I understand. And it is, so over the next fifteen minutes I'm going to prove, beyond any reasonable doubt, that these words were inspired by God, not made up by men. I'm going to demonstrate that God is not only knowable, but also that he wants us to know him.

"To do that, I'd like start on familiar ground. You know the story of Abraham, Isaac, and Ishmael, right? We've talked about how Ishmael was Abe's illegitimate son through Hagar, his wife Sarah's Egyptian slave. Isaac's birth was a miracle. Sarah was ninety at the time." She smiled. "That's a good *wife's* name, don't you think?"

"Are you suggesting something?"

"Who, me? I'm not that kind of girl."

The Admiral gave her a sideways look. "So Isaac became the father of the Jews, and Ishmael, the Arabs."

"Right."

"Well?" Thor implored, pointing to his cheek. "You promised."

"This may take *twenty* minutes," she scolded him, tugging at his ear. She kissed his cheek anyway.

"A promise is a promise."

"That's right. Thanks for the segue. A dress rehearsal is like the promise of something to come, right?"

"Sure."

"Then let me tell you a story." Sarah turned to the 22nd chapter of Genesis. "Isaac had grown into a fine young lad, the spitting image of his father when God called. 'Abraham,'" Sarah intoned in her best godlike voice. "'Here I am,' Abe answered.

"God said, 'Take your son, *your only son,* Isaac, whom you love, and go to *Moriah.*' Abe was in Beersheba at the time, about twenty miles south of where Jerusalem is today. The Jewish Temple would later be built on Mount Moriah, Thor. Jesus was crucified on its slopes. The Muslim Dome of the Rock is there now."

"Okay. I know that place."

"Then God said something that must have brought Abe to his knees. '*Sacrifice* Isaac there as an offering for the *forgiveness of sin.*'" She emphasized the phrases she wanted him to remember. "This morning, I heard this really cute guy say that nothing good happens without sacrifice."

"That would be me," Thor smiled.

Raindrops began to pelt the window next to the small table. Flashes of lightning and distant thunder added to the drama.

Sarah returned to her story. "The next morning, Abraham, being the faithful guy that he was, got up early and saddled a *donkey.* He cut enough wood for the offering and set out with his son. 'On the *third day* he looked up and saw it in the distance.' *Mount Moriah.* He told his servants, 'Stay here with the donkey while Isaac and I go and worship. We will *return* to you. Abraham took the *wood* upon which Isaac was about to be *sacrificed* and placed it on *his son's back.*'"

"It's not a very nice story so far." Thor complained. "Can you imagine being Abe? You're a hundred and something years old and finally your cute-old-hag-of-a-wife gives you a son. Then God tells you to sacrifice him! What's up with that?"

"You'll find out, but for now just imagine the faith required to follow such orders."

The Admiral shook his head slowly.

Sarah loved sharing things with him. "As the two climbed up the slopes, Isaac, ever the trusting and obedient son, asked dear old dad, 'I see we've got the fire and the knife, but where's the *lamb* for the sacrifice, pop?'

"Abe answered, '*God himself* will provide the lamb for the offering, my son.' Yes, indeed he will." Sarah editorialized.

"So he *doesn't* sacrifice his son," a relieved Adams said.

"Oh, yes, *He* does, but *Abe* doesn't."

"Huh? Oh—of course he doesn't," Thor realized. "If he did, how could Isaac be the father of the Jews? *Duh.*"

Suddenly a lightening bolt struck a tree near their corner of the park, rattling the windows and startling Sarah. The crackling sounds of electricity bristled in the air. Thor touched her face.

Regaining her composure, professor Nottingly pressed on. "When father and son reached the place God had told them about, Abe arranged the wood. Then he *bound* his son and *laid him* on top of it."

Thor squirmed.

"Have you ever seen guys bound and strapped to wood before?"

"The crucifixions."

Sarah nodded, continuing the story from memory. "Abraham reached out his hand and took the knife, intending to slay his son. But as he did, the Lord called out to him from heaven. 'Abraham!'" she repeated in her pretend godlike baritone. "'Don't lay a hand on the boy. You have shown that you love me.'"

Thor looked a little pale. "That's a tough test, Sarah."

"You want everything easy, don't you sailor? Easy women, easy God...."

"No. But you made your point." Rain streaked down the window.

"Now for the good part. Abraham looked up, and there in a *thicket* he saw a *ram* caught by its horns. It was the same thicket that two millennia later would tear at the head of another only son, another sacrificial lamb, who would also be bound and laid upon a piece of wood, at the very same place. He, too, would ride on a donkey, endure three days of hell, and be totally obedient to his father, even sacrificing himself for us, bringing mankind back into fellowship with God."

"I get it. You're saying this was a dress rehearsal predicting how, where, and why Jesus would be crucified. Who wrote this story?"

"Moses."

"Moses," he repeated. He rubbed his chin. "Then I suppose Passover could have been another dress rehearsal. In Egypt, firstborn sons were spared when the blood of a lamb was wiped on the door frame."

"Yes."

"Then Moses leads his people out of Egypt and into the Promised Land. He writes down their history and starts what becomes the Bible." Tapping his fingers on the table, he added, "If I'm not mistaken, these same guys, Abraham, Isaac, Ishmael, and Moses play staring roles in the formation of Islam, too.

"Bingo."

As if on cue, the sky flashed with lightning; thunder shook the windows again. It was a good day to spend inside with a friend in front of a warm fire. "Like I told you," Sarah said, "there's a direct link between these words and terrorism, one that will become all too obvious."

"Then, speaking of obvious, anyone who died as described: on the slopes of Mount Moriah, with a thicket of thorns on his head, claiming to be the son of God, saying he was dying to forgive the sins of others...."

"...riding into town on a donkey, being gone for three days and then returning after being bound and laid on an altar of wood," Sarah completed Thor's improbable list, "would qualify as the fulfillment of this prophetic dress rehearsal. Abraham even called the place 'The Lord Will Provide'."

He gazed out the window. "Well beyond coincidence, I suppose."

"Yeah, ten billion to one, because only one man claiming to be the Son of God was sacrificed on this spot and in this manner. Actually, the most amazing of all of the Messianic prophecies is Daniel 9, but I want to save that one for last."

"Okay, but why?"

"In that prophecy, Daniel predicted the exact day the Messiah would enter Jerusalem, which in itself is pretty amazing. But he did it over five hundred years before it happened."

"Hey, speaking of Jerusalem, I made plans to visit the guys in Israel. Why don't you come with me!"

She didn't know what to say. Sure, she wanted to go, but the words didn't come.

He reached for her hand. His fingers interlaced hers. Smiling, they searched each other's eyes—green staring into blue, hazel into sapphire. "C'mon, Sarah. What do you say? The guys are great. You'll love 'em."

"You know I want to go. It's my favorite place. And I'd like to meet your friends, too."

"So, what's the problem?"

He looked so official, still wearing his officer's uniform. Thor had removed the jacket, but there was little question he was someone to be reckoned with. And who could turn down a man who was willing to smooch on national television? *Besides,* she thought, *I'd be a fool to let him go alone, surrender or no surrender.*

"Okay, I'll go but...."

"Separate rooms." He paused. "Sarah, about last night...."

"Yes, I know I can trust you. It's me I'm worried about, not you," she confessed. "I've never felt like that before."

"Me neither." That surprised her. He stroked her hand. "When we're done here, let's talk about how we're going to handle this, okay?"

"I'd like that."

"So teach," Thor said, returning to the lesson, "Lay 'em on me. The prophecies."

"Okay. Let's start with his birth."

"O little town of Bethlehem." Thor responded.

"Right, but did you know that Bethlehem was but one of two thousand towns in Israel at the time?"

"No."

Sarah opened her Bible to Micah 5:2. "'But you, Bethlehem, so small among the clans of Judah, from you will come forth one whose origins are from long ago, from the days of eternity.'"

"Based upon the number of alternative towns, the odds that Jesus would be born in the right place are one in two thousand, " Thor figured assigning probabilities to each fulfilled prophecy might be a good way to keep track of their progress. "Y'know, it's really hard to arrange your birth."

Sarah smiled as she wrote down the number. "God being born into the world as a baby is interesting in itself. Isaiah 9 predicts, 'A child will be born to us, a son will be given, and his name shall be Almighty God.'"

Looking at her notes, she turned to Isaiah 40:3, reading, "'The voice cried out in the wilderness, 'Prepare the way of the Lord. Make smooth in the desert a highway for our God.' How many rulers or kings do you know of that had an advance team proclaiming their mission before they even began their public life?"

"None. There have been thousands of revolutionaries, thousands of rulers, generals, and kings, but I'm not aware of any that were proclaimed in advance. Propagandists *follow* coronations. They never precede them. So who was this voice?"

"You never went to Sunday School, did you?"

"No. Sorry. But I'm making up for lost time."

"John the Baptist. He's not only recorded as having done this very thing in the Gospels, but also by Josephus, the most famous...."

"Yes, I know Josephus," he said in a disgusted tone. "His work is respected by historians, but not by the military, 'cause he was a traitor.

Anyway, I suppose the odds of having predicted hundreds of years in advance that Jesus would have a publicist proclaiming him to be God, is also better than a thousand to one. Never happened before or since."

Sarah wrote it down. "Jesus was the only religious teacher who claimed to be God, Thor. And he's the only one eyewitnesses claimed to have performed miracles."

"I suppose you're right. Moses was a liberator. Confucius and Buddha were just teachers. Muhammad was a messenger, and the founder of the Hindus is all but mythological. None of 'em claimed deity.

"But Jesus did. He said he was the one the prophets had foretold. She thumbed to Second Samuel 7:11 and paraphrased. "Here the prophet Nathan is speaking. He tells King David that one of his direct descendants will be God's son and have an everlasting kingdom; in other words, he'll be the Messiah."

"Okay. The Jews were a fraction of one percent of the world's population at the time Jesus was born, just like today. That would make the odds against any one man fulfilling the bigger part of this prophecy approximately five hundred to one. But let's be generous and call it a hundred to one."

Thor started to analyze it. "Now the fact he had to come from one of the twelve tribes of Israel is obviously twelve to one. But the odds that he would be able to show that he was a direct descendant of one particular man in that tribe, namely David, is a big deal. If we knew how many folks were in David's tribe at the time...."

"David took a census," she shared. "There were five hundred thousand men in the tribe of Judah who could handle a sword, in other words, half a million adult males of 'reproductive quality.'"

"Reproductive quality. That's pretty clever."

"I thought so." She winked. "And there's more to this than meets the eye. Not only were both Mary and Joseph direct descendants of King David, at the time of Jesus' birth, the records to prove it were available in the Temple."

"The same Temple that was destroyed after Christ's crucifixion?"

"Yep. Jesus was born in the last generation that could actually prove Messianic lineage. If he had been born later, the prophecy would have become meaningless—impossible to verify."

"All right, Miss Cleverness, that would make the odds a person could prove he was a direct descendant of David one in five hundred thousand. But I'm sure you know it's much more extreme than that. Odds are cumulative, meaning that the likelihood of all of these things happening is 2,000 x 1,000 x 100 x 12 x 500,000. That's a bunch."

Nottingly reached into her purse and pulled out a tiny calculator. She was prepared. She used the tip of her nail to punch in the numbers. The result was already too big for the display.

"Try this," Thor suggested. "Punch in 2 x 12 x 5."

"That's 120."

Thor had already done the math in his head but didn't think it would be good form to outshine the teacher. "Now add thirteen zeros," he said.

"That makes the odds against these five things happening by chance to any one man, 1 in a 120 followed by thirteen zeros." The number even surprised Sarah. "What's that, a thousand trillions, a million billions? It's almost laughable."

"That's right. A scientist would note it as 1.2×10^{15}. Also known as impossible. But I'll bet you've got more."

"How about this one?" she said. "Zechariah 9:9. 'Your king is coming to you, endowed with salvation, humble and riding on a donkey.' How many of your revolutionary types came into town on an ass proclaiming salvation?"

"None. So he was a humble guy. A humble God—it sounds like an oxymoron. Let's say the odds are a measly ten to one that such a person would humble himself this way."

Sarah jotted down another note. "He'll be betrayed by a friend, Psalm 41. Sold out for thirty pieces of silver, Zechariah 11. The betrayal money will be thrown down in the temple and then used to buy a potter's field."

"If those things happened, the odds for all of them occurring as predicted would be better than a hundred to one. How do we know they did?"

"Everything we're talking about was preached by the disciples to the citizens of Jerusalem immediately after they occurred—and there were tens of thousands of witnesses. Many converted from Judaism to Christianity during a time when the Jewish rulers, the Sadducees and Pharisees, would have done anything to snuff out the new faith because it was a threat. All they would have had to do was correct the record—demonstrate that Jesus missed fulfilling *any one* of the required prophecies. But they didn't, because they couldn't."

"Did you know that archeologists have found a bunch of tombs in Jerusalem that date back to the time of Christ? Many have crosses carved into them, proclaiming Jesus to be their savior, their Messiah."

"Crosses, huh. If nothing else, those tombs tell us that Allah's a liar. He claims that Jesus wasn't crucified."

Sarah agreed but stayed focused. "There's even more to it than that. Much of this was recorded by eyewitnesses and passed along in writings that became the New Testament, some within a decade or so of Jesus' crucifixion and resurrection. They've discovered twenty-five thousand ancient manuscripts confirming the accuracy of these accounts."

"Yep. Even secular historians like me know that the Bible was the most frequently copied and most widely circulated book of antiquity."

"The second most prolific is Homer's *Iliad,* isn't it?"

"Yes, but we have very few old manuscripts of that available to us. And the time lapse from the events they describe to the oldest parchment is ten times as many years as for the New Testament." Thor spoke from a position of knowledge. "You're on solid ground here, Sarah. The Bible is the best preserved, the most accurate and detailed account of ancient history. However, being detailed and accurate doesn't mean it's inspired."

"No, but Biblical critics have worked overtime trying to disprove its validity by pointing out historical discrepancies."

"Yes, it's true. But they all seem to embarrass themselves instead. They said that there was no evidence the Jews were ever in Egypt. Then we found inscriptions proving they were. They said there were no Hittites as described by Moses, but recently we've found ample evidence of their existence. The critics even said that there was no historical precedence for Mary and Joseph having to come to Bethlehem for a Roman census. But archeologists have found those records too."

"You do love your history." Nottingly checked her notes and scanned Psalm 22. It described the manner the Messiah would die. "Listen to this, Thor. 'I am poured out like water; my bones are out of joint. My heart has turned to wax. It has melted away within me. My strength is dried up and my tongue sticks to the roof of my mouth. Evil people encircle me; they have pierced my hands and my feet, yet none of my bones are broken. People gloat and stare at me. They divide my garments among them and cast lots for my clothing.' Does that sound familiar?"

Thor looked stunned. "My guys' arms were all pulled out of their sockets. They said it felt like their hearts had melted, depriving them of the strength they needed to get the others down. Like the Psalm said, fluids poured into their lungs, leaving them so thirsty their tongues were literally stuck until we gave them water from our canteens.

"I'll never forget it, Sarah. The Muslims encircled my men, gloating, hurling insults at them. Of course, you know they pierced their hands and feet, but did you know they stole their garments too, the SFGs? It happened exactly this way to my men. Who predicted this guy was going to be crucified, and when?"

"David did, one thousand years before it happened. Five hundred years before crucifixion was even *invented.*"

"Good grief." Thor rubbed his head. "Okay then, how do we know he's talking about the Messiah?" Adams asked.

"Listen to the rest of the Psalm. You tell me if this sounds like your average unlucky schmoe hanging on a cross in Nowheresville. 'Praise him, all you descendants of Jacob; glorify him, stand in awe, Israel. Those who seek the Lord will praise him. All the ends of the earth will remember and turn to him, and all the nations will bow down before him, for he rules over all.'"

"Okay, you win. Sounds like God hanging on that cross. Not the kind of thing you'd expect."

"Oh, it gets better. 'Those who cannot keep themselves alive will kneel before him. Posterity will serve him. Future generations will be told about him. They will proclaim his righteousness to a people yet unborn—for he has done it!' Psalm 22, my dear."

"Goodness. Hard to misinterpret that one."

"Sounds pretty clear to me, too," the beautiful agent proclaimed.

The Admiral loosened his tie. "There are no odds for this sort of thing. A hundred million to one wouldn't do it. And it's hard to misinterpret what you just read. Heck, with the Dead Sea Scrolls I can't even claim the Psalm was later altered to fit the facts."

"That's why I'm a believer. So what do you think, sailor?"

"It's like Psalm 102, only worse, in a better sort of way. It's hard to find a rational answer apart from...." It was hard for him to say.

"I believe God inspired David to write these words so we'd be able to recognize who Jesus was—who he is."

"Recognizing it is one thing. Dealing with it is something altogether different."

Sensing that Thor needed some breathing room, a little time to reconcile recognition and acceptance, Sarah returned to familiar ground. "Why don't we complete our probability calculation?"

Thor appreciated the gift. "Okay. But I've gotta tell you, that Psalm 22 hits pretty close to home. Prior to a week ago, I'd only heard of two mass crucifixions," he said, "the Spartacus slave revolt outside Rome and the one in 70 A.D. at Jerusalem, again courtesy of the Romans. I'll bet fewer than one in a hundred million people have been crucified, especially with nails in the hands and feet. The Assyrians invented crucifixion, but they tied their victims. It was the Romans who increased the pain by using spikes." Thor agonized over those he had cut to free his men.

"The Prophet Isaiah said the Messiah would die alongside criminals. His appearance wouldn't be anything special, that he would be truthful and never do anything violent. Yet the empowered would despise him. Isaiah said he would suffer and be pierced for our sins, and by his wounds we would be healed." Sarah read from Isaiah 53. "'All of us like sheep have gone astray, each has turned his own way; but the Lord laid on him the iniquity of us all.'" With each word, Thor's heart softened.

"'Oppressed and afflicted, he didn't complain or try to defend himself. He was led like a lamb to the slaughter.' Now catch this, 'After the suffering he will see the light of life; his days will be prolonged.' He's predicting the resurrection. 'By knowledge of him, my righteous one, many will be saved, for he will bear their sins.'"

"That sounds just like that John, what was it, the sports-stadium verse—John 3:16, doesn't it? I thought you said this was from Isaiah, not one of the New Testament guys.

"It is, Thor. Everything I've shared with you is from the Hebrew Bible. It was all written five hundred to fifteen hundred years before Jesus was born. The Prophet Isaiah made his predictions *seven hundred and fifty years* before any of these things happened. The New Testament writers didn't make this stuff up. They were witnesses to it."

"Y'know something? I expected this to be a fair fight. Sure, I thought I might lose. But this borders on overwhelming."

Sarah smiled. "In other words, proof beyond a reasonable doubt."

Thor took a deep breath, letting it out slowly. "So you want odds on a guy never doing anything wrong being executed as a criminal. A thousand to one. That he'd do it for this specific reason, that a guy would be willingly die on a cross to save humanity, is preposterous unless he's the real deal, but why don't we give that a one in a thousand chance, too."

Sarah wasn't done. "The prophets also promised that he would be beaten, that he would be silent before his accusers at his trial, that his bones wouldn't be broken—like your friends—that they would gamble for his garments, that his side would be pierced, that the earth would shake, the sky darkened, and that he would be buried in a rich man's tomb. They even said that his body would not decay. All of this happened the way they predicted."

"The last one alone is the whole deal, isn't it?" Thor observed.

"Yep."

"If he rose from the dead, then he's God. It's a lay-down hand from that point on. Frankly, it is anyway, Sarah. I don't now how I've managed to run from this all my life—how anybody confronted with these prophecies could deny...." The Admiral searched for the right phrase, but it didn't come.

Sarah nodded. "Mankind's fate hung on that cross. Yet our eternity was born in the empty tomb."

"I suppose you're gonna convince me of that too."

She just smiled. It had been enough for one day. "Let's just finish your probability calculation. We'll deal with resurrections another time. So what are the odds that one fellow could fulfill Isaiah's prophecies?"

"One in ten on silence at his trial. Knowing the Romans, the same odds on broken bones. I'd say half that on gambling for clothes, and the same for the pierced side, although that was uncommon. And no decay? These guys let their victims hang so long, the birds would peck them to the bone. They'd throw the remains into a common burial pit. Thus a rich man's tomb and a body that would not see decay, for a crucifixion victim, is a bazillion to one, but let's just say a thousand to one on each to be ridiculously conservative. But coordinating your crucifixion with an earthquake and darkness in the middle of the day, well, that would take some doing; it's a million-to-one shot, Sarah. I presume there's evidence of that."

"The prophecy is in Amos 8. God swears by the 'pride of Jacob'— that's the Messiah—'I will never forget their deeds. The land will tremble for this.' Amos says that God 'will make the sun go down at noon and darken the earth in broad daylight.'

"Matthew reports the fulfillment. 'Now from the sixth hour'—that's noon—'there was darkness over all the land unto the ninth hour.' Then he says, 'The earth shook and the rocks split.' Two Greek historians from the first century, Thallus and Phlegon, both independently reported that a strange darkness blotted out the sun for three hours during Passover in the year A.D. 33—the year, day, and time of Jesus' crucifixion."

"Let's face it. The odds against all of this happening as predicted are astronomical." Thor didn't need to be a math major to figure it out.

Nottingly added up the score. "That's 10 x 100 x 100,000,000 x 1,000 x 1,000 x 10 x 10 x 5 x 5 x 1,000 x 1,000 x 1,000,000, which is twenty-five followed by thirty-one zeros to one."

"Now," Adams suggested, "multiply that by.... Actually multiply 25 by 1.2, our first figure, and then add the original 14 zeros plus another 31 zeros." He wrote it out. "That's going to give us odds of one in, wow... 30,000,000,000,000,000,000,000,000,000,000,000,000,000,000,000 that your Jesus could have fulfilled them all by chance. That's thirty billion trillion trillion trillion, I think. It's three times ten to the..." Thor started counting zeros. There were an awful lot of them. "Three times ten to the 46th power. If you add in the odds of Jesus fulfilling every aspect of the Abraham-Isaac dress rehearsal, it's 10^{56} power. Just to make the odds a crapshoot—you'd have to have...." Again, Thor wrote the incredible number on her notepad: 10,000,000,000,000,000,000,000,000,000,000,-000,000,000,000,000,000,000,000,000. "That's how many people you'd need to have lived on planet earth for it even to be possible."

"Maybe he just got lucky," Sarah quipped.

"A lucky crucifixion. Now there's a thought."

Sarah chuckled. It was all so absurd, in a majestic sort of way.

"It's hard to believe there are any agnostics," Thor said. "Not with odds like these. Especially when you combine all of this with what we talked about on the airplane, about the Jews returning to Israel.

Adams tapped his fingers on the table. "Speaking of returning, Sarah, where is that predicted? Isn't that the rift between Christians and Jews?"

"Isaiah 11:11 is one of many. He says God will return and gather the remnant of his people."

Thor thought about his Jewish friends. "You said all this stuff was from the Hebrew Bible, yet Jews don't recognize Jesus as the Messiah. Amazing."

"Yes, but when they do, they actually become more complete Jews, by forming a relationship with their Messiah. And when we gentiles accept the Messiah as our savior, we become grafted in to the living tree that is Israel. According to Paul in the book of Romans, Christian roots are Jewish roots. In a way, Thor, I'm an adopted Jew.

"So because the Jewish religious leaders were threatened by Jesus, the Jews have been estranged from their own Messiah for centuries."

"Right. And what's even more amazing is today, those who accept him are Israel's greatest supporters. Christians are more committed to Israel than are most liberal Jews—especially secular Jews. Your friends should read this stuff if they want to understand why."

"I agree, but they're going to find these prophecies real uncomfortable," Thor said.

"Yet with so much at stake, they need to know. The validity of their scriptures, the war on terrorism, the future of their nation is tied to their prophets' words."

"Maybe even their souls."

"And yours, my dear."

"You're probably right, but give me time," he added, turning to look out the window. "I'm halfway there, Sarah. I'm no longer an agnostic. There is a God, of that I am certain. These prophecies alone prove it. As for the rest, dealing with the boy from Bethlehem..." Thor shook his head. "I've got a lot of old baggage I need to discard—forty years of living in a very different..." he wanted to say "world," but he couldn't. It was obvious that God had his fingerprints all over this one. He didn't even know why he was resisting.

11

FOOD FOR THOUGHT

Amerca's prince and princess boarded the El Al 777. They would soon be winging their way toward the most contested place on earth: the Promised Land. The Admiral was on the mend, now able to walk, albeit with a pronounced limp. His right arm and hand were healing.

Yet to his chagrin, he still wasn't up to being a beast of burden. The slender Sarah was hefting both their carry-ons, heavy cases packed to the brim with books, notes, and even a gun or two. Okay, four. The powers that be had given them a special dispensation.

Thor's reading list was similar to Sarah's. Slowly but surely, they were homing in on the enemy, coming to understand the events that had led to the world's most recent Waterloo.

"What's your pleasure, oh cute one?"

"How about a back rub followed by an hour or two of smooching? No, wait," he teased, "the smooching should come first."

She shook her fist, pretending to clobber him on the chin. "You've got a one-track mind, flyboy. I meant what would you like to do first: relax, read, eat, or grapple with one of the three subjects we planned to cover?"

He smiled. "Grappling sounds good."

"You're hopeless."

"And you, princess, have more energy than any ten guys I met at BUD/S, Stanley included."

"Last week you called me ugly and retarded. Now you say I remind you of ten smelly guys at camp. You're a tough one to please. I don't know why I put up with you."

✡   ✞   ☾

THEY HAD GIVEN almost as much blood as a suicide bomber. Anwar Abu and Aymen Halaweh were having a time of it. Working day after day, late into the night, inside these revolting beasts had tested their mettle and tried their resolve. As they struggled to install their creations, the dark, dank confines of these monsters haunted them. They had battered and beaten their knees, elbows, and heads into submission. They began to view themselves as martyrs, earning their tickets to Paradise.

Unfortunately, their leadership didn't see it that way. Half a world away, they salted their wounds with criticism. While each day's call provided an opportunity to crawl out of the stench-mobiles, it was hardly a reprieve. Impatient, Kahn and Omen began their conversations by chastising their American operatives for delays and cost overruns.

"I'm sorry, but the trucks you've given us are garbage. They're beat up, so worn out we can't get the access we need. Everything's rusted tight. And the bolts that aren't rusted are stripped." Aymen wasn't having fun. "We can't even weld our machinery in place. The metal's too fatigued."

"I've *had it* with the two of you complaining." Kahn wasn't pleased. "Allah's got a special place for women who whine."

"We are not miracle workers," Aymen protested in his most masculine voice. "Handling something as small, and *deadly*, as this confetti is difficult. We're trying to spread something infinitesimally small evenly over many kilometers. Don't you see how impossible this is?"

"There are no failures in Paradise. Either succeed or prepare to explain your shortcomings to Allah. *Personally*." Haqqani liked being able to intimidate others in the name of God. It made him feel superior.

"We will not fail," Anwar returned bravely.

"Weren't you pleased by Anwar's success, sir? The office conditioners were effective. They infected far more infidels than you'd planned, thanks in no small part to Abu's handiwork."

Omen responded curtly. "Did he conceive the brilliant idea? No. Did he raise the capital to make it possible? No. Did he arrange for the manufacture of the insidious disease? No. Did he install these devices? Answer these questions and I will tell you who is worthy of praise."

There was no winning with these people. Quagmer had just made that abundantly clear. If the boys complained, they would be replaced. There was no shortage of disgruntled Muslims in search of excitement.

✡   ☫   ☾

TRIXI LIGHTHEART was having the time of her life. Having clawed her way into the anchor's chair, she was a happy girl. Off camera, that is.

"The death toll from the most recent terrorist attacks keeps rising." She reported, "34,667 people have tested positive for inhalation anthrax." The media's fascination with body counts and their disdain for investigative journalism were all too evident. It was as if the disease was more interesting than the vermin spreading it.

"According to healthcare workers, half of those stricken may die over the next two weeks. Anthrax is particularly hard on seniors. The majority of those over fifty may succumb."

To a medley of horrible visual images Lightheart went on to chronicle what the victims could look forward to. "The first warning signs of inhalation anthrax typically appear within five days, although the spores can lie dormant in the body for months. The symptoms begin with muscle aches, fever, chills, headache, and a general feeling of malaise."

That sounded bad enough, but she wasn't through. "As early as the second day, victims awake feeling exhausted, often with a dry, hacking cough. Their sputum is tinged with blood. Then it gets worse. By the third day, those infected endure an acute shortness of breath, nausea, and tremendous pain in their chest as fluids begin to collect in their lungs."

Graphic images of people suffering through each progressive stage of the disease continued to be shown as Lightheart reported the grim news. "Vomiting begins as victims enter their third day. This phase is accompanied by a scorching fever and horribly labored breathing. The body slips into shock if treatment isn't well underway by this time. Death follows."

America had come to realize it knew precious little about this disease. Experts had thought that it took ten thousand spores to trigger a case of anthrax. They believed it had to be puffed into a breathable cloud to permeate the lungs. Neither factoid was true. Anthrax didn't have to be inhaled to kill, as previously thought. Simply touching a spore-covered surface was sufficient. Cross contamination was common. No one had a clue how few of the little critters it actually took to bring an unlucky victim down. And then there was the Houdini factor. The spores managed to travel in unpredictable ways—popping up inexplicably in the oddest places. The disease, it seemed, made no more sense than the Muslims spreading it.

✡   ✝   ☪

ON SCHEDULE, the El Al jet passed roared over the Atlantic on its Great Circle route to the Holy Land. The dinner dishes were cleared. "Are you ready?" Sarah knew that Islamic terror could not be understood apart from the Bible. Originally based upon an odd recasting of Biblical accounts, Islam ultimately turned and attacked its heritage. This bizarre reversal was at the heart of Muslim militancy.

"We're gonna discuss the resurrection, right?" Thor returned. "You believe the miracle man rose from the dead after he was beaten to a pulp by the Romans and nailed to a cross."

"Right."

"Sure. Why not? Up to this point the odds he wasn't God are a thousand million billion trillion to one. Why not beat death?"

"Speaking of odds, Thor," she said, clearing her throat, "have you ever thought about how impossible we are if God isn't?"

"Yeah. That's why I was an agnostic, not an atheist. It's impossible—about the same odds as Jesus just being lucky."

She shared some of what she knew. "Everything starts with stars, but stars are just gigantic nuclear furnaces, turning hydrogen into helium—the lightest elements."

"Yes, but we're made of heavier elements. Carbon, for example, is created during the death of *second-generation* stars. Once formed, these heavy elements have to coalesce into planets and orbit the proper distance from a *third-generation* star. That process takes up about two-thirds of the time evolutionists say is needed to make the impossible seem possible." Adams loved physics and astronomy. He was a geek with muscles.

"Very good," Sarah said, a little surprised. "Then all of these heavy elements need to bang together in just the right way. Scientists figure the chances against this happening in the precise manner and place it needs to is about one in ten to the sixtieth power. And that's a problem, statistically. There aren't that many particles in the entire universe."

"Yeah, but it gets worse," he added. "When the primordial life-form succeeds in beating the impossible odds, it needs something to eat to survive. Typically, it must consume *life* to live. And it needs a digestive system to process the nutrition once it finds it."

"Then it needs to figure out a way to reproduce itself—within that first generation—or all is lost and we're back to one chance in ten to the sixtieth power all over again." Sarah looked away, grappling with the immense improbability of it all.

Thor added fuel to the fire. "I think the biggest problem to the It-Just-Happened theory is DNA. It's a language, a code that tells every cell how it needs to play with the others. There is no way to explain its spontaneous generation." Thor was interested in the development of languages, believing, as did most historians, that the invention of written language was man's greatest achievement. Was DNA God's?

"The Second Law of Thermodynamics is another problem for the Abra-Kadabra theory. Without an outside source of energy, things *always* go from order to disorder. And even with a whole lot of added energy, if it's not controlled, things just melt down. The Twin Towers is a tragic example." She paused, looking for a better one. "If you were to drop a deck of cards out the window of an F-18, they wouldn't align themselves numerically in suits on the way down or play a game of bridge. They would simply scatter to the winds. Pulling them back together and organizing them requires an intelligent outside influence."

"I didn't know F-18s had windows."

"You didn't?"

He smiled. "Then tell me: how did we evolve from relatively simplistic life forms to vastly more complex organisms?"

"We didn't. Oh, there's micro-evolution within species, sure. And that's entirely consistent with a Creator. But spontaneous generation leading to us—machines more complex than any we can build or even imagine—takes a leap of faith beyond reason."

"Yes, because it requires mutations to be a positive thing. With evolutionary theory they're the only way viable new species can appear."

"Problem is, mutations are almost always harmful; in fact, they're usually *deadly*."

Thor nodded, soaking it all in.

"There are few—if any—transitional species in the fossil record, and there would have to be hundreds of thousands, if not millions, of them for global evolution to be plausible."

"Right, and there's little evidence of upward or macro-evolution either between differing life forms or *en masse* from less complex creatures to more complex ones. In fact, the fossil record shows explosive and sudden appearances of all kinds of related groups—like crustaceans, fish, dinosaurs, or birds—but huge gaps between these groups."

"That is the *inverse* of what the theory requires to be valid."

"Smart girl."

"Evolution from ooze to humans is irrational. Yet it's preached with religious zeal. It's sad how easily delusions are perpetrated."

"You're going to find evolution a hard nut to crack, Miss Smarty-Pants. Too many isms depend on it. Marx credits Communism's rise to Darwinism. His theories were essential to the early success of Nazism. The secular humanists all preach it, 'cause without macro-evolution they don't have a leg to stand on."

"Funny boy," she laughed. "Bottom line? It takes a greater leap of faith to believe that we happened by chance, the haphazard offspring of the big bang, than to believe that there's a God who created us."

"Like I said, that's why I was an agnostic, not an atheist. In fact, the big bang theory itself only makes sense in the context of a Creator. The universe is otherwise missing ninety-nine point five percent of the energy or mass needed to make the laws of physics work."

He looked into her eyes. *Enough small talk.* "Now, since you think Jesus was the creator of the universe, tell me about the resurrection. Why did he come here? Why did he have to be crucified?"

Sarah interlaced her fingers and stretched. Easy questions, hard answers. "One can make, buy, or steal most anything—anything except the most important thing. Love. It's like nothing else."

"So I've noticed."

She smiled. "It can be given away and you'll never run out; it can be received and you'll never have too much." That made *him* smile. "But it cannot be forced on anyone or taken from them against their will. Even God can't force love. It requires choice."

Sarah swiveled in her seat. "Man was created out of a spirit of love. And God wanted his creation, us, to love him in return. But he knew that required the option *not* to love him."

"I'm with you so far."

"In the Garden of Eden, that lush land between the rivers—the very region that historians like you regard as the cradle of civilization—an option was provided. A tree was planted, the 'Tree of the Knowledge of Good and Evil.' It stood there providing man with a choice. That made him neither lapdog nor robot. We're told that on one fine day, perhaps a week, perhaps a hundred million years, after God breathed his spirit into Adam, he and his bride chose poorly. With a little demonic encouragement, they disobeyed. They *chose* not to love their maker."

"That's what unleashed hell's fury? Bad fruit?"

"No, silly. Adam and Eve turned their backs on God. Hell is simply what happens when we distance ourselves from him. If you want to know what that's like, go visit Auschwitz sometime, the Gulags in Siberia, or the killing fields in Cambodia. According to the Bible, that's all hell is— separation from God, nothing more, nothing less."

"Having read the Qur'an I can assure you that Allah's rendition of hell is far more colorful. A certain terrorist training camp in northern Afghan- istan serves as proof," he suggested.

Nottingly pressed on, trying not to remember. "We all have a choice to make: love God or reject him."

"Is that why God asked Abraham to sacrifice Isaac?"

"Yes. It proved that he loved God. And as you know, with the story of

Abe and his sons, God, the ultimate storyteller, choreographed a dress rehearsal."

"God's sacrifice of his own son," he acknowledged.

"Right. Now think about what followed—the resurrection. Why would the Apostles make up a story like that? I mean, if it wasn't true, why take the risk? No other religion claims that their founder beat death. How do you start a religion saying, 'Follow him—he was just crucified?'"

"You mean the Apostles didn't get to share in the plunder of raiding caravans or conquering villages, like Muhammad's clan?" he joked, lightening the mood. "They didn't do it for the booty?"

"No," she answered, darkening it again. "They got to be imprisoned, flogged, boiled, stoned, and crucified instead. And they did it without complaint because they *knew* they were going to be with the risen Jesus. All but one, John, died a martyr's death, and they say that even he was boiled alive in a vat of oil."

"Tough assignment. But you say there were no deserters? No one who said, 'Come on, fellas, he's dead. Let's get on with our lives'?"

"Nope. Well, initially they were scared spitless. Wouldn't you be after your leader was tried, beaten, and crucified? But then something happened. These guys went from cowering in fear to being willing to do anything, no matter the risk, to speak out about this guy, insisting he was God. Every single one of them was instantly transformed. How do you explain that?"

Thor was silent. He had studied human behavior under siege. None of this made any sense, unless....

"Their own people, the Jewish religious and political leaders," she continued, "had convicted Jesus of blasphemy. The Romans had ripped the skin from his back with their whips, spit on him, jammed a crown of thorns on his head, and nailed him to a cross."

She let that image sink in. "Sure, he was a nice guy. Sure, he did some pretty cool miracles, including bringing a fellow back to life. Sure, he said some remarkable things. Sure, he predicted exactly what was going to happen to him. Sure, every important aspect of his life had been foretold centuries before. But he was *dead*. Hope's once-bright light had been snuffed out. There was nothing left to do but go fishing."

"But," Thor realized, "it's an entirely different story if hope returns."

"You bet. It transformed their lives, and they in turn transformed the world. It's a simple story," she shared. "God became a man to show us what he's like and to restore his relationship with us."

"This is starting to make sense," Adams thought out loud. "If you're God, you'd want your creation know you and know that you love them. There's no better way to do that than to become one of them."

"And what else do you need to do if you're God?"

"How would I know? I didn't go to Sunday School, remember?"

"You need to build a bridge, a way to cross the divide from our sinful world to his perfect one. His death paid the toll." Sarah had shared the Gospel. "He made us a promise. He said that he'd meet us on the bridge, take our hand, and lead us to the Promised Land."

✡   ✝   ☾

"'ANTHRAX IS GOOD, but atoms are better.' That's what Mr. Ghumani told me. And then he instructed me to call you, Mr. Quagmer. Halam said you'd understand."

"And what am I paying you for this delectable tidbit?" Omen didn't like lawyers.

"The usual. He needs a good lawyer, and we're as connected as they come. He's in denial, you know. He told me that the Americans wouldn't have the pleasure of seeing him tried. I think you should talk to him."

"Sure. I'll just ring him up in prison, and chat long enough for the Feds to figure out where I am. That would be smart, wouldn't it? Now lose this number, pal," Quagmer said, hanging up. He turned to his compatriot. "Have I ever told you how useless I think lawyers are? If they'd been around in the seventh century, Muhammad would have put a *fatwa* on their sorry butts."

"What did your 'pal' say?" Kahn asked.

"Only that Halam said atoms were better than anthrax."

"Now you're talking." Haqqani jumped to his feet.

Quagmer was less excited. He knew that the problem the boys were having trying to make anthrax behave was nothing compared to working with nuclear devices. Unstable atoms had to be controlled until the last possible moment, and then they needed to misbehave all at once—when they would do the most damage. "To succeed, we're going to have to work together on this one, Kahn. And we're going to need help. That Pakistani nuclear expert, Bashiruddin Mahmood, was Halam's friend, not ours. He doesn't trust us. He says we're not Muslim enough."

"Yeah, but we're nowhere without him. We'll need the Russians, too, and either the North Koreans or the Chinese. Do you have Mahmood's number?" Kahn asked. "And since you're the accountant; how much sympathy can we afford to buy?"

"No, just his email. Sympathy? We can afford plenty—low ten figures.

But first, we've got to decide what we want to do, what we *can* do."

"We have three choices." Kahn had studied all the really neat forms of mass annihilation. "First, there's the really cool stuff—bombs sitting atop ballistic missiles—nuclear fission!" His eyes widened.

Both American and Israeli intelligence sources had known for years that al-Qaeda was looking in all the likely places for suitable nukes. They had met with unemployed Soviet scientists and nuclear security personnel from impoverished Uzbekistan all the way to Siberia. Many, if not most, were willing, even eager, to trade anything they had for dollars. But putting the whole package together had proved a formidable challenge. One needs a delivery vehicle, a firing mechanism, triggering codes, and, of course, weapons-grade plutonium, all wrapped in a shiny bomb casing.

"You know Iraq's mobile launchers aren't going to help us blast America. They don't have the range. Halam wants us to blow up Washington. He wants to die a martyr and take down the American government with him. And that means we don't have the year or two we'd need to finish overthrowing the Pakistani junta."

"Yes, but nothing says 'hello' like nukes atop missiles."

"Forget it, Kahn. Set your sights a little closer to earth."

"Why? The new Iranian missiles have a three thousand kilometer range. Combine that with what Castro said when he was last in Tehran and we're in business."

"I remember. Fidel told the Ayatollah, 'Working together, we can bring the Americans to their knees.'"

"Perfect."

"I suppose, but how are we going to work with the Iranians sitting here in Baghdad?"

"We're not," Kahn admitted begrudgingly.

"Well then, our next-best option is to use the Russian suitcase bombs," Omen suggested to a slightly less-dejected Kahn.

"That is, if we can get them to work. They're old."

This was an area where entrepreneurial Russians and zealous Muslims had been able to do business. With their nuclear security measures leaking like a sieve, the Soviets had managed to lose track of 134 mini-nukes. Rumor had it that some twenty of the misplaced suitcases had found their way to al-Qaeda. Informants in the sleazy underworld of the Russian mafia had claimed bin Laden had paid $30 mil for them, throwing in a couple of tons of opium as a tip. Although American intelligence had paid handsomely for the news, they'd ultimately laughed it off, not trusting the sources. Funny thing, though; they'd been right.

"Of the twenty cases, the best we can hope for is that one out of every two or three will actually work," Omen told Kahn.

"I thought that was why Halam had Mahmood here. Wasn't he supposed to be recharging the triggers?"

"I'm told he did some good, but that he didn't have the right equipment. Something to do with the life of tritium. It has to be recharged every six years for the bombs to be reliable."

"But he also said that even a partially detonated weapon could do a lot of damage if it went off in the right place." Kahn was persistent.

"Let's use 'em, but in clusters so we'll be more certain they'll light."

"What are you suggesting, Omen?"

"I say we put six sets of three together. Mahmood rated each bomb when he was here. We could put the one he said was most likely to detonate, based upon the condition of the tritium trigger, with the least likely. Then the second most with the second least, and so on down the line."

"I see. If one of them fails, another in the group will fire, igniting both. That means we could obliterate six or seven cities."

Omen rubbed his belly. "Or, at least bruise 'em real bad. But Halam likes doing things in twelves. What can we use to smack the others?"

"Dirty bombs! They're like the nail bombs we strap to kids; only they're nuclear."

"I've heard you and Halam talk about these things. How do they work?"

Kahn clapped his hands. "All you do is take some regular explosive, TNT or C-4. You wrap radioactive debris around it—the kind of stuff they discard from nuclear reactors is best."

"Then we'd be recycling in a way."

Kahn smiled. "There's no nuclear explosion. The radiation is spread when the lead containment vessel is shattered. Put in the right place, though, a dirty bomb is nasty enough to make a bunch of people real sick. Some will die right away. Others will take awhile, succumbing later to one form of cancer or another."

"Slow, kind of like your crucifixions were supposed to work."

"No, actually, more like Chernobyl," he said. "Our nuclear waste is Russian, and it's loaded with Strontium. It'll contaminate everything. The cities will be doomed for decades. It can't even be washed away. They'll have to demolish every building that comes in contact with it." Haqqani played with his long, straggly beard.

"And thanks to Halam, we have plenty of spent nuclear fuel. He had it stockpiled in a cave somewhere on the island of Jamaica, didn't he?"

"Yep. So, Mr. Logistician, how do we get it into America without being noticed? For that matter, how do we deliver any of this stuff?"

"I've got an idea," Quagmer said, thinking about Jamaica. "It just might work. What do America's largest cities have in common?"

"Umm, well, they're mostly on the coast, either the Atlantic or the Pacific. Come to think of it, others are on the Great Lakes."

"Yes indeed," the chubby little terrorist muttered. "Sailboats."

"But who do we know that knows how to sail?"

"Who did we know that knew how to fly?"

✡ ✝ ☾

THE TRIPLE-SEVEN skittered to a bumpy landing, taxiing for what seemed like an eternity toward Ben Gurion's Terminal 2000. The late-afternoon sun prepared to make its daily descent into the Mediterranean. As the shadows lengthened across the tarmac, they hefted their carry-ons and they scurried (limped, in Thor's case) down the gangway. While buses awaited other passengers, notoriety had its rewards; they were escorted via private van to the terminal's VIP quarters.

Passing a bronze bust of David Ben Gurion, Israel's first Prime Minister, their escort turned and asked, "I wonder if he'd still be proud of us."

"Sure he would," Sarah replied cheerfully. "Anyone would be proud of what you've built here."

"But at what price?" The man turned and looked at Nottingly. Strain and frustration were etched in his face. "I was a soldier. I was trained to kill. But not like what's happening now. Last night, we killed a little boy. It was an accident, of course. He was riding to school with his terrorist father, a leader in Hamas. Our rocket killed them both. It's hard. We're all so very tired of war. Our children, *their* children. We need to find a way to live in peace."

Inside the VIP lounge, they were offered food and drink and told to relax. Customs was handled by others. As they waited, they wondered if their escort's sentiments were as prevalent as he had made them sound.

The brisk air of an early spring evening greeted Sarah and Thor as they walked out of the customs lounge and into a private parking lot behind the terminal. Adams expected to see Isaac Newcomb's smiling mug; he didn't expect a crowd of familiar faces. But there they were, all four of his Israeli brothers in arms. Yacob Seraph, Moshe Keceph, and Joshua Abrams were still bruised and bandaged, but mobile, more or less, in their matching wheelchairs. Those fortunate enough to have them were accompanied by their wives. The Admiral was considered family.

Thor dropped his bag, let out a half-laugh half-shout, and threw a broad hug around Isaac. His arm hurt. He didn't care. The others wheeled themselves closer and got their own greetings in, laughing.

"Hey! Who's watching the country, anyway?" Thor quipped. "All the tough guys are here at the airport."

"Not to worry," Yacob teased. "If the Palestinians give us any trouble, we'll announce you're here, and they'll all run away, screaming."

"Well, I hope so, 'cause I'm the only military resource Madam President wants to send Israel—and that's just so she won't have to look at my ugly face on the network news. I don't think she likes me very much."

"That's okay, Thor," Moshe chimed in. "We like you. You c-can come to all our c-crucifixions."

"Absolutely," Joshua agreed. "If America won't send a division of Marines, Thor Adams will do nicely."

"Are you saying the American Commander-in-Sheets is a patsifist?" Yacob asked in mock horror.

Thor laughed. Yacob sometimes stumbled onto a good one.

All the while, Sarah hung back, sporting a silly grin, not wanting to interrupt the male bonding ritual. But she was never far from Thor's thoughts. He did a crisp turn and held out his hand. "It is my pleasure to introduce Miss Sarah Nottingly, CIA Bureau Chief and my, um...." Thor fumbled about for an appropriate word, trying to strike a balance between "traveling companion" and "love of my life," but he couldn't come up with anything that wouldn't get him slapped.

Isaac let him suffer for a few seconds, and then said, "Ah, yes, the infamous Ms. Nottingly! I'm afraid the whole world knows your smile by now, thanks to Cap...oops, *Admiral* Adams' greeting at National Airport a couple weeks ago. Welcome to Israel, Ms. Nottingly."

"Thank you. And please, it's just Sarah."

"I'm not here in an official diplomatic capacity," Thor explained. "But Sarah is scheduled to meet with the Mossad on Tuesday. They want to figure out what went wrong. She, as some of you know, helped plan our little excursion, but please, don't hold that against her."

"I'll be taking her in to the office," Joshua shared. His wife frowned. It wasn't that she didn't want her husband escorting Nottingly; it was just that every Mossad spouse had grown weary of the agency's headquarters being referred to so benignly.

"Do you think we could arrange a tour while we're here."

Yacob Seraph burst out laughing. "What is your expression? Be real! I'm afraid you've got all four of us as your guides."

"T-transportation is all arranged," Moshe added. "We have a van all w-week. It belongs to the Prime Minister." All four soldiers knew him personally. Israel is a small nation.

Isaac said, "Headquarters figured we weren't going to be of much use in our condition, so they gave us light duty—escorting VIP tourists."

He didn't mention that all four would be heavily armed, or that the van was armored, with bullet-resistant glass and a mine-deflecting steel bottom. Nor did he say that this had been their first and only assignment since returning home, other than mending in the hospital, studying Islam, and talking to an army of reporters.

All four "tour guides" had been cleared for weapons readiness at the Mossad rifle range. After all, no one knew if they could *lift* an Uzzi, never mind fire one, within such a short time of having spikes driven through their wrists. The Israelis were under no illusions about the emotional baggage their guests had brought into the country, without even declaring it through customs.

✡   ✝   ☪

THE HOTEL WAS IN JAFFA, a trip of a few kilometers and a few thousand years from Tel Aviv. They had decided to save Jerusalem for the morning. The Israelis wanted the Admiral to see it washed in the day's first light. They wanted him to love it as much as they did.

A dinner reservation was made for later that evening at one of their favorite restaurants. There was just enough time to check in, freshen up, and relax for a moment.

From Sarah's ninth-floor window, she surveyed the fading rays of the sun as it dipped slowly beneath the Mediterranean horizon. Looking in one direction, she could see the twinkling lights of Tel Aviv, a city as modern (and as tacky) as Los Angeles. In the other, the dim outline of Jaffa's harbor brought to her mind the misadventures of Jonah. This was where the Prophet had started running away from God 2,800 years ago. He had been told to go to the Assyrian capital, Nineveh, and turn them from their wicked ways. But you can't get to Nineveh from here, not by boat anyway.

The man in the adjoining room, she feared, had been running, or at least limping, from God too. But he was close; it wouldn't take an encounter with a big fish to get him to see the light. Sarah had a funny feeling that Thor Adams, like Jonah the Prophet, had been chosen by the Almighty to do something important—to deliver a message, perhaps.

Sarah had seen daylight through the chinks in his armor even before the long flight to Israel. But her Thor was a military man. He had an open mind but wanted to see concrete evidence, indisputable fact, *proof*. He wasn't about to commit to anything he didn't understand. That wasn't how he was built. But God, she knew, didn't work that way. He wanted people to *choose* him, to take a leap of faith, even if it was but a small step into the light. He would provide ample evidence, but he wouldn't make it so black and white it would all but force someone to capitulate.

And God had plenty of competition. Anybody could announce, "Thus says the Lord...." The monotheistic Jews, Christians, and Moslems all claimed to have the last word concerning God's revelation. Not to be out-done, followers of Hinduism, Buddhism, Taoism, Confucianism, and a plethora of others—including the oh-so-popular atheist faiths of Communism and humanism—all purported to be the true path to enlightenment. But whether they espoused one God, many gods, or no god bigger than themselves, their inspired writings all described, directly or indirectly, the object of their worship. Even atheists, whose actions proclaimed that they thought *they* were supremely important, had scriptures, and they varied from believer to believer, ranging from the *Communist* and *Humanist Manifestos* to *People* magazine. Man is a religious animal. He will always find something to worship.

Sarah reflected that religions all seemed to have one thing in common: they described how man could approach God or become godlike—whatever they took that to mean. Usually, it was what *you* did, how *you* acted that made the difference, whether that was being part of the Muslim's *Jihad*, achieving the Buddhist's tranquil state of enlightenment, or booking a week in atheist heaven, the ski lodge in Telluride.

Christianity was the lone exception, though many of its own adherents, those immersed in the politics of the pulpit, had lost sight of that fact. With Christ, God approached man, not the other way around.

Her hope for getting through to the once skeptical and now engrossed Thor Adams, strangely enough, was a principle she had come across in a freshman-level physics class. It was called Occam's Razor, "*Pluralitas non est ponenda sine neccesitate.*" In layman's terms: when two competing theories make the same prediction, the simpler one is better.

To Sarah, it meant that in matters of faith, you could demonstrate truth by testing scriptures *mathematically.* If it could be shown statistically that it was true, then it probably was. The best solution was the one it took the *least* amount of faith to accept.

The contrary would hold true as well. If things didn't add up, if there were serious inconsistencies, and the need for revisionist history, then the scheme was probably false—no matter how many adherents subscribed to the doctrine's methods and rituals.

Since the world's great religions invariably claimed to have prophets—

Moses, David, Isaiah, Jesus, *et al*, for Judeo-Christianity; the same list plus Muhammad for Islam; Lenin and Marx for Communism; and folks like Kant, Huxley, and Darwin for secular humanism—it was only reasonable to put their words to the test.

A weary Sarah lay back on the bed and closed her eyes. A pithy quote from a nineteenth-century scholar popped involuntarily into her head: *"There is a point beyond which unbelief is impossible, and the mind in refusing truth must take refuge in a misbelief which is sheer incredulity." Sir Robert Anderson,* she thought. *They don't write 'em like that any more, Bobby.* She smiled as she drifted off to sleep.

Startled awake by a loud knock on the door, Sarah hurriedly finished getting ready, enduring the catcalls of the five military men waiting impatiently in the hallway. Those with wives were more understanding.

"C'mon, S-sarah. We're hungry! Is she always this slow, Thor? What's she *d-doing* in there?" Moshe was obviously a bachelor.

"A minute forty-seven, gentlemen," Sarah announced as she opened the door. "That wasn't so bad, was it?"

Thor looked her up and down. "Worth the wait."

The Keren was a beautiful four-star restaurant in a restored nineteenth-century house on Rehov Eilat, between Tel Aviv and Jaffa. The group was escorted to a large table in the back. Isaac ordered a domestic Sauvignon Blanc to start things off. The menu was intriguing, but it was the conversation that held promise.

Over crabmeat with feta cheese, "lost bread" and hyssop, and a *foie gras* with vanilla sauce, the chatter explored the entire gamut of etiquette no-nos, roaming from Israeli politics to American, and from Judaism to Islam. The conversation, if not polite, promised to be lively.

The participants were all over the map, religion-wise. Sarah was a Christian. Evangelical, no apologies. Thor had recently migrated from agnostic to believer, but he didn't know in what, exactly. Moshe Keceph styled himself a secularist, kissing cousin to atheist, socialist style. This put him in the same class with a great many Israelis. But like them, he was plenty curious and open to divergent views.

Isaac and Josh were simply "Jewish," though from opposite ends of the spectrum. Isaac was "Reformed," which meant he took matters of faith with a grain of salt, a wink, and a shrug, but he'd wear a Yarmulke if the occasion called for it. Joshua (Yeshua, to his mom) was pretty much of the orthodox persuasion. He swallowed it all, including the two thousand years of baggage that had accumulated along the way. Not just the Law and the Prophets, but the Talmud, the Targums, the Midrash, and the Mishnah. You could study for a lifetime and not get to the bottom of it. The Jewish mind had managed to turn monotheism into a mountain of minutia.

But he was far from being a Black Hat, an ultra-orthodox Jew. The members of these rival sects, the Shas as they are called politically, turned most Jews' stomachs, refusing to pay taxes and expecting the government to support their indulgences. Yet they were unwilling to serve, especially in the Israeli army. They reminded Sarah of the Pharisees of Jesus' time—arrogant, self-serving, money-grubbing hypocrites.

And then there was the soft-spoken Yacob Seraph, that rarest of Jews, a true believer. Yacob took the Jewish scriptures, the Law of Moses—or Torah—the Books of Poetry, and the Prophets to be God's word. Period. The wisdom of the Rabbis, the commentaries, were all very nice, but they weren't any more *scripture* to Yacob than Matthew Henry's commentaries on the Bible were scripture to Sarah Nottingly.

As the main course arrived—saddle of lamb with lentils; ragout of veal offal with white-bean puree; lamb *carpaccio*; shrimp served with plump raviolis filled with mullard, goose liver, and bacon (or as Isaac called it, "short cow")—the conversation turned to what was on Thor's mind.

"What makes them so crazy, my friends? What is it about Islam that breeds terrorists like rotting garbage breeds flies? Oh, I know all Muslims aren't terrorists, but why are most all terrorists Muslims?"

"While I've studied Islam," Yacob said, "I know the most about the Arab branch, especially the Palestinians. For them it's jealousy. They covet what we have. It's an old family feud."

Sarah picked up on it. "Ishmael," she ventured. "Father of the Arabs."

"Bimbo," Yacob said.

"That's *Bingo*, you idiot." Isaac laughed hysterically at Yacob's disastrous attempt at American slang.

Sarah simply smiled and shook her head.

"Four thousand years is a r-real long time to h-hold a grudge."

"Yeah, but that's how this all started. Y'see, Sarah—Abraham's Sarah—was barren, we're told, so she offered her husband a surrogate, Hagar, her Egyptian slave," Josh began. "But her plan backfired. Once Hagar was pregnant, she started in with the flaunting and taunting. That made Sarah not so much fun, yes? So Hagar ran away. That's when an angel told her that her son's descendants would be, and I quote, 'wild asses of men.' Remind you of anybody we know?"

"Can't be," Thor chuckled. "Our terrorist pals are just misunderstood. I heard it on the evening news. It's not their fault. They *have* to kill women and children because…well, I don't *know* why, do you?"

"It's more than jealousy," Sarah noted. "The feud's ancient history, fellas. Get over it, already."

"They c-can't," Moshe answered. "Islam has rekindled old hatreds. It's all based upon a revisionist v-version of our Bible. But their adaptation is nothing but self-serving n-nonsense, and we know it."

Isaac chimed in. "That bugs 'em. Especially now that the Dead Sea scrolls confirm the precision upon which our scribes went about documenting these events. In a rational world, that find alone would have destroyed the illusion of Islam."

"'Illusion?' 'Self-serving nonsense?'" Adams repeated. "Isn't that a little harsh? Mistaken, maybe, but...."

"Admiral, all we've done since we were last together is study Islam. It's worse than you can imagine," Josh revealed. "It's wholly responsible for terrorism, *the* common denominator, motivating Muslim militants. It's why they honor suicide bombers. Allah, my friend, is as warped as his Messenger, as disturbed and violent as his followers."

"Strong words, Josh. I assume you've come up with something that justifies such an extreme position." Sarah shot back. "It's inconsistent with every nation's official view of things—including yours," she added, playing devil's advocate.

"Over the next few days, we're going to shatter some illusions. The peace-loving-Islam myth is one of them. We've been duped."

"And it's a powerful deception, one that serves far too many," Yacob added. "Corrupt as it may be, Islam is the source of Arab power. They'll stop at nothing to perpetuate the myth."

They all sat silently for a moment, chewing on their food and their thoughts. They were happy to be back together, especially in these surroundings, but they were still hurting.

Isaac got something off his bruised chest. "We want to offer our sympathy for the recent anthrax killings. Muslims. Disgusting."

"Do you know something we don't?" Sarah asked. "I mean, Omen Quagmer accepted credit, but we have no proof."

"We know these people better than you do. We've had more experience with them. They've made a career out of killing us. I'll make you a wager. If it's not militant Muslims, I'll...I'll kiss Yasman Alafat's ugly butt on the Temple Mount."

"Ugh," Sarah squirmed. Suddenly she'd had enough to eat, although she knew the Israelis had to be hungry. Watching their ravaged hands fumble with their silverware was painful.

Isaac changed the subject. "Anyway, welcome to Israel, my friends. Our Promised Land. After millennia of dispersion and persecution, we're still a nation, and we're back in our homeland. Met any Babylonians lately? Assyrians, Philistines, or Phoenicians?" He smiled.

Thor looked up. "I think there might be a few million Arabs who'd differ with your claim to having the title deed for this little patch of ground. No offense, but what right do you have to it that they don't? You lived here for thousands of years. They lived here for thousands of years."

Moshe bristled. "We b-bought this place with our b-blood, Admiral. The H-holocaust...." His emotions were clearly getting the best of him. He could say no more, nor did he need to.

"The Arabs sided with the Nazis," Joshua reported. "They cheered, as they do today, when we were slaughtered."

"I mean no disrespect," Thor said softly, "but the Holocaust was only the price of admission. It caused the British to honor a broken promise. Without having endured that trial, I doubt world opinion would ever have shifted enough for you to return. But that's not the same as being entitled to it. And it's a long shot from being able to hold on to it, outnumbered a hundred to one."

"You're right," Yacob agreed. "It's not our historic occupation of Judea, and it's not our suffering. It's not what we've done since 1948 to develop the country, to make the desert bloom. It's not even our love for this land that entitles us to it—no doubt the so-called Palestinians covet it too. What gives us the right to live here is that God gave it to us—to Abraham, to Moses. He gave the Arabs land too. And they're living in it."

"Won't hold up in court." Thor tested them. "Some folks don't acknowledge his sovereignty, or even his existence. What then?"

"Then," Moshe retorted, "it's the law the r-rest of the world abides by: 'p-possession.' We're here. The Arabs have done all they could to d-drive us into the sea. They attacked us in '48, in '56, '67, and '73. Truth is, they attack us every day. They've just g-gone from all-out war to non-stop terror. Y'know, Admiral, your nation's c-claims to California and Texas are *much* weaker than our c-claim to the West Bank."

"Possession is ten-ninths of the law, right?" Yacob observed. "And speaking of law, did you know that UN Resolutions 181 and 242, as well as Olso I and II, are illegal? They both violate the 1969 Vienna Convention on the Law of Treaties. It says, 'A treaty is void if its conclusion has been procured by the threat or use of force, or if it violates the principles embodied in the Charter of the United Nations.' The UN charter says that no right can grow from an injustice, i.e., you can't attack us and terrorize us as the Arabs have done and expect to be rewarded for it."

"Admiral, everybody wants what they call Palestine for different reasons," Isaac said. "Assad thinks it's Southern Syria. Mubarak sees it as a land bridge to the rest of the Arab world. The boy-king in Jordan sees it as a means to rid his own country of the dreaded Palestinians. The bevy of princes in Saudi know that their support for Palestinian martyrdom is a life insurance policy, keeping their people from killing them. Saddam Hussein used it to unify Islamic rage, to keep America from coming after him. Didn't work out all that well."

"And America wants to give it away to win the undying affection of these despots, so we can keep filling the tanks of our SUVs," Sarah added.

"And we only want it 'cause it's ours. It has been our home for four thousand years. Our enemies have attacked us and lost, that's all." Yacob was feeling his oats.

"Well, not always," Sarah said. "You've lost to some fairly formidable enemies. First, the Assyrians. Then the Babylonians."

This was Adams' beat. "Followed by Alexander the Great and the Greeks, only they weren't bearing gifts. The ultimate bad boys, the Romans, came calling next. As I recall, you guys yanked their chain one too many times. Titus' sent three legions. They reduced this place to rubble. Judea went desolate for centuries. Hardly anybody lived here."

"But as we left, someone must have said, 'I'll be back.'"

"Arnold?"

"No. God." Yacob had studied his prophets.

"And here we are. Six million Jews against a billion Muslims, all armed to the teeth and determined to eradicate us. I'd call that a miracle."

"Whether you're a math major, history buff, or soldier, it's hard to explain the lopsided victories any other way." Thor was preaching to the choir.

"No farce on earth is sufficient to evict us." Yacob grinned. "Looking at recent history, I'm surprised they even try." Even the skeptics, Thor, Isaac, and Moshe, military men through and through, knew that winning four wars in succession, outnumbered as they were, was unexplainable.

The dinner dishes were cleared. Isaac informed the overstuffed celebrants that dessert was coming as the waiter refilled their wine glasses.

"What do your scriptures have to say about gluttony?" Thor ventured.

"I don't know. But they do say we should respect our elders."

To which Sarah replied, "Happy fortieth, old man." She leaned over and gave Thor a kiss as his dessert arrived with a lone candle.

The wives smiled. Yacob's Marta and Joshua's Beth could see love in Sarah's eyes. These two were going somewhere. Isaac's wife had wanted to join her husband, but with both her parents and his in America, babysitters were few and far between.

"Okay," Yacob said. "Enough frivolity. Let's get down to business. The way I see it, the real miracle is not that we Jews are back, but that the prophets said we would be. If you'll indulge me, I'd like to share what they said would happen to civilizations in this part of the world. I don't have the scriptures with me, but I know the scenarios well enough...."

Sarah held up a finger and dove into her purse. She still had her compact Bible with her, right next to her 38. "Would this help?"

"Thank you." The first two thirds of the Christian Bible is identical to the Hebrew Bible. Yacob was in familiar territory. While most Jews didn't know their own scriptures as well as many Christians did, Yacob was an exception to the rule. He started flipping pages.

"Before you begin, Yacob, why don't we review the 'prophetic' support for the world's other basic belief systems. I'd like to start with Communism. After all, for all practical purposes, that started here, too."

"That's a strike out," Sarah jumped in. "They preached world domination, that religion was the opiate of the people, that folks could be made more responsible, more charitable, and tolerant through indoctrination. Although, I'll grant you, they'd call it education. They even said that their economic solution would triumph over capitalism."

"The best p-place to examine the failure is right here in Israel, at a Kibbutz. You'll be spending a night at m-mine. Most everything w-we predicted f-failed to materialize," Moshe confessed.

"Moshe's right. Communists dropped the bat," Yacob misspoke. "They hurt a lot of people. Hellish violence, just like our Muslim fiends. Deplorable conditions, too. Human wrongs, not rights. It was a bad idea."

Yacob's wife, Marta, corrected him. "Friends, Yacob, not fiends."

"Speak for yourself."

She did. "The secular humanists have struck out, too. Their desire to normalize behaviors that historically destroy nations is as faulty as their strategy to attain peace through appeasement." Marta, like most Israeli women, was bright and articulate, although she, like her husband, may have had a little too much to drink. Marta was seated next to Sarah. The two were becoming friends. They had bonded while the boys talked about their adventures.

"History condemns them, which must be why they feel the need to revise it." Adams explained. "They can't deal with the fact that the most 'enlightened' century, the most liberal, was also the deadliest."

Marta, having finished her dessert, toyed with her husband's. "Humanist philosophy penalizes success, rewards failure, and tries to redistribute wealth rather than create it. It's about politically correct rhetoric rather than intelligent debate, multiculturalism rather than patriotism, tolerance rather than truth."

"It's nothing but a self-inflicted death swirl into the abscess." Yacob took another swig of wine.

Sarah pushed her glass away. "In America, all of the Great Society programs have failed. Costs have spiraled out of control. And ultimately they have done nothing to bridge the gap between rich and poor." She held strong opinions.

"All right then, what about the great Prophet?" the Major asked. He looked around. "Any takers on how many prophetic predictions the Allah-Muhammad combo made or what percentage they got right?"

Josh sneered. Moshe raised his eyes heavenward. Yacob answered, "Zero, zipper, zilch."

"Calling Muhammad a prophet is like calling China a *republic*. It's nothing but political positioning," Joshua added. "We'll prove that while you're here, sir."

"That brings us to us," Yacob smiled. "Our prophets were confident enough to allow us to judge them by their predictions."

"Foretelling the future is a gutsy move," Isaac said.

"Yes. And there are thousands of prophecies to choose from." It was Joshua's wife this time. Beth was sitting across from Sarah. "One of my favorites is the story of Nineveh."

Yacob picked up on it. "Assyria: the first nation to force Israelis into captivity." Three of the five men involuntarily reached up and touched their noses. They were still smarting from the fishhooks. "It was at the height of Assyrian power that the Prophet Nahum denounced them—about sixty years after they had conquered the Northern Kingdom of Israel, thirty-seven hundred years ago."

Thor dove in. "The Assyrian capital was up the river apiece from Babylon, in present-day Iraq. It was well defended, with a seven-mile wall a hundred feet high and fifty feet thick. They had food and water to out-last a twenty-year siege. And they needed it. They were holy terrors—kind of like Muslims today. They had more than their share of enemies."

Beth grabbed Sarah's Bible away from Yacob. "The Prophet not only said it would go down easily, but that they would deserve their fate." She read from the book of Nahum, skipping from passage to passage: "'Nineveh, you will have no descendants to bear your name. While the Lord will restore the splendor of Israel, you will be laid to waste.' Nahum told us that God is slow to anger, but, if a nation is bad enough, long enough, 'the Lord will by no means leave the guilty unpunished.'"

Marta grabbed the book and read. "'Your river gates will be thrown open. Nineveh is like a pool and its water is draining away.' So God's explaining how it's going to happen. And then *why*. 'Woe to the city of blood, full of lies, full of plunder, never without victims!'"

"Sounds like G-Gaza," Moshe quipped.

"Sounds to me like Muhammad's rise to power, which is probably why," Isaac explained.

Sarah politely requisitioned her Bible from Marta. "'You will have many casualties, piles of dead, bodies without number, people stumbling over the corpses.'"

"You sure he's not talking about Afghanistan?" Thor interrupted.

Sarah ignored him. "'You are evil, for you have enslaved nations and used sorcerers and witchcraft. Nineveh will lie in ruins.'"

Yacob, retrieving the book from Sarah, continued the account. "'All your fortresses are fig trees with ripened fruit. When they are shaken, they will fall into the mouths of the eater.'" He took a bite before his wife had a chance to eat the last of his dessert. "'The gates of your land are wide open to your enemies. Fire has consumed your bars, for you are drunk,' like somebody else I know," he said, ribbing his wife.

With Yacob distracted, Beth stole the Bible. "'Fire will devour you, O king of Assyria, while you sleep.' Nahum goes on to say, 'Nothing can heal your wound—your injury is fatal. Everyone who hears the news about you claps his hands at your fall, for who has not felt your endless cruelty?' That sounds like Islamic terrorists, for sure—especially here in Israel."

"Okay," Thor said. "An easy kill, fire, flood, drinking, and no recovery. So what happened?"

Yacob answered. "Half a century after the prophecy, the Medes destroyed the city so completely that it was totally lost until archeologists unearthed it in the 1840s. There was evidence of arson.

"Funny thing, though. Folks had been trying on and off for years to breach the defenses and couldn't. But in the spring of 612 B.C., heavy flooding in the Tigris valley broke down a section of the city's wall, flooding the town and opening the gates for attack—exactly like we just read. Remember 'Nineveh is like a pool?' Yet the Assyrians, ever confident, kept on drinking and partying, according to the Medes. They were ripe for picking. Prophecy fulfilled."

Thor provided the analysis and then did the math, which surprised him. "One chance in sixty-four hundred of getting it all right."

"That's why I'm a believer," Yacob said. "The prophecies are so detailed, and in many ways so unexpected, the arithmetic proves beyond any reasonable doubt that our scriptures are inspired."

Sarah glanced at Thor; her smile silently preached, "I told you so."

"There's more to these stories than just predictions and history," Beth said. "There are also moral lessons. God is telling us that there's a limit to his patience. He allows nations to reap what they sow."

"Sometimes he even takes care of business himself. Sodom and Gomorrah come to mind," Yacob shared. "Their behavior became so deviant, God torched 'em."

"They've been found," Thor said. "Near the southern end of the Dead Sea."

"History, not symbolism," Yacob reminded the Admiral. "What they found matches the Genesis account perfectly: five cities near each other on the plain, dated right around the time of Abraham, 2000 B.C. All were destroyed in some kind of cataclysm—you know, walls knocked down, people buried in the rubble, not ordinary battle damage. And get this. There's sulfur everywhere—*brimstone*—like Moses said."

"Moses and Muhammad," Josh observed. "They covered a lot of the same territory, but as far as the archeologists are concerned, only our scriptures have history you can dig up."

"Speaking of prophecy and Muhammad," Thor said, "I'm sitting here with three distinguished members of the intelligence community, Mossad and CIA. Tell me, smart people, just how is Muhammad's fan club going to attack us next, and what can we do to stop them?"

Isaac was an expert. "To stop them, you must undo everything you've done thus far. Your nation's knee-jerk reactions have been worse than foolish. They're counterproductive."

"He's right, Admiral," Yacob agreed. "Our intelligence is the best in the world. And it's based on profiling. Your government, in refusing to profile, has declared that the rights of those who wish to kill are more important than the rights of those they want to kill."

"Thor," Sarah said, "Terror is a manifestation of Islam, just as the S.S. was a manifestation of Nazism. *Jihad* is to Muhammad as *blitzkrieg* is to Hitler."

Moshe explained it this way. "When a thief b-breaks into your home and kills your w-wife and son, you need to k-kill him before he murders you and your daughter. A c-crime has been committed, sir. On 9/11 Muslims c-came into your home and did this v-very thing. But your nation seems afraid to go after the real m-murderers—you're even afraid of accusing them of the c-crime."

The Major picked up where Moshe left off. "Why do you suppose civilized nations prosecute criminals and defend themselves when attacked?"

"To keep their people safe."

"Right. And to identify the murderers, to successfully prosecute them, what do you need to prove?"

"Sherlock Homes would say means, motive, and opportunity."

"The means was our Bible. Without it, Muhammad wouldn't have been able to form a sewing circle, much less start a religion. Islam's credibility comes entirely from the Judeo-Christian scriptures."

"Yeah. That's what I said back in Afghanistan. It's obvious."

"The m-motivation for killing is even more obvious. When we infidels called Muhammad on the c-carpet for the absurdity of his pronouncements, he got p-pissed."

"Sir," Josh interjected, "if you were to put the Qur'an in chronological order, you'd see that Muhammad started off as a wannabe Jew. In Mecca he prayed facing Jerusalem; he worshiped on our Sabbath. Most every character in the Qur'an comes from the Torah."

Yacob was eager to contribute. "The moment Muhammad was forced out of Mecca, his revisionist 'scriptures' were exposed to Jewish scrutiny. Our brothers in Yathrib were insulted, and that changed everything."

The Major pulled rank. "For example, there were over a hundred quasi-peace-loving verses 'revealed' to Muhammad when he was hanging with the Meccans. They were all abrogated—cast into oblivion, in Allah-speak—when the Yathrib Jews defied the Messenger. In Qur'an 9:5, Allah says, 'Fight and slay the infidels wherever you find them. Seize them, beleaguer them, using every strategy of war.' Hate is a powerful motive, my friend."

"And you gave them the third thing—opportunity." Josh rubbed his bruised chest. "By refusing to acknowledge who the murderers were, and failing to ascertain why they killed, you have made your family vulnerable. To use Moshe's example, it would be like leaving the thief in your home with your daughter while you go and consult with the criminal's friends and neighbors. While they confuse you with talk of peace, they tell one another that you had it coming. In their eyes, the killer was justified because their Prophet commanded him to terrorize you. Given the chance, they'd all slit your throat."

"That's a p-problem. The murderer has a billion neighbors, and they're taught to hate you. So what do you do? Do you brick up your doors and windows with the k-killer inside? How many bricks will it take before you're worn down and l-living in the dark? Or, I know, why not invite the murderer's largest benefactor over for a tour of your r-ranch? Tell him you like his plan to reward m-murders and abandon your friends."

"Okay boys. I get the point. We can't wall ourselves in any more than we could've prevented World War II by sealing our borders or randomly profiling non-combatants."

The Major agreed. "What would have happened if you had sent your fleet to South America and your planes to South Africa rather than to

Germany and Japan?"

"We'd be eating sushi and sauerkraut," Thor guessed.

"If you want to get serious and stop terror, then you need to take the battle to the source," Isaac concluded.

"That's not so easy. America doesn't have a leader capable of understanding these things, which means we're condemned to fight this foe on our soil," Thor acknowledged grimly. "So how do you suppose they'll attack next?"

"They're p-probably going to make you s-sick and then blow you to pieces." Moshe surveyed his battered hand. "Anthrax and nukes."

"Swell. Mind if Sarah and I stay here with you for a while? Suicide bombers seem a lot less menacing."

"Yacob smiled. "Me Ka'aba es su Ka'aba." His Spanish was no better than his English.

Thor sighed. "Do you think they can make enough anthrax to take the battle beyond mailboxes and office suites?"

"Sure. I wouldn't be surprised if they find a way to infect whole cities. You guys have already caught them studying crop dusters. Why do you think they did that? Seen any terrorist farmers recently?"

"You really believe they're gonna try to spray anthrax on us like it was a pesticide—infidel poison? You think they're going to drop it on us like it was confetti in some twisted tickertape parade?"

"Yep. Stock up on Cipro. You're gonna need it," Isaac prophesied. "But that's the least of your problems."

"Nukes?"

"Dirty bombs first, fission next." Yacob guessed.

"From what I've read, 'radiological dispersion devices' as the call them, aren't all that lethal." Thor raised an eye, checking Isaac's expression.

"If they use americium from smoke detectors, or barium from enemas, no. But cobalt 60, used in food processing plants, and cesium 137, used in X-ray machines, would kill a lot of people."

"Those elements are prevalent and available in America, sir. In fact," Josh warned, "your own Nuclear Regulatory Commission said that 835 devices containing radioactive material *disappeared* over the last five years."

"I don't suppose you're making this up just to make me feel better."

"'Fraid not," Josh continued. "Many contained cobalt 60, which is a gamma-emitter. It's highly radioactive, with a half-life of five-point-three years. It's especially lethal, permeating the skin and causing immediate cell damage, ionizing fleshy atoms. The rays weigh nothing and travel at light speed. Those who come in contact with cobalt 60 get cancer, mostly leukemia. Their immune systems will fail. The only good news is that it won't last long, so it has to be used right after it's stolen."

"But that's nothing compared to what would happen if they got their hands on strontium 90," Isaac said. "It's a beta-emitter with a half life of twenty-eight years. Beta rays are like light—they have both wave and particle properties. They're ideal for dirty bombs because they can be contained within relatively light aluminum vessels. Gamma-emitters like cobalt need several centimeters of lead to control the radiation."

"And how would they get strontium?"

"Russian power plants. It's a byproduct of fissionable uranium dioxide 235. They also produce plutonium," Yacob said. "Which is why energy-rich Arab nations are having the French and Russians build nuclear power plants. The first was Pakistan, followed by Iraq, Iran, and Libya. Anyway, a core reactor will have two hundred and fifty one-centimeter pellets per assembly and two hundred assemblies per core. The fission process of radioactive isotopes creates new substances like strontium. A measuring-cup load of this stuff would contaminate a city beyond salvation."

"The good news is, it's a s-suicide mission. Would-be t-terrorists exposed to the isotope apart from its shielding wouldn't live l-long. And the best materials are the hardest to h-handle. At 300 REMs they'd lose their hair and screw up their blood, hemorrhaging internally. At 600 REMs it would be all over. Eighty p-percent would die a miserable death."

"And as bad as all this sounds, sir, if they get their hands on a real nuke—fission—a million people could die. Especially if they put it in just the right place." Yacob looked down at the table.

Isaac explained another problem. "The two fissionable isotopes are uranium 235 and weapons-grade plutonium. They have half-lives of millions and billions of years. You could make a pillow out of the stuff and it wouldn't affect you. That makes 'em hard to detect."

"But they can't just waltz in here with it, can they? We have detection gear at critical points of entry. It's not like they're going to paddle up the Potomac and surprise us."

Moshe, the hardened warrior, looked pale. Unwilling to make eye contact, he seemed to be searching for something in his espresso cup. "I pray you're right," the atheist mumbled.

12

MOON GOD

They arose early, well before sunrise. Their destination this morning was twenty miles inland, a city set on fourteen hills. It would take them just thirty minutes to journey 4,000 years back in time.

"Whose idea was it to start before the sun?" Isaac tried not to laugh; his chest still hurt. But it had been his idea and everybody knew it.

"This better be worth it," Thor said, limping toward the van. "And before I forget to ask, since you're driving, are you still seeing double?"

"No," Isaac said, looking at an imaginary Thor standing to the right of the real one. He pretended to walk into the side of the van. "*Oops.*"

"I can't vouch for your pal's vision," Sarah chuckled, "but Jerusalem at sunrise? It's like no other place in the world."

Aboard the Prime Minister's van, they headed east. Purple and magenta rays chased the last of the evening's stars. The soft underbellies of a dozen clouds began to glow. As the van climbed steadily up through a narrow pass, Team Bandage saw that the slopes on either side had been newly planted with Jerusalem pines. In thirty years, this would be a forest again.

Breaking the monotonous sounds of travel, Isaac played tour guide. "During our War of Independence these hills were crawling with armed Arabs. They were ruthless, and we were defenseless. Taking a convoy through this valley was a bloody affair."

"B-but it was either that or let our p-people starve." Moshe, ever the courageous one, knew the 4,000-year history of his nation. Every Israeli did. They reveled in it. They always had.

Shifting into a lower gear, the armored van labored to make the grade. With each turn the sky brightened, silhouetting the rolling hills and lacy pines. Then, there it was, their first glimpse, up through the valley. But as quickly as it had appeared, it was gone, swallowed by the curvature of the pass. Teased again with another brief look, they saw white stone buildings descending the western slopes ahead of them. Even draped in the dawn's shadows, the city glowed.

Knowing what was to come, Isaac reached for the CD player. He cued up his favorite song. "O Jerusalem" burst forth. The words were uplifting. As the music reached its crescendo, so did the view. Reaching the final rise, they veered left. In front of them, bathed in the rosy light of the new day, lay the most coveted city in the world. The town that had known only war was named the city of peace; along with the music her very stones cried out—Jerusalem!

Even for those who had seen her a thousand times, the first glimpse was special. The city was spread out, undulating, clinging to the hills before them. At its heart was the most significant square mile in the world.

As the sun rose, Isaac sped eastward. "Mount Scopis or Mount of Olives? What do you think? One's a little higher; the other's closer."

"Mount of Olives," Sarah suggested. "It has more historical significance, both past and future. Imagine that," Sarah caught herself. "Future history. Only in Jerusalem."

The overlook was abandoned. There were no tourists here. It wasn't just the early hour. There had been too much killing in the recent past. There was no place on earth where death was more poignant than standing upon the Mount of Olives.

Moshe and Joshua were loaded into their wheelchairs and rolled into position. With pierced feet and broken legs, they were a long way from being ambulatory. "You all know we're in East Jerusalem, right?" Joshua asked. "This is an Arab sector. For example, see that hotel behind you?" he asked, turning round. Its arches loomed large on top of the ridge, just above them. "Now look down below you."

What they saw was an enormous cemetery, stretched out to the right and left. But unlike its counterparts in America, there was no grass, no trees. There were only white limestone tombs, set in tight rows one right after the other, descending all the way down to the valley floor.

"That hotel's entry and façade were built from the tombstones of our forefathers. Muslims seem to relish defiling anything holy."

"That's *disgusting*." The thought turned the Admiral's stomach.

"Tell Thor why there are so many Jewish tombs here, Yacob," Sarah suggested, "and why so many of 'em are so old. And tell him why the Muslims have tombs on the other side of this valley."

"This is the favorite cemetery for Jews," Joshua said, "or at least it was before the Muslims sullied it. That's because our scriptures say that the Messiah will descend from heaven right here, on the Mount of Olives, and then enter the city through the Eastern Gate. Those buried here think they'll be the first to rise when he comes."

"*Returns*," Sarah whispered in Thor's ear.

Yacob pointed to the blocked Eastern Gate. It was all so close, a matter of a few hundred yards. "The reason so many Muslims are buried on the rise leading to the old city, on the other side of the Kidron valley, is that they want to *prevent* the Messiah from entering Jerusalem. That's also why they sealed the gate with stones centuries ago."

"You're kidding, right?" The Admiral found himself staring at the gruesome scar Halam Ghumani's nail had gouged into Yacob's neck. "These guys are so stupid they think they can stand in the way of a divine being, one powerful enough to descend from heaven? 'Gee, let's fight God.' That's a swell idea." He was having trouble coping with the Muslims' tendency to abandon reason, even in death.

"Those boys are a few bricks short of a full deck."

Adams rolled his eyes at Yacob's disastrous vernacular. "That's the Dome of the Rock over there, isn't it?" It dominated the view.

"I think we should call it the Dome of the Hoofie Print," Sarah grinned.

"The *what?*" Josh asked, pretending to remove something from his ear.

"C'mon. We all know that the only reason it's here is for *naah-naah-na-naah-naah* value. Why not call it what it really is?

"For w-what...?" Moshe stared at her like she was losing it.

"For gloating rights. You know, to taunt Jews. It's there for the same reason they built that ugly hotel from your tombstones. It defiles your sacred site—your *only* sacred site."

"She's right," Josh agreed, rolling his wheelchair a little closer. "It's not only meaningless to their religion; it's an embarrassment." He involuntarily scratched at the scab on his nose where Kahn had inserted the fishhook. "So from now on it'll be 'The Dome of the Hoofie Print'."

"Is somebody gonna tell me this story?" the Admiral whined. He was sitting on the rock ledge that separated the overlook from the cemetery below. The viewing area, while not large, was nice. Curving stone steps cascaded down, producing a theatrical effect.

"One night in Mecca," Isaac began, "Muhammad was snoozing when, he alleges, the angel Gabriel, the archangel of the Hebrew Bible, offered to take him on a wild ride."

"Right up," Yacob interrupted. "Muhammad says the two hopped on an imaginary beast called al-buraq and scampered northwest to Jerusalem. This al-buraq thing, a donkey or jackass, or whatever it was, was flat-out fast. According to Muhammad, each stride soared as far as the eye could see."

"You flyboys would call it mach two," Joshua teased.

"They make it all the way from Mecca to the Temple that night, about nine hundred miles," Sarah shared, pointing. "But not to that bilious blue and gold number. To the Jewish Temple, although Muhammad called it a Mosque. *That* ugly thing was built to celebrate the Celestial Journey."

"Unfortunately for Muhammad, though, the story's got a hitch or two in its get-along." Isaac had spent enough time in America to pick just the right phrase. "For starters, his favorite wife Aisha—we'll talk about her later—claims the boy never so much as left his bed that night."

"And it gets worse." Sarah knew the story. "The Muslim revisionists, in trying to keep up with the Joneses, or the Jesuses as the case may be, felt the need to manufacture a miracle or two. They sort of embellished the nature of the mythical beast, right?"

"It's true," Isaac laughed. "Al-buraq changed from being a cross between a donkey and a jackass to a hybrid winged steed, with the tail of a lion, the back end of a horse, and the torso and head of a woman."

"I knew Muslims thought women were horses'…well, you know," Sarah chuckled.

Isaac smiled but continued. "Muhammad claims that he meets with Abraham, Moses, and Jesus in the Temple/Mosque. 'Course, Abe would have been twenty-seven hundred years old, Moses, a couple thousand, and Jesus, six hundred. And there's a slight problem with the building itself. As in, there *wasn't* a Temple at the time. It had been torn down in 70 A.D. by the Romans."

"Mind you," Josh remarked, "we're not making this story up. Muhammad's own account of what happened is dutifully recorded in the Hadith, and in his own words."

"Oops."

"Yeah. So anyway, after chatting for a while, big Mo thinks it would be really cool to go up to heaven," Isaac told the assembled.

"That in itself is intriguing," Sarah turned to face her boyfriend. "Since he never made a heavenly voyage from Mecca, it proves what I've suspected for some time."

"What's that?" the Admiral bit.

"You can't get to heaven from Mecca."

Thor, recovering from his coughing fit, asked, "So what happened?"

"According to Muhammad, Abe, Jesus, and Moses are all real timid. They'll go to heaven but not all the way up to the top floor," Josh said.

"Maybe that's because Muhammad's idea of paradise is drinking and great virginal sex," Sarah reported. "They may have stopped to shop for lingerie on the second floor to spice things up." While booze and sex with multiple virgins in paradise was orthodox Islam, her lingerie suggestion was merely the product of a fertile imagination.

Moshe carried on. "But our hero w-wants to meet the b-big guy."

"So Mo, confidently astride his mach-two buraq, gives him-her-it a kick in the side and bounds heavenward," Isaac said, waving his arms in the air. "The dome was built over the hoof print the magical beast is said to have left in the stone as it leapt skyward."

"The blessed hoofie print!" Thor exclaimed in mock wonderment.

"Oh, and don't forget Gabe's grip marks. They say you'll see them on the rock too."

"Huh?"

"Muslims claim Mo had a magnetic personality. The rock—which by the way isn't a rock but simply the top of Mount Moriah—tried to follow the Prophet skyward. Gabriel had to hold it in place so it wouldn't fly away, crash into heaven, and give Allah a black eye." Isaac shook his head. "If it weren't so sad, it'd be funny."

"Funny?" Thor said. "This is *hilarious*. Where'd you get this stuff?"

"I'm afraid most of it's right out of the Hadith of al-Bukhari, The True Traditions—Muhammad's own words."

Joshua rolled back and forth next to the ledge. "Oh, and catch this," he said. "The Prophet finally makes his way to the seventh heaven and meets Allah for the first time. What do you think they talk about?"

Most shrugged. They were hoping for something profound, like "Why are we here?" But no.

"Muhammad asks the Big Guy about what kind of mindless ritual he likes best. You know, butt up or butt down when bowing, how many times a day he likes it, and what words he wants repeated so often they become irritating and can be muttered without thinking."

Moshe, trying to keep a straight face, said, "Muhammad says Allah wanted to see a b-billion butts raised to him in p-praise fifty times a day."

"Gives a whole new m-meaning to the term 'moon god'," the Admiral joked.

"Yeah. It's a complete sentence."

"Now settle down," Moshe protested. "That's what Mo s-says Allah wants. So then on the way down from his chat with Allah, who *was* the moon god, by the way, he bumps into M-Moses—still in the lingerie department, I presume." He looked over at Sarah. "Moses t-tells Muhammad he's been ripped off—that f-fifty butt-ups is way too offensive, I mean oppressive, too b-burdensome on his t-terrorists."

"You mean the Islamic faithful," Sarah suggested.

Moshe could see little difference. And, in his defense, it was hard to miss the humor.

"Moses sends M-Muhammad back to negotiate. Allah, overwhelmed by the Messenger Boy's m-magnetic personality, changes his mind and cuts the number of butt-ups to forty. Back down in l-lingerie, Moses is not impressed. He shoos Mo off to do b-better."

Isaac took over. "They repeat this process until Allah's head is spinning. He's so impressed with the service Mo is providing his people, the Big Guy cuts the Prophet a deal he can't refuse. He acquiesces to being mooned a paltry five times a day."

He paused to catch his breath. His lung was on the mend, but it was far from healed. "I know it sounds ridiculous, but really, from virgins in paradise to mooning a god so dumb he changes his mind willy-nilly—it's what they believe." The Major had done nothing lately but study Islam. "Read al-Buhkari's Hadith, Book of Merits, Chapter 42. Prophet-Boy's got a vivid imagination. The story goes on for seven pages."

"And the other mosque? The even uglier one? Why is it there?" Thor had come wanting to learn. Yet this was not what he'd hoped to find. He was expecting a tragedy, not a comedy.

Isaac faced the black dome. "Aqsa Mosque is its name. Actually, the Dome of the Hoofie Print isn't a mosque. It's a shrine, like the Ka'aba in Mecca. The uglier one, the one under the black dome, is called the 'furtherest' place. Some Muslim conqueror was positively certain that as Muhammad stumbled around in the darkness that imaginary night, this was the 'furtherest' he ambled from Mecca. Naturally, they built a mosque over it."

"And it gave Muslims the opportunity to defile *all* of our Temple Mount rather than just some of it." Josh rubbed his bruised chest.

"But to add insult to industry," Yacob shared, "the Muslims are building another mosque in the southeast corner, over there," he said, pointing. "Not only are they obliterating great archeological sites that scream out not to be molested, but they are in danger of collapsing the southern wall of the old city. Right through three thousand years of our history." He looked over in disgust. "It really kisses me off."

"And for this elaborate t-tale alone, for this *dream*, they c-claim the right to p-possess Jerusalem. They call *our* Temple Mount their third holiest s-site, after Medina and the black p-pagan thing in Mecca." Moshe's anger only made the stuttering worse.

"Oh, yeah," Josh said, looking wistfully westward with his back to the rising sun. "According to the Muslims who live here, this place is so darn holy that infidels—that would be us Jews and you Christians—can't even set foot on our Temple Mount." Racism was alive and well.

"Y'know, I can almost guarantee that no Jew ever sold the Mount." Yacob had a point. "The last time ownership *legally* changed hands was when King David bought it from Araunah the Jebusite for six hundred shekels of gold. It belongs to Israel. The Muslims are trespassing. We bought it, we developed it, we own it.

"But not according to them," Isaac explained. "Arab textbooks claim that *they* built this city, not us. That lie is as obvious as Allah being called God or Muhammad a prophet. This is Moriah, Admiral, the very place where Abraham was asked to sacrifice Isaac. Our whole legacy is centered here. The Temple of Solomon was built here. This place is our heart and soul."

Now Yacob was mad. "Never mind that the only reason Muhammad even knew about Abraham in the first place was that we Jews were literate and we committed his story to writing—twenty *centuries* before the unProphetable Prophet was even born." Yacob hated seeing his heritage, his people's history, butchered by an uneducated seventh-century Arab with an inferiority complex.

"Maybe he just spelled it wrong," Sarah suggested, trying to cool him down.

"What's that?"

"Prophet. We know he was illiterate. And we know his new 'religion' faltered until he became a pirate, started robbing caravans, right?"

"Yeah."

"Then he's the 'Profit' Muhammad. Spelled P-R-O-F-I-T."

"That's it. That's the whole reason for this," Thor said just loudly enough to be heard. "Greed. They covet what you've built."

"That's why we brought you here," Joshua shared. "It's as obvious as that golden shrine."

Moshe got his licks in. "When Arabs learned th-that they, too, were descendants of Abraham, things got prickly, 'cause that made 'em bastard sons of a slave g-girl. In their quest for legitimacy, they lashed out at us."

"Muhammad found a void in Arab souls and filled it with hate." As he spoke, Yacob fingered the depression in his wrist left by Halam's spike. "He took Jewish history and convoluted it, recasting our patriarchs and prophets as Muslims. Then he put himself in the starring role. It's all revisionist history. And the fact we know better makes us the enemy."

"So you're saying that the more we learn about Islam, the more ridiculous Islam looks. And that knowledge, in itself, will cause Muslims to hate us because they'll know *we* know how foolish they are." The Admiral's search for truth was becoming a pain in the butt, not unlike sitting on the cold, hard limestone wall.

A brilliant spring sun broke through the low scattered clouds. Long streaks sparkled against the white Jerusalem stone. The mixture of new and old never looked better than it did here.

"Islam isn't alone, you know." Sarah sighed deeply. "All of the world's great religions have a dark side. Evil, self-serving men eventually rise to power and enrich themselves at the expense of believers. Jewish High Priests, Muslim conquerors and clerics, the Catholic Church during the dark days of the Inquisition and Crusades—all used God's name and authority to terrorize and plunder."

"And unfortunately, it's not just a history lesson, is it Sarah?" Thor asked, wishing it were. "The world is still grappling with holy hell. The Muslims are still at it."

"Yep." Moshe bristled. "But unlike the other religions, Islam started off bad. It didn't become corrupt—it b-began that way."

Adams raised an eyebrow and looked at Isaac.

"Yes, sir, it's true. And we'll prove it."

Joshua asked, "Do you know the story behind the Ka'aba, Admiral?"

"I know that it's more revered than the Dome of the Hoofie Print."

"One plays to their ego—one-upmanship. The other betrays their soul," Newcomb said.

Yacob began, "Thanks mostly to Christianity, which arose out of Judaism, the enlightened world was principally monotheistic by the time of Muhammad's birth. That is, with the exception of the nomadic Bedouins, the Arabs who roamed the Saudi Peninsula. In the center of their world was the backwater town of Mecca. And in the center of Mecca was the Ka'aba, one of the few remaining purely pagan shrines."

"The Ka'aba was just a small r-roofless building in a bad state of d-disrepair. It housed th-three hundred and s-sixty idols, mostly stones." Moshe sat in his wheelchair, squinting into the sun, his back to the old city. His friends occupied the stone steps or wheelchairs facing him.

"They *worshiped* these rock-gods," Isaac said. "Muhammad's clan, the Quraysh, had the responsibility of caring for the rock garden. And like the High Priests who once ruled here in Judea, being in charge of the shrine had its rewards. Pilgrims were charged fees to put their god-rocks inside. They had to pay to have their holy stones fed, watered, and dusted. And then they were charged when they wanted to visit them."

"If I may," Joshua interjected. He wanted to make sure the Admiral grasped the significance of the relationship between Muhammad, Allah, the rocks, and the Ka'aba. "Muhammad's father was the Ka'aba's custodian. His name was abd-Allah. It meant 'slave to Allah.' You see, long before Muhammad was even born, Allah was a pagan god. In fact, he was the moon god. That's why he lived in what some think is a meteorite—a rock that fell out of the sky. Allah's black stone was, and is, the top rock in the Ka'aba—the most exalted of the idols."

"That's right. Their moon god was believed to have lived in his own special stone, one that has quite a story."

"Wait a minute," Thor said. "You're saying *the* God of Muhammad's great monotheistic religion is a pagan moon rock, just one among hundreds of god-rocks? You're not serious, are you?"

"'Fraid so. Between us we've read dozens of books on Islam, including the big three: Ibn Ishaq, al-Bukhari, and the Qur'an," Josh said.

"Remember in the hospital aboard the *Ronald Reagan?* You asked to come here so you could learn why they kill, why they celebrate death," Yacob explained. "We decided the least we could do is figure it out. I mean, you *did* save our lives and all."

"You're not going to believe what we found," Isaac said.

Time was in short supply, so Josh jumped ahead. "The rock in which Allah, the moon god, lived had three daughters. The pebbles were named al-Uzza, al-Lat, and Manat. Ever hear of Salman Rushdie, Admiral?"

"The British novelist?"

"Yeah. The Ayatollah Khomeini put a *fatwa* on him for writing *Satanic Verses*, a novel about these goddesses. Rushdie retold the account, the *Muslim* account, mind you, of how the Prophet felt so dejected, so tired of constantly being harassed by the pagan rock worshipers of Mecca, that he had a brain fart. One day, he tells the Meccans that it's okay to worship the pagan goddesses in addition to the moon god, Allah. He even does so himself, setting a fine example. It's all chronicled in Tabari."

"Peace and harmony follow," Isaac continued, "because his tribe, the Quraysh, no longer see Mo's religion as a threat to their golden goose, the Ka'aba."

Adams scratched his head. "There's only one problem. If there are now *four* pagan gods, how's Islam monotheistic?"

Isaac burst out laughing. "Muhammad finally admits he screwed up. He claims Satan got to him, calling his earlier pronouncements 'Satanic Verses.' Rushdie didn't make this stuff up. If the Ayatollah had studied religion rather than revolution, he might have known better."

"So what happened?"

"He had these verses expunged from his Qur'an. Abrogated, in Muslim parlance. It means revoked and replaced by a newer, more rational explanation. There are a dozen direct or sideways references—excuses, really—for the Satanic Verses buried in the Qur'an.

Yacob explained, "According to Tabari, the angel Gabriel took big Mo to the woodshed. 'But when he longed [not to be harassed] Satan cast suggestions into his longing. But Allah will annul what Satan has suggested.

Then Allah will establish his verses, Allah being knowing and wise.' Muhammad annulled his claim that Allah's daughters were goddesses with these words from Qur'an 53:18. Yacob pulled out a copy and read. 'Indeed, he saw some of the greatest signs of his Lord. Have you considered al-Lat, al-Uzza, and Manat, the pagan deities? How can there be sons for you and only daughters for Him? These are nothing but names which your fathers gave them.'"

"Great," Thor said. "He went from being a pagan to being a sexist. How can a prophet be so stupid?" He shook his head. "I dunno. Stupid's not a crime. Maybe we should cut Muhammad a little slack here."

"Why?" Sarah asked. "He wasn't a miracle worker. There were no ten plagues against Egypt, no parting of the sea, no tablets from God, no virgin birth, no healing lepers or giving sight to the blind, no raising folks from the dead, and certainly no beating death himself. According to Muhammad, he never performed a single miracle other than deciphering the Qur'an. No prophecies, no cures, no signs, no wonders."

Thor scratched his head. "Let me see if I've got this right. Muhammad tells the Arabs around him that the Jews got their history mixed up, and so did the Christians who followed them. The guys that actually lived the events, did the miracles, and proclaimed the prophecies got it all wrong, and the guy who did none of the above got it right. What kind of a fool would believe such drivel?"

"Muslims. Considering one point four billion people say they believe this malarkey, it ranks up there with the biggest hoaxes in history." Yacob had said a mouthful. "But to be fair, I wonder how many Muslims are just pretending, going through the motions. It's like living in a Communist country. If you don't play along, somebody kills you. I wonder how many Muslims actually know what we've learned?"

"Admiral, we have just begun to pull back the layers of this onion," the Major revealed. "It's one wild tale, and rest assured, the terrorists all know it. But I think we have just enough time to finish the holy moon-rock story before your first interview. Who wants to go next?"

Moshe rolled forward. "Elevating the m-moon god, calling the pagan Ka'aba a monotheistic shrine, and his screw up with the S-Satanic Verses weren't Muhammad's biggest goofs."

"No." Josh agreed. " There's more to the special black stone—Allah's moon-rock. According to Tabari's Book of Creation, 'Adam brought the Black Stone down with him from heaven. It was originally whiter than snow.'"

"From heaven?" the Admiral repeated. "Why Adam? I thought Adam and Eve were in the Garden of Eden, in Mesopotamia. They're part of the Hebrew Bible, right?"

"Right. And wrong," Isaac laughed. "According to Allah's Messenger, Adam was ninety feet tall when he was expelled from heaven. He had been created from 'dust,' 'fermented clay tingling hard,' 'spurting water,' 'contemptible water,' 'a drop of semen,' 'an embryo,' 'a single sperm,' 'a single cell,' a 'chewed up lump of flesh,' 'extract of base fluid,' or simply 'weakness,' depending on where you look. There are thirty creation accounts and twenty-two variations in the Qur'an. 'Course, this must all make sense, because Allah insisted there are no contradictions."

"Was that before or after they dusted him?"

Isaac struggled to regain control. "Seriously, folks, Adam found himself not at the headwaters of the Tigris and Euphrates but in Ceylon. Missing heaven, the tall guy stood on a mountain so he could hear the angels sing. But he frightened them, so Allah shrunk him and shooed him away."

"If shrinking him eighty feet or so made a difference, their heaven must not be very high." Adams observed with a wry smile.

"You're right, but they changed that, too."

"They changed *heaven?*"

"Yep. Their new rendition of heaven is great sex. Depending on whether you die a martyr by killing infidels or just barely make it in by saying the magic words, you get anywhere from two to seventy-two virgins. Non-stop whoopee."

"And what about the women? What do they get?" Sarah asked.

"Bad news, I'm afraid. Quoting from the Book of Belief, Chapter 17, verse 27, 'The Prophet said: I was shown the Hell Fire and the majority of its dwellers are women who are disbelievers or ungrateful.'"

"Sounds like you can get to *Hell* from Mecca." Adams quipped.

"Ungrateful for what?" Sarah asked.

"I figured you'd want to know, considering how dismally Muslim women are treated today. You're about to learn how they keep them from complaining. I quote again from the same verse: 'It was asked, "Do they disbelieve in Allah or are they ungrateful?" He replied: "They are ungrateful to their husbands for the favors and charitable deeds they have done for them."' Their Prophet said that Hell is filled with Muslim women that complain. So today they're quiet, and live in hell as a result."

"Sick."

With broken ribs, Isaac struggled to join his friend on the wall. "According to Muhammad, Allah told Adam to search for the 'Divine Throne.' Adam, so his story goes, followed God's mandate and journeyed to the Mount of Olives—the place we're standing right now. Then, like

Moses, he wandered in the Sinai. There he found mountains with 'shiny black pyramids of rock.' *Eureka,* he must have said, or some such thing. Adam then claimed that the Sinai was the 'navel of the earth, round which it had spun as it came into being.'"

"Adam knew what a navel was? And I thought he was the only guy in creation without one." Sarah found that particularly humorous.

"So why don't they covet the Sinai instead of this place?" Thor asked.

Newcomb knew. "There's nothing there to covet," he said before returning to the story. "According to the Muslim account, one stone shone so brightly it illuminated all else—a perfectly white stone. Adam, of course, circumambulated it, in keeping with Islamic tradition."

"I thought the stone was black." Adams said.

"They have an explanation for that too, but first I need to relate the alternate version. See, Muslims have a second account of how they came into possession of the great Allah moon rock. This version starts the same way, but Adam brings the stone with him from Paradise. According to Tabari, he also brought the staff of Moses. The fact that Moses wouldn't be born for thousands of years didn't seem to matter. Tabari claims that the stone was the jewel of paradise upon which Adam wiped his tears— Eve wouldn't let him play with the virgins, I suppose. Adam put the stone on a mountain near Mecca, where it lit up the sky like the moon."

"Some rock."

"But there's even m-more to this pet rock story. And m-mind you, we're not just poking fun," Moshe was deadly serious. "Every Muslim is required to make a p-pilgrimage to the Ka'aba, to honor the sacred stone. They even make a big deal about kissing it. If we w-want to know why, understand their religion, this is important." Moshe shifted in his wheelchair. "According to M-Muslim tradition, Noah, another character out of our Bible, saw Adam's body f-floating on top of the magical stone. Being a good M-Muslim, Noah sailed his ark around it seven times." Keceph circled his splinted and bandaged hand in the air. It still hurt.

Josh chuckled. "That would be circumnavigating, not circumambulating. Does he still get points for that?"

Thor ignored him. "Why did it turn black?"

Josh read the passage from Sufi ibn al-Arabi. "'The Black Stone signifies the spirit... Its turning black is from the touching of menstruating women and signifies its becoming troubled and angry.' Some today say it became like Jesus and took on the sins of the world."

The Admiral couldn't believe what he was hearing. "Who'd kill for a religion as silly as this?"

"Oh yeah, and here's the good part. After a long absence, Muhammad returned to Mecca to perform his last *Hajj*. According to ibn Abbas in the Hadith, the Prophet ordered his followers to do as he did. He first kissed the Black Stone. Then he pranced around it and the Ka'aba three times. His followers proceeded to walk the remaining four circumambulations."

"Kissed it..." Thor just shook his head. "And then *pranced?*"

"Yeah. According to Abdullah bin Umar, he always pranced. And every time he passed the stone he pointed to it and exclaimed 'Allah is the greatest.' He worshiped Allah, the pagan moon god, and his special rock. This is the foundation upon which Islam is based. It's no wonder their behavior seems so irrational. Their religion is...is...."

"Lunacy?"

"It's 'The Three Stooges do Divine Revelation,'" Sarah moaned.

"And catch this." Isaac put his hand on his comrade's leg. "Umar bin al-Khattab was Islam's second caliph. According to an account in the Hadith, even he knew better. Umar was troubled by Muhammad's touching and kissing the black stone. It looked to him like pagan idolatry. So, Umar said, 'No doubt, I know that you are a stone and can neither benefit anyone nor harm anyone. Had not I seen Allah's Apostle kissing you, I would not have kissed you myself.' Mind you, he's talking to a rock. Muhammad evidently had that effect on people."

Yacob Seraph got up and marched—hobbled, really—around Moshe's wheelchair. "You see, Admiral, every Muslim is required to make at least one pilgrimage, or *Hajj*, to Mecca and circum...whatever they call it...prance around the Ka'aba, and pay homage to the rock in which Allah, the moon god, was once thought to have lived."

"You are Allah, and upon this rock I will build my mosque," Sarah paraphrased Jesus' remark to Peter. No one got it.

Looking at Adams, Isaac said, "I know, Thor. Promoting the pagan moon god doesn't make much sense to me either."

"But I know what will. Back in Afghanistan," Yacob reminded the Admiral, "you thought Isaiah 21 was an apt depiction of our plight."

"Yeah. It seemed to depict our mission and our enemy."

"Y'know, that wasn't all the prophet had to say about guys like this or about our situation. After the 21st chapter, Isaiah picks up our tale of woe with this verse: 'terror, the pit, and the snare await you.' Now think back to those boys singing praises to Allah while they're torturing us, as I read from Isaiah 57. 'Whom are you mocking; at whom are you sneering and sticking out your tongue? You brood of rebels, you children of deceit. You burn with lust...you sacrifice your children in the ravine and under the crags. The idols among you are smooth stones."

"With intel like that, who needs the Mossad?" Thor quipped.

"Sad but true. Now listen to this from Isaiah 59. 'Your hands are stained with blood, you have spoken lies and given empty arguments. You conceive trouble and give birth to evil. Your deeds are violent, your feet rush to sin; you are swift to shed innocent blood. Your evil thoughts create ruin and destruction. No one who walks with you will know peace.... Truth is nowhere to be found for whoever shuns this evil becomes their prey.'

"And finally from Isaiah 42 and 44. 'Do not tremble and be afraid. I will foretell what is to come. There is no God beside Me. There is no other Rock. All who make such idols and speak up for them are blind, ignorant in their shame. They will all come together and take their stand...but be brought down in terror and infamy.'"

Isaac pushed himself off the rock wall. Their discussion this brilliant morning had been like throwing a stone into a still pond. They had made an impression. "Gentlemen, we have told the Admiral the real reason for the Dome of the Hoofie Print and the sordid history of Allah, his Rock, and the Ka'aba. But I don't think he believes us."

"Oh, I believe you. I just don't believe *it*."

✡　✝　☾

YASMAN ALAFAT wasn't very cheery these days. He had come so close, only to be thwarted by his own people. While the crucifixions had been great for Arab morale, their brutality had become an impediment to infidel capitulation.

Both America and the United Nations had offered to fulfill Yasman's dream of a Palestinian state, one cut out of the heart of Israel. They had been willing to throw in East Jerusalem, including the Old City and the Jewish Temple Mount. What's more, they had been within days of taking the rest of the city away from the Jews, making it an international place of prayer under the benevolent auspices of the secularists at the UN.

But now the dream was teetering. A new plan had to be devised to turn the tide, regain the upper hand. They had spewed lies and sacrificed children, but now they were desperate.

Chairman Alafat knew the answer. The very thought brought a devilish grin to his aging face. His plan was so diabolical it caused his pulse to race, caused his Parkinson's-tormented face to stop quivering, if only for a moment.

✡　✝　☾

THE GARBAGE BUSINESS was proceeding apace. Anwar and Aymen had completed work on twenty of the twenty-four machines, transforming them from collecting trash to dispensing it. They were confident Allah would be pleased. At long last, the boys had assured themselves a brothel in Muhammad's Paradise.

In many ways this project exceeded the planning that had been required to orchestrate the suicide bombings of the Twin Towers in New York City. Rather than stealing planes, they had to buy trucks and then re-equip them to perform a function opposite of that for which they had been designed. Rather than using existing jet fuel to obliterate structures, the disease they would be carrying had to be manufactured, smuggled through customs, and properly loaded into the machines. Instead of eight pilots, there would be twenty drivers. And the machines themselves were plenty hard to handle. In addition, someone had to deliver the powder to just the right place, at just the right time, in cities spread across America.

No one was more full of himself this day than Omen Quagmer. He had arranged it all. While Haqqani's crucifixion spectacle had received mixed reviews, even among the Islamic faithful, there would be no such consternation when his plan, his leadership, his *genius* was revealed.

He had selected ten cities. Starting in the east, he would "condition" Miami, Atlanta, Washington, Philadelphia, and Boston. He had decided to spare New York, not out of sympathy but because *his* mob was afraid of *their* mob. The trash biz in the Big Apple was a dirty affair.

Moving west, he would roll trucks into Dallas and Chicago. The last cities to be conditioned would be San Francisco, Los Angeles, and San Diego. He had decided to skip Seattle. He had too many friends there. While he would have liked to condition a dozen cities, he would have to settle for less. It wasn't so much a problem of buying newer trash trucks to replace those that were too worn out to accept the blowers; it was the blowers themselves. The Feds were hot on their trail.

The newly formed Department of Homeland Security had identified several of the HVAC drivers from surveillance tapes. Both buildings in Washington had installed video surveillance cameras shortly after the Twin Towers were bombed. New Yorkers had purchased their systems within weeks of the first time Muslims had tried to blow up the World Trade Center—by detonating a truck bomb in the basement. One of the Islamic terrorists responsible for the initial attack had actually warned them of what was to come. Arrested in Pakistan and flown back to New York for trial, the terrorist had been all too eager to brag. When the helicopter carrying him to the court's jail facility flew past the Twin Towers his guards removed his blindfold, and said, "You failed. They still stand."

To which he had responded, "Not for long."

After searching their files, the FBI had found that the HVAC crew-members names *weren't* Carlos and Miguel. They were Mohamar and Assad. They had also discovered that they had no prior HVAC training, big surprise, and that they had spent time in Muslim hot spots around the globe.

Like the Twin Tower Twenty, these terrorists had been coddled by the German people, courtesy of their liberal student visa program. The World Trade Center bombing scheme had been hatched in Hamburg, planned and staffed there—not in Afghanistan, as so many had been led to believe.

The Feds claimed that these terrorists, like those before them, had also passed through London's most infamous mosque—the very same mosque whose clerics had insisted, while being interviewed on the network news, that 'Islam is a peace-loving religion.' It was eloquently spoken and *so* reassuring. Of course, during the interviews, news anchors always failed to ask the Islamic clergy why the preponderance of terrorists were young Muslim men. Or why the most bloodthirsty came from their mosque and from the al-Kod mosque in Hamburg. Must have been just a coincidence.

On top of their game, the Feds had determined that some of the anthrax had been manufactured in Iraq and was of extraordinary quality—similar to that which had been mailed in previous years. It shouldn't have been a surprise. With large and outspoken Muslim factions in their midst, Europe had become an impediment to America's "supervision" of Saddam Hussein's biological weapons facilities. And now, as so many times before, America was paying the price for Europe's blindness.

And then there were the blowers. As Aymen had feared they might, the FBI had traced the equipment back through the distribution channel to a facility in Research Triangle Park. It wouldn't be long before they came knocking.

Omen wasn't ready, but he had to pull the trigger. If he hesitated, the whole affair would be a dud. The confetti would be confiscated, the trucks dismantled, and worst of all, the Americans would gloat at his expense.

✡   ☦   ☾

"WHAT ARE WE going to do, Suzzi? Our approval numbers are in the crapper. Hell, *anthrax* is more popular than we are." The President was feeling blue. Feet up on her desk, Madam President was back in the Oval Office. Ditroe was sitting across the desk in a companion chair.

"Stay the course. Pull out of Saudi Arabia and give the Palestinians what they want. We won the election by promising to do just that."

"Yeah, but that was then and this is now. Sure, our Peace-In-Our-Time Resolution has the votes in the United Nations, but what about the sheeple? They want blood."

"You know our history. Americans never stay mad for long. Remember the Bushes? They both had approval ratings in the eighties when they were pummeling the bad guys, but they fell back to earth when the shooting stopped. The sheeple, as you call them, have a short attention span."

"So how do we regain the momentum we need to ram this thing through?" She took a drag on her oversized cigar.

Secretary Ditroe tried not to breathe. "Don't you know those things'll kill ya?"

The President took another puff. Taunting her Secretary of Defense, she blew the smoke in her face.

Thinking of killing, taunting, and smokescreens, Susan came up with a plan. "I've got an idea." She stood up and began pacing the elegantly paneled oval room.

The President put her feet back down on the floor. She leaned forward and placed her cigar in an ashtray, snuffing it out.

"Let's start a war."

The President didn't even move.

"Not a *real* war, you understand. Just threaten to start a war. We order the planes, the men, the ships to the Eastern Mediterranean, to the Persian Gulf. The anthrax dusters all hailed from there, right?"

"Yeah. Right-wing religious whackos. What's your point?"

"We tell people the truth. We tell them that even if we're not at war with the whackos, they're at war with us."

"Tell the truth? Why? We've worked so hard saying just the opposite. So did our predecessor. In case you've forgotten, we've insisted that the war isn't against Islam or Arabs—they've got the oil...remember? Besides, what makes you think people will accept the truth—or even that our friends in the press will report it?"

"Right now, they'll eat it up. War causes ratings to soar. That idiot Admiral of yours and his long-legged bimbo have them all stirred up. Let's give 'em what they want. Let's start a war."

"I understand it'll make us popular, at least for a little while. But how, pray tell, does it fulfill my campaign promise to bring peace?"

"Now you're getting sentimental on me? All of a sudden you think it's important to honor some old campaign slogan? Are you feeling alright? Last time I checked, you sold your husband out for a handful of votes."

"That's not fair. By dumping his sorry carcass, I got a *lot* more votes than that. He was yesterday's news."

"Right. So let's make *today's* news. Call up the troops. Send 'em off. Give the people what they want—patriotic we're-not-going-to-take-it-any-more speeches. You can do it!"

"Without throwing up?"

"Puke your brains out afterwards, if you want. Just *do* it. You're a politician. It should come naturally."

The President was starting to see the possibilities. "Okay, Suzzi, but what did you mean by, 'threaten' to start a war?"

"Just that. Send the troops, the planes, the boats, but don't let them fire a shot. Just rattle the saber."

"And then...."

"And then when everyone says were overreacting, that America is just a big bully, that we should give peace a chance—we do. Get up there on your soapbox and tell the world that life is precious and that you can't bear to have a single American boy shed his blood over the misguided adventures of others. As our Commander-in-Chief it is your sacred duty to protect our fighting men and keep them out of harm's way. Tell them that rather than following the failures of the past, ours is a more enlightened generation, one that has learned how to resolve conflict. Say international disputes can't be settled with violence."

"The media will love it. So will every leader in Europe. In fact, there probably isn't one nation in a hundred that wouldn't praise such a solution if it meant pulling our troops back." The President eyed her Secretary.

"Threaten war, give 'em peace. The whole trick is in the delivery. Your hawk charade has to be believable. You can do it!" the head of the Defense Department encouraged her Commander-in-Chief.

✡   ✝   ☾

THOR'S FIRST INTERVIEW was held in the courtyard of the American Colony Hotel, a charming old structure with a history worth remembering. Back in the late nineteenth century, a Christian man had planned a move to the Holy Land in hopes of serving God. He sent his wife and four daughters on ahead, but in a great storm, their ship went down. Though his wife's life was spared, his daughters perished.

Rather than giving in to despair and growing bitter, this man of faith sailed over the place where his children had died. There he wrote one of

Christendom's great hymns. Arriving in Jerusalem days later, he comforted his wife, and together they formed a colony of Christians devoted to serving others. Out of great tragedy, hope had been born.

"Hope. It is all I cling to these days," the former minister in the Palestinian Authority said. He was sitting with Thor and Sarah in a sunny courtyard. A lemon tree, a date palm, an olive tree, and a Lebanese cypress surrounded them. A cascading wall of dangling geraniums added fragrance and color.

"Why are you no longer with the Authority?" Adams asked. The man was so articulate, so well groomed, so presentable, it didn't seem reasonable that he would be a *former* member of anything.

"We didn't concur. I saw things one way; they saw them another."

"With whom was your disagreement?"

"It wasn't just with Chairman Alafat. It was with all his advisors." The dashing gentleman in his black suit, black crew-neck shirt, and charcoal-gray overcoat paused. "You see, they aren't very good at governing. Actually, that's not right," he corrected himself. "They have no interest in governing."

"Are you inferring that they prefer being revolutionaries?"

"Are you willing to keep what I say anonymous?" he asked, sitting uncomfortably in a black wire-mesh chair.

"Yes, we're here to learn, not to get anybody into trouble."

"Then let me tell you my history. I was educated in London. I have a Ph.D. I've lived around the world, including the States and throughout the Persian Gulf region. I came here because I'm an Arab, and because I hoped I could help."

"And...."

"And hope is all I have left. Now there is only despair and poverty. Worse even than that, there is no plan for change."

"No plan?" Thor asked. As an interviewer, Barbara Walters he was not.

"In all the time I served, no one *ever* developed a plan to govern, a plan to build our economy, a plan to create the necessary infrastructure. They didn't even try. They knew nothing of such things. They were all 'freedom fighters'."

"That's shocking!" Thor replied. "Those are baseline requirements. At one time, not so long ago, the Palestinians were considered the most free, prosperous, and best-educated Arabs in the world. There was plenty of talent. What happened, and when?"

"Oslo is the answer to both questions."

"Oslo? The European solution to the Palestinian problem? You got what you wanted—autonomy. The Europeans pressured the Israelis to give your people control over the Gaza Strip and some large metro areas like Ramallah, Bethlehem, and Jericho in return for a promise to squelch terrorism."

"That's right. We got to form our own government—the Palestinian Authority. We established our own police force and a source of funding for these things. It should have been our greatest victory. It turned out to be our biggest defeat."

Considering the ignominious defeats the Arabs had suffered at the hands of the Jews in 1948, '67, and '73, that was saying something.

"Why?"

"We have lost a quarter million jobs here in Israel and another hundred and fifty thousand on our side. No one is working."

"Walk me through the math, doctor," Thor said. "Back in 1948 there were a few hundred thousand Arab refugees. Today there are what, maybe three million Arabs living in Israel. Is that right?"

"Yes, but nearly a million of those are Israeli citizens and have not been affected. They're doing fine. The largest concentration of non-Israeli Arabs live in the Gaza Strip. About a million."

"The average family size is enormous, isn't it? Six or seven children per household."

"That's right," the doctor replied.

"And in the Muslim world, most women are prevented from working outside of the home, correct?"

He nodded.

"So with the loss of four hundred thousand jobs, that means some ninety percent of your families have no income."

Again he nodded sadly. "Extreme poverty."

"Why is Oslo responsible for this?"

"Separation."

Thor shook his head. "I thought that was the very thing your people were fighting for—independence, *separation* from Israel." The Admiral was confused.

"My people are wrong," the doctor shrugged. "So are the politicians—and the media." He drew a long breath. "An independent Palestinian state is the worst thing that could possibly happen."

Adams' prodigious jaw fell so low, it almost dislocated.

"I'll bet this isn't what you expected to hear from someone in the PA."

"No, sir. But in truth, very little of what I have learned so far squares with what I expected."

"Admiral, let me explain why separation from Israel hurt my people.

Perhaps that will help. In the world there is one economic bus. The driver is an American. The front seats are occupied by the G-8. There are lots of passengers in the back; others are hanging on the side. Israel is on the bus. We are not. *We* jumped out the window."

"Oslo."

"Oslo and *intifada*. Not knowing how to govern, the leadership in the PA focused on the one thing they knew how to do. Call it terrorism; call it freedom fighting. I don't care. Whatever name you give it, there is nothing about it that helps build a desirable economy or a nation."

"Is there anyone working?"

"Only those paid by the Authority to do public jobs."

Public jobs? Thor thought. *Does that include killing Jews?* But instead he asked, "Where does that money come from?"

"The VAT and import duties. The Israelis pass on about sixty-five million shekels a month to the PA. They have started to withhold some recently because they claim Alafat and his ministers are skimming."

"Are they?"

"Yes, but the Israelis have known that all along. They keep their money in Israeli banks, after all. There are no Palestinian banks or currency," the gentleman explained.

All the while, Thor wondered why the Israelis would pass on the revenues they collected, knowing that much of it would be used to kill them. He also wondered why the Europeans and the United Nations encouraged such behavior by making the PA their favorite charity.

"A recent poll showed that eighty-seven percent of my people think that their leaders are corrupt. Alafat has a thirty-percent approval rating. Yet the vast majority, seventy-five percent, favor giving his party, Fatah, more power by making Palestine an independent state. Doesn't make sense, does it?"

"No, but neither does *intifada*. From what you've shared, killing Jews makes even less sense than separating from them."

"The killing has taken on a life of its own. The *intifada* was supposed to be against the Israeli army and the settlers."

Yeah, but they can shoot back so where's the fun in that? Adams mused.

"My people have lost hope. The radicals are in charge now."

"And whose fault is that?"

"Oslo was oversold. It was a bad idea, and even more poorly executed."

No one ever blames themselves, the Admiral thought. Accepting responsibility and working to build things rather than coveting the possessions of others were attributes of another, more noble time and place.

"Would you characterize your people as being young and rebellious?"

"Seventy percent are under the age of twenty-five. They are half-educated, impressionable, and out of work. They have nothing but time on their hands. Time to hate. The situation is incendiary."

"The Jews have done what they had to do to protect themselves, it seems," Adams said. "They put up fences and barricaded the roads."

Before Oslo, there were no fences. Israelis had been responsible for policing the areas now under Palestinian control. With them gone, trouble was brewing. The PA police were fanning the flames of racial hatred rather than extinguishing them.

"Without access to the Israeli economy, there are no more jobs," the PA minister replied somberly. "My people have turned to violence."

The truth was a bit more complicated. When Alafat called for the first *intifada* against the Jews, the Palestinians had simply stayed home. It wasn't because they couldn't get to work; they just chose not to go. The barricades came much later, in response to a sharp escalation in terrorist activities. Jews didn't like being killed. Even crazier, when the Israelis went in to defend themselves and stop the attacks, their defense was called an "offensive" by those responsible for reporting truth.

The sun was growing warm. The doctor removed his coat. "We needed the Israelis to invest in our territories by improving roads and delivering more water and electricity. Instead they built settlements. Seeing the roads and power lines go around my people made them resentful. And after Oslo, there was diminished access to Israeli jobs."

Adams wanted to ask why an educated man would expect the Jews to invest in his autonomous region rather than their own, especially following a decree from Alafat to slaughter them—*intifada*. He bit his lip instead.

"The only solution for my people is for us to be integrated back into the Israeli economy, to be back on the bus, if only hanging on by our fingernails."

The Admiral raised his eyebrows. "This is the antithesis of what the Palestinian leadership has been clamoring for, the opposite of what the Western world has been demanding. Under former President Bush's direction, the UN called for Palestinian statehood. That would have made a bad situation intolerable. If I'm following you correctly, the Israeli-Palestinian meetings at Camp David in 2000 were a rotten idea. If the deal had been consummated, the Palestinian people themselves would have been worse off—*far* worse off—than they are now."

"That's right."

"It seems that rather than insisting that the Israelis trade land for peace, the world should be begging them to go in the opposite direction—to dissolve the boundaries and integrate the Arabs into Israel. That's what's in the best interest of the Palestinians, isn't it?"

"The Palestinian people, yes, clearly, but not their leaders. That's why you'll never hear anyone ask for such a thing. You know, the PA publicly hangs people who advocate peaceful solutions."

"I will honor my pledge not to reveal your name." Adams comforted a nervous minister, although he was troubled. He, too, had seen the public lynching of Palestinians courageous enough to speak out against Alafat's barbarism. "Can you tell me why your people don't find new leadership?"

The handsome engineer just smiled. You could see it written all over his face: *Americans are so naïve. Arabs may be blowing themselves up for virgins in paradise, but that doesn't mean they're suicidal.* "Oslo was like a test, a transition…call it an engagement period. It did not go well. Nothing worked as it should have."

"If the engagement is rocky, it's foolish to consummate the marriage."

Sitting up straighter, the good doctor looked directly at Adams. "This is my dream: I want statehood for my people, but a state without boundaries—a free exchange of capital, people, and ideas."

Imagine that. All the world together as one, without warring armies, living in peace as brothers. Each colorless and borderless realm unselfishly working to ensure that the fruits of their labors are shared with those in need. An unpolluted planet whose swords are turned into plowshares, making butter instead of bullets, where unambitious and virtuous leaders abstain from treachery, from coveting power, and from greed. A world where leaders are altruistic servants of their people. No problemo!

"You want *what?*"

13

LEAP OF FAITH

Sarah wanted Thor to herself. It wasn't that she didn't enjoy the company of the others; she was coming to love them. They were like him in a way—rascals. They were bright, funny, and opinionated souls, filled to overflowing with an exuberance for life. In short, they were Israelis.

But Sarah wanted some time alone with her man. What she wanted to show him was personal. Catching a cab, they drove the short distance to the Garden of Gethsemane, a walled grove of ancient and gnarled olive trees on the lower slopes of the Mount of Olives. Sarah walked with Thor among the ancient trees. "Some of these, they say, may have been saplings when Jesus visited this place. If only they could share what they witnessed on that chilly spring night."

Wandering between the trees, touching them as if his spirit might still linger, Sarah smiled. "Thor, last night we talked about how Islam was based on the Bible, and how Muhammad, being illiterate, goofed everything up. Naturally, those who knew better, Christians and Jews, ridiculed him." She sighed. "That in turn caused the thin-skinned Prophet to over-react, to hate the 'People of the Book' as he calls us."

"Strong words, Sarah. I trust there's substance behind them."

"I'm confident that between the Knesset meeting tomorrow afternoon, and the one scheduled with our guys the following morning, you're going to have more irrefutable evidence than you can handle. However, facts alone aren't sufficient. The Qur'an can't be understood apart from the Bible. And the Bible can't be understood apart from Jesus. But put it all together and you'll see Muhammad for the fraud he was and you'll understand why we're being terrorized by his followers."

"We're here to connect the dots, Sarah. And in dot to dot, if you want a clear picture, you have to go by the numbers. I've read enough to know that the first dot is Abraham; the second is Moses. The third, I suspect, is Jesus. The forth is clearly Muhammad himself, and if my radar is locked on, the final dot in this matrix is Muhammad's legacy—terror."

Sarah nodded. "With that in mind, I want to share what I know about the last twenty-four hours of Jesus' life." She found a comfortable spot. "Prior to his triumphant entry into the city in front of us, Jesus told his disciples what was going to happen. He said, 'We are going up to Jerusalem, where I will be betrayed. The religious leaders will condemn me to death and will hand me over to the Romans, who will kill me.'"

"Sounds like fun."

"Yeah. But in the same breath he told them, 'Three days later I will rise from the dead.' That all led to the last supper and later that evening to this place, the Garden of Gethsemane." Sarah walked around one of the older trees, brushing her hand against it.

The soldier smiled, intrigued. He was always fascinated by how great men handled adversity. He knew that this, above all else, provided the ultimate window into their souls, revealing their true character. He was also curious: having heard so many troubling things about Muhammad, he wondered if Jesus was any different.

"At the conclusion of the last supper, Jesus announced, 'A new commandment I give to you: Love one another as I have loved you. By this all men will know that you are my disciples.' Then he said, 'I am the way, the truth, and the life. No one comes to the Father except through me.'"

"Not through Allah's Messenger?"

"Nope. Sorry," Sarah said softly. "It just isn't rational to claim, as the 'Prophet' did, that Jesus is a source of divine revelation but not the gateway to God. Not after what Jesus said. One of them is lying."

She shared, "Muhammad's claim that Jesus was a prophet, a great moral teacher just like him—but not the Son of God—isn't possible. Jesus was either God, or he was a liar—a miracle-working lunatic who only *claimed* to be God. He left us with no other choices. On this one premise alone," Sarah told Thor, "Muhammad destroyed the credibility of Islam."

"Something just dawned on me. If the Bible is inspired by a real God, then Islam is a fraud because everything's different. But if the Bible is *not* inspired, then Islam is a fraud because Allah says it *is*. Either way, they lose." Thor clenched his fist.

"Lose, lose," Sarah repeated before refocusing on the account. "Philip said, 'Lord, show us the father and that will be enough.'" She alternated voices between characters to make them come alive. "Jesus answered, 'Anyone who has seen me has seen the father. Believe me when I say I am God; or at least believe on the evidence of the miracles themselves.'"

"'I will ask the Father to give you the spirit of truth.' Remember, he said *he* was the truth. So now he's saying that *his* spirit was going to live within them. That's what makes Christianity a relationship, not a religion.

There are no real rituals. Anytime you see them in the practice of Christianity—or any religion—run. You're looking at a scheme someone has concocted to manipulate people."

"What about that communion thing?"

"All Jesus said during the last supper was, 'When you eat bread and drink wine, remember my sacrifice. Where's the ritual in that?"

Sarah smiled. "Jesus said, 'Because I live, you will live also. My Holy Spirit will teach you all things and will remind you of everything I have said to you.' That's pretty clear, isn't it?"

"I think so," he nodded.

"Well, this is clear. Jesus' life had a bigger impact on the world than anybody's, so by getting to know him better you'll understand the world better, including Islam." Sarah smiled. "And who knows? You might even figure *me* out."

They sat on a white stone bench near one of the oldest trees. From their vantage point they could see the Eastern Gate of the old city, the Temple Mount, and the Muslim Dome defiling it. Sarah returned to the story. "'My peace I leave with you; my peace I give to you. Don't be troubled, and don't be afraid.' Comforting words, aren't they?"

"Amazing words from a guy who knows he's about to be crucified."

"Jesus was thinking of that when he told his disciples, 'I am going away.' That's a nice way of saying, 'tomorrow they're going to beat me to a bloody pulp and hang me from a tree,'" Sarah paraphrased. "'But I will come back to you,' he said. 'I am telling you this now, before it happens, so when it comes to pass you will understand and believe. I will not speak with you much longer, for the ruler of this world is coming.'"

"Who?"

"He's speaking of Lucifer, Satan, the Prince of Darkness." She faced Thor. "Jesus told his disciples, 'I have shared these things to make your joy complete. Greater love has no one than this, that he lay down his life for his friends.' You know something about that don't you, soldier boy?"

"Yes. We do it for one another."

"Precisely. But then Christ gave his disciples the bad news: 'If they hate and persecute me, they will hate and persecute you also. They will treat you this way because of my name,' *Christian*, 'for they do not know God.' Now catch this. He said, 'I have told you all of this so that you won't go astray. A time is coming when anyone who kills you will think he is offering a service to God.' Sound familiar?"

Thor looked stunned. "That's *scary*. The Muslims are doing exactly what he said would happen. The Qur'an is full of surahs that order them to kill Christians on behalf of Allah."

"Yep. Jesus told his followers to expect this. Muslims think they're doing God a service by killing us. It's one of the Qur'an's most dominant themes."

A warm breeze made its way up the valley, caressing them. She read from John's Gospel. "Then Jesus prayed, saying, 'This is eternal life: that they may know you, the only true God, and Jesus the Messiah, whom you have sent.' Then he said, 'My prayer isn't that you take them out of the world but that you protect them from the evil one,' Satan. 'And my prayer is not for them alone. I pray also for those who will believe in me through their message.' He prayed for *you*, Thor Adams."

"Yes." For Adams, this was timely. He was on a mission. He had come to the unshakable conclusion that he was on the verge of discovering something important.

Sarah stood and leaned against a tree. She touched its leaves, felt its bark. "When he had finished praying, Jesus and his disciples crossed the Kidron Valley, right there, in front of us. They went into this olive grove.

"Jesus asked his disciples to sit here while he prayed. Then he took Peter, John, and James aside. These were the same three guys he had revealed himself to in his *transfigured,* or heavenly form. On that day, God the Father spoke directly to them, personally telling the disciples, 'This is my son, whom I love. Listen to him.'"

"That would've gotten my attention."

With one hand resting on his shoulder, Sarah explained, "On the last night of Jesus' earthly life he knew what was going to happen. He knew he was going to be mocked by the High Priests and imprisoned in a dungeon. And that was the *good* part. The following morning he could look forward to flagellation, a whipping that ripped the skin from his body, followed by his coronation—with a crown of needle-sharp thorns. Then, just for fun, in the afternoon he got to attend his own crucifixion."

Standing behind him, she rested her arms on his shoulders. "And he could have willed it all away. He was God. He had the power to do that. Yet in order to demonstrate how much he loved us, he ignored every insult, felt every lash, endured every nail, and bore the agony of a suffocating death."

Thor reached up and grasped her slender wrists in his huge hands. He recalled all the anguish he had endured and witnessed during his life as a soldier. It paled in comparison.

"Jesus was grieved," Sarah explained. "Ultimately, the worst thing he had to suffer in order to make us right with God was to experience the pain of separation. And that process started in this place."

She looked at him. "Jesus said to his disciples. 'Arise! I am being betrayed into the hands of sinners.'" Sarah narrated the encounter. "'Who do you want?' he asked. "'Jesus of Nazareth.' 'I am he.'

"Peter, the impetuous fisherman, pulled out his sword and cut off the ear of one of the High Priest's slaves. Personally, I think he was goin' for his head. Jesus calmly picked it up and put it back on, healing him. He even scolded Peter: "If I needed help, I would have twelve legions of angels at my disposal." But bound to duty, those who came to seize Jesus simply tied him up and brought him to the High Priest.

✡   ✝   ☾

THE STREETS WERE DESERTED as they headed down the valley, south along the eastern wall of the old city. The cab veered right, then left, up the hill past some ruins. They arrived at a twentieth century Catholic church, one covering the site of what many believe to have been the house of Caiaphas, the Jewish High Priest.

With virtually no tourists, the cab driver was more than happy to wait. Making their way down from the parking lot, Thor and Sarah looked out at the remains of the City of David. The priest responsible for the church joined them. They were the first visitors he had seen in some time.

"Why did these Arabs built their homes right on top of the ruins?"

"Oh, there's no lack of archeological sites here. It's no big deal."

Adams was taken aback by the priest's callous remark. "I think the Jews might disagree. David was their greatest King."

"There are plenty of other places, that's all."

Sarah bristled.

The priest turned and started to walk away. "Don't you want to see inside?" he asked. "If so, you'd better follow me."

The priest stopped in front of the church's bronze doors. He delivered a prolonged dissertation about who built them, ending by saying, "Do you know why Jesus is depicted on our door holding up three fingers?"

"No," Sarah said hesitantly.

Boy Scout salute? Thor thought but had the good sense not to say it.

"It's because peoples of three different faiths, Muslims, Jews, and Catholics, had a hand in building these doors. It is our hope that we can all come together as one."

Sarah looked at Thor and whispered, "In essence, he just told us it doesn't matter what you believe, so long as you believe in something."

Inside, the priest bubbled happily about the stained glass and fancy mosaics. Sarah began to pace. When she couldn't take it any longer, she interrupted the priest by complimenting him. "The depiction of Jesus on this wall standing near Caiaphas is interesting—it shows him to be a tall man. If the Shroud of Turin is his actual burial cloth, and I think it is, then Jesus was five-foot-ten or eleven, a good five or six inches taller than the average Jew of his age."

The Priest's smile was short lived. Sarah said, "But your crucifixion scene is wrong. You depict him being nailed through the palm, not the wrist. That's not possible."

Allergic to constructive criticism, the young priest abruptly turned and walked away. Mission accomplished, Sarah took Thor down to the dungeon. It was enormous, carved out of solid rock. Secured behind bars, well under ground, prisoners would have been condemned to suffer in darkness, breathing stale air. Eyelets were cut into the stone where men had been suspended by their arms and legs, then beaten with whips.

"Want to hear something awful? The reason they know this was the house of the High Priest is *because* of the dungeon. Is that sick, or what?" Sarah had been here before. "Jesus was imprisoned in solitary confinement, lowered down this narrow hole into a ten-by-ten foot cell."

To accommodate modern-day pilgrims, the Church had constructed a set of stairs down into the limestone pit. "It was always night in this hole; there were no windows or doors," Sarah said. They noticed that the lower three feet of chiseled stone was badly stained. "The floor of this hellish place was covered with rotting straw, ripe with the urine and feces of prisoners who had enjoyed Caiaphas' hospitality during previous stays." Another dark stain, the silhouette of a man's upper body and head, was unmistakable in the southwest corner.

Thor rubbed his hand along the spot, feeling the texture of the chisel marks. He slumped down, his back leaning against the rough-hewn wall. On the other side of the dungeon, six or eight feet away, Sarah's graceful body stood in harsh contrast to the roughness of the cold stone that surrounded them on all sides.

"They took Jesus here," she said. "The Pharisees joined Caiaphas. They were of a single mind. Jesus had denounced them, and his rising popularity among the Jewish populace was an immediate threat to their tremendous power and wealth. They would do anything to stop him. For the better part of a year, these religious leaders had sent out emissaries to trap Jesus, provoking him to say something incriminating that they could use against him. But they had failed."

Sarah laughed, though it seemed sacrilegious in this dreadful place. "Remember when they challenged him about paying taxes to Caesar?"

"No. I never...."

"Yeah, I know; you never went to Sunday School." Sarah turned back a few pages and found the story. "The Pharisees were keeping a close watch on Jesus, sending spies who pretended to be earnest searchers. They hoped to catch him in something he said so that they could hand him over to the Romans. 'Teacher, we know that you speak and teach truthfully,' they began. 'Is it right for us to pay taxes to Caesar?'

"Jesus saw through their duplicity. If he said no, Rome would crucify him for reasons beneath his mission. But if he said yes, he would be tacitly endorsing emperor worship. Jesus said, 'Show me a denarius.' That's a coin. 'Whose portrait and inscription are on it?'

"'Caesar's,' they replied.

"'Then give unto Caesar that which is Caesar's and to God that which is God's.'"

"*Ouch!*" Thor laughed. "Busted their chops with that one, didn't he?"

"That's what it says here: 'They were unable to trap him.' Come time for the trial, they just made stuff up."

"Lacking real evidence," Thor said, "they manufactured it. That's a story as old as time. How To Be a Hypocrite 101. I could swear I've heard this story before."

"The Chief Priest and his cronies were looking for evidence against Jesus so they could put him to death. But they couldn't find any. Two tried to testify against him, but they contradicted themselves and each other. Somebody even asked him, 'Are you going to answer these charges?' But Jesus remained silent, fulfilling one of the Messianic prophecies. Then the High Priest asked the question *du jour*. 'I charge you under oath by the living God: Tell us if you are the Messiah, the Christ, the Son of God.'

"'Yes, I am,' Jesus said."

Thor smiled. "'Okay, thank you very much. That's all I wanted to know. Please don't zap me on your way out the door. And, oh, ah, have a nice life, sir.' Please—tell me that's what Caiaphas said."

"Not hardly. He wasn't that perceptive. He said, 'He has blasphemed and deserves to die.'"

"These clowns were so lost, so full of themselves, they didn't realize that they were in the presence of God?"

"'Fraid so. But don't be too hard on them. Folks are every bit as blind today. Including a certain Navy SEAL I once knew."

Thor got the point.

"Do you know what Jesus had to say about these people, the clergy, lawyers, politicians, and especially the religious leaders?"

"I'd guess that he wasn't real pleased with them. I know I'm not."

"He hated their behavior," Sarah said. "God knew—knows—that there are few things more vile than wickedness done in his name, especially when it's preached by politically motivated religious zealots."

"We're seeing that today in the Islamic states, aren't we, Sarah?"

"Yep. Religion preached by a politicized clergy is the damnation of the world." Sarah, in a single sentence, had explained much of mankind's pain—past, present, and future. "This very thing is what's fueling Islamic terror. So I think Jesus' view on the matter might be of significance. And from what I can tell, he wasn't terribly impressed with religious leaders. As I read what he had to say, think about all the holy robe wearers you've seen along life's way."

Sarah tried to find a comfortable place to lean in the dungeon. It wasn't easy. "By way of background, the Jewish government at the time was like the Islamic states today, or Europe in the Dark Ages. The clergy ran things and enforced religious laws. Those who didn't conform were condemned in the name of God.

"The Jews' supreme court," the agent explained, "was called the Sanhedrin. And like the Muslim nations today, it was a two-party system. In Islam you have Shiites and Sunnis. The Jews had liberal politicos, who didn't really believe in God—the Sadducees. They were the secular humanists of their day. And then there were, in today's parlance, the ultra-orthodox fundamentalist whacko types—the Pharisees. The closest thing to a Pharisee now is a Black Hat. The Sunnis are Islam's fundamentalists."

Sarah slipped down onto the cold floor. "As I read this, you'll understand why God allowed his Temple to be destroyed by the Romans and why he allowed the Jews to be dispersed for two millennia. But as you hear what Jesus said this day, two days before he was crucified, I want you to think about the Catholic Church with their priests, bishops, cardinals, and pope, especially during the sixth to sixteenth centuries. And then fast forward to today's Muslim clerics. The shoe fits them all. It even fits the Communist dictators as they, through grand parades, ostentatious statues, and long-winded speeches, seek to be worshiped as well."

Thor shifted, placing less weight on his still-aching right side. Getting comfortable would be important, because when it came to self-serving religious leaders, Jesus had a lot to say.

The intelligence officer opened her little Bible to Matthew, the twenty-third chapter. "Jesus spoke to the multitudes and to his disciples, saying: 'The Pharisees have seated themselves in the chair of Moses,' just like Muhammad tried to do. 'Don't do what they do, for they don't practice what they preach. They bind heavy burdens and lay them on the shoulders of others; but they themselves are not willing to lift a finger.' Seen any imams, sheiks, or politicos doing suicide bombings lately?"

The Admiral shook his head.

She read on. Jesus was just getting warmed up. "'Everything they do is done for men to see. They enlarge the ceremonial borders and tassels on their robes. They covet the place of honor at banquets, the most important seats in the synagogues. They love to be greeted reverently in the marketplaces, and to have men call them, rabbi, rabbi,' your eminence, your eminence, imam, imam, mullah, mullah."

Thor loved her improvisation.

"'But I say that the greatest among you shall be a servant. And whoever exalts himself will be humbled, and he who humbles himself shall be exalted. But woe to you.' Woe is not a good thing, Thor, and it doesn't mean *stop*. 'Woe unto you Pharisees,' politicians, power-grubbing thugs," she paraphrased. "'You are hypocrites! For you shut the kingdom of heaven in men's faces,' with false religion and demonic doctrines. 'Your pretentious prayers and long speeches are worthless. Woe to you,' men pretending to be godly and good."

"Power-grubbing thugs?" Thor asked, grinning.

"Yeah," she smiled sheepishly. "I threw that in. No extra charge."

"Insightful. Our Muslim friends need to hear this. After all, they claim that Jesus was one of their prophets."

"He certainly had a lot to say about them. 'Woe to you blind guides!' There's a world of them today. 'You blind fools,' priests, mullahs, and lawyers, 'you're hypocrites! For you have neglected the most important matters: justice, mercy, and faith. You strain out a gnat and swallow a camel!'"

"Eeyuu."

Sarah smiled. "Yeah. Jesus knew that there's nothing like a little exaggeration to put things into perspective. 'Woe to you,' preachers of damned doctrines, false prophets, you're *scumbags!*" Some of this was admittedly coming from the revised Sarah Nottingly World Experience translation.

"Catch this, sweetie, 'For you clean the outside of the cup, but inside it is full of extortion, greed, robbery, and self-indulgence. Woe to you, for you are full of everything unclean. You appear to people as righteous men, but inside you are full of hypocrisy, lawlessness, and wickedness.'"

"Jesus is speaking to us, isn't he, Sarah? Right here in this dungeon. He's telling us to expose evil, to condemn false doctrines, no matter the consequence."

"Yes. Some will malign our motives as they did his, and others will crucify our character as they did his body—but it's our duty."

"Why is a God I don't even know asking us to deliver this message?

Why would he do that? Why can't he find someone better?"

"I think he likes rascals. John and Peter were rascals. So were Abraham, Moses, and David. Saul, who became Paul, was chief in charge of killing Christians when God chose him. Rascals only know full speed ahead—and God loves that. They're equal parts head and heart, courageous to a fault. So long as rascals know their weaknesses, God's greatness is revealed through them."

Thor put his hand to his mouth as if he was afraid of what might come out. "So God uses rascals because self-righteous religious leaders and politicians are so full of themselves, they're useless to him. They're..."

"Wicked, lawless hypocrites," she finished his sentence. "I told you Jesus didn't like them very much. 'Therefore you are witnesses against yourselves,' Christ said. 'You snakes, you brood of vipers! I send you prophets, wise men, and teachers. Some of them you kill and crucify, and some you scourge. You pursue them and persecute them. And so I will stain your souls with all the righteous blood that has and will be shed on earth, from Abel to Zechariah.'"

"Where is this guy?" Thor asked. "Jesus had these guys nailed—ah, let me rephrase that—he understood what made them tick. The world needs to hear this speech. It's as correct as it is politically incorrect."

"Yes it is. And yes, he understands them because he made them. But the good news is that Jesus is right here in this dungeon, in my heart—and knocking at yours."

She looked at him lovingly. "I think he wants *you* to speak these words—use them to confront the modern-day hypocrites, the clerics and the politicians. Someone needs to hold them accountable for the terrible things they've done. Jesus' words explain the root cause of Holy War. It's *your* mission. I've known it for some time now."

Thor sighed. He sensed it too.

"Are you ready to go?" Sarah asked as she stood.

"Sure." He reached up for her hand, hoping for a lift. But trying to pull him up, she fell into his lap, laughing. Thor turned her around, hugging her. "How does a guy like me get a girl like you to take the relationship to the next level?"

"Physically, emotionally, legally? Or just back upstairs? What did you have in mind?"

"All of the above."

"Are you proposing?"

"What, here in this dungeon?" he asked, looking around. He could just imagine Sarah telling their telling their children, "Your daddy proposed to me in prison."

"You already know the answer. It's a two for one deal. But you've got to do it for the right reasons. It's about spending your life in heaven, not about spending the night with me."

"And I thought they were one and the same." He squeezed both her arms and winked so she wouldn't slap him.

"Very funny, sailor. If it wasn't for that cute little dimple, I'd sock you."

He gave her a peck on the cheek as he helped her to her feet. They walked out of the dungeon hand in hand, into the light of a fine spring day.

✡   ☦   ☪

BACK IN THEIR CAB, they headed to the archeological dig just below the southwest corner of the Temple Mount. They could have walked there, as Jesus had done his final morning; but with so many crazies on the loose, it was safer to ride.

The driver had been listening to the radio in their absence. He glanced over his right shoulder as they climbed back into his cab. "Two Arabs were just arrested for planning a chemical attack on a kibbutz. When confronted, they said they'd received an explosive device containing chemical agents and nails from a Fatah terrorist. They even said that they were paid twenty thousand shekels, about five thousand U.S. dollars, to plant it in the middle of a Jewish crowd. Be careful, friends. It ain't safe out there."

"The Fatah is just another name for the PLO, right?" Sarah asked.

"Sad but true," the driver replied. "They also use the name al-Aqsa Martyrs' Brigades, but a thorn by any other name still pricks as deep."

By the time the story was done, they had arrived. Nottingly took the Admiral's hand and walked him down to what had once been the entrance to the Temple Mount. There were five giant gates, each of which had been sealed shut by Muslim marauders in centuries past. Yet the giant steps under their feet, those cut into the stone face of Mount Moriah, were clearly evident, as were the Herodian stones that comprised the frame around each ancient arched passage. The two thousand-year-old stones Herod had quarried from this hillside were unmistakable. They all had beveled perimeters about three inches wide. It was his signature.

What wasn't as certain was which stones belonged where, especially those piled in giant heaps along the southwestern corner of the most important site in the Judeo-Christian world. Many could have been part of the magnificent Temple itself, one of the wonders of the ancient world. It was certain, however, that they were all still here, some in piles, some still buried, and others hidden under the city itself.

From this vantage point, Thor could see the Wailing Wall. The Black Hats were bobbing at its base, clustered in groups of ten. Sarah pointed out that they didn't pray unless they had a quorum, a group they called a minion. When the Israelis recaptured Jerusalem during the Six Day War, this place, the western foundation of the Temple Mount, became accessible to the Jewish faithful for the first time in almost twenty centuries.

But the same could not be said for the Mount itself. IDF General Moshe Dayan felt badly for his defeated foe. An atheist himself, he decided to soothe the Arabs by allowing them access to the Mount—all thirty acres of it. But they returned the favor by banning all infidels, Jews and Christians alike, from the historical cornerstone of their faiths. So much for the "we-all-worship-the-same-God" and "we're tolerant" theories.

Directly above Sarah and Thor stood the al Aqsa mosque. It, too, had its history. Aligning himself with the Arabs against the Jews, Mussolini, the Italian despot who fought alongside the Nazis, had donated the mosque's marble columns. The ceiling was the gift of Egyptian dictator/King Farouk, Israel's most frequent enemy. It was here, in the doorway to the mosque, that an enraged Palestinian had assassinated Jordan's King Abdullah in front of his grandson, the future King Hussein. Had the young Hussein not been gilded with all manner of ceremonial garb and decoration, he too would have been slain in this spot. The incident explained the late King's distrust for Palestinians.

As he looked down the long southern wall of the Temple Mount, Adams could see a conspicuous bulge in the stonework. Another mosque was being built, and it was clearly playing havoc with the site. The old stones looked like they were ready to topple.

"We cannot go up on top, infidel," Nottingly told her companion, "so why don't we sit here for a moment. I'll read what happened on Friday, April 3rd, 33 A.D. But before I do, let me share the most amazing of all of the Messianic prophecies."

"You're telling me I'm going to have to revise my he-just-got-lucky number up from one chance in ten to the fifty-sixth power?"

"'Fraid so. Just a tad." They were sitting on cool limestone steps that had been carved into Mount Moriah a hundred generations before them. Facing south, they were bathed in the warmth of the afternoon sun.

"The angel Gabriel, the same angel who brought the announcement of Jesus' imminent virgin birth to Mary, gave the prophet Daniel a timeline to the Messiah. Gabe tells Dan, 'Know and understand this: From the issuing of the decree to restore and rebuild Jerusalem until the Messiah comes, there will be seven sevens plus sixty-two sevens.' A 'seven' is a seven-year period. 'The city will be rebuilt. Then there will be times of trouble. The Messiah will be cut off. The city and the sanctuary will be destroyed.' It's all recorded in Daniel 9."

This was exciting if you were into 2,500-year-old news. "Daniel's vision of the sixty-nine seven-year periods begins with a decree which was made on March 4, 444 B.C., in the twentieth year of Artaxerxes' reign. The event is recorded in Nehemiah 2:1."

She opened her Bible to the place. "'In the month of Nisan in the twentieth year of King Artaxerxes, I, Nehemiah, was sad. The King asked me why, and I told him it was because the city of my fathers, Jerusalem, was in ruins. I told him that I'd like to return to the city in Judah where my fathers are buried, so I could rebuild it.' Artaxerxes granted Nehemiah's request, announcing his decree publicly."

She set down the Bible. "To be fair, some say that the decree of Artaxerxes to rebuild Jerusalem was in 445 B.C. You see, Xerxes' death, that's Art's pop, was in 465 B.C. Adding twenty years takes you to 445. However, these folks fail to account for a rather interesting drama that took place following the death, murder actually, of Xerxes.

"An ambitious fellow named Artabanus killed Xerxes while he was sleeping. Knowing that the crown would pass to Xerxes' son, Darius, Artabanus killed *him* as well. This left Artaxerxes, a teenager at the time. He must have thought he could manipulate the boy. But this little arrangement only lasted seven months. Artabanus decided to kill Artaxerxes, too. Only it didn't work out quite like he planned. In a scuffle the knife pierced Artabanus the Bad.

"Meanwhile back in Camelot, another son of Xerxes, Hustaspis, who'd been gallivanting in some exotic spot out of town I suppose, scurried back to claim his throne. But he should have stayed on vacation, 'cause the teenager killed him too. As a result, Art wasn't able to claim the throne of Persia for himself until 464 B.C. Thus the twentieth year of this charming lad's reign, and the decree to rebuild Jerusalem, was 444 B.C."

Thor looked at Sarah with wide-eyed admiration. "Have I ever told you you're really smart?" he asked.

"No," she replied curtly. "You called me retarded, remember?"

He laughed.

"Alright, smart guy, here it is. Sixty-nine times seven years equals 483 years, or 173,880 days using the 360-day prophetic calendar. That was how long after the decree that the Messiah would come. To get the arrival date on today's Julian calendar, you'd start with March 4th, 444 B.C., the day of the decree, and add 173,880 days. That works out to 476 years and twenty-five days. So, what do you get?"

"Well, since there is no year zero, it has to be sometime in the spring of A.D. 33, right?"

That's right. March 29th is the date Daniel was told that the Messiah would come. What do you suppose happened right here on that day?"

"I have a funny feeling you're about to tell me."

She read, "'The next day a great crowd had gathered, for they had heard that Jesus was on his way to Jerusalem. They took palm fronds and went out to meet him where the road comes down from the Mount of Olives. They shouted praises to God,' it says, 'in loud voices for all the miracles they had seen.'"

"That's counter to what the anti-Semites have been preaching," Thor noted. "If the Jewish people were singing his praises, then only the establishment was threatened by him."

"To be fair, the common folks may have been more interested in the miracles, the free wine, fish, and bread. You know, dinner and a show." Sarah explained before continuing. "'Now the crowd that was with him when he called Lazarus from the tomb and raised him from the dead continued to spread the word.' Jealous, the Pharisees snarled, saying, 'Look how the whole world has gone after him.'"

Sarah's legs dangled out two steps below. "Doing what bureaucrats do best, the Sadducees and the Pharisees called a meeting. They grumbled, 'This Jesus fellow is performing so many miraculous signs, if we let him go on like this, everyone will believe in him. Then the Romans will come and take away our positions.' Anything but that."

The Admiral shook his head. "Those bozos were no brighter than the Muslims buried outside the Eastern Gate. 'I've got an idea! Let's kill the guy performing all the really cool miracles. Since we can't perform any ourselves, that'll make us even.'"

"Truth isn't always pretty." Sarah recounted what happened. "So Jesus, on the day upon which it was prophesized, rides triumphantly into the troubled city of Jerusalem. Four days later, the 14th of Nisan 33 A.D., that's Friday, April 3rd on the Julian calendar, he was crucified, cut off, in Daniel's words."

Looking over at him, she said, "This April 3rd crucifixion date is confirmed, I'm told, by a document in the British Museum in London. The Governor, Pontius Pilate, sent a letter to the Roman Emperor explaining the reason for crucifying Jesus, dating it two days after the event."

"The odds of predicting the exact day Jesus would enter Jerusalem claiming to be the Messiah, is better than…well, 2,600 years since it was made times 365 days—a million to one. But it's more than that. He predicted when his people, who were slaves at the time, would be freed.

Daniel said Jerusalem would be rebuilt, the Messiah would be 'cut off', and 'the city and temple would be destroyed'. That increases the odds considerably, say a thousand to one." He did the math. "Ten to the sixty-fifth power." He rolled his eyes skyward. "Only a fool...."

Thor rubbed his chin. "You wanted me to have a comparison, didn't you, Sarah? Based upon what you and the guys have told me about Muhammad, he was a scoundrel. If I was only exposed to him I'd probably have gone from agnostic to atheist."

"Yes, that was one of many reasons. Another pertains directly to the Daniel prophecy. A surprising number of Jews stayed in Babylon; many others migrated no farther than the Arabian Peninsula."

"Thor figured it out. "So that's how Muhammad got access to the stories he usurped from the Hebrew Bible."

"And why he grew to hate Jews. They took their scriptures seriously. Muhammad's revisionist liberties were heinous crimes to them. Crimes worthy of condemnation."

"Being insecure, the Messenger Boy couldn't handle the criticism, and we have *Jihad* today as a result. It's all tied together."

"Just connecting the dots, my dear."

"This is the most amazing story I've ever heard. So tell me, Sarah, what happened next? How black *was* Friday April 3rd, 33 A.D?"

"They led Jesus from Caiaphas' posh dungeon to the Praetorium, Pontius Pilate's hangout when he was in town. To keep the Romans happy, Herod had built the Governor a palace of sorts. It was so massive, it towered over everything else, including the Temple he'd enlarged to appease the Jews."

"Some things never change."

"Anyway, with Jesus in tow, the priests and their pals in the Pharisee party made their way to the Governor's pad, but they didn't dare set foot inside, or they'd defile themselves. You see, pious Jews thought we Gentiles were unclean and that their souls would be stained if they touched us or even set foot in one of our homes. Kinda like the Muslim belief today that we infidels are defiling their holy lands by our presence."

Thor noted the similarity.

"The Roman Governor, Pilate, went out to the entourage and said, 'What accusation do you bring against this man?' To which they answered, 'We found him undermining our nation and refusing to pay your taxes. If he were not an evildoer, we would not have delivered him to you.' Loosely translated, 'Trust me.'"

"Oh, sure." Adams knew better. So did Pontius Pilate.

"'Then you take him and judge him according to your law.'

"'We would if we could but with you in charge, we don't have the authority to put him to death.' *Poor babies,* Pilate must have thought as he began the first round of shuttle diplomacy. He marched back inside and asked Jesus, 'Are you really King of the Jews?'

"'Yes, I am. But my kingdom is not of this world. If it was, my servants would prevent all of this from happening.'

"'So you *are* a king then?'

"'You say rightly that I am a king. For this cause I have come into the world, that I should bear witness to the truth. Everyone who knows the truth hears my voice.'

"'What is truth?' Pilate asked, obviously not knowing. He rushed back out to the Jewish ruling elite and said, 'I find no basis for any charge.'

"But all the clerics could say was, 'Crucify him.' So Pilate took Jesus and scourged him. He had his soldiers use special leather whips embedded with bone and metal to rip the skin off of his back. Then, ever the clever ones, the Romans twisted a crown of thorns and put it on his head. Just for fun they covered his now-mutilated back with a purple robe and taunted him. They even punched him in the face."

Thor took a deep breath and let it out slowly. Kahn Haqqani's performance had been civil in comparison.

"Pilate said, 'Behold, I find him not guilty.' Although just for giggles I've beaten him to a pulp. He didn't say that but I've often wondered what he was thinking.

"Jesus came out wearing the crown of thorns and the purple robe. But the hypocrites' vocabulary had shrunk to match their character. They cried out, 'Crucify him!'

"Pilate said, '*You* take him and crucify him, for I find him innocent.'

"The Jewish religious elite answered, 'We don't have the authority, but we do have a law that says he ought to die, as do you, for he called himself the Son of God.'"

Sarah frowned. "That was a bit of a problem for ol' Pontius. You see, the Roman Caesars claimed that *they* were gods, and anyone else asserting similar status had to be, well, eliminated. This put Pontius Pilate in a pickle. He went back inside and asked, '*Where* did you say you were from again?' Jesus just shook his head. *Men.*

"'Why aren't you answering me?' the pompous Roman Governor asked. 'Don't you know I have the power to crucify you and the authority to release you?'

"'You would have no power or authority at all over me unless it had been given to you from above.' Meanwhile, the Jewish bigwigs pranced outside. Wrapped in their elegant robes, full of themselves, and steadfast in their desire to maintain their lofty positions, they shouted, 'If you let this man go, you are not Caesar's friend. Whoever makes himself a king opposes Caesar.'

"'I was afraid of that,'" Sarah read between the lines. "'So Pilate brought Jesus out and sat him down in the judgment seat.' Looking at his beaten body, he just gave up, ignominiously etching his name in history."

"And let me guess," Thor interrupted, "ever in character, the politicized clergy cried out, 'Crucify him! We have no king but Caesar!' In the choice of faith *versus* politics, they had just voted. Then Pontius washed his hands of the whole bloody affair. Rather than standing up to evil, Pilate turned his back and walked away. He had the right, he had the might, but like so many before him and since, he failed to act and the Romans and Jews paid a horrible price."

"It wasn't Rome's finest hour."

"Nor the Jews'. In less than forty years, Jerusalem was toast, and the Jews were banished from this land for nineteen centuries. Then, for good measure, mighty Rome was brought to her knees," Sarah shared. "God doesn't forget."

"So the moral of the story is: don't mock, imprison, hit, whip, reject, or crucify the son of God." Thor was just guessing.

"Or fail to stand up to evil when destiny calls." Sarah did some guessing of her own. "Actually the moral of this story isn't about retribution—it's about salvation. This story has a happy ending. While there are no more Romans, there *are* Jews, and God loves 'em."

With that she stood up, grabbed Thor by the hand, and pulled him toward her. Closer than they had been since their encounter in the dungeon, they just stared into each other's eyes. Time seemed to slow. Thor didn't know if he should hug her, kiss her, thank her, or propose.

He closed his eyes, then slowly opened them again, staring straight into her sapphire blues. "I love you, Sarah Nottingly." Then he looked up as if to God. "Thank you, sir."

Sarah didn't know if she should hug him, kiss him, or just fall apart right there in front of, well, there was no one around. Muhammad's legacy had managed to kill tourism along with a significant portion of the Israeli populace. So standing on the rocky steps of Mount Moriah, she simply enjoyed a warm embrace.

"Come with me. I want to take you to the Damascus Gate, and then on to Golgotha," Sarah said at last.

"I'm with you, but what's a Golgotha?"

"The place of the skull. It's where they used to kill people around here."

"Swell. Maybe I should plan our next date."

✡   ✞   ☾

IT WASN'T VERY FAR, maybe a quarter mile. The Cardo, a narrow alleyway dissecting the old city, passed back through time and cultures as they walked north. First, the Jewish Quarter, so elegant, yet deserted. Then what's known as the Christian Quarter. In these troubled times it was quiet; the shops were all closed. But as they reached the Arab quarter, the place was abuzz with activity: unemployed men kibitzing, busy women shopping, laughing children playing, cheap merchandise everywhere, strange-looking food, and exotic smells. As they progressed, Thor grasped Sarah's hand more firmly. The Americans were out of place here, and the glances they received were hostile. He felt uncomfortable.

"Just a little farther," she promised as they threaded their way between the shops, across the uneven stones, and through the anthill of humanity. Emerging from the Cardo, they turned left. There it was, looming above them: the Damascus Gate. Climbing the stone stairs as Jesus had done two thousand years ago, Sarah said, "Over this way." She steered him off to the right.

"You know this isn't safe," he observed. "We're surrounded."

"You're with me," she said calmly. "Nothing is going to happen to us. I want to show you something." She headed across the street. Thor hobbled along, struggling to keep up.

"I don't know if you're packing, but even if you are, it isn't enough. We're outgunned. Just look at these people. They'd kill us both for a cup of coffee. Actually, I think they'd kill us just for the fun of it."

"Oh, stop it." Sarah was unfazed. She was on God's errand. Up the hill about a hundred yards or so, just past the city's main bus terminal, she stopped abruptly. "What do you see?"

"Um, a crappy old bus station and an asphalt parking lot—oh, and a whole lot of angry-looking Arabs."

"No, silly. Past all that, on the cliff."

"It looks like a pair of eyes, a nose, and maybe a mouth. Why?"

"Golgotha, the Place of the Skull," Sarah smiled. "Let's go."

Why are you smiling? he thought, but said, "Are you sure about this? Look around. There are no Americans, no Jews. Only Palestinians. I've already seen my quota of crucifixions."

"You're such a baby. It's not our time to go. God's got some unfinished business." With a reluctant Thor in tow, Sarah scampered to the face of the cliff, behind the bus depot. It was three o'clock in the afternoon.

"Like I said, this is called the Place of the Skull—Golgotha—where everything changed. The sacrifice was made right here on this spot." Sarah bent down and picked up a small white stone that had fallen from the bluff. She slid it into her purse.

"One gun and one rock still aren't enough." Thor tried to stare down the angry crowd of Palestinians that had gathered at the entrance to the open-air station, less than fifty paces away.

Sarah winked, reaching into her purse again.

Adams flinched. *She's going for her gun? No, thank God!* He breathed a sigh of relief.

Sarah pulled out something she found more powerful: her Bible. Calmly, she explained, "'And he, bearing his cross, went out to the Place of The Skull, which is called in Hebrew, Golgotha. A great multitude followed him, mourning and lamenting. But Jesus turned to them and said, "Jerusalem, stop weeping for me, but weep for yourselves and for your children."'

"Here," she glanced down, "they forced him onto his now shredded back, aligned his arms on the patibulum, and drove crude spikes through his wrists." Sarah faced the white limestone bluff. Its haunting eyes returned her gaze. "The Roman executioners raised the beam with Jesus attached and pounded nails into his feet. As they crucified him, Jesus said, "Forgive them for they know not what they do."'"

"I thought it was on a hill. That's what you see in all the pictures."

"I know. Somebody wrote it in a hymn. An artist painted it that way, and one thing led to another. Now everybody thinks he was crucified on a lonely hill far away. But the Romans didn't do things that way. They crucified their victims along major roadways, like the one in front of us. This was the road to Damascus. They wanted as many people to witness their cruelty as possible. It increased the deterrent value and made the punishment that much more humiliating. There were maybe a million people in Jerusalem for Passover. This would have been the ultimate spectacle."

"Nothing's changed. Look around you. Now we're the spectacle."

Sarah ignored them. "Hard to believe Allah was foolish enough to say Jesus wasn't crucified."

"Or just as foolish, to say Abraham went to Mecca to sacrifice Ishmael rather to this place with Isaac. Like you pointed out, it was a dress rehearsal for this very moment."

All too aware they were being stalked, Sarah was eager to complete the story of the passion that had played out in front of the skull-like orifices. "'And the people passing by looked on, hurling abuses at him, shaking their heads. The rulers sneered at Jesus, saying, "He saved others; let him save himself." Even the Roman soldiers mocked him."'

"But Jesus neither engaged them in debate nor condemned them; he simply forgave them. After all, he was hanging there for all mankind, including those who were torturing him.

"'It was now about the sixth hour, and darkness fell over the land until the ninth hour, the sun being obscured.' Fulfilling prophecy and experiencing the pain of separation, Jesus said, '"My God, my God, why have you forsaken me?" Then Jesus cried out with a loud voice, "It is finished!" he said, and breathed his last breath.'"

Facing the cliff of crumbling white stone, the impression of a human skull was striking. The sun's lengthening rays cast dark shadows into the recesses that formed the eyes, nose, and mouth. With their backs turned to the old city, the Damascus Gate, and the gathering horde, Sarah read, "Now, because it was an hour before the start of Passover, dying men could not be allowed to remain on their crosses. So the Jews asked Pilate to have the legs broken of those being crucified with Jesus so that they might be taken away."

"Pretty sick." Thor projected himself into their thoughts. 'Let's kill God quick so we're not distracted. We've got a religious holiday to celebrate.'"

Sarah pondered what he'd said. "Passover—they were unable to connect the dots. The religious hypocrites were about to thank God for using the blood of a lamb to spare *their* first-born sons, while they killed *his*."

"It's clear to us but for some, dots are still just clutter."

Sarah continued to connect them. "'Roman soldiers came and broke the legs of the two thieves who were crucified with Jesus. But when they came to him and saw that he was already dead, they didn't break his legs. But one of the soldiers pierced his side with a spear, and immediately blood and water oozed out.' Then John says, 'He who has seen this has borne witness, so you also may believe.'"

"The ultimate eyewitness," Thor mumbled. He was staring at the bluff, imagining the scene on that day. It was all so real. He could hear the crowd behind him; taunting him, as they had Jesus. He could see their eyes crying out, "Die." He felt Christ's pain as few in this world could. He saw it all happening, in this very place, almost two millennia ago. For a moment, it was as if he were there. He heard the hammering, the tormenting, the forgiving. Thor shuddered as he looked upon his face. His eyes called to him.

Sarah spoke softly. "'After this, Joseph of Arimathea, being a disciple of Jesus, but secretly for fear of the Jewish establishment, gathered up the courage to walk back into town and asked Pilate if he could take the body of Jesus down from the cross and bury him.' He had to ask permission because the body of a crucified man was the property of the Roman

Government. Fortunately, Pilate was more than willing. So Joseph came back here, along with Nicodemus, another secret disciple of Jesus and also a member of the Sanhedrin.

"On their return, John says, 'They brought a mixture of myrrh and aloes'—things they would need to prepare Jesus' body for burial. With the help of the Roman soldiers they pulled the nails from his feet, raised the cross upon which his wrists were affixed, and lowered his body to the ground." Sarah looked at the very place. She fell to her knees, as the Romans must have done. "The soldiers pried the nails from his wrists and, working together with Nicodemus and Joseph, they carried his battered corpse to a rock tomb less than a hundred paces from here."

Thor looked around. "Where?"

"Up there," Sarah stood and pointed to her left. "We need to go around the corner. His tomb is on the other side."

"I didn't think he had a tomb," he said. "But if we don't get out of here, *we're* gonna need one." The scene had grown very tense.

As they made their way through the crowd of Palestinians and around the corner, Sarah told Thor the story of how Joseph of Arimathea broke the news to his wife: "I know our tomb was built for our family. But not to worry, dear. I have it on good authority, he's only going to need it for the weekend."

Thor laughed in spite of his apprehension. They were being followed. Glancing over his shoulder, he asked, "How much farther?"

"We're almost there. Come on, gimpy. You're so slow," she chided him. "It's just inside that green metal gate."

As the barrier closed behind them, the atmosphere changed immediately. They were now in an old olive garden, a working garden in its day. A cistern and olive press were clearly visible. Sarah kept walking, more slowly now, along the gravel path. She knew right where she was going.

They soon found themselves standing at the top of a series of curved stone steps. These led down to a cliff about ten meters high. An opening had been carved near the base.

One last time, she pulled out her favorite book. "'Now in the place where he was crucified there was a garden, and in the garden was a new tomb cut into the rock, in which no one had yet been laid. They took the body of Jesus and bound it in strips of linen with spices, as was the custom of the day.' Finished, they closed the tomb by rolling a stone across the doorway. They only had forty-five minutes to complete the burial, because it was a crime to work on the Sabbath, particularly *this* Sabbath, Passover. And Passover began at sunset."

Sarah encouraged Thor to walk with her, down the steps to the doorway of the rock-hewn tomb. He was reluctant. She didn't know why.

He did. The only life he had ever known was about to end. He was about to trade it in for a new one. He was certain, yet hesitant. Clearly, there was a God. And certainly Jesus was much more than merely the greatest teacher who ever lived—he was God come in the flesh. He didn't understand how that could be, but the prophecies proved it. So did his words. Thor now knew that he had died for him. And he knew that he still lived, for he could see him in her, feel his presence as she spoke his words. Yet he was uncertain as to what his new life would bring. The old one hadn't been perfect, but it hadn't been so bad, either.

Nottingly gave him a tug. "The story doesn't end here. Come on," she said, pointing at the tomb. "Please."

He walked to the opening, bowed down and followed her inside. He had never seen anything so empty. It was as empty as he felt.

The burial section of the tomb was against the far wall. It was a little over six feet long. A wedge of stone at one end formed a pillow. There was a recess for the feet at the far side. There were several places to sit, all chiseled into the white Jerusalem limestone.

As Thor knew she would do, Sarah opened her Bible. In the dim, lingering light, she said, "'Now it was the first day of the week, Sunday. Mary Magdalene went to the tomb early, while it was still dark. She saw that the stone had been rolled away. She ran to Peter and John, shouting, "They have taken away the Lord. He's not in the tomb, and we don't know where they have laid him."'

"'Peter and John went to the tomb together, running all the way. But John outran Peter,' or so it says in *John's* Gospel," she chuckled, "'and got there first. Stooping down' as we had to do, 'and looking inside, he saw the linen cloths lying there,'" Sarah pointed to her left.

"Peter, the more impulsive of the two, went right into the tomb. 'And he beheld the linen cloths lying there, and the face cloth that had been around his head, not lying with the linen, but folded in a place by itself.' Y'know something, Thor? As impressed as these guys were by the burial linen, I'll bet you dollars to bagels they didn't just leave it lying there."

"You're talking about the Shroud of Turin, aren't you? You mentioned it when we were in the Catholic Church, the one over Caiaphas' dungeon."

"Yeah. It's either real or it's a magnificent hoax. It shows the image of a crucified man, but like a photographic negative, not in the positive. The image wasn't painted or stained. There are no traces of any natural pigments. It's like the image was *radiated* onto the surface of the linen. It's even three dimensional. Moreover, contrary to every painting of the day, the bloodstains from the nails were in this man's *wrists*, not palms."

At the mention of pierced wrists, Thor involuntarily shivered.

"His arms were elongated, as were your men's, as would be any crucified man's, about five inches. Not only was there a puncture wound in his side, but the blood flow was correctly shown coming down his back and pooling under his spine, not as it often is, pictured dripping down his abs. The man whose image was mysteriously left on this burial shroud had been beaten unmercifully with a Roman flagram. The places where it ripped his skin were clearly evident. There were over seventy contusions on this crucified man's back, buttocks, and upper legs. They nearly killed him before they killed him."

"I thought they carbon dated the Shroud and determined that it was made in the eleventh or twelfth century."

"Actually, it now appears that the date was for the mold that grew on the Shroud. Linen is a natural fiber. Over time stuff grows on it. The carbon 14 dating machines can't differentiate between the linen strands and the molds or fungi growing on them. Besides, there are other problems with the twelfth-century date. For one, the Shroud has a history going back to the *second* century. And it's covered with pollen from flowers and spices indigenous only to this region, some of which no longer existed by the time it was alleged to have been forged in medieval Europe. Even the soil particles found around the crucified man's feet were from the Jerusalem area, not Europe."

"That's one clever forger if he was smart enough to place pollen from another continent and another millennium on the shroud before science even knew things like that existed."

"No kidding. And there's more to it, Thor. There's blood evidence that this man wore a crown of thorns."

"So you think the Shroud's authenticity is important?" Thor asked.

"No, I don't. But if it's the real deal, then we know what he looked like. Viewed in the negative, his face and body take form, like a picture— the world's first photograph. He was five foot ten or eleven, fit and muscular, about a hundred and sixty-five or seventy pounds."

"That's *unimportant?*"

"Interesting, but unimportant. My faith is based upon his promises, his sacrifice, resurrection, and most importantly, his still being alive and living in me." She let that soak in.

She completed her story. "As for John and Peter, Mary and Mary, and the rest of the disciples, they still didn't know he'd risen." She read, "'All of the disciples scattered, going away to their own homes.' Just as Jesus and the prophets before him had predicted. The boys were frightened, but not Mary. Women are tougher than men," she editorialized. "'She came to the tomb, looked in, and saw two angels.'"

Thor could see the carved recesses where the angels had sat.

"Just then Jesus appeared outside. She didn't recognize him, in his resurrected body. Can you imagine how different he would have looked from the ghastly, dead, bloodied pulp of a man that had been removed from that cross a few days before?"

Sarah and Thor were still sitting against the back wall of the garden tomb. The sun was beginning to set, but there was still enough light to make this place the most magnificent on earth. She painted the scene for Thor. "Jesus said, 'Mary!' at which point she must have reached out and hugged him for all she was worth.

"'Please do not cling to me, for I have not yet ascended to my father; but go to my brothers and say to them, 'I am ascending to my father and your father, and to my God and your God.'

"Mary ran to the disciples and told them that 'she had seen the risen Lord, and that he had spoken these things.' Poor boys. Imagine living in a man's world and being told by a *woman* that Jesus had risen. It was the zenith of his ministry, the act they would all spend the rest of their lives proclaiming, for which they would all suffer, even unto death. Yet Jesus humbled the guys, letting a woman be the messenger."

"He hasn't finished using women as messengers. I'm sitting in a tomb with one."

With goose bumps making their way up her body, Sarah stayed the course. "Later that evening, with the doors shut, the disciples assembled nervously, agonizing over what the Sanhedrin was preparing to do to them. It was then that Jesus came and stood among them, saying, 'Peace be with you.' Then he showed them his hands and his side."

Thor smiled. "And there was much joy in Rockville."

"Then Jesus said, 'As the Father has sent me, I send you.'"

"Not the most fun set of orders ever issued."

"No, I don't suppose. Every one of the eleven was martyred as he proclaimed the simple truth that Jesus was God, that he had died for our sins, and then had risen." She smiled. "'And when he had said this, he breathed on them, "Receive the Holy Spirit."'

"'Now Thomas was not with them when Jesus revealed himself. So John told him, "We have seen the Lord."' But you know men," Sarah said, "ever the stubborn ones. The doubting Thomas said, '"Unless I see the print of the nails and put my finger in them I will not believe.'" 'So Jesus returned, stood in their midst, and said, "Peace to you."'"

"He didn't say, '*Jihad* on those infidels? Look what my critics did to me? I want revenge! A *fatwah* upon them,' perhaps?"

"No," Sarah laughed. "Muhammad and Jesus have absolutely nothing in common." She could see a dimple forming in Thor's left cheek as he thought about how awesomely different they were. "'Jesus said to Thomas, "Reach your finger here, and look at my hands. Do not be unbelieving, but believing."'"

"I suppose standing among them after having been bludgeoned, crucified, and buried, would qualify as a miracle."

"It sure got the boy's attention."

"That's what he told you to do with me, isn't it Sarah? Show Adams the facts. Get his attention, and give him reasons to believe."

"Yes." Sarah didn't miss a beat. "'And Thomas answered, "My Lord and my God!" "Thomas, because you have seen me, you have believed. Blessed are those who have *not* seen and yet have believed.'"

"John finished by saying, 'Jesus did so many other signs in the presence of his disciples, which are not written in this book, that if they were, the world itself would not be big enough to contain them. But these things I have written that you may believe that Jesus is the Christ, the Son of God, and that believing you may have life in his name.'"

Alone with Thor in the garden tomb, she asked, "Who do *you* say he is?"

He looked down, *inside* really, closing his eyes. His face tensed. He breathed deeply. Then he relaxed. "He's God. I know that."

"Do you want to know him as I know him?"

"Yes." The tomb was aglow with the reddish hues of the setting sun.

"The Bible says, 'We are sinners, having gratified our cravings. And so it is by grace that we are saved, through faith, not as a result of our works; it's a gift from God, so no one can brag.' Do you want to receive this gift?"

"Yeah, I do."

"Then you may want to tell him."

"Talk to *God?* You can do that?"

"Sure. I know him. Would you like an introduction?"

"Well, I umm, ah, I mean....yeah!"

Sarah tried valiantly to suppress a grin. "God, this is Thor. He wants to know you."

"Umm, h-hi, God."

"That's a good start. You're doing fine. So, now that you've got his attention, what do you want to tell him?"

"Uhhh...."

"How 'bout, 'Thanks for loving me.'"

"Right."

"You might want to tell him that you've sinned a time or two. Y'know, your life hasn't measured up."

"A time or two?"

"Okay three. I've seen your file, remember?"

"Yeah, and so has he," Thor added sheepishly.

"Then since he already knows it's been at least four, you could accept his charity. He's already paid your fine."

"Good thing, 'cause that's exactly what I want to do."

"Then tell him. And while you're at it, tell him you want him to be your Commander-in-Chief. He'll probably get a kick out of that."

"Alright." Thor looked at the place Jesus' body had once laid. "God, thanks for being the first to love me. I haven't known much of that." Adams swallowed hard. "I haven't done much to deserve it. I'm sorry."

He looked out the door. "I'm sure grateful for your gift." He collected his thoughts. "And I'll do my level best to follow your orders, sir."

Thor smiled. "Now, about this first mission...."

14

BOOM

"Nothing's going right." Omen complained to Kahn. The two were still in Baghdad, reluctant guests of the Iraqi regime. "This anthrax thing is killing me."

"You sound like that engineer kid of yours, Aymen Halaweh. Stop bellyaching. I've got my own problems."

"Like what?"

"I just spent an hour with a bunch of sheiks. Praise be to Allah *that's* over."

"Be nice. Without them, well, you know...."

"Yeah, don't remind me. We'd have no people, no money, no bombs."

With Halam Ghumani behind bars, the leadership of al-Qaeda was floundering. Omen lacked charisma and Kahn lacked self restraint. And while they could have managed the far-flung international network if they had combined forces, they had succumbed to bickering instead. Other Islamic clubs were now prospering at their expense.

"Work with me, Kahn. Once we finish the city conditioners, we can deal with your atoms."

"But I'm ready. Between sweet-talking our Pakistani members and kissing up to the Iranians, I've got everything I need to make the dirty bombs work. And after I switched from rubles to dollars, even the Russians came through on tuning up the hot ones."

"One mission at a time, Kahn."

"But yours is taking *forever*. And here we sit in this pit of a country. Everybody hates everybody here. Iraq loves Pakistan like Alafat loves Jews. And Iran? Let's not go there," Haqqani snarled at his comrade.

"Not my problem. I'm out of here, off to Egypt, then Palestine," Omen said to a dejected Kahn. After letting him stew a minute, he put him out of his misery. "I've arranged for you to follow me in a few days."

That was enough to make the terrorist smile. The women were prettier in Palestine. "But first things first. After all, compared to my blowers, your atoms are a piece of cake."

"Yeah. We just sail 'em into the yacht harbors. From what you've told me, the U.S. Coast Guard only inspects a sailboat if the skipper calls 'em in advance. And even if they checked ours, the cargo's hidden. A little of this stuff goes a long way."

Although Quagmer was preoccupied with his own problems, he thought that spending a little time with Kahn might be good for the cause. "Listen, in my spare time, I've done what you wanted. I've found plenty of Muslims in the Bahamas. They've already identified the customs officials they think can be bribed. They say it's no big deal. The big, bad Americans are on the lookout for drugs, not nuclear weapons."

"Good, 'cause like I said, I'm ready."

"Look, I've made the arrangements. The guys in the insurance sector bought twelve sailboats. They're in slips in the Abacos, on Andros, Grand Bahamas, Bimini, Exuma, Eleuthera; there's even one on San Salvador."

"As in Columbus' San Salvador? The New World was discovered in the same place we're gonna sail from to blow it away?"

"I thought you'd like that. See what I do for you? I've even had our Florida contacts buy registration numbers and decals so your boats won't look out of place when they cruise in."

"You know, for a terrorist you're not a bad guy." Kahn yanked his chain. "And I'm sure you heard, I've got the sailors lined up. Twenty-four of them. Half of 'em speak English. Some even claim they can sail. I found them in Indonesia, the Philippines, and Turkey."

"My, my." What about our Palestinian brothers?"

"Sorry, no. No yacht clubs in Palestine."

"What do your sailors know? You haven't said too much, have you?"

Haqqani gave him a condescending look. He didn't like Omen very much, and he hated it when he talked down to him. "Please."

"Alright then, with your nukes ahead of schedule we can focus on distributing my anthrax." Omen was worried. "We're set to roll in three, but the boys are acting up. They say the trucks are hard to drive. Something about air brakes and ten-speed transmissions. I've got a conference call with Halaweh and Abu," he said glancing down at his Rolex. "They'll be calling any minute. Help me out. Put the fear of Allah in them. You're better at that than I am."

"You sound troubled. You don't think the Americans are gonna find the trucks before you're ready, do you?"

"I'm concerned, that's all. Nothing's going like I planned. Two cities had to be scrubbed because the supplier wouldn't ship any more blowers. Even the weather is working against me. It's expected to rain in three of the ten cities, and in three others the wind is howling. The spores won't stay airborne long enough to...."

Before Omen could finish, the phone rang. The voices on the other end sounded panicky, just as Quagmer had predicted.

"They've been to the mosque!" Abu said, in high-pitched voice. "They found our warehouse. We barely got out in time."

"Did you move everything, like I told you?"

"Yes, we leased the new space in the Shenando...."

"*Don't say it*, boy," Haqqani interrupted.

"Sorry. We're all here in...where you asked us to go."

"We used different names." Aymen, being more religious, was less frightened. "The trucks are all inside. Most left yesterday. The last of them went out before dawn. Two had to be towed in. They broke down en route. The air brakes are giving our men fits, sir."

"And the confetti?" Kahn inquired in a derogatory tone. He was miffed at Anwar Abu's lack of discipline. He shouldn't have said where he was.

"It's here too," Anwar assured him, "I rented a U-Haul truck. Drove it myself. We loaded mine with the confetti and our tools. Aymen drove another. He carried the powder."

"We had some girls from the mosque sanitize things after we left. Then we had a couple of our guys drive the rental trucks on to Kentucky. They turned them in there to throw the Feds off."

"Did you leave the rest of the office blowers?" Omen inquired.

"Yes, we...."

"But they're *on* to us," Anwar interrupted Aymen. They know we were there. I'm sure of it."

"Shut up, you worthless piece of garbage! You sound like a girl." Kahn was just doing his job.

The boys were stunned. Abu was afraid, Halaweh intimidated.

Quagmer took over. "Here's what I want you to do. Go to a local WalMart. Buy a sleeping bag, towels, and bib overalls for each of your twenty crews. I don't want them or my trucks outside the building—period. You go out to McDonalds. Buy 'em bacon cheeseburgers for all I care. Just don't let 'em out." Omen had it all figured.

"Rent some prostitutes," Kahn suggested. "Keep 'em busy. Tell 'em they can use what they learn on the virgins. Read the babes-in-paradise verses from the Qur'an. Sprinkle in some of the 'infidels will roast their weenies in hell' surahs, especially the good ones that tell us to hurry them on their way. Give 'em the Prophet, peace be unto him, pep talk. My personal favorite is: 'I have been made victorious with terror!' But there are so many good ones to choose from."

"Yes! I know them all, sir," Aymen boasted.

"But nobody calls home, nobody so much as moves outside that warehouse until I say so. Is that clear?"

"Yes," Anwar Abu said sheepishly.

"Sir," Aymen began with some trepidation, "do you want us to get gas masks for the crews?"

"Are you crazy, boy?" Kahn kind of enjoyed this 'bad-cop' role. "That'll give us away for sure."

"*No?* They're gonna die. They'll inhale enough...well, you know. It's going to *kill* 'em."

"So?"

"And you don't want us to tell them they're gonna be martyrs?" Halaweh was considerably braver than he should have been.

"Allah will sort it out in the end," Haqqani said callously. "The Prophet says Allah's always ready to harvest martyrs."

"Praise be to Allah." Aymen swallowed hard.

Omen got back to business. "Did you deal with my fax before you left, Anwar?" He had provided the boys with the paint schemes and logos of the various refuse companies in each of the ten cities. Now that much of the deliveries needed to be made during the day, when people were at work, they would have to look official.

"Yes sir. I bought the paint, the spray guns, and the masking materials yesterday before we left. But we're not gonna fool anybody putting new paint on old trucks. They may pass from a distance but the crews will need to get in and out in a hurry." Halaweh was envisioning all sorts of evils: speeding, forgetting to use turn signals, rolling through stop signs. Air quality violations.

"Sir, I'm worried," Aymen confessed. "The drivers need more practice. They're awful. These things aren't like driving Toyotas. And we need to test the mixers and blowers, especially with the spo...confetti. They aren't all going to work." Halaweh desperately wanted more time to tune and debug the beasts. He, like any engineer worth his pocket protector, realized that things went wrong when management pushed too hard. Complex equipment got cranky when forced to do new things.

"Enough already." Omen held up his hand as he spoke, silently telling Kahn to lay off the boy. He sensed they had pushed him to the breaking point. "Finish up there, son. Then it's time you came back home. We're working on another project...."

"One that's a whole lot more exciting," Haqqani interrupted.

"And we need you back here," Omen concluded, glaring at Kahn. "I booked an e-ticket. Your flight leaves tomorrow afternoon, four o'clock. It's under your school name. Use that passport."

Still in the mood, Kahn got in a few parting shots before he hung up.

✡   ✝   ☪

THEY WERE NOT altogether comfortable entering sections of the West Bank or venturing toward Israel's northeastern border with Syria and Lebanon. While Adams feared no man, there was something in the air, something that caused him to cringe inside. It may have been the game the Palestinians had made of randomly ambushing unsuspecting infidels.

But throwing caution to the wind, Adams, Nottingly, and friends decided to hit the road in their borrowed armor-plated van. Shortly after sunrise the more ambulatory crusaders crawled into their seats while Moshe and Joshua were rolled into position. They began their journey with a long decent along the slopes east of Jerusalem down toward the Dead Sea, the lowest place on planet earth.

This was to be a two-day excursion. Isaac had warned them that there would be places along their route where they would not be welcomed. They were entering the breeding ground of Muslim militants.

Adams was astounded at how quickly the vibrancy of the city faded into the bleakness of the desert. Moments after leaving the vitality that permeated the reborn Jerusalem, the cheery glow of its white stones, they were confronted by the starkness of the Judean wilderness.

Suddenly there was brown, an all encompassing brown, punctuated here and there by a patch of tan. The bold mountainous terrain looked as invincible as the spirit of the Jews themselves. But there were no Jews here, only the occasional Bedouin, living as they had for centuries.

Large flocks of sheep under the watchful eyes of young shepherds carefully traversed the steep slopes. What they found to eat was a mystery to all aboard the van.

The Bedouins lived in shanties, though they were people of some affluence. Hastily erected near springs, their homes were as tasteless as they were temporary. Yet their children seemed happy, as did their wives, often four to a man. While they were all Muslims, none were militant. They were at peace with themselves and this land.

In the distance far below, Team Bandage occasionally caught glimpses of the valley floor. The bleakness was overwhelming. A lot can change in 3,500 years. When Moses led his people here, it was called "the land of milk and honey." Now it was the land of silt and Hum-vees.

Moshe recounted the Exodus story. "M-moses had a s-stuttering p-problem, y's-see. So when G-God asked him w-what land he wanted, he had a little trouble saying it, 'C-Caa, C-Caaann....'

"'Oh,' God said. 'I understand. You want Canaan.' But w-what he was trying to say was '*C-Canada.*'"

Isaac shook his head. He had heard it before. Thor, riding shotgun, doubled over laughing.

"What *really* happened," Sarah chuckled, "was that Moses, being a guy, got lost in the wilderness. But rather than stopping to ask a woman for directions he wandered around until he ended up here, in this place."

"*This place,*" Isaac repeated. "The Promised Land. Our sweat and blood has turned deserts into gardens. Without that, no one would want, much less fight over, this pile of rocks."

It was a bleak, dry, and foreboding place. There were no trees, no shrubs, no grasslands, no softness to bring pleasure to the eye. Only brown. Here, a scorpion would starve.

Reaching the valley floor, they were 1,300 feet below sea level. Yet the Mediterranean shoreline was only forty miles distant. Turning north, they found themselves within a deep rift, one formed by tension between three great continents, Asia, Europe, and Africa. This is where the world had come together, and this is where it was being torn apart. Politics and geology made strange bedfellows.

"Isn't it magnificent?" Isaac said cheerfully. "The most beautiful place on earth." The Israelis all seemed to agree. Thor thought it must be something in the water until he recognized that the only water here was undrinkable. The Dead Sea wasn't called dead for nothing.

"Beauty must be in the eye of the beholder," Adams said, searching out the window for something to compliment.

"What's that over there?" Sarah asked. "Is it Jericho?"

"Yes, b-but we can't go there. It b-belongs to a fellow named Jube," Moshe shared. "He's the local w-warlord."

"Following the Oslo accords," Isaac explained, "towns like Jericho were turned over to the Palestinian Authority. As you've heard, it didn't work out so well. Their leadership was better at terrorizing than they were at governing. They built slums, so we built fences. They made terrorists, so we made barricades. Had no choice, really."

"We took this road around the town," Josh explained. "Then we dug a trench. There's only one way in and out, a checkpoint. See it up ahead?" A series of concrete barricades blocked the two-lane road, not to stop traffic, just impede it, slow it down to a crawl.

"Hey, didn't you guys tell me at dinner that we couldn't stop terror by walling ourselves in?"

They said nothing as they headed toward a half dozen soldiers dressed in green IDF uniforms. They were patrolling the checkpoint with M-16s strapped to their sides. Like those in the city, these men and women were well armed. Unlike those in the city, they were ready for trouble. Their ammunition clips were inserted rather than just strapped to the sides of their weapons.

As Isaac approached, he rolled down his window and spoke to one of the border guards in Hebrew. Thor thought he heard his name and Sarah's mentioned. All eyes turned in his direction. They were heroes to these folks. Not knowing what else to do, Thor snapped an appreciative salute, but his admirers simply stared. In Israel, authority is earned, even admired, but it is not acknowledged in this way.

"We don't salute," Josh said. "But I'm sure they'd like an autograph."

Adams rolled down his window. With Sarah sitting on his lap, more or less, they shook hands, exchanged greetings, and signed something for each soldier. Then they were on their way. There was no perusal of passports, no checking of identifications, only a good word and a wave.

That experience, however, would not have been true if the car belonged to a Palestinian. Their license plates were different. At the insistence of their own leadership, Palestinian plates bore the letter "P." Adams thought maybe the "P" stood for patience—something they needed.

"Why are *they* being delayed?" Thor asked, looking at the long line heading in the opposite direction.

"Just to harass them," Isaac responded abrasively. "The more difficult it is for them to travel, the less they'll do it. The less they travel, the less they'll molest us. Simple as that."

"Maybe," Sarah observed, "all you're doing is making them mad."

There was no answer. The Jews had grown to distrust Arabs. Bitter experience. The hatreds were old, deep, and unforgiving.

As the comrades sped northward, Jordan's mountainous terrain loomed large on their right side. Closer still was the famed River Jordan, now just a trickle. No one would have mistaken it for the Mississippi. In fact, calling the Jordan a *river* was an exaggeration.

Gradually at first, the validation of Israeli pride began to emerge. An elaborate system of submerged drip irrigation and moisture-retentive tenting had transformed the arid surroundings into something remarkably productive. This was a wasteland worth owning, albeit one they were being told to give away.

Everything imaginable was being grown here. If Henry Ford had been into gardening, this would have been his idea of a plant plant. Farm after neatly aligned farm was being run with mechanical precision. Men and women in equal numbers, mostly young, worked the fields with equipment that would have turned a John Deere dealer green with envy.

"The land of milk and honey," Yacob announced with considerable pride. "There was nothing growing here prior to the Six Days War. After we reclaimed this land, we made this happen."

"I've been noticing," Sarah interrupted from the back seat, "that every few kilometers or so, there are a couple of farms that don't look like these. They're messier, less organized. What's up with that?"

"What else did you notice, Miss Intelligence Analyst?" Isaac posed.

"Um, women and children. There are mostly children working in the fields. The men are all sitting around off to the side."

"Very astute. Those are Palestinian fields. They have copied our methods, our irrigation systems, but not our work ethic," he shared. "Nor our love for the land."

Then why are they so bent on killing you to possess it? Sarah wondered as she pondered the all-too-obvious contrasts.

Team Bandage drove on in silence as they made their way north through the West Bank. Thor wondered just how yesterday's decision would change him.

There was less to see now. Their view was impeded by electric fencing, razor wire, and signs warning of minefields. Whatever alliances had been formed with Jordan were uneasy ones. But none of this compared to the war zone that awaited them on the rise ahead. Looming above them along the eastern shore of the Sea of Galilee was the Golan.

The life-giving substance that makes this desert bloom originates in here—a third of Israel's water supply. Recognizing that water was more valuable than gold, the Syrians tried to divert these sources in the '60s, starving Israel. But in the '70s, they grew impatient with that plan, and....

"Back in '73," Isaac broke the silence, "on Yom Kippur, Syria caught us off guard. Knowing ninety percent of our armed forces were on leave with their families, they attacked with over 800 tanks."

"Syria, like every Arab nation surrounding Israel," Josh said, "is a dictatorship. They've never recognized our right to exist."

The Syrians had attacked the fledgling nation in 1948 and again in 1967, losing badly both times. But that didn't deter them.

"From independence through the Six Days War, Syria has made a hobby of provoking us; they kill Israelis as if they enjoy it."

And it wasn't for elbow room. Syria and Jordan are relatively small for Arab countries, yet they dwarf Israel. The nation is tiny, just 8,500 square miles, *including* the Golan. It's about the same size as Massachusetts. Syria is massive by comparison at 71,000 square miles. Even Jordan, at 35,000 square miles, is four times larger. Saudi Arabia and Iraq combined are giants, a hundred times bigger. When the Middle East was partitioned between Arabs and Jews, the Jews were cheated, getting only one five-hundreth—two tenths of one percent—of the land occupied by Muslims. Yet as history had proved, even that wasn't acceptable to the Arabs. This made trading land for peace a fool's proposition. Considering how many were still trumpeting the "Peace Process," the world apparently had no shortage of lemmings.

Moshe charged in. "Syria's dictator, excuse me, *P-President* Hafez el-Assad, ruled the Sunni m-majority because he was more r-ruthless than anybody else. He, and his s-son after him, headed one of the world's m-most evil regimes—more oppressive than you can imagine."

"And that's saying something in this part of the world." Seraph held little regard for the drug-dealing, terrorist-supporting, bloodthirsty Syrians.

Sarah had read the mountain of files the CIA had collected on these bad boys. "The President's brother, Rifat Assad, and T'llas, his Defense Minister, have made big bucks selling heroin in the States."

"We give them nearly a billion dollars in foreign aid, and they thank us by selling our kids *heroin?*" Thor turned around and looked at Sarah.

"'Fraid so. The DEA says that their rulers are directly involved in about twenty percent of the heroin trade in the U.S."

"We are *soooo* stupid. Makes me crazy."

"Well then, this'll toast your cookies," Yacob said. "Did you know that in February '82 the Syrian army, at the direction of the President himself, carried out one of the most gruesome mass murders in history?"

"At least it w-wasn't on us," Moshe said. "The g-government of Syria m-massacred its *own* citizens. They k-killed everyone in the city of Hama. Twenty thousand men, women, and children were m-murdered."

"The Muslim Brotherhood, the same group that ran afoul of Nasser, was unhappy with his regime, so he had the Army of the free, peace-loving democracy of Syria seal the doors and windows of every house—with the families inside. Then, in full compliance with Islamic Law, they filled each home with cyanide gas. Does that remind you of any other freely elected, legitimate-government leader in the Muslim world?"

"Saddam Hussein." Sarah knew more than she was at liberty to say. This was her beat. "Mr. My-Heroes-Are-Hitler-and-Stalin gassed his people too. Even King Hussein, in September 1970, slaughtered seventeen thousand innocent Palestinians in a series of attrocities. You sure know how to pick your leaders in this part of the world."

Yacob explained it by paraphrasing the Torah. "'They will be wild asses of men; their hand will be against everyone, and everyone's hand will be against them; and they will live in hostility with all their brothers.' God said this of Ishmael's descendants, the Arabs, forty centuries ago. They're just acting out their part."

"It's true," Thor observed. "They really do live in hostility, and with most everyone, even their brothers.

"Think about that for a moment, Admiral. You're a historian. Has there ever been a people that have risen up against *everyone*, or a people that have had *everyone* against them? *Ever?*"

"No. Well, not until today."

"Interesting, isn't it? While the Muslim death machine can find plenty of rogue nations willing to partner with them for a buck, they have no real friends. Their 'wild-ass' terrorism has made enemies the world over. It's Islam against the infidels. In fact, the Muslim view of the world has only two parts: the house of Islam, *dar al-Islam,* also known as the 'house of peace' or *dar us-salam,* and the house of war, *dar al-harb,* which includes every as-yet unconquered nation, in other words, non-Islamic states. The house of war will continue until it is consumed by the house of peace."

"Starting with us, right here in this van." Isaac reminded them. "Americans and Jews are at the top of the 'Infidel Hit Parade.'"

"Let m-me give you an example. In a s-speech to the Syrian Parliament, Defense Minister T'llas p-praised a Syrian soldier who, and I quote, 'annihilated t-twenty-eight Jewish soldiers, s-severing several of their heads with an ax.' He was particularly p-proud to report, 'The heroic Syrian soldier *ate* one of the Jews in the p-presence of his c-comrades.'"

"It was all reported by the *Algerida Rasmiya* newspaper," Josh said.

Adams quietly sent God a line. *Lord, if I'm supposed to love 'em, you've got to give me somethin' to work with here.*

Isaac chuckled. "I still laugh when I think of what Bush had to say. Remember his 'Provisional Palestinian State'—the one without borders? Bush wanted neighboring Arab nations to help establish their democracy and work to ensure human rights. Since every Arab state's a dictatorship devoid of human rights, how was that supposed to happen?"

"Yeah. The only f-freedom they have is the right to h-hate us."

"And free elections?" Sarah smirked. "Look at their political parties. I can almost see the campaign slogans: Fatah—I like Yas. Hamas—A Bomb in Every Bus. Aqsa Martyrs' Brigade—A Few Good Boys."

Mercifully, Isaac interrupted Sarah before she embarrassed herself further. "I hope you appreciate just how absurd America recognizing a Palestinian state inside Israel really is. Imagine Mexicans in Texas and

California terrorizing American citizens. It gets so bad, Mongolia tells the terrorists that they'll give them those states if they'll swear off killing for a month or two and promise to elect one of their gang members president. That's not unlike what Bush proposed."

"Now, that's not nice. We stole Texas and California fair and square."

"Swell. And I suppose when Jefferson bought the American West from Napoleon, he checked the title deed to see if he'd paid the Sioux for it?"

"Isaac," Nottingly said, wanting to change the subject, "you were going to tell us the story of the 800 Syrian tanks." The van rumbled up the southern slopes of the Golan.

"Oh yeah. On Yom Kippur, 1973, eight hundred state-of-the-art Syrian tanks, Russian-made, of course, crossed the border and surprised thirty-six outdated Israeli machines."

"Tough odds even if God is on your side," Adams remarked.

"Worse than that, they had air cover, Russian MIGs. We had none. All of our planes were down south in the Sinai trying to keep the Egyptians at bay. As they had in '67, the Arabs coordinated their attack."

"So they had the element of surprise, they held the high ground here on the Golan, they attacked on a Jewish holy day, you had to fight two enemies on two different fronts, they had total air superiority, they had better equipment, and they outgunned you twenty-five to one. Is that about it?"

"No, not quite. As the battle raged into night, we learned that all of their tanks were equipped with infrared night vision. We had no such thing. So after dark, we were blindfolded, fighting an enemy with twenty-twenty vision." The Mossad Major pulled the van into a small gravel parking lot. "This," he said, surveying the land before him, "is where it all took place."

"Then why are *we* here, not them?" Thor asked the obvious question.

"We won." With that Newcomb put the van in gear and drove away.

"Good God...." Thor caught himself thinking out loud.

"It got my attention, too," Yacob said. "I had read all the Bible stuff about God giving us this land and his prophecies about bringing us back. But this was more miracle than I could handle. Here we are, surrounded. Six million Jews against a billion Muslims. Roughly ten times the odds of the Syrian tank battle. And their religion specifically tells them to hate us—to kill us. Just being here is impossible."

"But the odds have made no difference," Thor observed. "Come hell or high water, nobody but nobody is going to boot the Jews out of this land." Adams was becoming an expert, but more importantly, he was now a believer. "When God makes a promise...."

"He keeps it," Yacob knew. "But we're a stubborn, hardheaded lot. It's amazing he puts up with us."

"After all the promises, after all he's done, you'd think we'd get it by now." Joshua just shook his head.

The newly ex-agnostic Admiral expounded, "The greatest mysteries to me are that so many Jews remain agnostic; that so many Arabs have been conned into believing Allah wants them to kill; and that we Christians are so tepid about it." He smiled to himself. *Good grief! I'm sounding as evangelistic as an ex-smoker!*

Once again, Isaac pulled over to the side of the road, this time just above an old Syrian bunker. A thousand feet below, the Sea of Galilee sparkled in the midday sun. "With the high ground, the Syrians used to shell us from up here." He pointed to his right. "The ruins of Capernaum are over there. Your Jesus spent more time there than anywhere else. The Mount of the Beatitudes is to the right of the old city." He was back in tour-guide mode.

"The most revolutionary speech ever given was spoken on its slopes," Sarah explained to the un-Sunday-Schooled Admiral. "Jesus found his disciples here, fishermen and tax collectors. He calmed the seas, walked on water, fed multitudes with a few fish and a couple loaves of bread. Here he healed lepers, cured a Roman Centurion's son, returned sight to the blind. Just below us, he drove Satan's demons into a herd of swine— or as Isaac calls 'em, 'short cows.' It was here, right here in front of us, that he lived the life and proclaimed the message that forever changed the world."

✡   ✟   ☾

"THE WITCH HAS DECLARED war on us. I can't believe it," Alafat told his henchmen. "After all the promises, after all the times I kissed her rear. After all the times I had to grovel at the White House, now *we're* the enemy." The Chairman was fuming. "You can't trust Americans, especially politicians."

Secretary Ditroe, on behalf of the administration, had just announced that America was suspending the peace negotiations and was preparing for war. She said, "Those responsible for the anthrax attack will soon feel the sting of American retribution." The CIA had learned that these terrorist acts had been the handiwork of militant Muslims, though the Administration had been careful not to report their findings in such precise words for fear of upsetting the fragile sensibilities of America's oily

Arab friends. Nonetheless, she had said, "The American flotilla is steaming east."

"We're going to have to take matters into our own hands," Alafat snarled. "If the American infidels won't hold the bat in the middle, we need to punish them with the fat end."

He was in his element, ranting and scheming all at the same time. He raged, "We must make the American Government pay for betraying us." Pacing like a caged badger, he nearly wore a hole in his Persian carpet.

"And how do we achieve this goal?" queried Mamdouh Salim. He was the senior PA Minister, Alafat's most loyal lieutenant. "We've called the third *intifada*. Under your leadership we have united the parties. Hezbollah, Islamic Jihad, and Hamas are working with our Fatah and Aqsa Martyrs' Brigades—at least here in Palestine. We're killing Jews faster than ever."

"What more could you want?" Talib Ali asked the boss.

"The PLO was once international," Alafat reminisced. "Remember the Muslim Brotherhood and Black September? We called the shots around the world. We struck wherever and whenever we wanted. Airplanes, cruise ships, the Olympics—we hit them all. We were al-Qaeda before there was such a thing. Bigger, even." Alafat loved to muse about the good old days. "But now we are only equipped to fight here, in this godforsaken place."

"But this is *our* land," Talib protested. "Our Muslim brothers, the Iranians, the Syrians, the Iraqis, and especially our Saudi kinsmen support our cause. They give us the munitions we need to kill Jews. Thanks to Allah, we have rifles, anti-tank rockets, surface-to-air missiles, land mines, and plastic explosives." Talib Ali, unlike most at Alafat's side, had swallowed Islam whole. He was a true believer.

"Yes, but we're no longer equipped to carry our battle elsewhere," the Chairman complained.

"Even so, sir, our people are in power. Al-Qaeda was started by a Palestinian and now, with Halam Ghumani in prison, two Palestinians head the network again. They will soon be here, here with us—in your country."

"Yes, Mamdouh, I know, but it isn't the same. I have known what to do for some time. I have just needed a reason." Alafat spoke through the quivering of Parkinson's. "I am dying the death of fools." He lowered his eyes. His massive lips followed. Looking up again, he said, "I wish to die as I have lived."

"Your legacy is assured, my leader," Mamdouh protested. "Your people love you for having fought the Jews. You have united the Arab world around our cause. Don't do whatever it is you are contemplating."

Ali didn't agree. "The Prophet says that the best places in paradise are reserved for martyrs." Having memorized the Qur'an, he quoted from his favorite surahs: "We are to 'seize them and fight them wherever they are...banish them from the land. Fight in the way of Allah...until they grow weary of fighting.' 'Allah commands us to fight the allies of Satan.' He tells us to 'prepare against them whatever arms we can muster to strike terror into the hearts of His enemies.'"

Mamdouh Salim rolled his eyes but the Chairman listened intently. He found Allah's words stirring.

"How do you wish to do this, my leader?" Talib Ali placed his hands together in prayerful fashion. He recognized the look that had swept across Alafat's face. His suicide bombers had worn the same smile as they prepared themselves for entrance into paradise.

"*No!*" Salim screamed. "This is nuts. You don't *believe* that."

"Look at me, Mamdouh. Am I not hideous? This infernal disease has stripped me of what little dignity I once had."

"No!" he lied.

"With Jewish occupation, I'm but a prisoner here. The situation is impossible. If I rein in Hamas or Hezbollah, or even my own Fatah Party, they'll kill me. If I don't, the Jews will. We have no economy. We survive on charity. This is no way to live. Look around you, Mamdouh."

"We've just received our first shipment of C-12 from the Iranians, Mr. Chairman." Talib wanted to seize the opportunity.

"How much?" Alafat asked.

"Seventy-five one-kilo bricks," Ali answered. C-12 was like C-4 plastic explosive, only on steroids. Pound for pound it was fifty times more destructive. "Would you like us to prepare a suit?"

"Yes. Then use the rest to make four additional bombs," Alafat growled. "Something that can be carried in a backpack."

"Five? That stuff's powerful. Are you planning on blowing up the whole city?" Mamdouh snorted.

"Five, sir," Ali responded. "No problem. I'll make the suit in your size." Talib Ali was the most devoted Muslim in the Chairman's cabinet. Suicide bombers were his specialty. While Alafat ruled over his Fatah terrorists, Force 17, and al Aqsa Martyrs' Brigades, he used Ali to impose his will on the real crazies, Hezbollah, Hamas, and Islamic Jihad. The job brought Talib great satisfaction.

"There will be two targets, two missions." The Chairman placed both hands on the conference table and stood up. "I am a tired old man. I will take out the first target myself," he said to an astonished Salim and supportive Ali. "With the American Government, it's personal. I will have my revenge."

"No! Ali has boys for that." Mamdouh Salim didn't understand.

"We are accused of being cowards, of sending our children."

"So?" Ali questioned.

"But Mr. Chairman, we only have one of you," Mamdouh pleaded. "There are many boys. Remember your last election? You received eighty-seven percent of the votes." The PA was a one party system, like Communist states. Alafat's "election" had been as popular as Stalin's. The party, Fatah, ran the schools, the media, the courts, the military, the police, the government, and the constitution—as well as the terrorists, the flow of money, and most every job. Imagine running against their "candidate."

"Spare me. I ran against a seventy-five-year-old woman."

"Next time then, how about a seven-year-old boy? A Jew perhaps?"

Alafat laughed. "As my critics in Ali's circle of friends like to point out, I'm an Egyptian, not a Palestinian." He didn't know that as descendants of Ishmael, all Arabs were at least three-quarters Egyptian. "Hamas is more popular than I am." Still standing at the end of the sleek black conference table, the portly leader folded his arms across his chest. "You all sound like you want to vote on this." He looked sternly at both of them. "I suppose you think this is a democracy!"

Neither Salim nor Ali dared speak out further. Poles apart, they simply stared blankly at their leader, awaiting his instructions.

"I know that the Shin Bet has been killing our engineers as fast as we can recruit them. Do we have anybody who knows anything about C-12?"

"Omen Quagmer of al-Qaeda recruited one of ours, a Palestinian. An MIT graduate," Talib explained. "I know him. He's a good boy, a smart engineer, and a devoted Muslim. His name is Aymen Halaweh."

"Aymen Halaweh," Alafat repeated. "Isn't he the boy that made the cameras work at the crucifixions?"

"Yes. Why?"

"Al-Qaeda captured some high-tech Israeli uniforms, didn't they?"

"There were nine crucifixions. I suppose they did."

"See if we can buy the Jewish ones from al-Qaeda. Call Quagmer. Offer him whatever he wants, and have him bring them with him when he comes. Ask for the boy, too."

"Yes, sir. Word is he's currently in America, working on something big. But I'm told he's about to be recalled. Haqqani's on the warpath."

The Chairman wasn't listening. His mind was elsewhere.

✡   ☦   ☾

THE DAY ENDED with a tour of Moshe's kibbutz. The children's wing had been converted into a motel of sorts, and the Israelis thought their guests might enjoy a taste of commune living.

"Nothing's the same," the director grumbled as he began the tour. "When I came here we were all so idealistic."

"What's changed?" Sarah asked as they strolled through the grounds.

"Many of us came from Russia. Like Lenin, we were Communists, secular Jews, ready to change the world."

"And now?" Thor led the witness.

"We've had to change to survive. For example, when I was younger, the children lived together, apart from their parents, in the buildings you're in. Moshe grew up there. But today, kids live with their families. Back then we were all atheists; now most attend synagogue."

"You sound saddened. Why?" Nottingly inquired.

"Kibbutz members were once eight percent of Israel. Now we are less than three percent. This isn't as popular as it used to be."

"What else has changed?"

"We don't eat together anymore. Every family has a food allowance, and they prefer to cook at home. Most everybody is married, too. We used to just live together. Today, we even earn wages, and they differ depending upon the importance of the job."

"So much for, 'From each according to their ability, and to each according to their need.'"

"'Fraid so. Didn't work. We used to have communal cars, but now everybody owns their own. Once our clothes were provided, but now we get an allowance and buy whatever we want. It just isn't the same."

"Excuse me for being blunt," Thor said, "but it sounds to me like the same things that caused Communism to fail in Russia caused it to falter here in your kibbutz."

The director just stared grimly. Old dreams died hard. He managed an affirmative nod, nothing more.

✡ ✟ ☾

"MADAM PRESIDENT, Chairman Alafat just called." The President was on the phone with her Secretary of State.

"What does that foul creature want now?"

"He wants a meeting with you, me, the Vice President, your Cabinet, and the leaders of Congress, both sides of the aisle."

"He does, does he? What makes him think we're all going to drop what we're doing to listen to him whine? *I'm so mistreated. You just don't understand my problems. The Jews are the real terrorists.'* It gets old."

"He wants to be a peacemaker. Says he's ready to deal."

"Who got to him?" the President asked.

"Maybe he got religion. Then again, it could be the armada sitting off his coast."

"You think he's allergic to aircraft carriers?"

"I don't know, but I'll tell you this; he and his staff are dialing all the right numbers. They're looking for a crowd, and they're gonna get it. Nobody wants to miss out."

"If he actually signs something, it's the photo op of the century."

✡   ✟   ☾

TEAM BANDAGE was headed back toward Jerusalem, by way of Nazareth. The night's stay at the Kibbutz hadn't been comfortable, but at least they had learned something. They had been reminded that, even without a homeland, Jews had managed to stay at the center of world events. As the nineteenth century crashed into the twentieth, atheistic and idealistic Jews, liberal, secular, and well educated, had led the world to Communism, which had in turn provided much of the impetus for World War II. In an ironic twist, Hitler had been empowered by Germany's corporate elite in an effort to thwart the growing red menace to free enterprise. As it transpired, the top positions in Germany's Communist Party were held by Jews, amplifying the Nazis' rage. And now, at the dawn of the twenty-first century, Communist Jews were admitting defeat. The kibbutzim were in full retreat, or at least their founding ideals were. Another myth had died an ugly death.

Isaac, Moshe, Yacob, Joshua, Thor, and Sarah took a long last look at the Sea of Galilee as they climbed the hills on its western shores, making their way southwest. The conversation, not surprisingly, turned to the news report they had all read in the morning's paper.

"Another ship full of bombs and rockets. Can you imagine what would have happened if we hadn't stopped it?" Isaac drove on, frowning.

"No, but I'm amazed the Mossad found it," Sarah said. "You guys are good. How'd you know it was carrying death?"

Isaac just smiled.

"Death. That's a g-good name for it. Why don't we j-just call a spade a spade?" Moshe asked.

"No one believes us, that's why," Yacob said. "The Associated Press story today looked identical to the one several years ago. They can't seem to put two and three together. Let's see, why would Yasman Alafat need that kind of weaponry if he's a peacemaker, not a terrorist? Fact is, he's signing the checks that buy the explosives his boys strap to their bodies."

"Remember the first of these ships?"

"I do." Thor had a memory for such things. "Fifty tons of weapons— about the same amount that was on this one yesterday. The ship was owned by the Palestinian Authority, and had a Fatah captain and crew."

"That's right," Joshua replied. "The captain didn't much like the idea of spending the rest of his life in prison as a terrorist so he squealed, said he was a military man, just following orders."

"The PA begrudgingly acknowledged that they owned that vessel, as they will this one, but said that it was just a cargo ship. They admitted that the captain worked for them, but they denied any knowledge of what he was carrying, right?" Sarah shook her head.

"Sure, I believe that. Just like I'd trust Alafat's signature on a peace accord. The peace wouldn't last thirty seconds," Newcomb moaned.

"But if he gets statehood, this will be the last of these boats you'll ever seize," Sarah observed.

"Makes me sick. The Iranians said they were blind, deaf, and d-dumb, too, though all of the m-munitions were made by them. In fact," Moshe added, "Hezbollah t-terrorists loaded the boat on the Iranian coast."

"I read the CIA files on the Karine A. The shipment was coordinated by Hajj Bassem. He works for one of Alafat's pals, Imad Mughniyah. He's the guy who engineered the attack on our Marines in Beirut."

"Imad? I'd be mad too if my last name were Mughniyah."

"Yeah, me too. But the moral is, there's no distinction between Palestinian terror and international terror. I've never understood why your government is willing to negotiate with Alafat."

"The rockets, missiles, mines, sniper rifles, mortars, rocket-propelled grenades, and C-4 explosives were given to Yasman to kill Jews," Joshua explained, itemizing the inventory. "But Iranians claimed the whole thing was staged by the *Mossad*, of all people, to derail the peace talks."

"That's the story. And that's the way it was reported. Screw the facts. If it wasn't for lies, your Muslim friends wouldn't have much to say." Thor sat up a little straighter. Today he was sitting in the back and Sarah was riding shotgun. "Truth is, we're fighting the same enemy."

"If I recall, that first ship carried three thousand pounds of C-4, similar to the cache on this one. Aside from a perverted religion and a gullible young man, isn't that the main ingredient in making a modern suicide bomber?" Sarah's question was rhetorical.

"That's enough explosive for several hundred boy bombs," Isaac explained. "And that wasn't the worst of it. There were sixty Iranian Katyusha rockets on that boat. They would have killed thousands of Jews."

"But the world stuck its head in the sand. Rather than recognizing that Iran was ground zero for terror, we chose to pretend that they were on our side, reforming their repressive Islamic government and fighting terrorists. Bull *pucky!* Excuse my French, Sarah."

"No apology necessary, Thor. But the correct technical term for this kind of deception is 'camel dung'."

"*Excuse* me." Thor shook his head. "Y'know what bugs me? After 9/11, America could have rid the world of terrorism, but Bush lacked the courage to take the fight beyond the easy targets. Bombing the Twin Towers was no different than bombing Pearl Harbor. Have we sunk so far in sixty years that we no longer care about defending ourselves?"

"Some might protest that the bombers came from different countries," Sarah said, "but that's not a valid excuse. Muslims call themselves the 'Nation of Islam.'"

"It's just that our war got in the way of Bush's war," Isaac shrugged, "and his war was making him popular."

"What's really sad about that, sweetie, is that the people who live in countries like Iran, Iraq, Saudi Arabia, Syria—the list goes on and on: Egypt, the Sudan, Somalia, Libya, Morocco, and God knows how many others—would have been better off if we *had* gone after the terrorists running the Nation of Islam."

"When will we learn? Dictators, whether Communists, Fascists, or Islamic, never respond to dialog or embargoes. They only respect power and the will to use it." Thor was thoroughly disgusted. "Like you said at dinner, Bush even invited terror's biggest benefactor to his ranch!"

Sarah was miffed. "We aid and abet our enemies. It doesn't seem to make any difference whether the administration is liberal or conservative. I'll give you an example. The dictators in China knocked down our planes, stole our nuclear and ballistic missile technology, murdered Christians, denied their citizens human rights, and we just smiled. Then we rewarded them with permanent most-favored-nation status because some bright-eyed idealistic fool in the State Department said we could use it to influence them. That worked great."

"About as well as giving Hitler Czechoslovakia. As I recall, appeasement made the world a *whole* lot safer." Europe's democracies were unwilling to face Nazism until the fight cost the world fifty million souls."

Thor didn't much like fighting, but he, like his hero Douglas MacArthur, knew that when you had to fight, you lost fewer men when *you* chose the time and place of the battle. "Dictatorial megalomaniacs just love the 'peace process'."

Isaac shifted the van into a lower gear as they coasted down the western slopes and into the valley. There was a lull in the conversation. The rhythmic vibrations of the drive soothed their wounded bodies. But these were gabbers, not a shy one in the bunch. By the time they were rolling up the northern outskirts of Nazareth, the dialog was back on full boil.

"Sure, this thing began as a family feud, but thanks to the legacy of Muhammad, it's grown well past that now." Joshua wanted to share what his studies had revealed. "The more you learn about the Prophet, the more similarities you'll find between him and the worst terrorists today."

Thor had more questions than answers. "How do you really *know* that, Josh? Sarah said that Ibn Ishaq was Muhammad's first biographer. But he didn't compile his bio until a hundred and twenty years after the Prophet's death. I'm told there are no surviving copies; all we have is Ibn Hisham's edits, done eighty or more years later. By that time, four or five generations had come and gone. He could have made everything up."

"In a way, you're right," Josh agreed. "But the best they've got is this bio, the Hadith, and the Qur'an. And even then, there's only one Hadith that all Muslims seem to trust, the one by al-Bukhari. It's called the True Traditions. If they're not accurate, everyone's clueless."

"But let's face it," the Major said. "Since Muhammad has been sandals up for fourteen centuries, all we really care about is what the terrorists read and believe today. And when you read this stuff the message is crystal clear. Muhammad and Allah speak the same language: death."

"And y-yet, Muslims tell us infidels that their religion is p-peaceful. They know we're too lazy to read and think for ourselves. It's a r-recipe for disaster."

"Islam," Isaac moaned. "It was born ugly and grew up hideous. What you're going to learn, my friend, is that Islam will never be popular among rational men."

"Swell."

"Let's begin by examining Arabia at the time of the Prophet's birth." Josh was itching to get down to business. "A few years before the Messenger began to see and hear things, they knew it was high time to stop worshiping the pagan stones in the Ka'aba. The rest of the world had long since gone monotheistic, thanks to the Jews and Christians."

"That's r-right. They said that the Allah s-stone 'was of no account.' They c-claimed it 'could not hear, see, hurt, or help.' The Bedouins told their p-people, 'Find yourselves a religion, for by God, you have none.'"

"So even before the Messenger gets started, the Arabs figure it out. Their moon rock is no better than moonshine. A source of money and false hope—nothing more."

"According to w-what I've read, Admiral, we Jews told the Arabs that they were d-descendants of Abraham."

"Muhammad sure took *that* rock and ran with it," Sarah agreed. "As you know, he changed most everything Abraham did to fit Arab sensibilities. With a flourish for revisionist history, Mo claimed that Abe was 'neither a Jew, nor yet a Christian,' and that he offered to sacrifice *Ishmael,* not Isaac. He even told his followers that the almost-offering took place at the Ka'aba in Mecca, instead of on Mount Moriah in Israel."

"Actually," the Major said, "the revisionist history is a great deal more sinister than it appears at first blush. Muhammad didn't bastardize our history by accident. He didn't do it because he was illiterate and didn't know any better. He was purposely trying to cover something up." This was getting interesting. "What do you suppose it was?"

There were no takers. "Okay, let me tell you a story from the annals of Islam. Abdul Muttalib, a wealthy pagan worshiper born two generations before Muhammad, was the custodian of the Ka'aba. One day he vowed to the rock gods that if given ten sons, he would sacrifice one to the stones. Bad move, 'cause eventually he *had* ten. Foolishly faithful to the rocks, he rolled the dice to determine which son would die. His youngest, Abd-Allah, lost. By the way, who remembers what the name Abd-Allah means?"

"Slave to Allah," Sarah answered.

"Clever girl. But now, ask yourself why would someone name a kid 'slave to Allah' a generation before Muhammad claimed Allah was the supreme creator-god of the universe?"

Sarah again: "Because all Muhammad did was *promote* the Moon God. Allah had been the top pagan deity for centuries. He not only lived in the biggest rock, but as top dude, he was said to have been the father of the rock goddesses al-Lat, Manat, and al-Uzza, that's why. But all of that is embarrassing to Muslims because it means their religion is regurgitated paganism."

The Major was impressed. "How do you keep up, Admiral?"

"Hey, I thought you were telling us a story," Thor grumbled.

"Yes, well," Isaac said, clearing his throat and winking at Sarah, "Papa Muttalib started having second thoughts. So he goes off and consults with a sorceress, hoping to get the 'right' advice."

"*Sorceress*, as in devil worshiper?" Sarah asked.

"Bimbo," Isaac grinned. "And she turns out to be worth her weight in camel dung."

"That much?"

"Yeah. She tells the proud papa to offer the pagan gods camels instead of his son, Abd-Allah. She says that he should keep increasing the number until the gods say *enough already*."

"Is this story going somewhere?"

"We're not getting testy, are we, Admiral? Just because I said your girlfriend was smarter than you were."

"I already knew that. But I need to take a leak. Pull in there, would ya?"

"Yes, sir," the Major answered, steering the van into a service station. In about as much time as it took to top off the van's tank, Adams emptied his. "Thanks," he said, climbing back in. "Now, where were we?"

"Camels," Isaac smiled. "This whole charade was played out at the Ka'aba itself. Abdul Muttalib followed the sorcerer's advice and started offering camels in groups of ten. But by the time he'd sacrificed several sets, not a single rock had so much as stirred. Not even a wiggle."

"Do tell."

"Then a diviner, another occult fellow, says, 'The gods want a hundred camels to release you from your vow.' So Abdul Muttalib acquiesces, and the stones, diviners, and sorcerers come to an understanding. Abd-Allah's life is spared. Still with me, Admiral?"

"Yeah, what you're saying, if I read you, is that our pal Muhammad isn't comfortable with the truth, with the real almost-sacrifice story that took place at the Ka'aba, because it's a pagan ritual, probably Satanic, or at least stupid, right? So he decides to convolute the story in the Hebrew Bible instead, to vindicate the Ka'aba."

"Oh, I'm afraid that the truth is much more sinister than that, my friend. You see, Abd-Allah, the boy who was nearly sacrificed—*he* was Muhammad's father."

"Oh...my...God."

"Oh, yes. Muhammad knew the truth. He knew exactly what happened at the Ka'aba—pagan sacrifices, rock worship, sorcery—yet he chose to continue worshiping there, bastardizing Jewish history to justify the practice. There was no misunderstanding. The deception was purposeful—and that's really bad when you're trying to start a religion."

"So he knew all along that Allah wasn't a real god." Sarah was suddenly short of breath. "He...he had to know that Allah was just a...a *rock*. His own father was named 'slave-to-the-rock.'"

"But it was an easier sell, a slipperier con, because Arabs already loved the moon rock."

"Oh, no. Please, no." Thor was in misery. "Good God, please don't let

Islam be like this." He didn't know if he was talking to himself, God, or his friends. *I can't tell this story to the American people. They'll think I'm looney.* "If I tell 'em this, they'll say I'm a hateful narrow-minded bigot with an over-active imagination. There has to be another explanation."

"No, sorry. Actually, it gets even uglier. You don't know the half of it yet." Josh pulled out a copy of the Qur'an from his daypack. He opened it to surah 21:57. "Allah is speaking for Abraham. 'I swear by Allah I will do something to your idols when you have turned your backs and gone. He smashed them to pieces, *with the exception of the biggest one*, so they might turn to it.'

"Situational scriptures, sir. First, in the context of history, Abe could never have done such a thing, and Muhammad *did* this very thing. When Mo stormed Mecca at sword point at the end of his life, he tossed every rock except Allah's from the Ka'aba. That one he kissed. Then to make his silliness look Prophet-like, and to make the Allah-rock look god-like, he invents a similar story for Abraham."

No one could speak for the longest time. They all wanted answers, but not *these* answers. The words of Muhammad's biographers—his own words—even Allah's words in the Qur'an, had condemned him. They revealed that from the very outset, Islam had been a hoax. Muhammad had just cut and pasted his religion together, combining his own pagan past with a purposely altered version of Jewish traditions.

Yacob gazed out the window. "Before Muhammad started his 'I-want-to-be-important scheme,' he married money—a twice-married woman about twice his age."

Thor chuckled. "There you go. My dad used to tell me a boy could marry more money in five minutes than he could make in a lifetime."

While the others laughed, Sarah simply turned and stared. She wasn't pleased. Her folks were rich, but Thor didn't know it. Or did he?

Sensing that his remark had somehow landed him in Sarah's doghouse, Thor backpedaled. "Wasn't somebody talking about Muhammad?"

"Yes, like I was saying, Muhammad was forty years old, which means his wife was in her sixties, when he received his first vision. Guess where it happens?" Isaac asked his friends.

"In a cave," they answered in unison.

"Right."

Team Bandage was downtown Nazareth. The city reminded Sarah of San Francisco, only without the bay. Every house seemed to be clinging tenuously to one hillside or another. Even its pastel tones and sense of energy were similar. So was the eclectic mix of people.

The one thing that really struck Sarah, though, was how much this place had changed over two millennia. It had once been a hick town, a social backwater, the home of zealots and nobodies. It was said that nothing good ever came out of Nazareth.

The heroes-turned-tourists, quickly paraded into a church that had been built over the town's well. As the only well, it had to be the place where the angel Gabriel told Mary that she, an unwed virgin, would bear God's son. But the well was now encrusted with tasteless religious décor. Sarah sighed. What she wouldn't have given for the site to be unmolested, a simple well still open to the sky.

As they stepped outside, criers were calling the Muslim faithful to prayer. The sound was mournful, depressingly off-key. And as the various mosques vied for attention, the cacophony seemed out of place, out of character, with the town where Jesus had been raised.

Fortunately, the irritating melody was short lived. Within minutes Team Bandage was out of town, headed down into a valley, one encompassing a broad plain and stretching as far as the eye could see. It was anchored by Megiddo, a four thousand-year-old battle-ravaged town. According to the Hebrew Prophets, this place was ground zero for the final war to be fought on planet earth: Armageddon.

It had been prophesied that as a prelude to the final battle, the descendants of Gog and Magog, from a land far to the north of Israel—Russia, according to the ethnologists—would launch an attack on the tiny nation. And it, like those of the Arabs, would fail no matter how badly the Jews were outgunned.

"Look." Sarah observed, "It's the perfect battleground for men, tanks, and aircraft. There's plenty of maneuvering room."

The revelation of John was well beyond them, and Sarah knew it. The Bible predicted that seven years after a peace treaty was signed with Israel guaranteeing her sovereignty, an army of 200,000,000 men would march into this valley from the east, from the land where Muslims now live. God would even dry up the Euphrates, making it easy for them. Sarah quietly pondered the horror of it all. The battle would be so horrific, only Jesus' return would save the world from total destruction—an unfathomable concept when the prophecy was written.

The prophetic descriptions sounded to her like a combination of nuclear and biological war. Sarah knew that both Muslims and Jews had these weapons. Pakistan had developed theirs several years before, and it looked to all the world, certainly to the CIA, like Iran was on the cusp. What's more, the Muslim nations could rally a couple of hundred million men with ease. What had once seemed impossible now looked downright likely.

Sarah quietly pondered Thor's mission. Was his, like that of Jonah before him, to delay the inevitable judgment?

By late afternoon they had made their way back to Jerusalem. Their next meeting was scheduled to begin promptly at five o'clock, downtown in the Knesset. There would be no time to freshen up.

Boom!

A thunderous explosion ripped between the buildings in front of them. The shockwave and shrapnel shattered the surrounding storefronts. Cascading shards of window glass began to rain down, adding to the terror. People screamed. Cars rammed into each other. As the debris and smoke began to clear, they all saw what had happened.

A bomb had detonated on the sidewalk, not thirty feet from them. The area was littered with broken bodies. There was blood everywhere. Sarah opened her door and rushed out; Thor ripped open the sliding side door of the armored van and ran after her. The only other ambulatory members of Team Uniform stayed put. It wasn't that they were cowards. But they knew better. At the top of their lungs, they screamed out, pleading with the Americans to stop.

Sarah's head told her that what she was doing was foolish. Suicide bombers often operated in pairs. And there were usually trigger men milling in the crowd just in case one of the boys came to his senses, got religion, grew a heart, changed his mind. There had been one blast. There might be another.

Yet her heart, like Thor's, could not resist helping. Innocents lay shattered, splintered, and bleeding, right in front of them. They knew from the way their van had collided with others following the explosion that rescue workers would be delayed. And a delay could cost a life.

Thor caught up with Sarah as she made it past the bloodied spectators, those who had been far enough away to escape death. Then it happened. The second boy bomb blew up among a group who were desperately trying to flee. The blast knocked Nottingly off her feet. Adams, still holding her hand, looked down in horror. Blood covered the front of her dress.

"*Sarah!*" he screamed.

She didn't answer. Sarah looked shocked, hollow, as if the life had been blown out of her. "*Sarah, no!*" he screamed again as if he could will her back to life. *This can't be happening.*

Thor fell to his knees at her side. She made a horrid gurgling sound, struggling to breathe, gasping for air. He didn't know whether to pick her up or leave her lying on the sidewalk. She was covered with blood. Thor's anguish was more than he could bear. His soul felt pain greater than anything he had ever known.

Slowly, agonizingly, signs of life started to return. Air entered her lungs in short, gasping breaths. She began to move and moan. Just looking at her nearly killed him.

Sarah tried to tell him that she was going to live, but she couldn't form the words. She tried to push herself up, but didn't have the strength. Thor was frozen, useless, unable to move. Sarah closed her eyes.

"*Noooo!*" He reached down and hugged her for all he was worth. If she *had* been near death, his squeeze would have killed her.

"Thor," she whimpered, letting him know that she was still alive.

"Oh Sarah, Sarah, don't die. Please."

"*Oh, God. No!*" she cried.

He lightened his grip, moving her far enough away to look into her eyes. They had grown large, staring blankly over his shoulder. He tried to analyze the look. Was it pain, horror, shock? He turned around. Not ten feet away were the mangled bodies of a woman and her child. This was unlike any war he had ever witnessed.

Sarah tried to wiggle her way out of Adams' grasp, falling as she lunged forward. Crawling on her knees she reached the child—a beautiful little girl, perhaps seven or eight years old. Thor, still in shock, knelt down next to her mother. Neither of them were moving.

Adams turned her over. The woman looked horrible. Her body was lifeless. He now knew the source of the blood on Sarah's face and dress. The woman was young and beautiful, but she was bleeding profusely from the chest, throat, and mouth. Her body had taken the brunt of the bomb's shrapnel. Parts of nails protruded from her skin. She reminded Adams of men who had tripped a mine. There were no words to describe the horror, the terror that unfolded before his eyes.

Gradually regaining his wits, Thor instinctively felt for a pulse. There was none. He moved so that he could administer CPR, but as he placed his hands on her chest they found little to press upon. Her chest cavity was a crater. His hands were soaked in her blood. The precious little girl now lying near death in Sarah's lap was motherless.

"She's dead," he whispered into Sarah's ear, making sure the child couldn't hear him. Nottingly had had the good sense to turn the little girl away from her mother's shattered and nail-ridden corpse. Even if she lived, the sight of her mother's shattered body would haunt her.

Adams turned his attention to the child. One of her arms was bleeding and appeared to be broken. He removed some of the shrapnel from her arms and legs. She had contusions and deep gashes on her head and face. Her breathing was labored and sporadic. She was too terrified to cry.

The first of the sirens could be heard in the distance. Thor looked toward the sound—it seemed to be coming from behind their van. Isaac and Yacob were out, tending to the sea of wounded bodies. Joshua was yelling into a cellular telephone. Moshe sat in his wheelchair, staring straight ahead, seething. Rage consumed him. The memory of this happening to him, disfiguring his parents, rose inside like molten lava.

"I need to carry her out of here," Thor said.

Sarah looked up with a mother's gaze, one that pleaded with Thor to be gentle. He picked her up, making sure not to put any strain on her injured side. She tried again to cry, but couldn't.

Thor looked at Sarah. "Can you pull yourself up by grabbing hold of my arm?" He turned so that his left side was nearest her. He was running on adrenaline.

Using Thor as a brace, Sarah slowly rose to her feet. The three hobbled in the direction of the sirens. Sarah was now cradling the little girl's wounded head. Slowly, trying not to jolt the child, they made their way past the growing crowd, past their van to the first ambulance. The medics jumped from their seats and rushed to the back of the vehicle. Opening the doors and quickly removing the gurney, the paramedics motioned for Adams to set the child down. They looked at his bloody hands, then stared at Sarah, spattered red, her hair, face, and arms, all soaked in blood. And they noticed what Thor had missed—nails protruding from Sarah's arm and leg.

Their eyes screamed, *What demented doctrine causes such pain?*

"One of you can go with us and ride in the back with your daughter. The other is going to have to follow in another ambulance."

This wasn't the time to explain what had happened to the mother. Nor was there time for a debate.

"I'm going," Sarah said. "I'll see you after the meeting, at the hotel. Don't worry. I'll be fine."

"I'm not going to the meeting, not after all this!"

"Yes you are! If we're going to be a couple, then we need to act like one. I can do more to comfort her than you can. And you need to find out what causes bastards like these to maim little girls."

"But...."

"But nothing. That's an order, Admiral. Go."

15

BAD NEWS

Experienced in this sort of thing, it didn't take Newcomb long to extract the van from the tangled wreckage. The windshield had been cratered by the force of the blast, yet because it was bulletproof, it had remained intact. "The Prime Minister is not going to be pleased when he sees his van," he observed with a wry smile.

With Isaac behind the wheel, the five men ascended an inclined drive and entered the VIP lot across from the main entrance to the Knesset. The guards studied the damage, but recognizing Adams and his Israeli escorts, they allowed them to pass. Although the Parliament building sat on a prominent knoll, it wasn't much to look at—a low, modern, poured-concrete construct without form or style.

Some time ago, Thor had asked his friends to schedule a group meeting with an academician, an economist, a politician, a rabbi, a journalist, and even a historian. He wanted to learn. But now he wasn't so sure. With each passing day, the enemy was becoming more sinister.

Sarah had planned to join him this afternoon, but now she had more pressing problems. Even when she finished attending to the little girl's wounds, she would need to change from her bloodied clothes and shower—to do what she could to wash the stain and stench of death away. Thor, who was no stranger to mutilated flesh, simply removed the nails embedded in his side and wiped his hands. It was another day at the office.

Entering the security checkpoint, Team Bandage set off every alarm in the Parliament Building. As usual, they were armed, but no one seemed to care. Isaac pushed Joshua. Thor drove Moshe. Yacob hobbled on his heels. They looked more like an ad for a hospital supply company than valiant warriors. Strolling down the covered pathway, they took a couple of right turns and entered the Knesset's main lobby.

Their hosts took them down, or rather around, a short flight of stairs. On the wall to the left, flanking them, was an enormous Chagall tapestry depicting the long history of the Jews. As they walked the perimeter of the square building, a wall of glass followed them on their right.

Reaching the southeast corner, they entered a small door. The legislative chamber for the nation of Israel opened before them. The room was modern, paneled in warm, dark woods set in angular strips. Its western wall was white stone. Although there were some 120 seats on the main floor, arranged in the shape of a *menorah*, and another hundred for the media on the balcony, very few were occupied. The presenters were all sitting in the Ministers' chairs around a conference table, up front, in the center of the room. They had saved a seat for the Admiral at one end.

"What happened to you?" the eldest of the attendees asked Thor, holding out his hand and introducing himself.

"Couple of suicide bombers. Not very far from here. We're all okay, but Sarah, my CIA associate, elected to ride to the hospital with an injured girl. Her mother was killed in the blast. Sarah was wounded too, but not badly. So I'm sorry, but she will not be joining us."

"And you?" a concerned woman asked, staring at a nail Thor had somehow missed. "Are you okay? Wouldn't you like to reschedule this for another time?"

"No, ma'am. Seeing my friends here hanging from crosses was horrible, but seeing the look of terror in that little girl's eyes was even more frightening. We must learn why they kill. We must stop them. Now!" He took a labored breath. "They murdered my people in the Pentagon and in the Twin Towers. They killed us with anthrax. They've hijacked our planes. They shot us in Somalia as we tried to feed them, and they blew up our barracks as we tried to bring peace. They maim innocent little girls and kill their mothers on the streets of Jerusalem. I've had my fill of Islamic terror. *Enough*, already."

As the Admiral motioned for the group to sit down, the economist pointed, saying, "Did you know you have a nail in your arm?"

Thor looked at his previously-injured right arm. "Oh, so I do," he said nonchalantly, plucking it out and placing it on table. It became a symbolic reminder of the importance of their mission.

The ice was broken. This wasn't an academic exercise. Thor quickly discovered that the experts surrounding him were as frank as they were informed. All told a story of a world poised on the brink of war.

"They despise most everything we represent," the journalist began. She was a beautiful, bright-eyed, blonde woman. Her "we" was collective. It included most of the West, but especially America and Israel. "They blame our very existence on America. Hating us has become the cause celeb of the Muslim world." Her "they" was even larger. It covered dozens of nations and hundreds of millions of enraged youth.

"We stand for freedom, which they disdain. There are few places on earth more repressive than those controlled by Islamic regimes. Our success gives rise and substance to their envy. The Arab nations are among the world's most destitute. They resent our prosperity, and they view us as arrogant, for they have experienced only failure and defeat."

The politician stepped into the fray. With olive skin and graying hair, he had lived in Israel for forty years. "There are no free Arab societies. The citizens of Egypt, Lebanon, United Arab Emirates, Morocco, and Kuwait enjoy few human rights. But in Syria, Iraq, Iran, Tunisia, Algeria, Libya, Yemen, Sudan, and Saudi Arabia, there are *no* human rights—*none*. Their citizens are little more than prisoners. While the Iranians are mostly Persians, the same can be said for them. Tunisia and Algeria are no better. There is no freedom of the press in any Muslim nation. Only two even make a pretense of it. Freedom of religion is nonexistent. The penalty for discussing the merits of another faith is life in prison. Criticize their Prophet or renounce Islam, and you die. Truth frightens them. If it wasn't for lies, they wouldn't have much to say."

Thor swallowed hard. His friends shared an uneasy glance. They knew that the Prophet and his faith were at the root of all of this. Ignoring his legacy would doom the world.

"Their treatment of women is deplorable." The beautifully attired journalist was well spoken. "In most Arab nations they are denied rights we award our pets. And there are no SPCAs looking after their interests," she said. "Where else can tens of thousands of women and children be killed, as they were in Syria, without consequence? Or a hundred thousand in Algeria? Where else can they be gassed with impunity, as they were in Iraq? Or butchered by the tens-of-thousands as they were by the Taliban. Where else could one hundred *million* young girls be savaged by their fathers. Without anesthetic, held down by family members, as men mutilate their daughters' privates. This savagery guarantees virgins who will never sense pleasure. Even in this more-enlightened age, sir, Muslims are still barbaric, and their governments are brutal."

"With all due respect, having spent time here, you can't tell me that Muslims living in Israel are anything but second-class citizens." Adams had made a good point, although considering what he had been through, it was hard for him to say it.

"Perhaps, but by comparison," the Knesset Member returned, "Israeli Arabs have more rights, freedoms, and opportunities than they do in any Muslim nation. So why criticize us? The Palestinians, at least when they were integrated into Israel, were better off here than they would have been under any Islamic regime." His assessment was accurate, yet few outside Israel understood this.

The economist, a pleasantly plump woman in her fifties, waded in. "Their economies rank as the world's most inefficient. This is particularly bothersome because in the same region, from the same desert, we have been able to build a thriving high-tech economy, feed our people, and defend our borders. Arab nations can't do any of these things. Egypt and Syria have per capita GDPs of less than a thousand dollars, one twentieth of Israel's. Not surprisingly," she said, "they find this embarrassing." Listening to her, Thor wished Sarah were here.

It was the historian's turn. "But all of this pales in comparison to their biggest problem. Over half the population of every Arab nation is under the age of twenty-five. It's sixty percent in places like Syria, Jordan, Iraq, Iran, Oman, Yemen, Saudi Arabia, and Libya. It's nearly *seventy* percent among the Palestinians." An author of several books on Middle-Eastern peoples, the middle-aged historian even *looked* "authorish" with his crew-neck shirt and wire-rimmed glasses.

"Why is that such a problem?" one historian asked the other. "In America they say we're in trouble because a large percentage of our population is *over* fifty."

"There are few things more incendiary than youth in a troubled land," the dapper gentleman offered. "In the context of the despair these youths experience and the indoctrination they endure, it's little wonder they envy us, or that their envy has given rise to hate."

Adams looked down at the blood encrusted on his shirt.

"Any large influx of restless youth is a challenge for a culture, sir. You're too young to remember, but America in the sixties was awash in youth—the result of the baby boom that followed the war. It was a tumultuous decade for your country. It became the 'me generation', and soon thereafter, the age of entitlements was born.

"Societies overrun with impetuous young people fall prey to revolutionaries. France went through a similar proliferation of under twenty-fives just prior to the French Revolution, as did Iran in the late seventies before their revolution. It's one of the reasons why the Palestinians are so out of control today."

"Young people are more impressionable," the rabbi added, "especially during difficult times. As you saw today, they can be impulsive."

Thor looked down at his hands. *So that's what they're calling mass murderers now—impulsive.*

"The educational systems in Muslim nations are failing." It was the first time the academic had entered into the fray. It had been a lively table. "They teach Arabic grammar so that students can study the Qur'an.

Children memorize the Prophet's speeches in class. It's little wonder these nations breed unthinking terrorists. Uneducated people are easily stupefied. Fact is, if you read their textbooks, you'll see that they are actually *taught* to hate.

"Upon examination of a hundred and forty PA textbooks, scholars found three principal themes: hate Jews, wage war, revise history. These themes are consistent, pervasive, and repetitive. Here's something from a third grade textbook: 'Jews and Israel are the enemy of Arabs, of Islam, and people in general, since the Jews are evil and dangerous. They are killers and robbers, and have stolen Arab land. Zionism is a synonym for Nazism, a prototype of racism. One must be aware of the Jews, for they are treacherous and wage racial cleansing wars against innocent Palestinians with appalling massacres of women and children.'

"The 'Song of the Martyr' is presented in a fifth-grade textbook: 'I shall take my soul in my hand and hurl it into the abyss of death. I see my death, and I am marching speedily toward it....'

"From the seventh grade: 'Islam will defeat all other religions, and will be disseminated by Allah through Muslim *jihad* fighters.' And how's this for revisionist silliness? 'Jerusalem was built by Arabs,' 'the Jews are not the Israelites of the Bible,' and we 'Jews lived in Yemen, not Israel.'"

"How do they account for the fact that the Bible is the most accurate and detailed history of a people and their attachment to their land?"

"Truth is not popular here," she answered.

The historian had studied this. "The biggest problem is in Saudi Arabia. The royals are viewed as American puppets. They're gluttonous and detached. They garner just enough popular support to keep from being assassinated by funding the most extreme madras schools. That's the devil's own bargain. They deflect attention from their shoddy record by breeding terrorists, the very people who want to bring them down and install an even more intolerant regime in their place. The population has now been indoctrinated beyond hope. There will be no peaceful transition to a freer, more responsible government. Thanks in large part to a collusion of media, mullahs, and madrases, the people have become more radical than their leaders. By funding these schools, the Saudi ruling family is responsible for killing Americans and Jews. They build the factories that manufacture terrorists. If it gets any worse, terrorism will surpass oil as Saudi's largest export."

"But they are not alone, Admiral Adams," the Knesset Member added. "These terror-manufacturing facilities exist in every Muslim nation in both public and madras schools. The failure of their dysfunctional political institutions gives rise to Islamic fundamentalists, who in turn create schools that breed like-minded individuals. Over the past twenty years, the Saudi ruling family, the Iranians, Egyptians, Pakistanis, *et al.*, have funded 'schools' that have turned out millions of fanatical half-educated Muslims who view America as the Great Satan and Jews as their mortal enemy. They have taught an entire generation to hate."

"Muslims, sir, seem eager to believe deceptions rational people would consider laughable." The rabbi sounded more learned than pious. "In spite of what you've been told, Admiral, Islamic political leaders are complicit in the deaths of Americans."

The economist spoke next. "The Muslim killing machine runs on money, oil money." She stared directly into Adams' eyes. "The killing will continue until you cut off the fuel. If you want to derail this thing, you've got to start with the basics. Stopping the flow of money is more important than shutting down the madras schools, which in turn is more important than eradicating individual terrorist leaders. It's money to madrases to murder. They flow from one to the other. Eliminate the murderers and the madrases will simply manufacture more. But if you stop the flow of money from Iran, Iraq, and Saudi Arabia, you'll stymie the schools and emasculate the killers."

The aging Knesset Member tapped Adams' arm to gain his attention. "If you intend to make a difference, you're going to have to take the battle to the real source, which is not Afghanistan. It's Arabia. When you send foreign aid to Egypt and Syria, when you support the monarchies in Saudi and Kuwait, and when you simply tongue-lash Iran for its behavior, you fashion a future too frightful for words. America buys a quarter of a billion dollars worth of Arab oil *a day,* for crying out loud. You're funding your own execution."

"Do you know the history of Islam, sir?" the author asked.

"The basics," Thor answered. "I know that the Prophet's closest friend, Abu Bekr, unified Arabia under Islam at sword point within a year of Muhammad's death. In the warrior mode, Muslims immediately lashed out at Syria and Persia. In a genocidal rage, they decapitated 70,000 Persians. The following year they started a war against the Byzantines. They conquered Egypt next. Then under the Umaiyid dynasty, they invaded the greater part of the civilized world. A hundred years after the Prophet's death, territorially, they had reached their zenith."

Adams gestured as he spoke. "They prevailed because there was a vacuum of leadership at the time. The Byzantines and the Persians had bludgeoned each other into bankruptcy. Europe was crumbling—in the Dark Ages. And there was something about Islam that motivated otherwise-peaceful Bedouins to wield a merciless sword."

"Right, so far," the historian acknowledged.

"Then the Muslim capital moved from Syria to Baghdad, resulting in what I would call the orientalization of Islam. With the Arabs out of power, they reached their cultural zenith between 750 to 850. It's all been downhill from there. Centuries later the Turks built the Ottoman Empire using Muhammad's original three-part formula: demanding that the conquered either surrender to Islam, pay a tax, or die. They didn't much care which option their victims chose—which in a manner of speaking made them the most tolerant regime on the planet for several hundred years."

Thor continued, "The Turks were defeated by a coalition of British and Arabian warlords in the First World War. That in turn led to the establishment of 'kingdoms'. The French and British drew lines on a map and rewarded the warlords who had fought against their Muslim brethren by giving them their own fiefdoms."

"Very good," the author said. "And more recently they've flirted with Communism. The Arabs, following Nasser's lead, chose poorly. They established modified Communist states that were especially inept."

The economist barged in. "The result was burdensome bureaucracy, stagnation, and repression. Central planning allowed dictators to entrench themselves by incarcerating their opponents. Yet craving the reassurance of the Russians and coveting their weaponry, they toed the Soviet line," she said. "Muslims were the mouthpiece of the pro-Communist 'non-aligned' movement of the sixties and seventies."

"If you look beneath the surface, there are remarkable similarities between Islamic and Communist regimes, Admiral." The dapper historian adjusted his glasses.

"How so?"

"Each prefers to conquer with the sword. They use evangelists only to undermine the culture they're about to attack. Both systems target young people, who display more idealism than wisdom, and the poor, who are more desperate than discerning. Prisons and gangs are fertile recruiting grounds, Admiral." He shot him a harrowing look. "Communist and Islamic governments are totalitarian. If you don't agree with the ruling junta, they kill you. There are no civil liberties, no freedom of religion, no freedom of the press, no freedom of expression. It's their way or no way."

The historian continued. "The justice system is a sham under either regime. In both Communist and Islamic states, children are indoctrinated rather than educated. Typically, only five to ten percent of the people are zealots—Communist hardliners or Islamic fundamentalists—yet they always manage to impose their will on everyone. Brutality is common, but with their borders sealed to independent journalists, their internal terror goes unreported. There is evidence, for example, that Muslims in the Sudan have murdered or enslaved nearly two *million* Christians—making it the most horrific genocide since Hitler's and Stalin's."

"And in case you don't think religion is at the core of a Communist society, just read their books, visit their schools, gaze upon their statues and billboards." The rabbi's dark eyes were fixed on Adams. He knew. He had emigrated from Russia in 1965. "Lenin and Marx became godlike. So did Mao. The people memorized their sayings in the identical way young Muslims memorize Muhammad's. In one regime you're a 'comrade', in the other, a 'brother'."

"In North Korea, the Communists celebrate their leader's birthday by singing songs that worship *him*," the professor interjected. There were ten times more pictures and statues of Saddam in Iraq than mosques.

"For both groups, the ends justify the means, and the agenda is always set by zealots." The author tapped the table as he made his points. "They think nothing of killing innocents, viewing them as mere collateral damage in a clash of cultures. They use propaganda to shape public opinion. Those with the courage to stand up and confront the lies, to hold leaders accountable, are silenced—brutally tortured.

"Interestingly, Communist and Islamic states have both found a willing ally in the media," the politician intoned. "Anyone who dares call their behavior evil is publicly humiliated. Yet they seem eager to give the thugs a free forum." He had learned much along life's rugged road.

The young journalist slouched in her chair, frowning. She wasn't comfortable having her profession critiqued. She and her associates were good at applying labels but didn't much like wearing them.

"If you do as you've promised, Admiral, if you expose them for who they really are, you'll be brutalized by your own media. By exposing the extremists, you'll be labeled an extremist. You're a historian," one said to the other. "You know what I'm saying is true."

The Knesset member agreed. "Our Prime Minister stole one of Ronald Reagan's best lines. He told the Palestinian Chairman, 'We share something in common. In your country you control the press, and in my country you control the press.'" He paused, looking directly at Adams. "The media will hate your words, so they will hate you. But then, sanctimoniously, they will label *you* the hater." With age had come wisdom.

The beautiful blonde reporter lowered her eyes. It was a lot more fun dishing it out than it was being the object of scrutiny. It would be a while before she spoke again.

The historian rapped his knuckles on the conference table. He hadn't finished his comparison. "In both Islamic and Communist societies, those preferring freedom to tyranny are far more numerous, as you might expect. But the masses are completely powerless to effect change. Dissenting opinions are viewed as treason. Stating them publicly, in either culture, is a death sentence."

"Communist and Islamic leaders despise each other, and one another," the professor proclaimed, "yet their nations band together because they have a common enemy."

"The outward manifestations of both systems—their propensity to terrorize their own people and their willingness to export terror in the name of their doctrine—are frighteningly similar." The distinguished gentleman said, "Admiral, if you want to defeat this deadly foe—state-sponsored terrorism—you have to start by recognizing that their belief systems and politics are similar and inseparable. Muslim and Communist doctrines are woven inextricably through every nuance of their societies."

Thor raised his bloodied hands and stood. He wanted to assimilate what he had heard. The implications were staggering. As he thought, he stared up at the enormous white limestone wall before him.

"Prior to 1967, Jerusalem was a divided city, sir, severed by a wall, not unlike Berlin," someone said behind his back. "We Jews were not even allowed to see our holiest of places, the Temple Mount. So we built this, the Western Wall of the Knesset, in remembrance."

"Why are politicians so interested in creating divisions?" Adams asked the wall, himself, everyone, and no one, all at the same time.

"Nowhere are divisions more apparent, sir. This very body is a prime example," the Knesset Member answered. "Divided left and right between Labor and Likud, the real power is held by the Shas, Socialists, and Arab minority parties. They are appeased to form temporary coalitions. Political enemies serve as ministers. Rather than weaving a durable fabric, our nation is pulled apart at the seams."

Adams turned back around.

"Divided or not," the educator said, "we are not at war with a mere handful of bad guys, those openly calling themselves terrorists: al-Qaeda, Hamas, Hezbollah, Fatah, or Islamic Jihad. The resentment, the jealousy, I dare say, the hate, runs deep and cuts a broad swath through Muslim societies. Have you ever read an Arabic newspaper?" the professor inquired. "Especially after the September '01 attacks?"

"No. My Arabic's a little rusty."

She laughed. "Well, they all pretty much say the same thing. They renounce the killing of innocents, saying they're peace-loving, and then in the same breath they say we had it coming, that our occupation of their lands justifies what they've done, and are doing. And then they encourage more of it. Not too long ago, the state-controlled paper in Saudi Arabia said that we Jews are so perverse, we kill children so we can drink their blood as part of our religious rituals."

"Come on. No way."

She reached into her folder and found a clipping. "A Saudi columnist, Dr. Umayma al-Jalahma, wrote this for the nation's leading newspaper: 'The Jewish people must obtain human blood. And for Passover there are some special requirements: the blood must be from Christian and Muslim children under the age of ten.' She went on to describe the procedure. 'A needle-studded barrel is used. The victim suffers dreadful torment that affords the Jewish vampires great delight.'" Her point made, the academician set down the clipping. "You'll can find the same kind of lie in every state-controlled newspaper in the Muslim world."

"The Saudis made the execution of Daniel Pearl into a recruiting film. It was played religiously on Arab TV and Muslim Internet sites."

That was enough. The reporter needed to redeem herself. "It's true. The governments in this part of the world encourage America-bashing in their state-run media outlets. They glorify suicide bombings. Even the 'independent' station the Emir launched in Qatar, Al-Jazeera, plays along. They are the devil's cheerleader."

The portly brunette professor removed her glasses. "The more Muslims focus on how horrible your country is, the less they have to face their own reality. 'The Great Satan is *out there*—not around here.' Their leaders, especially the terrorists, are presented as righteous freedom fighters in Allah's Cause. It's like throwing gas on an open flame."

"Although you don't know it, *you're* responsible for everything bad," the politician concurred. "By perpetuating this myth, the ruling juntas absolve themselves of responsibility."

"If there is a Satan, as they claim, he's alive and well—living quite nicely in the delusional world of the Muslim militants, within the Arab dictatorships themselves," the rabbi noted.

Isaac spoke for the first time. "The terrorists are not demented loners, contrary to what you've been told, my friend." As a Mossad agent, he was privy to information few others had. "They are prolific and popular. That's why eliminating bin Laden made so little difference. As murderous as Alafat's PLO was, and his Fatah is, Hamas is far worse, and worse still, Hamas is more popular than Alafat. Islam has created sewers that breed terrorists like rotting garbage breeds flies. It creates 'em faster than we can swat 'em, Admiral."

"But not all Arabs are bad," Thor protested. "America has good relations with Egypt and Saudi Arabia. They're considered 'moderate'."

"You pay Egypt over two billion dollars a year for Mubarak's tacit support. Carter *bought* the Camp David Peace Accord." In her thirties, the economist wasn't old enough to remember, but she'd read the accounts. "Bush forgave Egypt twenty-nine and a half billion dollars in foreign debt in return for their verbal support during the Gulf War. And what did they do with the money? Feed their people? Improve their schools? No. Twenty-eight percent of their GDP goes toward armament—nearly twenty times what most nations allocate—over fourteen billion dollars last year alone! And since they claim to have but one enemy, why do you suppose they bankrupt their country to buy these weapons?"

"Because the peace accord wasn't worth the paper it was printed on," the historian interjected. "Muslim nations have violated every agreement they've signed—in fact, they take pride in doing so. By way of example, in '98 Yasman Alafat said on Egyptian Orbit TV, "My signature on the Oslo accords was a setup, just like Muhammad's non-belligerence pact with Jewish tribes at Hudaibiya.' Alafat told his audience, 'When Muhammad's forces grew strong enough, he reneged on the pact, and surprised and slaughtered the Jews. Muhammad established the principle that lies and the disregard of signed agreements are legitmate acts if they are committed for the glory of Islam.'"

"Why would anybody trust the survival of their nation to peace treaties signed by those who brag about using them to destroy you?"

"Admiral, this quote from Shimon Peres, leader of the Israeli left and the driving force behind the 'Peace Process', says it all: 'The past interests me as much as the snows of yesteryear. There is no greater mistake than learning from history. We have nothing to learn from it."

"That's suicidal!" Thor said, staring blankly ahead.

Isaac stood and circumambulated the table. "The leaders of the Islamic states lie awake wondering which night will be their last." The Mossad agent passed menacingly behind the participants' backs, making his point.

The historian leaned forward. "They have many more zealots in their midst than Hitler had Brown Shirts during his rise. Yet because their tactics are so similar to Hitler's, the Arab dictators know they're but a breath away from an assassin's bullet."

"And when that happens," the professor added, studying the room, "these nations will be plunged into even more barbarous rule. So many have been brainwashed, assassinations would serve to expand the rule of Islamic clerics, the fundamentalists. Why do you think the elder Bush didn't let your troops march into Baghdad?"

"Fear of the unknown. He knew that as bad as Saddam was, his replacement might be worse." The Navy had briefed the Admiral.

The rabbi twisted his beard. "Those with access to the pulpits and the guns are as rotten as they are numerous. Kill one and you just elevate another. They may publicly claim that they and their faith are nonviolent. They may want us to believe that their culture does not condone terrorism. They may even find it useful to infer that we all worship the same God. But none of it's true."

The historian pulled out a pipe and lit it. Thor, though a non-smoker, enjoyed the pungent aroma. The reporter coughed, but said nothing.

Taking a thoughtful puff, he said, "Their faith and their governance seem to require an enemy, someone to hate. We ought to know."

"Yes. We 'infidels'," the rabbi proclaimed, "are considered a sub-human form of life, one unworthy of sharing Allah's planet. They want us dead." He stared holes through the Admiral. "All of us."

"And don't delude yourself," the historian warned, puffing away. "Their societies breed terror. They fuel fanaticism. To say that al-Qaeda is a fringe group may sound reassuring, but it is false. If nothing else, I hope you understand that." This was the crux of the matter.

Brushing aside a stray blonde hair, the reporter said, "I will never forget the sheik's opening line in the bin Laden video tape, the one where he was caught bragging about bombing the Twin Towers. The sheik said, and I quote, 'Everybody praises the great action which you did, which was first and foremost by the grace of Allah. This is the guidance of Allah and the blessed fruit of *Jihad*...a beautiful *fatwa*. May Allah bless you.'"

"I remember bin Laden's response." The author held his pipe to one side. "His words are etched on my soul. He said, 'We calculated in advance the number of the casualties the enemy would suffer, and who would be killed based upon the position of the planes as they hit the towers. I,' he said, 'was the most optimistic of all. Due to my experience in this field, I was thinking that the fire from the gas in the planes would melt the iron structure of the buildings and collapse them. This is all I had hoped for.'"

"To which the sheik answered, 'Allah be praised,'" the reporter said. "Then the sheik shared how Egyptian families watching the attack on television 'exploded with joy.' He explained it this way to bin Laden: 'Do you know when there is a soccer game and your team wins? It was the same expression of joy.' He said that the Egyptian TV station ran a subtitle that read: 'In revenge for the children of Al Aqsa, Osama bin Laden executes an operation against America.'"

The author finished the sorry tale. "Bin Laden shared his sentiments, telling his fellow Muslims, 'The brothers that conducted the operation all knew that they were on a martyrdom mission. Allah bless their souls.'"

The table fell into a troubled silence. Al-Qaeda was clearly a symptom of a much more serious problem—Islam.

The reporter could sit no more. She pushed back her chair with a heavy sigh, stood, and paced. "When America first focused her energies on annihilating al-Qaeda, you elevated their prestige."

"Yes. They revel in one of their own gaining respect, tweaking the nose of the Great Satan," the historian growled, threatening to bite through the end of his pipe. "Fact is, despite the line they fed your gullible media, Admiral, bin Laden wasn't an extremist. He is loved throughout the Muslim world. You made him a hero; then you made him a martyr. Your actions swelled the size and resolve of his army."

It was time for a short speech from the Knesset's point of view. This was his room, after all. "In this part of the world, they make no pretense of hiding their admiration for al-Qaeda or any other group committed to *Jihad*, to killing infidels."

The Admiral held up his bloodied hands. "I know you mean well, but you're wearing me out. This sounds hopeless. I'm tempted to just give up."

"You wouldn't be the first." Isaac said, making his way to Thor's end of the table. "The problems are horrendous, my friend. But you cannot quit. It's not in you to quit. You have earned the ear of the world. You may be our last hope." He placed his hands on Adams' shoulders.

Thor stood and walked toward the imposing stone wall, pausing at the speaker's platform. Every eye followed him. He placed a calloused hand on either side of the rostrum, bracing himself. "This is a suicide mission," he said. "You have described a collusion of influences that make this battle unwinnable with words. The state-controlled media is promoting a violent and delusional doctrine. Politically empowered mullahs are preaching a violent and delusional doctrine. State-supported madrases are teaching a violent and delusional doctrine. And repressive, dictatorial governments are enforcing the same violent and delusional doctrine. How can reason seep in, much less prevail?"

"Islamic fundamentalism is virulent throughout the Arab world, sir," the journalist proclaimed. "You're right. There is a raw, violent, and hateful anti-American, anti-Israeli sentiment that permeates the place. It's pervasive. Too many characterize Islamic terrorists as 'extremists', as if they're rare, isolated, and out of step with their societies. That's dangerously delusional. Politicized Islam is a doctrine of arms, Holy War in Allah's Cause, *Jihad*. It allows no rival, no alternative. This is the land of flag and effigy burners. It is the place where hatemongering mullahs inspire impressionable youth to heinous acts, where suicide bombers are revered and idolized. Murder is celebrated here."

"Delusions cloud their thinking—and ours." The Knesset Member liked seeing Thor behind his bully pulpit.

The historian concurred. Looking up at Adams, he said, "Not a single Afghani has been tied to terrorism. The Taliban merely turned their nation into a campground for the Islamic army that is battling America. Sure, they were brutal and repressive. But they were no different than other Muslims."

"Then I suppose the Afghanis have already forgotten that we freed them from the abuses of the Taliban?"

"Yes, because that only made it possible for other warlords to brutalize them."

"What about the fact that we fought on the behalf of the Muslim minority in Yugoslavia?"

"That wasn't reported here."

"But surely they know Americans shed their blood to free Kuwait and save Saudi Arabia from the same megalomaniac that was willing to use poisonous gas on his own people!" the Admiral protested.

"Did you know that, per capita, the greatest number of Taliban prisoners hauled to Guantanamo Bay were Kuwaitis? The very nation you saved. Here they think you rescued these nations for the ruling families and for the oil. They despise their dictators, seeing them as corrupt puppets of the world they hate. There's a big difference."

"As for what was once Yugoslavia," the rabbi interjected, "they simply discard facts that don't fit with their conclusions. Islam is not a religion that is popular with rational men." He rubbed his forehead.

"What makes them so irrational?" Thor's frustration was showing.

"What makes *anyone* irrational? Seductive lies. Half truths. Self-serving agendas. Hate. Despair. Poverty. Greed. Lust. Paranoia. Oh, and don't forget gunpowder. It levels the playing field, emboldening the timid and empowering the weak."

"Testosterone and gunpowder—quite a combination," Thor said, leaning against the rostrum.

"Your nation was befuddled, sir. You sought revenge for 9/11 by killing Afghanis because they harbored al-Qaeda. And then you negotiated with the founders of al-Qaeda—the Palestinians—right here in Israel," Mr. Knesset explained.

"If you haven't figured it out yet, Admiral, you soon will," Isaac predicted as sat back down at the far end of the wooden table. "Islam encourages, even rewards killing. Read the Hadith, if you haven't already."

"The Qur'an itself," the rabbi cautioned, looking up at the Admiral. "It's a vague and repetitious book filled with plagiarism and contradictions. You can find expressions of tolerance next to passages that openly condemn Jews and Christians. Its words, like those found in Judeo-Christian scriptures, have been the motivation for a great many things, both good and bad." *While this view was popular, it was errant. The rabbi had said it just to appear tolerant.*

"I'm really getting confused here." Adams decided to play devil's advocate. "There are some imams who sound peaceful, even reasonable." I've heard Muhammad Othman quoted on the news. He says that Islam forbids killing innocents."

"He's wrong," the overly nourished professor declared, squinting through her glasses. "He needs to study his own scriptures, especially The True Traditions, Muhammad's own words. Othman is a lonely man, a cleric without a congregation. He even admits that there's no other Islamic scholar in all of Egypt who shares his view."

The rabbi added, "Militant Islam is nothing more than a return to the religion's roots. Islam hasn't been twisted by those bent on violence; it *is* bent on violence. The more one tries to emulate the life of the Prophet—the more one follows his advice—the more like bin Laden one becomes."

"He's right, Admiral," Isaac said. "I know it's not what you wanted to hear. But that's what we found too. Reality is grim."

"Then," Adams put the pieces together, "fundamental Islam and fundamental Christianity are polar opposites."

"Yes, Admiral." The politician leaned forward at the near end of the table. "Interpreting the Qur'an is a matter of politics, not scholarship. The religion is not believed; it's *used*. It's used by power-hungry men to replace secular governments with Islamic ones, repressive and ruthless enough to ensure that once they're empowered, they'll stay that way. Touting Islam is politically expedient. Even Saddam Hussein acted religious—building mosques and carrying his prayer blankie everywhere."

"I believe," the reporter said, "that the attitudes men like him display toward women, toward education, their economies, toward personal freedoms, and human rights tell us more about them than their scriptures do." *She obviously hadn't read them, for they were the same. Muslim women exist solely to make and pleasure men. But men are slaves as well: submission is required of all Muslims.*

The historian fiddled with his pipe. "Nasser, the Lion of Egypt, roared into power courting Soviet-style Communism. While he was a Muslim, the Muslim Brotherhood didn't see it that way and opposed him—violently. So Nasser, like the good despot he was, cracked down on their dissent. He threw the bums into prison, where they were ceremoniously tortured. One of those jailed was Sayyid Qutub. He wrote a book in prison that has become the modern 'Muslim Manifesto.' It's entitled *Signposts on the Road.* This fiery work became the inspiration for radical Islam—a terrorist guidebook."

The parallel wasn't lost on Thor. Making his way back to his seat, he said, "Sort of like another guest of the state, a guy named Adolph. He wrote a book in prison too, called it *Mein Kampf.* You may have read it."

"Six million Jewish voices snuffed out during the Holocaust warn us today," rabbi said sternly. "They implore us not to tolerate a doctrine that advocates racial violence." He flicked away the nail that had once pierced Thor's body. "As costly as that lesson was, it doesn't appear that we've heeded it."

Signifying his agreement, the author said, "In his book, Qutub condemned Nassar, saying he was a bad Muslim. Mind you, Muhammad expressly forbids any Muslim to judge another's faith. But Qutub didn't let that stand in his way. He went on to say that *every* Arab regime was un-Islamic and therefore flawed. The solution? Create a new state, an *Islamic* State, governed by Islamic principles and based entirely upon the Prophet's sayings. He wanted Muhammad's speeches, like those recorded by al-Bukhari in the Hadith, to become law."

"The Nation of Islam is a political desert," the Knesset Member explained, rubbing his gray and balding head. "There are no political parties, no free expression, no open debate. From the Muslim Brotherhood to Hamas and Islamic Jihad, from Hezbollah to al-Qaeda, the most religious groups control public discourse; they shape the national agenda. Cleric and crackpot become one, as do mosque and state. And like the Nazis, the most devout adherents make their people feel good by telling them they're superior, and that others, the infidels, are subhuman. They stir the faithful by proclaiming that they will ultimately rule the earth. They call them to war."

"That should sound hauntingly familiar. The Nazis proved that a small, vocal, and especially violent minority, properly indoctrinated, could bring the world to its knees. Muslims are told by the madmen, the media, the mullahs, and in the madrases that it is good to eradicate the infidels. After all, we're just infesting *their* planet. We have no right to soil their holy places. You *worm*, you," the author concluded, puffing his pipe.

"A moment ago," Adams said, returning the historian's gaze, "you very effectively compared Islamic states to Communist states. But Nazis are usually placed on the far right of the political spectrum, not the far left."

"It's a circle, not a line. The Nazi Party was the National *Socialist* Worker's Party. Communism and Nazism are very similar. Most productive assets are either controlled or nationalized, and the governments loom large in the form of totalitarian dictatorships. Even the ruthless manner in which their adherents claw their way into power is similar."

"In your studies, Admiral," the professor inquired, "have you discovered how Muhammad salvaged his career? Do you know what he did after he squandered his wife's money, when he was being humiliated on all fronts, after he had been driven out of Mecca?"

"That's when he started robbing Arab caravans and Jewish villages, right?" Thor answered.

"*Ja vol.* And how did he get his followers to go along?"

"He gave them an equal share of the plunder." The Admiral paused. "Sounds pretty socialistic, doesn't it?"

"*Da,*" she said. "He taught his followers that family and country were immaterial. Allegiance had to be sworn to *him* and his doctrine—just as the Nazis did with Hitler, and Communists do today with their party oaths."

"So what can be done?" Enough about the problems. Adams needed a solution. "Don't they need to clean up their own mess?" he pondered. "Why should we do it for them."

"Some say we must. Others argue we can't." Mr. Knesset knew all about dissenting views. "*Newsweek*'s editorial staff presented a chilling portrayal of the Islamic world after 9/11. They said America should get into the business of country making. They said your nation should free Muslims from those who have convoluted their faith into 'a manifesto for killing'. They wanted America to rebuild the Muslim economies, moderate their governments, and change their people's attitudes."

"Gimme a break! Rebuilding Afghanistan cost the American taxpayers twenty billion dollars, and all we got for our investment was a black eye. Iran spent bupkis and picked up a satellite nation. We drove al-Qaeda into Pakistan, where they promptly destabilized the government. Now they're but a breath away from having atomic weapons. So I suppose *Newsweek* said we should establish their governments for them and correct their religion, too."

"Yes. Seen one megalomaniac, seen 'em all."

"Good grief. Aren't these the same people who wanted us to capitulate on Israel? They would have you trade your land, which you have too little of, to thugs who already have too much, for a 'promise' of peace. And all this from people who abhor it. Aren't they the same folks who mocked Reagan when he stood up to Communism, calling it what it was—evil? What Islam is too, by the way."

"They are. Maybe they got religion," the rabbi quipped. "'Cause now they say America must do all these things: stop the political, educational, economic, and religious collapse that underlies Islamic rage—or else...."

"Or *else?*"

"Or else the world as we know it will cease to exist. Like other armed doctrines before it, fundamentalist Islam must be defeated."

"A clash of cultures. The mother of all battles. World War III— Armageddon."

Mercifully, the presentation had come to a conclusion. Politely, the distinguished panel of presenters waited for Adams to rise. Yet he didn't, not right away. Finally, he brought his blood-stained hands up, placing them firmly on the table.

"I think I have a better plan." He looked slowly around the room. Nobody moved. "It all makes sense to me now."

✡   ✟   ☾

THOR HAD ASKED ISAAC to call the doctors for an update every thirty minutes since Sarah had climbed into the ambulance. He knew she was sore, riddled with wounds where nails had punctured her skin, but otherwise uninjured. He had also learned that the little girl was going to live.

"When did you say she was going to be here, Isaac?"

"I didn't, 'cause *she* didn't." The question had been asked and answered a dozen times.

Miserable, Adams paced back and forth past the large fountain in the lobby of the Jerusalem Hyatt. With each turn he looked expectantly at the door, hoping to see her. He was dying to hold Sarah, to comfort her, to ask her all she knew about Mary. But beyond all that, he had arrived at a solution to Islamic terror. He wanted her to know.

Thor's friends were in knots. Just watching him pace was making *them* nervous. The pain of separation was chiseled all over him.

The second the ambulance pulled through the hotel's circular drive, Thor ran out the door, found Sarah, and wrapped his arms around her still-bruised body. She let out an uncomfortable gasp and pulled back.

"I'm sorry. I missed you."

"I know. I needed a hug, too. I'm just a little sore, that's all."

The moment Sarah had wiped the blood from her face, the paramedics had recognized who she was—*and* who she wasn't: the injured child's mother. Nottingly's transition from CIA Agent to mother hen had touched them. So they had stayed with her at the hospital, hoping they could help. Now they were standing by the door.

"Please, come in," Adams said, motioning for them to sit. A number of large couches and overstuffed chairs were arranged near the entry.

The paramedics provided them with an update. "They killed five, injured thirty. The little girl's mother was one of the victims."

"Did you find her father?" Adams asked. "Did he get to the hospital?"

"No," one of the drivers said, looking at the floor.

"Mary doesn't have a father," Sarah said quietly, sitting next to Thor.

"He was killed, sir, about six months ago," the paramedic explained. "He was serving in the IDF near the Gaza Strip. Some Hamas gunmen cut through the fence and threw a grenade. Killed him, along with two of his comrades. He was a reserve officer, only twenty-eight years old."

"What about her grandparents?" Isaac asked.

"No family. The hospital checked. They wanted permission to operate. Mary had shrapnel embedded in her neck and face," the medic shared. "Suicide bombers cover themselves with nails."

"Yes, I know." Thor brought his hand to his mouth, rubbing it, as if by magic it would help him say the right words. He turned to Sarah. "I know we're not married, not even engaged yet, but...."

Her eyes widened, encouraging him. *You can do it; just say the words.*

"If it's all right with you, Sarah, I want to adopt her."

Team Bandage was shocked. This was not the Thor Adams they knew, the tough guy. This was a kinder, gentler Thor.

Sarah couldn't have been happier. Next to "will you marry me," these were the words she most wanted to hear. Since the moment Mary had told her that she didn't have a daddy anymore, Sarah had prayed for this very thing, though she didn't think it would occur to Thor.

"You're really something." Her eyes had grown moist. Sarah knew she looked awful, but she didn't care. Her dress was still soaked in blood. She bit her lip. No one else said a word. They didn't even move.

"When I told Mary that her mother had died...." She paused, trying to collect herself. "I told her that I would be her mommy. I know I had no right to, but I couldn't help myself. She was so fragile, so alone, so...."

She buried her head in Thor's chest and began to cry. He stroked her blood-spattered hair, looking up at the paramedics. "Can you take us to see Mary?"

They nodded, too emotional to speak.

"Guys, can I have a moment, please?" Adams asked.

His friends all moved toward the lobby door with the ambulance drivers. They wanted to give him space, but they also wanted to stay close, to know where he was going, what he was going to do.

"Sarah," Thor said, reaching for her hands. "I want you to know...." He paused to make sure she was looking directly at him, "I love you, and I'm going to propose." He waited again. "But not now, not here tonight.

I want it to be special."

Tears rolled down her still blood-smeared face. She freed one of her hands and pushed a crusty section of hair out of her eyes. She was so happy she couldn't stand it, so emotional she couldn't express it. She wanted to scream, "I do," but he hadn't asked a question.

"What we have to tell Mary is forever. I just thought we should be forever too, that's all." He gave her a hug, more gently this time, and a kiss on the cheek. "Shall we?"

✡   ✚   ☾

THIRTY-SIX HOURS. That's all that remained. Anwar Abu could no longer sleep. Camping on the warehouse floor, though uncomfortable, wasn't the reason. Nor was sharing a bedroom with forty smelly guys, twenty-four trash trucks, and a few gazillion anthrax spores. He was nervous. The brilliant and compulsively religious Aymen Halaweh was no longer at his side. He was winging his way toward a whole new adventure.

The trucks were painted, fueled, loaded, and ready to roll, although none had been tested properly. The drivers were no better prepared to handle these beasts than their counterparts of 9/11 fame had been to fly. A special license and training was required to drive vehicles of this weight and size, but there hadn't been sufficient time for any of that. And Anwar knew that with Aymen gone, there was little he could do about it.

The first machines would be dispatched in three hours. With drivers and crewmembers sharing time behind the wheel, the trek west would be completed just as the trucks were ready to roll in the East.

Although no one had the courage to ask, Anwar was sure they had figured it out: this was a martyrdom mission. They weren't going to live long. His first clue was the wild expression in their eyes. The second was how readily they had accepted the notion of bringing in prostitutes. Ten high-priced call girls had been limo'd in from Washington.

But what really gave it away was the kibitzing among the boys, the eager exchange of ideas on positions and techniques. After sharing, the newly initiated would run off gleefully to one of the private offices to practice what they had discussed on the girls. Once in paradise, the virgins would be so impressed with what they had learned.

✡   ✚   ☾

AFTER SPENDING the evening at the hospital, Sarah and Thor returned to the hotel, weary, excited, and apprehensive, all at the same time. The Hyatt had offered the Admiral the Presidential Suite on the ninth floor. It came equipped with a kitchen, a dining room, two seating areas, and a pair of large bedrooms at either end of the opulent complex. He had slept in one, she, in the other.

They both needed a shower, so they headed for their respective rooms. But try as they might, they were unable to wash the evidence of the day's events away. Thor came out wearing one of the white terrycloth robes the hotel had provided. Either it was too small, or he was too large. He quickly turned off all the lights and opened every drape. The suite had a wall of windows overlooking the old city and the Temple Mount.

The sky was black, yet a billion points of light burned in its vastness. As if envious of the grandeur of the heavenly canopy, the city sparkled brightly. On its rolling hills a million lights shined from buildings, homes, and streets. From Thor's vantage point on the balcony, Jerusalem looked like a wrinkled magic carpet. A crescent moon lingered directly over the golden Dome.

Dazed by the day's events, his mind wandered as his eyes stared blankly off into the distance. In the space of twenty-four hours, Thor Adams had gone from what he had been all of his life—his own master, free and independent—to none of the above. He now had a really big and powerful boss, the God responsible for all he could see. He was as close to being married as a single guy could get. And for good measure, he was now a dad. Then he thought about Sarah: a semi-betrothed virgin with a child. It reminded him of another story.

She walked quietly out onto the balcony, reaching her arms around his waist and placing her chin on his shoulder. She, too, was wearing a terry robe. Thor could feel it against his arms.

"I love you, Thor Adams," was all she said.

I love you, too wouldn't have been nearly enough, so he said nothing. She didn't mind. She already knew.

They stood that way for quite some time—eyes open, taking in the view, then closed, replaying the day's events. Life for them had become a perilous journey.

Finally, they turned, faced each other, and kissed. This time it was more love than passion. There was time for both, they knew. And both, they had discovered, were equally good.

"I don't want to be alone tonight, sweetheart. Would you sleep with me?" she asked.

He stroked her hair, kissed her forehead, rubbed her back. "I think I can." He wasn't trying to be cute. This night he wanted to comfort her even more than he wanted to make love to her. And he knew that the only way he could do the one was *not* to do the other.

They walked inside, toward her room, hand in hand. Upon reaching the bed she let the white terry robe slide from her shoulders. She was wearing a silky nightgown that clung to her body, neither seductive nor matronly. Washed by the soft glow of the city lights, she was even more spectacular than he had imagined.

"Oh my God," he gasped. He prayed for strength.

She smiled as she reached out and undid the tie on his robe. Placing her hands on his chest, she pushed it off his shoulders and let it fall to the floor. He was wearing only a pair of boxers and a smile he couldn't repress. She kissed him softly and slid gracefully into bed, still looking at him the whole way down. But he was frozen. Everything and nothing wanted to move, all at the same time.

"Thor, come here and hold me." She patted the bed next to where she was lying. She had no idea how hard this was for him.

Somehow he mustered the strength and complied, wrapping his arms around her sender waist. Cuddled together, utterly fatigued, emotionally drained, they just fell asleep.

✡   ☨   ☾

TRIXI LIGHTHEART was back on the air. She arched her back and repressed an unprofessional smile. "Last night, FOX News lost one of its very best. Blaine Edwards, the anchor made famous around the world by his revelation of the crucifixion tapes, has died." Trixi read an obituary that had been prepared by the staff. She hadn't known Edwards as anything but a rival. There was no emotion in her voice. It was just business.

"Including Mr. Edwards, the death toll from the most recent round of anthrax attacks has reached nine thousand four hundred seventy six. A total of forty-eight thousand four hundred ninety five people have been infected." FOX showed file footage of overwhelmed hospitals and overstuffed morgues.

"In related news, the Secretary of Homeland Security has announced that the CIA and the FBI, working together with the new administration, have discovered what was behind these attacks. We go now to the news conference they held an hour ago. CIA Director James Barnes is speaking from the podium of the National Press Club."

"NSA agents intercepted a suspicious-sounding phone call between al-Qaeda operatives in Iraq and here in America. Although they did not identify themselves, experts have determined that the Iraqi voices are those of those of Kahn Haqqani and Omen Quagmer. These are al-Qaeda's two highest-ranking officers now that we have Halam Ghumani in custody."

Director Barnes looked down through his bifocals onto the briefing notes he had placed on the rostrum. "The HVAC blower attacks on our commercial buildings in Washington, Baltimore, Philadelphia, New York, and Boston were coordinated out of a group of small warehouses in North Carolina's Research Triangle Park. Our agents, working with the FBI and the Department of Homeland Security, have raided these facilities in a coordinated and cooperative manner. But unfortunately, it appears that the perpetrators escaped only hours before our arrival.

"I am pleased to report, however, that this administration has confiscated thirty blower devices, identical to those we found here in Washington. That means that there will be thirty fewer office buildings contaminated with anthrax. We may have saved the lives of a hundred thousand Americans. The terrorists are on the run. We have given America some breathing room."

He looked back up at the audience, mostly reporters, in the enormous old room. "That is all I have to report. Are there any questions?"

"Yes, Director Barnes. Do we know where the perpetrators have fled?"

"No, not exactly. That's all I'm at liberty to say."

Another reporter shouted. "Do you know if they're planning any more attacks?"

"They seem to be struggling with whatever they're doing. The conversation we intercepted was an unpleasant one. And now that our agents have confiscated their blowers, I think we'll be okay for a while."

"Can we have a copy of the tape? Where will the next attack take place? What are they going to do?"

"We don't know, and I can't say. Some of that information is classified. Our agents, working with other departments in law enforcement, are trying to track down these fugitives and bring them to justice."

"Was your agency guilty of illegal wire taps or racial profiling as it has been in the past? If you find the terrorists, will they be released as a result?" a reporter from the *New York Times* asked.

"That is all the time we have for questions."

16

PROPHET OF DOOM

THE MORNING'S SUN poured through the eastern windows of the Presidential Suite. Sarah rolled over onto Thor's side of the bed, kissed him lovingly, and thanked him for being there. Just as quickly she stood, walked into her bathroom, and began to ready herself for the day ahead. Their guests would be arriving within the hour. Thor had invited the Israeli contingent of Team Uniform to the suite.

Breakfast was served by the hotel staff—Palestinians—around the black dining room table. It was next to his room, not hers, but they had shut both doors, trying to be discrete. Sarah wasn't embarrassed, for nothing inappropriate had happened, but she didn't want others jumping to conclusions. They would anyway, Thor knew.

With the Arabs present, they watched what they said more closely than what they were eating. The four Israelis were obviously eager to learn what had happened at the hospital. Thor and Sarah both wanted to know if Newcomb had made any progress with the authorities.

Turns out he had. Isaac had managed to reach the Prime Minister at home. After apologizing for the condition of his van, he had told him about Mary, Sarah, and Thor. He in turn placed a call to the head of Israel's Adoption Services. There were advantages to celebrity.

The breakfast dishes were cleared, and the Palestinians made their way back down to the hotel kitchen. The Admiral called the meeting to order.

"Thank you for coming. I know how diligently you've prepared, and I'm grateful. We have a serious problem," he announced, looking at each of them. "And there is no painless solution. Thousands more will die before this is resolved." These were not encouraging words. "My hope, however, is that we can prevent the deaths of millions. And make no mistake; that's our fate if we hesitate, if we're afraid to deal with Islam. There is no chance our present course will lead to peace."

He placed both hands on the table. "I believe I know the answer," he said as their eyes widened. "But before I share it with you, I need to understand Muslims better." He studied their faces. "While I am certain more Marys will be butchered by these deluded fools, we must do every-thing in our power to limit the carnage."

They all reached for their books and notes. They understood that this was why they'd been gathered. They had dedicated themselves to this very thing, and they were ready, although not eager, to report what they had learned.

Isaac got down to business. "In our opinion, Islam, Allah, and Muhammad are one. When you understand Muhammad, this whole sorry mess comes into focus."

"That's right. So yesterday afternoon, moments before those two boys tried to blast their way into paradise, we were talking about the Prophet's first vision," Josh said.

"It was in a cave, late one night. He was forty, married to a sixty-year-old woman—a rich widow from two previous marriages. She was in the caravan biz, right?" Adams recapped.

"Yes. And w-we know that Muhammad's dad was n-named Abd-Allah, 'slave to Allah,' after the Ka'aba's m-moon-rock god. His life had been spared b-because his father negotiated a deal w-with some occult types."

"Before we move into new territory," Sarah interrupted, "there's so much to say, I suggest we set some ground rules."

Thor, Isaac, Moshe, Yacob, and Josh nodded in agreement.

"I propose that we review Muhammad's life in chronological order, and limit our source material to the Qur'an and the Sunnah—the Traditions or Hadith, and the oldest biographies—no speculation."

"Agreed. The p-portrait is hideous enough." Moshe stared at his shat-tered hand as he spoke.

"Okay, then. By way of recap, our first day here we discussed the embarrassment of the Dome of the Hoofie Print. There are two things I want to add to that story. As recorded in the eighth chapter of the Hadith's Book of Creation, Aisha, the Prophet's youngest wife, said, 'Magic was worked on Muhammad so that he fancied himself doing things that he never did.' She said the Prophet told her he was 'bewitched' by devils. Second, in chapter five of the same book, she declared that Muhammad *never* saw Allah, *ever*, and that anyone who claimed he had was a liar. Therefore, Muhammad's Celestial Journey to meet Allah was a fantasy, and the shrine commemorating it stands as a monument to that deception."

Thor stared out the window, watching the morning sun glisten off that very same delusion.

Sarah looked down at her notes. "Next, we discussed the absurdity of Muhammad's revisionist account of Adam and his search for the navel of the earth, the white Ka'aba stone that turned black from being fingered by menstruating women. He said Noah, as you may recall, circumambulated the stone seven times as Adam's body floated on it. Mind you, the Ark was a barge, rudderless, propulsion-less, totally unnavigable, stones don't float, and Adam had been dead for centuries."

She glanced down again. "Third, we discussed the nature of the Ka'aba. It was a small, crude pagan temple with over three hundred idols—most of them rocks. The Black Stone was Allah's. Muhammad was born within a quarter mile of the shrine. His father and his father's father were custodians of the Ka'aba, and Muhammad himself worshiped the pagan gods, observing their rituals. He incorporated all of them into Islam. So he knew the truth, but instead he chose to deceive."

Sarah was wound up. "By saying Abe nearly sacrificed *Ishmael*, he purposely recast Jewish history and Hebrew scriptures to give a pagan shrine and his fledgling new religion credibility. There is no chance that Abraham was ever anywhere near Mecca. Not only was the deception purposeful," she said, "giving us an insight into the soul of the perpetrator, but this very act later caused Muhammad to hate Jews, and ultimately led the world to the fix we're in today."

"Right on the dollar," Yacob misspoke. "A billion people bow toward a rock that Muhammad elevated to the status of supreme deity." He rubbed the gash on his neck.

"The downfall of Islam begins with Muhammad's birth," Isaac began. Muslims say the would-be Messenger was born in A.D. 570, right after his dad, Abd-Allah, died in Yathrib. His 'loving' mother, Amina, immediately gave him up to be suckled by a stranger, a Bedouin woman. So the fatherless infant boy was carried off into the desert."

"Don't tell me," Adams said. "His biographers conjured up some miracles to make all of this look more prophet-like."

"Oh, yeah.." Josh, sitting in his wheelchair to the Admiral's right, was buried in books and notes. His body had been bruised by Islamic terror, but not his spirit. "The biographers claim that a couple of shining white beings threw the boy onto the ground, cut him open, ripped out his heart, washed it, and then stuck it back into his chest. If only they had," Josh mused. "Muhammad, by the way, says the same thing happened to him again, right over there." He pointed toward the Temple Mount." His notes read: Book of Merits 42:1589.

"That," Isaac interrupted, "is a triple whammy for the Muslims.' First, it's utterly ridiculous and makes them look silly. Second, it's Satanic, since the removal and washing of organs is an important part of occult ritual worship—the kind of thing his father and grandfather were into. And third, Muhammad admitted that he was not capable of any miracles."

"In fact," Yacob jumped back in, "in Qur'an 21:5 we read that one of the many arguments used by Muhammad's critics at the time was that he *couldn't* do miracles. Since the Judeo-Christian Prophets could, and did, they said he didn't measure up. If he had been involved in a miracle, or could do one, all he would have had to do to silence his critics was to explain the ones that had taken place, or simply do one. But no."

"Isaac finished the story of his childhood. "The Bedouin woman brought the boy back to his mother in Mecca when he was six. But before the year was out, she died. A slave girl took care of him for a while before his grandfather finally took an interest. And even that is potentially disturbing, for the biographers say that Abdul Muttalib was, and I quote, 'extremely fond of him and used to constantly pet him and play with him.' But he died a couple of years later, and Prophet-to-be was handed off to Abu Talib, an uncle, his father's brother. Needless to say, Muhammad had one whacked-out childhood. It's not hard to understand why he was so insecure."

Sarah was sitting to Thor's left with her back to the window, enjoying the sun's warmth. "Long story short, he grows up, and at twenty he marries a rich forty-something widow named Khadija, his employer no less. They have six kids, nearly all dying young. Both sons die while still infants. He spends a lot of time at night hanging out in caves over the next twenty years, which isn't surprising, considering his life up to this point. Then it happened: one night in the month of Ramadan 610, he claimed he had a vision."

Joshua and Moshe rolled their wheelchairs in a little closer.

"He says that out of nowhere, deep in this cave, while he's all alone, a 'vision' told him to read. 'But I cannot read,' the illiterate Mo replied. Must have been a case of mistaken identity."

"So what happened next?" Thor asked.

"It got n-nasty." Moshe had the Hadith open to the first chapter of the Book of Revelation. "Unlike real prophets before him, Mo got p-pummeled. He couldn't b-breathe. He was told to r-read a couple more times, each time insisting he couldn't, followed by another b-bout with the belligerent vision. It nearly squeezed the life out of him. He was a-agitated, mentally confused, to the point he—in his own words—said, 'I will go to the top of the mountain and throw m-myself down, that I may kill myself and be at rest.'"

"The first suicide bomber." Thor exclaimed. "No wonder they're so screwed up.

"Oh, it gets worse," Yacob said. "In terror, he starts hallucinating. He sees a man so tall, his feet straddle the horizon. More worried than ever, he hightails it back to momma, his sixty-year-old wife. Again in his words, 'I went into Khadija and sat by her thigh and drew close to her.' Mind you, he's forty at the time. Afraid he's going out of his mind, he tells her that he's being possessed by an evil spirit, a jinn—what we'd call a demon. As we've learned, sorcerers, diviners, and other forms of occult worshipers were very common in Mecca, and Mo was quite familiar with the idea of paranormal phenomena like this. He was convinced he'd had an encounter with the Dark Side of the Farce."

"That explains a lot of things, doesn't it?" Thor laughed.

"Unfortunately for little girls like Mary and thousands before her, Khadija convinced her hubby that it wasn't a devil after all." Normally a fan of strong women, Sarah wasn't very impressed by this one. "After a while Muhammad calmed down, pacified to the point that Khadija could get up and wrap him in her cloak. Then she darted out the door and ran to her cousin, a fellow who Muhammad claims translated the Christian Gospels—at Allah's bidding—into Hebrew.

"That makes no sense at all. Hebrew was a dead language by then, and the Gospels were spoken in Aramaic and written in Greek. Translating them from Greek into Arabic would have at least made sense. But Muhammad was illiterate, so what did he know? Unfortunately, Khadija's cousin, a blind geezer named Waraqa Abdul Uzza, was so old his tombstone had to be backdated. This poor guy gets an earful from Muhammad's hopeful wife and says, 'If all you have said is true'—fat chance on that—'the spirit has appeared to him, as it appeared long ago to Moses.' Alzheimer's maybe."

"C'mon, Sarah, there's just no way. The beginnings of Islam can't be that full of dumb mistakes. You're improvising, right?"

She found her copy of the Hadith and read, "The Book of Revelation; Muhammad is speaking about the first man to identify him as a prophet. He says, 'Waraqa Abdul Uzza, who during the Period of Ignorance became a Christian, used to write with Hebrew letters. He would write the Gospel in Hebrew as much as Allah wished him to....'" She handed the book to Thor so he could read the rest of the account.

Adams shook his head. "Okay, you're not improvising."

Sarah returned to her notes. "Several things bear mentioning. First, Moses met directly with God, not some menacing vision. Second, the biographers, Ibn Ishaq and Tabari, claim that the spirit Mo encountered was none other than Gabriel, the angel who played such a large role in Jewish revelation. Unfortunately, Mo doesn't say anything about Gabe being in the cave in his Qur'an. And third, if it *was* Gabriel, why was he squeezing the life out of him? And why would someone want to commit suicide after meeting with an angel, a messenger sent from God?"

"It's because to Muhammad, angels are instruments for killing, not compassion," Josh said. "But we're getting ahead of our story."

Isaac, sitting at the far end of the table, shook his head. "What we're saying is that *Khadija,* not her husband, was the first Muslim. Muhammad was *her* first convert. In fact, Khadija's so important, within weeks of her death, Islam goes from being a silly religion to a menacing doctrine."

Adams breathed heavily. "Muhammad strikes out in the first inning. He has a deplorable childhood. His father and grandfather are occult idol worshipers, bigwigs in the local pagan religious establishment. Then he strikes out again in the second inning with the revelation from hell. This is a disaster, so far."

"The third inning's not much better," the Major shared. "After the initial vision, it's years before Muhammad's plugged in again. In fact, he never has another wrestling match."

Adams stared at him. "*Wait* a minute! I thought that's all the Qur'an was—hundreds of pages of alleged revelations."

"They weren't exactly 'revelations,' Thor. Muhammad claimed he received impressions he had to unscramble. He described the experience as the 'ringing of a bell'. It clanged in his head. He typically climbed under a cloak when it started, shaking and sweating profusely."

"Sounds a lot like epilepsy."

"Well, who knows what it was, but there were no more bouts with the supernatural. That one nasty experience in the cave was all she wrote. From that point, on it's all about the ringing of bells. He says they continued until he was able to decipher the message. Unfortunately for his credibility though, his unscramblings seem to be timely justifications for whatever he was scheming to do. As a matter of fact, my friends," Isaac said, looking around the black dining table, "I'm convinced he just made them up. And those he didn't invent, he plagiarized from Jewish oral traditions. But as we get into his story, I want you to be the judge."

"I'll give you a classic example," Yacob said. He was sitting next to Sarah, his back to the window. "After it becomes apparent he's not going to get any more of these cave visions, he becomes despondent, or as his biographers say, 'fearful' and 'anxious.' After all, his sixty-five-year-old wife has been bragging to everybody in town that her hubby is a prophet—*just like Moses.* So what do you think he does? Right. He makes one up. After three years of being ignored by Allah, he claims that he's deciphered a message that says, 'Your Lord has not forsaken you, nor does he despise you.' Qur'an 93 goes on to say that Mo will be 'content' and 'enriched'. Pretty convenient, I'd say."

Sarah interrupted, "Again, no godly insights, just 'you're my guy, and working together, this gig's gonna be profitable.' Muhammad says it this way in the Hadith, number 224, 'The booty has been made lawful for me, yet it was not lawful to anyone before me.' A bit full of himself, in the same passage, he also claimed, 'The earth has been made for me.'"

"Good grief." Thor gazed out the window.

"The majority of the surahs that follow tell us that the Apostle's critics, the Meccans, are stupid for not buying into his Prophet act, and as a result they're going to roast in hell. In various forms, there may be a thousand such verses. Then we have a series based upon Judeo-Christian themes and events, positive, yet positively butchered versions of Biblical characters and accounts. If we were to reorder them chronologically, these would be followed by some rather nasty surahs, ones that say Christians and Jews should be hurried on their way to hell. Allah's Messenger goes from trying to emulate and win over the 'People of the Book,' as he calls us, to wanting us dead."

"For e-example, in Qur'an 98, Allah s-says, 'Surely the unbelievers among the People of the Book w-will abide in the h-hell fire. They are the worst of creatures.'"

Josh had something to add. "By the way, Mo's Allah has a thing for hell. One hundred and nine of the one hundred and fourteen surahs in the Qur'an speak of punishment. Over ninety-five percent of 'em. Somebody obviously had an unhappy childhood."

Moshe moved on. "What's the h-hardest part about t-telling a lie?"

"Remembering what you said," Sarah answered.

"Well, that's w-what happened to the Messenger Boy. Muhammad regularly f-forgot the text of p-past revelations, or s-simply changed them. At times he c-conjured up new ones that contradicted others, c-canceling them out. But he had a ready excuse for that too."

Sarah smiled. She knew it. "Qur'an 2:106." She quoted it from memory. 'Whenever We cancel a verse or throw it into oblivion, We bring one which is better.' Of course, Muhammad had a more colorful explanation. When he was chided for forgetting what he'd said, he explained that the Qur'an was more fleeting than a runaway camel."

"But seriously," Joshua laughed, regaining his composure. "Since the Qur'an is alleged to be divine revelation, it means that over the course of twenty years, the all-knowing creator rock of the universe changed his mind a bunch of times."

"The second problem is his use of 'We'. The plural pronoun is used throughout the Qur'an when speaking of Allah, yet Mo makes a big deal of the fact that there's only one God—no Trinity. He says *that* would be paganism. So what's up with 'We'?"

"Maybe Allah's schizophrenic. He's got multiple personalities 'cause he speaks in first, second, and third person, singular and plural. He refers to himself as: Lord, Allah, I, Me, We, Us, Him, He, My, and Our."

Sarah laughed. "He also makes a really big deal about Jesus not being God, saying fifty times that it is beneath God to beget a son. Yet then in Qur'an 66 he says that the virgin Mary was 'filled with God's spirit.' Allah says 'We breathed into her a new life from Us.' Sounds like a direct contradiction to me. He also says, by the way, that he and Jesus have different mothers but the same father. It seems our hero was easily confused. Want proof? In Qur'an 2:136 Allah calls Jesus 'Christ'—Greek for Messiah."

"Is this a religion or a comedy?" the Admiral asked.

"It's a Greek tragedy," Sarah moaned. "There are only flawed characters and a lifetime of losing. Even when these guys finally win, they do it the wrong way."

Sarah had commandeered the conversation. "Speaking of losing, the only guarantee of paradise is to die a martyr, fighting for either Allah or Muhammad. In surah 47, Allah says, 'When you meet with the unbelievers in battle, smite their necks until you overpower them, then hold them in bondage...taking a ransom. Allah will not allow the deeds of those who are killed in His Cause to go to waste, and will admit them into Paradise.' And then, Qur'an 61 says, 'May I offer you a bargain which will save you from a painful punishment? Come to believe in Allah and His Apostle and struggle in the Cause of Allah with your property and your lives. He will forgive you your sins and admit you into Paradise.'"

"Believe in *him?*" Adams asked.

"Oh yes. It was, and is, all about *him.*"

Papers and books were shuffled feverishly on the table.

Isaac spoke first; his hands had worked better than the others. "Admiral, do you recall what Hitler did as he made the transition from loser to appointed figurehead, to dictator, to *fuhrer?*"

"Yes. He forced Germany's military to pledge their allegiance to him."

"To *him*, not Germany." Isaac paused. "It was the same with Mo."

Joshua waded in. "From the lips of Muhammad: 'I invite your allegiance, on condition that you undertake to protect me as you would your own families.' For this, Admiral, he guaranteed them a free pass, direct admission into paradise. Read it and weep. And I ain't Joshin'."

"No," Yacob chuckled, then coughed in pain. His throat still hurt. "He's speaking of what's called the Pledge of Aqaba. The leader of an armed gang said this to Muhammad, and I quote: 'I will war against all those who fight against you and be at peace with those who are at peace with you.'" Yacob looked back up. "And just so that there's no confusion, he says that his gang will protect the Apostle with their weapons just as they protected their own women."

Joshua twisted his chair slightly to face Adams. "*Der Fuhrer* and the Messenger have a great deal in common. They were both compelling orators, charismatic even. Their followers said of each that they were so persuasive, people would swoon in their presence. Yet they were both mercilessly heckled by the establishment, and failed miserably until they plotted a series of violent acts against Jews and other political opponents. They used treaties initially to lull their enemies to sleep before turning, in the end, to all-out war. As you'll see, both convoluted pre-existing beliefs and preyed on the people's phobias, jealousies, and prejudices. Muhammad's 'struggle in Allah's cause' and Hitler's *Mein Kampf—My Struggle*—are frighteningly similar."

Adams looked stunned. He knew his friends wouldn't make something like this up. But comparing the founder of a religion to the most diabolical character in history was hard to swallow.

"Let's f-forge ahead." Moshe turned to the next page of his notes. "Right from the b-beginning, the Meccans, especially Mo's Quarish tribe, see our hero and his message as m-madness. Many, if not m-most, believe he's possessed by a *jinn*, a d-demon. The Qur'an itself is full of such allegations."

Sarah tried to bite her lip but spoke anyway. "Muhammad was *real* insecure—paranoid even. He thought everybody was out to get him. The evidence for that in the three books of Islam—the Hadith, the Biographies, and the Qur'an—is overwhelming. He's constantly attacking his critics, condemning them to hell. The Prophet, like most delusional people, elevated himself by cutting his opponents down. For Muhammad, Islam was all about power and plunder—not faith."

Thor Adams stood and walked to the window. These were words the world wouldn't want to hear.

She shared, "As God's Messenger, you'd think he'd try to save folks in his home town, especially his kinsmen. But no. When they criticize him he goes berserk. Insecure people love to dish it out, but they can't take it. There are forty consecutive surahs in the Qur'an about how Mo's critics are going to be roasted and toasted. For giggles he condemns their offspring too. He even condemns their ancestors, *his* ancestors mind you, saying that they're already burning in hell."

"Sarah's not making this stuff up, Admiral," the Major said, turning around. "His fixation with hell and punishment is all consuming."

"One of the wealthiest merchants of Mecca said that the Prophet was a magician, a nice way of asserting that he, like his father, was into the occult. So in Qur'an 74:24, a revelation comes to Mo from his spirit friend: 'The spirit said, "This is nothing but enchantment, the magic of old. This is only the speech of a man. I will cast him into the fire of hell."'"

The Admiral nodded as he returned to the table. "So the Prophet is ridiculed; he bears the brunt of some sarcasm from the normally accommodating people of Mecca. It's hardly persecution." As he talked his gestures became more animated. "But you're telling me that he cracks under the pressure? Rather than correcting them, trying to win them over, even forgiving them, he condemns them to *hell?*"

"You've got it. The fourth inning is no better than the first three. On the character scale, they're all strikeouts." Isaac had played ball in America.

Sarah picked up the thought. "The continual sneers exasperated our boy, according to Ibn Ishaq. What I'm going to share with you should tell you all you need to know about the nature of the Prophet. In fact, most everything he does from this point on betrays the character flaw revealed in this story." Nottingly opened one of the books she had brought. "'While they,' the Quraish leaders, 'were discussing him, the Apostle came toward them, kissed the Black Stone and then passed by them as he walked round the Ka'aba. As Muhammad passed, they said some injurious things about him. I could see his expression darken. He passed them a second time and they once again attacked him verbally. Then he passed the third time and they did the same. He stopped and said, "Listen to me, O Quraish. By Him who holds my life in His hand, I bring you slaughter."'"

Thor shook his head. "They taunt him and tease him, and he responds by saying he's going to *slaughter* them? Not much of a Prophet. Certainly doesn't sound like God's guy to me."

"'By Him who holds my life in His hand,'" Sarah repeated thoughtfully, "'I bring you slaughter.' Who do you think 'Him' is?"

Moshe started to laugh.

"What's so funny?" Yacob asked.

"Oh, it's just this w-whacked-out verse I found in al-Bukhari's Hadith. Muslims m-must have a sense of humor."

"What'd you find?"

"Enough s-stuff to keep a p-platoon of comedians employed for a year, but the bit about the 'Lord of Slaughter' reminded m-me of a great one. 'The Prophet was told that a person had k-kept on sleeping till morning and had n-not gotten up for the early morning p-prayer. Allah's Messenger said, "Satan urinated in his ears."' As sick as that s-sounds, I didn't take it out of c-context, and that's the whole thing. It's number

605," he said, looking at the paper.

Glancing up and still trying to suppress the urge to laugh, he added, "I wrote it d-down at first because I thought it was so w-weird—so un-prophet-like. But one-handed, it took awhile, and I began to think. Why would Satan be "pissed" about a fellow missing a p-prayer to Allah, since they're s-supposed to be enemies? So it d-dawns on me—*they aren't.*"

"Can I get ya'll a drink?" the Admiral asked, feeling uncomfortable. He took the team's orders as he shuttled to and from the small kitchen.

Josh jumped back in. "Listen, Satanic or not, the Messenger Boy was just an irritant to the Meccans, nothing more. His reshuffling their god-rocks in the Ka'aba would only have been costly to them if his newfan-gled way of looking at things caught on. And that didn't happen. By the time he was fifty, he had less than a hundred converts."

It was Yacob's turn. "But with us Jews, it's different. Muhammad went from being an irritant to...well, being *lethal.* He starts off by basing Islam on Judaism. Most every important Jew makes an appearance in his book. Yet every account is twisted. As an example," he looked down, "in the nineteenth chapter of the Qur'an, Muhammad claims Allah told him that the mother of Jesus was a virgin named Miriam. Simple mistake? In verse 28 he specifically calls her the *sister of Aaron.* That would make Mary, or Miriam as he called her, thirteen hundred years old when Jesus was born."

"At least it proves the virgin birth was a miracle," Sarah laughed.

"I don't get it." Adams said, "How can Muhammad say Jesus was vir-gin-born, and still insist he was just a regular guy?"

"Oh, Allah even claims he spoke in the cradle and from it predicted his own resurrection."

"Well, I'm glad to hear that, 'cause it proves something else."

"What's that, Admiral?"

"Islam's not satanic. Satan would have told a more believable story."

Moshe set down his Coke before he choked. "It's pretty weird that this thing caught on, 'cause Mo c-claims that he, an illiterate m-messenger, has the stories r-right, but that the Jews and Christians, whose history it actu-ally was, g-got them all wrong. His explanation: *w-we* corrupted our scrip-tures! Since he couldn't r-read, how do you suppose he f-figured that out?"

"The blind fellow with Alzheimer's probably told him as he was trans-lating the Gospels from Greek into Hebrew."

Between laughs, Sarah said, "Y'know, guys, in the Book of Judges the Bible says that the Ishmaelites, within six hundred years of Abraham, a good two thousand years before Muhammad, were already worshipping a moon god. It speaks of the gold crescent ornaments that hung from their Camels' necks."

That caused Thor to remember something. "Well, at least Mo got one thing right. He said Islam was the original faith of Abraham. Abe came from Ur, in Sumeria, where everybody worshiped the moon god—Sin.

"The moon god, as in Allah, was named *Sin?*"

"Yep. But I ask you, if Muhammad's mission was to bring back the religion of Abraham, why didn't the Muslims roll up their tents and go home, admit that Mo was wrong, when that Bedouin boy found the two-thousand-year-old scrolls at Qumran? The Dead Sea Scrolls prove that the Hebrew scriptures haven't changed one iota in over twenty-one centuries. Those scrolls prove that the very foundation of Islam is a lie."

"As does the Septuagint," Yacob said. "That was a widely distributed translation of the Hebrew Bible into Greek, produced in Alexandria about 275 B.C."

The Admiral calmed back down. "I dunno. Maybe we should cut the Messenger Boy some slack. He admitted he was illiterate, and the Bible is a written account. Furthermore, it's God's relationship with his people, the Jews, not the Arabs. Why should he know these stories? And why should we care if he got them all wrong?"

Josh rose to the occasion. "You can't cut him slack when he tells his followers to kill us."

The Mossad Major said, "When Muhammad started spewing this rubbish, the Jews in Yathrib laughed at him. Heck, when I read what he said, *I* laughed at him!"

"Want some examples?" Josh asked, as his friends nodded. "Hadith 1732, or Qur'an 9:30, take your pick. 'The Jews will be called. They will say they worshiped Ezra,' of all people, 'the son of Allah. It will be said, "You are liars"...whereupon they will be gathered into the Hell Fire destroying each other. Afterwards the Christians will be called. They will say, "We worshiped Jesus, the son of Allah." It will be said, "You are liars, for Allah has never taken anyone as a wife or a son"...and they will be thrown into the Hell Fire with the Jews.'"

"Allah has never taken anyone as a wife or a son," Sarah repeated. "Then I suppose Allah's three daughters were bastards."

"*Ouch,* girl." Joshua shook his head. "How's this for revisionist silliness? 'Allah will ask Noah, "Did you convey Our Message of Islam?" Noah will say, "Yes."' Or this, 'We went out with Allah's Apostle to receive captives...because we desired women and loved to do *coitus interruptus.*' I swear, I'm not making this up. Okay, how 'bout this? Muhammad, struggling with his propensity to lie, gave us this little gem. 'I have never intended to lie...I hope Allah will save me from telling lies the rest of my life. So Allah revealed this verse: "Allah has forgiven the Prophet."'"

I suppose that means, 'You can lie all you like, because I like you.'"

"Or in Allah's case, *I'm* like you." Sarah had stumbled onto the truth. "You know, Allah is as different from God as Muhammad is from Jesus."

"Yeah," Josh said, "Muhammad is a veritable treasure trove of hate speech. There are hundreds of hate verses." He glanced down at his notes. "'The Prophet had their warriors killed and their women and children taken as prisoners.' And, "'O Allah's Messenger, do you want us to kill or fight anybody?'" To which the Prophet replied, "'Proceed on, in the name of Allah.'" Or perhaps you like this peaceful little pearl from number 1629. Speaking about a village of four thousand people, the Prophet said, "'These Jews have agreed to accept your verdict. Kill their men and take their offspring captive.'" Impressed?"

"No. Not surprised, either. The leading imam in Saudi said the same thing recently, as did the Saudi Ambassador to Great Britain. I've just learned why."

"The Jews," Isaac added, "didn't care much for the Prophet. And when it came to his scriptures, they knew that he was making a fool of himself. Naturally, when they corrected him, it made him angry. So, ever in character, Prophet-Man made them pay—made *us* pay—for his delusions of grandeur and paper-thin skin. We're still paying today."

"Admiral, if I may," Joshua interjected, "from what I can see, our notes are in chronological order. But Muhammad's beef with the infidels, especially Jews, is the single most important part of his life as it relates to the fix the world is in. I think we should cover it last."

"Agreed," someone said as all heads nodded.

The Major moved ahead. "Let's skip the story about how the little clan of Meccan Muslims snuck out of town and headed to Yemen in hopes the Abyssinian Christians would protect them."

"Okay, but it's important to share what Muhammad told his entourage to say to their Emperor." Sarah looked down and read, "'We say about Jesus what our Prophet says about him, namely that Jesus is the Servant of God, and an Apostle. God implanted in Mary, the Blessed Virgin, His Spirit and His Word.'"

Thor hit his forehead. "That line alone renders Islam ridiculous. If God implanted his spirit in a virgin, Jesus is God and Islam is a sham. Their position is preposterous. Don't these people *think?*"

"Apparently not." Sarah shook her head. "Muhammad says, and I quote, 'I am the nearest of all the people to the son of Mary...and there has been no Prophet between me and Jesus.' Then he says, 'Jesus will judge people by the law of the Qur'an and not by the law of the Gospel.' First, that's embarrassing. Being illiterate, Muhammad doesn't know that the Gospel is the life and lessons of Jesus, not a collection of laws. Second, how can Jesus be nearest to Muhammad as Allah's prophet if Mo discards and discredits everything he said and did? Finally, how can this second-best prophet judge people by the Qur'an, a book that goes out of its way to call him a liar and his ministry bogus?"

"Speaking of s-stupid," Moshe charged, "listen to this. According to Tabari, the Apostle was reciting chapter f-fifty-three of the Qur'an around the Ka'aba, which at the time was still a wholly-pagan shrine. He reached verse eighteen, and 'He s-saw one of the greatest signs of his Lord. "Have you considered al-Lat, al-Uzza, and M-Manat?"' So Tabari says, 'Satan put into the Prophet's mind to insert the words, "These are exalted females, whose intercession is to be hoped for."' The recitation complete, Muhammad prostrated himself. The i-idolaters, delighted at the mention of their three g-goddesses as i-intercessors, prostrated themselves also. So everyone around the Ka'aba was b-butt up to the sky. 'Muslims and pagans alike, bowed down worshiping together.'"

"Oops," the Admiral chuckled. Then the grin fell from his face. He became serious as he processed the implications of what he'd just heard. This was no laughing matter. "The first part about seeing the greatest signs of *his Lord* followed by the fact it was *Satan* speaking says a lot more than I really want to know."

"Oops indeed. The ultimate brain-fart." Sarah hadn't said it to be funny. Her tone was depressed. The fact that it didn't sound like her was evidence that she was becoming cynical.

"After t-the Satanic Verses were r-revealed, Muslims hiding out in Abyssinia came scampering b-back, for all was happiness and joy again in Ka'abaville. But Gabriel, we're told, is m-miffed. He has our boy expunge the S-satanic Verses, blaming Satan himself for infecting the Messenger's m-mind and putting the heresy in his mouth. The w-words were summarily struck from Allah's Message, and as a result, the Quraish resumed their v-verbal abuse."

Nottingly concurred. "With the Satanic Verses repealed, the war of words got prickly. Then Islam's matriarch, Khadija died, leaving Mo all alone with his tormentors. Unimpressed with his demonic indulgence, many of Muhammad's initial converts started to heckle him. So with the going tough, Mo got going. He skedaddled out of town—decides he needs a little vacation. Anyone want to venture a guess where he went?"

"Right here. Vacation paradise of the world. Book me a flight to the Temple on a mythical buraq, he told his travel agent."

"I guess you've heard this one before."

"Yeah, but when the Meccan pagans heard it, they laughed themselves silly. And when his fellow Muslims heard it, many of those who hadn't already bailed over his brush with Satan recanted their faith. There are dozens of Muhammadisms in the Hadith trying to make sense of this whole affair, but the harder he tries, the more ridiculous he looks."

"Okay, now things start to fall apart," Yacob shared.

"Whoa," Adams interrupted. "*Start* to fall apart? So far he's looking like an overturned truckload of camels—humps and bumps everywhere. Nothing but strikeouts through the fifth, according to my scorecard."

"Oh, this is the good part, sir. We're now in the year 619. Our tarnished and tattered hero is fifty. With his seventy-year-old wife gone, he's a wreck, totally unable to cope. Like I said, things unravel in a hurry."

"What fool would follow such a fool?"

"Arabs. Within two weeks of Khadija's death, Mo's married again. But then his uncle Abu Talib dies. That's bad, because he was a bigwig in the Meccan community and did a lot to mute some of the criticism that otherwise would have been hurled at Prophet-Man," Isaac explained.

"And w-wouldn't you know it, even though he was Mo's p-principle benefactor, he's burning in h-hell. He was never willing to say the magic words, 'There is no g-god but Allah and Muhammad is His Messenger.'"

"I guess you're going to Paradise, Moshe. All you've got to do is say the magic words."

"Yeah, b-baby, bring on the virgins."

Sarah feigned a displeased look. "Mo's bummed," she pressed on, "so he flies the coup. He heads to Talif, fifty miles north, and meets with their honchos. They double over laughing when he tries to convert them, saying, 'If God needed a messenger, he would have found someone better than you.'"

"Smart boys," Thor suggested.

"Muhammad is crushed, embarrassed really," Sarah went on. "He pleads with the rulers not to tell anyone what he'd tried to do for fear he'll be ridiculed. They, of course, ignore his request and proceed to lambaste him, stoning him on his way out of town. But he lives through it, 'cause its hard to throw rocks when you're laughing so hard."

Joshua picked up on the story. "Scared spitless to go back into Mecca, our intrepid Hero sends off a message to some leading idolaters pleading for their protection. Any port in a storm may work for a sailor, but it's not so good if you're pretending to be the Messenger of God. They blow him off too. But finally a couple of clansmen in Mecca get word of Mo's predicament and agree to protect their hometown boy. They march into the Ka'aba square fully armed and announce that the big Mo is under their wing. They're pagans, mind you, but what's a Prophet to do?"

"Actually, Josh," Yacob said, "it was the devil's own deal. In order to earn their protection he had to shut up—no talking. He became the Silent Prophet. Things were looking bleak. He had gone from the embarrassment of the Satanic Verses, to the embarrassment of the Celestial Journey, to the embarrassment of being the first stone worshiper to get stoned, to being the Mute Messenger. His fiftieth and fifty-first years were the pits. There were no new converts. He had blown through the money he'd inherited, blown through his followers, blown his credibility."

"His life was in shambles." Isaac recounted the sorry tale. "Twelve years after the initial cave vision, Islam is looking more like a fiasco than a religion."

"Desperate, Muhammad tries the conversion thing on some pilgrims from Yathrib. Unlike the men of Talif, they don't laugh in his face. So he presses them for protection, and they trade it for a free pass into paradise. They go back and tell their pals that the Mad Merchant of Mecca is prepared to hang with them so long as they vow to guard his sorry butt. Why someone didn't ask the obvious questions I'll never know. Why on earth did the Prophet of the mighty Allah need protection? If Allah likes you so much, why doesn't *he* take care of you? Or, if he's so afraid to die, how can he be our ticket to paradise? But they didn't, and as a result we start a new chapter."

Moshe shook his head. Lest we f-forget, the Qur'an now needs to be amended to j-justify violence, right? The p-pledge was a call to arms. For the first t-time, Muhammad claims that he gets it on d-divine authority that it's good to f-fight against anyone who has wronged him. It's the birth of *Jihad*."

"You're making this up, right? If this was a Broadway play, it would've closed on the first night." The Admiral thought he had studied Islam, but with every word it was looking like the greatest con ever sold.

"Oh, ye of little faith," Sarah chided him. "We've done our homework. With the world hanging in the balance, I'm surprised everyone hasn't. Now, who wants to read Qur'an 22:39?"

Moshe's mangled paw went up. "'Permission is granted to take up arms and f-fight because we have been oppressed. Allah is able to give victory to those who have been expelled from their home.'"

Sarah explained, "The last part's the killer. He had left Ka'abaville in disgrace because he couldn't handle the humiliation. Now, according to Allah, the head rock of that same pagan Ka'aba, it's okay to fight the tribe that created him, worshiped him, and diligently dusted him for centuries—Muhammad's own tribe, by the way."

"Tail between his l-legs, Messenger Boy sends his entourage, what's left of it, two hundred and fifty miles north, to Yathrib. It's a v-veritable garden compared to Mecca, an affluent agricultural c-community. Yathrib has five t-tribes, three of which are Jewish. They're smart, l-literate, and very p-prosperous. We're now on a collision course with d-destiny."

"But our hero hangs back for a while," Yacob said. "He lets his pals put their toes on the water. It's not the best idea he's ever had, 'cause by this time the Quraish have had their fill of him. They decide—just like today's consensus-building politicians—that one clansman from each tribe should simultaneously plunge their sword into the weasel. It's a multinational alliance—so modern of them. But with so many people involved in his assassination, word gets out to the Mighty Mo. Ever the coward, he has someone dress up like him and lie in his bed. Then he slithers out of town and hides in a cave."

"He doesn't mind murder, so long as it's not his," Thor moaned. "This guy goes from bad to worse."

"You don't know the half of it," Yacob snarled. "His stand in, the stooge, is his own adopted son. Some father, this one,"

"Oh, and Admiral," Sarah smiled, "guess where the cave is?"

He just looked at her.

"On Mount Thor."

"Please. Say it ain't so."

"Look on the bright side. You've got a mountain named after you."

"And a weasel hiding in it."

"So the Prophet, after cowering in the cave for three days, finally decides it's safe to head north, to the Jewish community of Yathrib. While the Muslim accounts are considerably less critical of his behavior, the facts are as we have reported them, sir," Josh said, fingering the depression in his left wrist.

"In Yathrib, he has the followers who preceded him, the 'emigrants' as he calls them, build him a home and mosque—Islam's first. Although in al-Buhkari's Book of Stories, Muhammad tells a whopper. When asked about the first mosque, he tells his fellow militants that it was really the pagan Ka'aba in Mecca. The second, he said, was built forty years later: Aqsa mosque in Jerusalem. Mo was evidently allergic to truth.

"But not to young girls," Josh continued. "He goes to his best friend, Abu Bekr, and tells him he wants to screw, I mean *marry* his six-year-old daughter. Mind you, he's fifty at the time. The biographers say she was a really cute kid, and Muhammad waited until she was nine, but there's something altogether sick about a fifty-three year old doing it with a nine-year-old girl."

"Yeah," Nottingly cringed. "There's a word for it—pedophile."

"So Catholic of him."

The Major rolled his eyes. "Even though there are only some seventy Muslim emigrants in Yathrib, they decide to rename the place Medina, the Prophet's City, in guess-who's honor. Then Prince Charming tells the Jews in town that the religion he's selling is the original faith of Abraham, and that he is a Prophet in the line of Moses, Abraham, Adam, Noah, and Jesus. Unfortunately, he doesn't know which one came first, or that most of those on his list never held the office of Prophet."

"Undeterred," Isaac continued, "Muhammad confirms his 'Jewish-ness' by telling the locals that Muslims bow five times a day facing the holiest place on earth, the Jewish Temple on Mount Moriah. Since he's been ostracized from Mecca, Ka'aba worship is evidently on the rocks. Not surprisingly, the Jews aren't impressed, knowing there hasn't *been* a Temple there for five and a half centuries."

"Unable to woo converts, *der* Prophet proposes a non-aggression pact," Sarah said. "Kinda like the one the Nazis offered the Russians. And it worked out every bit as good for the Yathrib Jews, but we're get-ting slightly ahead of our story."

"Immediately after f-forming this alliance. Mo gets up on his s-soap-box and tells the Jews his favorite Bible s-stories, b-butchering them all. They laugh and call him s-stupid."

"It gets so ridiculous, the Jews start to make a game out of it. Before Mo even gets settled into his new digs, and with his new, *real*-new wife, he's right back were he was in Mecca, a laughingstock."

"For example," Joshua offered, "according to the Hadith, one day Abu Bekr was out begging for money. He said, 'Who will give Allah a good loan?' Whereby a passing Jew exclaimed, 'If your god needs a loan he must be in pretty bad shape,' or words to that effect. Being the most Muslim of Muslims, Bekr decked him."

"A few days l-later in Qur'an 9:61, Mo is annoyed by s-someone who says he's g-gullible. The divine voice rushes in to s-save the day, rescuing our hero's pride. 'There are some of them who a-annoy the Prophet and say that he believes everything he hears.' Followed by, 'There is a painful p-punishment in store for those who a-annoy Allah's Messenger.'" Moshe's expression betrayed no amusement.

"Situational scriptures," Josh observed.

"Being an agricultural town," Sarah dove in, "the Prophet often found himself in a pickle, or 'on a date', as the case may be." She laughed. "Mo found the process of pollinating date trees repugnant, so he made it a for-bidden act for Muslims—part of his religion. The trees, of course, bore no fruit after that, causing the Jews to mock him once again."

Sarah smirked as she shook her head. She knew what happened next. It was so typical of Muhammad. "Tired of being played for a fool by the Jews, the Prophet figures its time for Allah to change his mind. He tells his followers that the bit about Allah wanting five daily prayers and prostrations facing the holy Jewish Temple in Jerusalem was all wrong. So was worshiping on their Sabbath. Now Allah wants them to face his special rock pile, the Ka'aba, and to worship on Friday. Loosely translated, that means, 'The Jews have yanked my chain one too many times, and we aren't going to play with them anymore.'"

Moshe, shuffling through his notes, started chuckling to himself.

"More potty talk, Moshe?"

"How'd you know? This one c-comes from al-Bukhari's True Traditions, verse 119. '"Whenever you sit for answering the c-call of nature, you should not face the Ka'aba or Jerusalem. But I saw Allah's Messenger answering the call while sitting on two b-bricks facing Jerusalem."' First, the b-boy is *way* too into the details, and second, it sounds just a touch p-petty, don't you think?"

"Must sound like scripture to them. They've been dumping on the Jews for centuries."

"Good one, Yac."

Moshe wasn't done. "While on the s-subject, I enjoyed th-this. The Book of Wudu, chapter 3. 'Muhammad was asked about a person who he imagined to have p-passed wind during the morning prayer. Allah's Apostle replied: "He should not leave his prayer unless he hears s-sound or s-smells something."'"

"Words to live by." Sarah shook her head. "No question in my mind he was doing Allah a real service."

"Actually, Sarah, service was something Mo *got*, not *did*. You know what happens next?"

"Yeah, he was flat broke, so he concocted the perfect revelation. He said that Allah wanted his people to pay a tax—called it 'alms.' Then, making sure he would get *his* even if his faithful starved, he instructed his followers to start observing the pagan tradition of fasting during the idolater's holy month of Ramadan. Ever in character."

"Unfortunately," observed Yacob, "the Islamic community in Yathrib wasn't any more productive than Muslims anyplace else, before or since. Taxing them wasn't the answer. So Allah's man comes up with a most 'Profitable' idea. 'We're busted. Others aren't. Why not steal from them?'"

"Because it would be armed robbery? Because it would be wrong?" Isaac gritted his teeth.

"Mo didn't look at it that way. He didn't seem to have a conscience. So he and his 'faithful' set out to rob caravans. They became pirates. Failures in the religion thing, they reshaped Islam into an economic doctrine by plundering the wealth of others at sword point. It became the precursor to Fascism and Communism."

"Sad but true," the Major moaned. "And all too soon, the grand scheme of redistributing wealth led to the battle of Bedr."

"Wait, Isaac," Sarah burst in. "Before you tell Thor the story of the grand skirmish in the sand, I need to clarify something. Raiding caravans, plundering, and killing were all rare in Arabia, considered bad form."

"Are you sure about that?" Thor asked. "Muslims claim Muhammad was only doing what every red-blooded Arab did."

"Positive," Yacob pointed out. "There were tribal alliances just to make sure it didn't happen. Caravans were the foundation of their economy. Heck, Muhammad's first job was as a salesman on a caravan."

"But there's more," Josh said. "While the Arabs of Mo's day thought it was great sport to raid a neighboring village and steel a camel or a goat, they would do anything to avoid killing a person. Murder in the Arab world had to be avenged. It was, and continues to be, a messy business. When Mo did it, it was a criminal act. And because the victims were always civilians, it was a *terrorist* act."

"But it was hardly the most ungodly thing he ever did," Adams said.

"No, but it was w-wrong. He knew it, and yet he did it. In fact, until he became a p-pirate, his prophet gig was on the r-rocks. Afterwards he really was a P-R-O-F-I-T."

"So rare was raiding caravans," Yacob laughed, "the Profit's first nine attempted robberies were a bust. Then finally, in the pagans' sacred month of Rejeb, his armed marauders found and attacked a small caravan, murdering one man and taking two more hostage. They carted the booty and prisoners back to Muhammad, who was horrified when he discovered they had done the deed during the idolaters' holy month. He was so upset, he refused to accept the plunder."

"Imagine that."

"Yeah, but then the heavenly dinner bell rang in the Profit's head," Sarah suggested. "It said, 'Are you stupid, or what? You're busted, flat broke. You're our boy; we'll cut you some slack. Create a loophole for conscientious objectors.' Okay, that was a paraphrase," she grinned. "Rocks can't talk." So she quoted directly from the Qur'an: "'If they ask you about fighting in the sacred month, say: Fighting in it is an important matter, but preventing men from following the way of Allah and denying access to the sacred mosque and turning people out of it—with Allah, these are more important still, and schism is more important than killing.'

"The mosque Allah's speaking of is his rock garden, the Ka'aba, in which he's still the biggest of some three hundred and sixty stone idols. According to Mo, Allah's saying it's a-okay to pocket the loot because those bad boys down in Mecca shooed him away from his rock. And that just isn't fair. The rift, or schism, is so dastardly, in fact, Allah says that it's good to kill them. How's that for situational scriptures?"

"Bottom line," Josh offered, "is that Chairman Mo, now with the rock's blessing, pockets his share of the booty, dividing the rest up equally among his comrades. Muslim militants had scored their first kill. But, it wouldn't be their last. *Jihad* was born. Holy War. Check this verse out. It's from The True Traditions. 'Allah's Messenger was asked, "What is the best deed?" He replied, "To believe in Allah and His Messenger." "What is next in goodness?" Muhammad answered, "To participate in *Jihad*—to fight in Allah's Cause."'

"One would think," Adams offered, "that if you were to go about creating a religion you could do a whole lot better job. Heck, this sounds more like the gospel according to Attila the Hun. 'Hitler's Helpful Hints' would be better than this garbage."

"*Hitler's Helpful Hints?*" someone repeated, laughing.

"Fact is, sir, it's not a religion. It's a doctrine, like Communism and Fascism. Worse still, it's a manifesto for war."

With so much to cover, Moshe just looked down at his notes and plowed ahead. "The b-big one was just on the horizon. In January 624, the Moon-God's fifty-four-year-old Messenger Boy c-coveted a colossal prize. He knew that if he could snag a full-fledged c-caravan carrying goods from a variety of m-merchants, he would instantly solve his financial w-woes and properly equip his arsenal. That first score w-was just an appetizer.

"But he failed. So the f-following March, he and three hundred of his marauders h-headed out again. Eighty of them were 'Emigrants,' Muslims from Mecca. The remainder were 'Helpers,' as he called them. They were along for their share of the l-loot. Together, Helpers and Emigrants all shuffled off, battle flags flying. But they looked better than they felt. The Emigrants were troubled about the prospects of k-killing their fellow Quraish tribesmen. Even p-pagans abhorred killing—especially k-kin."

Sarah took over. "God's Messenger, however, didn't mind. He was trying to break down tribal and family loyalties replacing them with total devotion to himself. In the Book of Belief, Allah's Boy said, 'You will not have 'faith' until you love *me* more than your parents and children.'"

"Well," Isaac pressed on, "living in poverty, the young men jumped at the chance. They had nothing to lose. All they owned was a sword, and they were more than ready to wield it to avenge their grievances and line their pockets."

"Some things never change. They sound like today's bad boys."

Sarah nodded. "As focused on plunder as he was, Muhammad on the battlefield was something of a problem. So on the eve of the skirmish, they built the 'general' a shelter out of palm fronds, allegedly so he could be comfortable and make a rapid escape should the festivities not go according to plan. Of course, it may just have been to keep him out of their way. We'll never know."

"Thor, the battle of Bedr is the turning point for Islam. It explains why we're still dealing with his followers today."

"Alright, Isaac. Tell me how war made a religion."

"A doctrine, sir, not a religion." He looked stern. "It began with a test between champions. The defeated Islamic swordsman's dying words were, 'Am I not a martyr, O Messenger of Allah?' To which Muhammad replied, 'Indeed you are.' We have our first applicant for Muhammad's rendition of paradise.

"Then to rally his troops, der Prophet promised them all the same thing. He cried out, 'Every man killed today will instantly be admitted into Paradise.' To which one of the youngest swordsmen replied, 'What! Is there nothing between me and Paradise but to be killed by these men?' He seized his sword, plunged himself into the battle, and was killed.' Guess where he is today," Isaac pondered.

"Scratching his head with all of the other boy bombers," the Admiral grumbled, "trying to figure out what went wrong."

Isaac returned to the Battle of Bedr. "Not accustomed to fighting, the overly accommodating Quraish, the peace-loving Meccan Merchants, put themselves at a disadvantage. They faced a blinding sun in a valley, looking up at their adversary. They tried to advance over soft dunes. And then, to make matters worse, they were downwind. A squall whipped up some sand, blasting it in their faces.

"Muhammad, as you might have guessed, sitting back in the comfort of his palm-frond hut, cried enthusiastically, 'It's Gabriel! He, with the help of a thousand angels, is falling upon the enemy! He is throwing sand in their faces.'"

"Oh, good grief."

"Can you imagine a god so destitute he had to send his top angel to help pirates steal other people's money? Or angels so feeble it takes a thousand of them to subdue a hundred merchants?"

Thor shook his head in amazement. He prayed they were making this up. His prayer was not answered.

"When the sand finally settles, about fifty Meccans are dead, and a similar number are taken prisoner. The Muslims admitted losing fourteen. It was a meaningless skirmish by any standard. Yet it transformed Islam. Over three years it had evolved from an egotistical charade, to a silly religion, to plundering-pirate gig, to a killing machine. Which is where it remains today.

"Muhammad reveled in killing. It got so bad, he sent one of his servants out to search for the corpse of a man who had upset him when he was in Mecca. Finding it, he severed his head and tossed it at the Prophet's feet. Muhammad cried, 'The head of the enemy of God. Praise Allah.'"

"The enemy of *God?* This guy's beyond belief. It's no wonder they celebrate killing," Adams noted.

"The prisoners were carted off, Admiral. They would be ransomed—all but three anyway. A couple said that their stories were better than *der* Prophet's, so he cut off their heads too. Another was hacked to pieces by a vengeful lad who viewed him as an unworthy infidel.

"The victims cried out in anguish, 'Who will look after our children, O Muhammad. But Hitler's mentor was unmoved. 'Hell Fire,' he said. Do you think our boy may have been a touch vindictive?" the Major asked.

"Perhaps just a smidge. But still, associating the leader of a 'religion' with *der Fuhrer,* may be a bit over the top."

"He earned it," Isaac shot back. "Now back in the pirates den, the rebels started to quarrel about who was going to get the most booty. It was a mutiny in the making. Those who killed a man felt that they were entitled to his sword and shield. However, those in the rear guarding the Mighty Mo felt left out. They hadn't come along for the fun of it, and they demanded their share. So the Prophet, displaying the wisdom of Lenin, had all the stolen loot piled up. After taking twenty percent for himself, he distributed the rest equally among his bloody, sword-wielding 'religious' stalwarts."

Looking up from his notes, Isaac summarized, "So it was and so it would be. Muslim raids from that time on would divide the spoils in like fashion. It was great for recruiting. The workers' paradise for those who died, loot for those who lived."

"Sure beats trying to do it the old-fashioned way, evangelizing. You know, trying to convince people that your faith is worthy of their soul."

"As you might imagine, my friend, Muhammad's alter ego, Allah, condoned the whole sordid affair in a revelation to his Profit." The Major read in the Qur'an's eighth surah: "'They ask you about the spoils of war. Say: The profits belong to Allah and to the Apostle. So fulfill your obligations to Allah, settle your disputes, and obey His Apostle.' Then the Qur'an says, 'I am reinforcing you with a thousand angels.' And, finally,

'He who turns his back in battle shall meet with the anger of Allah and his abode shall be hell.'

"You like probabilities, Admiral. What do you think the odds are that the creator of the universe actually revealed any of this to Muhammad?"

"About one chance in ten to the sixtieth power?"

They all nodded their heads.

"Bedr. In an hour's time, a ragtag gang of misfits were transformed into military conquerors. Their pride swelled, and so did their numbers. A failure as a prophet, Chairman Mo was now victorious as a terrorist."

Isaac looked back down at his notes. "They stole a hundred and fifty camels, ten horses, and a considerable stash of weaponry. The ransoms paid for the prisoners were even more valuable."

"It's enough to make you puke," Adams said.

"Well, if you liked that, you'll love this. The most prolific poet of her day wrote something critical about Profit's new career path. Muhammad didn't like it, so he had her murdered in her bed, surrounded by her children. A week later, he did the same to another poet. How's that for press censorship? When anyone wrote about the inappropriateness of his behavior, he had them assassinated. Hitler had nothing on this guy. Even today, threatening writers remains standard operating procedure for Muslims the world over. It all started with Muhammad."

"No wonder they're terrorists. Their *Prophet* was a terrorist." Thor pounded his fist on the table. "I don't know how much more of this I can stomach," he confessed to his friends.

"I'm sorry," Isaac replied, "but we can't stop now. This is too important. Of the billion Muslims, over half are young, impressionable, and *indoctrinated*. They're old enough to fight, and foolish enough to die. If someone like you, someone people trust, isn't willing to speak out against this demented doctrine and rally others to stand up, we're going to find ourselves embroiled in world war."

"It looks inevitable." Thor closed his eyes. He wanted to wish it all away. He had so much to live for. He said a prayer, barely audible.

Everyone realized what Thor was up against. Those who had clawed their way to power in the Muslim world would treat him as their Prophet had treated his critics. They would make Thor Adams' life a living hell, if only to dissuade others from rallying to his side, from telling the truth about Islam. Even if they didn't kill him, they would most certainly assassinate his character.

"The next thing Muhammad does sounds a lot like Islamic dictators today. He uses the money he's stolen from productive people to employ his own journalists. We have our first official state-run media. Needless to say, these poets have only nice things to say about Chairman Mo, and flaming arrows for anyone with the *cajones* to criticize him."

Moshe was the next to speak. "There's something y-you ought to know about his f-first encounter with his house poet. When the Apostle asked Thabit if he could d-defend him from the verbal attacks of his enemies, the p-poet stuck out his tongue and said, 'There is no armor which I cannot p-pierce with this weapon.'"

"You're not making this any easier."

"Hang in there, my friend. It only gets worse."

"As you might have guessed, things get nasty between the Prophet and the Jews," Sarah shared. "They don't buy into his warmongering-kidnapping-terrorist-pirate thing any more than they do his bogus Biblical accounts. Immersed in their scriptures, the Jews continued to snicker at Messenger-Man. Unfortunately, they had no idea how evil he was, and they were ill prepared to fight him."

"Good grief. This sounds like a prelude to Hitler and the Holocaust."

"Yep." She went on. "A carbon copy, *exactly* thirteen hundred years in advance. You could call it a dress rehearsal."

"Enough to make you triskaidekaphobic," Thor noted wryly.

Sarah smiled. "Running low on cash again, Messenger-Man tuned in to his spirit friend for this handy Qur'an revelation: 'Say to those who disbelieved,' in me and my doctrine is the inference, '"You will be defeated and driven into Hell, an evil resting place."' So with Allah firmly in his pocket, Mo and his mercenaries march against Yathrib's first Jewish tribe, the Beni Qainuqa. They lay siege to their settlement. After two weeks, the Jews, without anything to eat or the means to fight back, surrender.

"Ibn Ishaq tells us one of their supporters, with the unlikely name of Abdulla, goes to the Prophet and says, 'O Muhammad, deal kindly with these people,' but the Apostle turned his back and became so angry, Ishaq says, that his face turned almost black. Then what do you think happened?"

"Prophet Vision?" Thor ventured.

"Bimbo." Yacob said, winking at Sarah.

"Surah 5:51." She quoted, "'O you who believe, do not take Jews and Christians as allies. They are friends of one another. Whoever takes them as friends is one of them. And their hearts are affected with sickness....'"

"Oh, man! Like the Nazis telling folks, 'If you stand up for the Jews you'll share the same fate!"

"Sounds like hate speech to me," Joshua proclaimed.

"Then fasten your seatbelt," Nottingly said. "Verse 57 is pure unadulterated, insecure, thin-skinned Mo-babble. Speaking of the Jews, the People of the Book in Yathrib, he claims the bell tolls for them: 'O

Muslims, do not take as allies those who received the Books before you, those who make a sport of your faith and treat your religion as a joke.'"

Yacob looked at Thor. "Like we said, sir, Muhammad was a wannabe Jew who embarrassed himself with silly renditions of our history and faith. If he had just invented his own religion, instead of coveting ours, the Jews in Yathrib would never have teased him. He wouldn't have lashed out, and we wouldn't be having this conversation today because there would be no Muslim militants."

The latest in the group to have been injured by Islamic terrorists stood and faced her friends. "In Qur'an 3:3 Allah 'confirms the Books revealed before; indeed Allah has revealed the Torah and the Gospel.' Mo said he was just one of the Jews—one with Abraham, Noah, Moses, Jacob, Joshua, David, and Jesus. A fellow prophet. Then he usurped their stories. In fact, if you were to remove four things from the Qur'an—Hebrew Bible stories, pain for anyone who makes a game of Mo's version, Muhammad's un-prophet-like behavior having the Good-Ka'aba-Keeping Seal of Approval, and mindless repetition—you'd have nothing left."

Sarah brushed her hair back, gazing deeply into each of her friend's eyes. "Muhammad condemned himself when he said that the Hebrew Bible and Christian Gospels were both God's word and wrong. Thinking men and women of his day knew he was crazier than a bed bug, a fraud who was just making it up as he went along, in today's parlance, a con artist. But rather than admit he was wrong when he was challenged, he killed thinking people instead. He even ordered his followers to do likewise, to the end of time."

Every member of Team Uniform was focused on Sarah. "Muhammad was the inverse of Jesus. He turned what should have been a simple relationship between God and man into a hate-driven, money-grubbing doctrine, replete with befuddling ritual and repressive laws. His line, 'The retribution for those who fight Allah and me, for those who commit such horrors, is to be crucified,' defined him and his doctrine. In that light, let's examine what Muhammad did next."

Moshe took the floor. He was an expert when it came to Muslims torturing Jews. "Thanks to some fortuitous 'scripture', Muhammad now had Allah's permission to kick the Jews out of their h-homes and into the desert. At sword point he commanded the d-defenseless Jewish tribe of Beni Qainuqa to leave all that they owned to *him*. They were perhaps three thousand strong, outnumbering their assailants many times over. They had l-lived peaceably in Yathrib all their lives. They had built things w-worth owning. Yet it was all t-taken away by a hateful man and his ragtag assemblage of well-armed m-misfits. They had waltzed into *t-their* town because they had been laughed out of their own. Muhammad's Muslim militants proceed to s-steal every Jewish possession."

"They were forced to leave their property behind," Josh said. "True to form, the peace-loving and tolerant Islamic faithful confiscated everything, dividing their homes and wealth among them. This was particularly sad because up to this point, the Muslim emigrants from Mecca had been flops in business. They had survived on the charity of their hosts. Now they were celebrating their departure, rolling in the plunder, sleeping in their benefactors' beds."

"As the Communists and Fascists proved, it's still possible today. A tiny minority, properly armed and motivated, can bring any nation to its knees." the Admiral muttered to no one in particular.

"In May 624, Muhammad storms off again," Newcomb told the assembled. "He leads a raid on two nomadic tribes, stealing some five hundred camels. I bring this up because a Jewish poet named al-Ashraf criticized the Prophet's despicable behavior. Perturbed, Maniacal-Man asked his fellow raiders, 'Who will rid me of al-Ashraf?' A boy replied, 'I will kill him for you.' To which Muhammad said, 'Do so if you can.' 'I will have to tell lies to get it done,' the would-be assassin confessed to his religious leader. 'You are authorized to lie,' Muhammad replied."

"A license to kill—a license to lie. This is some religion. It certainly explains their behavior though, doesn't it?"

Josh finished the story. "We're told that Muhammad's hit man—okay, hit *boy*—goes off and spends a pleasant afternoon reciting poetry with his intended victim. After dark he slits al-Ashraf's throat. When Muhammad heard this, Ibn Ishaq says, he told his faithful to, and I quote, 'Kill any Jew who falls into your control.'"

"But I keep hearing, 'Islam is peace-loving religion—we all worship the same God.'"

"Must be the Nazi god, 'cause he wants 'em to k-kill Jews."

Thor looked around the room, studying everyone's face. "They have a clear mandate from Muhammad to lie, steal, and kill."

"I'm afraid we're not done, Admiral. When one of Muhammad's followers heard him say this, he immediately went out and murdered a Jewish merchant in Yathrib. His brother protested, saying, 'Why did you kill him? He was your employer!' To which the terrorist, Jewish blood still dripping from his hands, boasted, 'Had the one who told me to kill him ordered me to murder *you* instead, I would have cut off your head.'"

"Sounds just like *intifada*."

"That's because they're all singing from the same hymnal."

"One of life's great ironies," Sarah suggested, "is that those who take what rightly belongs to others have no appreciation for its value. Muhammad's gluttonous marauders always seemed to need ever-larger and more frequent fixes. So with the Great-Religious-One at their side, they set off with reckless abandon, raiding caravans and villages. The richest caravan ever seized was robbed by Mo's adopted son. Stealing was considered such a good thing, in fact, the Prophet eventually stole his son's wife. There's even a verse in the Qur'an condoning his incest."

"Mo's Marauders became a different breed. Something in his life and words changed the hearts of boys, turning them into killers, thieves, and kidnappers. He convinced Arabs that Allah not only condoned this behavior, but actually rewarded it. And they bought it, which is more insane."

The Major moved on to the next battle. "The merchants in Mecca had finally had their fill of caravans being plundered. So they sent out another assemblage of sword-wielding shop owners to Yathrib—or Medina, whatever you want to call it—to do battle. We're told Mo wanted to hide, hoping they would go away. But the youngest men in his emerging terrorist network wanted to go out and play. They believed their fearless leader would call in a thousand angels again to throw sand in the merchant's faces, as he had at Bedr. But it didn't quite work out that way. Muhammad's mob was defeated.

"The Muslim militants were massacred. Mo was knocked unconscious early on and left for dead. Unfortunately, he wasn't," Isaac said. "And the Meccans, being as good at this as Bush One, simply left. They thought they had taught the bad boys a lesson, so they packed up and went home."

"There's a line from this battle I just love." Josh smiled. "One of the biographers writes, 'Seized with sudden panic, the Apostle's warriors rush past him in full retreat.' To which Muhammad cried out passionately, 'Where are you going? Come back here. I am the Messenger of God.' But no one, he says, took notice."

"'The Messenger of God'—sure you are, pal."

"I think I know the reason they lost." Sarah had studied this. "When Islam was a just silly religion, only 'true believers' followed Messenger-Man. Darn few, it turns out. But when Islam became the ticket to paradise and plunder, the sincerity of the adherents was less genuine, although their numbers swelled. At the first sign of trouble, the hypocrites, as Mo called them, ran. The same is true today. Remember Iraq's Republican Guards? They couldn't surrender fast enough. The same could be said of the Taliban."

Yacob looked up from his notes. "The two most interesting tidbits here are Mo's stirring words, 'I swear I will mutilate thirty Quraish in revenge.' And in chapter 3 of the Qur'an, Mo, ever in character, justifies the fact that Gabe and his angels stayed home. 'We cause days like this to occur so that Allah may know who the believers are and that He may harvest martyrs from among you.' The ultimate situational scripture."

"Well, s-so as not to make Muhammad l-look like he got run over by the M-Merchants of Mecca, Bukhari reports, 'I saw Allah's Messenger on the day of the battle accompanied by two men f-fighting on his behalf. They were dressed in w-white and were fighting with extreme bravery. It is said they were the angel Gabriel a-and the angel Michael.' 'Course, since they lost, what does that say about Allah's angels?"

Isaac continued without comment, "Now purely a terrorist, Maniacal-Man sends out one raiding party after another to assassinate his political enemies, principally chiefs and poets. When each assassin returns, Allah's Apostle praises him for his devotion. Nothing has changed, my friends. And if you don't think so, listen to al-Jazeera sometime."

Moshe flipped pages. "Here it is in his own w-words. 'Allah's Messenger said, "I have been made victorious with t-terror."' You'll f-find this in Bukhari's Book of Jihad, 56:1279, if you want to look it up yourself."

"I think I need a drink."

"Shaken, not stirred?" Nottingly teased. "Sip on this. Mo needs an easy score to reclaim his tattered reputation, not to mention bucks to keep his little band of thieves together. So *der* Prophet turns his attention to the second Jewish tribe living in Yathrib/Medina. First, he surrounds them. Then he cuts down their date palms, their food supply, something even his own people know is insane. But Mo's cool with it. See, he had Allah's blessing. Qur'an chapter 59 says so. 'Whatever palm tree you cut down or leave standing up, it is by permission of Allah, that He might shame the evildoers.'

"After a siege of two weeks, the defenseless and starving Jewish Beni al Nadheer tribe surrenders, expecting to be driven at sword point into the desert. Muhammad feels a twinge of embarrassment. He's done this trick before. So he comes up with a handy scripture, 'It was Allah who drove out the unbelievers, the People of the Book, from their homes in the first banishment.' Either he forgot about *his* armed assault and siege, or else he's admitting what I've known for some time: *he's* Allah."

Moshe glared down at his mutilated hand. "With the p-productive people gone, the p-parasites sucked up the spoils. As was the custom, they divided the land, homes, farms, shops, and personal b-booty between them, as always giving Pirate-Man his twenty percent c-cut off the top."

"I hate to correct you, Mosh," Yacob interrupted, "but this time, because Muhammad was able to confiscate the Jew's property without fighting, the Prophet took *all* the spoils. It's a story as old as time. If you want to know what's happening or why—follow the money." He turned to Adams and quoted surah 59. "'You did not charge with horse or camel so whatever booty Allah gives his Apostle from the [Jewish] tribes is for Allah and His Apostle.'"

Sarah took the last sip of her Diet Coke. "Insecurity is the root cause of all this. Mo's grew out of his troubled childhood. Like all who suffer from insecurity, Muhammad simply manufactured whatever lie was necessary to take what didn't belong to him. Allergic to criticism, he was fixated on punishing his tormentors. He would stop at nothing to satisfy his sexual appetite, his craving for power, and his lust for money."

Adams cringed. He knew about insecure people. They were the most destructive parasites on the planet.

Sarah continued. "Insecure men are trouble around women. They're either abusive or insatiable. The latter was the case with our man-child. He had as many as a dozen wives at a time. One was twice his age. Another was less than one fifth as old as he was. He married a cousin and stole his adopted son's wife. Plus, he had a plethora of concubines, sex slaves from his conquests."

"He's forgiven for such indulgences, of course," the Major told the Admiral. "Muslims like to point out that both David and his son Solomon eventually had harems."

"While true," Yacob said, "God withdrew from them when they did. Their lives became unproductive, and they died in sorrow. Solomon's book, Ecclesiastes, is a treatise on the vanity, the futility, of such a lifestyle."

"Although the Qur'an prohibited much of what Allah's Messenger did, there was always a new scripture," Josh knew. "He was an exception to his own rules. In one place the Qur'an limits the number of wives to four. In another it says, 'O Prophet! We have made it lawful for you to possess as many wives as you wish, but that this is a privilege for you alone.' To which his youngest wife, Aisha responded, 'Your Lord certainly seems anxious to gratify your desires.'"

"She's *so* perceptive! I'm getting to like her."

"Ah well, *he* liked the girls, too. In fact, Muhammad once said, 'I like women and perfume better than anything else,'" Sarah quoted.

"Great. Allah likes fights and Muhammad likes sex. War and Booty."

Isaac laughed. "We have one last episode to share with you, Admiral. And as you might imagine, it isn't pretty." Once again, the Major led the charge. "Muhammad ran into Gabriel, who said, 'The angels have not laid down their arms. Allah commands you, Muhammad, to go to Beni Quraidha,' the last remaining Jewish tribe in Medina. 'I am going there myself.' So with orders from 'god' to harass his chosen people, *der*

Prophet lays siege to Yathrib's last remaining Jewish tribe—*his* final solution. Starving and defenseless, they, as those before them, ultimately capitulate, expecting to be deported from their homes."

"But this time Allah's boy is in a f-foul mood." Moshe completed the story. "He says y-yes, but then at the same moment d-draws his forefinger across his throat, signifying that they should all be m-massacred." Moshe tried to act out Muhammad's signal, but his mutilated hand wouldn't comply. "The Prophet said, 'Allah gives the judgment that the men should all be killed, their p-property divided, and the women and children shall be sold into s-slavery.'"

Isaac related the grim aftermath. "Trenches were dug during the night near the main market of Medina. The Jews were led out in small batches, we're told. Their hands were tied behind their backs. They were made to kneel down beside the trenches." He paused, unable to go on.

Yacob picked up the story. "Muhammad ordered his men to sever their heads." He involuntarily touched the gash Halam Ghumani had gouged into his throat. "The peace-loving Muslims did as their Messenger instructed. They drew their swords and raised them to the sky as the manacled men awaited their fate. One by one, they did the despicable deed. Heaving their swords down, they hacked off each head, laughing as they tossed one after another into the trench. Others pushed their mutilated bodies into the pit, singing *'Allahu-akbar.'* He bowed his head.

"He taught them to be t-terrorists. Surah 8:60—'Prepare against the infidels whatever weapons you can muster, that you may strike terror into the enemies of Allah.'"

Josh groaned as he moved in his chair. His chest still hurt. "Eight hundred Jewish men were slaughtered that day. Many times more than that were sold into slavery. The money from the slave trade, along with what they confiscated from homes and businesses, was used to buy more weapons to continue the rule of terror."

Thor sat there, stunned. "Holocaust."

"Yes, one justified by Islamic scripture."

"So Allah approves mass murder."

"Indeed. In Qur'an, chapter 33 Allah said, "'Remember the blessing of Allah. We sent a wind against them, invisible troops.' Then, 'Allah drove back the unbelievers in their rage and they gained no advantage. Allah was mighty and glorious. He brought low the People of the Book, and filled their hearts with dread so that you could kill some and make many captive. Allah made you inherit their lands, mansions, and wealth.'"

Yacob put his hand to his mouth and doubled over. He stood, stumbled off to the bathroom, and lost a perfectly good breakfast. Moshe was paralyzed, consumed with rage. His life bore the scars of Muhammad's legacy. The Admiral was nauseous. Sarah wept.

Isaac gritted his teeth, mustering the strength to continue. "Mo's marauders went on to exterminate and rob other tribes, all with the Prophet's blessing. Muhammad pursued the Beni Nadheer—the second Jewish tribe he'd exiled—killing every male above the age of twelve, raping the women, and selling the children into slavery. Tabari says that Muhammad even ordered their chief tortured hoping to find hidden treasure. In December 627, a raiding party captured some women and children. They raped them as the Apostle watched. They became sex slaves. A new form of booty."

"According to Ibn Ishaq, the Prophet took the most beautiful woman they captured for himself. In the Book of Prayer, number 243, it's reported this way: 'Muhammad came with his army and conquered, taking captives and war booty. A follower asked, "O Allah's Messenger, give me a slave girl from the prisoners." The Prophet answered, "Go and take any one you desire." He picked a beautiful Jewish princess.' But, we are told, the Prophet coveted her. He reneged on his gift, and took her for himself. The story goes on, but I think we've said enough."

"Did you ever wonder why no Muslim nation allows anyone to criticize the Prophet? Why they'll kill you if you do?" the Major asked his friend.

"I did. Not anymore."

"You may think, sir, that we've only given you one side of the story, that Muhammad's got to have some redeeming qualities. Am I right?"

"Nothing is black and white," Thor admitted. "But I'm afraid there's more than enough black here to condemn this guy a hundred times over." He stood and faced the window, contemplating the Dome of the Rock.

"Gentlemen, Sarah, you've given me all I need to know to see the stone that became Allah, the snatch-and-run that became Islam, and Muhammad, the Prophet of Doom, for what they are—a false god, the surrender to a false doctrine, and a false prophet—a terrorist. You documented everything you've said from their scriptures. And you've traced the deviant behavior of the Muslim militants directly to Muhammad. The world needs to hear this: Islam itself is the putrid spring from which terrorism flows."

17

TEA WITH TERRORISTS

"C'mon, Isaac, is all this necessary?" Thor was being made up, but this time it was to make him look bad, not good. Or more precisely, it was to make him look like a nobody, *anybody* other than who he really was.

"This has got to be the dumbest idea I've ever heard," the Major grumbled. "I think you've lost your marbles, pal." They were at Mossad headquarters, known as "the office" to insiders, trying to disguise Thor's appearance.

"Maybe. But it's something I've gotta do. I need to crawl into this enemy's head. Figure out what makes 'em tick. How can I do that without talking to them?"

"Talking with terrorists. I don't believe it. You're supposed to *kill* 'em, remember? Now you want to chitchat." Isaac was struggling. "This makes what Danny Pearl did look like a walk in the park, and in case you've forgotten, they *killed* him. They invited him to lunch, then they cut off his head. Do you want to see the video?"

He continued to nag his friend. "Say you get into trouble, say they figure out who you really are; there's nothing we can do to save you. You go in there, you're on your own. We're talking about Zone A. There are more terrorists per capita in there than any place on earth."

"I understand the risk. No guns, no wires, no cameras, no nothing. You drive me to the border and I walk across on my own."

"This is insanity. Why not meet with some more Shin Bet agents, IDF Intelligence, our Mossad guys, even with the PA, for cryin' out loud. How much more do you need to know?"

"Plenty. Listen, Isaac, you've been great. I've learned more than I thought possible. But it's not enough. Agents grow callous, military intelligence is an oxymoron, and politicians all have agendas."

"Sharon's friend, the Director General, was plenty candid. He knew every Arab dictator personally. He laid it on the line, told you all you need to know about them. So did everybody else I introduced you to, including the Generals and Knesset Members. You don't need to do this!"

"You sound like Sarah," Adams complained. "She's already given me an earful. She's starting to sound more like a wife than a girlfriend."

"What you need is a mother," Isaac moaned. He gave up, unable to dissuade his friend from going forward with his foolhardy adventure.

"I've been called to do this, Isaac. I'm following orders."

Makeup finished, an agent snapped a picture. Adams looked positively average. His hair was now black, not brown, streaked with gray, making him look ten or fifteen years older. He sported a wispy, graying goatee that he'd swear was real if he hadn't seen it glued on. They'd given his skin a grayish pallor that made the older man's hair believable. His eyes were hazel and somewhat hidden behind thick-rimmed glasses. He was considerably heavier, sporting love handles and a bit of a gut. His dress was sloppier too, wrinkled and uncoordinated, something totally incongruous for a military man, especially an officer. They even dirtied his nails. As Thor looked at himself in the mirror, he saw an author, a nobody.

Satisfied, he was led downstairs to a waiting cab. Isaac joined him in the back seat.

"The driver's Shin Bet. They're in charge, because technically you're not leaving the country." The Shin Bet's beat was domestic intelligence, not unlike America's FBI. Isaac's Mossad was strictly international.

"*Technically* is the operative word, sir," the driver said. "You're entering the twilight zone. You're headed to a place without laws. It's the domain of terrorists, a place where they use Islam to justify murder."

"Forget the media's pictures of us rolling tanks into defenseless civilian areas. These people are better armed than, well, you-know-who." Newcomb explained, referring to their prior adventure.

"They'd kill you for a shekel." It was the driver again. "Be careful what you say. And for heaven's sake, don't provoke them."

"Whatever you do, don't let them take you in too far. And make sure you're out by sunset." Isaac had no idea how the Admiral was going to influence either of these requests. His hosts would be armed to the teeth. Adams was only carrying a pen. Mightier than the sword, perhaps, but no good at all for hostage extractions.

"Unless you're on God's errand, my friend, I'll never see you again."

"I am."

The driver took a deep breath and let it out loudly, expressing his frustration. "We'll drop you off in no-man's land and then we'll have to turn around. You'll need to walk a hundred yards west. On the left side of the street, the driver of a green minivan will flash his lights three times. When you acknowledge the signal, he'll make a u-turn. You get in. The driver will ask if you're a friend of Niam's."

"Niam is the restaurant owner, right?" Thor asked.

"Yes, that's right. He thinks you're an author and that you're writing a book on the Palestinians' struggle for independence. Niam's a Palestinian Christian, which puts him in a bad spot." Isaac explained.

"His people hate him because he's not a Muslim. He thinks we hate him because he's an Arab. He wants out but he's got something we want."

"Niam bought into the PA rhetoric, Thor. The leadership said that they were fighting for all Palestinians, Muslims and Christians alike, and he believed them. So he signed up for Force 17," Isaac said, looking at his unfamiliar friend.

"That's Yasman Alafat's palace guard, his personal bodyguards. Kinda like your Secret Service except that they, like Fatah, are terrorists."

Adams shook his head. Getting an intelligence briefing from a cab driver was odd. He was beginning to feel like James Bond. "So what's he have that you want so bad?" he asked. Adams was as out of character as the cab driver, not looking the least bit like the warrior he was.

Isaac answered, "To stay alive, Niam has had to befriend the crazies. That, shall we say, makes his Christmas card list *real* interesting. We told him that we'd scratch his back if he'd scratch ours. Give us his pals' names and addresses and we'd let him and his family emigrate."

"He said no. Something about not wanting to be a traitor. So he's stuck." Stopped at the light, the driver was even more pensive.

"I'm guessing that the folks on his Christmas card list don't celebrate Christmas." The Admiral was sharp today.

"No," the cabbie snickered. "They're all Muslim militants."

"And they're in some rather interesting clubs." The whole world had come to know their names. "Islamic Jihad, Hamas, the PLO's el-Fatah, Aqsa Martyrs' Brigade, Hezbollah, and al-Qaeda. No Boy Scouts or Indian Guides."

"The Shin Bet called Niam a couple of days ago—after you got this wild idea of yours, and, well, we told him we'd appreciate some intros. No names, no addresses, no reprisals—just conversation. If it all works out, we'll cut him a deal."

He'll treat you right, but his 'friends,' that's a different story. They're heavily armed, and, well, let's put it this way: they're a few Black Hats shy of a minion." Isaac was worried, but he hadn't lost his sense of humor.

"Niam will provide introductions and will be your translator. He's well educated and speaks Arabic and English fluently."

"He thinks your name is Curt Smith."

"You'll find a wallet and passport in your pants. We used your old address in Missouri so it would be easy to remember," the Shin Bet cab driver explained. "You're married. Two daughters."

"This is it, pal, your last chance. The border is just over that rise. I'm begging you. Don't do this," the Major pleaded. "This isn't your war."

Adams slapped the top of Newcomb's leg. "I'll be fine. I've got way too much to live for to be yanking these guys' chains. I'm just going to ask some questions. I'll be nice, pretend I'm sympathetic, then bail."

Both men looked at Adams with pleading eyes, shaking their heads. They prayed he wouldn't open the door. But the man-of-war turned man-of-faith followed his calling. He lifted the latch and strode bravely toward hell.

Thor did his best to conceal his limp as he made his way through no-man's land. It was a foreboding world of desolate buildings, barbed wire, cement barriers, armed guards, and spindly olive trees struggling to grow through rubbish-laden piles of rock.

In the distance he spotted the green van. On cue it flashed its lights. Adams gave a coy wave, acknowledging the signal. The van turned around in front of him. A moment later he opened the door.

"Friend of Niam's?" the driver asked as Thor climbed inside.

"Curt," he offered, holding out his hand. "Yeah, I am."

"We're closer than brothers," the driver said, speeding off. That would be the extent of their conversation for a while.

Thor gasped as he got his first glimpse of the war-ravaged town. Buildings had been destroyed. The IDF, the Israeli Defense Forces, had done what armies do—kill people and break things.

The experience was surreal. Thor found himself flinching as children, some as young as seven or eight, darted out of boarded-up buildings into the street. Seeing Adams' non-Arab features, they turned and pointed their guns at the speeding van. *Are they toys?* He couldn't tell. They looked real, even to a trained eye. The youngsters, all boys, pulled back the actions on their weapons, giving the appearance they were chambering a round. All the while Thor wondered why they had been left unsupervised in the streets. *Why aren't these kids in school?* There wasn't an adult in sight. It seemed bizarre. *Where are their mothers? Why so many guns?*

As they turned the corner, the driver slammed on the brakes, bringing the car to a screeching halt. The Admiral flew forward against the dash. Face pressed up against the windshield, Adams saw why he'd braked so violently. Four boys, ten to twelve years old, were climbing out of a storm drain in the middle of the road. As they emerged, they rolled up their sleeves as if they wanted to pick a fight. With the van stopped, they walked menacingly toward it, shoulder to shoulder. They too were armed.

They may have been children, but Thor knew that the guns they were packing didn't discriminate based upon the age of the finger pulling the trigger. It got worse. Two of the four boys unsheathed their pistols, raising them so that they were aimed directly at his head. He saw them smile, as if it were a game. Adams was too bewildered to duck. They just stared at each other, eyes and gun barrels.

The driver took his foot off the brake, accelerating ever so slowly. As he crept forward, the boys reluctantly moved aside. Two young gunmen were now standing within a meter of Adams. The business end of their pistols scraped the window. Thor turned, looking into their eyes, trying to read their thoughts. *What on earth is happening here?*

With the road clear ahead, the driver accelerated. But the landscape didn't change. Block after block, it was the same eerie scene. They passed through a shopping district, but it was abandoned, locked up. Giant steel doors now barred what had once been a beehive of activity.

"Where are the adults? Why so many kids? Why are all the shops closed?" Adams asked. "Is it a holiday?"

"There is no business. No jobs. No money. Nobody works anymore." The driver said it matter-of-factly, like it shouldn't have been a surprise.

"And those boys back there—were the guns real?"

"Yes, but they didn't kill you."

Is that good news or bad? Adams wondered, thankful to be alive. This was unlike anyplace he had ever seen. Passing street after street of sealed doors gave the now-pudgy Admiral a sinking feeling. Poverty breeds nothing but trouble, he had come to learn.

The driver headed toward an open square. The buildings on all sides were blown apart. Once-proud signs now teetered in the breeze. Black smoke had stained their faces. Rubble covered the sidewalks; concrete and broken glass lay strewn everywhere. A desperate clash of cultures had turned this place into a war zone. And it was no distant memory, no haunting reminder of battles long past. These wounds were still open and raw; the injuries hadn't had time to heal.

The damage had been left unrepaired. Each building told a story, not unlike the burned-out villages in Vietnam. They were silent spokesmen, screaming out, "You have an enemy."

They turned a corner and suddenly everything changed. The square was alive. While there were no cars, and certainly no tourists, it was now evident where all the adults had gone. With their shops closed they had acquired a new vocation. Like the children before them, they were playing army. But this time there was no question as to whether the guns were real.

It was a motley collection of souls. Some were dressed in army fatigues, while others had stepped right out of *GQ*. Many wore tattered civilian clothes. There were no flowing robes or turbans so reminiscent of the Arabs Thor had fought in other parts of the world.

The guns they played with were an eclectic mix as well. Russian Kalashnikovs, multi-national Galiels, Israeli Uzis, and American M-16s, all with clips inserted. This spelled trouble. The glares Adams received as he sped past the townsfolk needed no translation. He was an infidel, defiling their holy ground.

A few hundred meters past the town square, the van came to an abrupt stop. Without a word, the driver opened his door, stepped out, and walked away. As he did, another Arab man rose from behind a wall, walked around the van, and climbed into the driver seat. Without saying a word, he put the car in gear, turned right, and accelerated away from the square.

"Are you Niam?" Thor asked.

"No Inglish."

They drove on in silence. Thor was beginning to think that this might not have been his all-time brightest idea. The sporadic scenes of milling gunmen added to his consternation. He shot God a line. *I'm doing this for you. Keep me safe.*

After a ten-minute eternity, the van with the stoic at the wheel stopped suddenly in front of a three-story stone building. A large man, every bit of six foot five and three hundred pounds, opened the passenger door.

"I'm Niam." He reached out his bear-like paw, grinning.

"Curt Smith."

"Follow me," His voice was reassuring. Niam wore a disarming smile.

They entered the large stone fortress of a building through a set of thick steel doors. At each turn they passed men who looked like bodyguards. Niam, with Thor a step or two behind, turned right, descended a narrow set of stairs, turned right again, and entered a large room in the basement. The scene was right out of the movies.

An eight-foot-long green Formica table occupied the center. Rugged and massive, the table was surrounded by eight utilitarian metal chairs, the kind one might expect to see in a prison. This was the only furniture in the room, giving it the appearance of an interrogation cell. The ceiling was uncomfortably low, barely six feet. The light fixtures were broken, with bulbs and wires exposed but operational. The floor was concrete, as were the walls. The only window was a small slit, up high, covered with iron bars. If the steel door was closed, no one would find him. Ever.

Maneuvering around the light fixtures, Adams plopped down, pulling out his pen and a small notepad. As he always did, he managed to find a seat facing the only exit. Men in high-risk professions never sit with their backs to trouble—or in this case, freedom.

Niam set the stage. "Your first interview will be with Fatah and their Aqsa Martyrs' Brigade. I've arranged for you to meet their Captain. He's in charge of the military wing for this region, the second largest in the country. He said he was bringing his top lieutenants. You'll have two hours to question them. After they leave, you'll meet with Hamas, Hezbollah, called Islamic Jihad here in Palestine, and al-Qaeda."

It sounded like a terrorist delicatessen.

The first contestant entered the room hesitantly, checking the darkened corners of the basement. It was as if he were walking on eggs. He was clean shaven, with short, dark hair. His dress was a cross between military and business casual. As he cautiously made his way to the table he began barking commands into a small handheld radio. In Arabic, they made little sense to Adams, but his tone was one of authority.

By the time he had reached the table, he was joined by an officer, a diminutive man dressed in smart-looking military fatigues. Seconds later a third man, tall and rugged, also in a jungle-green uniform, slid in behind the other two. He was Hollywood handsome, with a strong chin, curly hair, broad shoulders, and a near-perfect smile. He canvassed the room like a professional.

It was obvious to Adams that the leader didn't much like his strategic disadvantage, having his back to the door. Though they were in his territory, Fatah had enemies.

Niam introduced the leader by name, saying that he was a Captain. But he did so with a warning, a stipulation. He said that repeating his name would constrict the scope of the interview.

Adams acknowledged that he understood, making a pledge to keep all parties anonymous. Unlike Jews and Arabs, the Admiral had no use for reprisals; he simply wanted information—he wanted to learn.

With a nervous grin the diminutive leader reached out and accepted the Admiral's extended hand. He had a surprisingly weak handshake. His hands were thin, even frail. There were no calluses.

Sitting with his back to the door, across the table and to Adams' left, he said, "I am the most wanted man in this country." Bragging, he continued, "The Israelis' Shin Bet has me at the top of their list."

"Why?"

"They think I'm responsible for the deaths of many Jews, including the most recent killings."

"Which killings?" Thor asked, wiping his right hand on his pant leg. It was as if the urge to kill was contagious.

"The settlers on the bus to Emmanuel." He smiled, turning to face his lieutenants. They seemed equally pleased.

"That was done with rifles." Adams had read the papers.

"Yes, we prefer not to use suicide bombers. We are soldiers."

"Were you responsible for killing those eleven people?"

The leader's face erupted into another uncontrollable grin. He wiggled in his chair and tried to look away. "I will not tell you how many Jews I have killed." They had disabled the bus with explosives, then over the next few minutes had lobbed grenades at the passengers and shot them with assault rifles as they tried to escape.

"There have been *many?*"

He looked away again. He could not hold the Admiral's gaze.

Niam translated, turning the rhetorical statement into a question. The Captain nodded.

"He says yes." Niam proclaimed, almost laughing at himself. A nodding head was universal. So was the delight that was written all over the "soldier's" face.

The lieutenants shuffled in their chairs. They would have preferred to pace. They, like their leader, were very uncomfortable. Thor decided to change the subject. He already knew that terrorists killed civilians; the question was why.

"I noticed the uniforms. What organization are you part of, and why did you join?'" Niam translated seamlessly.

"Fatah. The majority of Palestinians belong, that's why."

"What is Fatah, and who is its leader?" Adams asked.

"It's a political party. We're part of the military wing of the PA. Alafat is in charge. I report to him," the leader said in a manner that questioned "Curt's" intelligence.

"I thought the PA had a police force, not an army."

The PA, or Palestinian Authority, was the sanitized and politically expedient new name for what had once been the world's largest and most heinous terrorist network, the PLO. Another acronym, it stood for Palestine Liberation Organization. More correctly, it stood for murder, kidnapping, and mayhem. Its name betrayed its Communist roots, as did the one-party system that supported it. In fact, as in the Soviet Union, the party, Fatah, preceded and superceded the government.

"Think of the PA as the government and Fatah as the party. The party has a political wing and a military one." The Captain seemed surprised by "Curt's" questions. Real journalists knew Fatah's roots and purpose.

"These gentlemen are all from the military side. They are army men." Niam stated what was clearly obvious.

"But we are not killing now," the leader said in a disappointed tone.

"The bus shooting you said you are being sought for—it was just a few days ago, wasn't it?"

"Yes. That was then. This is now. Alafat hadn't asked for a cease-fire."

"Were you involved in planning the ambush and shooting?"

"Yes, but not alone. We worked with Hamas and Islamic Jihad."

"Hamas? I thought Alafat ordered you to put Hamas members in jail."

"Yes. That is why we are looking for them."

"Yesterday they were your partner, today they're your enemy? Next week are you going to ask them to join the PA?"

"Sure. Why not?"

Following this line of reasoning, Thor asked, "If Yasman Alafat wakes up tomorrow and asks you to start killing again, will you?"

"Of course."

The Admiral was dumfounded. He had been told that Yasman Alafat was now a diplomat and that even if he had once been a terrorist, he had left that life behind. Now he was a peace-loving man, interested only in serving his people by negotiating a political settlement. He was the winner of a Nobel Peace Prize. His tools were words, not bullets. Or so the world had been led to believe.

"Why did you agree to meet with me?"

"Talking to writers is important. I did a TV interview before coming here. The world needs to understand our situation."

"What do you want us—Americans—to know?"

"That it's your fault," the diminutive leader responded crisply. It would not be the last time Thor would hear this.

"Radical Islam is America's fault—you and the Jews."

Why did he begin by pointing a finger at Islam? But this was *the* question, Adams knew, so he asked it: "Why?"

"First, you must know we are not like them. Fatah is not extreme. We do not want to push Jews into the sea. We only want them out of Palestine—out of our land." Although he didn't say it, his superiors defined Palestine to be all of Israel. It's what their maps showed. It's what they taught their children in school. Even the logo of the PLO shows *all* of Israel. "I was raised in occupation." The Captain's tone was defiant. "Our goals are reasonable; so are our methods. We only want what is rightfully ours. We want to occupy our land, to live in peace in our own state, with our own people, and our own passports. *They* are the crazy ones."

"They? You mean Hamas and Islamic Jihad?"

"Yes. They are still in the minority here, but their numbers are growing rapidly—very, very rapidly."

"Why is that?"

"You saw our town. No one is working. People are starving. And they, the leaders of Hamas and Jihad, have all the money."

"What money?"

"Before I answer, you need to know how we are suffering. No one has worked for almost sixteen months."

"Since the start of the last *intifada*, right?"

An *intifada* is a call to arms. Alafat had told his followers to terrorize the Israelis into submission. The blood bath that followed had left the parties deeply divided, each wary of the other. Barricades had replaced roads, rhetoric had replaced reason, and death had swallowed hope.

"Yes, *intifada*. Since that time we have suffered. The only way we can feed our families is with the help of other Arab nations. But their money comes with an agenda—one that causes our people to think bad thoughts—very bad thoughts."

"What do you mean?"

"They promote radical Islam. That leads to Hamas and Islamic *Jihad*."

"Islam? How does that lead to terrorist groups like these?"

"I am a Muslim. So are my men. We observe all of the holidays with our families. We adhere to many of the rituals. But they do not think like us. They are crazy, more violent."

When men crazy enough to gloat over killing a busload of innocent people call *other* people crazy, they *must* be, Thor reasoned. "Does this violent form of Islam focus on the Prophet's speeches? Is it political?"

"Yes. It is not the same as what I believe."

"Is it popular?"

"Yes. It will soon be the majority. We have very little time."

Adams had found his answer, but switched gears as he saw Fatah grow uncomfortable with the previous line of questioning. They did not want to talk about the influence of Islam.

"If you could have one or two of the following things, but not all three, which would be your biggest priority: possession of this land, political autonomy, or a productive economy—an end to poverty?"

The Captain looked at his Lieutenants. They appeared to be having a heated conversation. It was as if they wanted to give the approved answer.

"They say they want this land." Niam translated. "It is where they were born. It is the most important thing to them. Autonomy is next, followed by the economy."

"Curt Smith" scribbled notes furiously as he talked. "If you could have your own state with a vibrant economy somewhere else nearby, you'd give that up to fight over this pile of rocks?"

"Yes." He had heard them right.

Israel was little more than a rock-strewn wasteland with a violent history. Much of the land was hostile and mountainous. It was dry, and rocky to a fault. While the Jews had transformed small sections of it into productive garden oases, there was better land almost everywhere.

"You said they—the Islamic groups, Hamas and Jihad—have the money. Is that why they are growing?"

The Captain and his lieutenants looked at Curt Smith like he was from another planet. "It's the *only* reason the crazy groups are growing. Money is at the root of everything."

"But who wants groups like Hamas and Islamic Jihad to grow? Where is the money coming from?"

The Fatah leader explained, "We get money, food, and supplies from Saudi Arabia, Egypt, Kuwait, the Emirates, Iraq, and Ir...." He stopped abruptly, mid-sentence.

It appeared that the Captain had started to say Iran but had caught himself. Niam's translation had stopped at Iraq too, but the slip had not escaped Thor's notice. The truth was as obvious as the fifty tons of bombs on the Karine A. Yet denying unpleasant realities had become part and parcel of everyday life in the twilight zone.

"These countries used to just give us money, but now it's supplies and money."

"What kind of supplies do they send you?"

The Fatah Captain had to look away. As much as Adams wanted to know about the "supplies," the leader's body language made two things clear: he knew, and he wasn't going to say.

"What is the problem with giving you money?"

"With money there's too much skimming."

"What do you mean 'skimming'?" The Admiral knew the answer. He just wanted to see if the Palestinians would own up to their problem.

The combatants just stared at each other. Niam answered. "In every sector there is what you would call a mob boss. The most famous is Jube in Jericho, but they're everywhere. In Bethlehem there are many 'Jubes.' They skim money off of the top and spread the remainder among those who are the most loyal." It was shades of Mogadishu. There, Muslim warlords had skimmed food, medicines, and supplies, causing hundreds of thousands to die needlessly.

"Are supplies and money coming from the ruling families and the governments, or are they coming from more secret sources?"

"Both. The Saudi Royal family provides hundreds of millions." In truth, Saudi was the PA's single biggest supporter, to the tune of $400 million dollars a year.

"I have heard that these governments reward the families of the suicide bombers. Is that true?"

"Yes, of course."

"How much, and who pays?"

"We do not like to use suicide bombers."

"Yes, I know. You use rifles. You are soldiers." *Targeting civilians,* he thought, but didn't say. "But do you know how much is paid to the families of suicide bombers? Do you know who pays it?"

"The government of Iraq pays fifteen thousand, the Syrians, ten thousand. Iran also pays ten thousand. The Saudis have no set price, but they pay the most."

"Dollars? Shekels? What?"

"Dollars. They have lots of dollars. Your dollars."

"But there is more," the diminutive Lieutenant added. "The families are taken care of for the rest of their lives. They are given the best housing, all the best things. Other sons are even offered the most beautiful women. The rest of their children get free university educations." He sounded jealous. His people had been taught to hate, and they were being rewarded for it. The Palestinians had become mercenaries.

"Sometimes they get even more," the tall Lieutenant said. "You know the story of the Palestinian girl and mother who were shot by the Israeli soldier?"

Thor nodded. He had seen the film on CNN five or six years before. It was a haunting example of what fear can do to a man's judgment in the stress of combat. To their credit, Adams recalled, the Israelis had put the soldier in jail and apologized to the world for his behavior.

"The woman's husband received over one million dollars from Saudi's King Fahd, King Hussein, and the Sultan of Brunei. It was a reward for the good it had done our cause."

"The money from Iran and Syria goes to Hezbollah mostly, then Hamas," he claimed, supporting the party line. "The Syrians and the Iranians do not care so much about the Palestinian people. But it is good for them to have agents here who will follow their orders."

"You Americans are often fooled by the Iranians, I think. You did not know why they offered to support the U.S. in Afghanistan."

"Why did they?"

He smiled. "They knew that as soon as you were gone, they would step in and control the government. Last time the Pakistanis financed the Taliban. Now it is the Iranians' turn to control Afghanistan. They are all neighbors, you know."

The moment the Americans had lost interest, that very thing had happened. Warlords had crawled out of the ruins and swarmed down upon the people, all too eager to use their Iranian weapons to kill their brothers.

"Is there a relationship between Hezbollah and Islamic Jihad? Are these the favorites of the Iranians?"

"They are the same, really. Yes. You should know the Syrians and the Iranians are very close. They do many things together."

"You said earlier that these groups were growing very fast—Hamas, Hezbollah, Islamic Jihad. When did they start growing, and will they become the majority?"

"Radical Islam started to grow with the first *intifada* in '88. It took off following the Oslo accords. It became much worse after the failed Camp David meetings with Clinton. That's when Sharon came to power. Now it is all about the money. You buy support here with dollars."

"How?"

"Everyone is out of work. There is no economy. Would you let your children starve, or would you accept their money?" the Captain asked rhetorically. "Do you think they just give it away out of kindness?"

Niam talked with them in Arabic and summarized in English. "If you accept their money and their food, you must accept their authority and their way of thinking—their form of Islam. They all have people. They assign someone to every family that accepts their money. Soon everybody is thinking the same way."

"You go along or starve," one of the Lieutenants added.

"You get what you pay for," the Fatah Captain interjected. "If you had money, you could buy loyalty too," he said with a devilish grin. "Support comes from dollars. Sometimes it's even *your* dollars."

"What do you mean?"

"Your government gives the Egyptian government two point seven billion dollars a year. Some of that money comes right here, through tunnels into Gaza. The Egyptians don't like the Palestinian people either. Their money goes to Hamas and Islamic Jihad."

What he had said was true. The Israelis had offered to give the Gaza Strip back to the Egyptians, but they wouldn't take it. What wasn't true was Egypt's promise. Israel had returned the Sinai in exchange for peace. Yet the Egyptians were among the largest suppliers of war materials to the Islamic militants, including Russian-made SAM missiles. Worse, their schools, mullahs, and media were the most vitriolic—openly preaching and teaching that Jews and Americans should die. A dollar doesn't buy what it used to.

"What about the Oslo accords caused militant Islam to grow?"

"The Israelis cheated. Their government was taken over by the radical parties, the Shas and the Likud. They built more settlements on our land."

"Did you know that we were trained by the Americans?" the most handsome of the terrorists asked.

"We not only pay you to kill Jews, we train you too?" Adams asked.

"Yes," the Lieutenant replied brightly. "My friend and I were trained in the United States, in Virginia, by the CIA."

"We were there forty days. There were nineteen of us," the other said.

"As we got ready to land, they made us put our window screens down. We were blindfolded during the drive, too." The first Lieutenant smiled.

"You said it was in Virginia. What part?"

"It was a base of some kind. There were many trees, giant trees, and a big body of water, a sea or a bay."

"Fatah gets help from America. We are good friends," the terrorist said. "You pay us about a hundred million dollars a year."

Adams lifted his mock glasses to rub his eyes. He was trying to comprehend what he had heard. *How could America be so stupid? Who was making these decisions?* "What does Fatah want?"

"We want pre-1967 borders. UN Resolutions 181 and 242."

Thor scribbled down another note. He was thinking. If all they wanted was pre-'67 borders, why did they attack in '67? This made no sense. Not only was the West Bank part of Jordan at the time, and Gaza part of Egypt, Alafat's PLO was at war with Jordan. *I just don't get it.* The fact that Nasser had said the object of the '67 War was to destroy Israel might have been a clue.

But the Admiral knew that line of questioning would lead to trouble, so he tried a different approach. The angels were already working overtime. "Back at the end of the Clinton administration in 2000, the Palestinians were offered most everything they wanted. Why did your Chairman turn it down?"

"Not *everything*," the Captain said. "We were not given Jerusalem."

"You were offered *east* Jerusalem, including the Jewish Temple Mount. The agreement would have given you ninety-five percent of the West Bank and all of Gaza. Statehood. This land we're in right now."

They conferred among themselves in Arabic. "The refugee problem. That's why we turned it down."

Alafat wanted Arabs to flood back into what he called Palestine. The more the merrier. While those who were here were breeding like rabbits, with an average of seven children to a family, they were still outnumbered by Jews two to one. But if the immigration floodgates were opened and another five million Arabs were allowed to enter, they would instantly be in the majority. Mind you, Alafat's PA couldn't take care of those who lived under its domination, so wanting more was clearly political. And there was one other little detail Alafat failed to mention when he cried for the "right of return for Palestinian refugees." Any of the few hundred thousand adults at the time of "exile" would be seventy-five today.

"Those claiming to be Palestinians already have a state in which you are the majority. You represent seventy percent of Jordan, and thanks to the Syrian invasion, you control Lebanon as well. Why aren't those Palestinian states? Or why not go to Egypt, Iraq, Iran, Saudi Arabia? They have plenty of land. And they all say they love you—the Prince, the Ayatollah, the King, Emir."

"Don't go there," Niam suggested. "I don't think it is wise."

Thor sighed. He knew the real answer anyway. There really was no such thing as the "Palestinian People." It was a myth, a marketing ploy. They were just Arabs with an attitude. The chip on their shoulder was the only thing that made them different from the other hundreds of millions of Arabs surrounding Israel. And it was why no one wanted them.

The land had originally been called Canaan, named after Abraham's uncle twice removed. When Abe had settled there, about 2000 B.C., the Canaanites, Perizzites, and a few other tribes inhabited the land. By the time of the Exodus, in the mid-1400s, they had been joined by the Hittites, Jebusites, and Amorites. Between Joshua's conquest, begun in 1406, and Israel's golden age under David, about 1000 B.C., these peoples had all but disappeared.

But as the Jews had risen in numbers and power, two coastal nations had reigned in small niches in the north and south of the Promised Land. The Philistines were located near today's Gaza, and the Phoenicians, in today's Lebanon. The Assyrian conquest in the seventh century B.C., followed by the Babylonian invasion in the sixth, had not spared these seafaring peoples. They, like the Canaanites before them, had vanished without a trace.

Unlike the now-extinct Philistines, the Jews returned to Judea after seventy years of Babylonian captivity, only to witness successive waves of conquest. In 70 A.D., however, the Jews were once again exiled from their ancestral homeland. Finally, in a desperate attempt to sever the Jews' emotional attachment to Judea, the Romans invented the name "*Palestinia*" in 135 A.D. However, Israel's national memory was not so easily obliterated. They never forgot that this rocky piece of ground between the Jordan River and the Mediterranean Sea was their homeland, no matter what their overlords insisted on calling it.

After the fall of Rome, the moniker *Palestinia* was largely forgotten, a mere historical footnote. That is, until the end of World War I. Following the defeat of the Turks, the British dusted off the old Roman epithet, incorrectly referring to Judea as "Palestine." The indigenous Arabs, who until that time had called the place Syria, took the name upon themselves, though they were genetically unrelated to the Philistines of old. But by calling themselves Palestinians and the land Palestine it caused the world to think it was theirs and that the Jews were trespassing. However, there have been no "Palestinian" people for the last 2,600 years. And there has never been a Palestinian state outside of Gaza.

Niam was getting progressively more nervous, constantly looking at his watch. The second set of terrorists had called him repeatedly on his cell phone, asking if the coast was clear. The first meeting had run a little long, and thanks to recent events, there was discord growing among the Muslim militants. The PLO's Fatah was now *hunting* Hamas and Islamic Jihad. The first group had to leave before the second could arrive.

Adams knew that it was all a charade. In previous days he had talked to enough Arabs to understand the game they were playing. Alafat had come under pressure from America and Europe to diminish terrorist killings. Reining in terror was his sole responsibility. His promise at Oslo to do this very thing is why the Israelis gave Alafat what neighboring Arabs would not—territory and autonomy. But as time would prove, his promise was worthless. With Jews out of his autonomous regions, terror increased rapidly. And rather than admit that his own party, Fatah, had been responsible, Yasman blamed the atrocities on Hezbollah, Hamas, and Islamic Jihad—and even on the Jews. He had promised the West that he would put the offending parties in jail.

In actuality Fatah jailed but a handful of foot soldiers. They were taken from their homes with a promise of good food, a comfortable stay, and a quick release. According to Thor's Palestinian sources, the terrorists were even told that the only reason they were being jailed was to appease the gullible Americans. This reality became painfully obvious moments later. When Niam told Fatah that they had to go so the meetings with Hamas and Jihad could begin, they laughed.

And so it was. Within seconds of Fatah saying goodbye, Thor found himself shaking hands with an entirely different breed of terror. These fine folks were introduced as Islamic Jihad, Hamas, and al-Qaeda. Unlike their predecessors, their uniforms were not coordinated. They had evidently not been trained by the CIA, nor were they supported by the U.S. Government or the European Union, the PA's most vocal benefactor.

The Hamas representative was a tall, lean young man. Clean shaven and soft spoken, he carried an assault rifle, clip inserted and safety off. He proceeded to place the weapon on the table before him.

"How did you get your M-16?" was Adams' first question. Although he was intimately familiar with the gun, it looked different, somehow larger and more deadly, from this vantage point.

The M-16 was America's rifle. Born in the Vietnam conflict, it was considerably more sophisticated than the venerable Russian Kalashnikov, the AK-47, of which 50 million were in circulation worldwide. While Thor had fired both, he preferred the M-16. With its tighter tolerances, it was lighter and more accurate. But its precision was also its downfall. The heavier Kalashnikov required little or no care while the American gun was temperamental and required careful maintenance. An AK-47 could be buried in a swamp, dug up, and fired without missing a beat.

"I can't buy an M-16 and I'm an American," the "author" exclaimed.

"Made in America," the Hamas member said proudly, patting the menacing rifle. "Would you like one? I sold my land to buy this gun."

Although the line, "I sold my land to buy this gun," betrayed an incredible lack of devotion to this land they were willing to kill for, Thor, for safety's sake, ignored the relevance.

"Sure, I'd like one. How much?"

"I paid twenty-five hundred dollars for mine," he said. "But since the last *intifada,* the price has gone up. Now they're seven thousand dollars. The Jews sell them to us—black market."

Adams knew that M-16s were manufactured in Israel, under license. They cost but a few hundred dollars to make. "Why do you need an assault rifle?"

"To protect myself from Israelis."

"But I don't see any Israelis here, not on this side of the border. So why are you armed?"

"I must be ready to protect myself. The Qur'an says that we have to fight. But we should prepare ourselves first, and not hurry into battle."

"I have read the Qur'an. I don't recall that verse."

Surprised that an American had read the Qur'an, he admitted, "Although the Qur'an says something similar, my quote is from one of the Prophet's, peace be onto him, speeches."

"I see. Is it from one recorded by Ibn Ishaq, his earliest biographer, or is it in the Hadith, Al-Bukhari's True Traditions perhaps?"

"No. It's from a much newer source. But it's proven to be accurate. Hamas maintains a large library of Islamic books, and they are used to compile and prove the newer ones."

"Ah! What is the most popular of these 'newer ones?'" Adams inquired.

"*Ryad Elsalehin,*" he said. "It has many of the Prophet's speeches."

Thor asked Niam for the spelling to make sure he had written it down correctly. The Hamas member, attired in his finest bluish-green quasi-military jumpsuit, replied, "I'll buy one and send it to you."

"Thank you. You're most kind."

"You know killing is not a hobby for us." The smaller of the two Islamic Jihad members spoke. Both looked rather scraggily, sporting rough, short-cropped beards and curly, ill-mannered hair. If you called central casting asking for terrorists, these boys would fit the bill.

"Then why do you do it? I assume you do. I mean, after all," the "writer" said, pointing to the M-16, "those things have been know to hurt people."

They all nodded, sporting menacing grins. "They have killed far more of us than we have them. The Jews have murdered sixty-eight Palestinians in Bethlehem alone, many of them young."

Maybe they're better shots, Adams thought but said, "They've got bigger guns."

"They fight with *your* guns," the al-Qaeda member finally spoke. He had been quiet, surveying the situation. He was an unattractive man, older than the others, with a pitted face, crooked teeth, and thinning hair. "They kill us with your tanks and Apache Gunships."

The tanks the Israelis made themselves. They would have made their own aircraft as well, but the U.S. insisted they buy American.

The more aggressive of the Islamic Jihad members said, "You Americans need to learn how to hold the bat."

"Hold the bat?" Adams had no idea what he was talking about.

"Yes. Rather than beat us with it, you need to learn how to hold it in the middle. You need to understand our problems."

"Why is that? Why are the problems of Hamas, Islamic Jihad, and al-Qaeda America's problems? Why should we care?"

"We all have many members in America. Abu Marzook is the head of Hamas. He lives in America."

"Why doesn't America support our people, understand our problems?" the al-Qaeda terrorist asked. "You only support Israel."

Adams couldn't resist the urge to teach—to see if truth would find fertile ground. Besides, he figured answering a question or two might take the conversation in interesting new directions. So he replied, "It's because Israel is the only democracy in the region. Every Arab nation is a dictatorship. America sides with freedom, with democracies. We were against Russia when they were Communists, but supportive when they became a democracy. We share common values with Israel—freedom of speech, freedom of religion, freedom of the press." *Rational behavior,* he thought but didn't say. "There are no such freedoms in any Arab nation. That's why we Americans support Israel."

The assembled had no pre-set response to Adams' explanation. The Jihad members were silent, arms crossed. Al-Qaeda glared. The Hamas gunman began reciting Muhammad's speeches in Arabic again.

Niam told "Smith" that his guests were growing progressively more irritated. "Considering who is holding the guns, that isn't good."

"If you want us to hold the bat in the middle and support your cause, why kill Americans? Tell me, why did Muslim militants fly those planes into the World Trade Center?" It probably wasn't the best question Thor could have asked under the circumstances.

"You deserved it," the al-Qaeda member shot back defiantly, displaying his hostility. His eyes narrowed. His face tensed. His hand moved ever so slightly toward the nine-millimeter bulge in his coat.

"Your government's policies caused it to happen." The Jihad members agreed. It hadn't been their doing.

"We have no quarrel with the American people, only the government," Mr. Hamas said, stroking his rifle.

Thor's blood was boiling. He wasn't much of a poker player and didn't know if he could hide his emotions. "There were no government officials in those buildings—just innocent people. Why did you kill them?"

"You allowed it to happen. Al-Qaeda was used by the Americans and the Jews," the Hamas terrorist explained as al-Queda snickered.

"*Used?*"

"Yes. The Mossad used the attack like a man uses a hammer."

"The *Mossad?* What evidence do you have of any of this?"

"It is common knowledge here. We see such things on the TV."

"Al Jazeera?" the Admiral asked.

"Yes. But on all the other Arabic stations too." The Jihad members took turns answering.

"How do you explain the fact that five thousand Jews who worked in the World Trade Center were told to stay home the day of the attack?"

Adams was stunned. "I'll tell you what. If you believe that bull, then you need to produce some evidence to prove it. Saying that the Jews were responsible for using al-Qaeda to kill Americans has got to be the dumbest thing I've ever heard." *Next to Islam,* he thought.

Although Adams couldn't be sure, he guessed Niam's Arabic version of his inflammatory statement lost something in the translation.

Welcome to the twilight zone. Reason was dead. Long live rage. Arabs were as willing to be duped today as they were during the days of Muhammad.

"The Jews started Hamas, you know," the slender fellow in the blue jumpsuit said, turning the tables on the Admiral.

It was true. They had done so to control the PLO by providing them with an antagonist. But it hadn't worked out exactly as they'd planned.

In an earlier discussion with a former Force 17 member, Thor had learned that Alafat had formed alliances between his Fatah, Hamas, Hezbollah, and Islamic Jihad. The informant reported being present when Alafat planned joint operations to terrorize Israelis. According to the Force 17 member, they all accepted Yasman's orders without complaint. Alafat's signature on orders to kill Jews and reward their murderers had been made available to the Admiral, confirming this. It was hardly a secret.

"And the Americans started al-Qaeda," one of its members said, now trying to rub it in.

That wasn't true, even though it was interesting that he had said it. America had used the *Mujahadin* to fight the Russians. Al-Qaeda also supported the *Mujahadin*, which made the U.S. a brief ally. And it had served America's and humanity's interests. Seeing thousands of Russian boys come home in body bags had jolted Russian mothers, causing them to rebel against the war. This contributed to freeing them, hundreds of millions of people, from the shackles of Communism. In reality, a Palestinian had started al-Qaeda.

"I still don't understand," Thor said. "Why did Muslim militants, mostly from Saudi Arabia, fly those planes into our buildings?"

"We did it to lash out at your government for its policies." They were unable to see the conflict between accepting credit and blaming the Jews. They wanted it both ways.

"Then why attack commercial buildings?"

"Because they are an economic symbol. We wanted to hurt America's economy," the al-Qaeda terrorist snarled.

"Why?"

"The economy pays for the military, and your military is killing our children."

"Killing your *children?* Where?"

"America is killing babies in Afghanistan, in Somalia, and in Iraq. The American government wants to kill our children. That is why we had to take revenge. We had to make America pay."

"America went to Somalia to *stop* the warlords from killing children! We brought food to feed starving Muslims. What on earth are you talking about? We did the same thing in Lebanon and in Afghanistan. How can you say that America wants to kill innocent children?"

"Because it is true. We have all seen it on TV," one of the Jihad members insisted.

"But I have seen the baby killing with my own eyes. I was trained by al-Qaeda in the Sudan. I served in Somalia. I was headed to Afghanistan before the bombings. They sent me here, to Palestine, instead."

Maintaining his composure was the battle of his life. Adams would have liked to have ripped these deceptions from their minds. The hateful lies they had been fed would surely fester and grow until they resulted in the deaths of more innocent people. But the battle could not be won in this room.

The delusion would have been bad enough if it had been limited to this one absurdity, or just to terrorists. But sadly, the insanity was contagious. It had infected the masses. Millions had swallowed the lie. It had been broadcast by the Arab media, preached by the Islamic clerics, taught in Muslim schools, and reinforced by their dictators. They had been conditioned to hate and to blame their violent acts on their victims.

During an earlier interview with a Palestinian businessman, Adams had been told—with a straight face—that terrorist suicide bombings were all directed by the Shin Bet. Dumfounded, he had laughed out loud at the absurdity. But now these Palestinian terrorists sat before him justifying their outlandish claims by saying that they were not alone in their belief. It was as if a lie had become true simply because it was seductive enough to fool so many. "All Palestinians believe the same thing," they said. "So it must be true."

Arabs, apparently, were responsible for nothing, including the suicide bombings they were celebrating. Their rationale was that their attacks ultimately hurt the Palestinians more than the Jews. Therefore, it must have been the Jews that arranged them. They said that when Israel's Prime Minister needed an excuse to roll tanks into Palestinian areas, he simply told the Shin Bet to direct Hamas to send out another bomber. Thor couldn't believe his ears. *Nobody* was this dumb.

"Can you boys handle the truth?" Thor asked four blank faces. "When I landed here in Israel, I was greeted by a nation in mourning. The Shin Bet had sent a missile into a car, killing a Hamas leader, a murderer, but also killing a small child riding with him. This brought everyone I met to their knees, nearly to tears. What you've told me couldn't be farther from the truth."

"It is what we see. It is what we hear, what we read. It is what happens here. It is what we believe." Goebbels would have been proud.

"In Gaza, Israelis targeted a group of little girls on their way to school. They murdered them," the murderer said.

"You're saying that Israeli soldiers specifically sought out little girls and shot them in cold blood?"

"Yes."

"What I've seen here is just the opposite. I see Americans and Jews saddened when innocents are injured, while I see your people celebrate in the streets. The coffins of suicide bombers responsible for killing Jewish children are carried in great celebrations. You call the murderers martyrs." Thor was not making friends. He was putting himself in harm's way. He was making Niam very nervous.

"Well, if America's goal is not to kill children, then it is to test their newest weapons. You are using the World Trade Center as an excuse to test your weaponry on our people," the al-Qaeda operative said.

"And it is good for American arms sales too. That is another reason."

"You think Americans purposely look for reasons to kill Muslim babies so that we can test and sell our weapons? Did I hear you correctly?"

"Yes. That is common knowledge here. We all know it." They were nodding their heads in unison. Their eyes cried out, "I hate you!"

"America needs to prove that it is the most powerful nation. You Americans want to conquer and dominate the world," Hamas said.

Clearly uncomfortable with the direction the discussion had gone, Niam suggested they all have a cup of tea. The idea somehow seemed totally out of character coming from this huge man.

The scene was surreal. An elegant flowered china tea set with matching cups was brought down to the basement by a bodyguard. Looking at the elegant tray, Thor continued to ask questions, but Niam simply ignored him, focusing on serving the tea instead. He knew the conversation had gotten out of hand, too heated for anyone's good.

"He's ignoring me," Thor said to the terrorists. "I don't think our friend Niam can do more than one thing at a time." They laughed, understanding everything Adams had said.

Mr. Hamas was in a zone all his own. He busied himself reciting scripture, thumbing something that looked like prayer beads while stroking his M-16. This one image was worth a thousand words.

"Would you like one lump or two?" the taller of the Islamic Jihad members asked "Curt Smith" as he held the silver sugar spoon above the ceramic bowl.

"None, thank you." Adams had already received enough lumps.

As Niam had hoped, the tea had a quieting effect on the room. It's harder to say hateful things while holding a delicate porcelain teacup with your pinky out.

Sipping his tea, the Admiral asked a more genteel question, the same thing he had asked Fatah. "If you could have this land, a vibrant economy, or your own independent state, which would you prefer?"

Once again this question stirred a lively debate.

"We want our land." They all nodded.

"What makes this *your* land?" Good question, Thor.

"Because it is mentioned seven times in the Qur'an." Not surprisingly, this response came from the most religious terrorist, Mr. Hamas.

"Jerusalem alone is mentioned hundreds of, maybe a thousand, times in the Hebrew and Christian Bibles. So why isn't it *our* land?"

"I won't translate that statement." Niam said. "Why don't you have some more tea?"

"This is our holy land. The Prophet, peace be onto him, flew here on his Night's Journey. Therefore, it belongs to us."

By that logic, the Admiral thought, *Paris should belong to Lindbergh.*

Quoting from speeches again, the Hamas member said, "Muhammad told us that it was our duty to own a piece of Jerusalem. According to our religion, any land that we have occupied is *our* land. We must fight for our land. We must do as he instructed. Palestine is part of *dar al-Islam.*"

"I understand that he said these things, but why fight with suicide bombers?" He looked directly at the man in the blue jumpsuit.

"There are seventy virgins waiting for me in Paradise as my reward."

The "me" and "my" were of concern to Adams, as was the smoldering twinkle in the terrorist's eye. But nothing was as chilling as the man's smile—a serene, thin smile, between a smirk and a sneer. It screamed that he was ready, even eager, to die. For Mr. Hamas, paradise was calling; the virgin whores were whispering his name, motioning for him to slip into their lair. It was all so real to him. He faded inward, seeing himself in their midst. His eyes glazed over. The conversation stalled. The room grew still, cold, deathly silent. The only things growing were the size of his grin, a gloating attitude, and his arousal. The martyr-in-waiting reached down into his pocket and adjusted his gun. Thor closed his eyes and prayed, *Oh God, no!*

Paradise for these disturbed souls was nothing more than a place of sexual exploitation, a fleshy world of exotic fantasies. Adams had heard about such things, but seeing and hearing them from one on the cusp of the illusion was mortifying.

More chilling still was that this bizarre promise of virgins was universally known, pervasive in this culture. Islam's leading Egyptian cleric had proclaimed that men would have everlasting erections in Paradise. Suicide bombers, captured when their devices had failed to explode, had revealed that they were doing it for the promise of incredible sex. Most had even wrapped their privates with considerable care so as to protect them from the blast of the bombs they were carrying on their bodies.

Sadly, the promises that had driven so many young men to madness, the promises that had killed thousands of Americans and Jews, had come from the Islamic clerics themselves, from the imams, from the mosques, from the Islamic scriptures.

"It is our reward for fighting the infidels, for martyrdom." The more diminutive member of Islamic Jihad revealed. As a leader, he had most certainly gotten his fill of sexual pleasure from prostitutes here on earth and was therefore less attracted by the lure of otherworldly desire. He knew, of course, that Allah condoned such behavior in the 70th surah. Islam indeed, had something to offer everyone. The media had even studied such things and discovered that the most frequent users of prostitutes in the Promised Land were ultra-orthodox Jews and devout Muslims.

"Those who fight should receive a great reward; for we are suffering," The al-Qaeda member snarled vengefully. He resented, envied, and hated America and Americans all at the same time. Thor's very presence disgusted him. The only reason he had agreed to come was the prospect of getting his views published in the Western media.

"Our Prophet has promised paradise to every martyr."

"You cannot blame him for being hostile, for feeling as he does," Niam said of the Hamas member. "The Israelis beat his brother. He is angry and seeks revenge. In Islam it is part of his religion." Niam pointed to the terrorist seated to the Admiral's right. "His father was also beaten. He too is seeking revenge. It will burn inside until it is satisfied."

"So Islam requires them to kill—a life for a life. As I understand it, the Israelis say the same thing. But who shot first? Does anyone remember?" Thor asked Niam as he canvassed the faces of the assembled mob.

Again Adams knew the answer. Again the terrorists were silent. They knew as well. In 1948, the moment the UN resolution had passed, awarding the Jews two tenths of one percent as much land they had given the Arabs, the Arabs had attacked, wanting it all. 99.8 percent had not been enough. *They* began an unprovoked massacre of Jews. On May 15th Azzam Pasha, the Secretary General of the Arab League, predicted, "A war of annihilation, a colossal massacre that will be remembered alongside the Crusades." *They* had drawn first blood.

So as not to spill any of his own on the ugly green table, "Curt Smith" shifted gears. "Before the Oslo accords, the Palestinians were the freest and most prosperous Arabs in the world. I am having trouble understanding why you'd prefer this land and statehood over returning to a decent way of life for your people."

Niam wrung his giant hands nervously, but he translated the question.

"The Qur'an says...." The Hamas terrorist stopped, recognizing his error. "Muhammad, peace be onto him, taught us that he has no use for a nation that eats the bread of another."

"If we have our own land and our own state, we will make our own economy," one of the Islamic Jihad members agreed with him.

"Your position is not consistent with the facts. At Oslo you were given autonomy over cities like Ramallah, Bethlehem, Jericho, and Gaza in return for ending terrorism. The Israelis removed their police protection, and the PA was put in charge. But autonomy has brought poverty, anarchy, and violence to your people. Do you want more of these things?"

"I do not wish to translate this," Niam said.

"I want you to. Please...." Adams motioned in the direction of the al-Qaeda member. Niam refused.

"We are suffering because the Israelis have cheated on the Oslo Accords," one of the terrorists blurted out, absolving himself and his people of responsibility. It was one of only two things they seemed to be good at. Their latest deception in this regard was the politicizing of suicide bombers. If they were a political response, and not inspired by Islam, then someone else was responsible—the Jews, perhaps.

"How has their cheating hurt your economy?"

"They built tunnels under Jerusalem when they weren't supposed to. They built new settlements on our land, and did not expand our borders."

"I can understand how these things might make you angry, sir, but how do they impact your *economy?*"

That stumped the killers. Following an Arabic discussion, they tried a different tack. "The reason is because they have blockaded our borders. There are no tourists."

"I don't understand. I was not questioned as I came through the checkpoint. Tourists are free to come here. There are no tourists here because there are no tourists *anywhere* in Israel. Your *intifada* caused that. You have to be crazy to come here. Besides, you have bombed our buildings, poisoned our people with anthrax, and killed Jews and Americans with suicide bombers. That tends to discourage tourists."

"We had to call *intifada.*"

"Why? And is its purpose to kill Jews?"

"Yes, they occupy our land. We had no choice. Sharon marched into al Aqsa mosque with ten thousand troops. Our leaders called for *intifada* the next day. The Likud party and the Shas, the black hats, are radical...."

"He marched into your mosque, you say? Why would he go into al-Aqsa? It is of no significance to the Jews."

"He went into the Dome of the Rock." The terrorists were obviously making this up as they went along.

"Are you sure?"

"It was the Temple Mount. He went there to prove that Muslims were under his control."

"Isn't the Temple Mount the holiest of all places for Jews? After all, it's called the *Temple* Mount, not the *Mosque* Mount."

"Tea! We need more tea," Niam pleaded. "Please, Mr. Smith," he said, "do not go there. They have guns."

"By calling the *intifada* you ended any chance for a peaceful settlement. Both sides have become hardened by the killing." Thor demonstrated his point visually by pounding his closed fists together. "Now what?"

"More killing, if that is what it takes. We will never give up. We will always fight for our land."

"Tell me, you are constantly quoting from the speeches of Muhammad, yet he was not a Palestinian. Most Muslims don't even like the Palestinians. So what's more important to you, following Islam or fighting for this land?"

"Islam is more important, much more important than anything else." They all nodded in unison. "We are *dar al-Islam*—the Nation of Islam."

"Then why do you kill? I was told Islam is a peaceful religion."

"The Prophet, peace be onto him, commanded us to kill."

"Do you fight in the name of Allah?"

As they spoke Adams studied their body language, he gazed into their eyes. He could see that they were restless, troubled. They seemed out of touch, detached from reality.

"Yes. *Jihad* is fighting in Allah's Cause."

Thor had just confirmed why Muslim terrorize and kill. But he knew that showing his disgust, his righteous indignation, would be lethal. And he needed to live long enough to report what he had learned to the world. So Adams returned to a previous line of questioning. "How else did the Jews hurt the Palestinian economy?"

The taller of the two Islamic Jihad members offered to pour him another cup of tea. Once again he asked, "Sugar? One lump or two?"

Thor just shook his head.

"They slowed the flow of European money to our people."

So much for the Prophet's admonition not to eat the bread of another nation, Adams thought. *Now they want charity.*

In reality, the reason for the brief suspension of European charity had been their frustration with graft. Thor had met with regional development leaders who told horror stories of French, British, and German officials giving money, only to have a PA warlord confiscate it.

"They also ended our jobs. Two hundred and fifty thousand Palestinian jobs were taken away."

"Imagine that," the admiral/writer said. "You kill their women and children with suicide bombers, and all of a sudden they don't want you to work for them any more."

Niam didn't bother translating.

"They need us and we need them. We need their jobs and they need us to do their work."

"Based upon what has happened after Oslo, returning to an economic interdependence is impossible. In fact, if you are given statehood, the roadblocks will turn into massive gates; gates that will never open. The fences will become enormous walls. There will be less freedom of movement when you are left to police yourselves, not more. In fact, there will be none. I don't know if the Jews will put the walls around you or around themselves, but there will be walls, I can assure you of that. Giant, impenetrable walls. Walls that will make the Iron Curtain look like a curb."

The truth was clear. Autonomy was not in the Arab peoples' interest. All things Israeli were better than the best of Arab thuggery. The Palestinians had become murdering parasites, killers who needed to be contained.

"They have hurt us in more ways than taking away all of our jobs. They do not give us the chemical fertilizers we need for the land."

And I thought there was enough mental manure here to go around. "Curt Smith" scribbled down another note. "How do you survive with no one working?" the pretend writer posed.

"We get money from the Syrians and the Iranians. We also get some from Iraq, Egypt, and Saudi Arabia."

"Money buys loyalty here. We get money from America, too, from charities, tax free," they smiled. "But not enough."

"They have cut down our olive trees, you know." Actually they were Israeli olive trees, and they were only cut down alongside the roads because Fatah snipers were hiding behind them shooting Israeli citizens. But it made the Jews sound mean spirited, and that was the point.

"They have not paid their taxes to us. They have withheld over two hundred million shekels."

"Sorry," Thor answered. "The Israelis *have* paid the lion's share of the import duties they collected. Your own PA Ministers have told me this. They also acknowledge that PA officials got their hands caught in the cookie jar, skimming." Alafat himself had skimmed over five hundred million.

The terrorists ignored the affront to their collective character. They simply plowed ahead with their grievances. "They have stolen our water."

"The majority of the water Israelis use comes from the watershed around the Sea of Galilee. How is this yours?"

They just stared at him. This wasn't as much fun as they'd expected. They had become accustomed to the press letting them bellyache. They didn't like being challenged.

"They have expanded their settlements!"

"I'll grant you this. Building settlements in Gaza is brain dead. But I have seen those in the West Bank. They are built on the top of rocky hills—a security measure—not on fertile land. How does this hurt your economy?" There was no answer, only animosity, so the Admiral continued. "Who provides you with electricity, fresh water, roads, the gas you put in your cars? Whose currency are you using?" The Israelis provided all these things.

"When we are independent, we will do it all ourselves."

"If you *can* do these things, why haven't you?" Adams asked four blank stares.

The Palestinians simply returned to their tale of woe. "They have bombed and ransacked our hotels. All for what?" the al-Qaeda member asked. "Just because we shot our M-16s and Kalashnikovs into some of their homes. They were very far away. How much damage can be done by an M-16 at the range of five hundred meters?"

"Who lives in those houses you were shooting at?" Adams asked.

"Israelis."

"Do they have children?"

"I suppose."

"When you aim at their windows, don't you think you might kill them?"

"Very few. Less than six have died from this shooting. It is not an excuse to roll tanks into our cities."

"I thought you said you bought these rifles to protect yourselves. Isn't that what *they* are doing?"

They didn't answer, so Adams posed another question. "Will you accept responsibility for any of your problems? Or is everything the fault of the Jews and the Americans?"

Niam let out a heavy sigh.

"Yes, I know, my friend. You wish I would shut up and have some more tea." The Admiral had done enough damage for one afternoon. "No, actually it's late," he said. "The sun has gone down. I must be going."

With that everyone stood. They collected their weapons and escorted

Adams out the door. As they did there was a considerable amount of Arabic chatter in the background.

"We have trouble," Niam whispered in Thor's ear. "They don't think you're a writer. They think you are with the CIA."

The Admiral tried his best to hide his fear. "Tell them...."

"I already have." Niam interrupted. "We must get you out of here. I have called for the car." An uneasy quiet followed as al-Qaeda, Islamic Jihad, Hamas, a former member of Force 17, and an American hero disguised as a pudgy author milled about in the darkness.

The van provided little relief. The taller of the two Jihad terrorists jumped into the seat behind Adams. The other three Muslim brothers, guns bristling, hopped into a chase car. Together, they sped off into the night. The Admiral looked up at the reddish crescent moon hanging low in the sky. *How appropriate.*

The silence was deafening as both vans sped through the deserted and potholed streets of Bethlehem. In a confusing series of right and left turns, they made their way up and down the hilly roads, past cratered and barricaded buildings.

The lead van, the one carrying the Admiral, stopped abruptly. The driver got out, as did the accompanying member of Islamic Jihad. A new driver emerged, said nothing as he got behind the wheel, and drove away. Adams looked back. Thankfully, the chase car was gone. He knew from familiar landmarks that he was close to the border. It was the longest drive of his life. His heart pounded; his pulse raced.

Then he saw, off in the distance, the lights of Jerusalem. The border was less than two minutes away. The street was torn up where tanks had recently passed. Power lines were down. This was clearly a war zone, one in which the Admiral was ill prepared to fight.

Speeding along the rim of an exposed canyon, the van made a series of abrupt turns. Finally he saw it: no-man's land was less than half a mile ahead. The driver eased forward, then stopped suddenly. He looked panicked, motioning for "Curt" to get out.

Fearing that he would be shot in the back before reaching the relative safety of Israel, the would-be author hurried as fast as his wounded body would carry him. He thought of Sarah and Mary, of his Jewish comrades, of his nation, of the world. In a moment he would be back in the land of reason, but Thor Adams was a different man from the one who had crossed this barren divide five hours earlier. He now carried a burden heavier than he could have imagined.

18

OFFENSIVE

If he hadn't been such an emotional wreck, Anwar Abu would have engaged his ten prostitutes and had himself a ball. After all, the boys were gone, delivering the goods. The girls, however, were not. This was a matter of prudence, not perversion. Back on duty, Omen thought the lusty ladies might climb into bed with the authorities and tip them off.

Abu knew that five cities were going to be dusted just before dawn. The remaining five would have to wait for the arrival of their people. The timing had been based upon the nature of the towns. Most folks commuted to places like Los Angeles and San Diego. But they lived in Boston and Chicago.

The weather was a concern. Wind was not his friend. It had blown all afternoon in Miami, San Diego, and, of course, in Chicago—it wasn't called the windy city for nothing. Dispensing the spores up and down Michigan Avenue would be a grand endeavor but wasted if they simply blew into the lake. Nightfall was expected to bring some relief, but there was no question death would be seriously impaired.

Thank Allah it was spring. The stifling humidity of summer would have made the mission impossible. Rain was his worst nightmare. Showers would wash his dreams away. Anwar knew Echo 4 was already in trouble in Atlanta and Dallas. Storm clouds were on the horizon. Abu watched the Weather Channel religiously.

The night deliveries were supposed to be fairly simple. The trucks would come and go without being noticed, without being suspected of foul play. That was the plan, anyway. They were scheduled to arrive at two o'clock and be gone by five, before most arose from their final night's peaceful slumber. Within hours, life would be a nightmare. Within days, death would be a reality.

The excursions into the workday were expected to be considerably more difficult, especially in Los Angeles and San Diego, where they had scheduling conflicts. In those cities, an elaborate plan had to unfold: the real trucks had to be hijacked, hidden, and then replaced.

There was also the problem of the dust plume. The spores were microscopic, but the particulate they were hitching a ride on was not. It was quite possible that one or more of the daylight deliveries would be stopped before they were through.

Worried to death, but with nothing to do, Abu looked over at the prostitutes. They were calling him, and he was tense. Perhaps a back rub would be just what the doctor ordered.

✡   ✝   ☪

HOLDING A FLASHLIGHT in one hand and a map in the other, the crewman in Echo 4 Chicago 2 was having a tough time. He was a long way from his programming cubical in Research Triangle Park. It was even farther from his madras school in Pakistan. No matter which way he rotated the paper, he was lost.

"We need to find the Ritz. Our first set of barrels is hidden behind the hotel," he said to his compatriot. The driver thought it was miracle enough that they had found Chicago.

They had been spewing death for twenty-five minutes. If they didn't find the powder soon, they'd be out of business. And it was all he could do to keep the three-axled, ten-wheeled behemoth on the road.

"That thing over there," the driver pointed, "it's all lit up. Must be some sort of a landmark."

"Are we going north or south?"

"South, I think." Looking for signs, the driver had lost his bearings.

"I know where we are. Turn left!" the crewman screamed.

The driver slammed the airbrakes to the floor, overdoing it. Man and machine skidded to the outside of the turn. The old tires lost their bite, screeched, and then bumped abruptly into the curb. Now rolling precariously along the sidewalk, the driver spun the wheel to the left, taking out a streetlight before regaining control. Sparks lit up the night sky as a transformer exploded. The crackling and popping sounds of ripped high-voltage lines shook the windows.

Even light on powder, the garbage truck's weight was sufficient to ride up over the pole, pulling wires behind it. They were hardly inconspicuous.

Hoping to find a place to hide, the crewman bellowed, "I think the hotel's on the left."

Ducking in behind the Ritz, they parked the truck and caught their breath. Relieved, they looked up as if to Allah. The grand hotel loomed before them in unsuspecting majesty.

The tall tower was nestled between the black pyramid-shaped offices of Hancock Insurance and the white elegance of the Standard Oil Tower. The pricey shopping center nestled in the hotel's bottom floors was quiet at this hour, as were the guestrooms above. Good thing. They felt as if their hearts were pounding loudly enough to wake the dead.

Re-focusing on their task, they discovered the trash cans exactly where they were supposed to be, around the back of the building.

"Praise be to Allah. There they are." The driver did his best to back the truck into position. It took so long its "beep, beep, beep," reverse warning had become obnoxious. "Close enough." He took it out of gear and set the brake, but forgot to push in the lever stopping the blower. As they stepped out to feed the machine, a swirling gust of wind roared between the tall buildings. The two "trash men" were immediately blanketed with enough spores to wipe out a score of villages back home.

"Push in the lever, stupid. You're going to get us killed."

"Shut up and help me lift this can. We're going to die anyway. What's the difference?" Religious piety didn't necessarily bring peace and harmony.

Standing in the predawn air, covered from head to toe with anthrax spores, the crewman of Echo 4 Chicago 2 pondered what his partner had said. *He has a point.* The faster they became martyrs, the sooner they would be in Paradise practicing what they'd learned in their Shenandoah Valley truck stop/brothel. And the way he was driving, they'd be there soon enough.

✡   ✝   ☾

THE OLD NARROW STREETS of Alexandria were tough on a rookie driver. The first two ten-square-block sections of town had taken Echo 4 DC 1 almost twice as long as Omen had planned. Not knowing how to sweep wide into the cramped turns, they'd had to stop and back up, then move ahead again what seemed like a hundred times. Their reverse gear was getting a workout.

Looking at their watches, they started to worry. "Our next pickup is behind a church, right?" the driver asked, arms shaking with fatigue.

"Right. It's between here and Georgetown." Then the crewman laughed. "The place is called Foggy Bottom."

"Foggy Bottom," the driver repeated. "You're joking, yes?"

"No, I swear to Allah; look here," he said, holding out the map.

Distracted by thoughts of bottoms yet to come, the trash pilot veered across the street.

"Look out!" the crewman shouted, covering his face with the map.

"*Nooooo!*"

Desperately trying to find the brake and clutch, the driver found neither. The giant beast surged forward as his panicked foot stomped the accelerator instead. Pushing harder and instinctively jerking the wheel to the right, bad things began to happen. The left bumper clipped the rear of a parked car, tossing it into a storefront, shattering the glass façade.

Bad got worse. The accelerating machine snapped off a fire hydrant, sending a cascading fountain of water forty feet into the night air. Enough of the torrent found its way into the collection bin at the truck's rear to thoroughly gum up the works. The mixing device ground to an ignominious halt as the towering plume of water washed the diabolical machine of all obvious signs of its offensive cargo.

Now completely out of control, the truck raced across the street precariously balanced on its left-side wheels. Finally succumbing to gravity, it bounced and rumbled toward the shops on the far side of the street.

The impact of 20,000 pounds of steel going from fifty to zero in a microsecond was horrific. The truck slammed into a brick and glass storefront, flipping onto its left side and coming to rest upside down. The bearing wall separating a drugstore from the neighborhood watering hole next door instantly crumbled, turning everything to rubble. Three stories of bricks, merchandise, glass, drugs, steel, and booze fell upon them in a tremendous crash. Fire erupted from broken gas lines as smoke, dust, and debris mushroomed skyward.

Through for the night, the boys were immediately whisked into Allah's presence. Still surrounded by fire, the scenery hadn't changed.

✡   ✝   ☾

ALLAH MAY HAVE been pleased. Omen Quagmer was not. The moment the disaster was reported on FOX News, he exploded in rage. The Alexandria truck had been assigned one of the most important routes. Its final two ten-block grids were in the District of Columbia, right downtown. The highlighted route of their now-burning map had been Constitution and Pennsylvania Avenues.

When the news hit, Omen was half a world away, preparing his lunch.

For some reason, the Islamic organizer and fundraiser extraordinaire lost his appetite. He now knew that the spores he had so carefully nurtured to infect the very lair of the Great Satan were themselves dead. He mourned, as for a lost child. Far fewer would suffer. He felt ill.

✡   ✞   ☾

THE WINDS were still strong in Miami. But it didn't matter anymore. Hardly anything was working. Even though it was early spring and still before sunrise, Florida's legendary humidity had fouled things up. The powder particulate had swollen, seizing the blower's impeller. The only thing that kept the mechanism functioning, even sporadically, was the power of hydraulics. An electric blower would have burned up hours ago.

"What do you think?" the driver asked his partner, struggling with the ten-speed gearbox.

"The gauge shows we've still got most of our second load. We're supposed to be done, you know."

"I say we dump what's left and bail."

"Sounds good to me. If we stay out much longer, it'll be light."

"Let's head downtown, toward those tall buildings. We'll do the most damage there."

Returning from the casual yet elegant decadence of South Beach, they crossed the Venetian Causeway Bridge. Yachts bobbed in the marina off to their right. Lights from the hotels, apartments, and office windows sparkled in the quiet waters of Biscayne Bay. It all looked so peaceful. Of all Muslims, they were closest to Paradise.

✡   ✞   ☾

ATLANTA AND DALLAS were rainouts. The drivers had pulled their trucks off to the side of the road, hoping for a break in the weather. They prayed to Allah, whom Muhammad had said was responsible for rain, but to no avail. Cooped up in his depressing black cube-like shrine, Allah didn't get out much. What did he know of the American South? Life would go on in Dixie. Heaven would have to wait.

The two San Francisco teams were down to just one. Crossing the vast continent had been harder on both man and machine than they had expected. Not up to the challenge, the older of the refuse haulers coughed, choked, and sputtered to a stop just below the Eisenhower Pass. In the rarified air of the Rockies just west of Denver, the beast died.

The fatigued crew of Execution Team Echo 4 SF 1 was having problems of their own. They were antsy and jumped the gun, prematurely ejaculating their spores into a city that was still asleep.

They got lost near Beacon Hill and again in the fog along the wharf. Their sleep-deprived minds were so numb, they drove their second grid without the mixer engaged. The particulate barrels weren't where they were supposed to be following the third section. But it no longer mattered. Their driving technique was no match for the challenge of San Francisco's fabled hills. The clutch was all but shot.

At least the crew was having a good time. Even in these pre-dawn hours, there always seemed to be something entertaining to gawk at as they prowled the back streets. Although the boys dispensed their full quota of jeers at the decadent infidels, their words were considerably less deadly than the spores they were *not* dispensing. Hate speech wasn't lethal, after all. San Franciscans would live.

The operations in Philadelphia began simultaneously with San Francisco's. Four in the morning in the city by the bay was seven in Philly. One city was cloaked in darkness; the other was wide awake, with the long shadows of the morning's first rays streaking across its proud boulevards.

In Philly, the boys behaved themselves, and so did the spores. The air was dry and still. Both machines worked perfectly, spewing great plumes of anthrax-laden powder high into the air. Unfortunately, as the morning sun poured down the east-west streets, its light fell upon the deadly clouds, making them glow.

✡ ✚ ☾

CARLOS AND MANUEL, the real ones, were half asleep at this ungodly hour. As they had done a thousand times, they picked up their BFI trash truck from the depot and were heading north on Wilmington Boulevard. The streets were deserted. By the time the coffee kicked in, they would be in downtown Los Angeles, the City of Angels.

Stopped at the last light before their 405 Freeway onramp, they were still dazed, listening to a Hispanic station, rocking to the music's beat. Suddenly, they were startled by men in jumpsuits similar to theirs. The intruders stood on the running boards, hammering the windows with the butts of guns. They looked like the crazed Islamic militants they had seen on TV, but without the turbans. *Que paso?* they wondered. *What do they want with us?*

Carlos was slow to roll down his window, so Abdul simply shot him. Frightened half to death, Manuel was taken the rest of the way by Mohamar's bullet seconds later. The windows shattered, the Muslim brothers lifted the latches and opened the doors. They scooted inside, pushing the dying men to the center of the bench seat.

At this early hour, 6:15 A.M., there was no one around. It was barely light. Abdul put the truck in gear and made an illegal u-turn. Several hundred meters south of where they had exterminated the crew, he drove the trash truck into the staging area of a large warehouse. Several football fields long, it must have been nearly a half million square feet. The gate to the ramp area was wide open. They were expected. Some local al-Qaeda operatives, those who had been responsible for the particulate deliveries, had bribed a security guard.

As they drove alongside the vast facility, the murdering Muslims honked their horn. A drive-in door at the top of a cement ramp flew open, allowing them to take the refuse truck into hiding.

The idea was to exchange vehicles. There was no way to dust cities during the day without being noticed. However, if they looked like they belonged, like they were making their appointed rounds, no one would be suspicious.

Once inside, Abdul drove the beast to the back corner of the giant building. His partner removed a tarp from his pack and placed it over the nearly lifeless bodies of Carlos and Manuel. Pleased with their work, they jumped out and climbed into the truck they had driven across the country. They were impressed by how similar they looked. But there was no time to gloat. Within moments, they were back on the road again.

Across the Southland three separate hijackings were unfolding simultaneously. The others, however, hadn't been as effectively choreographed. Things were beginning to unravel.

In San Diego, gunshots had alerted a policeman just ending his duty shift near the eastern shores of Mission Bay. Spilling his coffee and donut as he sped in the direction of the menacing sound, the officer motored north on Morena Boulevard. Within moments, lights flashing, he found himself trying to pass a painfully slow trash truck. He flicked on his siren for a second, hoping to catch the driver's attention, hoping he would notice the lights, pull over, and let him by. Instead, all he heard was the grinding of gears. The transmission of the stolen truck was different from the one the hijackers had driven west. They were struggling and confused.

Frustrated, the cop hit his siren again as he tried to nose alongside. It was difficult because the driver, focused on the gearbox, was taking his half out of the middle of the road.

Finally catching a glimpse of the lights in his side mirror, Hassam swerved to his right, hoping the officer would pass. He tried to look cool, but as he did, he went too far, scraping the left side of a parked car. Unnerved, the navigator pulled out his gun and leaned over the two murdered men to see what was happening. That just made matters worse.

Unable to see, and with the crewman's weight pressing on him, Hassam lost control. The truck careened into a corner gas station. Heading directly toward the pumps, the driver's eyes became round as full moons. Leaning into his murdering friend, and against the lifeless bodies of his victims, Hassam yanked the wheel right for all he was worth. Launched up on three wheels by striking the concrete island that supported the gas pumps, the giant machine rolled, tumbling over onto its side. They braced themselves for an explosion. But miraculously, the rear end of the massive machine missed the pumps. *"Allahu-akbar!"*

Although the truck was now skidding on its side, the terrorists breathed a sigh of relief. Even as they lay against the crewman's door in a tangled mass of dead men's arms and legs, they relaxed, believing disaster had been averted. Still sliding and spinning across the asphalt, the truck continued toward the back fence. They never saw what killed them. The belly of the beast slammed into a propane tank. The explosion and fireball that ensued lifted the ten-ton monster into the air, cartwheeling it backwards, hood over fender, then slamming it to earth a few feet from the pumps it had missed on its way in. The officer held his breath.

✡   ✝   ☾

ALL WAS NOT WELL in the City of Brotherly Love. There were no route conflicts with other trucks this morning, so the crudely painted vehicle moseyed down the sun-drenched boulevards in broad daylight. It didn't fool anyone. While people don't usually notice trash trucks, these looked plenty peculiar. For one thing, they weren't stopping to pick up any trash. Besides, they were out on the wrong day, and speaking of day, they were supposed to be doing this at *night* when they were less of a menace. And then there was this little issue of a glowing four-story dust plume following them down the street.

Some nervous-nellies had called the cops. The dispatcher tried her best to keep a straight face as she took their reports. She knew she would catch lip from the units who responded. Even in Philadelphia, there's something odd about asking an officer to check out a suspicious trash truck. But she did her job and so did they. Racing off, nearby police units searched the streets for the offensive vehicle.

Mahoney was the first PPD officer on the scene. As he approached the refuse hauler, he saw nothing out of the ordinary, other than the timing being unusual. He was as unaccustomed as anyone to seeing trash trucks roaming city streets during the day. The officer uncradled his radio and pushed the talk lever on its side. "Dispatch, this is Unit 13. I have the suspect vehicle in sight. I can't see anyth...." His eyes widened.

"Oh my God," he said, dropping the mike into his lap. The officer turned on his lights and activated the siren. Heading south, the truck had crossed an east-west intersection. Sunlight hit the plume of doom, and it became immediately apparent. Mahoney's gut told him what his mind begged him to deny. Philadelphia was being introduced to the legacy of Muhammad.

✡ ☩ ☾

ADAMS CLOSED HIS EYES. So many conflicting thoughts vied for his attention. He had just converted to one faith and was about to justly condemn another. He had fallen in love with a woman and had come to hate a man. He was now a father, yet he would never know the mother.

Along the way, the Admiral had found what he was looking for. He was prepared to deliver on his promise. But he had also discovered something he hadn't expected, something that would make his proclamation sound hateful to many, bigoted to some, though it was neither. Perhaps strangest of all, he had found peace at a time when America was awakening to war.

The new parents had reluctantly left their new daughter behind. The hospital needed her to stay another few days. So did the authorities. Yacob's wife, Marta, had risen to the occasion. She was on duty, virtually living at the hospital. She even volunteered to escort young Mary to America when she was ready.

The lovers had elected to stop in London on their way home. The Brits wanted to talk, to share what they had discovered, and hear what the Admiral had learned. But they still had plenty of time. Heathrow was three hours away, although it wouldn't seem that long. They were flying west, so by the clock they would land shortly after they took off.

Sarah began, "Back in the suite you said that you knew the answer. What is it?"

"Do you have that little Bible with you?" Dumb question.

"Yes. Why?"

He had the strangest feeling.... "Uh oh!" he chuckled.

"What's so funny?"

"I think I'm being told to *read*."

"Well, at least you *can*," she laughed, making her own sideways reference to Mo's encounter with the molesting cave critter.

"I'm not sure this is the smartest thing I've ever done. Tell me I'm not crazy, Khadija."

"So now you're calling me old? Or are you just begging for some cuddle time like Muhammad did?" She played along.

He seemed agitated. "Y'know Sarah, I've never run from a fight. But this mission...a guys gotta be *nuts* to do this."

"Yep."

"*Yep?* I was looking for a bit more inspiration—maybe even a little support." Now he was begging.

"Taking on Islam will be the fight of the century. You're gonna get pounded from every side. It's not politically correct."

"No. It's just *correct*. That used to count for something."

"It still does. But not with the people who have the microphones."

"That's scary, isn't it? The most irresponsible folks are the ones with the biggest responsibility."

Sarah shook her head. "Journalism attracts more zealots than most any other profession."

"And they're not gonna like what I have to say."

She sighed. "Problem is, by telling the truth, even by using the term evil to describe Islam, you'll be taking on evil's principal advocate."

"*Evil* has an advocate?"

"The Devil," Sarah said. "But fortunately, *his* adversary is going to be with you all the way."

"*God?*"

She nodded.

"But I'm not prepared. I'm a rookie at this faith thing," Thor confessed. "I'm going to get creamed."

"Yep, but you've got no choice."

Thor shook his head. "I used to think I was pretty good at what I did. I made a career out of taking on bad guys. And I've even seen my share of devils out there, but not *the* Devil."

"He's a formidable foe. And he fights dirty." She gently stoked his arm.

It was her way of telling him he wasn't alone. "Satan's the ultimate counterfeiter."

"Smart. I can't think of a better way to fight God than deceiving people with *this* bogus bill."

"Islam?"

"Yeah. So how do we beat the beast?"

"What do you mean 'we,' paleface?" Sarah said, trying to keep a straight face. "Okay, just kidding…. 'We.' Are you asking me how we beat Islam, or beat Satan?"

"Satan." Adams smiled, not knowing why. His enemy had just grown wings. "Muhammad created Islam all on his own."

"You're right. If Satan had helped write the Qur'an, it would have been coherent."

"I guess this blasts another perfectly good illusion to smithereens."

"What's that?" she asked.

"The Devil's not a cute little red guy with horns and a pointy tail."

"No, not hardly," she laughed. "And virgins aren't all ugly gradeschoolers. Do you know who he was? Satan, I mean?"

"No."

"He was the most beautiful being God created—the highest of the angels. But that wasn't enough—not for him."

"The insecurity thing again."

"Right. He became jealous, coveting what didn't belong to him. He wanted to be like God, so he rebelled."

"By deceiving man." He rubbed his forehead.

"I was right about you."

"How's that?"

"You *are* on God's errand."

"Great. The best mission I've ever had has the lowest chance of success. Heck, my adversary won't even come out and fight like a man."

"Be thankful for that. You can't kill him with bullets. Without God's help, he'd eat you for breakfast."

"I feel better already."

"He doesn't want to be seen because he's most effective when he's misleading people, corrupting the truth, chipping away at the edges. And he's done a great job. Even the terms good and evil have become suspect—they're considered narrow-minded, judgmental, and moralistic."

"If people really knew what he was up to, they'd hate him." Thor was starting to get it.

"Yes. But he'll do anything to keep that from happening."

"Then by reporting the obvious, that Islam is merely recycled occult practices, streamlined paganism, and a purposeful counterfeit of Judaism, I'm going to be labeled a fanatic. When I say that it's only being touted because men profit from the delusion, they'll slime me."

"Yep. Just another hatemongering, narrow-minded religious nutcase morbidly preoccupied with a relic of a less inspired and enlightened generation," Sarah agreed, smiling.

"That sounds bad," Thor groaned.

"Your new enemy doesn't like the spotlight. He's much more effective lurking in the shadows. He wants people to be tolerant, open minded, and most importantly, deceived. Heaven without hell. Indulgence without guilt. That's why there are so many religions, so many isms. They're his best camouflage."

"They're his SFGs," Adams quipped. "Satan's Fallacy Groups."

"He's hiding in plain sight," she laughed. "But just because you can't see him doesn't make him any less real. Thor, Muhammad was fixated on Satan. And that's because from beginning to end the Bible tells us all about this bad boy, the Prince of this world. Remember, Jesus said his kingdom was not of this world."

He nodded, recalling what little he knew. The battlefield was taking shape.

"Bottom line: if the Bible is inspired by God—and I think we've established that—then Satan exists, and he's a formidable foe."

"Once again, being correct and being *politically* correct have nothing in common."

Sarah squeezed his hand. "In this battle of values, reason will triumph. Truth wins out. The last chapter has been written. No matter how loudly those with the microphones whine, God prevails in the end. Besides, you're not being called to convince people—just warn them."

"So how do we survive in the meantime?"

She looked at her leather Bible. It had been sitting in his lap. "With that, and with this." She pointed to his heart. "There's a reason you were told to read. Your bullets are words. But they have to be 'fired' in love."

"In the Garden of Gethsemane, you said that Jesus in his last prayer asked God to protect us from this guy." Thor shifted in his seat. "Can I count on that?"

"Read," she said in her best "God" voice.

They both laughed as she helped him find the book of John, where he read, "My prayer is not for you to take them out of the world but to protect them from the evil one. Sanctify them...." He stopped.

"It means to make holy, to set apart."

He nodded. "'*Sanctify* them with the truth. Your word is truth. Just as you sent me on this mission, I now send them.' And here's the good part. 'My prayer is not for them alone. I pray also for those who will believe in me through their message.'"

"Sounds like you're in good hands."

"Are there any more of these?" Adams asked naïvely. "That's cool."

She bit her lip, nodding. "There was one that leaped to mind the moment you were asked to read. I think maybe he had you in mind when he inspired King David to write these words." From memory she recited the Psalm: "'He who dwells in the shelter of the most high shall abide under the shadow of the Almighty. I will say to the Lord, "He is my refuge and my fortress; My God, in him I trust. For it is he who delivers you from the snare of the trapper, and from the deadly pestilence."' Does that hit close to home, or what?'"

"Yeah. Isaac and I were the only ones spared from the trap. So is he now saying we're going to be spared from deadly pestilence—anthrax?"

"That's pushing it. Although I'll grant you, the correlation is a little freaky. But I'm sure it's just a coincidence. Let's not read too much into this."

She did. "'Under his wings you will find refuge. His faithfulness is a shield and bulwark. You will not be afraid of the terror by night, the arrows that fly by day, the pestilence that stalks in the darkness, or the destruction that lays waste. A thousand may fall at your side, and ten thousand at your right hand; but it shall not come near you. No evil shall befall you, nor will any disaster come near your dwelling; for he shall give his angels charge over you, to guard you in all your ways.'"

"Deadly pestilence is repeated. I wonder if that's important? We've already been hit once with anthrax. Do you think there may be a second attack—also at night? Is this a clue?"

"What do you mean?"

"Can we put the pieces together and figure this thing out? David was predicting terror. We've got terror. He predicted deadly pestilence. We've got that too. Arrows by day could be military hardware, a missile, a bomb, or some such thing. Then in the second pestilence attack he gives us two more clues. It stalks in the darkness. That means it's moving, unlike the first blowers which were fixed inside the HVAC ducts. And this attack lays waste, killing thousands right near us—as in Washington, perhaps."

"Whoa, big boy. You're reading way too much into this."

"Waste," he repeated out loud. "Stalking—moving waste. Pestilence a second time—anthrax. In darkness."

"You think we're going to be trashed with anthrax?"

"I need to call somebody. Warn the authorities."

"Forget it. You're being impulsive. If you tell people where you came up with this idea they'll put you in a white jacket and carry you away."

"Alright. I'll let it lie for now. But just so I know, what does he want in return for this protection thing?"

"Love. He only really gave us two commandments: that we love God with all our heart, soul, and might, and that we love one another as we love ourselves."

"That love thing," he said, looking at her. "Even Muslims?"

"*Especially* Muslims. Love is the most irresistible force in the world."

Sarah reached for her Bible. She found her favorite passage, reading it slowly, lingering over every phrase:

"'If I speak in the tongues of men and of angels, but have not love, I am only a clanging bell. If I have the gift of prophecy and can fathom all mysteries and knowledge, and if I have a faith that can move mountains, but have not love, I am nothing. If I give all I possess to the poor and surrender my body to the flames, but have not love, I gain nothing.

"'Love is patient, love is kind. It does not envy, it does not boast, it is not proud. It is not rude, it is not self-seeking, it is not easily angered, it keeps no record of wrongs. Love does not delight in evil but rejoices in the truth. It always protects, always trusts, always hopes, always perseveres. Love never fails.'"

"So what I have to do is love Arabs while hating Islam and the evil that flows from it."

"Bimbo!"

Bimbo. Thor's mind involuntarily raced back to that night, to Sarah lying next to him in bed, holding him. He smiled.

"Don't go there," she said, reading his mind. "I was vulnerable. It had been quite a day."

"Are you always going to be able to read my mind?"

"Yes."

"Then what am I thinking now?"

"That you'd like to fall asleep in my arms more often. And...."

"And..." he said looking around, "if you really can read my mind, keep it to yourself."

She reached for his hand again and squeezed it gently. They flew that way for some time, imagining.

"The Crusaders weren't Christians," Thor said, interrupting the silence.

"I beg your pardon."

"They couldn't have been."

"What in the world are you talking about?"

"Well, I went from thinking about loving you to thinking about love. Then I thought, if God is love, how did the Crusaders go off and conquer in his name. Then it dawned on me. They weren't Christians."

"I presume you're going to explain this.

"To be a Christian, you have to know what Jesus said and did. And then you have to act upon that knowledge, right?"

"Right."

"For a thousand years the Bible was unavailable. Most people had no way of knowing these things. The scriptures were translated into a dead language, Latin. The sermons were delivered in the same dead language. Only the clergy had Bibles, and their goal was to suppress the people, keep them ignorant and dependent so they could rule over them." Thor was out there, thinking.

"The clerics told the people that the bad guys, the Great Satan, was *out there*, not among them. And how would the people know? No serf, tradesman, farmer, teacher, or soldier had a Bible. They had no way to know what it actually said. They were kept in the dark, purposefully duped."

Sarah stared at him. She was impressed, although it was a little weird that he'd transitioned from thinking about falling asleep in her arms to sending misguided soldiers off on some bloodthirsty crusade.

Thor continued to unravel the mystery. "There are striking parallels to Islam here, Sarah. The preponderance of Muslims haven't read Ibn Ishaq or al-Bukhari any more than the medieval Catholics had read the Bible. I'd bet my life on it. Religion for them is just like it was for the poor saps in the Dark Ages. Ritual, ritual, and more ritual. Just mind-numbing repetition, group bowing, and mass mind conditioning.

"Nonconformity is treated now exactly as it was then. People are Muslims only because in their situation, *not* to be one is fatal. But remove the threat of death, give Arabs access to the truth, and a great many will discard the delusion. Of course, thanks to centuries of conditioning, it won't happen as readily as Germans discarded Nazism, or even at the pace the Russians said *nyet* to Communism. But it *will* happen. And when it does, a great pall of oppression will be lifted from their lives, and from the world."

"Wow. That's pretty profound, for a flyboy. That may be the most rational explanation I've ever heard." Not to be outdone, Sarah reached into her carry-on. She pulled out a page she had photocopied from an old book written by Alexander Hislop. "I'm going to read a paragraph and you tell me who this sounds like: 'If it had appeared at once in all its hideousness, it would have alarmed the consciences of men and defeated the very purpose for which it had been conceived. The object was to bind all mankind in blind and absolute submission to a hierarchy entirely dependent on the clergy. In the carrying out of this scheme, knowledge, sacred and profane, came to be monopolized by the religious leaders, who dealt it out to those who were initiated in the faith exactly as they saw fit. Thus the people, wherever the doctrine spread, were bound neck and heel to the clerics. They were the only depositaries of religious knowledge; they had the true tradition by which the writs and symbols of the public religion could be interpreted. And without blind and implicit submission to them, what was necessary for salvation could not be known.'"

"That's a dead wringer for Islam, but I suppose the author could have been writing about the kind of Catholicism that led to the Crusades."

"Actually, it was written to describe the original Babylonian religion. It was the ultimate manifestation of the occult. Satan was king"

"Well it sure explains the hows and whys of organized religion."

She nodded. "And based on that, I think the Dark Ages were dark because God's light was hidden, covered up by a politicized clergy. It's remarkable Christianity survived."

"What's more amazing is that Islam survived. Think about it. It grew out of idol worship. Allah was the *Moon God*, for cryin' out loud."

"But surely re-marketing rocks does not a religion make, at least one persuasive enough to fool so many," Sarah protested.

"No. Delusions are never that simple. They need to be infused with just enough truth to make the lies seductive." Thor's mind was churning. "That's why Muhammad ripped off Judaism."

Sarah was right with him. "In his search for legitimacy, he latched on to the world's best documented, most credible monotheistic faith, Judaism," she agreed. "He usurped its moral lessons, its laws, and theology—just enough to make Islam seem rational at first blush."

"Finally, he turned his faith against its foundations, against itself, claiming that the Jews got it all wrong. He said that the scriptures upon which Islam was based were corrupt." Thor was connecting the dots.

"Then in typical megalomaniac fashion, Muhammad had a tizzy fit when his silly 'revelations' were scoffed at. He retaliated, as is the custom among maniac types, by killing, raping, enslaving, and plundering. Then for good measure, he imbued his demented doctrine with the gift that keeps on giving—terror," Sarah said. "Muhammad's character fell while his 'religion' rose."

"When you read this bad boy's biographers or his speeches, it becomes obvious that he was a pathological liar, a pedophile, a womanizer, a rapist, a coward, a kidnapper, a thief..." she paused for a breath.

"...a murderer, an assassin, a slave trader, a warmonger. He was even genocidal, although," Thor observed, "by the time his bio was edited, these may not have been considered bad things."

"In short, he was a terrorist," Nottingly concluded. "It shouldn't be a surprise that those who follow him, those who know what he said and how he lived, are terrorists, too." It was all starting to come together.

Sarah looked up at Thor. "His 'religion' gained substance through war. It spread at sword point; it's maintained at gun point."

He reflected, "We've been told that Muslims who kill are following a corrupted form of their religion. We've been told that that terrorists are criminals who have perverted Islam. But the truth is just the opposite: the religion condones, even *commands* deception, fighting, and murder."

"You're right," she said. "From Muhammad's own lips."

"In our folly we have gone after the terrorists, not the thing that makes them terrorists. We've made more of the very thing we were trying to eradicate."

"By obfuscating the source of the problem, we have allowed it to grow out of control. This is one of those times when doing something, the *wrong* something, was worse than doing nothing."

"Yes," he squeezed her hand. "But doing nothing isn't the answer either. The cancer of terrorism will infect everything unless we kill it at the source."

"So the questions are," Sarah said, "does America have the will, or even the ability, to wrestle with this unexpected reality? And do we have the courage to stand up and deal with it? Islam is a deadly cancer. And it's growing at an exponential rate."

"The surgery to remove it, the chemotherapy needed to drive it into remission, will be painful," Thor knew. "But it's the only treatment that has any chance of preventing this disease from consuming everything."

He turned to Sarah and confirmed his mission. "The thugs that rule the Muslim world must be neutered. Islam must be exposed. And we now know that this disease thrives on money. Money allows mullahs to build madrases that manufacture murderers."

✡   ✝   ☪

THEIR FACES said more than words could have.

"Guys, what's wrong. What happened? I thought you'd be happy to see us," the Admiral was puzzled.

"You don't know, do you?" Major Huston asked.

"Know what?" Sarah searched their eyes.

"First things first." Blake opened his arms and gave Adams a hug.
Stepping back, he asked, "May I?" nodding toward Nottingly.

Thor smiled, so Huston enveloped Sarah as well, squeezing her as if
they were long-lost friends. "Any friend of this bloke's a friend of ours."

"Who ever said the British were reserved?" Adams chided his pal.

"By Jove, it's good to see you." His face brightened. "Every morning,
the first thing I do is thank God for Thor Adams. If you hadn't saved our
sorry assets we'd still be hanging on those infernal trees."

Before he could finish, the other three hobbled forward. Although
hurting, they were ambulatory. Group hugs and warm smiles were the
order of the day.

"For dead men you guys don't look half bad, especially you, Sullivan.
For a while, I didn't think you were going to make it."

"For a while there, I wasn't sure I wanted to make it, Cap...I mean
Admiral. Don't mind telling you, crucifixion hurts."

"Right," Cliff agreed. "But that's ancient history. We survived, which
is more than...."

The Major held up his hand, asking Powers to wait. As he did, Sarah
fixed her gaze on the scar on his wrist.

"We've sequestered a private room, down the hall a bit," Lieutenant
Sullivan said. He motioned in its direction.

"How long do we have with you, Admiral?" Lieutenant Childress
inquired. They had plenty to discuss.

"Layover's an hour and a half."

"What aren't you telling us?" Sarah tried again.

Blake explained as they walked. "We've known for a couple of hours
now, but now I think it's beginning to hit the telly."

"What?"

"They've gone and done it again."

"Who?"

"Muslims, of course. This time they may have killed millions."

"How?"

"They've enlarged their anthrax blowers. Put 'em on wheels."

"Where?"

"America. Six cities for sure, maybe more."

Suddenly ill, Adams stopped in his tracks. "'The pestilence that stalks in
darkness, the destruction that lays waste,'" he said just loud enough to be
heard. "Trash trucks, wasn't it?" The sheer enormity of the evil his people
were enduring overwhelmed him. It was as if a million voices were crying
out for help. He felt his strength evaporate. With his back against the wall,

the Admiral slid to the floor.

"Thor!" Sarah screamed, kneeling beside him. Expressionless, he just stared across the hall.

Mustering the strength they had displayed freeing their comrades from the crosses, the injured Brits lifted his limp body. Halfway up, he seemed to regain consciousness.

"The pain...," he tried to explain.

"Right," Major Huston said, pointing. "A few more meters. We're nearly there."

Once inside the private lounge, Lad Childress soaked some napkins in water and placed them on Thor's forehead. Ryan Sullivan found the remote control. Turning the television on, he scanned the channels. They were all reporting the story. He settled on FOX Satellite News.

Their anchor, Trixi Lightheart, had already begun her report. "...initial details are sketchy. We know that at seven fifteen eastern time this morning a Philadelphia police officer arrested two men driving a refuse truck. The vehicle had allegedly been reconfigured for distributing inhalation anthrax. The suspects have denied responsibility, saying they had no knowledge of what they were dispensing."

She held her hand to her left ear. "A second truck, I am told, also in Philadelphia, was apprehended just a few minutes ago. The driver and crewman have been taken into police custody."

The studio cut to video. Viewers were getting their first look at what appeared to be the rear end of an overturned trash truck buried under a pile of bricks, glass, and other debris. "This morning, in the Alexandria suburb of Washington, D.C., a third trash truck, similarly equipped, went out of control and crashed. Authorities believe these incidents may be related."

"Brilliant deduction, Sherlock," Sullivan interrupted.

"...another truck was detained in downtown Chicago after toppling a street lamp and dislodging power lines. The Chicago Police Department has confirmed that this vehicle was loaded with what may be anthrax spores. Two suspects are under arrest.

"Moving on to San Diego, we bring you this live report. Monique, good morning."

"Good morning, Trixi. I am here at the Exxon service station on Morena Boulevard just north of San Diego. In a bizarre story, a Western Refuse truck was involved in what witnesses are calling a high-speed police chase. The driver apparently lost control blasting into this gas station. The garbage truck blew up after colliding with a propane tank. Moments later, as you can see, the truck careened back over to these pumps and ignited a second fireball. It's a scene right out of hell.

"This is Captain Frank Finley of the San Diego Fire Department and Steve Mathews of the SDPD," Monique said. "Captain Finley, Officer Mathews, what can you tell me about what happened here this morning?"

The British contingent of Team Uniform listened intently even though they were privy to more than FOX was reporting. They knew that a truck had been discovered in a Carson, California, warehouse. Blood dripping on the floor and the arm of a dead man hanging out a window had caused an observant security guard to investigate. Alerted, the LAPD had detained two trucks spewing spores in downtown Los Angeles. They had found one in San Francisco. The Brits knew that the San Diego truck had been hijacked and that its crew had died along with the perpetrators. The police were scouring the city looking for the converted death truck, one they now knew had to be hidden somewhere.

The Brits had been on the line with MI-6—England's famed intelligence agency. The Major had been informed, not only because he was Britain's leading expert on Islamic terror, but also because he was now the Tory Party candidate for Prime Minister.

MI-6 had been briefed by the CIA. They knew that anthrax had been found in eight cities. But pending absolute confirmation, the agency didn't want to release the tragic news, fearing residents and workers would panic and try to flee these metropolises, putting even more lives at risk.

The Brits filled in the details, none of which made Adams feel any better. Sarah didn't know if she should throw up, give up, or simply cry. She chose option three.

"Sorry to be the bearer of such awful news, sir." The Major rested his arm on the Admiral's shoulder. "But at least I've got *some* good news."

"Please," Thor begged his friend.

"My party, the Tory Party, has asked me to run for PM. The polls say I might give it a go."

"A *go?* Unbelievable." Cliff laughed. "The Major is leading Labor by twenty points."

The Admiral stood up. Wearing the biggest smile that would fit on his rugged face, he held out his right hand. "Mr. Prime Minister, congratulations. Now, sir," he said as the smile vanished, "let's save the world from this scum."

✡ ✝ ☾

BACK ON THE PLANE, they were headed home. Their heads were spinning, their stomachs were churning, but their resolve was never stronger.

The Admiral reached for the phone alongside his seat. From memory he dialed the Pentagon and asked to speak with Chairman Hasler. There was a long delay. Adams knew that meant he wasn't in his office. From experience, he knew that the boys in the basement were scrambling to track him down. A smallish room jammed full of computers, electronics, and sophisticated communications systems was manned twenty-four seven. Their only job was to keep track of the nation's most important souls. Hasler was high on the list. They would find him.

In less than a minute they patched him through. "What can I do for you, Admiral?"

"I'm headed back to Washington and thought you might like a briefing. I know what's behind the killing, sir."

"Sure, I'll meet with you. But it won't do much good. I'm not exactly Madam President's favorite General, you know."

"I heard she asked you to relieve me. Thanks for...."

"My pleasure, son. It's about the only thing I've done right since I took this job. When do you arrive?"

"Fifteen thirty at Dulles, sir. British Airways. I've got Agent Nottingly with me."

"I'll have someone pick you up and bring you to wherever I am. As I'm sure you know, we've got a crisis brewing here. I'm headed to the White House now."

"Tell them it's not over, sir. The next attack will come during daylight, a bomb or a missile. Just don't ask me how I know. But if Secretary Ditroe pins you down, tell her I met with al-Qaeda." Caution wasn't Thor's long suit.

"You did *what?*"

"I had tea with terrorists. Met some swell boys: al-Qaeda, Hamas, Fatah, Hezbollah, Islamic Jihad, Aqsa's Martyrs' Brigade."

"You're nuts, Admiral."

"Yes, sir."

Meeting arranged, Adams returned to reading Sarah's Bible, taking notes as he did. He had to be productive. Wallowing in the moment, no matter how painful, wasn't going to do anyone any good.

"Sarah," he said, rhythmically tapping his pencil on the paper. "It's all here. Yacob was right—a four thousand-year-old-family feud. The motivations, the very nature of everybody involved in this calamity was laid out chapter and verse. In the beginning, no less, in Genesis."

"I know. It's been there all the time."

"All the time, as in forty centuries. Why didn't you tell me?"

"You weren't ready to hear it, or at least understand it."

"You're probably right." He looked back down. "The first time this feud rose its ugly head, Isaac's mom sent Ishmael's mom away into the desert empty handed."

"But God sent Hagar back. He didn't like the idea of her being treated so callously, sent off to die. You know, like Muhammad banished the Jews from Yathrib."

He read on. "I'll be." He pounded his fist on the armrest.

"What?"

"The answer. God gave us the answer."

"Separate the warring children," she knew.

"Yeah, but not just *separate*. Supply them. Help them. As much as I hate what they do—God still loves them."

"He told us how to solve this problem. First, he doesn't want them together 'cause he knows they'll hurt each other. Second, he's picked out places for both Jews and Arabs. But the third thing, and the most important, is he wants Arabs treated kindly in spite of their behavior. Here, read what God said to Abraham." He handed Sarah the Bible.

"'Do not be distressed about Ishmael and Hagar. I will make the son of the maid into a nation also, because he is your offspring. So early the next morning Abraham took some food and a skin of water and gave them to Hagar. Abraham set them on her shoulders and then sent her off with the boy.' Oh, and it also says to 'listen to your wife Sarah and do whatever she tells you.'" A big grin erupted on her face.

"Yeah I know. I saw that part, too. Man, this is a tough religion. But nothing some situational scriptures couldn't fix. Where's Mo when you need him?" Thor deflected a feminine fist. "I know, I know," he said, holding up his hand, laughing. "It's a relationship, not a religion."

"I didn't know you were so easily trained," Sarah smiled. "This holds promise." She gazed down, continuing to read. "'Ishmael's descendants settled in the area from Havilah to Shur, near the border of Egypt, as you go toward Asshur. And they lived in hostility toward all their brothers.'" She handed the Bible back to Thor, pointing out the passage.

"The *answer* is: South of Gaza, going southeast along the Sinai. For five billion dollars, what is the *question?*" Thor loved *Jeopardy.*

"Where does an independent Palestinian state belong?" she answered.

"We have a winner. The Genesis account gives us the answer."

"But love," she added, "If we flip back to the end of Numbers...." She held out her hand. "May I have my Bible back?"

He pretended to covet it, and then thought better of it. She might find another "mind Sarah" verse.

"While I'm looking, remember God told Abe that his offspring would have all the land from the Great Sea to the Euphrates River."

"Yeah."

"Well, these accounts are different. Here, read this," she said, pointing to the 34th chapter.

"The Lord said to Moses, 'Command the Israelites to pee facing Mecca.' No, I read that wrong. Must have gotten it confused with the Hadith."

If looks could kill, he would have been wearing a toe tag.

Thor looked down. "He tells Moses, 'Command the Israelites, "When you enter Canaan, the land that will be allotted to you as an inheritance will have these boundaries: Your southern sector will include the Desert of Zin along the border of Edom. On the east, your southern border will start at the end of the Salt Sea, cross south of the Scorpion Pass to the ascent of Akrabbim and continue on to Zin. It shall go south of Kadesh Barnea. Then it will go to Hazar Addar and over to Azmon, where it will turn, join the Wadi of Egypt, and terminate at the Sea."'"

He thought for a moment. "This sounds real specific, Sarah, like a sur-veyor was laying it out. And, what's more, archeologists have to know were these places are, or were."

"You're not done." She pointed back down at the book.

"'Your western boundary will be the coast of the Great Sea. For your northern boundary, draw a line from the Great Sea to Mount Hor and from Mount Hor to Lebo Hamath. Then the boundary of your nation will go to Zedad, continue to Ziphron and end at Hazar Enan. This will be your boundary on the north.'"

"Go on."

"'For your eastern border, draw a line from Hazar Enan to Shepham. The boundary will go down from Shepham to Riblah on the east side of the Ain and go down along the slopes east of the Sea of Kinnereth,' that's Galilee, right? 'Then the boundary will continue along the Jordan and end at the Salt Sea. This will be your land, with its boundaries on every side.'"

"No question. No ambiguity at all."

"None. God intended the Jews to have all of the land that they cur-rently occupy, *including* the West Bank and much of the Golan."

"Exactly. That northern border falls just a little north of Beirut, Lebanon, but it doesn't include any of Syria. The boundary goes right down the eastern slopes of the Ain mountain range. The current Jordanian border is right on the money, as is the border with Egypt." Sarah had worked all this out.

"A couple of decades ago, when Ariel Sharon fought the Syrian-backed Palestinians in Lebanon and took a big hunk of the country as a buffer from the Hezbollah terrorists...."

"Yes, he was not overstepping his bounds. Never should have given it back. They *were* correct, by the way, giving the Sinai back to Egypt. Anyway, now flip back to Genesis. Read the last few verses of chapter 15."

Thor read, "'The Lord made a covenant with Abram and said, "To your descendants I give this land, from the Wadi of Egypt to the Euphrates."'"

"All right, smart boy. What's up with that?"

Thor smiled. "Thought you had me, but no. It all fits. Abe's offspring include the Arabs *and* the Jews—Ishmael *and* Isaac. Notwithstanding Muhammad's confusion, Moses was a Jew. Israel was God's gift to the Jewish people. The rest—the lion's share, by the way—was his gift to the Arabs, it belongs to them—all the way to the Euphrates."

"And it's still that way," she shared. "Between the Mediterranean and the Jordan River, it's mostly Jews. Between the Jordan and the Euphrates, it's Arabs. East of the river, there are still are still bazillions of Muslims, but racially they're Persians and Indonesians. The Muslims in the north are Turks, and in the south they're Egyptians and Africans."

"So that means the area south of Gaza running diagonally southeast toward the Gulf of Aqaba is not only where God sent Ishmael, and where Muhammad claims the Earth's navel was found; it's *not* part of Israel's inheritance, although the Gaza Strip may be within those boundaries."

"So, separate the warring children and provide the means for them to prevail. We even know where he wants them."

The Admiral laughed. "Y'know something, Sarah?"

"I like to think so. Why?" she smiled.

"Our boy Muhammad left his faithful high and dry."

"In more ways than one," she chuckled.

"Muhammad not only said that he was a prophet just like Moses. He also said that the Books of Moses, the Torah, were inspired by God. Moses wrote both Genesis and Numbers."

"Read it and weep." Sarah smiled. "They can't claim that Israel is their land without making a mockery of their Prophet's revelations."

"Worse, they can't even claim foul play. Muhammad waltzed into Yathrib and systematically booted out the Jews. Two mass migrations and a mass murder."

"So you help them leave Israel. Give them everything they need to be successful. Including the means to feed themselves and a source of water."

"It shouldn't come as a surprise, Sarah, that the Jews are the foremost authority on growing crops in the desert and the leading manufacturer of water desalinization equipment. Nor that the Arabs have plenty of oil to power the energy-thirsty machines."

"When they scream bloody murder, you politely explain that you're just following the fine example their Prophet set."

✡ ☦ ☾

"MADAM PRESIDENT, what are we going to do?" Secretary Ditroe was a mess. She had spent the night at the White House and thus hadn't been contaminated. But it didn't seem to make a difference. She and her President were dying—if only politically.

The President stared at the report. Stared through it, really.

It was late morning, the day of the Great Offensive. She and her Secretary of Defense had been joined in the Oval Office by Chairman Hasler from the Joint Chiefs and Director Barnes of the CIA.

"How many are we going to lose, Director?" she asked.

"Here in Washington, officials, elected or otherwise, probably twenty percent. All they missed in town was the area around the mall. They dusted most every important residential area except Georgetown. Those bastards knew that Congress was in session. They got us good this time."

"How many Americans, Director Barnes?"

"We don't have an estimate yet. Hundreds of thousands have been, or at least will be, infected. It's really bad."

"The worst part is, now we have a refugee problem. Everybody's packing up and leaving the cities," the General said.

"But nobody wants them. They think that they're covered in anthrax spores. It's like when the Irish came here after the potato famine." Ditroe was in her usual position, swallowed by the large burgundy sofa.

"I've got an idea, Madam President."

"Yes, General."

"Why not open some of our bases for them. We've pared down our military to the point they're just sitting empty."

She stared at him. She hated the military, now more than ever.

"It'd make you look generous, ma'am. Like you're giving the people something. Since we're dying in the polls, it couldn't hurt."

"All right. What else. How are we going to survive this thing?"

"The disease or the political fallout?" Barnes didn't really have to ask.

"The disease will take care of itself. All we can do is give people drugs and clean up the mess. The politics could be far more deadly."

"We've already threatened war. What else can we do?" Susan asked.

Just then a voice came over the intercom. A secretary announced that the Speaker of the House was on the line.

"Mr. Speaker," the President said, "what's happening over there?"

"Best we can tell, nearly two hundred Members were poisoned. They've all been given Cipro. But based upon the office experience, the majority may die—most are over forty."

"And the Senate?"

"Even worse. More than a third of the Senate was exposed."

"Do you have a party breakdown? How many were Republicans?"

"We got it worse than they did, I'm afraid. Our guys seem to prefer the commotion of living close to the District. The way it looks, they're going to regain control of both Houses."

"Then we need to hold some special elections, don't we? It's not right to let people go unrepresented."

"Of course not, Madam President. And it's a brilliant strategy. I'll set the wheels in motion, then find some way to justify it Constitutionally."

"Good. Report back when there's something I can announce."

"All right. But Madam President, I'm afraid I have some disturbing news. Admiral Adams is returning from Israel. He's ready to deliver his report. Republicans are proposing a Joint Session of Congress."

"When? Can they do that?" She cast a quick glance toward the General. If her instincts were correct, his fingerprints were all over this.

"Yes, sure they can," the Speaker said over the phone. "In fact, it's scheduled for Friday afternoon. But you can order us to boycott the speech. Or better yet, you can upstage him. Give a speech yourself—announce something big."

"Boys and girls, you heard the man. We need a big kill. We've got to upstage that meddling Boy Scout." She opened an ornate box on her desk, extracted a cigar, and lit it. The smoke wafted through the air. "I think I may have just the ticket." She took another puff. "Suzzi, call Chairman Alafat back. Tell Yasman we're willing to sign his peace accord. And then arrange to have everybody that's anybody at Camp David—first thing Friday morning."

Turning back to face the speakerphone, she said, "Mr. Speaker, invite the whole Hill, what's left of it. You can even invite the Minority leaders. Let's make this look bipartisan."

✡   ✝   ☾

IT WAS LATE, but the aging Chairman was still up. He was rehearsing, trying to look casual with the additions to his wardrobe. But try as he might, it wasn't happening.

His team had been unable to blend ten kilos of C-12 and an additional five of skin-piercing shrapnel into a garment without compromising its tailored appearance. Looking into the mirror, the portly terrorist saw an ugly man, flabby and stiff, not the least bit comfortable. He was disappointed, knowing he wasn't going to look good in the pictures.

"Call for you boss," Mamdouh Salim said, rushing into the room. "It's from the White House. Susan Ditroe."

The old terrorist moseyed over to the phone. He waited a good long while, picking at his nails. Quietly, he was sending a message. "This is Chairman Alafat," he finally muttered in his most demeaning tone.

"Mr. Chairman, the President asked me to call to invite you to Camp David. She wishes to sign your peace accord. You and your ministers will be our guests, starting tomorrow, Wednesday, if you wish." Even talking to Alafat on the phone turned the Defense Secretary's stomach. She didn't know how she'd endure the better part of three days in his presence. "We'll be holding a dinner in your honor Thursday night. The President has scheduled the signing ceremony Friday morning."

It's not enough, the veteran terrorist thought. After all, Bush had promised the Saudis, Syrians, and Egyptians this very thing, including withdrawl from the Golan and all of Jerusalem, in return for their support in the Gulf War. *But with a return to the '67 borders, Tel Aviv, with seventy percent of the Jewish population, will be trapped between our pincers. Yes. Another step toward the total annihilation of Israel.*

"Who's been invited?"

"Every Congressional leader will be there, sir, including the committee chairs." Although most hadn't been called yet, it didn't take a rocket scientist to know they'd all be there. "All of us on the President's Cabinet, the Vice President. Oh, and um, with your permission, I would like to invite Israel's Prime Minister."

"Yes, by all means. Perfect. And the press?"

She wanted to say, "Like fleas on a camel," but didn't. "Every major news anchor. Pretty much the entire Washington news corp."

"I'm sure no one will leave disappointed," the Chairman said.

"I hope not. The President is counting on this peace accord putting an end to the violence. I trust you've received our acknowledgement of your most recent requests."

"Yes. I've gone over the final draft, and it's better, but it's less than my people deserve." Secretary Ditroe's heart fell a foot.

"B-but, Mr. Chairman. We're counting on you to honor your pledge."

Alafat laughed. *Americans,* he thought. *They're so trusting. What is it with them?* "Yes, Secretary Ditroe. I will sign it. Someone has to put an end to the killing, don't you think?"

"Yes. This morning we awoke to the horror of war."

"Today your people tasted what my people have endured for decades. Ten of your cities have been infected with anthrax, just as all of mine have been infected with Jews. We Palestinians understand your suffering."

"I'll pass your sympathies on to the President. She, like you, is committed to stopping the victimization of innocent people. We too have suffered from radical right-wing hate groups. It's time we gave peace a chance."

"I couldn't have said it better myself."

"Mr. Chairman, you are one of the world's great peacemakers," America's Secretary of Defense told the once and future terrorist.

"Yes, I know. I'll see you tomorrow afternoon. I will be flying in with several ministers. We will be expecting full diplomatic status while we're in America, status befitting my people as their elected head of state."

"Yes, Mr. Chairman, of course. As President of the soon-to-be sovereign nation of Palestine, you and your ministers are entitled to such standing."

Hanging up, Alafat danced an ungainly jig. It was quite a sight, especially since Talib Ali and Mamdouh Salim knew what he was wearing. The dance of death had never looked so bizarre.

"One plan hatched. One to go," he said, rubbing his hands together excitedly. "Now where is that Palestinian engineer you promised me?"

"Waiting outside. His flight from Hamburg arrived in Tel Aviv about three hours ago. I was planning to meet with him this evening and check him out. But if you'd like, I'll invite him in." Salim walked toward the door.

"We can trust him," Ali added. "I know this boy. He's a good Muslim."

"And a good terrorist. Remember, he was in on Kahn's crucifixions."

"I've just learned he was the genius behind today's anthrax trash trucks," Talib shared. "Credentials like that speak for themselves. He's one of us," the Palestinian Muslim told the Egyptian Communist.

"Splendid. Bring him in." The Chairman sat at his sleek black conference table, a bit out of breath.

Aymen Halaweh walked nervously into the Chairman's office. He was in awe. While the office was nothing to look at, Alafat was his hero.

"Sit down, boy. May we get you some tea?" Alafat motioned toward the porcelain pot on his left.

"Thank you, sir. Meeting you is such an honor," he gushed. Talib Ali poured him a cup. Aymen shook, spilling half of it into the saucer.

"Do you know why you're here?" Talib asked.

"To do Allah's work."

"Yes. And let me show you what Allah wants." The Chairman unrolled detailed blueprints of the Dome of the Rock. He wiped his hands across the sheets, flattening them. Feeling proud, he smiled as he saw his darkened reflection in the table's mirror finish.

The founder and Chairman of Fatah reached down into one of the three large boxes at his feet. With a dramatic flourish, he lifted the contents. He could see Aymen's eyes grow large.

"That's one of the Special Forces uniforms we captured in Afghanistan," the young engineer exclaimed. "Do you have the backpack and helmet-cam?"

"Three of them," the Chairman said as he dove into the box a second time. He set the Israeli SFG helmet next to the suit. Both bore the symbol that inflamed his rage—a small, blue, six-sided star.

"That star cursed the Jews in Europe and now, thanks to you, boy, it will curse them again, this time in Jerusalem.

Growing more comfortable wearing twenty pounds of C-12 explosive, Yasman Alafat explained his intricate plan for turning the tide of public opinion.

✡   ✝   ☾

"DID ANYTHING go the way you planned?" Haqqani teased his partner.

Omen Quagmer was miserable. For a guy so obsessed with detail, he was a mess. Only eight of the ten cities he had planned to infect had been dusted, and none had lived up to his expectations. Only one truck made every particulate pickup and actually finished all five ten-block sectors.

"What do you say we have some fun, loosen up, give atoms a try?" He slapped him playfully on the back. "Maybe they'll behave better."

Kahn's sense of humor was as twisted as his mind. But neither was a match for his soul.

Omen was still shaking his head. "I understand. To keep our alliance pieced together, we need victories."

"That's my man. Now you're back in the game." Kahn Haqqani was the devil's own cheerleader.

"I'll tell you what: give me a few minutes to clean up after the boys. I need to work the press. Before we begin Alpha 5, Bravo 4 needs to look like a rousing success."

"Just tell them that the angels didn't show up. Tell 'em Allah wanted to scavenge for martyrs."

"I'm afraid that joke's a little inside for my friends at the AP."

Quagmer reluctantly turned to the phone. He reached out and dialed the Jerusalem offices of the Associated Press from memory. They had a symbiotic relationship. Next to CNN and al Jazeera, they were his most stalwart supporter. But even they, he felt, couldn't always be trusted in times like these.

"Were you responsible, Omen?" a familiar voice asked hopefully. The scoop would be sensational, a great coup for his career.

"Yes, my friend, we were responsible. It was a beautiful *fatwa*," he choked out. He wanted to claim credit himself, but that wasn't how the game was played.

"Did you plan it?"

"Yes. We wished to punish the American government for killing our children, for defiling our holy lands, and for supporting our enemy." That line was sure to earn him the donations he so desperately needed.

"Does that mean you and the American President are in agreement? She is on record saying the solution to terrorism is the removal of Jewish settlements from the Occupied Territories and the withdrawal of American forces from Saudi Arabia."

"Although we share these goals, America's foreign policy is corrupt. Americans are responsible for the stalled peace talks; they are responsible for killing our babies in Palestine, Iraq, and Afghanistan. They sail their ships into our waters because they want to dominate the world. This was Allah's just punishment for their wickedness."

"Some of your trucks, sir, never delivered their anthrax. Others didn't complete the grids you established for them. Aren't you disappointed?"

Omen swallowed hard. He knew he had failed, but he forced himself to smile, knowing his countenance would be reflected in his voice. "On the contrary. We exceeded our expectations, my friend. As with any new technology, we expected glitches. That's why we targeted eight cities and had two trucks in each. This mission was much more sophisticated than the Twin Tower bombings. Yes, we exceeded our expectations," he lied. "Thousands of Americans will suffer for what their government has done to my people," he ranted, lowering expectations.

"The authorities are saying that hundreds of thousands may die."

"Praise be to Allah. He has made this great victory possible."

19

BAD BOYS

"I'm told Islam is a peace-loving religion and that Muslims are busy worshiping a merciful god." There was a touch of sarcasm in the General's voice.

"Our last two Presidents preached that same sermon, so it *must* be true," Adams scoffed. They were in the Pentagon, having dinner in the Officer's Mess.

"Sure," Sarah answered, "if by 'peace-loving,' you mean they'd like a *piece* of Israel and a *piece* of America."

"And not only are they happy to kill us for it, they do it all for a piece of aa...." Adams looked over at Sarah and thought better of it.

"What he meant to say, General, is that their minds are twisted. They believe they get seventy virgins as a reward for terrorizing us."

"Then what I've heard is true." Hasler was beginning to lose his appetite. He brought his linen napkin up from his lap and tossed it on the table.

An attentive waiter in a perfectly pressed uniform grew worried. "Can I get you something, General?"

"No, I've had more than enough." The others followed Hasler's lead, telling the waiter he could clear their dishes. It was a shame really. The food was as magnificent as the setting. The Officer's Mess is anything but. It's a small, private dining room in an inner ring of the Pentagon, replete with crystal, silver, china, and white tablecloths. It's a far cry from eating an MRE in a Quonset hut in northern India.

Sarah and Thor pulled out their notebooks. "It's worse than you can imagine, Mr. Chairman," Adams resumed. "Their 'religion' not only promises paradise to anyone who dies killing infidels for Allah; it's the only guaranteed way to get in, as far as I can tell."

"Some god."

"Actually, I don't think so," Thor said. "Not unless you know a god that lived in a rock. One that had three daughters who also lived in rocks."

"Not unless you know a god so small he changes his mind, one who

craves monotonous ritual, and wants to be mooned fifty times a day."
Sarah smiled at the thought.

"But will settle for five," Thor elaborated.

The waiter poured everyone coffee and retreated a discreet distance.

"Do you know of a god who condones—actually *encourages*—lying,
stealing, revenge, rape, kidnapping for ransom, terror?" Adams looked
Hasler directly in the eye. "How about selling women and children into
slavery, or the assassination of innocent people? What did I leave out,
Sarah?"

"Just the usual stuff: pedophilia, bigamy, money grubbing, mass murder, and genocide. Do you know any gods like that General?"

"No."

"Do you think there's any chance God's like that?"

"No."

"Congratulations, sir. You've just joined the world's smallest club.

"Club?"

"Yep. There are now three Americans and four Israelis who know that
Allah isn't God. Seven people who know Muhammad was a fraud."

"If Allah isn't God, what is he? And more to the point, who are his followers following?"

"Well, sir, Allah's rock was worshiped as the Moon God. And if you
forget to pray to it, *Satan* gets angry. How's that for a clue?" The Admiral
marched onto the battlefield of the mind, a place where as often as not,
truth gets trammeled and messengers are maligned.

"Islamic scriptures promote war, lying, thievery, rape, bigamy, genocide...well, you know the list. That's the kind of fun stuff Allah busies
himself with. And Allah's angels are killers, fixated on pain and punishment." Sarah followed Thor into the "mind field." If they were going
down, it would be together.

"That's like the opposite of the God I know—the God who wrote the
Ten Commandments and gave them to Moses, the God who inspired the
Pilgrims to come to America, the God who guided the framers of our
Constitution." The General, it turned out, was a closet Christian. He
believed, but he kept quiet, knowing that being typecast in the military
wasn't good for his career. *Don't ask; don't tell.*

"Allah didn't inspire such things, sir."

"And as for his Apostle," Sarah said, "he was...." She shook her head.
Nottingly didn't like Muhammad very much. "You're a military man,
General. You must be aware of the parallels between *der Fuhrer* and *der
Messenger*, between the rise of Nazi Germany and the rise of Islam.
Surely, you've studied this adversary."

"And more importantly," Thor added, "have you contemplated the parallels between Europe in the early 1930s and the fix we're in today?"

"No. What did I miss?"

"Our destiny." Sarah was about to share some unpleasant history with the man who had saved her almost-fiancé's job. "Let's begin by comparing the bad boys: *der Fuhrer*, 'the Leader,' and the Messenger, a title which Muhammad interpreted as 'leader'.

"Hitler, not unlike the Prophet before him, started by asking his compatriots to view him as their long-awaited savior, a prophet called by fate to save Aryans, or in Muhammad's case Arabs. Hitler, like Muhammad, capitalized upon the people's pre-existing beliefs, their jealousies, and prejudices. Both feigned support for prior religious sentiments in order to form bonds and to smooth the transition."

It was Thor's turn. "Just like Allah's Messenger, halfway through Hitler's life, he had managed to lure only a hundred or so followers into his ranks. As in Muhammad's Arabia, the *Fuhrer's* motley group meandered aimlessly until their insecure leader imbued them with his spirit, a sense of rage. In both cases, when the leaders demonstrated a willingness to employ violence and thievery, the number of adherents grew at a geometric rate. In less than a decade, both causes expanded from less than three percent of the local population to a controlling presence. This was a direct result of Muhammad and Hitler providing youthful wannabe-warriors with a sense of adventure, giving them the green light to savage others." Adams paused. "Their story is the same."

Hasler sat stone-faced.

"'None but Germans may be members of the Nation,' Hitler announced from a cellar below a beer hall in Munich—seems they both liked caves. The *Fuhrer* screamed so eloquently, 'The Nazi Party will free you from the power of the Jew. My aim is a thorough solution, the removal of the Jews from the midst of our people.' His mentor must have been Muhammad," Sarah hypothesized. "It's what Muslims want today.

"Did you know, sir, that Allah's Prophet removed the Jews from the midst of *his* people four times? The first two instances were forced mass deportations; the last two featured mass executions of Jewish men; their women and children were sold into slavery. He blamed all his people's woes on the Jews. And, like Hitler, he even came up with some pithy sayings that soothed whatever consternation the pious bystanders may have felt at the time, an antidote for whatever discomfort their consciences may have caused them. Those that supported Jews in either culture found themselves sharing a similar fate."

"The god of the Qur'an calls Jews his enemy, senseless, vile creatures, donkeys and apes. He says that they are destined to burn in His flaming fire. It could have been where Hitler got the idea for his crematoriums. The Prophet's biographer, Ibn Ishaq, claims Muhammad directed Muslims to, 'Kill any Jew.' Not very ambiguous, is it?"

"This is getting creepy," the General moaned.

"Yes indeed," Adams agreed. "These were men on a mission. Focusing on the young and capitalizing upon their impetuousness, Hitler and Muhammad formed bands of armed marauders—Storm Troopers and Caravan Raiders. These men were encouraged to attack, to terrorize, and loot for *Lebensraum*—living space. They were especially keen on killing Jews and political opponents. Both were racists, preaching that their people and their doctrine were pure, superior, and undefeatable. All others were beneath them, infidels or non-Aryans. Jews in particular were evil, deserving to be exterminated."

"*Der Fuhrer's* inspiring speeches and Nazi doctrine motivated the Hitler Youth just as the Messenger's speeches and Muslim doctrine inspire a plethora of youth organizations today, clubs with names like al-Qaeda, Hezbollah, Islamic Jihad, Jamaah Islamia, Fatah, and Hamas," Sarah said. "The sermons haven't changed, nor have the results." The agent and the Admiral were taking turns enlightening the General.

The waiter's eyes were as big as his ears. Standing near the galley door, he was but a few paces from the table.

"Violence was the key to victory for both men," Thor said.

"Thin skinned and paranoid, Hitler had his Storm Troopers, Brown Shirts as they were called, attack anyone who annoyed him, beginning as early as January 1930." Sarah explained.

"With that first kill, they developed a taste for blood. They reveled in the spoils. So did the Prophet's pals. They called it booty. The Qur'an says 'the spoils of war are lawful and good. They belong to Allah and His Apostle.' He also said that anyone who 'annoys' him will receive 'a painful punishment.' So with Allah's blessing, Muhammad's killing and plundering started, as had Hitler's, ten years after his doctrine was conceived, just as Islam was faltering, on the brink of extinction. It was as a direct result of his peers calling him a charlatan."

"How have we missed this?" the General pondered quietly. "What are the implications?"

Sarah plowed ahead, knowing what she was going to say would answer the General's questions. "Because no one had either the foresight to recognize what they were about or the fortitude to stand up and stop them, they made it through the lean times. They signed their treaties, forced their annexations, stirred their followers with dramatic speeches, and wielded ever-sharper swords. They seduced some, forced their will on others, and ultimately impacted much of the world. They both said that treaties they had signed were not binding on their people. In this, sir, their lives and their movements are identical. And by recognizing this, we can predict what will happen tomorrow."

"General, early on, the destruction they caused could have been nipped in the bud with minimum bloodshed. But it was not to be—in either case." Thor paused. "As a result, the world has paid and will continue to pay a horrible price." Adams let that sink in.

Nottingly marched on, making certain to provide sufficient evidence to transcend the gulf between opinion and truth. "Both men maintained their grip on their followers by manufacturing an enemy, *inventing* someone to blame for their pain. Poverty breeds thugs like cesspools breed maggots, Bill. Its stench gives rise to all kinds of warlords and prophets, charlatans with charismatic charm and spirited speech. Hitler and Muhammad propelled their parasites out of poverty, if only temporarily, by finding someone productive to rape and plunder. They used the spoils of war to equip and reward their followers. It instantly swelled their ranks. Two leaders, one victim: the Jews."

Adams looked at Sarah as she spoke.

"On January 30th, 1933, President Hindenburg gave Hitler the break he couldn't win at the ballot box, making him his Chancellor. Hindenburg had given him an inch, but Hitler took a mile, quickly changing the rules and becoming Germany's dictator."

Now Thor picked up the torch. "As thugs are wont to do, the Nazis intimidated the electorate in the March elections, just five weeks later. Then for good measure, they counted the votes themselves, announcing, not surprisingly, that they were the overwhelming winner. *Four days later* they started killing Jews in earnest, opening the first concentration camp in Dachau, outside Munich.

"It was no different with the early Muslims. After their first 'win,' they took control of Medina and began killing and expelling Jews. Think of it, General, with Jews less than one percent of the world's population, what are the odds that both men would blame their problems on *this* tiny minority, confiscate their wealth, and slaughter them in genocidal rage?"

"Not good," the Chairman of the Joint Chiefs muttered.

"The media played a starring role in the ascension of both men," Sarah continued. "They had their thugs kill anyone who said bad things about them, a move designed to dissuade their peers from likeminded foolishness. Then they used the plunder they'd stolen to enthrone their own personal 'journalists.' These upstanding men and women condemned any attempt to critique their leader and his methods: *Jihad* or *Blitzkrieg.*"

He gave an example. "The German newspapers reported in November '33 that 99.5 percent of the inmates in the Dachau concentration camp voted *in favor* of a plebiscite, a referendum designed to solidify Hitler's power. When others protested the obvious prevarication, they labeled their objections 'Mad Jew Propaganda' in banner headlines. With the press in his pocket, Hitler initiated a blockade and boycott of Jewish areas; he created ghettos. His craving for death yet unsatisfied, *der Fuhrer* sent those who survived off to forced-labor and extermination camps. He called anyone who befriended a Jew a 'traitor'. The propagandists justified it by quoting from Hitler's inspired speeches."

Sarah picked it up. "Muhammad, in like fashion, created blockades of Jewish settlements. But starving and robbing them was insufficient to satisfy his bloodlust. *Der* Prophet sold the women and children of Beni Quraidha into slavery and massacred the men. Then he justified his violence against these defenseless Jews with this verse from the Qur'an." She looked down at her notes and read, "'Allah drove back the unbelievers.' 'He was sufficient for the believers, so that they did not have to fight.' And 'Allah brought low the People of the Book, the Jews, some of whom you killed and some you made slaves.'"

"See any similarities so far, sir?" Adams asked.

"I'm starting to believe in reincarnation," the General professed.

"Perhaps it was just the same character flaw, raging insecurity."

"Both Muslims and Nazis based their new pseudo-religions on the pagan practices of their forefathers. They both relied on ritual to stupefy the masses. When conflicts arose they simply revised history to suit their agendas. Call it situational scriptures."

She added, "In Germany, burning twenty-thousand books in a massive bonfire was merely a good start. Goebbels' propaganda machine turned out to be the perfect antidote for everything that ailed their bruised egos. Working together with Hitler, Goebbels helped compose the Third Reich's inspired doctrines. As in Muhammad's day, the best and brightest were either driven away or exterminated, so the dummies who were left thought it all sounded perfectly reasonable. In similar fashion, Muslims burned conflicting versions of the Qur'an. The Bible, the most influential writing of Muhammad's time, was condemned as errant and unenlightened. He called its rise in influence the 'Period of Ignorance.' The Qur'an was the only acceptable antidote."

Thor took over. "Unrestrained egos caused both men to claim that the message and the messenger were one, equally worthy of acclaim. Muhammad said, 'Believe in Allah and his Messenger,' and, 'You will not have faith until you love me more than your own family.' Hitler said, 'The *Fuhrer* is the Party and the Party is the *Fuhrer.*' These guys were two peas in a pod. Both were gifted orators. They had a way with words."

The uniformed waiter moved in closer, refilling all three coffee cups.

"They created a cult," Adams said. "Their zealous fervor was manifested in militarism, violence, terror, heroism, martyrdom, banners, flags, mysticism, ritual, inspiring rhetoric, and all kinds of religious symbolism."

"But it didn't start off that way," Sarah shared. "In Munich, those in power initially viewed Hitler as little more than an irritant, a vulgar crybaby, a petty demagogue. In Mecca the empowered viewed Muhammad pretty much the same way, as an irritant—an insecure and thin-skinned whiner, a harmless but annoying charlatan."

Thor continued. "But their followers saw them as other-worldly, god-like, supreme. They became blindly devoted, pledging in the form of an oath to protect their leaders personally as they would their women and children. For this, both leaders promised utopia, a paradise of their own making, one in which their followers' every craving would be satisfied." It sickened the Admiral, and wasn't doing much for the General, either.

"And speaking of cravings, they both had an unnatural desire for young women. Hitler's young cousin was his first love. Muhammad's favorite was six when they were betrothed. He was a nifty fifty."

"I have been told," the General confessed, "that the church, both the Catholic and Protestant branches, supported Hitler. Is that true?"

"The truth," Sarah said, "for both the Prophet and *der Fuhrer,* is far more revealing." She let that linger for a moment. "In Germany, the Nazis—the National Socialists Workers' Party—were atheists, just like their counterparts in Russia, the Communists. As a result, there was a tremendous conflict between the Nazis and the church, Catholic and Protestant. But Hitler, being a master of deceit, lured them to his side by incorporating their symbols into his movement and by falsely presenting himself as one of them. During his rise, when the movement was fragile, he promised to protect them—not kill them—if they agreed to be passive about his atheistic and militaristic ways."

"You're familiar with how the *Fuhrer* cult grew out of the Goebbels-inspired Leni Riefenstahl propaganda film, *The Triumph of the Will,* right?" Adams asked.

"I've seen it. If you want to understand the mindset of megalomaniacs, it's a must-see," Hasler answered. "Most every rally in 'support' of a dictator tries to emulate Hitler's success. Similar displays of adoration became commonplace in the old Soviet Union, in today's China, North Korea, Iraq, and Iran."

"If you recall, the film begins with Adolph's airplane descending out of the clouds like the Messiah, casting a cross-shaped shadow over a sea of elite troops in ceremonial garb. They're all shown waiting reverently, in eager anticipation of his arrival. The Party faithful were gathered in Nuremberg to praise their exalted leader, *der Fuhrer*. Hitler was only filmed alone, and only from below. The camera looked up at him as he looked down on his people. Remember Heb's stirring words? 'Hitler is Germany just as Germany is Hitler. *Sieg Heil!*'

"Islam's story is the same, though not so high-tech. Muhammad incorporated the Ka'aba, an old pagan shrine, into his religion. Then he added Allah, its Moon God, and his stone. He followed this by telling his faithful to celebrate the idolaters' holy month of Ramadan. Then he announced that he *agreed* with their theology, via his brush with the 'Satanic Verses.' Finally, after he was empowered militarily, he handed down laws which said in essence, don't annoy me and I'll let you live.

"Now, as for the Meccan merchants who had a vested interest in the Ka'aba, the source of their wealth and power, Muhammad took care of them the same way Hitler took care of the clergy, especially the Catholics. Muhammad kept the Meccans in business. All of the stones in the Ka'aba were removed except Allah's. Then he made the Ka'aba the center of his religion, which left the Meccans financially whole. In Hitler's Germany, so long as there was an ostentatious display of Nazi symbolism and prayerful respect was shown for Hitler himself, the churches continued to fleece the flock."

"Ultimately, Bill," Sarah added, "the biggest difference between these guys was that Muhammad didn't have Germans working for him, and no modern technology, so it took his followers a little longer, although Muslims ultimately managed to conquer as much territory as the Nazis did."

"In either day," Thor jumped back in, "with either thug, you were perfectly free to express your concern over their assassinations, mass murders, thievery, or their brutality toward their citizens and neighbors so long as you didn't value your life. Critics were few and far between. Interestingly, in Germany, while the Cardinal capitulated early for political reasons, the lower-ranking priests were defiant for a good long time."

"The Protestants, however," Sarah said, "were pretty much a lost cause, top to bottom. Germany was crawling with liberal theologians who viewed the Bible as moral mythology, a pick-and-choose smorgasbord sort of affair. Their faith had become meaningless. It wasn't so much that the church *supported* the atheistic Nazis. It's that without a vibrant, grounded faith, parishioners lost the ability to tell right from wrong. And equally important, they lost the courage and character they needed to stand up and thwart the evil that had grown among them."

"How's that any different from America today?" the General asked.

"It's not," Sarah replied, flipping through her notebook. "I'd like to pose a riddle. The 'faithful' said of one of these men, 'We believe that Fate has chosen him to show the way to his people. Therefore we greet him in devotion and reverence, and can only wish that he may be preserved for us until his work is completed.' Was that spoken of the Messenger or the Leader, the man of faith or the man of politics?"

"Sounds religious. I'd say it's Muslims speaking of Muhammad."

"Nope. Goebbels, 1929. Okay, how about this one?" She looked down at her notes again. "'Salvation can only come about through a leader/messenger selected and blessed by Providence, who can rescue his people from their plight, restore them, make them honest, and serve as the embodiment of their longing, the bearer of Godly power, destiny, and grace; an organ of a power transcending him.'"

"'The bearer of Godly power?' *That's* Muhammad, for sure, God's Messenger."

"Wrong again. This stirring wisdom was conceived by Sontheimer in Munich, not Muslims in Medina."

"*Good grief!*"

"Which one do you think changed the rules," the Admiral queried, "so that he could justify assassinating his political opponents, kill anyone who uttered something critical of him? Who was it who murdered the media in their beds to silence them?"

"Obviously Hitler."

"Obviously *Muhammad*."

Hasler shook his head, frowning.

"Who 'worked the miracle of faith, enlightening the people like a meteor before their astonished eyes, instilling in them a belief that eliminated despair?'" the Agent asked the General.

"Um, Muhammad, right?"

"Hitler," Sarah revealed. "You're not very good at this game, are you, sir? That was propaganda from Goebbels. *Der Fuhrer's* brand of socialism was propelled by a religious zeal. His inspired vision became doctrine; *der Fuhrer* became godlike, commanding great reverence. The '*Heil Hitler*' was similar to Muslims being required to add 'and Muhammad is his Messenger' every time they ritualistically repeated 'There is no god but God.' The Qur'an even instructs the faithful to 'salute the Prophet with a worthy greeting.' Both portrayed themselves as selfless servants of the people, but they lived and acted like kings—above the law."

"As with the Muslims' Pledge of Aqaba, Nazis pledged their loyalty:

'Friends, raise your right arm and cry out with me proudly, eager for the struggle, and loyal unto death, '*Heil Hitler!*'" The Admiral thrust out his palm in mock praise.

The waiter jumped, asking his only customers if he could be of service.

Sarah held her hand above her cup, as did the others. "They both required unwavering devotion from the faithful. In Goebbels' words, Hitler was 'The Leader of a new, young Germany, *der Fuhrer*, the Prophet, the Fighter…the last hope of the masses.' It was a leap into the darkness, just as it was following Allah's Prophet."

Sarah gazed down at her notes. "Rudolf Heb, a Nazi big shot, embodied the spirit of both movements when he wrote, 'The Leader must be absolute in his propaganda, in his speeches, and words. He must not weigh the pros and cons like an academic, he must never leave his listeners the freedom to think…The great popular leader is similar to the great founder of a religion: he must communicate to his listeners an apodictic faith. Only then can the masses be led where they should be led. They will then also follow the leader if setbacks are encountered; but only if he has communicated an unconditional belief in the absolute rightness of his cause.'"

"Although that was written by a Nazi for Hitler, it's a flawless description of Muhammad and Islam."

Hasler scratched his head. "Are you reading too much into this? I mean, the similarities are shocking, but aren't all dictators the same?" the General wondered.

"Not *this* similar, sir, but think about what you said." The Admiral wanted to make a point. "Muhammad didn't portray himself as a political dictator. He said he was on *Allah's* errand. There are over a billion people who trust this bad boy with their soul."

"They *can't* be that naïve."

"Sure they can." Sarah knew. "Like Heb said, propaganda sells. In a vacuum of truth, lies are irresistible. And remember, General, these people have been fed nothing *but* lies for fifty generations."

"And lies that speak to our preconceived notions, our deepest longings, can be very seductive, sir," the Admiral reminded him. "That's especially true when there's collusion. Today, in the Muslim world, Arabs are bombarded from all directions, but with the same message. They hear it repeatedly in the media, learn it in their schools, have it preached to them in the mosques, and have the same rubbish dictated to them by their leaders: we are worthy of hate. It is their duty to kill us."

"Hitler and Muhammad both knew that the best way to deceive an audience was to include just enough truth in their lies to make them seem plausible, *believable*," Sarah pointed out. "I could give you a million examples, from yesterday and today."

"The source of such deceit is often insecurity." Thor knew from experience. "It's a monstrous cancer that causes its victims to attack everyone who doesn't submit. The insecurities of the Prophet and *der Fuhrer* are revealed in their cravings. They coveted power, sex, and wealth.

"These people religiously, hypocritically, tear others down to elevate themselves. They can't tolerate being criticized. You see, Muhammad and Hitler were both ridiculed by Jews," Thor added. "In Medina, religious Jews made a game of teasing Muhammad after he'd embarrassed himself by convoluting their heritage and beliefs. In Munich, secular Jews, members of the Communist Party, mocked Hitler. They said he was a *prima donna* with his rehearsed gestures and pathological vanity, a sham and a coward. They made a game of tormenting him with sarcastic caricatures, slurring him with reckless abandon. In both instances, they kindled a rage that devastated Jews and eventually impacted the whole world."

Hasler leaned forward. "Even though the Jews were right about these creeps, it would have been prudent for them to keep their yaps shut."

"Yes, sir. Speaking out against evil is only effective if you're willing and able—if you have the character and means—to do something about it."

Bill Hasler put his hand over his open mouth as he processed the implications of what Thor had just said. He sensed its importance.

"Both Muhammad and Hitler became anti-Jew and anti-Christian," Sarah resumed as the two men stared at one another. "Yet they both began their mission by identifying themselves with, even embracing, Jewish inspired doctrines. Hitler did so when he drew rhetoric and inspiration for his National Socialism from Lenin and his people's revolution in Russia. Hitler called himself 'the People's Leader' and 'head of the Worker's Party.' And Muhammad drew similar inspiration from Moses, another Jew. He regularly compared himself to the Great Liberator. They stole their ideas before they stole their possessions."

She took a sip of her coffee, now cold. "For a while, both men tailored their pronouncements to appease the establishment. Muhammad lapsed from monotheism, worshiping three pagan goddesses to appease his tribe. Hitler appeased the Catholic clergy by claiming he was 'deeply religious'."

"In both cases, the deception worked," Adams said, staring intently at the General. He saw in his eyes the look for which he had been searching. The General understood. "The lies bought the madmen time. The opposition was lulled to sleep, only to awaken to a nightmare. Both promised peace while plotting war. Both signed non-aggression pacts with those they later attacked. Think about that in today's context, sir."

"Two men, one footprint." Sarah touched the General's hand. "They craved and obtained absolute power and dictatorial control. They desired and achieved complete submission and unquestioned obedience. At the head of killing machines, they spoke and people died."

"Sir, these men, and their missions were identical," Thor said. "And fortunately both were egotistical enough to leave us a memoir so we could get to know the better. Their books speak of their megalomania, their fixation with punishment, and, of course, their hatred of Jews."

"Why would anyone want to know what these nutcases had say?"

"Because their demented doctrines led directly to the world's worst wars. And *that's* because they had the same motive: racial hatred. Their tactics were similar as well: terror and deception," Sarah concluded.

"Muhammad's Austria was the Jewish settlement of Beni Qainuqa in Yathrib. His Czechoslovakia was the Jewish clan of Beni al Nadheer. Both were annexed and plundered, with the Jews expelled from their homes. Beni Quraidha was his Poland. Those that weren't killed were forced into slave labor. It was the beginning of genocide."

"Oh my God," the General said softly as the lessons of history began to close in upon him. "How have we missed this?"

"The nature of man has not changed in four thousand years," the Admiral admonished. "If we do not learn from past mistakes, Palestine will be our Czechoslovakia, our Beni Qainuqa. And America will be the next Poland."

✡   ☥   ☪

"I'VE ARRANGED for the shipment," Omen grumbled, upset that he was still stuck in the shifting sands of Iraq.

"And as you know, I've had one of the Imam's boys make our suitcase nukes look like scuba gear. He made the other cases look like they were holding photographic equipment."

"That plays nicely into the sailing theme."

Kahn was thrilled that his comrade was playing with his atoms. He was actually being civil. "Hey, did you know they have a terrorist school here in Baghdad? They gave me a tour—they've got a Boeing jetliner to practice hijacking, classes on bomb-making, kidnapping, even how to play the media. You should check it out, Omen, maybe take a class or two."

"Some other time. I'm leaving to escort our bombs to Egypt. As a country of origin, it sounds more benign than Iraq, don't you think? And

I'm going to pick up Aymen's bomb launchers. He had his contraptions fabricated by our agents in Cairo."

"*Holy moon-god,* this is fun," Kahn squealed, rubbing his hands together. "We've got missiles after all."

More restrained, Omen explained, "With the help of our Bahamian faithful, I arranged for someone to modify the v-berth on each vessel to conceal the cargo. We've also enlarged the forward skylight. The design allows us to catapult the weapons through the hatch and launch them a hundred meters into the air. " Omen suddenly burst out laughing.

"What's so funny?"

"Blacks submitting to Islam and helping us out. They have no idea who sold them into slavery. It's delicious."

Kahn nodded, smiling. "Yes, and there's something equally elegant about using a sailboat to deliver nuclear holocaust, don't you think?" Haqqani waxed poetic. "Gliding on Allah's breath, the Devil gets his due."

Omen was unimpressed. "It'll take a few weeks for all of the sailboats to pass through Paradise Island and pick up their gear. Six will stow three cases up front, one will get just two."

"What about the other five boats? The dirty ones."

Omen raised his hand, quieting his friend. "Take it easy. The following week five more are scheduled to sail for Jamaica, also one at a time. Each will pick up ten kilos of our nuclear material."

"Yes. It's not weapons grade, as you know. But that makes it better for dirty bombs. I've had our isotopes tested, and the stuff is plenty nasty, half-lives of five to thirty years. Eighty percent of those exposed are gonna die."

"And the explosives? Are we going to use Iranian C-12?" Omen asked.

"As you wish. I've been busy kissing up to the Iranians, and I found that envy is a beautiful thing," Kahn said gleefully. "I told the Ayatollah that the Iraqis were getting all the credit. After all, they were *their* anthrax spores. He darn near forced me to use his nuclear technicians to recharge the triggers. And I swear, he would have given us enough C-12 to blow up America even without the nukes."

✡ ✝ ☾

ON A STARBOARD TACK America's couple glided down the Severn River. They were headed toward the Chesapeake Bay. Annapolis was fading out of view off their stern. The chapel dome at the Naval Academy was the last discernable landmark.

It was a glorious day. Just enough clouds drifted across the sky to make it interesting. The late spring sun warmed them. And they had a sailor's wind: a steady blow from the southwest filled their sails.

Thor scanned the horizon. "Sarah, if you had your choice between being First Lady or Vice President, which would you choose?"

"Are you running for something, proposing, or recruiting? Or are you just waffling?"

"Are you always this much trouble?"

"Yes," she smiled.

He shook his head. "Prepare to come about," he said, finding his next point. "About ho."

He gave the command an instant before he pulled in the main and pushed the tiller toward the sail. Sarah released the jib sheet, winching it in on the other side. Thor eased the main as the boom crossed above their heads. They were now running downwind, on a port tack.

"I just want to make sure I understand the question," she said. "And I want to know why there are only two choices."

"How many do you want?"

"At least two more—'all of the above' and 'none of the above.'"

"Would you just answer the question?"

"No."

"No what?"

"I don't like having a multiple choice. If you want to know what I think you'll have to ask them one at a time."

She wasn't making this easy.

Once again he picked a point, one ninety degrees from their present heading. "Prepare to come about." He paused a moment, pulling in the line he was holding in his right hand. With the boom more amidship the jolt would be less severe. "About ho." Thor pushed the tiller toward the sail, again changing course. Sarah released and then re-cleated the jib sheet on command. Adams, like his first mate, shifted to the port side of the boat, providing ballast.

The old but meticulously maintained wooden sloop swung through the stiff breeze, settling in on a new tack. Her sails filled, pulling her forward. She was Adams' pride and joy. He had christened her "*Sunrise*."

"Should things continue to progress as they are, and should I be encouraged to accept the Republican nomination at the next election, as the Senate Minority Leader suggested, would you want to be Vice President?"

"Yes, but I'm not old enough."

"Now, see how easy that was? Why didn't you just say so?"

"You didn't ask."

He sighed. "If I were to win, would you rather be First Lady?"

"No hypotheticals on that one. Sorry, sailor."

Distracted, the wind went out of Thor's sails. They luffed, making a terrible racket. Fortunately, he knew just how to recover.

Adams reached into his pocket and removed a small box. He opened it. Inside was a beautiful stone standing proudly on an elegant platinum mount. Sitting tall and strong, it reminded him of her: brilliant and multifaceted, breaking down whatever illumination it found into its most basic elements.

The ring had been a gift. The Israeli contingent of Team Uniform had been so moved by the way Thor and Sarah had reached out to Mary, they'd bought it in anticipation of the big event. Not by themselves, mind you— they were mere men. Yacob's wife, Marta, had helped them pick it out.

"Sarah Nottingly, will you marry me?"

Forgetting where she was, Sarah leapt into Thor's arms, knocking the tiller out of his hand. The boat responded appropriately, spinning out of control. No one cared.

"I'll take that as a yes," he grinned.

Alternating glances between her eyes and her new ring, Thor couldn't decide which sparkled more. Their boat was adrift, but *they* were going somewhere. The sun, sea, and warm breeze all smiled in agreement.

✡   ✝   ☪

"BEFORE I BLOW out of here, I need to know if you're ready," Yasman Alafat questioned his young engineer.

"Piece of cake, sir," Aymen answered. "The Dome's only got four primary support columns. They're huge rectangular structures, but you've given me enough C-12 to take out twenty buildings its size."

"Down boy, careful now. This is not about sending the shrine to Allah. It's about sending the Jews to hell. Implicating them. Politics, boy."

"Yes, sir, I understand," Halaweh said. "We're bribing Jews to carry the bombs inside our SFG packs. But they'll get caught before they can set them off. He looked over at the high-tech gear. "Mamdouh told me to disable their triggers. So I've created a short that will cause them to fail in a way no one will ever detect. Mr. Salim also asked me to make an operable one for him just in case." Aymen Halaweh was much more comfortable working with Alafat than with Kahn.

"Good, son. But we won't have to bribe the Jews. There's a gang of right-wing radicals called the Temple Faithful who are committed to the destruction of the Dome. I plan to use them."

"Why?"

"They want to rebuild their Temple on its original site. Something about it having to be there for their Messiah to come. They're religious zealots. They say they've already made the Temple furnishings to God's exacting specifications."

"How do they know what God wants?"

"They claim Moses told them."

"Moses? Moses is *our* prophet. He met with Muhammad, peace be unto him, here in the Temple during the Night's Journey."

"They don't seem to think so."

"Then they're wrong!"

"Well, they're just Jews. What do you expect? They don't see it our way, which is probably why they've already tried to blow up the Dome."

"They did? When?"

"About ten years ago. They lied, said they were from National Geographic doing survey work of some sort. What they called 'measuring devices' were really bombs. We caught them in the nick of time."

"As we will with this operation, won't we, sir?" A giant grin swept across Aymen's small face. "When they set the bombs against the columns, our brothers will 'discover' them. The Jews will be caught red handed."

"That's right, boy. Then the world gets steamed at the Israelis for trying to desecrate our Holy Shrine. It's despicable behavior."

"Ahh, but it's a brilliant plan, sir."

"Thank you, Aymen. But for the plan to fool the media, the bombs must actually work. The size of the explosion and the placement of the packs needs to be such, that if they *were* ignited, they actually would bring the Dome down. It can't look like a setup or the Shin Bet will smell a rat."

"That's the way I've designed them."

"And Mamdouh Salim's remote triggering device must work as well."

"I understand. I've combined a remote trigger to the telemetry and video data coming from the SFGs. It's all on a laptop PC."

"You know the reason for that, don't you?"

"Yes, sir. You want a second set of triggers in case the Jews get second thoughts, become cowardly, and start to run. As soon as they're in the clear, far enough away from the Dome—boom! No evidence, no tattletales."

"That's it. And with the computer link to the SFGs, Mamdouh will know exactly where they are at all times, right?"

"To the meter. The SFGs have built-in GPSs with transponders.

There'll be live pictures from the helmet cams, too, so there won't be any question as to where they are or what they're doing."

"*Or* who tried to perpetrate this heinous act," the Chairman smiled. Then he got serious. "I've invited Omen Quagmer here. He's going to help out with the organization after I'm gone. Like you, he's a Palestinian. My top ministers are going to work with you as well. Mamdouh Salim will be in charge after I'm gone. Talib Ali will help with recruiting."

"I'm going to miss you, sir. But I know there will be a great reward for you in Paradise."

"Yes, I'm sure."

"Your plan to implicate the Jews will work, sir."

"Praise be to Allah," Alafat mumbled as he headed out of his office for the last time. At the door he stopped, turned, and looked at the boy sitting at the far side of the dark conference table. He could see his reflection along with the blueprints of the Dome of the Rock. Three Israeli SFGs were hanging against the far wall, helmets mounted above them, packs to one side. Politically speaking, this was Alafat's Holy of Holies. And soon his Ark of the Covenant, the SFGs themselves, would be proclaiming his message to the world: the Jews are *my* chosen people.

✡ ✟ ☪

SARAH COULD HARDLY WAIT to tell her folks the great news. They hadn't even met Thor, not in person anyway. Life had been a swirl.

Likewise, Thor wanted to ask Sarah's father for her hand in marriage. Although he knew almost nothing about him, he wanted to meet the man who'd helped mold the woman. Sarah had described him as a wonderful dad and a great husband. Living up to his standard wasn't going to be easy.

And then there was her mother. What would she be like?

Fortunately, Thor wouldn't have to wait long to meet them. Sarah's parents lived on a narrow peninsula nestled between Harness Creek and the South River. It was a leisurely sail from where they had lost control on the Severn. As the seagull flies, Sarah's home was but a few miles south of Annapolis.

The bride-to-be told Thor as much as she could about her parents as they sailed toward them. To his surprise, she said she had been adopted and was an only child at that. Dad, she explained, had been a hard-charging businessman, but he now spent his time writing books. Like Thor, he was a pilot and a sailor. He liked to scuba dive, ski, and play golf in his spare time. He had made a shekel or two in his lifetime, setting enough aside to buy a private airplane.

Mom, she told him, was *mom*. She was the organizer, German through and through, a nice contrast to dad's more relaxed Irish nature. Leisel Nottingly had given up her career as a banker to raise her daughter.

The newly engaged couple entered the mouth of the South River and sailed alongside the picturesque Quiet Waters Park. Inside Harness Creek the wind became squirrelly, requiring the crew to lower the sails and motor the last hundred yards. Negotiating their way around a series of submerged sandbars, they arrived at an old wooden dock. Sarah handled the lines as Thor carefully managed the tiller. Bumping into one of the pilings would have been easy enough, but repairing the damage to the brightly polished mahogany hull would have taken days.

Surviving their first crisis as an engaged couple, they safely secured the *Sunrise* to the pier. Sarah smiled as they walked up to the house from the dock. This was home. Adams smiled, too, for it was *some home*. Sarah was evidently rich, or at least her folks were.

The home looked like it belonged in New England, along the coast, perhaps in Nantucket or on Martha's Vineyard. It had cute written all over it. Shingle style, it came complete with white columns, impressive stonework, brightly colored gardens, and a plethora of ornate flower boxes, one beneath every window.

And then there was the view. Framed by an old red barn on one side and magnificent centuries-old trees on the other, panoramic snapshots of the South River loomed large. The setting sun danced off their private pond, one strategically positioned between home and the sailor's paradise beyond.

"The Muslims are right," Thor said, provoking a response.

"Right about what?" she asked as she rang the doorbell.

"There are virgins in paradise."

Sarah laughed, but hit him on the shoulder all the same.

"Ouch," he said as mom opened the door.

"Nice to meet you, too."

"I'm sorry, ma'am. Not you. Your daughter just hit me, that's all."

"Sarah, play nice. She's always been hard on the boys."

"Yes, ma'am," he said, "I know."

She hit him again.

"Is she always this much fun?"

"'Fraid so." She smiled, opening the door wide. It's good to finally meet you, Admiral Adams," Mrs. Nottingly said, holding out her hand. "Our daughter has told us a great deal about you. And then, of course, there's the TV news."

"Well, you can't believe everything you hear. Those folks with the microphones have been known to make stuff up."

"Come in, Admiral. What brings the two of you by?"

"We were out sailing and thought we'd say hello," Adams said, stepping inside. "I'd sure like to meet Mr. Nottingly. Is he home?"

"Yes, in his usual spot...."

"He uses the study above the garage to write," Sarah interrupted her mom. "It has the best view."

"It's so good to see you, sweetheart." Mom gave her daughter a hug. "I want to hear all about Israel. Did you have a good time?"

"Ma'am," Adams said. "Excuse me for interrupting, but could you point me in the direction of Mr. Nottingly's study? It'll give you girls a chance to catch up on things, chat about our trip."

"Sarah, go and introduce your...." She wanted to say boyfriend but didn't. Adams was way too much man for that. "...Admiral Adams to your father. I'll make some tea."

"*More tea!*" they laughed in unison. It was an inside joke, they explained, without really explaining.

Climbing up the curved stone stairs, the Agent and Admiral found themselves on a large balcony knocking at the door. A tree loomed overhead.

"Sarah!" her father exclaimed, not even seeing Thor by her side. He gave his daughter a warm embrace. "You're back!" he added, finally noticing she had company. "Admiral Adams," he burst out, half in surprise, half in admiration, "to what do I owe this honor?"

He wanted to say, "Her," but settled for, "Hello, sir." He extended his hand. "Please, call me Thor."

"I'm Troy," he responded with an enthusiastic vice-like grip.

"Come in, come in. Please. Does your mother know you're here? She'd be so excited to meet you, Admiral—Thor."

"Yes daddy, she does. She's making us some tea right now."

"Then let's go down and help her out."

"I'll go, daddy. We've got stuff to catch up on, girl stuff. Why don't you and Thor get to know each other. Talk about airplanes or sailboats. Or whatever guys talk about when you're together."

"She's pretty bossy, don't you think?" Troy said.

"Cute, though." Thor could have said more but thought better of it. She packed a mean right hook.

"Sit down." Troy motioned to his future son-in-law. "I converted this place into a study. That couch in the corner makes into a bed but I only use it when I'm in the doghouse," he chuckled. It wasn't true, but it made for a good story.

Adams scanned the room. It was littered with memorabilia, personal encounters with some of the world's best and brightest. There were family photos as well. Some were shot underwater, some in the clouds, others on golf courses in exotic tropical locales. There were also a myriad of business treasures, announcing one success after another. Then there were books on all manner of subjects. Thor felt right at home.

"I understand you're a pilot."

"Yes, but not like you. No carrier landings, no mach two, no bombs or guns. But that notwithstanding, I've gotta pretty sweet ride, a Pilatus."

"Swiss-built. Pratt and Whitney PT-6, right?"

Troy nodded. They were bonding, sharing something in common—something they both loved. "You know your airplanes. Cruises at nearly three hundred knots, flies at thirty thousand feet—coast to coast nonstop. Yet it's nimble. Able to take off and land from strips as tight as Lee Field here in Annapolis—it's only twenty-four hundred feet."

Troy studied Thor over the top of his reading glasses. "I suppose we could talk about flying all evening, but that's not why you're here, is it?"

"No, sir."

"I couldn't help but notice."

"The ring?"

"That and the smile she was wearing. You know she's my pride and joy, but she's a handful, that one."

"Yes, sir, she is."

"Got a mind of her own."

"Yes, sir."

"She intimidates folks. Drives 'em crazy. She may be too smart for her own good."

"Yeah, she's smart, smarter than me, I'll give you that. And she drives me plenty crazy, but in a nice sort of way."

He just listened, smiling.

Thor got down to business. "I'm in love with your daughter, sir. With your permission, I'd like to marry her."

Troy Nottingly smiled broadly, stood, and reached for the Admiral's hand. "Welcome to the family, son." He pulled Adams up, giving him the official Nottingly family greeting, an all-encompassing hug.

"I'm sure her mother has noticed the rock. Fair warning: she's into jewelry."

"I suppose there's something special about an engagement ring. Particularly one on your daughter's finger."

"Yeah, but don't worry. Leisel's too classy to ask about it, not with us up here anyway. All the same, she's dying to know, so we'd better go down before she explodes."

Downstairs in the living room, the announcement was made. The champagne was opened. Well wishes filled the elegant room.

"Have you set a date?" Leisel asked.

Thor looked at Sarah. That was her job.

"Soon," she answered. "We're expecting our first child—a daughter."

They both looked at her stomach, and then at each other. *Where did we go wrong?*

"No, it's not like that, ma'am, sir. I'm not responsible."

That sounded even worse. "I mean, I'm not the father."

That was worse still. Alarmed, Leisel and Troy looked back at their daughter.

Sarah put them out of their misery. "We adopted a little girl in Israel. She's eight years old. Her name is Mary."

Thor explained. "She lost her father in a guerilla attack while he was on duty. Her mom died right in front of us. Victim of a suicide bomber."

"Where is she, little Mary," Troy asked, relieved and worried all in the same breath.

"She's still in Israel, in a hospital in Jerusalem. Friends of Sarah's and mine are with her. She's doing great and should be here Friday morning."

"Because of Mary we'd like to get married as soon as we can."

Thor agreed. "Sir, my life has stirred up quite a squall, and I'm afraid it's going to get worse before it gets better. We'd like a small wedding, out of camera's view. That is, if it's all right with you."

"It's your wedding. We're happy with whatever makes you happy." In truth, Troy was happier about it than Leisel was. She had dreamed of planning the perfect wedding for her little princess.

"Soon, as in the next *week* or next *month?*" Leisel asked.

"Early June, mom."

"And where are all of you going to stay in the meantime?"

Thor scratched his head. His apartment was perfect for one, awful for three. Sarah's was in the middle of the anthrax zone.

With no answer forthcoming, Leisel volunteered, "Then you'll stay right here with us. Sarah can have her old room back, and Mary can have one of the guest rooms. Thor, you can have the room over the garage."

"But that's...." His protest was cut off at the knees.

"It's all settled." It was easy to see where Sarah got her assertiveness....

"We're *grandparents,*" Leisel said, squeezing Troy's hand.

...and where she got her love.

✡ ✝ ☾

DIPLOMATIC IMMUNITY was Chairman Alafat's ticket in. His private jet, a gift of the Saudis, wasn't even inspected by the American authorities. As with all senior diplomats, he didn't pass through customs. Even his luggage was considered state property, hence off limits.

It was good to be out of the depressing sewer of Gaza. While the Chairman acted more like a weasel, he felt as proud as a peacock. After all, he was carrying a secret, one that would make him a legend in his own time. Further, he was a celebrity here in America. The press treated him like royalty, hanging on every word he muttered.

And then there was the ride that loomed large behind him. This was no humble Gulfstream or Challenger. The Saudi Princes knew how to live. Their private airlift included 757s, 777s, and 747s, like this one. Well rested and out of Palestinian purgatory, life was suddenly good again.

Under the glaring eye of the media, the Chairman's luggage was carefully loaded into one of the three stretch limousines that had pulled up under the mighty plane's wings. Speaking into the microphones the press had provided, Alafat complained about everything he could think of, especially about how unfairly his people were being treated—how they were suffering as a result of America's corrupt foreign policy and Israeli occupation. And while he did the obligatory, "I'm sorry a million of your people were poisoned" speech, he was quick to add, "America had it coming," or words to that effect.

He even played the political card, sharing how neither he nor his people were responsible for suicide bombers. "Palestinians are angry. We have been oppressed too long. My people's response to Israeli occupation is only natural. The Jews are the real terrorists."

Asked if he thought he would share another Nobel Peace prize, this time with the current President, he scoffed. "This is *my* initiative."

Lip shaking, Yasman Alafat snarled, "Coming here, we flew over an armada of American warships. Every gun was pointed at my people."

With that, the cameras flashed and the stories were filed. The Chairman and his entourage headed off into the darkness.

20

THE MESSAGE

Thursday morning's headlines screamed, "ANTHRAX ATTACKS!" Trixi Lightheart delivered the bad news. "According to an Associated Press story out of Jerusalem, al-Qaeda has taken credit for the most recent attacks on America. An unidentified spokesman said they were 'a direct result of America's corrupt foreign policy.'" File footage was run of the arrests of the truck drivers and the mass exodus from the cities.

"A spokesperson for The Centers for Disease Control predicted that as many as four hundred thousand people may have been infected with anthrax. As many as half of them could ultimately die from the disease."

Trixi continued, "FOX News has learned that the al-Qaeda network targeted ten cities. Boston, Philadelphia, Washington, Miami, Chicago, San Francisco, Los Angeles, and San Diego have been turned into virtual ghost towns." As she spoke the network showed eerie pictures of deserted streets. Atlanta and Dallas were spared due to inclement weather."

She turned to face the center camera. "We are told that the early morning showers along the eastern seaboard following the attacks have significantly reduced the risk of infection. According to the CDC, the number of people exposed is half of what it would have been had it not rained. In moist conditions the spores are unable to stay airborne long enough to find a host. Rainstorms washed exposed surfaces of buildings and vehicles, carrying the deadly spores down storm drains, and in many cases, out to sea. Speaking from their headquarters in Atlanta, a CDC official told FOX News that the high humidity in South Florida and fog in San Francisco caused blower malfunctions, saving even more lives. Environmentalists, however, are outraged by the potential impact on sea life."

The studio cut to a file photo of Ghumani, AK-47 at his side. "Even with their ringleader, Halam Ghumani, in a Federal prison, al-Qaeda was able to attack America," Lightheart said, as if one person was solely responsible. "An anonymous spokesperson told the Associated Press in Jerusalem yesterday that 'the attacks were designed to punish America for sending its aircraft carriers to the Middle East.' Al-Qaeda claimed that 'America's unilateral support of Israel and Israeli war crimes against the Palestinian people are to blame.' Speaking from the White House, Secretary of Defense Ditroe replied, "These statements underscore the urgency of the President's planned withdrawal from Saudi Arabia and her upcoming summit with Israeli and Palestinian leaders at Camp David."

With the camera back on Miss Lightheart, she smiled. "Amid the killing, the only real hope for a lasting peace may lie with Palestinian Chairman Yasman Alafat. He arrived in Washington last night, flying into Andrews Air Force Base. He and his aides were taken by car to Camp David. At a press conference, the Chairman said he was prepared to sign his Palestinian Peace Initiative. The ceremony is scheduled to take place tomorrow morning. According to the White House, the President's Peace Initiative removes America from the Middle East, bringing a true and lasting peace in our time," the info-babe proudly proclaimed.

She continued, "Chairman Alafat expressed regret that Americans were poisoned. In his remarks to the media, he also criticized the use of military force in the Middle East, saying, 'Coming here we flew over an armada of American warships. Every gun was pointed at my people.'"

The studio broadcast a picture of Hasler in uniform. "Unable to protect Americans from terrorists, William Hasler, the Chairman of the Joint Chiefs, said today that he will resign as soon as the President names his successor. Insiders say that the President lost confidence in the General.

Trixi moved to other news. "Republicans, upstaged by the President's remarkable diplomatic coup, are calling on Thurston Adams to address a Joint Session of Congress tomorrow evening. Democrats are calling the speech 'irrelevant.' The Admiral could not be reached for comment."

✡   ✝   ☪

IN THOR'S MIND, the Lincoln Memorial was America's Temple Mount. He asked his fiancé to meet him there. He needed some inspiration—from both Abraham and Sarah.

He had worked on his speech all day, pecking away at a laptop in Troy's study. Sarah had shifted gears. Having finished her written report on Islam and its founder, she had gone out with mom to look at dresses. They had picked a date and a place for the wedding. It would be held in three weeks, in a beautiful chapel called the Belfry. The church adjoined a nineteenth-century mansion. Friends of the family had restored both buildings, making them perfect for the wedding and reception. High above the Severn River, it overlooked Annapolis and the Naval Academy.

Surrounded on three sides by the massive memorial, Thor and Sarah were together again. They looked up at the back wall. He read the Gettysburg Address. The words were powerful, moving, almost majestic.

Holding her hand, he turned to his right, mouthing the words of Lincoln's Second Inaugural Address as if he were giving it. Finished, he and Sarah gazed up at the statue.

"If only he could write my speech."

"If only he were still *President*."

"Yeah. Slavery was evil and he knew it."

"Fortunately," Sarah said, "he had the courage to stand up and fight it. He wasn't into appeasement."

"In a way, we're fighting slavery today, Sarah. Do you know that?"

"Yes. A billion people are slaves to Islam. In fact, the very word 'Islam' means submission. They're slaves to those who use it to stay in power. We need to help free them—for in freeing them, we free ourselves from the terror their masters inflict on us. Win-win."

Thor agreed. "The dictators who control these governments are no better than the worst slave owners. Their people have no freedoms. If they step out of line, they're lashed."

"A billion people are slaves to a false doctrine, a doctrine that legitimizes—actually glorifies—terror. How on earth did something so bad get so big?" she asked as they walked away from the statue and toward the open end of the Memorial.

"I think I've figured it out, Sarah," Thor said, sitting down on the steps. He motioned for her to do the same. "I've been thinking about this since I heard them praising Allah while my men hung on those crosses." He touched her knee. "The Prophet died in 632. And surprise! Arabs rejected Islam. They refused to pay the I-love-Mo tax. Afraid he might actually have to go out and earn a living, Abu Bekr started the War of Compulsion instead. The bloodiest battles in the already violent history of Islam were fought between Arabs. But by year's end, the anti Islam rebellion was squashed by the military wing of the fledgling 'religion'.

"Now the new caliph, Muhammad's best friend and father-in-law, has a bit of a problem," Thor said as Sarah rested her head on his shoulder. "Bekr knew Islam's gains had come as a result of turning peaceful Bedouins into a warmongering horde. With the war over, he had to either change the spirit of the new Muslims, change his religion, or find a new enemy. He chose the latter. In 633 Muslim Arabs invaded Judea and Syria. Three years later they attacked the Byzantines, and the year after that, they massacred the Persians—occupying all of Iraq. In 640 they invaded Egypt. *Blitzkrieg* on camels."

Sarah suppressed a smile. "Seven major wars in less than that many years. There's a pattern developing here."

"You think so? Yep, Islam's as peaceful as the Third Reich," Thor moaned. "So then the Prophet's cousin, Ali, became khalif in 656, but the Muslim governor over now-occupied Syria and Judea refused to recognize him. Cousin Ali was assassinated, bringing the Umaiyid dynasty to power. Then there was *another* civil war, this one lasting five years. It ended with the killing of the Prophet's grandson. This led to a blood feud, a schism that still exits today—between the Shiites and the Sunnis. With me so far?"

"You do love your history." Sarah reflected, "Up to this point, Islam makes the Nazis' rise look like a Sunday School picnic."

"Yes. And why? Because the Arabs who'd rubbed shoulders with Allah's Messenger, those who knew him best, acted just like him. Within one hundred years of Mo's death, Islamic warriors had conquered most everything from the borders of China and India in the east to Spain and a good bit of France in the west. There was something about Muhammad's new doctrine that turned peaceful nomadic Arabs into aggressive warriors."

"Yeah. That's 'cause killing for Rocky and Hoodwinker was their ticket to plunder and paradise."

"Rocky and Hoodwinker—now there's a twosome." He gazed out upon the great reflecting pools and Washington's crippled obelisk. "They became as fond of violence as they were addicted to booty."

Long shadows descended across the mall as evening drew near. "So then how, you ask, did this violent, money-grubbing 'religion' become relatively peaceable and tolerant? Why was it assimilated into the conquered cultures? And why, after all these years, did it revert back to the warlike ways of its forefathers?"

"You plucked the questions right out of my mouth."

"As the Arabs advanced, they gave their victims three choices: die, pay a debilitating tax, or say the magic words."

"The magic words?"

"There is no rock but Rocky and Mo's da Man," Thor paraphrased. "But that's about all the conquered knew about Islam. You see, the Prophet *forbade* taking the Qur'an to infidel lands. Not that it would have made much of a difference if they had, you understand. The preponderance of Arabs were illiterate."

Thor looked toward the Vietnam Memorial, drawing strength from the courage of those who had gone before. "Muslim warriors had expanded the Arab Empire to its maximum size by 750, a hundred years *before* Al-Bukhari compiled his Hadith or Ibn Ishaq's biography was edited by Ibn Hisham. Therefore, during the hundred years of conquest only the Islamic warriors themselves knew anything about the life and sayings of the Prophet. And they knew it only by virtue of oral tradition."

"Ah," Sarah said as the light dawned, "so if by saying the 'magic words' you got to keep your money and your life—well, why not? Nobody had a clue what they meant. It would be more than a hundred years before an account of Muhammad's life was written or his speeches compiled, and another *millennium* before these were available to anyone except for khalifs and clerics."

"Precisely." The lovebirds watched as a pair of white doves flew in front of them, seeking shelter. Thor finished his tale. "Now, uncomfortable living in the lands they'd conquered, the nomadic Arabs returned home, leaving a void. The conquered found that, for all practical purposes, they had surrendered to a religion they knew nothing about. Its founder, his message, and his hatred for Christians and Jews, was a mystery. As a result, the conquered continued to be the same tolerant people they had always been. All they knew for sure was that giving Islamic 'alms' was cheaper than paying the heavy taxes imposed on non-Muslims and a whole lot less painful than losing their heads."

Sarah nodded. "I get it. There were no printing presses to publish the Qur'an, and Arabs were really snooty about it needing to be read in Arabic. That made it both inaccessible and incomprehensible."

"It's perfectly clear, Sarah. When Arabs were influenced by the Prophet, they were militant. Those who didn't know about him were tolerant. This was never more evident than during the glory years of the Islamic Empire, the period between 750 to 860. The cultural high-water mark *followed* the period of violent conquests and *preceded* the advent of 'reliable' information on the Messenger and his message. The good times were literally sandwiched in between the bad. The decline of Muslim tolerance, culture, prosperity, and intellectual curiosity coincided with the publication of Al-Bukhari's True Traditions and Ibn Hisham's edits of Ibn Ishaq's biography. It was no coincidence."

"You have a gift, love."

"Then you agree," he said, pleased by her response.

"Sure. In fact, I know right where you're going with this." She brushed a stray curl away from her eyes. "Fast forward to the fifteenth century. Guttenberg invents the printing press and everything changes. The first book he publishes is the Bible, and for the first time in a thousand years,

Christians could actually discover for themselves who Jesus was, what he said, and what he did for us. It transformed the world, gradually depoliticizing the clergy and eroding their power. Thus began the Reformation and with it the dawn of Western civilization."

"But," he said, stealing her thunder, "eventually those same printing presses that did so much to liberate the West made their way to the Middle East. There they had just the opposite effect. At the dawn of the sixteenth century, the Turks became the first Muslims since the time of Muhammad to actually know their Prophet. Imbued with this new understanding, they became terrorists again, acting as he had acted. The Ottoman Turks conquered Syria and Egypt, starting in 1517. Then they moved on to Iraq and Algeria." Thor stood, pulling her up by the hand.

"Now Sarah, fast forward again—to the twentieth century. The world finds itself running on oil, and, thanks to the Brits, Arab Muslims find themselves back in power. What's more, their schooling focuses on teaching children all about the life and times of Muhammad, the Prince of Destruction. Arabs get it from all sides, their madrases, their mosques, their media, and the maniacs in charge. So what do you suppose happens?"

"They begin to act like the Mighty Mo."

"Yep. Muslims once again begin emulating *der* Prophet. Terror reigns. The scourge of *Jihad* commences anew."

✡   ☦   ☾

FRIDAY MORNING DAWNED fraught with portent. The international media had joined the Washington press corps at Camp David. The place was abuzz; the world was changing before their very eyes.

Limousines were stretched out as far as the eye could see. If you were somebody, *anybody,* you were here. Or at the very least, you were stuck in traffic trying to get here. Identification badges, all proudly proclaiming, "I'm important," were being flashed at every enlisted man and Secret Service agent within miles of the historic, normally tranquil retreat nestled against the Blue Ridge Mountains.

Inside, still cozy in the nicest cabin, the President prepared for the day. Secretary Ditroe had slept alone. She had a job to do. On this chilly spring morning, other cabins were coming alive as well. One was occupied by the Chairman of the soon-to-be state of Palestine, another by the leader of the soon-to-be-smaller state of Israel.

These two statesmen had come to Camp David for different reasons.

For one, it was a command performance. Show up and sign or be completely abandoned, orphaned, if you will. By signing his nation away, Israel's Prime Minister saved face in the arena of public opinion. And hopefully, as a result, he would weather the storm, endure long enough to reach more sane times. Half of his nation was crying out for political compromise, for caving in to terrorist tactics, for trading land for the promise of peace. The other half was *right*.

But as sad as he was, he had to laugh. His son had packed his favorite t-shirt. It featured a picture of an American Indian sitting cross-legged next to conservative Israeli Prime Minister Benjamin Netanyahu. The caption read, "Bebi, let me tell you about trading land for peace."

Down the path a bit, the other contestant was yawning. His being here was a horse of an entirely different color. This was to be his crowning achievement. His nation would be born this day. And while the agreement failed to cede all of Jerusalem to his people, as he had promised them, he was no longer afraid of the political fallout.

The last time he had been here was in July 2000. He had been a guest of his friend, Bill Clinton. During that stay, liberal Israeli Prime Minister Ehud Barak had offered him the keys to the kingdom—*his* kingdom. But it wasn't enough. With terrorists, thugs, and other lesser life forms, it never is. Alafat knew that signing a peace accord that didn't have Arab flags flying proudly over *all* of Jerusalem was akin to signing his own death certificate. Having seen Yitzhak Rabin assassinated by his people shortly after initialing the Oslo accords, he knew exactly what awaited him. And to his credit, he'd admitted as much to Clinton at the time.

But now, that little annoyance was no longer a problem. He had taken destiny into his own hands.

At seventy-something, body racked with Parkinson's and character assailed by those even more militant than he, the Chairman was ready. He would die as he lived. Within an hour he would be the most famous person on the planet, his legacy assured. And if Allah was the god the Messenger claimed him to be, if Paradise was how he had described it, then he was within minutes of ecstasy. If not, then at least he had the satisfaction of having lived the Marxist/Leninist version of paradise—dictatorial domination over the masses.

With curtains partially drawn, he calmly and ever so carefully strapped the burden to his ill-shaped body. It was heavy and uncomfortable. It chaffed, was stiff, and a bit awkward, he thought. The deed done, he lay back on the bed. Shadows filled the rough-hewn room. The fire he had built the night before had died. Only the smell of soot remained.

Fanciful imaginings danced through the old man's head. He read tomorrow's newspaper headlines in his mind's eye, listened to the news anchors eulogize his life and struggle. He saw his people carrying his wounded body through the streets in a massive celebration, the biggest ever. Then he saw the virgins—the most beautiful of all. Perhaps the Prophet was right. They seemed so real.

He sat up and reached for the gauze he had packed for this moment. Like a kamikaze warrior enveloping his head with slogans stirring his soul, as if he were drinking one last ounce of liquid courage, the Chairman reverently wrapped his privates, protecting them from what was to come. He knew this was how it was done.

How having a penis in paradise would do him any good after the rest of his body had been blown to bits took a leap of faith he couldn't quite muster. But at times like these, terrorists tend to ponder such things, although suicidal Muslims muse with the wrong head.

With a few minutes to spare, Yasman Alafat reviewed his magnificent life. He thought back through the decades to his youth in Egypt. Following the Six Day War, he, a devoted Marxist-Leninist, had been hand picked by the head of Soviet Intelligence, General Aleksandr Sakharovsky. It had been such an honor. He was viewed as the perfect terrorist. That brought a smile, for he knew he had become the best in the world at his chosen profession.

Lounging in the quiet of his cabin, Alafat remembered the joy of co-founding Fatah and then being elevated to the Presidency of the PLO. It had all been arranged by General Sakharovsky and supported by his ally, Egypt's Marxist-Muslim President and PLO founder Nasser. The gullible Americans had never understood Egypt's role in his life as a terrorist, Alafat mused. For the last two decades, the only national leader he had felt obliged to seek counsel from was Egypt's "moderate" Hosni Mubarak. The PLO's plans for the annihilation of Israel, even the PLO's Covenant had all been conceived, approved, and implemented in Cairo.

Stretched out on the unmade bed, he thought of the trip he had taken to the Soviet Union for training. He and his KGB mentor had so much in common. They lived to rid the world of Zionists and other rabid dogs. He had done so much to keep America's infected fangs out of Arab lands.

Then his smile broadened as he relived the early seventies, the siege he had so cleverly planned with the PLO and KGB. The American diplomats in Khartoum, deep in the Sudan, never knew what hit them. They had been invited to a reception hosted by the Saudi embassy, he remembered. The Americans were to be held hostage, he reminisced, pending the release of Sirhan Sirhan, the Palestinian assassin of Robert Kennedy. Nixon had refused. Alafat clinched his fist. Then he replayed in his mind how he had given the order to murder his hostages. First blood.

He thought about his role in the kidnapping of the Israeli athletes at the Munich Olympic Games. It too had been a murderous affair. All those plots he had planned—all those he had denied. He laughed out loud. They were the same. He was the master of deceit. It had been so easy to fool the stupid Americans. They were all so naïve.

And then there had been the uprising. September 1970. He and his fellow PLO militants had nearly overthrown King Hussein in Jordan. While he had been expulsed, he had managed to turn that dark hour into a tremendous victory. He smiled as he remembered leading his troops into Lebanon, subverting the government, starting a civil war, and destroying the country just six years later. Yes. Those had been the golden years. His friendship with Syria had led to the occupation of Lebanon which continued to this very day. *I shall be remembered as a great warrior.*

Friends he thought. He had so many. Any enemy of the Jews or Americans was a compatriot. Cuba, Iraq, Iran, North Korea. That brought his reflections around to his comrade, Romanian dictator Nicolae Ceausescu, like himself a devoted Marxist. He had successfully murdered 50,000 of his own people, yet the gullible Americans had congratulated him following each 're-election' by the Communist party. *The American State Department,* he thought. *What a joke.* For twenty years they wallowed all over Ceausescu, believing that he could be used to breach the Iron Curtain. During the Cold War, two American presidents had traveled to Bucharest to grovel at his feet.

For him, it had been the same. He too had deceived the Americans, and for just as many years. He had convinced them he could bring peace. That deception brought a smile. Alafat shook his head, remembering the times he had been a guest at the White House, for a while more than any head of state. Secretary Colin Powell had even come calling a few years back. The Americans groveled so nicely when Arabs threatened to withhold their oil.

Then he recalled how his pal, Ceausescu, had died at the hands of his own people, executed after being accused of genocide and tyranny. That wouldn't happen to *him.* No, not to him. He was about to write his own history, take his legacy into his own hands.

He patted the bomb wrapped around his torso, donned his military fatigues and artistically arranged his headdress. He was a soldier, doing his duty, he reassured himself. Rabid dogs were about to become extinct.

There was a soft knock at the door. "Mr. Chairman," the voice said respectfully. "Are you ready? The President and the press are waiting for you." It was Secretary Ditroe. She had been asked to escort the man of the hour to center stage.

He said nothing, sucked in his gut, and buttoned his jacket. He looked official. He checked himself out in the mirror one last time. Pleased with what he saw, he turned and walked out the door.

"You look splendid," the Secretary lied.

"Thank you," the Chairman answered. "And how have you and the President been doing?"

She ignored the veiled affront to her character. "She's waiting for you in the central cabin along with the Prime Minister." They zoomed off in their golf cart, Ditroe behind the wheel.

Bumping along the uneven path, the Chairman growled, "Slow down, woman. You're going to get us killed."

Driving more cautiously, Susan informed her passenger, "The plan is for you to leave the room together and sit at the head table—you on the President's left, the Prime Minister on her right. Each of you will have an original copy of the Peace Agreement granting total independence to the Palestinians. Congratulations, sir. This must be a very proud day for you." She rambled on as they rode, constantly encouraging Alafat for fear he might bolt, do something foolish, embarrass them.

"What about the others?" Yasman asked as they made their way through the towering trees and toward the prestigious gathering.

"Everyone important will be seated behind you. They all want to be included in the pictures. This is a momentous occasion."

"All as in *who?*" he asked, as they neared their final destination.

"The Vice President, our entire Cabinet, the Speaker of the House, Senate *pro tempore*, the minority and majority leaders, most all Congressional Committee chairs. Everybody who counts is here."

"Admiral Adams?" he questioned, as she opened the door.

"No. He wasn't invited. I hope that's okay. We didn't think you'd want him here. Not with all the killing."

"What's wrong?" the President asked pensively as they arrived.

"The Chairman was asking about Admiral Adams."

The President loathed that name. But after upstaging him today, she would never have to hear it again. She forced a smile.

"You fellas know each other, right?" the President asked, hoping the Chairman and Prime Minister might embrace each other.

They nodded grudgingly. They would shake hands only when required, once for the camera. That's all they had in them.

"Ready, boys?"

"No, not quite yet," Alafat replied, reaching into his jacket pocket. "I have something for you to sign. My people need a little bit more honey."

The President wanted to say, *You're getting nearly half of the land of milk and honey, honey. Don't push your luck.* But having anticipated what was coming, she replied, "How much more do you want, Mr. Chairman?"

"If I recall, Anwar Sadat received two billion dollars a year for signing the last set of peace accords initialed in this place. Don't my people deserve at least that much?" No one ever said terrorists were stupid.

The President called Ditroe over to the corner. This had been expected. "I *told* you he'd hold us up—force us to buy his signature."

"You were right," she whispered. "He'd have us over a barrel if you hadn't seen this coming. It was shrewd getting Congress to take it out of my defense budget. We were planning on a peace dividend anyway."

"Yeah, but I wanted to spend it on *our* people, not his."

The President looked down at the paper. Seeing no way out, she asked Susan to bend over. She placed the agreement on her back and scribbled her name. It was written in a hasty, illegible scrawl, but on the right line.

"Thank you," Alafat said politely, retrieving the paper from her.

Less than amused, the President walked outside, followed by the Prime Minister and the Chairman. The cameras were rolling, the tapes were recording, the pens were flying. This was the big moment, the moment the whole world had yearned for. Peace was at hand.

Three abreast, they made their way through the sea of political dignitaries. A professional-sounding voice proclaimed, "Ladies and gentlemen, please welcome the President of the Palestinian Authority, the Prime Minister of Israel, and the President of the United States of America."

They were hailed with reckless abandon. Even the squirrels ran for cover. Arriving at the elegantly carved mahogany table, they sat, staring at the crowd. The President wanted the agreement signed first, self-congratulatory speeches later. It left less to chance.

"Gentlemen, we have given each of you a commemorative pen and an original agreement. There are three signatory lines. It is time for each of us to sign, for each of us to etch our names forever in history."

They all lifted their pens. The President was the most dramatic, then the Chairman, followed by a dejected Prime Minister. They put pen to paper, and in their nicest writing, they spelled their names. By so doing, they each committed their peoples. Exchanging papers, they repeated the process two more times. As they placed the elegant plumes back in their receptacles, the audience broke out into a spontaneous roar; even the impartial press joined in the frenzied celebration.

Ministers from each nation took their respective copies, placing them into blood-red commemorative portfolios. The Chairman slid the multi-billion-dollar annuity the President had signed into his binder so it could be carried away for safekeeping.

It was time for the speeches. The President went first, proclaiming how wonderful she was. Her speech was filled with all her best words. They represented the very height of tolerance, multiculturalism, political correctness, and compromise. It was forward thinking, not mired in the past. She was magnificent. Even the press was moved.

The Prime Minister followed. He was not nearly as optimistic. His words beseeched the ghosts of past generations to forgive them for not heeding the harsh lessons of history. His speech was utterly forgettable. It was all about yesterday, not tomorrow.

Then the High Priest of Peace rose to his feet. The audience gasped. He was godlike, having with a single slash of his pen removed the last obstacle to a true, lasting peace for all mankind. They all rose to their feet, politicians and press alike giving Yasman Alafat the thunderous ovation his life's struggle had earned. This was his moment and they were reveling in it.

He walked confidently to the rostrum, placing a hand on either side. The world saw him smile. It was an odd sort of smile, the smile of a twisted mind, a subtle outward sign that he was about do something that would bring him great pleasure. Suddenly, inexplicably, all who saw it were chilled to the bone.

His left hand fell to his side and slipped into his pocket. Yasman Alafat turned and eyed the President. "Die!"

He pushed the button. It was over in an instant.

The world had no idea what had happened. Nor did those who had gathered at Camp David hoping to bask in the glory. Every camera was obliterated. Every life was extinguished.

✡   ✝   ☾

"MY FELLOW AMERICANS," Admiral Thurston Adams began his televised speech from the House Chamber. It was eight o'clock in the evening. All but two dozen seats were filled, including the balcony. The empty chairs belonged to souls now lying in state under the Rotunda, fifty paces from where Adams was standing. The day had not started well.

"I thank you for coming, and I thank you at home for listening—especially those whose lives have been ravaged by the scourge of terrorism. The horrific stench of terror has swept across our land once again. Many of our best and brightest have succumbed, dying needlessly to satisfy the ungodly cravings of deluded minds." He paused. "But we will survive." He looked around the mighty room, then at the camera. "We will wipe this plague from the face of the earth, so help me God."

The audience rose in agreement. The country, although depleted, was once again unified in its resolve. "We have lost our President, Vice President, their entire Cabinet, and many of the leaders who served in this august body. Our nation has been injured; we have been dealt a vicious blow." His eyes narrowed in righteous indignation. "But we shall endure."

The Admiral surveyed his surroundings. The giant chamber spread out to his right and left. The lower walls were a deep, dull red, the upper walls, above the balcony, a soft sky blue. Between them, white columns and trim majestically brought the hall's patriotic motif together.

"Tonight, I speak for the families who have lost loved ones to Muslim militants in Lebanon, Saudi Arabia, Somalia, Yemen, Afghanistan, New York, Pennsylvania, Washington, and now Camp David. It is my hope that their sacrifice gives us the courage to defeat this enemy."

He wasn't in a hurry. The message he had to deliver was going to make more enemies than friends. "America, we have made a tragic mistake. Al-Qaeda and the hundreds of terrorist organizations like them are not the enemy. Nor is this some new and malignant form of radical extremism. Groups like al-Qaeda, Hamas, Hezbollah, and Islamic Jihad are merely a symptom of a far more infectious and widespread disease."

He blurted it out. "The cancer is Islam itself."

The audience gasped. While it should have been obvious, no one had ever had the courage to say these words—not this bluntly. "America has paid a terrible price. Which is why I unabashedly call the perpetrators—and those who motivate them, harbor them, fund them, delude them, and celebrate them—the enemy. They and the doctrine that drives them are evil.

"Four years ago nineteen Muslim suicide bombers shattered the financial heart of our nation, robbing three thousand innocents of their lives. Since that time, Islamic lunatics have inflicted all manner of violence on our people. It continues on to this very day. In fact, every terrorist attack on America by a foreigner has been planned, funded, perpetrated, and celebrated by *Muslims*. Islam is the *only* common denominator."

He stared at the camera, making eye contact with millions. "I did not go in to this search with an open mind. I went in to find the enemy, to understand their motives, and to discover what we can do to eliminate the threat before they eliminate us." It was going to be a long night.

"I recognize that it is our nature as a people, as a nation founded upon freedom, to leave other peoples alone, to let them believe whatever they wish, to let them live however they choose. But today there are reasons why doing so will be at our peril—and theirs. The Islamic states have targeted us. We are *their* enemy, whether they are *ours* or not. We are the Great Satan, infidels worthy of death. They have demonstrated this hostility toward us with word and deed. I have not imagined this, nor can I ignore it. Nor can you, if you wish to live.

"The goodness within us cries out for tolerance and compassion, for dialog and even appeasement—but this course, though instinctive with us, is not in our national or personal interests. We must resolve to understand the madness that drives those who view us so malevolently. And we must use what we learn to stop them.

"Whenever totalitarian governments deprive their own people of basic human rights—the right to life, liberty, and the freedom to live in a manner worth living—Jefferson's 'pursuit of happiness'—we have an obligation to free the many from the tyranny of the few.

"Throughout the Muslim world, dictators are now depriving their citizens of these things, and to such an extreme that life is intolerable. Swamps breed disease. Despair gives rise to despots who terrorize.

"When we see leaders perpetrating heinous acts upon their people, we must act. Yes, *us*. Americans. Why? Because failure to do so reduces our humanity and separates us from the God in whom we trust. Failure to act actually endangers the freedoms we hold so dear, for racial hatred knows no borders. Yesterday, they killed their own. Today, they kill us.

"History confirms the merits of my warning. Hitler had no regard for human rights. He terrorized his critics, and viewed Jews as Muslims view us. The Marxists in Soviet Russia were equally tyrannical and similarly devoted to their misguided cause. But rather than understand these new emerging enemies of human decency, we ignored them, appeased them, did anything we could to avoid fighting them. As a result of our delays, our self-delusion, and the misguided 'peace process', fifty million souls were obliterated, and many times more found themselves imprisoned, impoverished slaves in their own land.

"We are facing the same referendum today with Islam. We can ignore, appease, and capitulate—or we can understand what motivates Muslims and eliminate the threat. The choice is clear. It is our minds that have become clouded. And to those who think it's immoral to criticize another's religion, I say Islam is no more a religion than Communism is, nor is it any more peaceful than Fascism was.

"Understand beyond all else that I share this harsh reality not because I wish to destroy Islam, but because Islam is trying to destroy us. Muhammad was more like Adolph Hitler than a man of God." A million mouths fell open. "And for this reason the world is in terrible peril. Not because he lives, but because his warmongering message survives in the hearts of *five hundred million* impetuous boys and girls of fighting age."

The chamber let out a collective gasp. Viewers across the nation dropped their remotes in astonishment. "We were not tolerant of Communism or Nazism when they proved to be barbarous. We fought them, even though many who lived under these regimes were good and decent. So, too, we must recognize the doctrine of Islam for what it is: a terrorist manifesto. We must deal with that uncomfortable truth."

The Admiral continued by explaining what the founders of Nazism and Islam had in common. "They told their people what they wanted to hear, made them feel racially superior, and blamed their woes on others, creating an enemy out of the Jews! Both rallied their people and funded their war chests by raping them. They were both guilty of genocide, killing a race of defenseless innocents to satisfy their own inadequacies.

"How can this be? You've been told that the Qur'an is a beautiful work, that it stirs the soul and inspires its followers to seek God and live in peace with man. That is a bold-faced lie. The Qur'an is repetitive and contradictory, fixated on hell and punishment. At its best, it's a poor attempt to present the great stories and moral lessons of the Bible. At worst, it's a call to war. But it's not only the Qur'an that incites Islamic violence. It's the Hadith as well—the Messenger's speeches—that inspire young Muslims to acts of terror. Unable to give his followers a reason to live, Muhammad gave them a reason to die.

"Fighting, by definition, is the antithesis of peace. Yet Muhammad says that the greatest rewards are given to those who die fighting. Allah agrees, commanding his followers to kill us. Since fighting in Allah's Cause is the highest calling for a Muslim, their religion can't be peaceful. Since Allah is fixated on banishing Christians and Jews to the fires of hell, it can't be tolerant or merciful. And since Muhammad is dead and Allah never lived, why do those who have been infected with this poison adhere to such nonsense and terrorize the world? Why do they lie about the essence of their perverse doctrine? And, more important still, why do we believe them?

"There are fewer than five surahs in all of the Qur'an that do not devolve into threats of pain and suffering. Fighting in Allah's Cause dominates the Hadith. The Prophet, as revealed by his earliest biographers, is arguably the most maniacal soul ever to have set foot on our troubled planet." Adams held a copy of the Qur'an high above his head. "I'm going to read one verse. But with the fate of the world handing in the balance I implore you to read this hellish book yourselves." He opened it to the fifth surah. "After speaking of the Children of Israel, Muhammad claims Allah revealed the following: 'The punishment for those who wage war against Allah and his Apostle is to *crucify* them, or banish them from the land. Such is their disgrace in the world, and in the hereafter. Their doom shall be dreadful.'"

Looking down and shaking his head, he closed the Qur'an and handed it back to Sarah. "Many of you tonight will choose to ignore what I have discovered, to deny reality. After all, it's easier to believe that one man is wrong than to deal with the fact that a billion have been deceived. But I say to you, although all have been indoctrinated, only a minority actually *believe*. Most profess this demented doctrine simply to survive.

I'm sure that sounds a bit harsh, but I am not the first to recognize that Muhammad was a fraud. Islamic scholar Dr. D.S. Margoliouth says this of the Prophet: 'The character attributed to Muhammad in the biography of Ibn Ishaq is exceedingly unfavorable. In order to gain his ends Mohammad recoils from no expedient, and he approves of similar unscrupulousness on the part of his adherents, when exercised in his interest. He organizes assassinations and wholesale massacres. His career as the tyrant of Medina is that of a robber chief whose political economy consists of securing and dividing plunder. He is himself an unbridled libertine, morally or sexually unrestrained, and encourages the same passion in his followers. For whatever he does he is prepared to plead the express authorization of his deity. It is, however, impossible to find any Islamic religious doctrine which he is not prepared to abandon in order to secure a political end. At different points in his career he abandons the unity of Allah and his claim to the title of Prophet. This is a disagreeable picture for the founder of a religion, and it cannot be pleaded that it is a picture drawn by an enemy.'

"Repressive regimes like those in the Muslim world have learned how to assure conformity. It's a one-word formula: *terror*. It's routinely directed at those who step out of line. Enemies of the state or faith—often one and the same—are imprisoned, beaten, and murdered. Such draconian measures diminish dissent. Call it coercion. Call it the deprivation of basic human rights. But call it on the carpet; call it what it is, and deal with it. If we eliminate the incentive to comply, we eliminate the threat. In order to prevail, we need only to defang thousands, not millions, and certainly not billions.

"You have been told by our leaders, some from this very platform, that Islam is not our enemy. But I stand here tonight and declare to you: *we are theirs.*" He looked around the House Chamber. Every eye was glued on him. "If you take solace in their comforting words, if you are a Chamberlain and seek peace through appeasement, dialog, and political compromise, understand this. Their spiritual leader *commanded* them to lie, to steal, to kill, to terrorize. His Qur'an even tells Muslims that treaties with infidels are not binding. It's no wonder they've violated them all."

Thor had nothing to hide. He had no agenda, not even his own. He wasn't running for or from anything. He simply had a message to deliver.

"I am going to read something to you out of the Hadith of al-Bukhari. It's but one of hundreds of similar verses that define Islam and reveal why its followers are dying to kill us today. This verse is from the Book of Faith, chapter 23, number 34. It reads, 'The Prophet said, "Allah assigns to a person who fights in holy battles in His Cause...to be rewarded with booty if he survives, or Paradise if he is killed in battle as a martyr."' The Prophet added, '"Had I not found it difficult for my followers,"' to do without me, is the implication, '"I would have fought in army units going for *Jihad*. I would have loved to be martyred in Allah's Cause and then made alive, and then martyred again in His Cause."'"

Thor let that sink in for a long moment. "Because Hitler and Muhammad are similar, mankind is in similar peril. The signposts along the road to oblivion are hauntingly familiar.

"With your indulgence, I would like to speak about the rise of Hitler's Nazism and demonstrate how it parallels the rise of Muhammad's Islam, for the best predictor of the future is the past. The character of man has not changed, nor have his methods, cravings, or delusions.

"World War II arose out of World War I. No one debates that today. It is simply understood. What the world does not realize is that just as assuredly, World War III will also emerge from the rubble, ashes, blood, and miscalculations of the First World War. That is, unless you and I have the courage to stop it here, in this place, tonight."

Thor Adams recounted the history. Too few knew it. "At the dawn of the last century, enough Muslims turned against their brethren for the British and French to defeat the Ottomans. Having no interest in vast reserves of sand and having too little regard for oil, the victors simply sliced and diced. They drew lines on a map and rewarded the warlords who had turned on their Muslim brothers by making them heads of state. They called some of the warlords Princes, some Presidents, Shahs, Sultans, even Kings. But Lebanon, my friends, was not ready to be a nation, nor was Saudi Arabia, Iraq, Iran, Syria, or Kuwait. Not surprisingly, it hasn't worked, nor will it work. The only winners in this doomed drama are the warlords, Sultans, and Princes—and, of course, the Islamic clergy. The dictators need them to manipulate the masses.

"And the loser in this game of evil thugs on oily thrones? Why us, of course—the very same nation that rescued the world from the tyrannical regimes of World War II. We're now faced with the same burden. And we must eventually fight in another war not of our making—either that or stop it from happening."

"For those listening who share my faith, the answer is Biblical. For those who profess no faith, it is historical. But either way, it's the same answer. As painful as this course of action may be, it will be infinitely less costly than any alternative.

"So having come to know this enemy, to know *why* they kill, what can we do?" Adams asked. "First, in Israel," he answered, "the flashpoint of the world, we must separate the warring children—separate Isaac from Ishmael, Jews from Arabs. The Arabs who wish to remain in Israel may do so, but only if they repudiate terror. They should be given all the rights and responsibilities afforded and required of Israelis, except for the right to vote. This course of action would make them the safest, freest, best-educated, and most prosperous Arabs in the world.

"But for those who prize independence even more than prosperity, for those who feel they must have the right to vote, the right of self-determination, a sovereign 'Palestinian' state needs to be established—but *not* in isolated little pockets of territory within the borders of Israel. I recommend that this state include all that is currently the Gaza Strip, plus a contiguous territory along the southern Israeli border with Egypt of similar width, for twenty miles or more. And while I'm no fan of the Prophet, we should deploy a more charitable version of Muhammad's own relocation strategy. The international community, for far less than it is currently wasting in the Middle East, for a fraction of the cost of fighting the war against terrorism, can help fund a prosperous new 'Palestinian' state—help make the desert bloom.

"Under this solution, every Arab living in Israel gets a choice: inclusion or independence, prosperity or self-reliance, the rocky, dry land of Israel or autonomy. The solution is as simple as the choices.

"As for Jerusalem, let us be perfectly clear. Jerusalem is Israel's. The only reason Muslims care about it is that the Jews consider it holy. Yes, I know. Muhammad dreamed about flying there one night from Mecca. Sorry. Dreams are not enough.

"I would like to shatter another illusion that has clouded our judgment: Palestine. The name itself was designed to deceive. The Romans derived it from the Philistines—seven hundred years *after* they had been obliterated by the Babylonians. Rome renamed Judea 'Palestina' in a vain effort to repress Jewish attachment to their ancestral homeland.

"The name went unused, even by the Muslims who conquered Judea, for fourteen hundred years. Then, with the intent of returning Judea to its rightful heirs, the British reprised the Roman name in 1920. 'Palestine,' a mandate that included all of present-day Israel *and* Jordan, was to be returned to the Jews. But the Arabs squawked, and the Brits backpedaled.

"Then, to influence public opinion, the Arabs living in Judea elected to call themselves 'Palestinians.' But calling them the 'Palestinian people' is like calling Sarah and me the Virginian people. It's a farce. We have been fed a lie. The land they claim, the West Bank, was occupied by Jordan as recently as 1967. During the Israeli War of Independence two decades earlier, the Jordanians conquered this territory—calling it the 'West Bank' for the first time. You see, it's really hard to sell the idea of it belonging to the 'Palestinians' if the world uses the ancestral name 'Judea.' History has been revised to deceive you."

The Congress was mesmerized. They had no idea. "I bet most of you don't know that Alafat's PLO was at war with the Jordanians while the Arabs occupied Judea. They were unable to live in peace with anybody, anywhere, anytime. No one wants them. The Palestinian terrorist group 'Black September' was named after the month the PLO was expelled.

"So I say, if the Arabs in Judea, today's Israel, want to be *Philistines*, then let them have the ancestral homeland of the Philistines—Gaza. The next time somebody whines that the poor 'Palestinians' are living under Israeli occupation, call that person a liar. The next time you hear people blame suicide bombers on Israeli 'occupation' or justify the mass murderer of innocents by labeling these butchers 'freedom fighters,' call them evil. Not only are they wrong, there's blood dripping from their hands."

With that off his chest, Admiral Adams continued. "Now as for the rest of the Arab world—that caustic mix of Islam and racial hatred, our choice today is no different than the decision the world faced in the years leading up to World War II.

"What do you think? What would it have taken to subdue Nazism and Communism when they were young and frail? Tens of thousands of lives? Hundreds of thousands? It's academic now, merely a painful lesson. The world hesitated and appeased them. The isolationists, "peacemakers"—those who controlled the public discourse—prevailed. We denied reality and as a result, fifty million people perished.

"Like it or not, we face the same referendum today. Islam can be curtailed and its infectious spread contained. This mind-numbing cancer *can* be sent into remission. Or we can sit here and watch it grow and do what cancers do—kill. Untreated, this disease will infect billions." He paused. "Oh, wait…it already has."

"But all is not lost, at least not yet. As we should have learned in Desert Storm and again in Afghanistan, it takes less than one might expect to free the world from this cancer. Though there is a cure today, there may not be one tomorrow. One Muslim state already has nuclear weapons; two others are on the cusp. Most have biological weapons. And all have an abundance of something even more sinister—suicide bombers—like those who flew into the heart of New York and Washington, like the one who showed his true colors this morning at Camp David."

He looked behind him. The loves of his life returned his gaze. "Sarah, would you please introduce our daughter and share how she found her way into our arms." Sarah rose, wheeling Mary to the front of the stage. Adams knelt down beside her, holding her hand.

Stepping to the rostrum, Sarah said, "America, this is Mary. She was the victim of a suicide bomber in Israel. By the grace of God, she is going to survive. But not her biological mother and father. They were consumed by this cancer the Admiral has told you about. They were just living their lives, doing what families do, loving and nurturing one another. How many more Marys are going to suffer before we wake up, before we act? A million Marys, precious little children, were murdered by the Nazis, bright and joyous candles whose flames were snuffed out before they had the chance to glow. Can you muster the courage, America, to prevent more Marys from suffering at the hands of militant Muslims? Or are you going to bury your head in the sand?"

Every eye grew wet. Even the hardest souls softened. In Mary, they were forced to face reality.

Admiral Adams again approached the podium. "Boy bombs happen because the despots we coddle, support, and enrich in Saudi Arabia, Iran, Iraq, Syria, and Egypt reward their families. These nations fund the Islamic schools that promise great sex in paradise to those they teach to maim little girls like Mary.

"The money that funds these schools and rewards the families of suicide bombers is beyond comprehension. And it's being used by those who view us as the enemy to indoctrinate the masses—to teach them to hate and terrorize. The four airliners hijacked in September 2001 became little more than big boy bombs. The terrorists who hijacked these planes had but one thing in common—Islam."

The Admiral studied the faces staring back at him. His message was beginning to resonate. "Unless we stop the flow of money and stop the racist indoctrination of impressionable youth, it will buy more terror than we can endure. The sources of terror that must be subdued are: Iran, Saudi Arabia, Iraq, Syria, Libya, and Egypt." He read the list slowly, letting every name sink in. "Removing the scum who control Kuwait, United Arab Emirates, the Sudan, Somalia, and other Islamic nations will also liberate their people from the scourge of this cancer. Simply stated: it would be good for the world."

Adams took his audience on an imaginary journey. "My fellow Americans, in your mind's eye, I want you to take a step back from the edge of this abyss upon which we are now standing. No, you're still too close. Please step back—all the way back to the dawn of the Dark Ages in medieval Europe. Imagine that you govern a powerful nation, one vastly superior to any feudal state. In your mind's eye, look into your crystal ball. What do you see all around you? Heartache and tyranny, extreme poverty. There are no freedoms of expression, no freedoms of religion, no means to escape the cesspool, no way to better one's life. For everywhere you look, life hangs by a thread, the thread of allegiance, obedience to cleric and king.

"Looking again into your crystal ball, you see the high priests. They're elegantly robed, rich and powerful, brutal and repressive. This politicized clergy is in lock step with the royals—symbiotically working to subdue the people, plundering them for personal gain, killing or torturing them when they step out of line.

"Now imagine these despots making inroads into your kingdom, sending raiding parties to sack your seacoast towns. They kill a few thousand civilians. But they get bolder, more vicious as time passes.

"So what do you do? Do you engage the empowered clergy and warlords in dialog? Ask them to behave better? Do you deny their existence? Close your eyes to the hell you know is coming? Do you turn away and let tens of millions suffer because you have neither the courage nor character to get involved? Remember, you *have* the means. The question is: do you have the will?

"Now, my fellow Americans, please step through time with me. You remembered to pack your crystal ball, right? Okay, now gaze into it. What do you see emerging in the motherland and in the fatherland, Russia and Germany? Revolution? I thought so. Do you see tiny minorities, less than five percent of the population, mobilizing? They're fanatical, aren't they? They're driven by doctrines that poison young men's minds. You see the masses succumbing. You watch in horror as they grow to worship their leaders. Then you see their names: Lenin and Hitler, ruthless dictators, thugs of epic proportions. Their followers, animals like Stalin and Goebbels, spread the false doctrines far and wide. Terror is their ally. Human rights are abolished. Anyone brave enough to criticize them is sent to the gulag, the concentration camp, or the grave. You hear them scream; you see their anguished faces. Life isn't worth living unless one spews the official rhetoric as if it were gospel.

"Now, my friends, you're still the leader of the world's only superpower. It's the early 1930s, and you know what's going to happen because you've got your crystal ball. Fifty million people are going to die. Eight times that many are going to live in relative slavery for decades, with no human rights. They'll be indoctrinated—told what to think, what to believe, how to act. They'll be taught to hate you.

"What do you do? Engage the socialists and fascists in dialog? Mind you, these doctrines are no more or less delusional or repressive than today's politicized Islam. Do you think it will be helpful to ask them to behave better? Or do you want to deny their existence, close your eyes to the hell you know is coming. Appease them by acquiescing to their demands? Turn away and let four hundred million people suffer because you don't have the courage or character to get involved?

"While you're pondering that question, turn your crystal ball around and gaze upon the dictatorial regimes of the Far East for a moment. Please indulge me. What do you see? Warlords and emperor worship in Japan, the rape of Nanking, the devastation of the Philippines, Americans pushed on death marches by Japanese bayonets. And only five years after we liberate the Chinese from a tyranny nearly as horrific as the Holocaust—what then? Do you see them storming over the horizon and slaughtering our young men in Korea? I thought so. And now—do you see it? Mao's little red book being lifted in praise.

"Now remember, you are supremely powerful—the world's only superpower. What do you do? You know what we *did*. We ignored the abuse. We closed our eyes to the genocide, the mass murder, the suffocating repression of hundreds of millions. We refused to fight until the battle was brought to us, and the price of victory was millions of lives.

"Okay, it's time to hand in your crystal ball. You wont need it anymore. In fact, you never needed it. You've always had something better—history. Some say hindsight is 20-20. With history as our ally, I say foresight can be just as clear.

"The evils that have led to the most painful chapters in human history are festering in the Muslim world today: delusional doctrines, revisionist propaganda, the rule of dictators, abject poverty, indoctrination of youth, a disregard for the value of life, and wealth beyond imagination. What's going to happen as a result?

"Should we ask them to play nice?" There was an edge to Thor's voice. "Should we try to convince them that they should allow their people to think for themselves, to choose a faith based upon its merits? If we ask them to stop killing us, to stop throwing billions of dollars at terrorists, to stop indoctrinating future generations in religious schools that teach racial hatred, do you think they will? What are the chances that the Islamic state-controlled media will stop lying, stop encouraging terror?

"Are you a Chamberlain who thinks we can appease them by giving them Czechoslovakia...excuse me, Palestine? Are you one who sees wisdom in denial? Do you think we should wait a few more years perhaps, and see what happens. Shall we continue to lavish dollars upon them for oil they did not create, hoping they will not turn our dollars into nuclear and biological arsenals? Do you suggest sitting back and merely hoping that they won't use these weapons against us when they have them?

"We have the means to stop World War III before it starts. Simply stop the flow of money, and the indoctrination will stop. But do we have the will—the character and the courage?

"It will be painful, but if I recall, when Iraq had the fourth mightiest army on the planet, we overwhelmed them in the blink of an eye. But we didn't finish the job. The second time, our mission was flawed. We sought regime change, not recognizing that Saddam was *meaningless*. He wasn't the enemy; Islam is. Al-Qaeda didn't go away because bin Laden finally died from failed kidneys. He wasn't the enemy either; Islam is.

"Douglas MacArthur knew something we must all learn. To minimize the loss of life, one must control the time and place of the battle. Using this simple strategy, he did more with less than any general in history. We must follow his lead in eradicating the source of terror, because its adherents will kill us if we don't. But then we must *finish* the job.

"The MacArthur Plan is precisely what the suffering masses in the Muslim world need. The MacArthur Plan is what the free world needs if we do not wish to die at the hands of Islam. And we can use the oil that flows from these sands to pay for it.

"MacArthur finished the job by putting the warlords out of business. In so doing, he spared the world, but he also improved millions of *Japanese* lives. He pointed out the obvious flaws inherent in emperor worship, freeing their souls. He wrote their constitution and helped revise their educational institutions so that they could eventually manage for themselves. He provided a model for free enterprise that enabled their middle class to grow and prosper. He gave the Japanese people a life worth living, eliminated despair and poverty, and thus the need to manufacture enemies—the need to hate, the need to terrorize others. And then, when they were ready to govern themselves, he left. The job was done.

"Everybody won. Everybody, that is, except for the warlords. They didn't think much of the idea. But why do we care what they think? The royal family in Saudi Arabia, the Ayatollah in Iran, the General in Iraq, the President in Syria—why do we care what they think? Why do we solicit their opinions or seek to form alliances with despots?

"The wisest man who ever lived said, 'There is nothing new under the sun. That which has been is that which will be.' From the historian's pen: 'Those who cannot remember the past are condemned to repeat it.' From my lips: 'The best predictor of the future is the past.' We must take heed; we must awaken from our collective trance and stop this menace now, while the costs are tolerable. If we do not, if we delude ourselves, if we ignore our past, we ensure a future consumed by terror.

"Throughout time, totalitarian thugs by any name—Pharaoh, King, General, Messenger, Chairman, or *Fuhrer*—have galvanized their power by lashing out at their neighbors. Kind words uttered in tolerance have never deterred them. Concessions have never appeased them. The only thing they respect is a strong shield, a sharp sword, and the will to use them. Harsh words and a puny stick only spur them on."

The hawks in the audience smiled, but their glee was short lived. "To the conservatives who may be celebrating these words, I say: this is not about conquest, not about flexing our muscles, and not about imposing our will and our ways on other peoples. Our mission must be to stop the flow of money, remove the thugs from power, demilitarize the region, stop the indoctrination, and establish the infrastructure these peoples will need to think for themselves, provide for themselves, govern themselves."

He looked to his left. "To the liberals in this chamber clamoring to squander our military preparedness by spending the peace dividend, I say: read your history. We disarmed after World War I, and we paid with our children's blood. We disarmed after World War II and encouraged the Communist incursions that led to the spilling of more American blood in Korea and Vietnam. We invited trouble. We were unable to fight effectively, to thwart sadistic and repressive regimes, so our boys died instead. They did not have to die.

"To the media watching this proceeding, eager to ridicule my message, I say think about how you chastised Reagan for calling the expansionist and repressive regime in Russia 'evil'. Despite your longing to revise history, he set the forces in motion that ended the suffering—the enslavement really—of hundreds of millions. You were wrong. He was right.

"When Winston Churchill criticized Neville Chamberlain's betrayal of Czechosolvakia, giving this democratic nation to the rising despot in Germany, the *London Times* liabled Churchill, saying, and I quote, 'The warmonger Churchill, who would make war without counting the cost, ought to be impeached or hanged. Mr. Chamberlain has achieved greater success in his agreements with Czechosolvakia, Italy, and Hitler at Munich than anyone in history.' Again, you in the media were wrong.

And your mistake was not without consequence. More people died as a result of this 'land-for-peace process' than in all prior wars combined. Please, I beg you, do not repeat the mistake.

"By the way, Churchill was not silent regarding our current enemy. At the end of his life, he left us a warning: 'The Islamic genie poses a greater threat than even the Soviet Union,' he said.

"For nearly a decade now, you have parroted the Islamic delusion. Unwittingly or not, you have fallen prey to their propaganda. Islam is *not* a peace-loving religion. We do *not* worship the same god. Their Prophet was anything but. Thus far, you have misled the American people. And while that in itself is wrong, it is inexcusable when it costs American lives.

"You are partially to blame for the rise of Islam. Your predecessors failed us during the rise of the tyrannical regimes in Japan, Germany, Russia, and China. Sometimes because you ignored them, enthralled with lesser stories. Other times because you failed to scratch below the surface. Mostly because you gave the lunatics a platform.

"I implore you to read, investigate, learn, think, and *then* report. I pray that there are enough real journalists among you to ferret out the truth, filtering what you find through the sieve of history and reason. Think about who killed the journalists in Afghanistan. Think about what motivated the assassins of Daniel Pearl. There is a lot at stake: the very freedom of mankind, the lives of millions of precious souls like Mary's hinge on you acting rightly.

"I have met with these terrorists. I know who they are. I have learned what motivates them, what unifies them. Our enemy is Islam. Everyone hearing my voice must come to terms with this reality: Islam in its purest form is a manifesto for war. We are their enemy.

"In closing, I would like to leave you with two of history's most important lessons. First, bad things happen when good people don't stand up. Second, peace never results from the toleration of evil.

"America, I have done my duty. I have fulfilled my promise. I have found our foe. The enemy is the perverse doctrine of Islam. I have presented a remedy, a painful yet possible solution. I say it is time to raise our shield and wield our sword. Destiny is calling. We must rid the world of this cancer before it consumes us."

21

POLITICALLY CORRECT

"That was incredible."

"Praise be to Allah."

"He brought the whole government down."

"He must have had a thousand angels fighting with him."

Mamdouh Salim, Talib Ali, Omen Quagmer, and Aymen Halawah were chatting over tea, celebrating yesterday's victory.

"Now that I'm in charge," Salim barked, "I say we keep the heat on."

"Death to the Great Satan," Ali agreed. "Death to the infidels."

"I know just what to do," Quagmer grinned. Visions of mischievous atoms danced in his head.

"Our Chairman, our great martyr," Halawah proclaimed reverently, "gave us a mission. He wanted us to turn world opinion against the Jews."

"And so we shall, son. But not today. Today is for celebrating."

✡ ✝ ☾

"THOR. ADMIRAL ADAMS," a familiar voice said softly through a crack in the door. He was fast asleep. The media's questioning had gone on well into the night. Then he had conferenced with Members of Congress, on both sides of the aisle. America was rudderless, desperate for leadership.

"Thor, wake up." Leisel walked over to the bed, shaking him gently. "You've got a phone call. Politicians."

"What time is it?" he moaned. It still looked dark outside, but then again, he didn't know if his eyes were open.

"Just after six o'clock. They said it's important."

Thor sat up, rubbing his face. "Good morning, Mrs. Nottingly."

"Good morning. Here, I made you a cup of coffee. It might help."

"Can I take the call in here?" he asked, reaching for his robe.

"Sure." She walked over to the phone on Troy's desk and pushed the speaker button.

Standing up, coffee in hand, Adams encouraged Leisel to stay. "Good morning," he said. "This is Thor Adams."

"Admiral, I have you on speaker. This is Senator Dodge. There are a good number of Representatives and Senators here with me. Some members of the media, too."

"Sorry for calling so early." The voice sounded familiar.

"That's okay. I was just sleeping." He winked at Leisel. She was sitting in the companion chair, her chair, just to the right of Troy's desk.

"We called this meeting to discuss our leadership crisis."

"In fact, Admiral, most of us remained here another three or four hours last night after your speech. We read Agent Nottingly's position paper on the nature of Islam, its history and politics. Then we re-read what you had to say. Hardly anybody went home."

"So you're saying *I'm* the sluggard, the hypocrite. I asked everyone to rise to the occasion, and I went to bed."

"That's pretty much the reason we called, sir. That's unacceptable behavior. No more sleeping." The room enjoyed a good laugh.

"Actually, sir, we were wondering. Oh, this is Congressman Macon speaking. Would you consider running for President?"

"Congressman," Thor said, trying to clear his head. He took a gulp of coffee. "I'm a bit confused. Senator Dodge broached this subject back on Wednesday when he asked me to address the Joint Session of Congress. That was back when we *had* a President, and the next election was three years away. And he's a Republican. You're a Democrat. I'm neither."

"There are no more Republicans or Democrats. Now we're just Americans," a confident voice boomed. "Don't know about 'Neithers'."

"You took us all to the woodshed last night," another added.

"I wasn't trying to scold anyone. I just wanted us to see the world for what it is, embrace our destiny—*make* some history for a change, rather than living to regret it." For a guy who had already fallen down on the job, he was making a decent recovery. He took another swig of caffeine. Leisel smiled; she was proud of him.

"You mean a history we'll be proud to tell to our children," one of the politicos proclaimed.

"Fact is," the Congressman said, "we all want you to run."

"But not as a Democrat or a Republican—as an American." It sounded like Dodge.

"Admiral, this is Congressman Macon. On instructions from the late President, we authored a bill calling for special elections of representatives and a referendum for senators in three weeks. We passed another bill last night to include the presidency in that special election. All of the Constitutional successors were killed yesterday morning," the Republican Senator explained. "In our zeal to get a peace accord, we somehow forgot that our real duty was to the American people. We're vulnerable."

"So if you'll agree to run as an Independent," the Democrat proposed, "neither of us will nominate a candidate to run against you."

"That's kind, but wrong," Adams said. "Americans deserve a choice."

"And they'll have one, sir. We believe the Reform Party will have a candidate, as will Peace and Freedom, and the Libertarians."

"You guys are *serious*, aren't you?"

"Never been more so, Admiral."

He took another gulp of coffee, emptying the cup. Fortunately, Sarah had found her way to dad's retreat, coffeepot in hand. Dressed in a robe and slippers, she made his bed, turning it back into a couch before sitting down.

"Ladies, gentlemen, I'm not a politician."

"Yes, sir. That's pretty obvious." Everyone chuckled again.

"None of us would have had the courage to present things as bluntly as you did last night. It's not politically correct."

"Alright, so you know I'm a lousy politician. But do you realize I don't *want* the job? Sarah and I came to the conclusion we could do more out of office than in—you know, speak more freely. Plus, it's real hard to raise a family when your character is being assailed in the media. No offense, but between you guys and the press, things can get pretty twisted."

"Admiral Adams, this is Tad Broadow. You're right." Tad worked for ABC. "I can't promise that we'll change, but if we fail and have to endure World War III as a consequence, I don't want it to be on my account."

"Mr. Broadow, I wasn't asking you to agree with me. All I wanted was for the media to scratch below the surface, to think, and to stop using inaccurate labels to obfuscate reality."

"We'll find things to disagree about, sir. But this isn't one of them."

"Now what? I've told you I don't want the job and that I'm a lousy politician, yet you don't seem to care."

"On the contrary, Admiral Adams. We do care. But more to the point, the political stalwarts, the leadership who put party ahead of all else, were killed yesterday," Macon said.

"We're not interested in political gamesmanship," Dodge offered.

Sarah rolled her eyes heavenward.

"I'll tell you what then," Thor said, glancing over at his fiancé. He sipped his coffee and prayed that his brain was sufficiently engaged. "You don't know me, and I don't know you. Not really. So, this is what I propose. I'll spend the day with Sarah composing what we think needs to be done to restore America."

Nottingly nodded. Having thought these issues through, she was ready.

"You're asking me to run for President. That's a political mission. Combating terrorism is but one part of that job. And to prevail, America must be united and strong."

"We agree."

"Then let's meet later and hash it out. 'Cause right now I think we've got the honeymoon before the marriage. I'd like it to be the other way around."

☆   ✟   ☾

"HOW DID WE get ourselves into this mess?"

"I botched the intelligence. You botched the mission."

"Oh, yeah, now I remember. That's great. So now they want us to run the country."

"Failure has its rewards," Sarah shrugged, spying a family of mallards meandering between the boats. "Although it makes perfect sense."

"Mind telling me why?" He was leaning against the cockpit of his sailboat. The *Sunrise* was moored along the seawall of the Annapolis Harbor, a place affectionately called 'Ego Alley'. They had thought the view up Main Street at the old church and Statehouse, with its majestic dome, might be inspirational. Besides, they both loved the cacophony of competing sounds—rigging clapping in the wind, flags waving, children playing, yachtsmen telling tall tales.

"We, well, you at least, acted heroically under pressure. There's a shortage of character up there," she pointed west toward Washington. You told people what you were going to do, and you did it. All politicians seem able to do is beg, borrow, bellyache, and blunder."

"The dreaded killer 'Bs'," Thor joked.

"It took guts to tell the truth—to tell the country what it *needed* to hear."

"You'd think figurin' somethin' out and proposing a plan would be a baseline requirement for 'blunderers'. Not an exception. Certainly no reason for recruiting an amateur."

"Well, they are," she said matter-of-factly.

"Sarah, can America be fixed? Or have we become too selfish, to complacent, too dependent and ignorant to work our way out of this mess? Can common sense be used to constrain government?"

"Maybe. We'd need to engage the American people and disengage their politicians."

"The Admiral opened his laptop and booted up. "We need to restore our nation's strength from the ground up. So I say we start at the same place we plan to destroy Islamic terror."

"Money."

"That's right."

"Then you'll need an economic policy. To win this battle we need to unburden our economy."

"That's precisely how Reagan won the Cold War. And that was the last time the world faced a similar foe. We're gonna need a lot more private-sector jobs. We'll need to encourage investment and increase spendable income. What we really need is to restore confidence in our economy."

"You're sounding pretty darn conservative for an Independent. Half the folks you talked to this morning aren't gonna like that."

"Good. One less suicide mission."

"Well, I don't think you're going to get off that easily. But you hit the nail on the head: the key to rebuilding our economy is confidence. Bottom line, that's all money really is."

"How do you increase confidence, make people more willing to invest their time and money?"

"You know the answer."

"Reduce taxes on the things we want more of?"

"Are you asking me or telling me?"

"Telling. It's obvious," he replied, more confident this time.

"You've got the first plank of your plan to revive America. Let's call it 'Opportunity,' she said, encouraging him to type it into his notebook PC.

The Admiral did as he was told, then rubbed his prodigious chin. "To accomplish this we must simplify the tax codes."

Sarah was enjoying the warmth of the sun on her face and legs. She was wearing a dark blue gingham blouse and lighter blue shorts, coordinated, of course.

"Right now, it's all set up to redistribute wealth. It's as if the killer Bs think giving away other people's money makes them charitable.

"No, it makes them popular. But to win we'll need to stop rewarding failure and start rewarding success."

The right-leaning Independent liked the way she'd put that. "Uh huh." Then he searched for a more "presidential" response. "We need to create incentives for the things that benefit our people and propose penalties for less desirable stuff." *Stuff* still wasn't a very presidential word, but heck, he was a rookie. "If the health risk that's associated with smoking a pack of cigarettes, for example, costs three bucks, tax it three bucks and spend the money on health care. Do the same with alcohol."

"Right. Then because we want people to have more money to spend, let's lower the income tax rate to twenty percent," Sarah suggested. "Make it the same for everybody. If you make ten times more money than your neighbor, then you pay ten times more tax. Everybody is in the game. Nobody gets anything for free, so everybody is interested in government being responsible, a good steward of *our* money."

"Now that's a revolutionary idea," he agreed, kicking off his shoes. "But while we're at it, we need to give taxpayers incentives to do the things we want more of."

"Such as?" she led the witness.

"There should be deductions for interest on home loans because home ownership is crucial—economically and socially. Healthcare costs should be deductible; that would encourage folks to take care of themselves instead of relying on government."

"There should be a big incentive to put money away for retirement. It would encourage investment in American business, and would wean the country off Social Security. You know that Social Security is just an elaborate pyramid scheme, don't you? There *is* no trust fund. The money everybody pays in is spent."

"That doesn't make it a pyramid scheme, just foolish."

"With Social Security, parents and grandparents force their children and grandchildren to pay for their retirement. The relatively little money they paid in while they were working was spent a long time ago on services their generation already received."

"That's embarrassing," Adams agreed. "And you're right; that does make it a pyramid scheme."

"Between payroll taxes and the FICA payments employers make, the government is confiscating fifteen percent of our nation's productivity, right off the bat."

"That's hardly holding it in the middle," he laughed, recalling an all-too-familiar line.

"I'd like to see a deduction for educational expenses, and one for donations to charity," Sarah proposed. "Community organizations, churches, and synagogues are much more effective than government agencies when it comes to helping people."

Thor typed it in as the economist flipped through her notes. Sarah had grown up with an entrepreneur and studied the subject at the University of Virginia. "We'd benefit from having a tax incentive for exporting goods overseas. That would go a long way toward solving our negative trade imbalance," she suggested, splashing some water at the mallards.

Thor laughed as the ducklings waddled toward the commotion. "What can we do to restore confidence in corporate America?"

"Establish an entirely different means of deploying auditors and analysts. Make accrual accounting illegal—it's responsible for most of the scandals. We also need to change the nature of corporate governance. Boards are clueless. But when you get right down to it, the reason we're in a pickle is the decline of corporate character. Our Supreme Court has made God illegal and immorality legal."

"In other words, the fix is hard but possible."

"Yes. And then we should create incentives to hire people," Nottingly continued, smiling at her new friends. "Your new tax code should encourage business investments by making the costs deductible rather than depreciable." Sarah had seen her father struggle with these very same roadblocks to productivity. "Business is the engine that propels America. It not only pays every bill, it's responsible for creating the lifestyle that's the envy of the world. It's a wonder business survives the liberal assault."

"With all these deductions for the things America needs more of, Sarah, I'll bet that a family making, say, thirty thousand or less would pay relatively little in taxes. Twenty percent of thirty thousand is six thousand," he said. "Once you make an allowance for retirement savings or home interest, one for an education allowance or charity, their tax burden would be cut to less than a grand. Heck, a deduction for health care alone could eliminate a poor family's tax burden."

"But with a rich gal," Sarah smiled, unbuttoning her blouse to soak in the sun, "it's entirely different. Say I make a million bucks a year."

"Yeah! Let's say that."

She winked. "At twenty percent, my tax burden would be two hundred grand. Once I make a deduction for Mary's education, including her computer, donate something to my favorite charities, take care of our retirement, and pay our health care, I'm still going to owe somewhere between a hundred and fifty and a hundred and seventy-five thousand. Your flat tax with incentives for things we want more of is plenty progressive."

"How'd you get to be so smart?" he asked, admiring her as she finished unbuttoning her blouse. She had worn a matching blue bikini. Sarah wanted to get some color. Thor wanted to get a look. Neither was disappointed.

As she slithered out of her shorts, Adams was about cooked. He had envisioned what she might look like, but seeing her, this much of her, was distracting.

"I'm not bothering you, am I? Your train of thought seems to have run off the track."

Eyes up, jaw down, he simply stared.

"Thor? Oh Thor, dear. Where have you gone?"

"Thank you, *God!*" was all he said.

That made her smile. "I'll take that as a compliment."

He bit his lip and nodded.

"I'm glad you like what you see." She stretched out her shapely legs on the wooden bench that ran alongside the tiller. She was leaning up against a pillow. Her chestnut hair fell down over her soft shoulders. Her eyes matched the sky; her skin was flawless, as perfect as her body.

Thor was in heaven.

She let her ring sparkle in the sun, "I reckon this says it's yours. But," she pointed at his laptop, "we've got work to do, honeybunch. If you're going to be President, you can't let little things like these distract you."

"Speak for yourself. Those are the most magnificent," he forced himself to look up, "distractions I've ever seen."

"Now, sailor, I know better, remember? I've read your file." She smiled and got back to business. "I think it's important to encourage companies to share profits with their employees—one wins, all win."

"Stock ownership. I agree."

"Then write it down," she said, trying to get him to reengage.

"Alright." He pecked at the keys. This was way more fun than it should have been. "Along those lines, I'd like to see us make *America* our most favored nation, not the Communists in China. Let's establish policies that put *our* people to work, not *theirs*. Enterprise zones, for example."

"Good thinking." It was all so obvious.

"With these things in place, our government will spend less, at least over time, right?" Thor posed.

"No question about it," the bikini-clad economist shared. "Collectively, our biggest expenses are entitlements: Medicare, Welfare, and Social Security. And last time I checked, our Constitution listed rights and responsibilities, not entitlements."

"In fact, the redistribution of wealth is unconstitutional."

"I'm glad *somebody's* read the Tenth Amendment. It was neither mandated nor approved. There's no provision for stealing what belongs to one citizen and giving it to another." This was Sarah's hot button.

"Yeah. Too bad the killer Bs who voted for these albatrosses, and the Justices that failed to overturn them, didn't read the Tenth Amendment," Sarah moaned. "You know, this is all a legacy of the Warren Court."

"General Eisenhower admitted that appointing Earl Warren Chief Justice was the biggest mistake of his presidency. We're still paying for it."

"Yeah. Between his concocting the notion of separating church and state and his failure to overturn Johnson's 'Great Society' boondoggles as unconstitutional, America's tombstone is going to read, "Thanks, Earl."

Thor sighed. "So how do we get out of the fix our parents' generation created before it breaks the bank—and our spirit?" he asked.

"Slowly. We've got to gradually phase it out. Those who relied on these things rather than taking care of themselves, need us to continue them. We have to honor the promises our government made, even if they were foolish, and even if the recipients themselves weren't willing to pay for them at the time."

She pressed ahead. "This isn't brain surgery. If people have an incentive to invest in their future, they won't be as dependent on government. If we tax them less, they'll have more to save for their retirement, more to spend on their education, their children, their health care."

"What are the numbers on the performance of private investment funds as opposed to Social Security?"

"No return at all, versus...well, let me put it this way. Even with conservative private retirement funds, most workers' contributions would grow to in excess of a million dollars."

"Oh, forget it, then. That makes too much sense."

"Are you trying to get yourself uninvited?"

"Could be a good thing."

"Then let's really give 'em something to hate. Point two of your plan to build an America strong enough to tackle terror: improve education."

"The best way to do that is to make schools accountable. America needs vouchers, school choice. We need to put parents back in charge, make schools perform," he said."

"If everybody gets a great start, we can curtail government dependence, especially among minority groups," Sarah observed.

"I'd like to see our public schools open earlier and stay open later each day. And since most have cafeterias, why not serve breakfast and dinner, especially to poorer families? Get rid of food stamps. Far too many are traded for drugs and booze," he added, typing away. "Stop paying farmers twenty billion a year not to grow things—buy food from them instead.

"Now there's an idea. Feed meals to people who need them in their communities. You could hire folks on welfare to serve and clean up; give 'em a job rather than charity." Sarah smiled. "You're pretty cute for a smart guy," she teased him.

Thor figured that if he was going to be judged for his looks, he might as well try to impress her. He lifted his shirt up over his shoulders. While most men would have sucked in their gut and puffed out their chest, Adams didn't need to. He simply carried on. "And another thing, we should reestablish the extracurricular activities schools used to offer—music, theater, sports, public-speaking tournaments, the sponsorship of civic-minded clubs. Those are the things that helped turn students into well-rounded adults."

"The more there is to do at school, the less time kids will have to get into trouble," she said, still eyeing the ducklings.

"We could even make schools fun by integrating corporately sponsored high-tech learning aids. And why not offer evening classes for parents—computers, job skills, even the 'three Rs'. The facilities are already there. Let's use them."

"An investment in our future," she said, nodding. "In the long run, it'll cost us less than welfare and a *lot* less than police and prisons."

"Uh-oh." Thor pointed. "I think we've just inspired a little trouble." *Paparazzi* were storming toward the boat faster than a summer squall. "Toss that bow line, sweetheart. I'll get the stern." Thor started the boat's small diesel engine. As it coughed to life he pushed off with one hand and managed the tiller with the other. Frustrated, the 'photo journalists' stumbled all over themselves trying to attach longer lenses. Sarah just smiled and waved goodbye.

"They used to get to you. Now you're teasing them. What gives?"

"I used to be the flavor of the week. Not anymore." She held her engagement ring aloft as they motored away.

A safe distance out, Thor asked Sarah to raise the jib. He turned the boat upwind. Holding the tiller between his legs, he pulled the mainsail halyard. Within seconds, they were sailing again. Adams cut the engine. The sound of water lapping lazily under the hull, the squawking of playful gulls, and the distant bellyaching of disgruntled photographers was all they could hear.

"Okay. We've got Opportunity and Education. I'd like our third initiative to be Service," Adams said as he stood, motioning for Sarah to take the tiller. He disappeared below. "Can I get you a drink?"

"How about a glass of that white grape juice you brought aboard?" Sarah would have preferred to join him down under. The finely crafted wooden confines of the sloop's interior were cozy and romantic. "I brought some cheese and crackers—cut some apple slices, too."

Thor opened the bottle, carefully pouring its golden contents into a pair of his finest plastic cups. He made his way back topside where they kissed, this time out of camera range. With cups in his hand and munchies in hers, it was all they could do to keep things right side up.

"To the Adams family," Sarah toasted, steering with her leg draped over the tiller. She had stretched back out, leaning against the stern.

"Pretty tough duty."

Thor lingered on the word *duty*. "I'd like to see America require a year of public service. It could be in the military or in some community program, mission, even the Peace Corps. And speaking of the military, we need to keep our troops busy, doing something productive. We could have them patrol our borders and provide security at airports. Let 'em wink at the pretty girls while they're keeping us safe."

She smiled. "Yes. It's hard to value something that isn't earned."

"And with the MacArab plan, we're going to need volunteers."

"Kennedy's 'ask what you can do for your country' idea."

Thor repeated the line, mimicking a nasally Boston brogue.

Images of JFK's indiscretions played in Sarah's head as he spoke. "You can talk like him all you want, cutie; just don't act like him. I won't be as understanding as Jackie."

"I may disappoint you every way from Sunday, but not that way."

She smiled. "You know, I like the idea of national service. Nothing of value is achieved without sacrifice."

"When you give somebody somethin' for nothin', you're killing 'em. That's why drug dependence runs rampant in inner cities. Narcotics are just an escape mechanism. It's the same with suicide bombers, too. Destitute in Muslim countries, boy bombers have nothing to live for. Suicide, like drugs, is a way out."

"Yes." The light flicked on in Sarah's head. "Let's give people a better way out. By restoring America we'll go a long way toward winning our most lethal war, the one killing our children—illegal drugs."

"It's all tied together, Sarah. "By creating opportunity, by investing in schools and communities, by encouraging service, we do what neither the Great Society nor Muhammad could. We give people a reason to live."

✡   ✝   ☾

IT WAS LATE AFTERNOON when the *Sacred Seas* arrived in the yacht harbor on Paradise Island. A grand pink casino, the Atlantis, loomed large in the background.

Among all the fine yachts in this tropical paradise, the scuba and photographic gear waiting for the crew looked perfectly natural. The jarring approach these less-than-proficient sailors made when attempting to moor their craft raised some eyebrows, however.

The Bahamian carpenters had taken their sweet time rebuilding the forward v-berth and overhead hatch. But now they were nearly complete, and ready to accommodate their cargo. Constructed from teak and marine Plexiglas, the work was of good quality, befitting a fine sailing yacht. Nothing looked out of place.

Most of the boats Omen had selected were forty to forty-five feet. This gave the crews ample room in which to hide their doomsday cases. And They were of sufficient size to cover the distances these would have to navigate—proper seamanship not withstanding.

Forty-foot yachts also had another feature that would play large in the scheme of things: tall masts. To comply with the mandated schedule, the triggers needed to be activated electronically. A special antenna had been mounted on each boat, just above the highest spreader, with the wiring hidden inside the masts themselves. Even the forward mast-stay cables had been moved port and starboard to accommodate the launching of weapons through the enlarged hatch and skylight.

"Hey, boys!" the dock master hollered. "That was quite an approach. I'm glad you're still afloat."

"We've got a big gash on the left side." Atta said, pointing to the port bow. "See it over there?"

The dock master knelt down and rubbed his hand over the massive wound. "You want some help with this?"

"Can you fix it?"

"I can't, but the boys over at the yard should be able to. I'll call 'em if you'd like."

"Yes, but, ah, do you have an idea how much this will cost?"

"Four, five grand, I'd imagine. Could've been worse. It's gonna take a while to do the work, though," the dock master explained. "More time to enjoy our hospitality here at the Atlantis, right?" He smiled. "Moored in the marina you're considered a guest of the hotel. Here are your cards. You can charge anything you want on them."

"Anything?"

"Most anything. Gambling, food, booze, all the ocean and pool toys."

"Thanks!" Atta said, accepting his pass.

With some unexpected time on their hands, the Islamic crew, Atta and his mate, Riza, were happy to indulge themselves in the full variety of Paradise Island pleasures. There was no need to rush martyrdom.

They soon found themselves splashing down the four-story waterfalls, teasing the sharks in the giant walk-through aquariums, and scaring unsuspecting swimmers to death on rented Wave Runners. They were about as inconspicuous as Muslims in flight schools.

Day faded into night, but the boys continued to play—this time indoors. Inappropriately inebriated, they found the lure of slots utterly irresistible. The flashing lights and festive sounds tantalized them. Their impulsiveness, however, was devastating to their wallets. Within hours, they had managed to lose most of their traveling allowance. Unless their luck changed, the eats would be slim en route.

That very same night, four less-fortunate sailors were anchoring off an isolated Jamaican beach. They were forced to use their tenders to row ashore, then climb the rugged slopes of the island. Retrieving two canisters of nuclear waste from deep within a cave, they alternated loads as they hefted their diabolical cargo back down the rocky inclines. One carried strontium 90, lightly encased in aluminum, while the other struggled with cobalt 60 wrapped in two inches of lead. Once back on the beach, they were required to row the encased atomic debris to their boats. It nearly scuttled them. There are few things more dense than spent fuel pellets—Muslim terrorists exempted.

While productive, in a destructive sort of way, moving the stolen cargo was considerably less titillating than piña coladas at poolside and prostitutes in Paradise.

✡   ✝   ☾

APPROACHING THE CAPITOL BUILDING, Sarah and Thor saluted the multitude of flags, all of which were being flown at half mast. America was in mourning. Inside, they paid their respects to the fallen. The floor beneath the rotunda was covered with coffins—the President's, Vice President's, Senators', Congressmen's, and Cabinet Members'.

Upstairs, there were plenty of places to meet. All of the larger offices were now vacant. While most in Congress work across the street and southwest of the Capitol in the Russell Office Building, the leadership gets to hang out, 'deliberate' in their parlance, in some pretty classy digs.

A quick peek down the mall, through the netting that protected the Western Balcony, reminded Thor and Sarah why they were here. Washington's terrorized monument stood between them and Lincoln's call for freedom.

Back inside, they got down to business, across the hall, in the Reagan Room, so called for the pictures of the Gipper at either end. The *de facto* leadership of the Congress and Senate—those who were left after the Camp David disaster, were assembled and ready to listen.

Thor began by explaining the obvious. "The fact that Muslim dictators routinely abuse their citizens is criminal. But that's not our problem. The fact that those who are willing to abuse their own people are also prone to abuse their neighbors *is* our problem. Most every Islamic state has publicly demonstrated that they consider us their enemy—Allah's enemy. They've picked a fight and we must defend ourselves. But before we do, we need to get our act together. Otherwise we'll lose."

"Along those lines," Sarah shared, "we've outlined a plan to save America."

Thor covered the first of five points: Opportunity. His thoughts were presented cogently. They were not, however, well received.

"The press will crucify you," Senator Dodge reacted. "They'll say you're giving the rich a windfall."

"We may not be able to support it either," Congressman Macon said.

"Then this is going to be a real short engagement. The press isn't responsible for saving this nation. Its elected leaders are. And I'm not going to play politics." The Admiral was not amused.

Adams couldn't help but wonder if the country was capable of being saved. Old habits, no matter how absurd, were hard to shake. The folks with the microphones had repeated their clever sound bites and applied their labels so many times, many had started to believe them.

"By taxing people less, we aren't *giving* them anything. We'd just be *taking* less from them. Confiscating less of someone's property is not a gift."

It was Sarah's turn. "Example: a thief robs you at gunpoint. He opens up your wallet and takes out seventy-five bucks rather than the hundred he normally steals. Using your logic, the twenty-five dollars he *didn't* steal would be a windfall for the victim."

"I dunno. This tax scheme of yours sounds like voodoo economics," Macon protested.

"Do you have a problem with supply-side stimulants, Congressman?" Sarah posed politely.

"It's just trickle down, all over again," the lawmaker moaned.

"Yes, I know, great line. The press ate it up. Too bad it wasn't true." Thor shook his head. "Congressman, even your most revered President, JFK, understood what you seem to miss. First thing he did was cut the capital gains rate. You ought to listen to his speeches sometime."

Thor pointed to the picture of Ronald Reagan riding tall in the saddle. "That man's supply-side plan took this country out of the most depressing period of stagflation in our history. It transformed the economy and led to the most robust peacetime expansion ever. It was a raging success, and everybody knew it except those with an axe to grind. You all hated it. Why? Because it made voters less dependent."

"Fact is, sir," Sarah said, "'Trickle down,' as you call it, did more for

the poor than any giveaway program you politicians ever concocted."
What is it about this place that makes people babble?

"You consistently distort the facts to serve your political ambitions."
Adams didn't want this job. "It's no wonder folks don't trust you."

"What about the debt Reagan ran up with his plan? Clinton fixed that
problem," one of the Democrats said.

"What branch of government has budgetary responsibility?"

"Congress," a Republican answered.

"Right. The debt rose because Congress continued to throw money at
everything under the sun. During Reagan's terms, if you'll recall,
Congress was controlled by the Democrats," Thor said.

"I think it was his tax cuts combined with his military overindulgence
that tipped the scales," Congressman Macon protested.

"Then you would be wrong. Again." Sarah challenged him. "First, by
cutting tax rates across the board, the government took in more money,
not less. Second, it costs less to maintain military preparedness than it
does to cut our forces—as both Carter and Clinton did—and then rebuild
when trouble comes. Trouble *always* comes."

"America borrowed less during the Clinton years for two reasons—one
good, one bad. Your man shortchanged the military, which left us vulnerable. That was bad. But then a Republican Congress was elected, and
they passed a balanced budget bill curtailing spending, which was good."

"In other words, Congressman, save your b.s. for someone gullible
enough to swallow it. The media perhaps." Such language was uncharac-
teristic for Sarah but nonetheless appropriate.

And I'm going to marry this firebrand, Thor thought. *Outstanding.* "Now,
can we move on, or shall we continue discussing the merits of returning
the nation's economy back to the people who built it?"

"And away from the folks here in this building who've nearly crippled
it." Sarah wasn't finished getting her licks in.

No one rose to the bait. She was a formidable foe.

The Admiral said, "Normally I wouldn't trouble myself with this stuff.
But you've asked me to run for President, so here I am." He placed his
hands before him. "The war against terrorism cannot be won if America
is divided, as it was during Bush Two. Legislatively, Daschle ground the
nation to a halt. Bush wasn't much better domestically or internationally.
We were rudderless."

The Reagan room was filled with a heavy silence. Deep down they
knew that economic revival had been a prerequisite for dismantling
Communism, just as it would be for battling this new foe. And they knew
that a house divided would not stand against an opponent a billion strong.

Over that hurdle, the Admiral and the Agent moved on to their second initiative: Education. It didn't go any better.

"The NEA is never going to support a plan that employs welfare recipients at their schools—even if it's only in food service and extracurricular activities," the Democrats protested.

"We've never been able to pass a school choice bill," the Republican Senator interjected. "Our opponents claim it violates the Constitutional guarantees separating of church and state."

"Can someone show me where the Constitution requires a separation of church and state?" Agent Nottingly had just reread the treasured document and knew there was no such clause. "What's wrong? Need a copy?"

"It's not there," Senator Dodge admitted. "In fact, it says just the opposite. 'Congress shall make no law respecting an establishment of religion, or prohibiting the free exercise thereof; or abridging the freedom of speech, or of the press, or the right of the people to peaceably assemble, and to petition their government for a redress of grievances.'"

"Since there can be no law prohibiting the free exercise of these things anywhere in America—separating church and state is unconstitutional." Sarah explained.

Impressed with his fiancé, Thor marched on. "Poor families need school choice. If we're to succeed, we have to make schools work for our *kids*, not the unions, although unions seem to to think otherwise. I'll give you an example. The NEA affiliate in New York recently negotiated a pay raise to $80,000 for tenured teachers. Not bad for nine months work. Yet even the concept of tenure is wrong. It breeds instant complacency. Suppose we gave it to pilots after three years of landing mostly wheels down. How safe would you feel?"

Sarah lowered her guns. "The NEA is against choice for two reasons. They'd lose control over the liberal agenda they're force feeding our kids, and they'd be out of a job. Given a choice, ninety percent of parents choose private schools with non-union teachers."

"How can you be in favor of giving a woman the right to choose an abortion but not in favor of giving a mother the right to choose how her child is educated?"

The Democrats were beginning to lose interest in Thurston Adams.

The Admiral presented the merits of national service. His audience had objections, but opted to table them.

Sarah took the initiative. "Our fourth goal is Justice. It's time we release all Americans from the shackles of prejudice and injustice. Our courts only serve lawyers. For example, if we don't do something to reduce malpractice and product-liability awards, we're going wake up with no healthcare system or manufacturers. I wonder," she said, "if your rich lawyer pals plan to take care of sick folks after they've bled the doctors dry? The Trial Lawyers Association may be a sacred cow here on Capitol Hill, as is the Teachers' Union, but gentlemen, it's time to fire up the barbecue."

"Now, if you want to do something worthwhile, let's conquer the digital divide," Thor added. "And by that I mean more than simply getting technology into the hands of all Americans. There's a far bigger foe that needs to be slain if our nation is to grow and heal. Most African Americans and Hispanics don't have credit cards, many don't even have bank accounts. Without electronic money, they're literally shut out."

"As part of our Justice initiative," Sarah rolled on, "we believe our nation should stop paying those in *want,* so we can care for those in *need.* If you're capable of working, you work. Simple as that. No work, no money. Politicians become accomplices to murder when you give able-bodied citizens something for nothing. It's poison, one that eats away at their soul until they die from an overdose, at the hand of another poisoned soul, or from an apathy-induced paralysis. It's not compassion or charity; it's murder. You're killing our nation."

"For those who can't work due to a physical or mental challenge, that's an entirely different story," Adams said. "There should be no limit to which our nation goes to help those who really need help."

"Besides, the Tenth Amendment declares every entitlement program unconstitutional," Sarah proclaimed to a roomful of blank stares.

"And finally," Thor shared, "we need to understand that freedom is not free. Every right is protected by shield and sword. Without a strong national defense we'll lose our freedom of movement, freedom of speech, freedom of religion, and our treasured prosperity—even our precious entitlements."

Congressman Macon was about to bust wide open. "Even if I could support your domestic agenda, I can't support your notion of nation building. I think it's ill advised."

"So do I."

That wasn't the response he expected.

"The only thing I hate more than meddling in the affairs of other nations is them meddling in ours. 9/11 was enough for me. I wouldn't have waited for them to distribute anthrax." The Admiral let that sink in. "If you know how to kill this cancer without surgery, without chemotherapy, speak up. If you can solve this problem with words—say them!"

"We can't afford to do half the things you're recommending—especially militarily," Macon protested. It wasn't the money. He was a big spender. He just had other priorities.

"What makes you think *we're* going to pay for them? Sarah and I are not proposing blasting rocks in Afghanistan or chasing bloodthirsty thugs around Somalia. The cancer of Islam doesn't grow on rocks or blood. It feeds on money. And the money comes from oil—oil that just happens to be under Iran, Iraq, and Saudi Arabia."

"No way. I'm sorry. I just don't agree with what you're proposing," the Democrat said. "I don't feel good about taking their oil."

Adams looked at him, eyebrows raised. He wasn't a touchy-feely sort of a guy. "You'd rather have them use their ill-gotten gains to *kill* us? You want them to write more million-dollar checks to the parents of suicide bombers? Do you think another oil boycott might be helpful?"

The Democratic Congressman shook his head. "This sounds a lot like Iran-Contra to me. Taking Arab money to support some pet project."

Thor was angry. "The Reagan Administration sold missiles to the Iranians and transferred the proceeds to the Contras so that they could fight for their freedom, fight the scourge of Communism. They were successful. However, the missiles were not," he said. "The Army had those missiles altered prior to shipment. I understand the investigation was classified, but you're elected officials and that was a long time ago. So just in case you don't know what happened, let me explain it this way. Are you familiar with the Elvis Presley song, 'Return to Sender'?"

"I'm glad you brought this up, Congressman," Sarah said. "Since you seem to have forgotten why Reagan needed to fund the fight for freedom this way, I'll tell you. The Democrat-controlled Congress passed a bill that tied the President's hands. Loving big government yourselves, you didn't see the problem with Communism. And you should have," she added, "because you made the same mistake in Vietnam. Once we withdrew, you cut funding to the South Vietnamese, so they ran out of bullets. The Communists overran them—causing the deaths of over fifty thousand American boys to have been in vain. The Communists massacred hundreds of thousands of defenseless civilians as a result of your carelessness. But it got worse. Next door, a nice Communist fellow named Pol Pot slaughtered millions more—one out of every five Cambodians."

It was Adams' turn. "The left has a legacy of making the wrong call when it comes to totalitarian dictators. MacArthur wanted to finish the job in Korea, but your pal Truman fired him instead. As a result, the world's worst rogue nation sells nuclear weapon technology to Islamic warlords. And the world's largest nation, after stealing our ballistic missile technology, now conducts its war games with us as its principal enemy. History has made it painfully clear: the price we've paid for not neutering

Communists when their regimes were young and frail is intolerable."

Adams stood and glared at the Democrats to his left. "FDR and Yalta," was all he said.

He paced behind them. "Do you want to make the same mistake again?" the Admiral added, testily. He was looking at the picture of Ronald Reagan on his horse, back straight, white hat, eyes focused ahead, wearing a smile that had rekindled America's spirit. "Today the Islamic states are young and frail. How long will that last? Today, only half of their citizens are brainwashed. Today, their nuclear programs are only half baked. But how long do you think it will take at half a billion dollars a day in oil payments before the Saudis, the Libyans, the Iraqis, the Iranians, *et al.,* buy what they need from Truman's pals, the North Koreans and the Chinese, or FDR's friends, the former Soviets, to ready a nuclear bomb?

"With oil money funding Muslim militants—their media, mosques, and madrases—how long do we have? When will this cancer kills us?" He glared at them. "You want to *talk?* Then say the words! *Economic embargoes?* Because you've forbidden us to drill, economic sanctions would destroy us long before they influence them. What's your alternative, gentlemen? I'd like to hear it."

"Good grief, you *are* a soldier," one of the Senators said.

"But aren't you unfairly singling my party out?" Macon whined. "The last Republican President's views were wholly counter to yours."

"I'm not a Republican, but you're right. When the Palestinians escalated their brutality, Bush thought it would be wise to *reward* their behavior. W sent his Secretary of State to negotiate with the head terrorist. Then he foolishly called 'Palestine' a state without borders." Adams laughed. "Imagine trusting the leader of any Palestinian political party— Fatah, Islamic Jihad, Hamas, Hezbollah, Aqsa Martyrs' Brigade, or even the Communist flavor of insanity, the Popular Front for the Liberation of Palestine. Even if you could find a responsible leader in one of those cesspools, the 'good' Muslims would kill the 'bad' one faster than he could say, 'terror.' What Bush did was irrational and immoral."

The Admiral shook his head, remembering. "Worst of all, Bush told another nation not to defend itself. He knew they were fighting the same enemy, the very same behavior, the same delusional doctrine that had caused him to send Americans off to Afghanistan. Yet Bush *ordered* Sharon to withdraw—to leave his people defenseless. And withdraw from what? From 'Palestinian territory.' He *had* to know there was no such thing." Adams took a deep breath. "But you're right, Congressman. Foolishness has infected both sides of the aisle."

"By my calculation," Sarah added, "America, in war making, homeland security, and intelligence gathering, has spent over *two hundred billion* dollars fighting terror since 9/11. And for what? There are more terrorists today than there were then, and they're more lethal than ever. Everything we've done has been wrong."

"Y'know, fellas, you used to be able to buy something *good* for two hundred billion," Thor noted dryly.

Sarah was still steamed. "And with all of your stupid restrictions you've punished the victims rather than the villains. Then you forced American taxpayers to fund your folly." Sarah, having delivered her knockout punch, folded her arms and glared at the assembly.

An awkward silence descended upon the room, broken at length by Congressman Macon. "Admiral Adams, after listening to you and Agent Nottingly, I think we agree on but one thing. America needs a choice." The politician paused. "I think I'll give them one. I'm going to run against you."

"Great. Like I said, I don't want the job."

"*Not* great," the Republican Senator groaned. "I still want you to run. I support most of the things you said—even the liberal ones."

"Good. Run against him, Senator Dodge."

"No. My party and I have done a miserable job of articulating our position. Sure, the press is united against us, but we couldn't market a hula-hoop. We need you."

"I'm not a politician. No offense, but I don't even *like* politicians."

"No offense taken. I don't like them either." That got them laughing, which was a good thing. The room had grown a little tense.

"Admiral, please. You can run as a Republican or as an Independent, either way. It doesn't matter. Even if we nominated a candidate, they'd vote for you. Frankly, if I were running, *I'd* vote for you."

The Admiral found his candor disarming. "Do you remember all the way back to the Contract with America, sir?" Adams loved history.

"Sure. Republicans told voters what they'd do if elected. They put it in writing. Apparently folks liked what they read because they threw the liberal incumbents out. We had the first conservative majority in decades."

"If Sarah and I were to put our plan to Save America into the form of a contract, could you get folks to sign it?"

"Yes."

"Enough to pass its provisions into law if they were elected?"

"I'm certain of it," he responded.

"Then let's give America a choice. Congressman Macon, commit your plan to writing. We'll do the same. Let the people choose."

22

OUT OF THE BLUE

"You need to call Quagmer." Riza rubbed his head as he spoke.

"You got a death wish? *You* call him," Atta retorted.

It was late morning. Both men were half asleep. Riza fumbled with the coffee pot, giving disheveled a bad name. Forward and rear, the cabin doors were open. The bunks, still unmade, were as unkempt as their current occupants—a couple of Bahamian prostitutes.

While the scene wasn't much of a testimony for the worth of Islam, it might well have served as a recruiting film for Muslim militancy. Hung over, groggy from lack of sleep, and completely broke, the wannabe terrorists were in deep water.

"We can't pay the girls. How are we going to provision our boat?" Atta complained, as if losing the money hadn't been his fault.

"Worse, whose going to pay for the hull repairs?" Riza whined. "You've got to call Quagmer. Make something up. Say we got rammed by another yacht—a Jew yacht maybe. Yeah. Or say we had to bribe the dock master to keep him from tipping the authorities off."

"You want me to *lie?*" Atta protested hypocritically.

"You've got a better idea?"

Atta's expression was as blank as his mind.

"On the other hand," Riza said, "you could tell him the truth. Tell Omen we drank ourselves into oblivion, gambled his money away, and whatever we didn't lose, we squandered on prostitutes. He ought to love that. With any luck, we might even live to see lunchtime."

The girls were beginning to stir. It was time to fish or cut bait.

"If the babes find out we're busted, they'll kill us before breakfast." Atta was slow, not stupid.

Riza's countenance brightened. "Our Atlantis cards are still good." He spied his sitting on the table. "The hotel doesn't know we can't pay."

"Yet," Atta warned.

"Then they're still good. I'll take the girls to breakfast. You call Omen.

That'll buy us some time." It was a heroic gesture.

Coffee done, they filled their cups and gradually brought their bodies back to life. Too bad it didn't have the same impact on their souls.

✡   ✝   ☪

"MR. NOTTINGLY, are you sure about this?"

Troy shook his head, smiling. "Son, I'm willing to trust you with my daughter. So why is trusting you with my airplane such a big deal?"

He had a point.

"Yes, sir, I understand. Thank you."

"You're welcome. Just take good care of her."

"I will, sir. But to be safe, let's make one more coupled approach."

"You *are* slow. Not her," Troy said, patting the glare screen. "*Her!*" He pointed to the rear of the Pilatus—to where Sarah was sitting.

That's twice, Adams thought to himself. *I'd better engage my brain before I crash and burn.*

They were flying northbound above the Eastern Shore, over the romantic little town of St. Michaels. The Chesapeake Bay glistened beneath them. Off to the west, Thor could see Annapolis out his side of the plane. A grand green carpet of open fields and old hardwoods spread out to the east, fading into the Atlantic.

Troy Nottingly had offered the Admiral the use of his airplane. Sarah was already certified in it, having earned her commercial pilot's license and instrument rating years ago. She had joined her father each year, in Orlando, getting recurring training in the simulators at SimCom's Flight School. Thor was just coming up to speed.

Having committed their Plan to Save America to paper, they were set to tour the nation. Seventy speeches, fifty cities, twenty states, fifteen days. It would be worse than taking flight instruction from Sarah's father.

Senator Dodge had delivered on his promise. Congressman Macon had not. There were eighty empty seats in the house, fifteen in the Senate. Every Republican candidate had signed the plan, as had most every surviving incumbent. While a smattering of conservative Blue Dog Democrats had pledged their support, most liberals were disparaging each of the five planks like they were a plague. They had even resurrected an aging James Carville to craft their "talking points."

However, the liberals had no plan of their own. Once the dust settled, or the spores, as the case may be, they merely returned to the status quo—

building a government of the politicians, by the politicians, and for the politicians. They had learned that there was no limit to what they could achieve spending other people's money.

Fortunately, Troy, a former dot-com founder, was well versed in the art of marketing. He brought the Admiral's ideas to life, making them accessible by crafting a multimedia presentation to complement Thor's stump speech. It came complete with stirring music, video segments, animations, spectacular photographic images, and, of course, text to support the Admiral's spoken words. He also produced a color brochure that helped communicate the plan with style and clarity. In addition, Troy built Internet sites to present what Thor and Sarah had learned about Islam and the substance behind their Plan to Save America.

As they had in their speech to Congress, Adams and Nottingly shared the stage. And, as before, they brought Mary along to give the horror of terror a human face. Between Thor's character, Sarah's intellect, Troy's marketing skill, and Mary's disarming tenderness, it was a *tour de force* in a teacup.

Americans were being given a clear choice. Would they choose left or right, liberal or conservative, more or less, a continuation of the same or something new? The only thing that puzzled Thor was how something so out-of-sync with the status quo could be called "conservative."

Since the opposition was reluctant to commit their schemes to paper, Nottingly and Adams took the liberty of doing it for them. They framed the issue by presenting the nature of the liberal agenda from a historian's perspective.

Adams explained it this way: "They want to intrude into your personal life. Why? Because they don't trust you to make decisions on your own. They want to increase your taxes. Why? So they can build bigger government programs to buy your unwavering support. They want to enact more regulations. Why? Because they think you're stupid and need to be protected from yourself. They covet control. Why? Because freedom is so untidy in the hands of others. They want to keep increasing their power. Why? So they can keep voters dependent on their wealth-reallocation plan. More government, more spending, more restrictions, more taxes. There is no wrong that can't be righted with a little more money."

Thor had become convinced that conservatives wanted less: less government intrusion, lower taxes, less spending, fewer watchdogs, fewer restrictions. Just as environmentalists implored Americans to conserve, to use less, he explained that political conservatives wanted America to use less government, to rely less on government resources.

However, he was prepared to acknowledge that in one place the roles were reversed. Conservatives wanted a stronger national defense. Sadly, the media miscast this debate, labeling conservatives "hawks" and liberals "doves." The unmistakable implication was that one wanted war and the other, peace.

Adams engaged the A-team, relying on Sarah to explain the economic wisdom of building arms so that they would never have to be used. While the concept was simple, Nottingly knew it was lost on many. In her view, the reasons were clear. Though liberals were willing to spend great piles of money to make problems go away, there was only so much they could take from productive Americans. Thus the military was a competitor—something that consumed money they wanted to spend on their constituents.

The left still seemed to think war could be averted through political dialog and were eager to rely on government negotiators. "Talk nice to people," Sarah characterized their approach. "Understand their problems, feel their pain, blame someone else, and buy the support of hostile nations the same way you buy votes here at home. Open the public coffers and grant them billions in foreign aid." It wasn't *their* money, anyway.

Nottingly, on the other hand, believed that a strong shield and a sharp sword were the best means of assuring peace, protecting what Americans held dear, and ultimately saving lives. Ready weapons were unused weapons. Freedom, she knew, was bought with coin or blood.

The battle lines were drawn.

✡ ✝ ☾

TRIXI LIGHTHEART looked depressed. The explosion at Camp David had blown out every camera, and without video, ratings were as depressed as the nation's mood. No amount of B-roll could make this disaster look sufficiently entertaining. And worse still, the anthrax attack had been a fiasco.

She began her report, "As few as a hundred thousand people may have been affected by the most recent anthrax attacks on America. It now appears that the spores the terrorists distributed were not effectively stabilized," she read. "Most, therefore, were not lethal."

It was a tale of woe. "Technical experts have analyzed the trucks. They claim that the mixing devices failed to properly combine the anthrax with the powder that is required to keep them aloft. This failure, in turn, substantially reduced their movement. Meteorological conditions were also unfavorable. The combination of wind, rain, and high humidity diminished the attack's effectiveness."

In other words, death didn't scale. The little buggers had been a bust.

This was *good* bad news. Lightheart was perplexed, not knowing whether she should be be smiling or stern in her presentation. She chose a non-committal grin. "The Centers for Disease Control in Atlanta confirmed today that antibiotics have been much more effective with this particular strain of biological weapon."

Trixi looked down at the papers spread on the desk in front of her. She knew that the network had decided to run file footage of the fifty coffins that still lay in state under the Capitol Rotunda. The video revealed color guards standing watch as long lines of Americans filed past, four abreast, showing their respect for the fallen.

The news anchor reported, "Mamdouh Salim, President of Palestine, expressed his sympathy for the families of those slain at Camp David. He went on to say, however, that former Chairman Alafat was justified in his actions because America invited the attack. The President, he said, created a state of war when she sent warships into Islamic waters. Salim also blamed Israeli occupation and war crimes. In his concluding comments, the President Salim told reporters that he expects America to honor its pledge to pay his new Palestinian State two billion dollars a year."

Each network was on a commercial-free twenty-four-hour news watch. As part of their coverage, they ran journalistic essays dignifying the plight of the Palestinian people and their struggle against "occupation." They had also prepared tributes to the life and service of each congressman, senator, and cabinet member that had been slain. Elaborate testimonials were aired, proclaiming the great accomplishments of the late President, presenting her as a selfless servant of the working people, a troubadour of the peace process. Ironically, she had become a martyr.

"Tomorrow, starting at ten o'clock eastern, a funeral procession, complete with horse-drawn carriages and military honor guards, will make its way through the Capital. Even in death, the President's family and party are trying to be inclusive, allowing every victim of the bombing to accompany her in the parade."

In the saddest expression she could muster, the new dean of the airways proclaimed, "One hundred and eighty members of the Washington press corps perished in service to their country. Their remains, along with the fifty political leaders now lying in state, will stretch the procession an estimated five blocks. Of course, FOX News will bring it all to you *live*." It probably wasn't the best word she could have chosen. "Pre-procession coverage will begin at eight A.M. eastern tomorrow morning."

✡   ✝   ☾

THEY WERE clearly uncomfortable. 4,000 years is a long time to hold a grudge. Confused, the men didn't know if they should pray for their lives or fight for them. In the end, they simply stared warily at their hosts, recognizing that four Palestinians and three Jews do not a minion make.

Talib Ali finally broke the ice, offering his unlikely would-be allies a cup of hot tea. Mamdouh Salim motioned for them to sit around the late Chairman's black conference table. They were in Gaza, in what had once been the headquarters of Fatah and the Palestinian Authority. It was now their nation's capitol, at least in their eyes.

"About a decade ago," Talib said, "several men from your organization, the Temple Faithful, tried to destroy the Dome of the Rock."

The Jews sat motionless, silent. There was no reason to deny responsibility for their previous failure.

"I am curious, gentlemen." Omen raised an eyebrow. "Why?" He hoped their answer would lead toward common ground.

"For the Messiah," the most diminutive of the Jews proclaimed. "Our prophets said he will rule the world from the Temple once it's rebuilt."

The response angered the believers, Talib Ali and Aymen Halaweh. Strangely, it seemed to please the more practical Omen Quagmer and Mamdouh Salim. They were fishing for volunteers. They were hoping these guys would take the bait.

"We too have an interest in seeing the Dome destroyed." President Salim's response shocked the three Temple enthusiasts.

Having been briefed, Halaweh and Ali knew this was a lie. They settled back down, knowing that the explosives would never be detonated. And there was little they enjoyed more than deceiving infidels.

Warily, the tallest Jew responded, "We're listening."

"Public opinion has turned against my people," Omen explained. "With the crucifixions, the anthrax thing, and now with the little incident at Camp David, we are struggling with our public relations." A lie is more seductive if you mix in a little truth.

"And you want *us* to help *you?*"

"No. We want you to help yourselves." Mamdouh turned the tables.

"Why are you doing something for us? We don't understand," the third Jewish man queried his lifelong enemy.

"We believe that the destruction of our third holiest site will help us regain the upper hand politically. That's especially true if the damage is done by radical right-wing Jews. No offense, gentlemen."

"None taken." He stroked his beard. "So you want to blame it on us."

"Give you credit," Omen corrected him. "Among your people and with your god, you'll be heroes. If you're caught, you'll be imprisoned, I suppose, but that's a small sacrifice for helping your Messiah, is it not?"

"And who knows?" Salim added. "Wearing the high-tech suits we're prepared to loan you, you might even get away with it."

"Then how would that help you?"

"After your last attack on the Dome, our people installed video surveillance cameras. The cameras will pick up the Star of David insignias on the uniforms you'll be wearing." Omen turned, pointing to the wall behind them. "See them over there?"

"State-of-the-art technology," Mamdouh interrupted. "You'll be nearly invisible in the midnight setting. But the suits will broadcast your position on a discreet transponder code, so we'll know where you are, and the world will know you're Israelis."

"Then what's to keep you from tracking us down after we've placed the explosives—I'm assuming you want us to carry C-12?"

"The C-4 will be stashed in the pack. That's where the transponder is so...."

"We know Alafat was carrying C-12. Don't lie to us."

Omen smiled. "You're right. I apologize on behalf of my colleague. We're all professionals. There's no reason to lie."

Aymen and Talib almost swallowed their tongues.

"These fancy suits...how did you get them, anyway?"

"Black market," Omen lied. "Your people will sell anything." That was true enough.

"They're called SFGs," Mamdouh burst in, sounding professional.

"So we put on these SFGs and tiptoe into the Dome under the watchful eyes of surveillance cameras. We take off the packs and set them against three of the four internal columns. Do I have this right?"

"Yes. You've obviously studied the construction of the Holy Shrine." Having earned their trust, Omen unrolled the blueprints. "Here, here, and here," he said, pointing to the three large support columns Halaweh had determined to be the most vulnerable.

"Then we hightail it out of the Dome, and push the trigger when we're clear," one of the Jews said. "If we're fast enough, we escape. If not, we go to jail. But either way, we both get what we want."

"That's the plan." Quagmer shot him an oily smile. "Are you in?"

The three Jews shared a glance. "Was Moses Jewish? Hell yes!" They were ecstatic. The Temple Faithful had committed themselves to doing this very thing.

✡   ✝   ☪

THOR WAS SITTING in the right seat, Sarah in the left. It was familiar territory. She was in charge.

Holding the checklist, Adams ticked off the preflight items. "Flight control lock?"

"Removed and stowed."

"Circuit breakers?"

"All in left," she said rubbing her fingers along them as she looked.

"All good right," he called out before lowering his thumb down to the next line. "Parking brake?"

"Set," she confirmed, pulling and twisting it as she tapped the pedals.

"AHRS one and two?"

"Slave."

"You *wish*," Thor joked. "Cooling, fans, and heat?"

"Off, low, and off," she said, looking down and to her left.

"EFIS?" he asked, moving down the list.

"Norm." Although she had no idea how it worked, she knew the acronym stood for Electronic Flight Instrument System. These glass tubes had become ubiquitous on high-priced aircraft, both civilian and military. The Pilatus had four of them.

"External lights?"

"All off except the beacon." She pressed the top of one of the large gray rocker switches, placing it in the middle position.

"De-Ice?"

"All off—probes, boots, and windshield heat. The inertial separator is open," she anticipated, pushing another switch.

"ECS?" The Environmental Control System was particularly handy if you wanted to remain alive at cruising altitude. He checked the position.

"Trim and Flap Interrupt?"

"Norm and guarded."

"MOR?"

"Less," she laughed, making sure the small red manual override lever was in its off position.

"PCL?"

"Power control lever is idle," she answered, pulling the large black throttle backwards.

"Condition lever?" he asked, moving his thumb down the plastic card.

"Cut-Off. Feather."

"Flaps?"

"At zero, indicating zero."

The lever was nearest him, so he confirmed what she had said. He then reached down to verify the stowed position of the emergency levers on the console between their seats. "Battery on. Fuel check?"

"Sufficient and balanced." They would need less than half of what they were carrying in the wings. The plane held 2,700 pounds of Jet A.

"Oxygen lever?" he asked, raising it himself. He loved the sound it made, filling the quick-donning masks behind their seats. Should there be a rapid decompression, these would save their lives.

"EIS Test?" It stood for Engine Instrument System.

"Eights and tapes," she shot back, putting the system through a self-diagnostic test.

"Daughter?"

Sarah looked back and checked on Mary. "Belted, supplied with semi-nutritious snack foods, and occupied with a big game book."

Adams smiled at Mary and then looked outside again to make sure they were clear. Shredding an unsuspecting lineman on the tarmac was considered bad form. With no one in sight he said, "Ignition."

She fired the starter. The giant one hundred-inch propeller slowly came to life. The turbine speed rose with Ng showing fifteen percent of its 30,000 RPM performance. As it did, she lifted the condition lever and pressed it forward, dumping kerosene into the turbine. It roared to life.

Eyes glued to the display, they saw an LCD jump to nearly 800 degrees when the secondary nozzles poured fuel into the hot section of the Pratt and Whitney engine, mimicking the afterburners on a military jet. This was all a far cry from the "kick the tires and light the fires" MO of Navy jet jocks. For Thor, learning to fly a complex general aviation aircraft was a study in personal discipline. Unlike going off to war, pilots often described the civilian experience as hours of tedium punctuated by seconds of terror.

"One victor alpha cleared for takeoff, on course." They were off to Florida, which meant they were within twenty-four hours of completing their fifteen-day marathon. Orlando and Miami were the only obstacles between them and a return to a normal life.

At altitude, they settled into the routine of flight. With the autopilot in command, the crew began to chat. "Last night, in...oh gosh, where were we yesterday?"

"Dallas, New Orleans, and Atlanta," Adams recounted.

"That's right. Last night in Atlanta, after I put Mary to bed, I did some more reading."

"What'd you find?" Thor was almost afraid to ask. The deeper they had dug into Islam, the uglier it had gotten.

Sarah confirmed his fears. "We didn't tell the General a fraction of the similarities between Muhammad and Hitler."

Thor looked at her. "Like what?"

"Like they both told the world they were peace-loving right up to the moment they butchered everybody in sight. Hitler said, 'My only great task is to secure peace in the world. I have a deep respect for the rights of other nations,' saying, 'from our innermost heart, National Socialist Germany wishes to live in peace and friendship.'"

"The friendship of *blitzkrieg*—death came so fast, it was relatively painless, I suppose. But did you know that the 'land-for-peace' terminology used in describing today's 'peace process' with the Arabs was usurped from Hitler? He said, 'The German minority in the Sudetenland must be autonomous.'"

"Germans in Czechoslovakia were corrupted by Nazism, just as the Palestinians are by Islam. Both comprised twenty-two percent of the population, and both were determined to undermine their democracy from within on behalf of neighboring dictatorships."

"Israel and Czechoslovakia: wealthy states with world class military defenses—defenses rendered useless by giving the high ground to a treasonous minority," Thor explained as he scanned the engine instruments.

"When Chamberlain gave Czechoslovakia to Hitler, he unwittingly unified Germany behind *der Fuhrer*. It was a stunning diplomatic coup. Awarding the Islamic terrorists with the heart of Israel will similarly galvanize their resolve and inflame their lust for war, won't it, Thor?"

"Yes. The 'peace process' is the most direct path to war. Giving Hitler Czechoslovakia ignited World War II; giving the Arabs Israel will be the opening salvo of World War III."

"Muslims say Islam doesn't support terror, yet the faithful terrorize. Muhammad even told them to lie to us."

"Unfortunately, the media has bought into the delusion. How many times have you heard them say Islam's a peace-loving religion?"

"A few thousand. They've spewed the garbage so often, folks have come to believe it. Makes us look crazy when we say it's untrue."

"Do you think it's purposeful, or merely foolish? Are the folks with the microphones lying, or just too lazy to figure it out?"

"Let me ask you this. What are the qualifications for being on television?" Sarah posed, scanning the instruments.

"You've got to look good and be able to read the teleprompter."

"Then since we know they can read, how is it possible they've missed something this obvious?" Sarah wanted to drive the point home. "If you were to pick up the Hadith, how long would you have to read before you knew that Islam was about war, not peace?"

"I don't know. Four or five hours at the most. Not very long, especially considering what's at stake. They've murdered thousands of Americans and pummeled our economy. Muslim militants have changed the way we live—so what's a few hours?"

"How about five *minutes?*" She reached behind the seat and dug into her flight bag, pulling out a copy of al-Bukhari's Hadith. "Give me five minutes, not five hours, and I'll find five Muhammadisms sufficient to prove that Islam is all about war—killing for Allah." Sarah opened the book.

Thor glanced at the cover. "You've got it upside down and backwards," he said, trying to help her out.

"No, I don't. It's written from back to front. Upside down is really right side up."

"Okay. Sounds perfect for Islam."

Sarah read what the Muslim scholars had had to say about the Hadith and their translation from Arabic to English. "'I am perfectly sure that the translation, with Allah's help, has approached perfection.'"

She turned the page. "Listen to this. 'It has been unanimously agreed that Bukhari's work is more authentic than all other Hadiths combined.' They said: 'The most authentic book after the Qur'an is al-Bukhari.'

"Since the Qur'an is supposed to be Rocky speaking, that would make al-Bukhari's Hadith *the* most authentic source for the words of Muhammad."

"The professor from the Islamic University of Saudi Arabia who oversaw this translation said, 'There is no doubt about the Hadith's authenticity.' He said, 'It's the most accurate account of the Prophet's sayings.' 'Al-Bukhari traveled to many places gathering the precious gems that fell from the lips of the noble Prophet.' I know you think I'm making this stuff up. But no, look here," she said, showing him the passage.

Looking back down at the book, she read, "'Many Islamic scholars'— now there's an oxymoron— 'have tried to find fault in the great collection of al-Bukhari, but without success. It is for this reason they unanimously agree that al-Bukhari is the most authentic book after the Qur'an.'"

"The best of Muhammad."

"Yes indeed—the best Islam has to offer. So if in the next five minutes I can find say, a half dozen places in which the Messenger promotes war, it would make the mullahs and the media either liars or fools, right?"

"If it's that easy, yes."

"Set the timer." She pointed to the top of the nav/com stack.

Adams pressed the far right button on the plane's RMI. "Go, girl."

She let the book fall open, flipping a few pages and scanning the subject heads. Finding what she was looking for, she read "The Book of Jihad, chapter one, number 1204. It says, 'A man asked Allah's Messenger, "Guide me to a deed that equals *Jihad* in reward." He replied, "There is no such deed."'"

Adams stopped the timer as she read each passage, starting again when she began her search for the next. "That's one. Although in saying this, Muhammad is condemning Islam outright. If fighting is *the* most important deed, Islam can't be peaceful. That's a direct hit."

"Listen to what the 'Islamic scholars' had to say about *Jihad*." Sarah's tone was deeply disturbed. She read, '*Jihad* is holy fighting in Allah's Cause with maximum force and weaponry. It is the most important part of Islam. By *Jihad* Islam is established, made superior, and propagated. If *Jihad* is forsaken, Islam is destroyed and Muslims fall into an inferior position. Their honor is lost and their lands are stolen. Their rule and authority vanish. *Jihad* is an obligatory duty in Islam on every Muslim.'"

"Whoa, or should I say, *woe*. What does that tell you about all the nimrods out there trying to convince us all that *Jihad* is a 'spiritual struggle'?" The question was rhetorical. He simply pressed the timer again. Twenty-five seconds had passed.

"They're lying." She flipped to the next page. "Number 1205: 'A man asked Allah's Apostle, "Who is the best Muslim?" The Prophet replied, "A believer who strives in Allah's Cause," i.e., *Jihad*, "with his life and property."' Humph," she said, "that one sounds suspiciously like an approval for suicide, doesn't it?"

"Yep. And there's a verse just like it in the Qur'an. You're forty seconds in, and you've found three."

"Okay. Same chapter, next verse. 'Allah's Messenger said, "Allah guarantees to admit the *Mujahadin* in His Cause into Paradise if they are killed; or Allah will return them home safely with war booty."'"

"What a scumbag!" Adams protested. "Paradise if you're killed fighting for him, booty if you're not. Good grief!" He shook his head. "Well, that's fifty seconds and four. One to go."

She looked down. "Number 1207: '"Paradise has one hundred levels which Allah has reserved for the *Mujahadin* who fight in His Cause."'"

"Five and fifty-five," he said pressing the timer again. "Either you're really good or Islam is real bad."

Almost instantaneously Sarah read, "'I heard the Prophet saying, "*Jihad* will bring about either a reward in the hereafter or booty in this world."' How's that for 'peace-loving?'" she asked.

"Well, now we know where they get this lame-brained idea of paradise being a reward for murder. You're six in sixty, seconds that is. You win—we lose."

"Not so fast, lover. I'm just getting warmed up," she said scanning the navigational instruments. After what seemed like an eternity, about twenty seconds, Sarah was ready. "'I heard the Prophet saying, "Paradise will be granted to the first batch of my followers who will undertake a naval expedition."' Then, '"The first army amongst my followers who will invade Caesar's city will be forgiven their sins."'"

"Seven."

"Seven it is. Chapter seven: 'Allah's Messenger said, "By Him who holds my soul, whomever is wounded in Allah's Cause, his wound will have the smell of musk perfume in Paradise."'"

"Eight."

She flipped forward. "You got it. Chapter eight: 'If Allah gives me a chance to fight Infidels, Allah will see how bravely I can fight.'"

"Nine."

"Yes, nine. 'Muhammad said, "Embrace Islam first, then fight." So he became a Muslim and was martyred. Allah's Apostle said, "A little work, but a great reward."' Sure sounds like a peace-loving religion to me—great rewards for fighting."

"That's ten in less than two minutes."

"Ooo! Here's a good one. 'Gabriel said to the Prophet, "Why have you have put down your arms? By Allah, I have not put down mine yet." The Prophet said, "Where does Allah want me to go now?" Gabriel answered, "This way," pointing toward the tribe of Beni Quraidha.' The Jews. 'So Allah's Messenger went out toward them.' Then, if you recall, the peace-loving founder of the peace-loving religion lined up all the Jewish men along a trench and cut their heads off. And just in case that wasn't peace-loving enough, he sold the women and children into slavery—all with Allah's blessing and a little angelic assistance."

"Makes me want to puke," he said.

"Please. Not in daddy's nice airplane."

He laughed. "So tell me, how does the media miss this stuff?"

"Like you said, it's either purposeful or irresponsible."

Still on a roll, Sarah read, "'A blind man said, "O Allah's Messenger! If I could see, I would take part in *Jihad*."' So Allah told his Messenger to give him a get-out-of-*Jihad*-free card," she paraphrased. "'A pass is given to the blind and lame.'"

"The blind and lame," Thor repeated. That sounds like *every* Muslim. Why don't they all take advantage of their 'free pass?'" He shook his head. "I think that's fourteen examples of Prophet-Man personally encouraging his followers to go to war, to kill infidels. In each case, the reward is booty or paradise. This is about as peace-loving as the Mongol Horde."

"According to this little treasure, paradise isn't sounding real special. 'The Prophet said, "If somebody uses a horse in *Jihad* in Allah's Cause...then he will be rewarded for what the horse has eaten or drunk and for its dung and urine."'"

"Well, that seems only fair," he quipped. "Paradise in his own image— a total waste."

"It says here, 'Allah's messenger fixed two shares for the horse and one for its rider from the war booty.'"

"This boy's too whacked out to be a founder of a fraternity, much less a religion."

"The fact is, Islam is all about war. This garbage goes on and on."

"Can I have a turn?"

"Sure," she said, handing him the book that was as backward as its message.

Thor scanned a few pages. "From the Book of Revelation, verse 6: 'Issue orders to kill every Jew in the country.' Must be Alafat's favorite. Or maybe it's 1261. Muhammad said, 'Muslims will fight Jews until they hide behind talking rocks. "There's a Jew hiding behind me. Kill him!" the rocks will proclaim.' Mo, in a fighting mood, says in the next verse, '"You must fight against the Turks; people with small eyes, red faces, and flat noses."' Nothing like a little prejudice to kick off a holy war."

He flipped the page. "'Once the Jews came to Muhammad and said, "Death be upon you." "So I cursed them," the Prophet said.'"

"Perhaps you'll like this one: Number 1268. 'Allah's Apostle sent us on a military expedition telling us, "If you find such and such a person, burn them with fire."' Oh, and catch this. It goes on to say, 'When we came to bid Allah's Messenger farewell, he said, "Previously I ordered you to burn so-and-so with fire, but punishment with fire is done by none except Allah, so if you capture them, kill them instead."'"

"See? Kill him, but don't burn him. Mo could be such a softie. Definitely peace-loving, as in 'rest in peace.'"

"Here's why they follow their thugs so blindly. 'The Prophet said, "It is obligatory for one to obey a Muslim ruler's orders." The Prophet also said, "To enter Paradise you must obey me, and he who obeys me obeys Allah. He who obeys the Muslim chief, obeys me. Muslims should fight for the Imam."' Islam is all about submission."

The Admiral had heard enough. Grabbing the book, he tossed it onto the floor behind them. It bounced, landing near Mary's feet.

"Careful, daddy."

"We need to let folks know this stuff," Sarah said.

"Yeah? How are we going to do that with the media being such a big part of the problem."

"Overwhelm them with truth. There's so much of this, and it's so black, even *they* can't...."

"Don't be so sure," the nattily attired Adams interrupted. He was wearing a suit and tie. Sarah and Mary were decked out in matching Laura Ashley prints.

"We've got another five minutes before we start our arrival into Orlando Exec." He looked out the window. Puffy white clouds decorated the brilliant blue sky, a sky that was mirrored in the glistening waters of the Atlantic and the distant deep colors of the Gulf. At 28,000 feet, they were high enough to see both coasts.

"One victor alpha, Orlando approach, descend and maintain seventeen thousand. Orlando altimeter is three zero one four," the air traffic controller said. Sarah reached up and turned the altitude pre-select counter clockwise. Pulling out the knob, she established a 2,000 foot-a-minute descent. Adams retarded the throttle so as not to overspend the machine.

"Sarah, did you do a similar search for *peaceful* Muhammad quotes?"

"I fell asleep reading al-Bukhari last night. I must have read for three hours. 'Let's-play-nice' sayings are few and far between. Muhammad was a real piece of work. And I'm afraid you're right. His condemning us infidels, his terror, all stems from him being insecure. I'll give you an example," she said, reciting a verse she had read the night before. "Insecure Boy is bragging about his trip to heaven. In the middle of his story, he somehow feels the need to cut Moses down to his own level, to make him appear to be as big a crybaby as he is. So Muhammad tells his followers this story: 'When I left Moses, he cried. Someone asked Moses why. "I weep because after me there is a Prophet whose followers will enter Paradise in greater numbers than my followers."' Pretty sad, huh?"

"Sarah, we've got a moment before they start vectoring us to final. I need to tell you a story—to explain why I know so much about Muhammad's insecurity and why it has created such a hateful legacy."

"Alright," she said with a mixture of curiosity and trepidation.

"Back when I was in my teens, my father was so insecure he wrote me a mountain of hate letters. Their tone and threats were nearly identical to the things we've read from Muhammad. Then one day dad's rage grew out of control. He called a minister friend of his and told him he was going to kill me. The pastor called and warned me, as he was obligated to do. I made copies of my dad's letters, looked up the name of a shrink in the phone book, and set an appointment. I delivered his 'love letters', along with an explanation of our 'relationship'.

"A few days later," Thor said, "after the psychiatrist had read everything, I met with him. I'll never forget this. He stood up as I walked into his office and told me not to sit down. He said that the man who wrote the letters had followed me there that first day. The shrink said that my dad had been threatening him and his family ever since." Adams stared blankly forward as he recounted the sorry tale.

"The psychiatrist told me that he would never meet with me again, saying that I couldn't even pay him for the visit, and that I was never to mention his name. Then he hit me with this. He said that the man who wrote those hate letters to me was *insecure*, to such a degree he was psychotic, delusional, and paranoid, just like Muhammad. He said my dad had lost contact with reality and that there was nothing I, or anyone, could do to change that. He told me that insecurity made him *insatiable*. Then he laid out the reasons why insecurity caused him to demean me, to lash out. He said he had to be in control, and that no matter what I did, no matter what I gave him, it wouldn't change a thing. Nothing would ever be enough. Again, just like Muhammad and his followers. He went on to tell me, 'With these letters, you will get a restraining order against him, but it will make no difference.'"

Sarah looked horrified. All *she* had ever known was love.

"What he said next was a shock: 'Buy a gun and learn to use it. The man who wrote these letters is violent and hateful. If you are not prepared to defend yourself, he will kill you.'" Thor sighed heavily. "So you see, Sarah, I know all about insecurity. I lived with it. I know exactly what caused Muhammad to be paranoid and delusional, violent and hateful. I know what caused him to kill, to deceive. And I know why his followers terrorize us today. Fact is, we can't appease those whom Muhammad's message has infected. A gun is the only thing that will stop them."

Thor's revelation stunned Sarah. She mourned for his loss.

"Pilatus one victor alpha, descend and maintain eight thousand." The air traffic controller's voice intoned over the intercom. "Turn right heading two seven zero. Contact Orlando approach on one three two point niner."

Thor tuned the number one radio to the new frequency. "Approach, one victor alpha out of seventeen for eight." Sarah switched the autopilot from Nav to Heading and reset the desired altitude.

Adams turned his attention to the number two radio, dialing in the ATIS frequency for Orlando Executive. The winds were light and variable, the sky clear. "One victor alpha turn left heading two two zero. Descend and maintain three thousand."

As they fell gracefully out of the sky, Sarah was inwardly troubled yet outwardly focused. Her left hand rested comfortably on the control yoke; her right was gently draped over the throttle. She had said nothing. She didn't know what to say.

Thor looked at his beautiful fiancé, now deep in thought. He placed his left hand on top of hers. In a little over a week she would be his wife. Then he thought of Mary, the precious little jewel strapped in behind them immersed in a puzzle book. Out of the greatest calamity of his life, he had found love, not once but twice. The Admiral reached behind him and pulled the shoulder harnesses forward, locking the tabs into place. For the first time in his life, he had something to live for.

"Orlando approach, one victor alpha has Orlando Exec," Sarah said looking out the left side of the airplane.

"One victor alpha, you are cleared for visual approach, runway seven. Contact tower on one one eight point seven. Good day."

Adams repeated the instructions as Sarah disengaged the autopilot. Foot on the left rudder pedal, ailerons deflected into a coordinated thirty-degree bank, she pressed the nose down, and throttled the power back.

"Pilatus one victor alpha with yankee five miles northwest inbound visual runway seven," the Admiral explained with military precision.

"Pilatus you are number two, left base entry, following a Cessna on extended downwind. Call traffic in sight," the tower instructed.

Nottingly spotted the small high-winged plane. It was obviously being flown by a student. The wobble in his flight path was the first clue, and the Sky Hawk's bright red tail identified it as belonging to a local flight school. Adams repeated the instructions, informing the tower that they had the traffic in sight.

"One victor alpha, you are cleared to land behind that traffic. Keep visual separation."

Adams checked the airspeed. Noting that they were below the requisite 177 knots, he lowered the gear. He wanted to slow their approach and give the Cessna plenty of room. "Three green," he said, noting the main and nose gear lights. "Flaps fifteen," he announced to Sarah on the intercom, pulling the flap lever back into the first position. The plane pitched down ever so slightly.

Sarah tried to make sense of the Sky Hawk's maneuvers. "Tower, is the Cessna landing or departing the area?"

"Sky Hawk six six whiskey," the tower said over the common radio frequency. "Turn left base."

After a few second's delay and without response, the controller came back on the radio. "Cessna six six whiskey, what is your intent?"

There was only silence as everyone watched the red-tailed Sky Hawk climb rather than descend.

"Cessna six six whiskey, how do you read?"

Once again, there was no reply.

"Pilatus one victor alpha, we have lost contact with the one-seventy-two. It appears to be departing the area, although it's been doing pattern work here for the better part of the last hour."

"Roger that," Adams replied, watching as the small plane began a gradual left banking turn. He put in thirty degrees of flap.

"Tower, what do you make of the climbing left turn?"

The tower responded, "The student pilot made some twenty touch-and-goes prior to your arrival. While his accent made him hard to understand, he's had no radio problems."

"Roger, tower. Do you know anything about the pilot?"

"The ground controller has the flight school on the line now."

Sarah pulled the power back to eight PSI and began her turn from base to final. "Flaps forty," she told Thor.

He started to put them in, but hesitated. "Tower, the Cessna is crossing the field. Do you have light signals?"

"Yes. We've been using them. We have tried to contact the pilot on ground and emergency frequencies. No joy."

"Did the pilot sound Middle Eastern?"

"Yes."

"Do you have his name from the flight school?"

"Just a sec...affirmative. It's Malamud Assad."

Thor and Sarah traded a glance.

"Sarah, I'm taking the controls." He wasn't asking. The warrior smelled foul play.

"Your plane," she nodded, immediately removing her hands from the yoke and throttle and her feet from the pedals.

The Sky Hawk had stopped climbing. It was now in a steep dive, heading directly toward the approach end of runway seven. It looked like a collision course. "Tower, one victor alpha is going missed."

Suddenly the T-CAS traffic avoidance system began bellowing, "Traffic, traffic, traffic!" The Sky Hawk was headed right for them.

"Tower, one victor alpha aborting right!"

With the skill of a 5,000-hour jet jock, Adams pushed the throttle full forward, raising the gear and flap levers in one fluid motion. He forced the right pedal full forward, swinging the rudder right as he deflected the ailerons. This pushed the Pilatus into a sharp sixty-degree bank. Instantly, they felt the G's accumulate, forcing them down into their seats. So he wouldn't stall in the steep turn, he forced himself to press the nose of the airplane into a shallow dive. It wasn't a move for the faint of heart. They were only 500 feet above the ground.

Mary let out a whimper as her puzzle book flew from her tray table across the cabin. She didn't like bumpy flights.

Sarah and Thor could both see the Sky Hawk bearing down on them, looking for all the world like a kamikaze. As the Cessna came closer, Malamud Assad and his wide-eyed smile became increasingly visible. He was staring—aiming—right at them. With the benefit of gravity, the Cessna was more than a match for the otherwise faster Pilatus. Each fraction of a second brought the high-winged attacker ever closer, causing it to grow steadily larger in the front window. Closer, closer.

Malamud's eyes focused as if he were looking through the sights of a gun. As quickly as they had banked hard to the right, he had turned left, pursuing them. It was a dogfight without guns.

In an ever-steeper dive, Adams gained speed, keeping the attacker at bay. He knew that a 172 falling out of the sky was faster than they were. The Pilatus was still a dirty bird, with flaps and gear partially extended. He had retracted the levers, but the cycle time for one was fifteen seconds, thirty seconds for the other. And this whole drama was being played out in a tiny fraction of that time.

"Hold on!" he yelled.

It was now a three-way game of chicken between attacker, ground, and airframe. They were all too eager to blink, of course, turn tail and run from the Muslim marauder. But to do so they had to descend quickly, and that created two new enemies. To delay the impact with the 172, which would be certain death, they had to give their systems awhile to react. The giant turbine engine required time to spool up, and the flaps and gear needed time to retract. Adams knew he had to dive, just as the Sky Hawk was doing, if they hoped to escape. But if he stayed in the dive too long, nature would finish what the kamikaze bomber had started. On the other hand, if he pulled up too abruptly or gained too much speed, especially in this extreme sixty-degree bank, he would rip the wings off.

Still slower than the rapidly diving Cessna, the Admiral had but one thing going for him. A slower plane turns faster than a fast one. If he couldn't outrun his adversary, maybe he could outmaneuver him. This tactic was not without risk, however. A sixty-degree turn doubles the aerodynamic load on the airframe. Pulling out of the steeply banked dive would stress man and machine right up to the breaking point.

The menacing propeller was now spinning in Sarah's side window rather than in front of them. And it was no longer growing, although the earth below them was.

The plane's ground proximity warning system was now squawking, "sink rate, sink rate, terrain, terrain, pull up, pull up." Annoyed, Sarah disabled the audible warning.

Thor was analyzing it all, calculating the pluses and minuses of every alternative. Properly trained and focused, the human brain is faster than any computer.

Military jets are stressed to handle more Gs than the human body can survive, but civilian planes aren't. Thor had noticed the overly engineered parts on the Pilatus, and he knew that the Swiss-made bird had been built by a military contractor. He was now praying that they had designed the craft to withstand more than the 4.5 Gs the FAA required. Their lives depended on it.

All in one motion, Thor raised the nose, smoothly yet firmly. It took a surprising amount of strength. He leveled the wings, trying to retard the dive and keep the airframe from breaking apart. The ground approached at an alarming rate. They were less than a second from impact.

With his wings nearly level, Adams pulled the control yoke back into his chest. The plane bottomed out just inches above the swampy Florida ground. Shrubbery exploded as the propeller trimmed the mangroves, scratching the undercarriage as it passed. Had the gear not partially retracted, they would have cartwheeled.

Sarah held her breath. Mary screamed.

Still pulling back, he felt the giant blades pull the five-ton craft forward, allowing it to rise, slowly at first, then at an ever-accelerating pace. The Pilatus' weight-to-thrust ratio was greater than a World War II P-51's but not nearly that of an F-18. He had beat death for the moment. Hope and adrenaline coursed through his veins.

As he climbed at 3,000 feet a minute, Thor began a slow bank to the right, hoping to see the crash site of their assailant. But no such luck. In a left descending turn, the Islamic warrior had missed both them and the ground.

Sarah, looking at the T/CAS traffic avoidance display, said, "Four hundred feet below us at three o'clock."

"Let's keep climbing. It can't climb at even half our rate."

"Nice flying, sir!" Orlando tower shouted. "That was *incredible.*"

"Do you have any more intel on our Mr. Assad?"

"Yes. The flight school said he's from Egypt, here on a student visa. They said he prayed religiously, even in class. A weird butt-up sort of thing."

"Why didn't they report him?"

"They did. But the authorities called it racial profiling. The Feds said it was illegal and actually threatened the school."

The Admiral shook his head. America had lost its way. In its desire to be politically correct, it had forgotten that its primary duty was to protect its citizens. Prudence had become a crime.

The tower continued, "The FAA has told us specifically not to profile anyone who looks Middle Eastern or anyone carrying Islamic books and such. We can only question little old ladies, small children, and white males—no terrorist types. They'd rather see Americans die than risk offending Muslims. Is that crazy, or what?"

Thor hoped that he was exaggerating. He wasn't.

"We've lost visual contact with the Sky Hawk. Do you have him on radar?" Adams asked.

"Yes, sir, we do. He missed you by as little as you missed the ground. We shot video of the whole thing. Right now, he's at your five o'clock and climbing, although not nearly as fast as you are, captain."

"He was trying to kill us, wasn't he?" Stupid question, but Thor had to ask.

"Yes, sir. No doubt about that."

"Okay, tower, listen carefully. I want you to switch to frequency: pitcher, first, catcher point center, second. I repeat. Frequency: pitcher, first, catcher point center, second." Thor didn't want the terrorist listening to their discussions. He hoped the tower understood baseball nomenclature.

Sarah dialed 132.84 into the number-two radio. Adams was impressed that she knew the positions.

"Pilatus, one victor alpha. This is Orlando tower. Do you read?"

"Affirmative, tower. This is Admiral Thurston Adams. I want you to call every military base within a fifty-mile radius. Bring them up on this frequency. But first, call MacDill and Patrick Air Force Bases and the Jacksonville Naval Air Station. Have them send whatever they have airborne."

"Yes, sir. I'll do it now."

"Admiral Adams," another voice came across the radio.

"Adams here."

"Admiral, we've closed the airport to all incoming traffic, but you are still cleared to land."

"Negative, Orlando. We will not be landing while the Cessna is airborne. We'd be a sitting duck on the ground. Where is he now?"

"Three thousand feet below you, heading southwest, away from the airport."

Sarah pointed him out on the "fish finder," as the T/CAS system is affectionately called. Adams pushed the GPS moving map overlay. With it engaged he could not only see their relative positions but could also determine where the intruder was headed.

"Tower, my track shows the Sky Hawk headed...oh *no!* Directly toward Disney World."

"Affirmative, sir. So does ours. He's twelve miles out."

"What *is it* with these guys?" the Admiral said to Sarah. Engaging the push-to-talk button on the yoke, he activated the radio. "Tower, close this airspace to all in-bounds. Have all current traffic land at the closest appropriate airport. Call Disney and warn them. They've got five minutes. Now, what's the status of the Air Force and Navy Jets?"

There was a short pause. The original tower controller returned to the mike. "Admiral, the Jacksonville Naval Air Station said they have two F-18s on a training mission over Cape Canaveral. That's thirty-three east. They will contact you on this frequency. And Admiral, the airspace has been closed. Disney has been alerted. They sound panicked, sir."

Adams banked to the right again. Descending at full power, he headed in the direction of the blip on the moving map display.

"What are you *doing?*" Sarah was alarmed.

"We can't just let him fly that thing into Disney World. He could kill a hundred people, maybe more."

"Thor, if we get near him again, he's gonna kill three people for sure."

"I just want to distract him, delay him long enough for the fighters to arrive." He flashed her a little grin. She did not return it.

"Pilatus one victor alpha. This is Hornet yankee seven. Come in."

"Hornet yankee seven, this is Admiral Adams. Where are you, son?"

"Thirty miles from your position, closing at mach one point two. Over."

"Do you have us on radar?"

"Affirmative, sir. Both you and the Cessna. Over."

"What's your ETA?"

"Five minutes, sir. No, make that six. We're going to have to slow down or we'll blow right past him. Over."

"What do you have for ordnance?"

"Guns and air-to-air missiles. Over."

"Do you have a wingman?"

"Affirmative."

"What's your name, son?"

"Lieutenant Commander Wilson, sir. My wingman is Lieutenant Kain."

"Have either of you ever flown combat?"

"No, sir."

"Well, then this is a good way to start. The Cessna can't shoot back."

"You want us to *shoot,* sir?"

"Affirmative. I want you to engage and kill the enemy before he kills the folks we're sworn to protect. That is an *order,* son."

"Yes, sir. We are four and a half out. Closing at mach one point one."

"Commander, we're going to distract the pilot. We're less than two minutes from overtaking him, but he's only three minutes from his target, Disney World. Get your tails in here and *engage.*"

Sarah pointed to the traffic they were following, first on T/CAS, then out the window. Thor veered to intercept. He wanted to pass on the left so that he and Malamud would be as close as possible.

"Gear extension is one seventy-seven, right?"

"Yes. Flaps fifteen at one sixty-three."

In a full power descent, they were at redline, flying at nearly 300 knots. Intersect was less than sixty seconds. Adams planned to fly past the red-tailed plane and then turn right, passing in front of him. He wanted to enrage the Arab pilot to the point he would recommence the chase in hopes of inflicting revenge.

"Two miles and closing," Sarah said. "Are you sure about this?"

"No."

"Oh, that's reassuring."

The Admiral pulled the power back. He didn't want to fly past Mr. Assad so fast that he wouldn't be sufficiently tempted. Thor grasped the yoke in his left hand so he could visually demonstrate his affection for his Muslim friend with his right. Smiling, he banked the Pilatus and cut as closely in front of the Sky Hawk as their relative speeds would allow. From his seat, Adams was able to enjoy a leisurely split-second view of the olive-skinned Arab turning white with fear. The panicked student pilot nearly jerked the 172 out of the sky trying to avoid the Pilatus. Being the attackee wasn't nearly as much fun.

With some effort, Assad regained control after flying through the Pilatus' wing vortex—violently turbulent rotating air. But rather than following the plane he had once pursued so aggressively, he merely turned back toward the theme park. Mickey Mouse couldn't fight back. A frustrated Adams slowed his plane and lowered the gear and flaps.

"*Now* what are you doing?"

"Math."

"*What?*"

"He'll be over Disney World in one minute. The Hornets are still two minutes out. We need to buy more time."

"So why the gear?"

"What do you think is stronger?" Thor asked, maneuvering the Pilatus back into position. "Our right main or his left wing?"

"I've always thought the left wing was lame." She laughed nervously. It seemed better than crying, which is what she really wanted to do. Suddenly, she thought of Mary. She spun around to see a very worried-looking eight year old strapped into her seat. She was not enjoying this one bit.

Adams flipped on the cabin intercom. "Hey, Punkin. You wanna see Disney World?"

"*Thor!*" Sarah was not amused.

"Commander, how long to intercept?"

"Ninety seconds, sir. But radar shows only one aircraft. Yours. Where is the one-seventy-two from your position?"

"Kissing our right main," the Admiral answered, slamming the gear down into the high-winged Cessna. Knowing that the bump would bank the demented Arab left, he pulled up and turned away.

Retracting the gear and moving back above the wounded Cessna, Sarah and Thor could see that the last two feet of his left wing was missing. Fuel poured from the ruptured bladder. Yet somehow, the rugged little Sky Hawk was still airborne, albeit slower and less maneuverable. Shaking, Assad was doing all he could to vector his crippled bird toward the center of the Magic Kingdom.

"Pilatus, we are ready to engage. Do you want us to fire?"

"I'd have done it myself, but my father-in-law didn't order the gun option."

"Roger that, sir. Lucky my uncle did."

"Can you waste him while he's over the lake?"

"Yes, sir. I think we've got him out-gunned," Wilson came back, lifting the guard and pushing the trigger. Just as quickly, huge portions of the Sky Hawk's red tail disappeared.

The relative speed of the 172 was now a problem. The first Hornet flew past the slower bird like it was standing still. But his wingman was further back than usual. "Admiral, I have missile lock. Permission to fire."

"Fire, Lieutenant." the Admiral ordered.

"Firing, sir."

From their vantage point high above Disney World, Thor and Sarah took it all in. The missile dropped. As the burst of flame shot out its rear, it lunged forward, picking up speed. A second later the Cessna was no more. Splintered into a million little pieces, it looked like confetti.

"*Yeah!*" Sarah shouted over the intercom, clinching her fist. "Splash one terrorist." She thought of all the families, chomping peacefully on their cotton candy, strolling obliviously with Minnie, Mickey, Goofy, and Dopey. They would live because Malamud Assad had died. This had been one of those rare occasions when killing saved lives.

"Good work, son."

"Thank you, sir. Do you want us to bug out or follow you down to Orlando Exec?"

"Follow us in. I'd like to meet you."

Adams turned to Sarah. "Your airplane. Put her down gentle like."

"Sure, now that you've used the gear for a battering ram and the propeller as a gardening tool," she winked. "So, sweetness, do you think the scratches are going to be covered under the warranty?"

He thought about how he was going to explain the damage to Troy.

"On second thought," she said, reading his mind, "let's not tell daddy about this."

"Orlando tower, this is one victor alpha. The air traffic problem has been eliminated. Request permission to land."

"You are cleared to land, Admiral. There is no traffic, other than the Hornets, that is, within twenty miles. Nicely done."

"It wouldn't have been possible without you, Wilson, and Kain. You all saved a lot of lives today."

"Yes, sir. But speaking of lives, shouldn't we dispatch a rescue op for the student pilot?"

"I don't think that'll be necessary," Commander Wilson said. "You can probably pass on the coroner, too. By the time the gators are done with their Muslim munchies, there won't even be a grease spot."

Sarah didn't know if she should laugh or cry. She turned around again to check on Mary, as did Thor. "You doing okay back there, honey?"

She looked a little green around the gills. "I want *you* to fly the plane, mommy. Daddy's not very good at it."

"Yes, I know, sweetie. So, Admiral," she asked, "are you always this much fun?"

23

PRESSED

Stories of the A-Team's narrow escape spread quickly, permeating the airways. The enormous crowd that had gathered at the Orlando Convention Center had heard them. Adams found himself a hero once again.

Not everyone was celebrating, though. The news crews swarmed around the threesome like mosquitoes, shouting questions so vociferously the buzz was deafening. Thor was annoyed, Sarah angry, Mary frightened. The way the reporters attacked with their cameras and microphones was a whole lot scarier than being assailed by a terrorist. She was used to that.

"Ladies, gentlemen," the Admiral misspoke, "calm down, please." He sandwiched Mary between himself and Sarah. "If you'll back up, I'll give you a statement."

The piranhas paid no heed, pushing their microphones into his face. They shouted inane questions like, "What right did you have to shoot down a civilian airplane? Isn't that a criminal act?" The Admiral finally lost his patience, brushed them aside, and walked into the auditorium.

The bands started playing and balloons were released skyward. The audience rose, bursting into thunderous applause. The media scurried to their positions. While Thor was running as an Independent, the festivities had been arranged courtesy of the Libertarian, Reform, and Republican Parties. All were without candidates of their own because they were endorsing the candidacy of one Thurston Merrick Adams. It had been the same everywhere they had gone.

"America, citizens of Orlando," he said, "we are pleased to be with you today." They all knew what he had just survived. "And in case you were wondering, yes, he was trying to kill us. Yes, he got within a mile of Disney World, and yes, he was a devout Muslim. Surprised?"

"No!" they shouted out in unison.

"From Pan Am 103 over Lockerbie, Scotland, to the Twin Tower Twenty, the murderers are always the same—they're always Muslims.

From the Syrian government being the largest exporter of heroin into America, to the Saudis being the largest exporter of terror, to Palestinian boy bombs on the streets of Israel, it's always the same cast of characters, the same *lack* of character. From our embassies in Tanzania and Kenya, to the USS Cole in Yemen, to the bloody streets of Mogadishu, the terrorists are always Islamic. From our barracks in Lebanon and Saudi Arabia to the Olympic Games in Munich, Jews and Christians are the victims, and Muslim militants are the perpetrators. Why?"

"Islam!" they shouted. They had listened to the Admiral's speeches.

"*No!*" he returned. "It's *our* fault!" He smiled and raised his hands, letting the audience know he was kidding. "I mean, it *must* be. Most every week I read a newspaper story or hear a network account of how we are to blame. The enlightened say we have failed to understand the Arabs, failed to solve their problems, and because of this we deserve our fate. I will never forget the AP story that took the Israeli Prime Minister to task because *he* couldn't stop Palestinian violence." The Admiral shook his head. "If you believe those with the microphones and printing presses, we're guilty because we haven't forced the Israelis to relinquish the spoils of war. But I say to you, those Arabs aren't Palestinians, it isn't their land, and more importantly, giving it to them isn't in anyone's interest."

"Back in 1948, if the Arabs had accepted the resolutions that gave a tiny sliver of land to the Jews—less than one percent of that which was given to Arabs—and lived in peace with their neighbors rather than killing them, they might have had a righteous claim. But they didn't. They drew first blood. They voided the UN contract, voiding any legitimate claim. Then, when Arabs *en masse* surrounded the fledgling state of Israel militarily in 1967 with the intent of destroying it, they lost."

Adams reached into his jacket pocket and removed a paper. Opening it, he read, "The Covenant of the PLO says, 'Armed struggle is the only way to liberate Palestine. It is the national duty of Arabs to repulse the Zionist, Imperialist invasion from the great Arab homeland and to purge the Zionist presence from 'Palestine.' By the way, you should know that they take 'Palestine' to mean *all* of what was once Judea. This would leave the Jews with nothing, treading water in the Mediterranean. The Covenant goes on to say, 'The partition of Palestine in 1947 and the establishment of Israel is fundamentally null and void.'"

He put the paper back in his pocket but repeated its most caustic phrase. "'Purge the Zionist presence from Palestine,' it says. The first Holocaust was not enough for these folks. Based upon what I have just read and based upon their actions, do you think giving Arabs the 'West Bank' will solve this crisis? Will it satisfy them? If your answer is yes, then ask yourself, if all they want is the '67 borders reestablished, why did they attack Israel in '67? Have the peace-loving Palestinians forgotten that the PLO was booted out of Jordan, the nation that occupied the West Bank in 1967? No, not likely, but they hope you have. Achieving their goals requires you being deceived.

"If you believe their deliberate propaganda, then they can con you into believing that they're helpless victims and that the suicide bombers are a natural consequence of being oppressed, of having their lands occupied. But if you know the truth, you'll see them as they really are: lying murderers."

The Admiral pulled a newspaper clipping out of a folder he had carried to the stage. "Now that I've explained why they have no legitimate claim to the land, let's establish why independence isn't in their interests. I found this story from the Associated Press particularly enlightening. They were reporting on how the Palestinian Authority had made a mockery of their court system, saying that verdicts were rendered before evidence was heard. In this case, they claimed that the bloodthirsty Kameel clan, a.k.a. rank and file Muslim militants, were displeased with the leniency of the court, so they stormed the building as an enraged mob and dispensed Islamic justice, vigilante style.

"But did you know it wasn't their fault? Oh, no." Holding the paper out before him, Thor read, "Since the *fighting* began three years ago, the legal system has become more chaotic." He stopped. "What the AP is suggesting here is that terrorist attacks are perpetrated by both sides. And while that's erroneous and purposely deceptive, it's what they *didn't* say that gives me pause. The Associated Press knows that the violence is the direct result of the *intifada*. For those of you who don't know, that's a call to war, Islamic War. It's Allah's Cause, *Jihad*. *Intifada* was not called by the Jews. It was not mutual. The call to arms came from the late Palestinian Chairman, Yasman Alafat. The AP knows—heck, *everyone* knows—that if the Muslims stopped their terrorist attacks, there would be no more killing—none. *Ever*." The Admiral eyed the enormous crowd.

"But the AP's omission wasn't careless. They thought it was somehow in their readers' interests to omit the real reason the Palestinian courts have failed. So I'll tell you, because it's crucial." Thor pounded the rostrum. "It is directly attributable to the autonomy the Arabs were granted by the Europeans at Oslo. Since that time, the PA leadership has had the responsibility to run their own courts, but they have failed to act responsibly. They have been more focused on promoting killing than they have been on prosecuting killers."

"*Intifada* has been more important than infrastructure to the leadership of the PA," Adams said. "But did you know *that's* not their fault either? No? The AP article says, 'The PA acknowledges the problem but claims restrictions imposed by Israel, combined with Israeli bombing raids, have made it impossible for them to be a proper government.' Can you say, 'Bull huey'?"

The audience obliged.

The Admiral's ability to make sense of the absurd endeared him to every crowd. "Now just to make sure you're sufficiently deceived, the AP thinks it's in your interest to hear a quote from a PA propagandist: 'The vigilante killings show that the Palestinian judicial system is weak and doesn't have the people's confidence,' said Ghassan Khatib, a Palestinian political analyst. 'This demonstrates that the Israeli restrictions on Palestinians are causing a semi-collapse of our system.'

"Yep, it's our fault." Thor stuffed the clipping back into the folder. "So much for the baloney. Now, how about some truth?" he said, flinging the folder to the floor. "Before Oslo, the Palestinians had a court system, and it worked. The Israelis managed it. After Oslo, the Jews pulled out of the Autonomous Regions, and the courts became the responsibility of the Palestinian Authority. They failed. They were given the responsibility and they bungled it. Face it, folks, they did this to themselves. Autonomy has led to more violence, not less.

"Oh, and just in case you haven't connected the dots…what else happened when the PA was given autonomy over these areas? The Jews were asked to withdraw their police. The responsibility for keeping mischief down was now in the hands of the Palestinians. 'They should be allowed to police themselves,' we were told by the Europeans at Oslo. And get this: American taxpayers even supplied the guns and trained the PAPD, a.k.a. Fatah. But the Europeans didn't act alone, so I'm not blaming them, well, not exclusively. Bill Clinton, the man who unwittingly helped Osama bin Laden unify Islamic rage, was in full accord." Adams was certain one of the Clintonites in the media would jump at the bait, come press conference time. He just let the insult dangle.

"Now, I ask you, what increased when Israeli police protection decreased?" The Admiral cupped his hand to his ear.

The crowd shouted out, "*Terrorism.*"

"You're right. So what do you think would happen if, rather than being an autonomous region inside the state of Israel, the Arabs were granted statehood, as our last three administrations have tried to do? It's obvious, right? If Israelis lose the ability to suppress terrorist acts by making them painful for the perpetrators, they'll increase." He scanned the room. "It's as clear as the bombs on their bellies—less will beget more!"

Most rose, applauding him. Adams was adlibbing this and they knew it. Nothing he had said so far this morning had been part of his prepared text, but his dander was up. Between the terrorist's attack and the media's poor behavior, Thor wasn't happy. He turned to look at Sarah and Mary, to see what they thought, hoping that by their expressions they would tell him whether he should stop or press on. Sarah winked, nodding affirmatively. Mary gave him a cute yet deliberate thumbs-up.

"Following the autonomy they gained at Oslo, the Palestinian judicial system failed, the economy collapsed, and Muslim violence soared. Stopping this violence, by the way, was the price the Palestinians were obliged to pay for autonomy. So I ask you: do you want more of this failure, more poverty, more violence, more killing…or less? Is anyone foolish enough to think that more autonomy will solve their economic woes, fix their judicial calamities, or bring an end to the butchering of innocents? Do you think these Muslim fundamentalists will be any different than the hoodlums who rule the Islamic states around them? Will the warlords swear off violence? Will the terrorists set down their plastic explosives? Will the Islamic clergy stop selling Paradise to impressionable boys and girls?

"What happened to Lebanon when the Christian-controlled government was overthrown by Syrian Muslims? Was not the paradise of the Mediterranean turned into a living hell? Why are we so blind to the truth? Why must we be taught the hard lessons of history over and over again?

"Has any thug ever been appeased? Has any dictator ever been satiated? Can you name a time in which doing more of a thing that *led* to chaos *ended* the chaos? What is to be gained by rewarding Islamic terror or negotiating with terrorists?"

The Admiral let that linger in the air. "And why does the media provide an audience for the people with this foolhardy agenda? Why have I never read or heard a single one of you say that it's not in our interest, *or theirs*, to give the militants greater autonomy?"

Adams paced across the stage. "I understand that Israel has at times been as disjointed as a two-headed gooney bird. Building settlements in Gaza was stupid. Signing the Oslo agreements was foolish. Rolling tanks only to withdraw them is counter-productive. Trading land for the promise of peace is nuts. But good grief, folks, there's no moral equivalence between the behavior of Jews and Arabs in this battle for the world's ultimate ground zero. And make no mistake; everything that happens there has a ripple effect on the rest of the world. There is a direct link between the suicide bombers in Israel and those who annihilated the World Trade Center."

He took a deep breath. "Many of you in the front row have accused me of sounding 'hateful and warlike.' Why? Because I have told the uncomfortable truth—that the only way to end this nonsense is to expose Islam for what it is, to cut off the money, to curtail the indoctrination of the youth, and then to demilitarize the region by rounding up the warlords. Like it or not, that's the most loving, rational, compassionate, and sane approach to this whole bloody affair. What's more, the biggest beneficiaries will be the citizens of these very lands. We didn't make this mess. And if it weren't for the fact that they are killing us, I, frankly, wouldn't give a rip what they believe, how they live, or even what heinous things they do to each other. Cleaning up their mess wouldn't be worth risking the life of a single American soldier. But they *are* killing us. And that leaves us with a simple choice: drain the swamp or die from the disease it breeds."

The Admiral picked up the folder he had tossed on the stage. "Here's another incriminating story. The 'impartial journalists' from the AP once again tried valiantly to prop up the PA's sagging reputation, this time claiming that they had 'incarcerated 195 militants, shut down 15 illegal munitions factories, blocked 56 suspect bank accounts, and derailed 79 unregistered charities.' Oh, and I almost forgot. They boldly proclaimed that the PA 'clamped down on militant mosque preachers.'"

Presidential candidate or not, Adams was in no mood for politically correct double talk. "The AP said they found these truths contained in a seventeen-page tear-smeared document that mysteriously made its way to their Jerusalem offices, although it had been 'officially' intended for our State Department. The report sounds so peaceful, doesn't it? So what did the branch offices of the PA, excuse me—the AP—forget to tell us? Not much really, except that everybody in Israel above the level of a worm knows that the incarceration of 'militants' is a ruse, a joke. It's all for show, like a weekend at the Holiday Inn.

"As for shutting down the 'illegal munitions factories,' that's laughable when proclaimed by folks who've just had a shipment of Iranian missiles, C-4 plastic explosives, and anti-tank rockets confiscated in the Red Sea. Blocking bank accounts? Just because there *is* no banking system in the 'Palestinian-controlled territories' doesn't necessarily make it a lie. But this does: even if they had been responsible enough to create a banking system, the only funds that could have been seized were held by PA warlords, 'cause they're the only ones with money. The economy is *kaput*.

"This may come as a bit of a surprise to those of you who haven't done your homework: the leadership of the PA were Marxist/Leninists. Like Saddam Hussein in Iraq, their heroes weren't the stalwarts of Islam, but history's other great peacemakers, Hitler and Stalin. How is it that we are now being told by the AP that the leadership has found religion, that they are attending mosque and 'clamping down on militant mosque preachers?' Even if this were true, which it isn't, take a moment and chew on the AP's words: 'militant mosque preachers.' They taste odd, don't they? If Islam is a peace-loving religion, why are their preachers so 'militant'?

"Then ask yourself, why didn't the brain surgeons at the AP point these things out—why do they gleefully give these absurd lies a vast international audience? I assume that to write for the AP one has to be literate." Somebody was definitely cranky this morning.

"I dunno. Maybe not. The Associated Press follows its eloquent admiration for the Palestinian Authority by sharing this timely tidbit," Adams said as he waved the clipping in the air. "'Meanwhile, a Palestinian teenager was shot and killed in the Gaza Strip by Israeli soldiers.' Witnesses inferred he was just playing ball with his friends. Mind you, the ball was a hand grenade, but who are we to pass moral judgments on what games they play?"

The Admiral shook his head in disgust. Through these otherwise meaningless stories, normally lost in the great ocean of irrelevant ink and destined for the bottoms of birdcages, Thor had connected the dots, painting a picture as clear as it was horrific.

"Buried deep in the article, the AP reported that those same murdering Israelis, in that same place, specifically targeted another boy. This one was also minding his own business, riding a bus to work, when he was arrested. Oh, incidentally, he happened to be wearing an explosive belt. A fashion statement, I suppose. He just wanted to fit in, be one of the boys, hit it off with the virgins. Although it seems hard to believe that in their earnest crackdown on Muslim militants, the PA somehow overlooked a Palestinian suicide bomber. But with so many of them, perhaps it's understandable. For some unexplained reason, there seems to be one on every corner. But that's a story that has eluded the progressives at the proudly independent, journalistically pure institution called the Associated Press.

"Oh, and lest I forget, on the same day, right under the noses of the peace-loving Palestinians, the Israelis managed to find what the PA had so diligently sought but had somehow missed—a *truckload* of rockets, rockets with the range to rain terror on Jerusalem or Tel Aviv. It was just bebopping down the peaceful streets of Ramallah. Oh, I know! They must have been transferring the inventory from *illegal* munitions factories to *legal* ones. Or maybe," the Admiral said as he hit his forehead, "just maybe, the rockets were being stockpiled to celebrate independence day."

The crowd laughed.

"Or maybe not. On the very day this story was filed, at none other than PA Headquarters, the late Chairman said, and I quote, 'I pledge that we Palestinians will defend our holy sites in the land of *Jihad.*' He led a chant, 'It is ours. It is ours. It is ours,' followed by the oh-so-peaceful second verse, 'And to Jerusalem we go, her martyrs in the millions.'

"And speaking of martyrs, Alafat went on to praise an Arab girl who grabbed a Jewish baby from its mother's arms and tossed it into a flaming bus, one a fellow Muslim had blown up with women and children aboard.

"Let's face facts. By definition, a 'terrorist' is someone who targets civilians for the purpose of achieving a political agenda. With the exception of the demented doctrines of Islam and Communism, such tactics are considered uncivilized, evil. There is no excuse for such behavior.

"Suicide is a cowardly act. Unstable individuals use it to escape life's realities. Terrorism is also cowardly. Civilians aren't armed, and cannot fight back. Suicide bombers are not freedom fighters; they are not martyrs. They are cowardly cold-blooded murderers."

That off his chest, Admiral Adams returned to the AP account. "The shocking truth was buried deep within the article. But the headline of the story I just shared was designed to deceive. It read: 'Palestinians Take Actions to Eliminate Terrorist Activities.' Yet on the same day it was written, AP reporters were on hand when the Palestinian Chairman called for the martyrdom of millions. I think we have a failure to communicate. How about you?"

The Admiral paused, then drove his message home. "This manipulation of facts is too reckless, too grossly negligent, too opinionated to be accidental. And be assured, it's not without cost. Let me give you an example. Back in January and again in March of 2002, Yasman Alafat arrogantly told the world in *public statements* that he wanted to die a martyr." The audience let out a collective gasp. They had no idea that he'd actually said such a thing. "Tragically, you in the media paid the admonition no heed. You brushed it off as hyperbole. I can only assume it didn't fit into your preconceived worldview, the view that the rantings of Communist and Muslim dictators only count when they say what you want to hear. *Then* you believe them. You think Alafat's signature on official PA documents paying terrorist families for sacrificing their sons is meaningless, but his signature on a peace accord would be meaningful." He took a deep breath and closed his eyes for a moment. Then with a pained expression, he continued, "So partly as a result of your irresponsibility, our nation was taken by surprise—our leaders and your media colleagues were butchered.

"America, I apologize for my diversion, but I'm tired of being told that *their* lunacy is *our* fault. I'm tired of hearing the peace activists wallow in pity over the plight of these people and their pathetic behavior. We're reliving the prelude to World War II all over again.

"Is it just me? Am I the only one who thinks that these misleading press accounts are part of the problem?" The Admiral shuffled through the folder. "Dateline Jerusalem. Quote: 'The rhetoric between Israel and Iran has become increasingly hostile following Israel's interception last month of another shipment of Iranian weapons to the Palestinians.' It goes on to say, 'Israel is especially concerned about Iran's plan to develop nuclear weapons.'

"But rather than say, 'And well they should be,' the AP closes with a denial from the Muslims, giving them an unwarranted platform. Listen to this: 'Iranian Foreign Minister Kamal Kharrazi *denied* that they supplied the Hezbollah guerrilla group in Lebanon with ten thousand rockets' all with sufficient range to strike at the heart of Israel. And then 'Iran's Defense minister warned of heavy retaliation for any Israeli preemptive strike.' After all, they didn't go to all the trouble of building these things for them not to be used. And used they were. The 'denied' rockets were shot into Israel in the spring of 2002." He tossed his folder full of articles back onto the stage.

With that, Thurston Adams dove into his stump speech. Stirring music played as the multimedia show was unfurled on giant screens behind him.

"I want our government to move out of the way, to unleash the full potential of our great nation and her citizens. It's time to stop coddling failure and to start valuing success. Redistributing wealth is not akin to creating it." He looked out. "We must free everyone from the oppressiveness of government control; trust our citizens enough to let them choose their course. I believe in empowering everybody with the opportunity to care for their families and better their communities. Together, we will build a better and freer, brighter and more prosperous nation through service and incentives, justice, and education.

"Ultimately, it all boils down to one question: whom do you trust? Here at home, do to you trust yourself, your neighbors, and your friends, or would you rather trust government administrators, bureaucrats, and politicians? Internationally, do you trust the warlords in Iraq, Iran, Syria, and Libya more than the men and women of our armed forces?

"War happens when good people don't stand up. It's most always the result of totalitarian thugs exporting the same violence they are all too willing to inflict on their own people. If we want to curtail the violence, we must remove these dictators from power. Take away their guns, dry up their funding, and cut off their means of indoctrinating children. Not only will we liberate their people from tyranny, giving them a reason to live rather than die, we'll also be freeing the world from the scourge of terror."

Gazing out, Adams said, "Some have said that I'm not an Independent. They paint me as having but one wing. Truth be known, we almost lost both of 'em this morning." The audience laughed. "I'm a practical man, not a politician. I'm not beholden to any political machine. I just want our nation to move as far from the abyss of world war as possible.

"I believe to do that we must move right, toward conservatism, a substantially diminished reliance on government. And while most of you may already be there, Washington is not. It has moved left of Moscow. That's a problem. Nations are born through toil and sacrifice, but they die from dependence and greed. For America to prevail against a doctrine with a billion adherents, we must be strong. We must save America before we save the world.

"Liberalism, the political manifestation of secular humanism, is a failed doctrine. As we take more from productive Americans to reward those who are not, the gap actually grows between the haves and have-nots. The more we penalize success, the less of it everyone has. As the incentive to be productive shrivels, so does productivity. As the incentives for failure increase, so does dependence. This is not rocket science. One wing or two, liberalism is a death spiral, and it's killing our nation.

"More government leads to more chaos, not less. Ultimately, the *most* liberal use of government is a dictatorship. In the end, it becomes a government that can impose its will, its views, its 'religion' on everyone, a government capable of pulling everyone down into the same pit.

"Our liberal leaders have gained what they covet most: control over your lives. But such power corrupts. That's why there are no benevolent dictators. Power is like a magnifying glass, turning minor character flaws into dangerous deficiencies with disastrous consequences.

"To the humanists listening to my words, those who think that we are nothing more than the byproduct of chance—an improbable life form that emerged over eons from the primordial slime—I say open your eyes. Judging by mankind's propensity to inflict violence upon ourselves, we haven't evolved very far from that slime. No matter how 'enlightened' man becomes, we move no closer to the utopian dream. The twentieth century was the most enlightened and liberal in history—*and* the most violent. And the century's most liberal societies were the most lethal to both man and the environment. The record is clear: a liberal use of government, concentrated power, leads to violence, the deprivation of human rights, economic collapse, and ultimately, war. Yesterday, it was Fascism and Communism. Today, it is totalitarian Islamic regimes, enslaving their people, and spewing death and destruction around the globe.

"Central to the failure of liberalism is its inevitable propensity to legislate one of the two extremes of human error. Islamic, Communist, and Fascist dictators have chosen either to separate their societies from God, making him illegal, or to politicize their clergy, making all views of God other than theirs illegal. Today, the most brutal enemies of mankind, Communist and Islamic states, represent these polar extremes. Ironically, however, the resulting outward manifestations, their domestic and international behaviors, are *identical*. And history proves that the only thing worse than the inclusion of politicized religion into governance is the separation of faith from governance.

"The framers of America's Constitution crafted a finely-tuned balance between *endorsing* a specific religion, empowering its clergy as Europe had done, and *removing* faith in God privately and publicly from our national existence. This is why we grew faster, stronger, richer, and more righteous than any nation on earth.

"Tragically, that balance was discarded by the Warren Court in the late nineteen fifties. They conjured up a non-existent clause in our Constitution separating church and state. Morality was removed from our nation's classrooms and was replaced with humanistic ideals. These have failed us, and as a result, our nation is failing. The boys and girls who were educated in the resulting godless schools of the '60s and '70s are today managing our corporations, leading our government, and speaking on behalf of our media. We have reaped what we have sown. You can't legislate morality, it's true, but our Supreme Court found a way to make morality illegal."

Thor went on to present his five-point Plan to Save America. Sarah explained the true nature of America's enemy, the delusion that is Islam. Mary brought it all home. She gave terror a human face. Adams tied it all together and opened the floor to questions.

Unfortunately, the reporters were still fixated on the moment. They were more interested in one unsuccessful terrorist than millions lurking in the shadows. After spending more time explaining the episode than it took to live it, Thor grew impatient.

"Folks, we've got less than thirty minutes before we have to leave for Miami. If you want to talk about the overall Muslim threat to our national security or our plan for national revival, I'd be pleased to spend it with you. If not, we'll be going."

The first to rise was a young man claiming to represent CBS. He said, "Many are saying that your Plan to Save America is too conservative, too right wing. They say that had it not been for your self-admitted failure in

Afghanistan, you wouldn't have any support at all." Finished with his 'question', he held out his micro recorder.

"My mission is simple. I am not running for anything. I don't want to be president. I'm here because I promised the American people answers."

"You didn't answer my question, sir," the reporter protested.

"You didn't ask one," the Admiral shot back, stating what should have been obvious.

"Isn't your plan just a scheme to reward the rich and punish the poor?"

"No. I just want to get government off everyone's back so we can all succeed. The failed agenda you in the media have so vociferously promoted is nothing more than a socialistic wealth re-distribution plan." Adams explained. "It not only makes the poor poorer, it makes them more dependent. Government needs to get its hands out of people's pockets. It's no accident that many states call their tax collection agency the Board of *Equalization*. Government paychecks are called *Unemployment Benefits*. Maybe it's just semantics, but all this serves to stifle productivity; it impedes progress and breeds despair. When a working man, scrounging to buy soup, has to watch a welfare recipient buy steaks with food stamps, something is wrong.

"When the income tax was initiated by FDR, it was two or three percent. Today it's fifteen to twenty *times* that amount. When Welfare and Medicare were proposed by LBJ, America was told that these programs would never cost taxpayers more than a few billion dollars. But today they cost a hundred times that. Social Security is a pyramid scheme, as inefficient as it is immoral. There are much more efficient ways to achieve superior results."

He continued. "Our Plan—Opportunity, Education, Justice, Service, and Freedom—benefits the poor more than it does the rich. But they will *earn* their rewards, as will every American. And I believe the disadvantaged, the poor among us, will treasure these achievements far more than they do your handouts."

He looked to his left and said, "By the way, I haven't been totally forthright with you. This five-point plan isn't mine." With that Sarah dug into her purse. Removing her small burgundy Bible, she opened it.

Thor reached back. "I'm not speaking for the author, you understand. He doesn't need me. He spoke quite nicely for himself." Adams looked down and read, "'Jesus went to Nazareth, where he had been raised, and on the Sabbath he went into the synagogue. Handed a scroll from the prophet Isaiah, he unrolled it, finding the place where it was written: "The Lord has anointed me to bring good news to the poor, and broken-hearted,"' that's *service*. "'He has sent me to proclaim *freedom* for captives, and enlightenment for the blind,"' that's *education*…"'to release the down-trodden and oppressed,"' *justice*, "'to proclaim the year of the Lord's favor,"' directly translated that means jubilee or economic *opportunity*. That was the inspiration for our plan. But before you go off and write that Adams is a religious whacko, please note that I said nothing about religion in any of that, nor did he."

The lone reporter from the AP shook as he stood. With a crackling voice, he posed his question: "Arabs claim that our reporting is slanted in favor of the Israelis. You claim that it's slanted in favor of the Arabs. It sounds to me like we're being objective."

"The Arabs all claim that the reason you're biased is because Jews control the American media. Do they?"

"No."

"Then, the Arabs are lying, are they not? Why would you use a lie to justify your behavior?"

A portly woman in the front row stood. Her thoughts leaped out of her like a viper attacking a rat. Her tone was ugly, enraged, hostile. "The Palestinians have struggled for fifty years under the brutal hand of Israeli occupation. Their women and children, their babies, have been gunned down with American weapons. The entire civilized world has been telling us that the solution to the refugee proplem a Palestinian State." She sat down so hard, it nearly knocked the snarl from her face.

"I didn't hear a question in any of that, but nevertheless I'll explain my position. Gosh, there were so many inaccuracies in there, I hardly know where to begin. So, I'll just dive in. Uniformity of belief is no indicator of truth. A thousand years ago, most everyone thought the world was flat. For many thousands of years, slavery was considered appropriate. Until the rise of Christianity, women were considered inferior to men—well, at least they were by men."

The crowd chuckled.

"I'm certain that giving Arabs large portions of Israel will lead directly to more poverty, more violence, more death, and ultimately to world war. I have explained my rationale and clearly presented my thinking on this. I've done so in a historical context, analyzing the economic, political, social, and religious implications. But now I'm going to share my feelings.

"I am against rewarding terror. I'm convinced that if the civilized world continues to dignify those who butcher innocents, we will lose our civility altogether. Less than three years ago, the first girl bomb exploded in the streets of Jerusalem. There were no soldiers killed or injured, just average people, young and old, men and women. The dynamite-laced shrapnel didn't discriminate. Nor did the young Palestinian woman who pulled the trigger. Over a hundred people were injured."

As he spoke these words, Mary reached up and touched the still painful scars on her face. A tear rolled down Sarah's cheek.

"The act was as rash and as inhumane as the delusions that encouraged it. It was murder, worthy of nothing but condemnation. Yet the murderer was praised with reckless abandon. Her death was celebrated by the Muslims. Her picture was carried aloft in the streets, emblazoned on placards. Smiling throngs of little girls waved it in parades, encouraging even more terror. Her image was enlarged and made into towering billboards. The girl suicide bomber became a martyr, her picture plastered on the sides of Palestinian homes. She joined other Muslim murderers on 'Martyr Trading Cards', and 'charm bracelets'. Her picture was nailed to classroom walls.

"Legitimizing this behavior by rewarding the Islamic clerics who preach killing, and empowering the warlords who trample human rights, is *wrong*. We do so at our peril—and theirs. Giving the Arab 'refugees' in Israel an independent state is a good idea only if you think the world needs another Libya, Somalia, Lebanon, Sudan, Syria, Iran, or Iraq.

"Your accusation of Israelis killing Muslim babies with our weapons angers me, ma'am. It is the terrorists who target babies, killing them purposely. Then, because they are cowards, they run and hide among their children and under the dresses of their women. It is their behavior, and theirs alone, that is responsible for the collateral damage.

"Let me share a quote from a distinguished source. In 1949 the United Nations established UNRWA as a provisional body to provide relief for the Palestinian refugees. The agency's director, Ralph Garroway, said, 'The Arab States do not want to solve the refugee problem. They want to keep it as an open sore, as an affront to the UN, and as a weapon against Israel. Arab leaders don't care whether the refugees live or die.'"

The silence was deafening but not lasting. One of the reporters jumped up, raised his hand, and shouted, "Admiral Adams, you began by referring to Muslim militants and the Twin Tower *Twenty*. There were only nineteen. And there are many good and decent followers of Islam. Don't you think it's unfair to label them?"

"When the Japanese bombed Pearl Harbor," Adams replied, "we called them our enemy. Not to be unkind, but to defend our nation. They were acting heinously, raping and plundering their neighbors. The Japanese government was a totalitarian regime, a psuedo-religious mix of emperor and warlord worship. And like the Islamic warriors today, their people were convinced that they were racially superior. They had no regard for their victims, not even women and children. They lashed out without provocation, like terrorists, thinking the world belonged to them. We called them our enemy because they had killed our people. We called them evil, as we should call Islam evil, because their behavior was reprehensible.

"Now, I am sure there were some good and decent Japanese, as there must be good and decent people in the Islamic world. But that did not stop us from defending ourselves, from fighting and defeating this enemy, nor should it today."

The reporter fired back. "But the Japanese, like the Nazis, were a clear enemy. The terrorists come from many nations."

"Four years and thousands of lives have passed since 9/11/01 and you still don't know *why* it happened. You don't know this enemy; you refuse to recognize what they have in common. *They* know who they are. Why don't you?" Adams said to a blank stare. "But you made a good point. The men who perpetrated the bombings share no national identity. In fact, they *hate* their governments. What they call *dar al-Islam*—the House, or Nation, of Islam—is the only thing that unifies them. Those who terrorize the world have not corrupted their religion, as many have claimed. The religion itself is a manifesto for war.

"By the way, thank you for holding me accountable. A moment ago, you called me on something. I said there were twenty suicide bombers, not nineteen—because there were. Zacarias Moussaoui, a French Moroccan, and a Muslim, had trained to be part of the team. But in late August the flight school he was attending called the FBI in Minneapolis, warning them that something was awry. You see, Zac was adamant about learning how to fly large commercial jets right at the outset of his training. Now, here's the amazing part: the FBI shunned them, saying there wasn't enough evidence to violate his rights, inferring that they were entering the politically tricky waters of racial profiling. So three thousand Americans died instead.

"French intelligence had said Moussaoui was known to have radical Islamic beliefs and ties to Muslim cells in Chechnya. They said he had fallen under the spell of Islam while attending business school in England. The French even warned the British about him, but they, like our FBI, ignored the warning. Zacarias came to the U.S. on a student visa. A fellow Muslim militant, Ramzi al-Shibh, wired Zac fourteen grand for flight school tuition.

"But Zac made a jerk of himself, was grounded, and moved on to Minnesota. A day late and a hundred billion dollars short, the Feds finally got around to searching his apartment. They found incriminating files on crop dusters and wind spreads of pesticides. He also had contact information for his fellow Muslim militant pals in Hamburg. So there *were* twenty. One was grounded. And there was a warning too. They planned to dust large cities with anthrax spores."

Adams rubbed his forehead. "Every one of the 9/11 pilots attended Al Kod mosque in Germany. Today the mosque still operates, still preaches hate, still inspires young boys to kill Americans and Jews. Every one of the suicide bombers was selected for their murderous deed by Islamic clerics preaching in Muslim mosques. You may want to ignore that reality, but that won't make you enlightened or politically correct—only dead.

"Let's review the facts. One of the pilots was born in Beirut, the home of the radical Islamic group, Hezbollah. The Lebanese pilot was said to be very religious. Another was an Egyptian. His father is an outspoken militant. He, too, was very religious. He, too, hated Jews and Americans. A third suicide bomber was born in the United Arab Emirates—an Islamic cleric's son. He had surrendered to Islam as well.

"Fifteen of the hijacking mass murderers were 'manufactured' in Saudi Arabian madrases. Like their Arab compatriots from Lebanon, Egypt, and the Arab Emirates, they shared a common faith, a common motivation, a common doctrine, a common rage. They were all devout Muslims. They all believed that America and Israel had to be destroyed. So I ask you, what does that make the Nation of Islam?"

Without thinking, another reporter stood. "Admiral, are you disturbed that progressive leaders in Europe, responsible religious leaders worldwide, and moderates in America are saying your MacArthur plan is hateful? They call it insane, murderous, foolhardy, unjustified, imperialist..." he looked down at his notes to see if he had left anything out. "Mean spirited, racist, intolerant, belligerent, pejorative, unenlightened...."

"That's a swell list of adjectives, son," he interrupted the young reporter. "And I'm convinced you can read, but can you think?" He paused. "What's your name?"

"Walt Clanduse. I'm a reporter with NBC," he answered, hoping it would cause the Admiral to cower. The media was a king maker and Adams wanted to be king, didn't he? It had worked on every other politician, no matter how vehemently they disagreed with the reporter's agenda. Even conservatives had been more interested in being liked and presented favorably than they had been in delivering a cogent message.

"Walter, do you agree with these 'responsible, progressive, and moderate' leaders?"

"It's not my opinion that counts here, sir; it's yours." *Touché*, the assembled reporters thought as they nodded in uniform agreement.

"Every question you ask, every article you write, every report you utter condemns you, Walter. Even the adjectives you used in your question betray your bias. You're just telling me that your opinions are more seductive when they're couched in the perception of journalistic independence, in the nobility of a free press. You know my position on Muslim militants. You know my opinion on the hell Islamic dictators are inflicting on their people and on ours. By asking the question, all you did was state your opinion. Moreover, please tell me: how is keeping what I have learned about Islam a secret in anyone's interest. How is covering up the motivation for their murderous behavior *good?* How is eradicating the scourge of terror at its source *bad?* Why is caring enough to conceive a plan to free people from tyranny, poverty, and brutal oppression *hateful?*"

Mr. Clanduse sat back down, humiliated. Another reporter rose. "Admiral, most are still touting the Saudi Arabian peace proposal. Even Bush favored it, recognizing Palestine as a state. Why not give it a chance?"

"For starters, because the Saudi Crown Prince is easily the most despised man in the Muslim world. His government is one of the most repressive. He has squandered his people's resources and only stays in power because his regime is ruthless, killing anyone who protests. Step an inch outside the strictest interpretation of 'Islamic law' and you're flogged. He and his cadre of princes are terror's biggest benefactors. They write the checks that encourage the murder of innocents. One of your own, a reporter for *USA Today,* broke a story which showed how a Saudi businessman linked closely with the royal family transferred billions, I said *billions,* of dollars to New York and London bank accounts controlled by fellow Saudi Osama bin Laden."

Thor retrieved his folder of news clippings and found one from *The National Review.* "The Saudi ruling family hosted a telethon for Palestinian martyrs. The imam they chose to promote this fund raiser, al-Buraik, said, 'I am against America. My hatred of America, if part of it was contained in the universe, would cause it to collapse. She is the root of all evils and wickedness on earth. O, Muslims, don't take the Jews and Christians as allies. Muslim brothers in Palestine, do not have any mercy, neither compassion, on the Jews, their blood, their money, their flesh. Their women are yours to take, legitimately. Allah made them yours. Why don't you enslave their women? Why don't you wage *jihad?* Why don't you pillage them?'

"Every word of what he commanded Muslims to do comes directly out of the Qur'an. This imam is not an extremist, nor is he out of step with Islam. Al-Buraik finished by calling the Jews monkeys, as did Allah twice in his 'holy book.' I reject the Crown Prince's demagoguery. What he is demanding is impossible, and what he's offering is improbable."

Adams cleared his throat. "Promises of peace from people whose leader encouraged his followers to lie, and who himself said, 'War is deceit,' is a fool's proposition. If the Saudi proposal is implemented, the only certainties are: Arabs will not be content, so the violence will continue; Arabs will continue to live in poverty and will blame it on us; Israel will be less secure and that will lead to war. Where's the good in that?

"Now as for Bush's about face on Israel, his condemnation of their war against terrorism, history has already spoken. The moment the Palestinians were within reach of their stated objective, they went berserk. Suicide bombings escalated exponentially because Arab leaders *don't want peace*. Hate is the only thing that keeps them empowered. Following Oslo, Palestinian terrorism increased four hundred percent."

An attractively-attired young woman jumped to her feet. "Speaking of President Bush, how do you plan to subdue the Islamic States without the kind of international alliances previous administrations have built?"

"Good question. What's your name?"

"Michelle Andre. I'm with *The Washington Post*."

"How? One at a time. Saudi first. They're the principle source of money and militants. Iran would be next, then Iraq. Back at a time when they were much better equipped than they are today, we were able to bomb them into submission fairly easily. As a result, the ground war was what, a hundred hours? Then I'd cripple Egypt's and Syria's ability to wage war, being careful to obliterate their weapons of mass destruction. I'd follow that by neutering Libya. Sadly, based upon the number of Taliban and al-Qaeda from Kuwait, I'd deal with them too.

"Then somewhere in that process, I'd cut the ruling thugs in the other twenty-some-odd-Islamic States a deal. I'd offer the Generals, Princes, Sheiks, Ayatollahs, and…what does that drug-smuggling warlord in Syria call himself? President Thug, I think, but it doesn't matter. I'd tell them all that they're free to leave, taking as much as a hundred million U.S. with them. Heck, let 'em steal a billion. They can wallow in their money in whatever country will have them. Or they can stay and die."

"But Admiral, none of these countries have attacked Americans. What right do we have to attack them?" Andre asked.

"Not a single Afghani had killed an American either. But freeing their people from the brutality of the Taliban was the best thing that ever happened to them. Albeit brief. The Iranians didn't waste much time destabilizing the region or reestablishing the rule of Islamic warlords. And the displaced al-Qaeda wasted no time in terrorizing their new hosts, the Pakistanis—putting them within a breath of having a nuclear bomb.

"As you know, Michelle, the Iraqis have killed Americans and Israelis. So have the Iranians, Palestinians, and Syrians. Together, they are Hezbollah. They killed scores of Americans in Beirut and again in Saudi Arabia."

"But why Saudi Arabia? Their ruling family is pro-America. And how are you going to pay for all of this?" the *Washington Post* reporter inquired.

"The majority of the Twin Tower Twenty were Saudis—fifteen of them. I'd say they've killed plenty of Americans—too many for my taste. More to the point, the Saudi ruling family funds the madrases. They manufacturer the Islamic terrorists who kill us." The Admiral wanted the media to assimilate what he had just said. "Listen, the only thing I want less than fighting them *there* is fighting them *here*. If there were any other way to stop the flow of money, stop the indoctrination of youth, stop the spread of this warmongering doctrine, to stop them from killing us, I would be the first to endorse it. But there isn't.

"Now, as for alliances, I believe they are counterproductive. Europe is useless. The French and Russians sold these thugs the nuclear reactors they use to make plutonium for their atomic bombs." For all his resolve, Admiral Adams was convinced that America would hesitate, that his nation would fail to muster the courage necessary to fight this foe while it was relatively weak. America, he felt, would cripple itself rather than cripple the enemy. He believed his nation would deny reality, giving the Islamic schools time to indoctrinate the preponderance of their people, and giving the governments time to acquire the final ingredients needed for more massive biological and nuclear weapons. While he did his best to awaken, enlighten, and warn his countrymen, deep down he knew he would fail. Millions would die.

Yet he pressed on. "Rather than going in, raising a ruckus, and then leaving these lands to a whole new gang of warlords, as we've done in the past, I'd stay for a while. I'd confiscate the oil—hold it in trust for the Arab people. It's the ultimate win-win scenario. Oil money would no longer be used to fund the madrases or the terrorists they inspire. And rather than our taxpayers footing the bill for cleaning up their mess, the beneficiaries would be held accountable—they'd pay their fair share. You all should love that," he said as everyone but the reporters rose in support.

"In a recent report to Congress, the Director of the CIA confirmed that 'Iran remains the most serious threat to the United States because of its across-the-board pursuit of weapons of mass destruction and missile capabilities.' The Director went on to report that Iraq and Iran were both close to developing nuclear weapons. He claimed that unsupervised, the Iraqis had increased his arsenal. Even more chilling, the CIA Director told the Senate that North Korea was selling nuclear and ballistic missile technology to Iran, Iraq, Libya, and Syria. But then he dropped the bomb. He told the Committee, 'Russia appears to be the first choice for nations seeking nuclear material, technology, and training. They are solidly behind the Iranian efforts.' Another report has them guarding nuclear storage sites with garden tools. The results have been predictable.

"But the Director wasn't finished. 'China,' he announced, 'was the key supplier of nuclear technology and missiles to other Islamic states.' He concluded the briefing by telling the Senate that 'U.S. intelligence routinely tracks Russia's, China's, and North Korea's efforts to sell missile and other weapons technology to countries that present a clear and present danger to the United States. Some of these,' he told the Committee, 'are overt weapons transfers, but some of the assistance comes in the form of a counterfeit—nuclear power plants for oil-rich nations or pesticides for those without the water to farm.' It's death by deception—plausible deniability until it's too late. Did you know that the state-controlled media in Iran publicly debates whether it will take two nukes or three to obliterate Israel?"

"The choice is simple enough. Would you rather strike now, *before* they annihilate millions, or later, *after* they have?"

The *Washington Post* reporter sat back down. Her question had been answered. And she didn't want to have to answer the Admiral's.

Another reporter rose. "Admiral Adams, earlier in your speech you said that Bill Clinton was more responsible for terrorism than Osama bin Laden. That sounds a little mean spirited."

"What I said was, 'Clinton unwittingly helped Osama bin Laden unify Islamic rage.' Let me explain by asking you a question. Did you see the CNN/al-Jazeera interview of bin Laden—the one shot a month after the September 11th bombings?"

"Yes."

"Do you remember what bin Laden said? Remember how he learned that America was vulnerable—what inspired him to attack us?"

"No."

"Excuse the historian in me. I do. It was Somalia—the Black Hawk calamity in Mogadishu. He told the reporter that America's retreat taught him that killing a few Americans would cause us to turn tail and run, because that's what Clinton did. Bin Laden said it gave him reason to bloody our nose. He used it to recruit boys into what otherwise would have looked like a hopeless cause. Clinton restricted our presence in Somalia, restricted our weaponry, sent Rangers in without armament, and put our boys under the command of the United Nations—bad decisions all. Then, when his failed policies resulted in the deaths of American heroes, he ordered a retreat, a retreat that was responsible for increasing terror, inspiring and emboldening Muslim militants.

"Do you recall what Clinton did next; do you remember the consequences? I'll bet none of you even knew who Osama bin Laden was before Clinton launched cruise missiles at him. Very few Muslims did, either. He was the head of an average terrorist organization—one of hundreds. But Clinton elevated him to the status of somebody important, somebody worthy of multimillion-dollar cruise missiles. His career as a terrorist took off courtesy of our President kicking a hornet's nest and walking away." The Admiral looked out upon the crowd. "The lesson here is that doing something halfway is all too often worse than doing nothing at all. We should have learned that by now."

"Admiral, many claim that there is no basis for your attacks on Islam, and especially upon their Prophet. They say you are no better than the church in the Dark Ages with your hateful opinions and derogatory tone."

Adams smiled. "Interesting. I have pointed out hundreds of condemning Islamic scriptures, any one of which is sufficient to explain why Islam breeds terrorists, why Muslims kill, and why we have been misled. If you think what I've reported is untrue, then by all means, use facts to refute me. If I have stated my opinion rather than revealed evidence, demonstrate where I've erred. If you can do so, maybe the problem is Thor Adams, not Islam. But if you can't, deal with reality. Now as for my *tone,* I dare say that the only rational response to their behavior is anger."

Although Adams had thrown down the gauntlet, there would be no takers. The purveyors of perverse propaganda assailed him, not his message. Rather than face facts, they distorted them. Rather than deal with history, they rewrote it. Rather than attack the real enemy, the made an enemy of Adams. It was easier.

"Admiral. You seem to be more intent on taking the battle to the Muslims than protecting us at home. Why?"

"One is possible; the other is impossible. One choice punishes the villains; the other punishes the victims. One cripples us, the other cripples them. As the world's freest society, there is little we can do to make ourselves safe at home. Our knee-jerk reaction to homeland security has done nothing but inconvenience our people, burden our taxpayers, stall our economy, and encourage our enemies—showing the world that they are winning. Most everything we have done in the name of protecting ourselves has been more harmful than beneficial. We interrogate little girls and confiscate nail files. How safe does that make you feel?"

Another reporter stood, this time a rather bookish-looking young man. "Haven't you unfairly singled out verses in the Qur'an to paint Islam in a bad light, as if they're promoting war? Couldn't someone do the same with the Bible? Don't the surahs you selected say more about you than they do Muslims?"

"Sir, what's your name?"

"I'm Samuel Woodman from the *New York Times.*"

"Hello, Sam. Would you do me a favor and come up here please?"

"*What?* No." He turned off his recorder and crossed his arms.

"All right. I understand. You lack the courage to discuss things openly. Anybody have enough self-confidence to discuss Sam's allegation?"

An attractive blonde woman stood and raised her hand.

"What's your name?" the Admiral asked.

"Paula Banks. I'm with CNN."

"Come on up, Ms. Banks."

As she made her way through the crowd, the murmuring rose, filling the room with a deafening buzz. This had never been done before. Back in their plush suites, even the studio executives leaned forward in their chairs.

Adams eyed a couple of stools off to the left, along one wall. He brought both center stage, setting them a couple of feet apart, facing each other, cheating out toward the large crowd. "Ma'am, you may set your notes down. You won't need them. I'll ask the questions."

Banks was suddenly riveted with fear. Panicked, she began to glow in front of the glaring lights. She never answered questions, never even offered an opinion that wasn't scripted.

"Relax. I'm not going to embarrass you, Ms Banks."

Some of the tension seemed to leave her face. "Please, call me Paula."

"Paula, do you agree with Mr. Woodman's position?"

She just stared.

"Let me help you. He asked, 'Have I unfairly singled out verses in the Qur'an to make Islam look bad, accusing it of promoting war?'"

"Yes. I'm told that Islam is a peace-loving religion and that the Qur'an doesn't encourage terrorism. The problem isn't Islam; it's just a small group of extremists—kind of like the radical right in our country."

"Ever read the Qur'an?"

"No," she admitted.

"What do you think? The Qur'an and the Bible—are they similar?"

"Yes." That was an easy one. She smiled, appreciating the softball.

"No, they're not. They don't present a similar god, or even a similar path to God. The Qur'an has a single speaker and a single author, while the Bible has forty authors and probably a thousand speakers. One is grounded in a historical context; the other isn't even chronological, much less historical. One was written over twenty years, the other over twenty centuries. Do you know who the speaker is in the Qur'an?"

"Muhammad," she said, knowing the answer.

"No. Actually, the Qur'an purports to be Allah speaking, never Muhammad. That's a problem. There's a quantum leap between the standard that must be upheld for someone speaking *about* God and someone speaking *for* God."

She nodded.

"Since it's Allah who is allegedly speaking in the Qur'an, do you think it's possible for God to forget?"

"No, but that's assuming there is a God, and he's it."

"Right on both accounts. Do you believe there is a god, Paula?"

"I don't see why my beliefs are at issue here."

"You don't? Don't your beliefs shape your opinions? Don't your opinions shape what you report?"

"I suppose so."

"Your program on CNN—it can be seen in how many homes?"

"Ninety-five million in America—several times that around the world."

"Then how can your beliefs *not* be at issue when they influence what you say to so many people?"

"I'm still not going to tell you what I believe."

"All right, let me ask you this. After the cameras are turned off, do you ever talk about issues like these with your colleagues?"

"Sure. We all gather at the same watering holes."

Adams knew they didn't gather at the same churches and synagogues. Independent polls taken of major media personnel revealed that over ninety percent considered themselves "atheists or agnostics." A similar percentage labeled themselves "liberal."

"You're immersed in politics all day long, aren't you, Paula?"

"You pretty much have to be a political junkie to do this."

"Are you affected by it, or do you just go through the motions? In other words, do you care? Do you form opinions of your own?"

"Of course. We all do."

"When you talk with your colleagues, do you ever find yourself on the defensive, trying to justify a position that's out of step with coworkers?

"No."

"Paula, have you ever called a liberal politician *radical?*" he asked to a blank stare. How about far left? Left wing? Liberal? Secular?"

Banks sat expressionless. She had never used such words.

"Have you ever used the term 'radical' in referring to conservatives? Religious right? Right wing? Far right?" he asked.

"Yes." There was no point denying the obvious.

"Do you recall using the term 'massive buildup' in describing Bush II's increase in military spending?

"Yes. It was."

"How about 'slashing' when it came to the decrease in the increases in social programs?"

She, like the audience, laughed at the absurdity of it. "Yes, I suppose."

"When Bill Clinton slashed military programs, did you refer to the cuts as 'slashing?'"

"No."

"Did you know, percentage *and* dollar-wise, the 'slashes" were larger than the 'massives'?"

Showing she was a good sport in addition to being biased, she smiled and shrugged her shoulders.

"Was that balanced reporting? Or did we see your opinions filtering into your words?"

"You've made your point, Admiral."

"And it's important." He smiled and softened his voice. "The media's bias is one of the reasons America is in the dark. It's the reason we don't know why Muslims killed our men in Somalia, or even why we had to go there. Or why Muslims killed our boys in Lebanon, or in Saudi Arabia, Iraq, or Afghanistan. Or why they killed us in New York. Shall I go on, or would you like to tell your colleagues why we were in Lebanon, Somalia, Afghanistan, and Iraq? Would you like to explain what those who murdered us had in common?"

Ms. Banks tightened up and looked defiant. It was easier to be an expert when reading a prepared script on a teleprompter.

"History is my bag, Paula, so let me help you out here." He smiled.

"We were in Lebanon because Arab Muslims, under the banner of Hezbollah and aided by the Syrians and Iranians, started a civil war on religious grounds. Their very name tell us who they are: Hezbollah means Allah's Party. The war they began destroyed a once-prosperous nation. They murdered tens of thousands. Our Marines tried to stop the killing but were killed instead—not by soldiers, but by truck-bomb terrorists.

"In Somalia, Muslim warlords killed three hundred thousand people, starving many to death. We felt compassion and delivered enormous amounts of food, only to have it stolen at gunpoint by these same Muslim warlords. The stolen food became their weapon of mass destruction; death became their ally. It was conform or starve. We went in militarily to help get the food to the innocents. The Muslim gunmen thanked us for feeding starving Islamic families by shooting our boys."

Banks nodded somberly.

"What nation kidnapped our embassy officials, Ms. Banks?"

"Iran?"

"What faith did they profess?"

"Islam."

"And was that faith central to their actions?"

"Yes."

"What is the state religion of Iraq?"

"Islam."

"Did the dictatorial thug in control there use poisonous gas on tens of thousands of his own people? Did he invade a neighboring nation and then torch the place when he left?"

"Yes."

"We've had three embassies bombed and we've thwarted another three attempts. Was there any connection between these six attacks?"

"Yes. Islam again."

"Why were we in Afghanistan?"

"To disrupt al-Qaeda."

"Are they Roman Catholics?"

"No."

"The suicide bombers in Israel, are they Baptists?"

"No."

"Did the twin-tower twenty have anything in common—faith perhaps?"

"They were all Muslims, mostly from Saudi Arabia."

"Were those things just coincidental, or do you think they were real important to them? Did they say five 'Hail-Muhammad-Allah-is-With-Thees' before slitting the throats of the stewardesses?"

"Their instructions were all about saying their prayers to Allah."

"The truth, Paula, is that Islam is at the root of all of this madness. So why are you and your colleagues so intent upon ignoring the obvious?"

"It's unfair to generalize that way, Admiral. I've had many Muslim clerics on my show who have clearly stated that Islam does not encourage war, that *Jihad* means spiritual struggle, not Holy War."

"In a moment I'm going to prove that the Muslim clerics are lying."

"Why bother, Admiral? It's a free world. They're entitled to believe whatever they want."

"First, their world isn't the least bit free. Second, when what they believe causes them to kill us, it *becomes* our business."

"That sounds like an opinion, Admiral," Paula charged.

"Does it? What do you call an opinion, no matter how harsh or unpopular, that's based upon irrefutable evidence?"

"Truth."

"Right. For example, the misguided nature of Nazi racial superiority, their willingness to trample their people's rights, to kill their neighbors, and slaughter Jews is considered historical fact, not opinion. So it stands to reason that if the evidence for the misguided nature of *Muslim* racism, their willingness to oppress their people, attack their neighbors, and exterminate Jews is just as apparent, it too would be truth, not opinion."

"I'll grant you that."

"In that case, Paula, the only reason you see one conclusion as truth and the other as opinion is that you know more about Nazism than you do about Islam. So since Muslim militants kill today based upon what their Prophet said and did, don't you think we should learn about him, find out what he was like, and most importantly, determine what he had to say?"

"Makes sense."

"Okay. Where would you go to find this kind of information?"

"I-I don't know." That was an embarrassing admission.

"Don't feel bad. You're not alone." Adams turned to the sea of reporters. "Does *anyone* know where to find these answers?"

No one stirred. It was like class, when the teacher asks a tough question and vainly searches the room for a volunteer.

"The answer can be found in three places. It's a real short reading list. You can read the Qur'an. It's allegedly Allah speaking, but I'm convinced it's just Muhammad ranting. You can read the 'official' Muslim biographers. The earliest is Ibn Ishaq. Or you can read the Hadith, which contains Muhammad's speeches. The most authentic, according to Muslim scholars, is al-Bukhari." He held up a copy and handed it to her.

"But before I have you read from it, I'd like to share some scripture from the Qur'an. I want you to come to terms with what I've learned: both the message and the messenger call Muslims to war. From the eighth surah: 'And Allah said to the angels: 'I am with you; go and strengthen the faithful for I shall fill the hearts of the infidels....' Infidels, by the way, are defined in Qur'an 5:72 as Christians. 'I shall fill the hearts of the infidels with *terror.*'" Adams wanted the audience to assimilate the direct link between Islam's god and terror. "Allah continued to rant, 'So smite them on their necks and every joint, and incapacitate them. For they opposed Allah and His Apostle; whoever opposes Allah and His Apostle should know that Allah is severe in his retribution. The punishment for the infidels is to taste the torment of Hell.'"

Adams read another verse from the same surah. "'Allah wished to confirm the truth by wiping the unbelievers,' that's us, 'out *to the last.*' The most prevalent theme in the Qur'an is Allah's caustic prescription of pain and suffering for Christians and Jews. The god of Islam and his Messenger want us dead."

Thor set the Qur'an down and looked at Paula, who was still holding the Hadith. She had it upside down. "I made the same mistake. Here," he said, helping her with it. "It reads from back to front. Now, remember how we got into this discussion—why I asked you to come up front?"

"Yes," she said. "You were asked, told really, that you unfairly singled out verses to paint Islam in a bad light, as if it was promoting war."

"Right. So before we begin, please read the editor's notes confirming that al-Bukhari is the most legitimate and respected source.

She did, and said, "Their own scholars say this is the best they've got."

"Right. Now please turn to any page and read something to us."

"Anywhere?"

"Sure. Anywhere at all."

She opened the book and began, "Number 891. It says here, 'During the conquest of Mecca, Muhammad said, "There will be no more emigration allowed from Mecca, but only *Jihad*. Whenever you are called for *Jihad*, you must go immediately."' Wow. This links the Prophet to the conquest of Mecca. Then it says he ordered *Jihad* as opposed to allowing emigration. That's quite an indictment."

"Maybe it was just a lucky fluke," Thor smiled. "Try again."

She opened to another page. "Verse 34. 'The Prophet said, Allah gives a person who participates in holy battles in Allah's Cause either a reward, or booty, if he survives; or he will be admitted to Paradise if he is killed in the battle as a martyr.' That's ugly. Worse, it confirms what you just told us."

"How does the verse end, Paula?"

"It says Muhammad wanted to fight in the army and become a martyr."

She continued to read one section after another, each condemning Islam, each explaining why Muslims terrorize. With each successive selection, she merely slumped lower in her chair. "We've been purposely duped," Banks said, just loud enough to be heard. "I had no idea. This is horrible. How could anybody buy into this...."

"Mean-spirited, racist, intolerant, belligerent, pejorative, unenlightened, delusional, perverse, hate-mongering religion?" Adams offered, borrowing his list of adjectives from the reporter from NBC. Thor winked at Mr. Clanduse. He did not wink back.

"Yes, it's obvious. Islam promotes war."

"Let's get one thing straight. The God of the Bible and Muhammad's Allah are not the same. In fact, they have very little in common. One wants us to forgive; the other seeks revenge. One says you shall not commit murder; the other says paradise awaits those who murder. One commands us not to covet; the other encourages plunder. One's heaven is all about love; the other's is about lust."

The Admiral asked Paula for the book, flipping through the pages. "Listen to this. 'Allah's Messenger said, "I have been made victorious with terror—casting it into the hearts of the enemy."' Sounds exactly like what *Allah* said in the eighth surah. Same speech writer, perhaps."

"Yes, and more importantly, it explains why Muslims are terrorists."

"It's little wonder they butcher women and children," he remarked. "'This headline from the Book of Jihad asks: 'Is it Permissible to Attack Enemies at Night with the *Probability* of Killing Babies?'"

Paula gasped. Her eyes widened. "He said no, right?"

"Sorry. 'Muhammad was asked whether it was permissible for Muslim warriors to attack infidels and disbelievers for Allah and his Messenger Muhammad at night with the probability of exposing their women and children to danger. The Prophet replied, "They, the women and children, are from them, from the infidels."'"

The Admiral reached his hand back, as Sarah drew a copy of the Qur'an from her purse. Opening it to the fifth surah, Thor read verse 72. "'They are surely infidels who say, "God is the Christ, son of Mary."' 'Disbelievers are those who say, "God is the third of the trinity."' I share that with you, Paula, just in case you didn't know that the infidels and disbelievers are Christians. That's why Muslims think they have authorization to kill American women and children."

"Then Osama bin-Laden was *right* when he said it was permissible."

"Yes, but the Islamic television network, al-Jazeera, had a conniption fit, insisting it wasn't, because they *knew* such evidence would condemn Islam. Your network was no better. CNN said bin Laden was an extremist, a radical, someone who had perverted Islam. But according to Muhammad, terror, the killing of non-combatants, is perfectly okay, so long as they're Christians or Jews."

Thor looked at Paula. "Having met personally with Islamic terrorists, I am deeply troubled by both the bias of CNN's reporting and by its relationship with al-Jazeera. You realize you used to share everything. You were aiding and abetting our enemy."

"But that's all behind us now. We stopped working with them a few months after the 9/11 attacks," Banks interjected. "Al-Jazeera got the only interview with bin-Laden and didn't share it with us."

"There's a reason for that. Al-Jazeera didn't want it to run, even claimed it wasn't 'newsworthy', because it proved Islam itself provides the motivation and the justification for terrorist attacks."

"That's clear to me now. It even explains why the reporter from al-Jazeera was so chummy with Osama. He gave him questions in advance, even interrupted him when he needed help with his answers."

"Paula, can you explain why CNN entangled itself in such a wicked web in the first place? You had to know al-Jazeera had done more to promote fanatical Islam than any organization on the planet. Without al-Jazeera, al-Qaeda wouldn't have been able to drum up enough support to sink a rubber ducky in a bathtub," Adams quipped.

Paula frowned. "They used us. It's embarrassing."

"Al-Jazeera's all about promoting the demented doctrine of Islam. That makes them terrorists. Thousands have died as a result."

"Thor returned to the Hadith. 'No doubt, I would have killed them, for the Prophet said, if somebody discards his religion, kill him.' Can you imagine a 'religion' so perverse you have to kill to maintain adherents?"

He looked back down and flipped a page. "'Allah's Apostle has ordered us to fight you till you worship Allah alone or give us tribute,' that is, convert at sword point or pay a tax. It goes on to say, 'And our Prophet has informed us that Allah says: "Whoever among us is martyred shall go to Paradise to lead a luxurious life beyond imagination, and whoever among us survives the battle shall become your master."' How are the it's-a-peaceful-religion folks gonna explain that one?"

Thor pointed to the headline above Chapter 73: *War Is Deceit*. That's how," he said, holding it so Paula could see. "These words, as much as any, encapsulate Muhammad's world view. His 'religion' is a lie."

Thor sighed heavily. "'The Prophet said, 'Caesar will be ruined and you will spend his treasures in Allah's Cause.' And, 'The Prophet appointed the commander of the infantrymen and archers, saying, 'see that we defeat the infidels.'" Shaking his head, he read the next pearl from Muhammad's lips. "'The booty! O people, the booty! Your companions have become victorious in the battle. What are you waiting for?' Allah's Messenger said, 'By Allah! We will go to the enemy and collect our share from the war booty.' The peace-loving Prophet goes on to say, 'Some of your casualties were mutilated. I did not urge my men to do so, yet I do not feel sorry for what they did.'"

"May I?" Paula asked for the book.

The Admiral was more than willing to give it up. The words of Muhammad were as disgusting as Allah's. It was obvious they deserved each other. It was obvious they were one and the same.

Paula read, "'Allah will endow a person with an understanding of the Qur'an, so that he understands the ransom of blood-money for captives, and the judgment that no Muslim should be killed for killing an infidel.' That's a license to kidnap and kill."

Flipping to chapter 79, she read, "'The Prophet on his deathbed gave orders saying, "Expel infidels in the name of Allah and His Messenger

Muhammad from the Arabian Peninsula.""'"

"Here," he said, reaching for the book, "let's try some other Islamic verses on for size. You tell me if Muhammad sounds like a Prophet. Heck, tell me if he even sounds *sane*." Adams flipped a couple of pages. "He testifies that 'the Qur'an is from Allah like the Torah.' How is that possible? Every account is different, including the god they describe. If the Torah is Allah-inspired, how can it contradict Allah's Qur'an?"

He flipped backwards. "This little pearl says that Allah's religion is so dimwitted, the only way to promote it is at the point of a sword. 'So Allah had brought about the battle for the good of His Messenger in order that they might embrace Islam.' Along those lines, here's one that says, 'Allah's Messenger took revenge for Allah's sake.'"

Thor continued. "Muhammad claims, 'Jesus is Allah's slave, His Messenger, and His Word.' Then the Prophet says, 'He was born of the virgin Maryam and was created by Allah's Spirit.' He even claims that the Gospels are Allah's word. But doesn't that make Islam a lie, since Muhammad contradicts *everything* Jesus says?

He turned a few more pages. "Muhammad has the roughest time understanding stuff. And unfortunately, his 'revelations' from Allah don't help much. For example, 'The Prophet asked me at sunset, "Do you know where the sun goes?" He said, "It prostrates itself beneath Allah's throne, and asks permission to rise again. It is permitted; the sun prostrates itself but it is not acceptable. Again it will ask permission to go on its course, but Allah will order the sun to return whence it has come, so it will rise in the west."' Let me ask you, Paula, would you be inclined to believe the promise of paradise from a guy who proclaims such drivel? In this one quote, he says the sun prostrates itself, it asks permission, Allah changes his mind, the sun—not the earth—has a course, and it rises in the west. Would you be willing to commit murder to attain this man's paradise?"

The reporter was visibly shaken. "No" was all she said.

"While we're on the subject of scientific accuracy, Muhammad reports that the Jews got lost and 'they were cursed and transformed into rats.' While I can't quite follow the connection, in the same speech the Prophet informs us, 'If a man has sexual intercourse with his wife and discharges first, the child will resemble the father, and if the woman gets discharge first, the child will resemble her.' I bet you didn't know that."

The reporters had finally relaxed enough to have a good laugh.

"Oh, and did you know that according to Muhammad, in Verse 71, 'Women will increase in number and men will decrease, so that fifty women will be looked after by one man.' Okay, settle down, folks, the Prophet is an expert when it comes to this sort of thing. 'Allah's

Messenger, the truly inspired one said, "In the matter of the creation, a human being is put together in the womb of the mother in forty days. And then he becomes a clot of thick blood for a similar period, and then a piece of flesh for a similar period."'"

They all chuckled.

"Who here, by a show of hands, wants to trust this guy with their soul?" They all stopped laughing.

"I wouldn't either. The Prophet revealed this little treasure from Judgment Day. 'Adam will ask: "How many people are suffering in the Hell Fire?" Allah will say: "Nine hundred and ninety-nine of every one thousand."' Sounds like terrible odds to me."

"Here's another pearl. 'The Prophet said, "Yawning is from Satan, and if anyone of you yawns, he should stop yawning as soon as possible; for if anyone of you, while yawning, exclaims, 'Ha,' Satan will laugh at him."' And we wouldn't want that, would we? 'Allah says a bad or evil dream is from Satan; so if you have one and become afraid you should spit on your left side.' Now you know which side of the bed to sleep on. 'Muhammad added, "If one of you awakes from sleep and performs the ablution, he should wash his nose by putting water in it and then blowing it out three times, because Satan has stayed in the upper part of his nose all night."' I hate it when he does that."

Now nearly doubled over, the crowd of jaundiced journalists were hysterical, rolling in the aisles.

"This one explains a lot. Aisha, the fifty-three-year-old Prophet's nine-year-old wife, said, 'Magic was worked on the Prophet so that he began to fancy himself doing things which did not actually happen. He has been bewitched.' Pretty much tells you all you need to know about Islam. And in case you doubt Aisha's credentials, Muhammad said, '"The superiority of Aisha to other women is like the superiority of the Tharid," that's a meat and bread dish, "to all other meals."' I mean, how can you top Tharid? Aisha went on to say, '"Anyone who claims Muhammad saw Allah is telling a great lie, for he only saw Gabriel in his genuine form, covering the whole horizon."' That's a problem, since her husband said *he* met with Allah.

"In the same chapter, she claimed that the Prophet said, '"Aisha, this is Gabriel and he sends his greetings and salutations to you." Aisha said, "Offer my salutations and greetings to him and may Allah's mercy and blessings be upon him." Then, addressing the Prophet, she said, "You see what I don't see."'"

The audience, especially the media, were beside themselves, hollering irreverently, laughing, some even clapping.

"Oh, you'll like this quote: '"O Allah's Apostle, this ordinary fire would have been sufficient to torture the disbelievers." But Allah's Messenger said, "The Hell Fire is sixty-nine times hotter than the ordinary worldly fire. It is so hot that the intestines will come out, and those thrown into Hell Fire will go around like a donkey goes around a millstone dragging them."'

"Now don't be laughing, ladies; this Hell's for you. In chapter seventeen, The prophet said, '"I was shown the Hell Fire and the majority of its inhabitants were women who were ungrateful to their husbands."' But for you guys, I've got good news! Talking about Paradise, Allah's Messenger said, '"There will be no spitting, nose blowing, or relieving nature. Sweat will smell like musk and everyone will have two wives; the marrow of their bones will be seen through their flesh out of excessive beauty."' That's a good thing, I guess.

"But you'd better hurry. Wonder why there's such a rush to get into Paradise, why there are so many suicide bombers? I'm going to read this exactly as it's written: 'The Prophet, peace be unto him, said, "Verily! 70,000 or 700,000 of my followers will enter Paradise altogether."' Think about that. Whichever number you use, the odds aren't good. There have been well over two billion Muslims. That means fewer than one in every *three thousand* Muslims are going to get their two translucent wives in paradise. It's a weenie roast for the rest of 'em, I suppose. Better stock up on the sunscreen, brothers—SPF 5,000 might do."

He turned the page and turned serious again. "I could read Mo-isms all day long, but I'm going to end with these. Verse 1294: 'The Prophet said, "If a Muslim discards his religion, kill him."' Chapter 18, the Book of Prayer, 'Allah's Messenger said, "I burned the houses of the men who did not present themselves for the compulsory prayer."'"

The Admiral was quiet for a long moment. "Folks, when I started on this quest, this is not what I was looking for. All I expected to find—all I *wanted* to find—was something that caused a small percentage of Muslims to become extremists, something that caused them to pervert their religion. What I found instead *was* a perverted religion."

He closed the book. "It's an unholy alliance of money, mullahs, madrases, and madmen. Working in cahoots with the Muslim media, they have force-fed this crap to millions. But the good news is, once the alliance is separated from the masses, peace will ultimately prevail. These people and their perverted doctrine are the enemy—not the billion people they hold in virtual slavery—at least not yet."

He turned again toward Paula Banks. "What do you suppose you'd do and say if you lived in Nazi Germany?"

"You'd go along and at least feign support for the Nazi agenda, or you'd be sent off as a slave laborer to a concentration camp."

"That's right, Paula. And if you lived in the Soviet Union, would it be smarter to toe the Communist line, or openly condemn it?"

"I suppose that if Stalin or any of his cronies thought you were critical of their, their...."

"Atheistic, totalitarian, murderous dictatorship?" Thor interrupted.

"Yes. If you disagreed with them, you'd be eliminated."

"Dissent was costly—you'd pay with your life. Everyone knows that Hitler was good at killing Russians. But Stalin was even better, murdering in excess of ten million of his own people, many of them for no other reason than he perceived them to be a threat. Atheistic governments are as tolerant and peace loving as Islamic ones. So what do you think happens if you criticize the Islam in any of their dictatorial states?"

"Same thing. Imprisonment or death."

"That's right, Paula. Population control is the only thing dictators are good at. Now, what happened to support for Nazism when Hitler, Goebbels, and others were put out of business?"

"It vanished."

The historian in Adams surfaced. "The expressed support for Nazism fell from ninety-eight percent to *two* percent. And what happened to the glitter of the Communist Party when Reagan exposed them for what they really were, evil, and when he forced them to compete with our revitalized economy?"

"It vanished too, a little more slowly, but it clearly waned."

"Correct again. Now, Ms. Banks, two final questions. What do you think would happen to the support that Muslims feign for this demented doctrine if we stopped the indoctrination of youth in the madrases, cut the flow of money, took away the guns, and freed them from their repressive regimes?"

"Support would vanish, just as it has in the past."

"Very good. And then, what would happen to terrorism?"

"There would be no more terrorism."

Thor smiled. "Class dismissed."

24

ROCKING THE WORLD

"Mary, do you have a little something for your mom?"

She reached into her right dress pocket, then into the left. Mary looked panicked, patting herself all over. Her eyes widened as she shook her head side to side, shrugging her shoulders and raising her hands. "Sorry." Then, unable to contain herself, she erupted into a playful laugh.

The guests, enjoying themselves, laughed along. Thor's nattily attired best man surreptitiously slipped Mary the elegant stone. She held it aloft with one hand, covering her mouth with the other, still trying to repress a mischievous giggle.

The pastor officiating the ceremony was more relieved than entertained. He cleared his throat to get the Admiral's attention, encouraging him to slip the jewel onto his bride's finger. Sarah gracefully lifted her left hand.

The minister breathed a heavy sigh as ring met finger. "Do you, Sarah Abigail Nottingly, take this man to be your husband? Do you promise to love him and cherish him, in sickness and in health, for richer or poorer, in good times and in bad, for as long as you both shall live?"

"I'm not so sure about the cherish part, but the rest sounds pretty good."

"I was looking for a simple yes or no," the pastor said. Turning to Thor, he asked, "Is she always this difficult?"

"'Fraid so." He smiled. Even behind a veil, "Abigail" was beguiling.

The pastor shook his head, suppressing a smile of his own. "If you don't find exception with not being cherished, I suppose it's all right with me. So do you, Admiral Thurston Merrick Adams, take this woman to be your wife? Do you promise to love her and cherish her for as long as you both shall live?"

"Yes, sir, I do. *Especially* the cherish part."

The pastor rolled his eyes. These two apparently deserved each other. "Then I pronounce you man and wife. You may kiss the bride."

"I'd thought you'd never ask," the former Miss Nottingly teased, freeing her face from the veil.

"Ladies and gentlemen, I present to you Admiral and Mrs. Thurston Adams. Umm, Mr. and Mrs. Adams? You can stop kissing now. Hello...."

✡ ✝ ☾

THE WEDDING PARTY had a decidedly international flavor. Team Tuxedo were all there, having a whole lot more fun than their first adventure together. This time the canteens were filled with champagne. There was romantic music, not angry shouting. The percussion came from drums, not Kalashnikov rifles. And although they were hanging out, no one was cross.

"Jolly good time. Thanks for including us, old chap." The British delegation was led by the man of steel, the former Major Blake Huston, now Prime Minister Huston. Lad Childress, Ryan Sullivan, and Cliff Powers were all decked out in groomsmen's tuxedos. Their ranks had also changed. They were now Majors.

"Are you kidding?" Adams responded. "You can't have a wedding without inviting your family!"

The Israelis never missed a party. They were led by the indomitable Isaac Newcomb, now a Member of the Israeli Knesset. Moshe Keceph, Yacob Seraph, and Joshua Abrams were ambulatory. They clearly looked better in black tie than in chameleon SFG.

Kyle Stanley was Thor's best man. It was a role he had played ever since that first cold day they had struggled together on the frosty beaches at BUD/S. And if the polls were any indication, it looked like he would soon be America's Secretary of Defense. Kyle had come a long way from being a crucified Lieutenant in Afghanistan.

The smiling Bentley McCaile and Cole Sumner rounded out the dashing dozen. Whatever uniform they found themselves wearing, they were a team, twelve men who'd bonded for life. They had faced the enemy, learned the source of their madness, and survived to tell the tale.

The boys had hosted Adams' bachelor party the previous night, commandeering the upper floor of Thor's favorite chop house. It had been a raucous affair, yet innocent enough to invite Troy Nottingly.

No stag flicks or scantily clad girls; instead, they'd roasted Adams. They even put together a Thor and Sarah highlights film, including the wheezing have-you-got-a-girl-back-home discussion taped when they were pursuing terrorists. The "Sarah!" outburst at the homecoming was a crowd pleaser. So was the infamous *Today Show* kiss. Had they not been judicious in editing, the film would have grown into a miniseries.

For his part, Troy compiled a too-cute-for-words video on the most embarrassing moments in "Abigail's" life. In between, Kyle kept the assembled in stitches, revealing enough inside dirt on the illustrious groom to keep Thor humble for a good long while.

After the ceremony, the wedding party moved from the private church into the elegantly refurbished old manor home for the reception. First chance she got, Sarah huddled with the Israelis in one of the reception rooms off the entry. "Thanks for the rock, boys," she said, proudly. She flashed the ice in their midst, making sure it caught the light. "While you shouldn't have, I'm glad you did. Every time I look at it I think of all we've been through. Thank you." She gave them each a kiss.

"Mrs. Adams?" Yacob said, hugging Sarah. "I found him—the Messiah," he whispered in her ear.

Sarah smiled, lovingly, like a mother.

"Thank you."

"Yacob, don't thank me. I didn't do anything. *He* did," she said, pointing toward heaven.

"Yes, but I saw him first in you. Then I saw him change the Admiral. Crucified men can't do that unless...."

"Unless they're God." Sarah's magnificent day had just grown brighter. Placing a hand on each side of Yacob's face, she kissed him again on the forehead. Joyful, she wiped her lipstick away. "God bless you, my brother."

It was the happiest day of her life. Better than any fantasy, she was living her dreams. Stunningly beautiful in her flowing white-pearled dress, her chastity was as pure as the gown's color. It had been worth the wait. She had a marvelous present to give the most grateful man in the world.

As for Thurston Adams, he was a new man. Dressed in black, his demeanor was anything but. He now had the best jobs in the world—Sarah's husband, Mary's dad, and God's messenger. And depending on what happened at the ballot box next Tuesday, maybe the worst job as well.

✡   ✝   ☾

AS THE PALESTINIAN LEADERSHIP had feared, America's mood had shifted decidedly in favor of the Israelis. These were dark days for the

Muslim brotherhood. Something had to be done.

They had tried blaming terror on Israeli occupation, but too few bought it. A result of the Admiral's national tour, the American people were galvanized. Enlightened, they shared a righteous indignation. While they harbored no animosity toward Arabs, or even Muslims, they had come to hate the behavior of those who used Islam to inflict their hellish views on an otherwise peaceable world.

Even the press had begun to see the light, or at least the glint of cold cash. Tipped off and ticked off, viewers were no longer as willing to put up with mindless sound bites and a transparent agenda. A dangerous trend seemed to be emerging: fair, thoughtful reporting. Viewers were switching channels in droves. The media was on the defensive, momentarily defanged, not dead but whimpering.

Info-babe Trixi Lightheart was not, however, ready to give up. She was at the top of her game. Bright and all-too-early on Saturday morning, she was on the air. "With the election just a few days away, a confident Admiral Adams has married his CIA-agent sweetheart, Sarah Nottingly. The gala affair was held in a private church on the Severn River in Annapolis, overlooking the U.S. Naval Academy. Our cameras were not allowed in, but as these FOX helicopter shots show, the Admiral has reunited Team Uniform. In black tie, they all served as his groomsmen. Mary, the Israeli girl the unmarried couple adopted while they were in Israel, was the ring bearer.

"No one is saying where America's Prince and Princess are headed on their honeymoon. But be assured, when we find out, we'll bring it to you live and unedited," she teased.

Trixi shuffled some of her papers. "On the political front, the most recent FOX News poll shows that the right-wing political neophyte is leading the more experienced and moderate Congressman Macon by a wide margin. The Congressman says he isn't worried, however. He is convinced the gap will narrow between now and Tuesday's election as voters view his latest round of television ads. In these commercials, the Congressman has assembled a prestigious team of international statesmen and clergy. Collectively, they condemn the Admiral's plans on all fronts: political, economic, and religious. They say that he is a dangerous demagogue, a racist, intolerant of other faiths, and a warmonger."

Lightheart looked down as long segments of the Macon commercials played free, as if they were news. "The Congressman's ads were provided to the Adams campaign staff," she said, "but they offered no comment. They seem content to let them air without providing any rebuttal. The Admiral's campaign manager and father-in-law, millionaire businessman

Troy Nottingly, said, 'We have stated our position and have no interest in attacking our opponent.' He went on to say that they will continue with their strategy of not running any ads of their own—positive or negative."

It wasn't for lack of money. The Save America campaign had received over one hundred million dollars in donations—though they had solicited nothing. Win or lose, they had decided to invest these funds as seed capital, supporting some of the initiatives they were promoting. A hundred million dollars would go a long way toward making credit available to those without it or computers more affordable to those in need.

Congressman Macon's war chest was overflowing as well. Those who would be the most negatively impacted by the Admiral's agenda, the dictators in China, Saudi Arabia, Iran, Syria, Libya, and Iraq, had sent the American Presidential hopeful and his party tens of millions. It was even more generous than the support the Chinese Communists had shown Bill Clinton and his presidency.

"In other news," Trixi reported, "the new President of Palestine, Mamdouh Salim, is trying to negotiate economic concessions from Israel. He blames his lack of success on the ultra right wing Israeli government and on the militant rhetoric of Admiral Adams. President Salim says the only hope for putting an end to violence is for Israel to pay reparations to his people."

✡ ✝ ☾

KAHN WAS BEING, well, Kahn. He was so antsy, he almost blasted his boats out of the water fooling with the remote trigger, a case of premature eradication. He nearly killed a million fish along with his hopes for a triumphant terrorist action.

Haqqani was fascinated by the electronic timers. Aymen Halaweh had used what the Russians and Iranians had provided and taken it to the next level. The triggering devices were state of the art. Kahn was thrilled with how his young M.I.T. engineer had tied all but one into Internet protocols. The lone exception was Washington. That one was particularly sensitive, since Halam Ghumani, in prison or not, was still the boss. He insisted on dying a martyr. Neither Kahn, Omen, nor Aymen were willing to risk their lives—or their standing in al-Qaeda—on something as potentially quirky as the Internet. D.C.'s dastardly deed was being done the old fashioned way—with a failsafe timer.

Aymen had arranged to have web cams installed at strategic locations in each of the twelve cities and on each of the twelve boats. This would give Haqqani the opportunity to witness the devastation in real time. Kahn smiled. He loved this stuff.

"Omen," he yelled, "when will the last of the boats leave Puget Sound?"

"Not for a couple of days. I want every yacht to arrive just before our little celebration."

He had already sent the San Diego and Los Angeles boats on their way. Omen had decided against sailing the three West Coast yachts from the Bahamas. Too risky. He had instead retrofitted sailboats already in the Pacific Northwest. Omen wanted to cruise into each city moments before Alpha 5's grand finale, on the theory that the less time the boys had to get into trouble, the less trouble the boys would get into. His experience with Atta and Riza had been a religious awakening of sorts. Muslims couldn't be trusted, he had learned.

Fortunately, money was the least of his problems. The war booty was coming in faster than even Muhammad, with his vivid imagination, could have dreamed. Candy sales had never been stronger. They were now a full-service provider, an evil version of 31 Flavors. They had heroin, cocaine, crack, ecstasy, date-rape drugs, uppers, downers, hallucinogenics, whatever the youth of America couldn't get along without. And while the fire and casualty insurance businesses were booming, nothing beat life insurance for encouraging compliance. Even the old standby, kidnapping for ransom, was bringing in millions the world over. It was enough to make Allah proud.

"Inauguration eve, my brother," Omen explained to Kahn. "If Adams wins, he won't live long enough to crow about it."

"You are a devil," Haqqani praised his comrade. "Elegant timing."

Quagmer was proud of himself. "Washington is scheduled to blow first, per Halam's instructions. Like he said, they won't live to see him die. Our boys have a transient slip in the Potomac Marina, near the Lincoln Memorial. They're scheduled to leave Paradise Island tomorrow. That puts them dockside D.C. on Sunday, eight days from now. In nine we celebrate. Monday afternoon, just before sunset."

"And then, poof—they all die." Kahn added, pounding his clinched fist into an open hand.

"The rest of the fireworks go off in succession, Tuesday morning, inauguration morning, about fifteen minutes apart. It's kind of like what we did in New York and Washington, with the planes hitting just close enough to prevent the Feds from doing anything about it, but far enough apart to prolong the agony. I call it 'rolling thunder'—a phrase I picked up from the Americans. It adds to the drama."

"Beautiful. Who's second?" Kahn asked impatiently. He was like a kid with a new toy on Ramadan morning. He couldn't wait to unwrap his presents and play.

"New York, New York. The city that never sleeps."

"Thanks to us." Kahn made a humming engine sound as he stuck out the thumb and little finger of his right hand, forming an airplane. He banked it into his left hand, fingers upright and split. The Twin Towers died again.

"The big apple gets sliced at nine o'clock Eastern Daylight Time, Tuesday morning. Yacht two, the *Serenity*, has a prime location right on the Hudson. Like the dock in Washington, it's less than a hundred meters from downtown." The terrorists were having fun. Terrorizing civilians and disrupting their economy was what they loved.

"Those boys left several days ago. Their transponder shows them…" Quagmer reached over to a laptop computer near where Kahn was seated. He clicked the mouse and stroked a few keys. "…in Savannah."

"Then?"

"You're insatiable, Kahn. Boston at nine fifteen."

"Did you remember to pack some tea?" Kahn loved symbolism.

"You're a sick man, you know that?"

"It's part of the job description, remember?" Kahn rubbed his hands together. "Well, did you?"

"Yeah," Omen admitted sheepishly. It was twisted enough to be embarrassing. "Those boys are aboard the *Carpe Diem*—that's Latin for 'seize the day.' They're in," he clicked the mouse again, "Cape Fear."

"No way. There's such a place?"

"Look here," Omen pointed to the screen, near Virginia.

"And…."

"Baltimore, followed by Norfolk."

"Norfolk," Haqqani repeated. "Perfect. There's a Naval and Air Force base there, a CIA training facility, Williamsburg, Yorktown, Jamestown. That's a good target."

"I thought you'd like it. Okay. It's ten o'clock on Tuesday morning, time for President-elect Adams to speak—pity, he's dead. Now where do you suppose the naughty little atoms are scheduled to misbehave?"

"Miami?"

"That would be a winner. Then we party in New Orleans."

"Mardi Gras? I can hear it now: Satan Sings the Blues!"

"Funny. If this terrorist gig craps out, you've got a future in stand-up."

Kahn smiled, envisioning himself delivering one-liners. He tried one on Omen, "A teacher at Suicide Bomber School looks around the room and says, 'Class, pay close attention. I'm only going to do this once.'"

"Real clever. On second thought, don't give up the day job."

Kahn feigned disappointment. "That's seven. We've got twelve of these little buggers. Where are the other five hiding?"

"Chicago at ten thirty, nine thirty Central Time. It was the first boat to set sail. Last time I checked, it was on Lake Erie. It's the *Great Balls of Fire*."

"You're kidding me. No, I don't suppose you are. And then...."

"Houston, we have a problem. It blows at nine forty-five local. San Francisco, San Diego, and Los Angeles follow in that order at eight, eight-fifteen, and eight-thirty Pacific Knockout Time. Like I said, 'rolling thunder.' Boom-Boom!"

"Which ones are carrying the good stuff? Fission, mushroom cloud, searing heat, wind, and radiation."

"Washington, New York, Boston, and Baltimore in the east. San Francisco and Los Angeles in the west."

In the best Hispanic accent he could muster, he repeated, "Los Ongheles." Kahn almost looked disappointed. "Bye-bye, beach babes. They don't wear enough sunscreen, you know. In the other cities they'll die more slowly 'cause our dirty bombs won't go thermo-nuclear. But that's good in a way."

"Sure. Nothing says terror like slow death. Everybody close gets cancer from the fallout."

"Mostly leukemia. The spent fuel pellets we stole from the Russians will kill eighty percent of those within a kilometer. At six hundred REMs, they'll puke their brains out. Their blood cells will mutate, and their immune system will be kaput."

"Since everybody's hair is gonna fall out we maybe should buy a wig business," the terrorist accountant mused.

"Chernobyl II. Shake and bake," Kahn predicted.

"Your dirty bombs have what, fifty kilos of Iranian C-12? Sitting under ten kilos of nuclear waste, right?"

"Grade A, prime-filet daughter products, my friend," Kahn explained in Haqqani parlance.

"Daughter products? As in the revenge of al-Lat, al-Uzza, and Manat —Allah's little girls?" Omen asked.

"Yep. That's what they call spent uranium fuel pellets. I looked it up on the Internet, and based on what I found, these ladies are really cranky."

Omen smiled as he walked over and stood behind where Kahn was seated. He was playing one of the computer animations Aymen Halaweh had created to demonstrate the features of his launching system. A series of four rocket-like devices built from jury-rigged RPGs were designed to

throw the bombs 100 meters skyward one second after the forward skylight hatch blew out of the way. At the highest point of their trajectory,
the C-12 would explode, spreading the radioactive debris far and wide.
The thermonuclear suitcase bombs would, of course, forego the plastic
explosive. They were plenty explosive in their own right. Kahn and Omen
watched the last sequences of Aymen's animation with considerable
pride. Washington, building by building, monument by monument, was
being turned back into the swamp from which it had arisen.

Aymen had also shown the pudgy terrorist and his insatiable sidekick
how to use the web-cam feature. With a few keystrokes and a click of a
mouse, the world's biggest rats were able to manipulate the cameras. They
switched to the Bahamas and scanned the marina. With its pristine, mul-
ticolored waters, bikini-clad babes, and virgin beaches, it looked a lot like
paradise.

"Oh, would you look at that? Why are we languishing here in this godforsaken desert?" Haqqani groused. "We signed up for the wrong duty
this time."

"Well, we *are* the most wanted men in the world. Don't you think people might get a little suspicious if we went on a yachting vacation?"

"Yeah, I suppose," he complained. "Besides, the delivery boys are
gonna get roasted. They know what they are carrying, don't they?"

"Of course. They wouldn't have it any other way."

Kahn rolled his eyes. "Don't tell me you're still selling them on the sev-
enty-virgin fairy tale?"

"Step right up. First to die, first served." He underscored his words
with an appropriately vulgar gesture.

"Do you write this stuff down for them like bin Laden used to, or do
you just have the clerics brainwash 'em?" Haqqani wanted to hone his
skills and become a more professional manager. Just because he was a terrorist, didn't mean he didn't have ambition.

"It's more complicated than that," Quagmer explained. He had given
this a lot of thought. His lucrative career depended on it. "Selling virgins
to boys wouldn't be possible if the clerics didn't support us," he admitted.
"We owe all this to Muhammad, peace be unto him. Without the
Prophet's, peace be unto him, speeches, we'd be living in a tent, yanking
a camel around by the nose."

"With our team floating on oil, the internal combustion engine didn't
hurt either," Haqqani observed. "But let's face facts; it's all a farce."

"Of course," he said, looking over his shoulder. He wanted to make
sure no one was listening. "But I suppose even the possibility of romping
with virgins in paradise is better than the reality of wrestling with vermin

in Palestine." Omen shook his head.

"Hard to imagine anybody believes this garbage." Kahn eulogized.

"Have you ever read Muhammad's speeches?"

"Only the good ones—you know, the stuff about *Jihad*, killing infidels, war booty—fighting in Allah's cause. Martyrdom: it's great for recruiting."

"Oh, just the peace-loving-religion verses."

They both doubled over laughing, nearly knocking Aymen's triggering notebook off the table.

✡   ✝   ☪

IT HAD BEEN WORTH the wait. They were in Paradise, literally. Thor and Sarah had chartered a sixty-foot sloop for their honeymoon. Actually, Troy and Leisel had chartered it. They had provided the transportation too. The newlyweds had been escorted. Sitting in the back, they had held hands for most of the three-hour flight from Lee Field in Annapolis to the Bahamas.

Having lost her taste for flying, Mary had moved in with Kyle Stanley for the week. The two had become pals.

The flight had been catered. Small fruit and vegetable platters had accompanied club sandwiches. Though the bride and groom had just left their reception, they hadn't eaten. They were too busy celebrating, cutting the cake, throwing garters, being photographed, dancing, and chatting with friends. Sarah had never been hungrier.

Moments after they landed, an aging white limousine pulled up next to the plane. A few seconds later, a lineman working out of the FBO in Nassau brought up a rental car. At the same time, a fuel truck swung around in front. It was poetry in motion.

Sarah opened the door. Wearing an attractive lavender sundress, she glowed as she stepped out into the soft warm light of the late afternoon.

The honeymoon itinerary had been arranged by Leisel. Thor and Sarah would take a small overnight bag to the Atlantis Hotel, where they had reserved the Presidential Suite. Although the room was often comped, they paid for it: Adams and Adams may have been risk takers, but neither were gamblers.

The bulk of their luggage was carted to the *Agape*, their sixty-foot floating palace. The Nottinglys had volunteered to do the schlepping. Chartering a smaller vessel, they had planned to stay a discreet distance away but still close enough to help out if needed—and more importantly, to remove the crew of the *Agape* when their presence was not wanted—no offense, but this *was* a honeymoon. The Nottingly's yacht had been chartered "bare boat," but the newlyweds' would have a captain and a cook, a crew that would make life easy when they could be of service and then conveniently disappear when their services were no longer needed.

Now, with the giant pink hotel looming above them, the Adamses had other things on their minds. Sarah had waited a lifetime for this night. Thor wished he had.

Finally inside, the newlyweds rode the elevator to the tenth floor, and floated down the hall. Thor removed the electronic key from its sleeve, and released the door. Propping it open with their overnight bags, he turned to Sarah. His smile broadened. He leaned over, placing his left arm under her thighs, his right behind her shoulders. She fell back, trusting him to catch her. As he carried Sarah across the threshold, Thor slid their bags away with his foot. The door swung closed. They were alone.

"Mrs. Adams, may I have the pleasure of your company?" Sure, it wasn't the best pickup line, but it worked well enough.

"I thought you'd never ask," she cooed, then said, "You remember that 'one track mind' stuff I used to bug you about?"

"Yes?" he replied, still holding her, spinning her around in the living room of the palatial suite.

"Forget it," she giggled.

Thor carried his bride toward the large panoramic balcony. He hoped she'd reprise that night in Jerusalem when she'd slipped behind him and wrapped her arms around his waist, her chin on his shoulder, hair against his neck. He wasn't disappointed. The romantic significance was not lost on her. As the sun turned a deep red and fell beneath the western horizon, the clouds began to glow. The view was magnificent. Sarah held him tight. A warm breeze caressed them. The sights and sounds of the Bahamas filled their senses.

Thor felt Sarah's arms rise beneath his, moving up from his waist to his chest. Her hands fumbled at the top button on his shirt, then the second and third. When she had reached his belt, she raised her hands again, this time rubbing them on his bare chest. She stood on her toes and kissed his neck. She dragged her nails softly across his pecs.

His breathing became labored. He closed his eyes. This was the moment he wanted to last forever, the moment he would never forget. Thankfully, she wasn't in a hurry. Her right hand was rubbing his abs just above his pants. Her left teased him, higher on his chest. Sarah reached down, pulling the remainder of his shirt free. She undid the last two buttons, dropping it from his shoulders, as she had done with his robe a month before on the balcony overlooking the Temple Mount.

They were outside, exposed to God's glory, surrounded by the passionate warm hues of his creation. Yet they were private, up high and tucked in behind a low curved wall that secured the balcony.

Naked from the waist up, Thor felt his skin tingle. It wasn't because he was cold. His hands were now on top of hers as they roamed freely. Just for fun, she occasionally let them drop, sliding across the top of his belt, sometimes below. Thor was in exquisite agony. Part of him wanted to turn and kiss his wife, unbutton her dress, return the favor. Yet the other part didn't want to move. He was relishing every moment. *In* love, he was learning, love was better.

Certain he was about to explode, he grasped his bride's arms, stopping her long enough for him to turn around. He held her hands for a long moment, down at her side. He stared longingly into her eyes. He could see her desire. He was sure she could feel his. Her hands still in his, he gently pulled them behind her back. Exposed and vulnerable, she wiggled closer to him, pressing her chest against his.

He closed his eyes, tilting his head slightly. She knew she was about to be kissed. Their lips met, softly, then more firmly. Hands still behind her back she leaned into him, opened her mouth and kissed him more passionately than she ever had, even in her dreams.

Thor maneuvered her hands so that he could hold both of hers in one of his. He sensed that she was too worried about pleasing him, about showing him that even though she was inexperienced, she could love him better than anyone ever had. But he wanted her to relax and enjoy being loved.

With his free hand he stroked her hair, the side of her face, her neck, kissing her as he did. Then he pulled her toward him again. She moaned. Thor stroked her side, flirting with her breast, just as she had done with the top of his pants. Each time his hand passed near her nipple, Sarah's breathing became deeper, more sensual. Releasing her hands, Thor used both of his to release the top button on her lavender sundress. She looked at him as he did, her eyes inviting him to continue. The second, third, and fourth took him down below her waist. He reached inside, holding her where she was narrowest. His hands were so large, they nearly encircled her. Kissing her again, he raised his hands slowly until they were just under the bottom of her matching lavender bra.

Thor pushed back just far enough to see what he was about to feel. Partially covered by a wisp of lace, he had never seen anything he liked better. The mother of all smiles erupted across his face. "How are my favorite distractions?"

"Never felt better." Her smile now matched his.

Dress open, revealing much of her beauty, Thor raised his hands and slid it off of her shoulders, letting it fall to the floor. Bending down, he picked it up as she lifted one leg and then the other. On the way up he tossed what little there was of it in the direction of a lounge, not knowing or really caring if he had hit his mark. He was far too enamored with the Sarah he saw between her matching lavender lingerie. All the way up, he caressed her tenderly.

It was hard to tell who felt better, more excited. Sensing her knees were about to buckle, knowing his were, Thor lifted Sarah off her feet once again. The warm breeze followed them as he carried his blushing bride to the bedroom, gazing down at her as he walked. He didn't bother closing the door. With an elbow he hit a light switch, illuminating the room ever so softly.

"Why did you do that?" she asked in a tone that seemed pleased.

"Seeing you," he answered softly, "is as exciting as feeling you."

"*Oooh,* good answer. That deserves a kiss."

"I was hoping for more," he replied.

Still in his arms, she agreed. "I'm all yours, sailor."

Hours later, exhausted, they fell asleep in each other's arms. But it wasn't long before Sarah awoke. She studied him, examining every detail. She ran her fingers over his chest, touched his stomach, and then laid her hand on his thigh. She let it linger there. He awoke, and they made love again.

Satisfied but hardly satiated, they fell asleep. As dawn's first light broke across the Atlantic, Thor rolled over and looked at Sarah for the longest time, examining each curve. She was still asleep, on her side; her back was closest to him. Unable to resist the temptation, he began to caress her. As he played, she began to move. At first, Thor felt a little embarrassed, but not for long. Sarah placed her hand over his, continuing to guide it wherever it pleased her. She cooed, letting him know that she was enjoying herself and all too happy to be Mrs. Thurston Adams.

✡   ☩   ☾

IT WAS NEARLY NOON before the lovers finally made their way down to the marina adjoining the hotel. Every time had Sarah tried to dress, Thor undid whatever she'd done. Somewhere along the way, she even managed to model a teddy, the one she hadn't gotten around to wearing the night before. That didn't last long either.

After what may have been a dozen attempts, Mr. and Mrs. Adams finally make it to the elevator. Half dazed, Sarah asked, "Are you sure you're okay with my parents?"

"Sweetheart, I love your parents. And Lord knows, as much as I'd love to make love all day long, we're going to have to come up for air sometime."

"Yeah, right, O insatiable one. You've got a one-track mind."

"You complaining?"

"Darn right. It wasn't nearly enough," she giggled.

Thor turned and frantically pounded the button for the tenth floor, but with the elevator already headed down, it didn't light.

Sarah turned and kissed him. "Have you ever made love while underway, sailor?"

"You mean in an elevator, or on an aircraft carrier?" Thor grinned.

She blushed.

"No, but now that I've found the right crew...."

Sarah was a complete woman, faithful, funny, loving, smart, spontaneous, and flirtatious. As she finished her you-won't-have-to-wait-long kiss, he offered a quick prayer. *God, please don't let this ever end.*

"You know," Sarah said, returning to the subject, "with as much attention as we seem to attract, my parents may actually assure our privacy."

The dock was but a hundred paces from the hotel and casino. Along the way, they spotted a pair of smiling faces lounging in the cockpit of the smaller of the two sailboats.

"Good afternoon," Troy chided them, looking at his watch.

"Shush up, sweetie. Remember *our* honeymoon?"

He reached for her hand, reminiscing.

"You two look positively radiant this morning. I trust the accommodations were to your liking?" she teased.

Accommodations? Thor had no idea what the suite even looked like. But that reminded him of something. "Oops," he said. "I forgot to check out."

"Already done," Troy said. "I took care of it hours ago.

"Thanks. That's nice of you."

"On the contrary, you've made us very happy. Letting us fly you down, seeing this moment, the two of you walking over here, oblivious to the world, brought us more joy than you can imagine." Troy squeezed Leisel's hand. "But this is the last you're gonna see of us until you're ready to go home."

"Home?" Thor repeated, glancing at his bride. "With all that's been going on, I haven't even thought about home. Where are we gonna live?"

"The way things look now, it's going to be 1600 Pennsylvania Avenue," Leisel laughed.

Thor shook his head. "Oh, man, I hope not."

It may have seemed like an odd response for a presidential hopeful but not for this one. His idea of winning was losing. He genuinely wanted the other Save America candidates to prevail; that's why he'd campaigned so diligently. And it looked like the majority were going to win. But just as fervently, he wanted to lose. He hated politics, hated what it did to people, hated what those with the printing presses and microphones did to those in it. Most of all, he hated the message he had to deliver. Islam was so much worse than he had imagined. Revealing its true nature, its history of violence and predilection for terror, was the last assignment he wanted. And then there was his solution. It was unimaginably horrible, and he knew it. The only thing worse was *not* implementing it.

That was why he had ignored the Congressman's vicious attacks on his character. It was why he hadn't responded to the most recent round of negative commercials. They had slimed *him*, not his plan.

Adams had criticized the legacy of the liberal agenda. But the liberals had attacked him, sanctimoniously and hypocritically labeling his analysis "hate speech." It was amazing, really. It never seemed to dawn on them that when they sullied his character because they hated what he had to say, they were actually guilty of the very thing they were falsely attributing to him.

Adams had studied the behavior and knew it would be coming. Power-hungry hypocrites had always risen by projecting their own faults on anyone standing between them and what they coveted. Muhammad was the best example he'd ever found. Yet knowing it was coming was a far cry from liking it. No, this was one election he *wanted* to lose.

"Son," Troy interrupted Thor's thoughts, "can I talk to you for a moment?" He stood and stepped from his boat onto the pier. He motioned for Thor to climb aboard the *Agape*. Sarah joined her mom.

"Thor, the Congressman's negative ads are taking their toll. Do you want me to arrange a news conference before you shove off? If we don't stem the tide, you may lose."

"No."

"I thought you'd say that. I admire you for it." He looked straight into Adams' eyes. "Son, I've found that the things I regret most in life are the things I did *not* do, not the things I've done. While I've got the courage, I want to tell you what you mean to me, to Leisel, to Sarah."

Thor had long since learned that becoming vulnerable, exposing oneself openly to another, took more courage than any battle he had ever fought. He purposely relaxed his body, softened his expression, trying to help Troy relax in turn, encouraging him.

"We never thought Sarah would find love, not like she's found it with you. For that we're grateful. She scared men off, intimidated them. She may be too smart for her own good. She's got more character than Leisel and I combined. She relaxes around you." Troy sat in the *Agape's* luxurious cockpit. He invited Thor to do the same.

"Since the first day I held Sarah in my arms, I've feared losing her, feared some man would take her away, someone who couldn't possibly love her as much as I did. Losing her to you," he said, almost in tears, "was one of the happiest moments of my life."

Thor wanted to say that he wasn't taking her away. He wanted to say that Troy and Leisel were always welcome, but Troy stopped him. He wasn't finished. "I was angry at God when I learned that Leisel was barren. I wanted children. Truthfully, I wanted a son. Thankfully, He didn't return my anger. He gave us Sarah instead, an angel, the greatest joy of our lives. And now, in a way, He *has* brought me a son."

"And a brother."

"Yes. I've enjoyed watching your faith grow. It's transformed you and your mission." He gave him the kind of hug only a father can give. "Son, I love you. Thanks for letting an old man babble. Now, we'll get out of your hair. Go get that bride of yours and have a great time."

Thor put his hand on Troy's shoulder. "I want you to know, sir, I look to you as the father I never had. I don't know if I'll ever be able to measure up, as a husband or as a believer, but I'm proud to be your son. And," he grinned, "I'm downright *thrilled* to be your son-in-law."

While the boys were baring their souls, mother and daughter compared notes. "Now Sarah, don't get mad at me when you see some of the stuff I packed for you. You weren't here, so I did the best I could."

"What did you pack?" she asked apprehensively.

Mom winked. "Honeymoon stuff. I looked through your things trying to figure out what you'd need, what you'd like, really. And well, you've got lots of cute outfits, but not the kind of things a new bride might enjoy having—you know, the kind of stuff a new groom might like his bride to have. Soooo...I went shopping."

"*Mom!*" She said it like it was a multi-syllable world. "What did you buy? What did you *pack?*" Sarah pretended to be mad, but she couldn't wait to look. Leisel saw right through her.

"Fun stuff, sexy stuff." She laughed. "But before you get all flustered, I packed plenty of your regular nightgowns and lingerie. You don't have to wear what I bought for you."

Sarah confessed, "Judging by last night, I'm not sure he's going to let me put anything on. I think he likes my birthday suit just fine. Not that I'm complaining, mind you. But mom," she paused, "I'm so crazy about him, I'm afraid I'm going to scare him away, love him too much, smother him. Is that possible?"

"Maybe. But not with that man," Leisel said as they watched Troy and Thor slowly making their way toward them. Her observation would have applied to either of them.

Leisel leaned over to whisper in her daughter's ear. "Have fun, sweetheart. Experiment if you like, be a little wild at times, take the initiative sometimes. Men love it when you do that—makes 'em feel wanted." A big grin formed on Leisel's face, matching her daughter's. "You might drive him away with too little, but never with too much."

Before climbing aboard the *Serendipity*, Troy motioned for the *Agape's* crew, its captain and cook, a husband-and-wife team, to join them. Introductions were made and the plan was reviewed.

"The waters in the Bahamas are thin, as you know, Admiral. We'll guide you through them, take you to all the best places, fix your meals, clean up, and then bail out, leaving the two of you alone. I know you're an accomplished sailor, sir, so just think of us as your crew."

It was the best of all worlds, Thor recognized. Paradise.

✡ ✝ ☾

"CAN YOU IMAGINE having your life depend on this stuff?"

"No way. I'm not gonna have any skin left by the time we're done."

"At least yours fits—sort of," he laughed. The smallest of the three Jews eyed his pals. They looked ridiculous. "You could fit two of me in this thing. I look like one of those wrinkly dogs. What do they call them?"

"Ugly."

SFG suits draped loosely around their undersized bodies, the Temple Faithful trio were preparing for God's mission. It was their own private *Jihad*, not against a people, but against a symbol.

More bookworms than combatants, the devout Jews struggled with their equipment. Their packs were loaded with twenty kilos of C-12 and a quarter that amount in heavy steel balls. They were designed to pulverize the large rectangular columns supporting the Dome of the Rock.

With unbalanced loads now strapped on their backs, it was all they could do to stand erect. Even without guns, ammunition, and water, the stripped-down SFGs tipped the scales at nearly forty pounds. Between suits and explosives, each beast of burden was condemned to carry nearly twice that amount.

"Good *grief*, this is heavy," one of the Jews complained.

"Hey, could you give me a hand?" another asked, trying to adjust the straps.

Although they were now in the best shape of their lives, it wasn't enough. Religious about their training, the Temple Faithful trio had met at the gym every afternoon since they had accepted the assignment. They had run five miles together each morning, that is, except Saturday. The Sabbath was holy.

Between pumping iron and pounding pavement, they had lunched each day at their favorite overlook. The devout Jews had discovered a landing at the top of some stairs about two hundred meters southwest of the Western Wall—the Wailing Wall. From this vantage point, they could see the thing that stirred them most, the foundation of the Jewish Temple Mount. They could also see, rising above it, the bilious blue and gold shrine, the Muslim Dome of the Rock—the object they loathed most in the world. The view inspired them, giving them strength.

Now, just after eleven on Sunday evening, they were as ready as they would ever be. Soon, a festering thorn would be removed from their side, from God's side. The Messiah would be delayed no longer.

Under their military garb, the three Jews had prepared themselves for battle. Yarmulke on top, phylactery in front, ritual threads down their sides, they looked plenty silly inside and out but not in their eyes.

Standing for a final prayer, they faced the Wall, barely visible from where they were standing. They could just make it out. The Faithful were in the Jewish quarter of the Old City. Praying, they began to bob, bending at the waist. It looked nauseating, especially since they were all reading a prepared prayer, as was their custom. The devout never prayed spontaneously to God. Only prayers written by learned men and approved by exalted rabbis were considered acceptable.

Ready at last, they hugged one another, kissing their companions on the cheek. Then they donned their helmets, tucked in their beards, and lowered their visors. Setting their SFGs to midnight black, they disappeared into the night.

Aymen Halaweh had been stationed at the gate leading to the Temple Mount. He was prepared to let the men pass. He knew that Talib Ali was a hundred meters away, near the doorway of the shrine, a shrine that had been locked much earlier in the day. As prestigious and devoted Muslims, they had managed to gain control of these important passages.

Though neither man knew it, they were not alone. Mamdouh Salim was on duty too—and close by. He had received his marching orders from the former Chairman of Fatah, now celebrated martyr, Yasman Alafat. President Salim was monitoring the proceedings from a notebook PC, connected via the Internet. Stationed in the Arab quarter, he had the best view of all.

Hoping that the suits might one day prove useful, Halaweh had broken the code sometime back. In his spare time he had programmed the SFG computers so that every image, every bit of data, could be seen remotely at the click of a mouse.

From the comfort of his private overlook, the President watched the Israelis bump Aymen as they made their way through the open gate. Halaweh, who hadn't seen them coming, nearly jumped out of his skin as they passed. Salim heard the men giggling, enjoying the fact that they were nearly invisible. He had clicked through the menu of visual images and data displays, discovering that he liked the enhanced light mode with image stabilization best.

For the new President, time was passing all too quickly. On his screen he could see the Jews struggling to walk up a long flight of stone steps. He heard their labored breathing. There was no chatter. These were men on a mission. They traveled through a series of open arches and into the large courtyard west of the Dome. Mamdouh smiled as he watched them move with stealth and haste across the last hundred meters of open space between them and their target.

In the helmet-cam view, Mamdouh Salim saw Talib Ali leaning against one of the red marble columns near the shrine's entrance. Ali's hand was over his eyes like the bill of a cap. He was trying to shield them from the glare of the spotlights that were illuminating the dome itself. Talib had no idea that the Temple Faithful were almost close enough to touch. Looking at his monitor, President Salim saw them pass between a pair of green marble columns to Ali's right.

Startled as the Jews opened the door, Talib Ali jumped back. Not trusting them, he wanted to keep an eye on their progress, although hints and shadows were all he could see. The devout Ali struggled to follow the sound of the trio's footsteps. From what he could tell, one of the Jews had turned right. He was walking across the red and gold octagonal hallway. The others veered left through the Dome's inner passage.

Ali was concerned. He wanted to be certain that the shrine's surveillance cameras caught the IDF insignias on the Jewish uniforms. The whole charade was being played out for that very reason.

Talib cupped both hands to his ears. Listening carefully, he thought he heard the first pack, then another, being set down on the floor. He prayed to Allah for guidance, then reached over to the light switch, feeling his way to just the right one. As he heard what he thought was the sound of the third pack being dropped, he flipped up the switch, flooding the interior of the giant shrine.

In the enhanced light mode, the visors on the Temple Faithful's SFGs were a whiteout. Each man staggered, his senses overwhelmed. Believing that the source of illumination had come from inside the dome, they spun around and faced the open area in the center of the shrine, raising their visors as they turned. The three men stared at the rocky top of Mount Moriah. What looked to be the Holy of Holies lay in front of them, carved into the stone. Their hearts raced; their eyes widened.

Then their world ended.

President Mamdouh Salim clicked his mouse three times, triggering the bombs. It was all over in an instant.

Aymen Halaweh went airborne, blown off his feet by the percussion. The sound was deafening, haunting, echoing as it did off of the graves standing guard on the Mount of Olives.

An eerie darkness followed. The light that had reflected off the golden dome a moment before had been extinguished. Now there was a void. No light, no dome. Instead, a towering plume of dust and debris rose from the center of the Temple Mount. With blood flooding into one eye and fragments of the shattered shrine obscuring the other, Halaweh struggled to see what had happened. As his vision grew accustomed to the dim ambient light of the surrounding city, he could see enough to know he was in serious trouble.

The young Palestinian engineer was aghast. This couldn't be. He had disabled the Israelis' triggers. The Jews were supposed to walk in, get noticed, drop their packs, and run for their lives. Sure, they would vainly press their triggers as they cleared the shrine, but nothing was supposed to happen.

Running, staggering, hobbling toward what had just moments before been the third holiest site in the entire Muslim world, Aymen fell to his knees in desperation. The weight of the world was on his shoulders. What had he done? He raised his hands to his face in shame and covered his eyes. "Oh, Allah, forgive me!" he cried.

✡ ✝ ☪

THE ADMIRAL was a happy man. Heading out of the channel, he had changed into a bathing suit, as had Sarah. She leaned up against him, cuddling in his arms. The sun was warm, as was the air and water. A stiff breeze had the *Agape* keeled over.

The captain's wife brought the pair a drink, frothy iced piña coladas. A reggae CD complemented the mood. Thor willed it to last but sensed it wouldn't. Nothing this good ever does.

The captain reached down and grasped his binoculars in one hand, holding the wheel in the other. His bright countenance soured. "I don't believe it. Those sorry sacks couldn't even make it out of the channel without running aground." He spoke as if he knew them.

Thor asked for the binoculars. Adjusting them for his face, he eyed the forty-five-foot sailing vessel, the *Sacred Seas*, marooned on a sandbar. Her crew was frantically trying to get the attention of more competent sailors. Anyone.

"Good grief," the captain moaned, shaking his head.

"You know them?" Thor asked.

"Not really. Well, sort of. They've been here the better part of two weeks. Bad news bears. Rude, obnoxious, obviously incompetent. They've made fools of themselves."

"Are we going to give them a hand?" It was the honorable thing to do.

"Sure," the captain answered. "Maybe they'll leave and never come back. Here, take the wheel. Steer a heading of two fifteen. I'll start the engine and have you bring her up into the wind. We'll lower sails, motor over to the edge of the channel, and bring 'em a line. I suppose it would be too much to ask for them to have one." The captain was clearly disgusted. "A couple of jackasses, those two."

Atta and Riza were waving their arms frantically, jumping up and down. It was hard to tell if they were screaming at each other or at the crews of other vessels, most which were doing their level best to ignore the fiasco.

Sails down, towline out, the captain said, "Admiral, I'll keep us on the edge of the channel if you'll lower the dingy."

Thor eyed the davit. It looked standard enough, but it was way too much of a hassle for a thirty-second ride. "Shoot, cap, I'll just swim the line over." He tied the bitter end off, throwing the loop into the water, stretching it out in the direction of motionless commotion.

"Be careful, sir. Nobody around here is sure if those boys have had their rabies shots. 'Course, since they're Arabs, maybe they'd prefer *rabbi* shots—you know, inoculation against Jews...." The captain started to laugh, but caught himself. Suddenly, he was embarrassed, recognizing his unfair generalization. Just because they looked like terrorists, spoke like terrorists, and acted like terrorists, didn't mean they *were* terrorists. *Did it?*

"They look more confused than vicious," Adams returned, jumping into the water. It was as warm as the air, about bathtub temperature. Swimming toward the loop, the SEAL expertly fastened it around his body, covering the remaining distance quickly. He handed the line to the nearest crewman. The Admiral flinched as they began to babble in Arabic. The last time he'd heard such sounds, he was having tea with terrorists.

Then he relaxed, in sympathy with their plight. These poor guys had no idea what to do with the line. Riza was holding it as if it were a snake, ready to bite him. Atta was staring wide-eyed at the Admiral. He looked like he'd already been bitten.

With his honeymoon temporarily marooned, Thor didn't have time for such nonsense. He took matters into his own hands. Swimming to the stern of the *Sacred Sea,* he climbed aboard. Riza tossed him the line, stumbling back as he did. Atta cowered, scared half to death. Looking at them quizzically, the Admiral simply walked the line to the bow of their vessel, tied it off, and motioned to the *Agape*. Slowly removing the slack, the captain expertly positioned his craft.

A quick tug was all it took. The *Sacred Sea* was free, bobbing peacefully in the channel, no harm done. The Admiral loosened the line, coiling up his end. He flung it toward the *Agape* before turning to the men he had just saved. They didn't look the least bit appreciative. They appeared more frightened than relieved. Thor shrugged his shoulders and muttered, "You're welcome," under his breath. The deed done, he jumped back into the water, etching the scene into his mind. His gut told him he hadn't seen the last of these two.

Free at last of all earthly distractions, the newlyweds felt the joy of having the wind at their backs. As they arrived at their private cove, the sun was dipping into the sea, making it come alive, celebrate, dance. It was as if it had all been choreographed by the great Celestial Playwright. The cove was totally secluded, surrounded by virginal white sand. The anchor was set and dinner was served. The lingering hues of the setting sun provided the ambient light, gracing the clouds nearest the western horizon.

Dining *al fresco*, they enjoyed an excellent chicken *cordon bleu* and an altogether too expensive bottle of French champagne. The dishes were cleared and the crew departed. They were alone again. The Admiral's heart raced. Sarah's skin tingled.

"Decisions, decisions," Thor said just loud enough for his bride to hear. "Should we go for a swim, then make love, or make love, then swim?"

"I know all you SEAL types love to swim, but I trust the other option hasn't grown so old-married-couple it's on par with *swimming*." She crossed her arms over her body, teasing him, like she wasn't interested. She had dressed for dinner—a sundress that was a bit short on fabric. Red, it was almost large enough to attract a bull's attention with its plunging necklines front and back. It had certainly attracted Thor's attention.

"C'mere, you."

"Ooh, what did you have in mind, sailor?" She wiggled her shoulder, letting one on the straps fall. "I seem to be having trouble keeping this thing on. Could you help me with it?" Sarah shot him a flirtatious wink. Thor wasn't much help. Seconds later Mrs. Adams was wearing little more than a satisfied smile.

Making love under the stars, warm breeze caressing their bodies, was the stuff of dreams. They never quite seemed to finish. Whenever one would stop to catch a breath, the other would rise to the occasion. By the time they were ready for their swim, they had no idea what time it was.

Lounging in his arms, Sarah asked, "Is this going to happen every time I suggest you might be bored with me?"

"Yes," he said, kissing her hair.

"In that case, remind me to complain more often."

As the lateness of today passed into the first moments of tomorrow, everything seemed to glow. A full moon washed the *Agape* in its majestic light. Then it happened. Almost magically, the sea beneath them came alive. Beneath the ripples, iridescent and glowing, the water was afire with a greenish-blue flame. Sea fire it's called, the aurora borealis of the deep blue, the ocean's Monet. It was as if God was happy for them, blessing their union, celebrating what he was—love.

As nature's light show faded, taking its curtain call, the two lovers looked heavenward, staring into the vastness of space. They were leaning against the soft cushions of the yacht's open cockpit.

Sarah went below and slipped into one of the little nothings mom had packed for such an occasion. Pawing through Thor's things before returning topside, she discovered just how busy Leisel had been. Silk boxers, made by *Hermes* in France no less, were neatly folded off to the side. She found a pair that coordinated with her blue teddy and brought it up, twirling them around on her finger.

Thor took another sip of *Monet Chandon*. There were things, he had discovered, that the French did right.

As their side of the earth raced into the darkness of space, another of nature's shows began to entertain the newlyweds. Shooting stars streaked across the sky in ever-increasing numbers.

"There's one," Sarah said pointing excitedly to her left.

"Did you make a wish?" he asked.

"Didn't have to. All of mine have already come true."

"Sarah?"

"Yes, sweetheart."

"Can we talk about something serious?"

"Sure. What?" she inquired, still surveying God's handiwork.

"I'm worried."

"About subduing the warlords?"

"Well, not exactly. Properly supported, we'll do fine. Our boys will prevail. Insecure bullies are the same the world over. They'll cower and run. They always do."

"What is it, then?" she asked. Another spectacular trail of light marched across the sky.

"Remember sitting around the table in Jerusalem?"

"The morning after?" The previous day had been one to remember.

"Yes, the day we outed the Prophet of Doom."

"You started us off by saying you already knew the answer. Like it had come to you during the meeting at the Knesset."

"That's right. I was convinced Muslims could be constrained the same way Reagan defanged Communists. He exposed them for what they really were. After reviving our economy, he outproduced them militarily. The Soviet Union imploded. Peace followed."

"But that won't work on these boys," Sarah knew. She hadn't been an intelligence officer for nothing—or an economist for that matter. "Exposing a warlike religious doctrine is much more difficult than exposing a warlike political doctrine."

Sarah shifted in his arms. "We have an even bigger problem economically. Reagan, in essence, bankrupted the old Soviet Union. We can't do that with Islamic regimes. They float on oil. The Soviets had some, but not nearly what these thugs possess, especially per capita. We're dependent on it, and they know it. Here's the rub: economic sanctions that restrict the flow of oil will paralyze *our* economy, but sanctions that allow it to flow will fail. Just a pinprick."

Her words were reasoned. The advice was wise. Her appearance, however, was another matter. Thor found it hard to look at her and think at the same time.

"And sweetie, there's one more thing. Mutually Assured Destruction, MAD. It worked with the Russians because they *weren't*—mad. Muslims are. They're crazy as bedbugs, and the closer they get to Muhammad, the nuttier they act. If they get their hands on nukes, they'll use 'em in a New

York minute, thinking paradise is their reward. Sorry, dear. You need to kill this viper before it kills us. Just calling it a snake won't do."

Thor loved the way Sarah felt in his arms. Even the way her hair tickled his neck brought him pleasure. He was willing to talk about most anything to prolong the moment. "I think I know how to ratchet up the stakes on these bad boys—give them pause, so to speak."

"I'll bite. How?"

"Rather than returning the bodies of suicide bombers to their families so that the lunatics can parade them around like martyrs, I'd declare them the property of the state. The next one gets scraped up with a spatula and fed to pigs. Muslims think swine are so unclean they'd be sent to the realm of flaming faggots instead of to the garden of black-eyed virgins. Take lots of pictures and let 'em know a similar fate awaits them all. Then, if they continue killing people, break out the para-porkers—swine in chutes."

Sarah giggled as Thor detailed his irreverent plan.

"Drop them on their biggest mosques. To quote Yacob, 'When you come to a pork in the road, take it.'"

"You're not serious, are you?" She looked at him, brows raised.

"I'll never tell. But I will tell 'em this. If they blow up one more American building, I'll blow up the Ka'aba. And if they nuke us, like Isaac thinks they will, Mecca will 'roast in Hell Fire'." He squeezed her tight. "You know the next attack is going to be a missile of some sort, don't you?"

"Psalm 91 again. Two by pestilence, one small, one large, followed by arrows by day." She eyed another shooting star. "You really believe God gave you that verse, don't you?"

"Yeah. In fact I'm counting on him protecting us. He promised." Thor rolled over onto his side so that he could look at his bride. "By the way," he said, "how'd you vote?"

They had both voted absentee, knowing they would be otherwise involved come Election Day.

"Are you asking who I voted for, you or the other guy, Congressman what's-his-name?" It was a pretty good question, actually. Sarah knew he didn't want to be president. "Not telling," she giggled.

"Are you always going to be this much trouble?"

"I get cranky when I don't get enough loving."

✡   ☦   ☾

THE SPECIAL ELECTION was a real nail biter. As usual, negative ads had had a negative impact. Americans knew more, but that was a far cry from acting differently. The constant assault on the Admiral's character had taken its toll. He'd been labeled a hater, a warmonger, and a racist. The nicest things the left had to say about him were that he was out of touch, an extremist, a right-wing hawk, someone ill prepared to govern.

The horrific images of tear-smeared faces wailing at the destruction of the Holy Shrine didn't help. Muslims the world over were calling for war—a war to end all wars—a war to end all *Jews*. Israel was on the defensive, as was its most stalwart ally, albeit in absentia—one Admiral Thurston Adams.

But there was some good news. Tuesday's elections had proved that provided with an intelligent choice, Americans would make the right choice. Most every candidate that had signed the Plan to Save America and the Plan to End Terror had prevailed. Their victories were of epic proportions—landslides demanding change. America and the world would soon be a freer, more productive, and safer place to live.

Thor's agenda, just as he had hoped, had won universal acclaim. But he himself had lost—by the smallest of margins. As a result, he was condemned to enduring four years in a fishbowl, 1600 Pennsylvania Avenue, Washington, D.C.

But there was a bright side. At least he wouldn't have to scrounge for a place to live, and he wouldn't have to borrow his father-in-law's airplane anymore.

✡   ✝   ☪

THE SIGHT OF F18 HORNETS off the wing was all too common for Thor, but not for Troy. And while the fighters looked menacing, the real deterrent came from what was flying behind them—a Lockheed C-130 Hercules, with the AC-U modifications. Its 28mm gun was good, the 40mm cannon was better, but for best it was hard to beat the 105mm howitzer mounted on the belly. Known as a Spectre Gunship, it was hardly lean, but it was definitely a mean fighting machine.

The Hornets were Navy. They had accompanied the Admiral everywhere he had gone, including his honeymoon. In that he wasn't a major party candidate, the air cover had been unofficial. The F-18s were on training missions, missions that just happened to coincide with the good Admiral's itinerary. How fortuitous.

The big turbine-powered gunship was a bird of a different color. It was

Air Force, and thus didn't normally run cover for Admirals, and never for wannabe presidents. But this Admiral was different. He was now president-elect of the United States, a single "So help me God" away from being Commander-in-Chief. With no current president, sitting, lame, acting, or otherwise, Adams was *de facto* the most powerful man in the world.

Unlike some who had served before him, almost-President Adams appreciated the value of overkill. The enormous four-engine, high-wing, bulbous-nose turboprop had a wingspan two and a half times that of the Pilatus it was tailing. And when it came to guns and payload, the PC-12/45 wasn't even in the same league as the AC-130U. It wasn't called Hercules for nothing.

The question was, would all of this foreshadow what was to come?

25

INTO THE SUNSET

The week had passed all too quickly. While they missed Mary, they could have stayed in the warm Bahamian waters forever.

The Adamses had splashed the fishes aboard wave runners, peered at them through scuba diving masks, and even eaten one or two during candle-lit dinners. Midnight skinny-dips off the *Agape*, midday plunges into Thunderball Cave, late morning picnics on deserted white-sand beaches, and early afternoon fishing excursions had filled their days. Love had consumed their nights.

But now, back home in Troy's study, it was time to go to work. Thor had another speech to write, this time an acceptance speech, his inaugural address. He shook his head. If he hadn't lived through it, he wouldn't have believed it himself.

At seven-thirty in Maryland, it was two-thirty in Jerusalem. This was the first chance the President-elect had had to check in with his old friend and new Knesset Member. "Isaac, tell me you didn't do it."

"I know what it looks like, but it wasn't us, I swear—at least it wasn't the Israeli government."

"But the uniforms! They looked exactly like your SFGs."

"Yeah, I saw the film too. Three of them. And the men were Jews; there's no getting around it. We've run the bombers' DNA. We've also checked their photos. Just before the blast, all three raised their visors. It was like they wanted to be seen," Isaac reported. "They were members of something called the Temple Faithful. They tried this stunt once before, ten years ago."

"Well, they sure didn't do Israel any favors, Isaac. The world is in no mood to listen to us now."

"I'm going to find out what really happened, my friend—and why. Something's fishy."

"Fishy?"

"Yeah. Doesn't smell right. Like where did these religious sorts get

Special Forces Gear? For that matter, why would they wear them? Where did they get hold of sixty kilos of C-12? How did they get onto the Mount? Jews are forbidden. If they hadn't been Jews, I'd swear it was an inside job. And tell me, why did the lights go on just before the blast? And why three bombers? There are—were—four main support columns holding up the dome. I've got more questions than answers."

"Keep me posted, will ya? Oh, and Isaac, I almost forgot. Thanks for coming. Thank all the guys for us. It was great to see you out of uniform."

"Are you kidding? We wouldn't have missed Sarah's wedding for the world. It's a wonder she married such a loser."

"Loser? Yeah, right. I couldn't even lose an election."

✡   ✝   ☾

THE WOUNDS to Aymen Halaweh's flesh would heal. His spirit was another matter. He had been shocked to learn that his own people had destroyed the Holy Shrine. Worse, it had been no accident.

Mamdouh Salim cut his protest off cold. "Forget it. The Dome was a political symbol, one built to annoy Jews. We used it as it was intended."

"No!" Aymen pleaded. "The Holy Shrine commemorated the Prophet's Night's Journey. His voyage to heaven began there."

President Salim placed a patronizing hand on the young man's shoulder. "Son, you don't *believe* that crap. Come on. You're a bright boy."

He looked him in the eye. "Ask yourself, why would the Prophet have to come here to the temple of the hated Jews to get to heaven? He was in Mecca, at the *Ka'aba*, for cryin' out loud."

Aymen's jaw dropped. He was speechless.

"Hey, I haven't memorized this stuff, but I know the Qur'an says that the big-eyed virgins are hangin' out in the Garden of Eden. This isn't the right direction, and you don't go up to get there. Islam's a farce, pal."

Aymen's brows raised in astonishment. Like a retreating tide, President Salim ripped the sand from beneath his feet, undermining the very foundation of his faith.

"That garbage is for the masses. Helps us keep them in line. But nobody on top actually buys into it. Open your eyes, boy."

Aymen's were. Wide open.

"Why do you think the Princes, the Ayatollahs, and the Sultans are such perverted bastards? Prostitutes, bestiality, gluttony—they do it all. Figure it out: they're not religious. Islam is for the sheep, not the shepherds.

Start living, kid."

"But what about Talib Ali?" Amen snarled. "You killed him. Why didn't you tell me? You planned to blow up the Dome all along!"

Mamdouh's gaze turned to ice. "You couldn't handle the truth. Ali's dead." Salim glared menacingly. "I can arrange for you to join him. Want to be a martyr, boy?"

The question wasn't rhetorical. The young and formerly naïve Halaweh could see it in Salim's cold, black eyes. It was the same look that had come over Kahn at the crucifixions. Aymen's shoulders dropped. Unable to speak, unable to look at his leader, he retreated clumsily from the room.

✡   ✞   ☾

"ALL AROUND THE GLOBE, political and religious leaders alike are pleading with President-elect Thurston Adams to abandon his plan for dealing with the Arab world." Trixi Lightheart was sitting tall in the saddle. Though less-than-idealistic behavior had gotten her into this position, she was now an ideologue—spewing the politically correct agenda with an evangelist's zeal. She knew the big networks were looking for anchors.

"Congressman Macon told his supporters today, 'In light of the wanton destruction of the Dome of the Rock by fundamentalist Jews, it's time to rein in the radicals. There is no room in a peace-loving world for religious zealots,' he said. 'We need to come together as a global community. The Admiral's criticism of Islam's Prophet is hateful, racist, and intollerant. His behavior has led us to the brink of war."

He had as much as said that freedom of speech was only for him and his supporters. "Hate speech," defined as anything they disagreed with, had to be silenced, muzzled, before the "unenlightened" hurt someone. Yet for the moment, the left was on the defensive, reeling, having been challenged and defeated at the polls by Thurston Adams and his coalition.

So following the commercial break, Trixi Lightheart wound herself up—for the good of the cause. "President-elect Adams' plan, many are now saying, is far too expensive and risky. Moreover, Islamic clerics worldwide are condemning the Admiral's attacks on their religion, saying that they are racially motivated and unjust. The Ayatolla has issued a *fatwa* on him for his inflammatory criticisms of the Prophet Muhammad. All moderate Arab leaders are saying that the *late* President's proposals, granting the Palestinians statehood and removing all U.S. presence from Islamic Holy Lands, is the only peaceful solution to the present crisis.

German and French leaders are objecting to calling Muslims terrorists, as the Admiral has done. The E.U. issued a statement condemning the Admiral's unilateral strategy and rejected the notion they were coddling terrorists. They say that by blowing up the Dome of the Rock, the Jews have shown that *they* are the real terrorists."

✡   ✝   ☾

FOR THOR ADAMS, watching the news was about as much fun as seeing his buddies crucified. No amount of fact, reason, or meticulous explanation ever seemed to quell their rhetoric. They saw the world one way; he saw it another.

"Truth is dead," Thor grumbled. "If it wasn't for talk-show hosts like Rush Limbaugh and Sean Hannity, America would be lost." The Admiral walked over to Troy's TV and turned it off. If he'd had a gun, he might have shot it, proving once and for all that he was a hawk.

"We have met the enemy, and he is us," Thor moaned. "Will these deceptions ever end?"

Sarah agreed. "Who would have thought that subduing the Islamic warlords was going to be easier than battling our own media. Good grief! You'd think we were responsible for what Muhammad did and said, for the legacy of Islam. Why get mad at us? We're just messengers."

"Yeah. Their emperor's got no clothes. Rocky and Hoodwinker are a farce. Islam is lunacy—literally. It's as obvious as the moon is different from the sun."

"Actually, Thor, all we're doing is what the Qur'an said to do, compare scriptures: 'Judge between them in the light of what has been revealed by God.' Well, from what I can tell, God revealed that the Qur'an is a piece of garbage. I read it again." She thumbed through her copy. It was covered with notes, a code of some sort. "Allah's primary theme is that everyone is 'mocking' Mo, 'scoffing,' and 'laughing' at him because they think what he's saying is ridiculous. Mo is called a 'liar' and a 'magician'. It's said he's 'possessed by devils', that he's just a 'crazy plagiarizing poet'. They call him a 'sorcerer', a 'lunatic', a 'farfetched forger', a 'fool', a 'specious pretender,' and 'deceitful'—in essence, a hoodwinker."

"I love you, and you're easily the smartest woman I have ever known, but there's no way that's all in the Qur'an.

Sarah patted him on the head and turned to the 38th surah. "'The unbelievers said: "He is a *deceiving sorcerer*, turning many gods into one deity."

"There must be a motive behind the Qur'an. It is surely a fabrication."''''" She flipped back one. "'They *laugh* at the Qur'an and say, "Should we abandon our gods for the sake of an *insane poet?*'''''"

She shot Thor a look, as she moved back a few more pages. "'Allah has not sent down anything. You are only speaking *lies*.' They rejoined, 'We feel you augur ill. If you do not desist, we shall stone you to death, and inflict a grievous punishment on you.' The Messenger responded, saying, 'The augury is within your own selves.'"

"Augury, huh?"

Sarah read on. "'When Our clear revelations are read out to them, they say, "This is only a man who wants to turn you away from what your fathers used to worship. This is nothing but a fabricated *lie*. This is nothing but pure *sorcery*."' Then, 'Those who do not believe, say, "Indeed, our fathers have been promised this before. The Qur'an is nothing but earlier peoples' *lore*."' In other words, plagiarism—stolen from Jewish oral traditions. 'These are *fables* of antiquity which he has reinvented.'

"'What sort of Prophet is this?' 'Why was no angel sent to him?' Then, from surah 21, 'Yet they say: "These are only confused dreams. He has invented them. Let him therefore bring a miracle to us as the earlier prophets did."'" Sarah looked over at Thor. "That no-miracle thing really burnt Mo's britches. At least twenty times in the Qur'an, his critics accuse him of being the only Prophet who couldn't do a miracle."

"Who said he couldn't do miracles? He made three Jewish tribes vanish without a trace."

"Yeah," Sarah laughed. "And he made blind men dumb." She read from surah 11. "'They say of the Prophet, "He has *forged* the Qur'an."' From the tenth, 'We find you full of *folly* and a liar to boot.' Then from the ninth surah, 'There are some among them who talk ill of the Prophet.' 'For those who offend Allah's Apostle there is a painful punishment. Have they not realized that anyone who opposes Allah and His Prophet will abide in hell forever?'"

"I will never doubt you again."

"That's good, because I marked over 400 of these I could have read to you. To give you an idea of Allah's propensity for repeating himself, three Bible stories appear twenty times each. Pharaoh gets pummeled because he didn't listen to Moses, everybody drowns because they didn't listen to Noah, and the townsfolk get scorched because they didn't heed Lot. Do you see a pattern here?"

"Yeah. None of these stories are about messengers, yet Mo twists them to scare his followers into submission. So how does Prophet-Man respond to his critics? I don't suppose he tells them he loves them, forgives them, and is willing to lay down his life to save them."

"No, no, no, no, no. Mo calls his critics liars, losers, evil, vile, lost, deaf, dumb, blind, dead, vain, conceited, shameful, sinful, slime, subversive, slanderers, hypocrites, insane, wicked, ignoramuses, conspirators, deceivers, malicious, oblivious annoyances. When he gets really miffed, he calls them mischief mongers, faggots, apes, nail biters, donkeys, and tongue twisters. But they're in great company. He condemns the deity of Christ and his message more than fifty times. He even says that Jesus was not crucified, but twice says Pharaoh threatened to crucify Moses, a thousand years before crucifixion was invented."

"A doctrine of death—Good grief."

"Grief, yes. Good, no. Allah was fixated on pain and suffering. I lost track, but there must be a *thousand* places in which Muhammad and his pet rock speak of hell, demons, and punishment in the Qur'an. It's an average of ten times per surah. Let me give you an example. 'Allah cursed the infidels and prepared a blazing fire for them.' Remember, in Qur'an 5:72 Allah defined infidels as Christians. 'They will live in it forever and will find no savior.' 'That day their faces will be turned on the fire as on a spit.' "'O Allah," Muhammad pleaded, "give them a double punishment and put a grievous curse upon them."' "'We have prepared Hell for the hospitality of the infidels.""'

"'We', as is in Allah, is providing this hospitality, right?"

"Yeah, according to Islam, but not according to Sarah. Y'see, Allah only lived in the mind of Muhammad. Allah is dumb as a stone 'cause, well, he *is* a stone. That's why Mo claims he says stuff like, 'Their requital will be Hell, because they disbelieved and mocked My signs and My Messenger.' There *were* no signs: no miracles, no prophecies, *nada*. And the Qur'an is easily the *worst* book ever written by most any criterion."

"And sweetness," she said. "In case you were wondering what hell is like, let me share how Allah describes it. 'There will be boiling water for them, and cold, clammy, fetid drink to taste, and other similar torments. They will roast in the fire.' 'They will wear iron collars and chains around their necks, they will be dragged through boiling water, and then burnt in the fire.' 'The food of sinners in Hell is like pitch. It will fume in the belly, as does boiling water,' according to Allah 'cutting their intestines to shreds.' 'Seize him and drag him into the depths of Hell, then pour over his head the torment of scalding water. Taste it,' Allah says. And just in case you wanted to know, 'The fire of Hell is kindled by Allah himself.'"

"How many times did you say Allah talks about demons, hell, and punishment?"

"I stopped counting at around *a thousand*. But to be fair, he does say,

'Allah is merciful and kind right after he tells Muslims he wants us to roast in hell. And he ought to know because hell's demons *love* the Qur'an. In 46:29, it says: 'We,' again as in the schizophrenic Allah, 'turned a company of jinns,' those are demons, 'toward Muhammad to listen to the Qur'an. They arrived when it was being recited, and said, "We have listened to a book which has come down after Moses confirming what was sent down before it showing the way to the truth and a path that is straight."'"

"Yeah. Straight to hell." Thor didn't know whether to laugh or cry. "While I'm convinced Satan didn't write it, I'm not surprised he likes it. It's right up his alley."

"It gets worse, love. Allah has several surahs dedicated to war, fighting, killing, booty, terror, and martyrdom. In them he says, 'If you meet them in battle, inflict on them such a defeat as would be a lesson for those who would come after them.' As you know, he tells them to break treaties, and he specifically says that treaties with non-Muslims are not binding on his followers. He even says that when confronted by unbelievers, Muslims are to say 'peace'. Muhammad says, 'They will find out soon enough'—what we're really all about is the implication.

"He speaks of killer angels 'drawing away people's souls, striking their faces and their backs, crying out, "Taste the torment of burning."' 'O Prophet, urge the faithful to fight.' Allah begins one of the War Manifesto surahs saying, 'If they ask you of the benefits of accruing the spoils of war, tell them, "The benefits belong to Allah and His Messenger."' Allah said, 'Wipe the infidels out to the last.' So no Muslim would be confused, in 8:60 Muhammad claimed Allah said, 'Prepare against the infidels whatever arms and cavalry you can muster, that you may strike terror in the hearts of the enemies of God.'"

"We went into this mess expecting to find some small flaw in Islam that caused radicals to corrupt their religion and turn violent. But it's just not true, no matter how many people say it. Islam *itself* is the problem."

"The historical facts, their own scriptures, all agree." Sarah breathed deeply. It saddened her. "The more Muslims learn about their Prophet, the more violent they become. The whole thing reeks."

"That's obvious, but listening to the media, you'd think *we* were the terrorists. It's so perverse." Thor shook his head. "It's little wonder so few decent people run for office. Now I know why nobody speaks out. By the time these buffoons get through mauling my character, even *you* won't like me."

Sarah couldn't help herself and burst out laughing. Her love was unconditional. Besides, she knew him; his critics didn't. To assail him they had to invent scandals, contrive motivations, cast aspersions onto him that mirrored their faults, not his.

Sitting in her mother's companion chair, Sarah said, "Come here."

The most powerful man on earth did as he was told.

"On your knees," she ordered, hitting the floor as well.

"Father, help us forgive those who have wronged us, those who have lied about us." With her eyes closed, she continued to pray just loud enough to be heard. "Lord, we pray for our enemies, for those who despise us, for those who wish to kill us for exposing them. Not that they'll get their wish," she chuckled, "but that you'll soften their hearts. Let them know that all we want is for them to know the truth—to be free from the deception that kindles their hatreds. Call out to them in love. It is the only thing that can extinguish their rage."

With his head bowed, Thor said, "God, please give us your wisdom, so we can tell right from wrong; your courage, so we'll do what's right; your love, so we'll do it for the right reasons; your faith, so we'll stay the course; and your protection, so that we might survive until this job is done. Let our enemies know we love them, in spite of what they've done. We pray this in your son's name. Amen."

✡   ✝   ☪

AYMEN'S WORLD was upside down. It was in no better condition than the dome he'd helped topple. All his life he'd been told—sold—the same story. The Palestinian leadership, the clerics in the mosques and madrases, the beautiful people in the media, had all sworn that Allah was God and that Muhammad was his messenger. They had told him that Jews were responsible for his problems and that America was the Great Satan. Every insult, every injury, was their fault. They were God haters, baby killers. They were infidels worthy of death.

He had just mortally wounded his own shrine, yet his brothers were celebrating the damage it had wrongly done the Jews. Worse, he was complicit in the murder of his own colleague, and no one seemed to care. He had nailed men to crosses his first day on the job. He had helped poison great cities, inventing the equipment to spew hideous spores of death into the air. He had crafted elaborate electronic triggers to detonate nuclear bombs, and launching devices to assure that they would kill more people than could be imagined. For the first time, he thought about his victims. Were they infidels or innocents? Were they evil, or was he?

Aymen slumped in his chair. He was all alone; the lights were out, the curtains drawn. He leaned forward, letting his head fall. Tears welled up in his eyes. The pain was unbearable. He was tormented. His heart, mind, and soul were fighting a holy war.

Truth! He had to know the truth. But where would he find it? Not from the media, not the clerics, not his leaders—they had all deceived him. *But why?* The question rang in his head like a bell, pounding, clanging relentlessly. *Why?* Aymen shook uncontrollably, alone in the darkness of his cave-like dwelling. Panic washed over him. He began sweating profusely. *Why?* An evil spirit seemed to be pressing upon him, squeezing the life out of him. *Suicide! Yes.* That was the only way out. He would take his own life—just as he had taken the lives of others. Inspired yet quivering, walking yet stumbling, certain yet unsure, he searched for a weapon.

Aymen flung every cupboard open, pulled out every drawer, throwing their contents onto the floor. Tears poured from his eyes. In anguish, his heart pleaded for mercy, for an end to the torment. But it was all for naught. The knives were too dull. He didn't have pills, nor did he possess a gun. In frustration, he fell to the floor. "God, *why?*" he screamed.

Curled into a fetal ball, he fell silent. He could hear his own breathing, feel his heartbeat. Then, out of the stillness, he heard a voice. Soft. Clear. Almost a whisper. "I love you."

He spun around, but there was no one. In the darkness, all he saw was his notebook computer, the one Mamdouh Salim had given him. The screen saver's shifting pattern provided the only source of light. He knew it was tethered to the Internet. *Is that where the voice had come from?*

Aymen was desperate to know who had spoken to him. And why *now*, when he was so unlovable? He crawled to the table and tapped the enter key. The screen came to life.

"*Noooooooooo!*" he screamed. The image that emerged had been the last he'd selected, the last thing he'd viewed before his talk with President Salim. The *Sacred Sea* filled the screen, floating malevolently in its slip near the Lincoln Memorial.

He had to stop the madness. But how? The only Americans he knew were as deceived as he had been. Then Adams' face popped involuntarily into his mind. He shook his head, trying to discard the image of his enemy, but it wouldn't go away. The more he tried, the more it beckoned to him. "Aymen. Aymen Halaweh." *The voice again! How does he know my name? Why is he calling me?*

Kneeling on the debris-littered floor, with tears lingering on his cheeks, the young Palestinian engineer typed, "ThorAdams.com." Nervously he tapped the enter key. Just then something started to orbit Microsoft's "e."

Was it Allah's moon, the American's evil influence, or just a harmless symbol? As Aymen pondered the imponderable, his panic seemed to ease; his pulse slowed from suicidal to simply frantic.

ThorAdams.com linked to a homepage Troy Nottingly had created to support Thor's candidacy. Halaweh now had choices. He could read Thor Adams' bio, register to vote, read the text of his speech to the Joint Session of Congress, review the Plan to Save America, or examine how the Admiral intended to scuttle terror. None of that seemed appropriate at the moment. Up off his knees, Aymen looked around for the chair he had tossed aside in his frantic search for a suicide weapon.

Sitting down, he saw something that piqued his interest, a link to "Delusional Doctrines—What's Wrong with Islam." His index finger trembled as he centered the cursor and clicked. A new page emerged.

The headline read: "God loves you and so do we." He shook his head, trying to clear his mind. *Those words again. Why?* Beneath the headline he saw, "However, He is not pleased with your behavior. Despite what you've been told, God isn't about hate, revenge, or lust. He doesn't condone holy war, the murder of innocents, or stealing what belongs to others."

Two links followed: "The History of Allah," and "The Life and Times of Muhammad." What he saw was no less shocking than Salim admitting he'd destroyed the Dome.

With each line Aymen's breathing became more labored. His eyes widened. His heart melted within him. He shook his head, trying to comprehend it all. He looked over his shoulder, making sure that the drapes were drawn. These were powerful words, make-people-angry words, change-the-world words. It was a catharsis, an exorcism, an apocalypse.

✡   ✝   ☾

"MR. NEWCOMB, you have a call on line six," the chief of staff for the recently elected Knesset Member said. It was nearly midnight in Jerusalem. Most everyone had gone home but not Isaac. Adams' parting words, "It was good to see you all out of uniform" haunted him. The uniforms, *their* uniforms, where had they gone, could they…?

Peeking around his office door, she added, "Normally, I wouldn't interrupt you with someone like this. I know you're trying to get to the bottom of the Dome disaster, but the voice sounds frantic. He won't give his name, but he says he knows you. Something about SFGs and Afghanistan."

Isaac pressed the speaker button. "This is Newcomb. Who is this?"

"My name is unimportant. What I know, however, is. I am a Palestinian. You would call me a terrorist. Until a few hours ago, you'd have been right. I was in Afghanistan when you were there. The SFGs that were worn by the Temple Faithful came from your men."

"How? Why? Who are you?"

"I brought them back with me. Why? To embarrass you. Who I am doesn't matter."

"Why did you call?"

Aymen blurted it out. "President Mamdouh Salim detonated the three bombs that brought the Dome of the Rock down."

"What! How do you know this?"

"I built the triggers."

"Oh, my God!" Isaac exclaimed. "How can I thank you for this?"

"Give me Thor Adams' number. You must have it."

"Why?" Above all, Isaac was protective of his friend. Handing out contact information to a terrorist, no matter how helpful he was, didn't seem like a terribly bright idea. "What possible use...."

Aymen cut him off. "There's an atomic bomb sitting in a sailboat just outside Washington. I built the trigger for it as well. It's set to go off in thirty minutes. *That* is why, Mr. Newcomb."

"Stay on the line, whatever your name is. I'll patch him through," Isaac answered with a calm only a Mossad Major could possess. "Ori!" he screamed at the top of his lungs. "How do I make the conference thing work?" Newcomb was afraid he'd disconnect the former terrorist as he tried to dial the almost President.

Ori expertly handled the controls, pressing the right buttons, although she too was trembling. With the door open, she couldn't help but overhear the extraordinary conversation. "Now dial your number."

Isaac did.

"Hello," an angelic voice proclaimed.

"Leisel, this is Isaac Newcomb. I need the Admiral. Is he there?"

"Hi, Major," she said. "It was such a pleasure to...."

"Mrs. Nottingly," he interrupted. "It's an emergency. I need Thor!"

"I'm sorry, Major," she said. "He and Sarah left here about forty minutes ago. They said they were going to the Lincoln Memorial. Thor was looking for some inspira...."

"Does he have a cell phone?"

"Yes, I believe he does. Let me see if I can find the number."

"Does *Sarah* have a cell phone?"

"Why yes, she does. That number is area code 410-555-1317."

Both Isaac and Ori scribbled it down. Newcomb dialed, forgetting to tell Leisel goodbye. If the terrorist was telling the truth, it wouldn't matter. If he wasn't, he could always call her back.

"Hello."

"Sarah. Where are you? Is the Admiral with you?"

"Hi, Isaac. You seem kind of stressed. What's up?"

"Sarah, please, if Thor's with you, give him the phone."

She looked crosswise at her cell. "Thor, it's Isaac. He sounds weird."

Adams was reading Lincoln's Second Inaugural Address for what seemed like the hundredth time.

"Hey, Isaac. What's up?" he said cheerfully.

"I've got a Palestinian on the line. He talks real good English but won't give me his name. He said he built the triggers for the bombs that trashed the Dome. He said the uniforms, the SFGs, were ours, Team Uniform's."

"So it was a setup?"

"Yeah, but *listen!* He says that there's a nuke in Washington on a sailboat. He says it's going to blow in thirty minutes. I've got him on the other line. He wants to talk to you. I'm going to conference him through."

I knew it! Adams thought as he walked toward the eastern opening of America's national shrine. Seconds later, the technology worked. Thor heard Halaweh's voice for the first time.

"Admiral Adams, my name is Aymen Halaweh. Until a few hours ago I worked for Omen Quagmer and Kahn Haqqani of al-Qaeda. I also worked for President Salim. I was in Afghanistan. I personally nailed Kyle Stanley and Bentley McCaile to their crosses. I set up the SFG cameras at the crucifixion that broadcast your ordeal home. I brought the suits back with me. Three of them, the ones with the star of David, were used by the Jews who were duped into blowing up the Dome. I also helped outfit the anthrax trash trucks. There were twenty-four of them, not twenty, like they reported on the news. You probably knew that."

Thor broke out in a cold sweat. "Why are you telling me these things?"

"So you'll believe what I am going to tell you next. Do you remember the sailboat you pulled from the sandbar on Paradise Island?"

"Yes. How did you know about that?"

"It's equipped with a web cam. We all laughed as we watched you do it. The crew knew who you were; that's why they were so scared."

"The *Sacred Sea*—a forty-five foot sloop, right?"

"Yes. It's in Washington, D.C., right now. Are you anywhere near the Lincoln Memorial?"

"Yes. Why?" The Admiral's knees were beginning to buckle.

"There is a marina, on the Potomac, southwest of the Lincoln Memorial. The *Sacred Sea* is in a transient slip in that marina. It has a nuclear bomb on it. I built the electronic trigger. It is scheduled to blow," he looked down at the display on his PC, "in twenty-seven minutes."

"Sarah, give me your car keys," Thor screamed, holding out his hand.

"It's my car. I'm driving. Where are we going?"

"Sarah, please!" he implored as he chased her toward the car.

Fortunately, the blue Jag was close, parked illegally, eastbound on Constitution Avenue. Sarah had figured if she got a parking ticket, she could get it fixed. Without even opening the doors, they both jumped in, Sarah behind the wheel.

The half-dozen Secret Service agents assigned to protect them were left in the dust. They scattered to the winds, first trying to stop them, then running for their cars, waving their arms and screaming into their lapels.

"Where to?"

"U-turn. Do you know the fastest way to the Potomac Marina?"

"Yeah. My last boyfriend used to keep his boat there."

"Step on it. We've got twenty-five minutes. Do you have your cell?"

"You're using it," she answered, whipping the XK-8 roadster around in impressive fashion. Two Secret Service Fords blew past them, going the wrong direction.

The Admiral reached into his pocket, handing his phone to Sarah. "Dial Director Barnes." Thrown side to side, he shouted into the other phone, "Aymen, are you still with me?"

"Yes." It was hard to hear. "The connection isn't so hot. Lot of static."

"It's wind. We're headed to the marina. Are you going to tell me how to disarm this thing?"

"Yes, but you must hurry. We don't have much time. And I'm not exactly sure...."

"Not sure of what?" Adams interrupted.

"I've never tried to disarm one. I built the electronic part of the timer. That's all I know," Aymen confessed.

"Sarah, watch out. You're gonna get us killed!"

She was driving on the wrong side of the street. The light was red, and there were way too many cars on their side. Weaving the Jaguar between oncoming traffic invited honks and one-fingered salutes.

She ignored Thor's critique. "Here, I've got Barnes. You talk to him."

"Director Barnes?"

"Congratulations, Admiral. My staff and I look forward to work...."

"Good. Start now. Who do you have who knows about nukes? We've got one on a sailboat moored behind the Lincoln Memorial. It's set to blow in...twenty-three minutes."

"I've got a team here at Langley, but even by chopper, it'll take 'em twenty to get there."

Send 'em. The boat's name is *Sacred Seas*. It's white with a dark blue and gold stripe. Forty-five feet. Sarah and I will be on it."

He hung up. "Still with me, Halaweh?"

"Yes."

"What did you mean, you only built the *electronic* timer? How many timers are there on this thing?"

"Two. Mine, the electronic one, only activates the failsafe."

"Failsafe? As in, if someone tampers with the timer, it blows?"

"Yes."

"Great. Hang on, pal," Thor said over the roar of road noise and horns. He pressed the first speed-dial button on his phone.

"Hello. This is the Pentagon. How may I direc...."

"Chairman Hasler. It's an emergency."

"Chairman Hasler's office. How may...."

"Judy, get Bill. It's an emergency."

"Yes, Admiral. He's right here."

"Hi, Admiral. Congratula...."

"Later. Can you get an anti-terrorism team with nuke training to the marina behind the Lincoln Memorial in less than twenty?"

"Without gear, maybe. Why?"

"We've got a nuke that's going to blow in twenty-one minutes. The boat is the *Sacred Seas*. Sarah and I will be on it, heading down the Potomac. Give 'em my cell number, Bill."

"You can't do this, Admiral! The country needs you. Get the out of there!" he said wisely into a disconnected phone.

Sarah, driving like Jeff Gordon on Sunday, made impressive time, especially considering the traffic. She drafted when appropriate, passed when not, and drove as much on sidewalks as she did on the wrong side of the road.

Holding on for dear life, they blew past a police car at seventy miles per hour. Thor looked over at Sarah. "And you call yourself a conservative?"

They were now less than a minute away. "Why are you helping me, Aymen?" the Admiral asked. A sinking feeling suddenly crept over him.

"I tried to commit suicide today." That wasn't saying much, considering he was a Muslim terrorist. "I was wrong." *That* was saying a lot.

"Wrong about what?"

"Everything. Al-Qaeda, the Palestinians, Islam, my life."

The Admiral stared at the phone like it was playing tricks on him. He didn't know what to say, so he prayed. *God, don't let me foul this up.*

Sarah saw that the marina's driveway was blocked by a security gate.

No longer having a keycard, she closed her eyes and turned the wheel hard right, gunning it. The Jaguar obeyed her command, leaping through the bushes that separated the parking lot from the street. Screeching around the sea of parked cars, it growled to a stop in front of the gangway. She threw the wooden gearshift into park as Thor jumped out.

"There it is!" he shouted, pointing to his right.

At a full gallop, the Adams family ran toward the gangway. An elderly couple was leaving, removing their keycard from the iron gate at just the right moment. Thor glanced at his watch as they blew past the startled seniors. They would have eighteen minutes by the time they reached the boat.

"Where's the bomb, the timer, Aymen?"

"Under the v-berth in the bow. But be careful. The crew's crazy."

Bouncing under the Admiral's weight, the pier made enough noise to wake the neighborhood. More to the point, it woke Atta and Riza from their sunset siesta. They had no idea the nuke was about to blow. Atta hesitantly peeked his head out the gangway door first. Then below him, Riza ventured a look. It didn't take them long to ascertain what was causing the commotion. To their great dismay, the man they feared most in the world was barreling down upon them.

Certain they were outgunned by the unarmed Admiral, the menacing Muslim marauders did what came naturally. They bailed, jumping overboard. Had time not been so limited, Adams would have preferred to deal with them up close and personal. Some other time, perhaps.

With the agility of an athlete, the six-foot-two man of steel made his way from dock to deck to cabin in three strides. Two more cautious steps put him in the forward berth.

"I'm in. Where's the timer?"

"I know. I saw you. There's a web cam onboard and it's online."

"The *trigger*, Aymen!"

"Top left drawer.

"Sarah."

"Yes."

"Get this thing out of here. You're going to have to sail it. They took the key with 'em. All right, Aymen, I've got the drawer open. There are two timers. Now what?"

"Are the LEDs illuminated?"

"Yes."

"Oh, *no!*"

"Oh no? What do you mean oh no?"

"The electronic timer wasn't supposed to activate the failsafe until T minus fifteen. It's at least three minutes fast."

"What are you telling me? How do we turn this thing off?"

"I don't know. Let me think," Halaweh anguished halfway around the world. "I built the electronic timers. The Russians built the failsafe and the tritium triggers."

Adams felt the boat rock. They were out of the slip.

"Can you turn the timer over?" Aymen asked.

"Yeah." Adams removed the wooden drawer, dropping it to the floor. He now held both timers in his hands. Turning each over he studied the wiring schema on their bottoms. "Hang on, Halaweh." He hit speed dial on his cell. "Hasler," he said.

"They're en route," the General answered.

"Good. Call the Russians. Find out who built the series four niner seven niner triggers. We've got a problem. We only have ten minutes fifteen seconds. Call me when you know somethin'."

"Okay, Aymen, I'm back. What do we do now?"

"The green and the blue wires are from my timer. Do you see them?"

"Right. There's plenty of light in here. What's with the huge hatch?"

The reformed terrorist thought it best to ignore the question. "The yellow and red connect the failsafe trigger to the bombs. The white and black wires are from the battery. Do you see them all?"

"Bombs? As in more than one?" the Admiral moaned, looking at the diabolical spaghetti.

"Three. They're wired in sequence. The device you're looking at isn't actually the nuclear trigger; it's a pre-triggering device. It's Russian but has Chinese, Iranian, and Pakistani parts."

"Swell, a regular terrorist potpourri," Adams grumbled. His cell phone rang, nearly scaring him to death.

"Adams."

"Thor, bad news. The Russians say the designers of that series are missing. They think several bailed to Iran. Big bucks."

Thor rubbed his forehead. He normally loved sailing, but this wasn't much fun. He braced himself as the sloop keeled over onto its side. Singlehandedly, Sarah had managed to push back and raise both jib and main. She had trimmed the sails and was headed out of town. But at eight knots, she wouldn't get far enough in eight and a half minutes to negate the damage of three nukes. Nonetheless, he was proud of her.

"Halaweh?"

"Yes, Admiral."

"You never told me why you're doing this."

"I was trying to kill myself when I heard this voice."

"Voice? What did it say?" the Admiral asked.

Normally Halaweh, being a terrorist and all, would have been embarrassed, but not today. "It said, 'I love you,'" he shared. "When I looked for who said it, I found your website."

"Then why don't we pray together, Aymen."

"Why not. I've tried everything else."

"God, it was you who spoke to Aymen. Please speak to him again and save us from this thing. In Jesus' name, amen."

In all of his life Aymen had never dreamed that a man he had once wanted to crucify would say such words. *Who is this man? Who is his God?*

"Okay, my friend. Time to save the world. I've found the ship's toolbox. We need to get down to business. Can I disconnect the battery from the trigger, or one trigger from the other?"

"No. There's a back-up battery built into the system. And if the failsafe system detects a broken circuit, it will arm itself automatically."

"What if I cut the wires from the pre-trigger to the bombs themselves?"

"No! That will just set 'em off."

"Can you reverse whatever you did with your electronic switch and shut this thing down?"

"Maybe."

"Any helicopters yet, Sarah?" Thor shouted, setting down the phone.

"No."

"Where are we?"

"Arlington."

Adams looked at the timer. They were down to their last three minutes.

"Admiral. *Admiral!*" Aymen raised his voice so it could be heard on the phone's speaker. "I've got an idea. I'm going to confuse the switch while you short the system. If we do it at the same time, it might work."

"Alright, let's try."

"Give me a minute. I want to send my timer a series of unanswerable commands. You may want to pray while I'm doing this. And when you're done, grab something from the toolbox you can use to short a couple of the terminals."

Aymen, still online, pounded the keys, programming the complex code. He was hoping to send his trigger a message, confusing it long enough to allow Adams to melt the electronic circuitry, keeping it from initializing its tamper-proof system. In the split second between being deactivated and the failsafe function engaging, Adams would have to disable the trigger by producing a timely short. It was possible, though not particularly probable.

"Can you find a short piece of wire in that toolbox?"

"Yeah."

"Cut the insulation away from both ends. You're going to need a piece ten centimeters long."

"Okay," the Admiral said, pulling out his Elmer-Fudd-meets-James-Bond miracle tool. He cut an appropriate section and then cut the plastic insulation from either end. "Done."

"Turn the electronic timer over and unscrew the base plate."

Thor found his Phillips attachment and did as he was told.

"Do you see the fuse?"

"Yes."

"Don't touch it. I want you to connect one end of your wire to each side of the fuse holder. For the short to work, the fuse has to be disabled."

"How'd you get to be so smart, Halaweh?"

"MIT. I'm an engineer."

"Great. Now it's time you pay us back."

"Is the fuse disabled?"

"Yeah."

"Do you have two conductors handy, Admiral—something to bridge the gap between the white and black wires and between the yellow and red ones?"

"Yes, two screwdrivers."

"Good. Now how about something to cut one of the wires with?"

"Sure," he said, grabbing his universal tool. "But I've only got two hands."

"Your wife," Aymen said, looking at her on the web cam.

"Sarah. Release the sails and get down here. *Hurry!* We've got," he turned the timer over, "forty seconds."

"Get ready." Halaweh executed his code, sending the message surging through the Internet. "When the green LED flickers, short the black terminal to the white one. When the red flickers a second later, short the other pair—the yellow and red ones."

The Admiral concentrated, trying to remain steady in the cabin of the moving boat. It was literally do or die.

"Here come the helicopters," Sarah shouted, as she made her way to Thor's side.

Thor heard them, but he knew the cavalry was arriving too late to save the day. He handed her his tool, having opened it to the needle nose apparatus. It came complete with wire cutters.

"What do you want me to do?" she asked.

"Halaweh, Sarah's got the wire cutters. What do you want her to do?"

Just then the green light flickered. Thor shorted the circuit between the black and white terminals as the former terrorist had instructed. A second later, the red LED blinked, but as it did, the rotor wash from the hovering helicopter pounded the boat's sails, knocking Thor and Sarah from the switch. Not knowing what else to do, the Admiral lunged forward, screwdriver in hand. Remembering where the contacts had been in his mind's eye, he pressed the tool against the trigger and prayed. It sparked. That was a good sign. The LEDs were extinguished.

"What now?" he shouted into the cell phone.

"Cut the black wire before the trigger figures out what happened. If you don't disable the power, the bombs are going to blow."

"The black wire. Are you sure?"

"No! Cut the white wire. That's safer."

"Halaweh, which one?"

"The white one. I've got a good feeling about this."

Placing the pliers around the white wire, Sarah closed her eyes and sliced it through.

Then it happened. *Boom!* The overhead hatch exploded, firing the four-foot-square skylight heavenward. Enveloped in the blinding light, Thor instinctively grabbed Sarah and did his best to protect her from impending doom. They closed their eyes and gritted their teeth, expecting to die in each other's arms. But nothing happened. Thor summoned enough courage to venture a look. Sarah was in one piece, as was he. *Could death be this painless, this slow?* No. It was over.

Adams sat up and pulled the white wires further apart for added insurance. They were going to live, as was Washington. Thor was relaxed for the first time in twenty-seven minutes. "Aymen, is it disarmed?"

Sarah wiggled out of his arms and climbed back topside. She wanted to get the boat back under control.

"Admiral, I'm showing disarmed on my display. Has the timer stopped?"

"Yeah, at three seconds. Cutting it a little close, don't you think?" Adams collapsed, sprawled between the bunks, staring skyward through the open hatch. The timers rested benignly on his chest.

Halaweh smiled. He felt good for the first time in his life. "Admiral Adams...."

Thor propped himself back up. "Aymen, what was that explosion all about? It nearly scared us to death."

"At T-minus-three, the skylight blows. At T-minus-two, the rockets fire, launching the device. It's in the v-berth you're laying on. You would have been the next John Glenn."

The Admiral jumped up and headed topside. "Hang on, Aymen. I need to check on Sarah." He climbed into the cockpit.

"Nice day for a sail, don't you think?" she said. The sun was now a bright orange disc hovering just above the western shore of the mighty river. A crescent moon loomed over the Capitol. It wouldn't be the last of these they would see, but sunsets and moonrises would never look quite the same again.

Sarah was on the phone with Director Barnes, waving the CIA helicopter off. Not only was it making an ungodly racket, the swirling wind was playing havoc with her sails. Uniformed agents dangled from rappel lines as the noisy bird made its retreat. In the distance, she could see the Secret Service officers. Two were swimming toward the yacht, another four were running along the Potomac's eastern shore.

"C'mere, you big brute, and bring your friend with you," Sarah cooed, holding the wheel steady in her hands. She had the *Sacred Seas* on a port tack, her sails full.

Thor gave his bride a hug, resting his exhausted head against hers. He handed Sarah the phone.

"Mr. Halaweh. God bless you," she said. "You saved our lives. If I book a flight, will you join us tomorrow morning at the Inauguration?"

"Tomorrow may not be good for me."

"Why not? What you did here today was heroic."

"Thank you, ma'am, but I'm afraid you may want to hold your applause. There are eleven more of these things."

She turned to Thor. "Sweetheart, I think you boys need to talk."

Also by Winn & Power

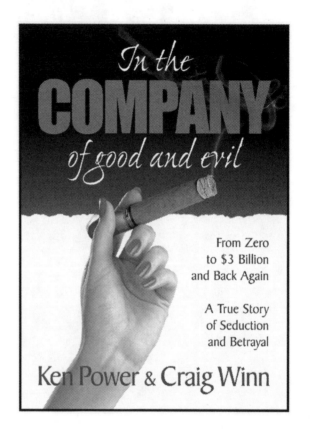

What's Killing Corporate America?

It was an idea whose time had come. In three short years, it grew from nothing into one of the largest businesses of its kind in the world, worth over three billion dollars. But sixteen months later it was bankrupt, a worthless shell of its former self. Through The Company's meteoric rise and fall, each of the calamities currently killing corporate America are revealed in chilling clarity.

In the Company of Good and Evil is the amazing true story of the Internet's second largest e-tailer. Who built it? How did it grow so quickly, and what made it fall even faster? What really caused the economic bubble that led to the rise of tech companies, and more importantly, what poisoned them all? The answers go beyond the story of a single firm. They shed light on both the entrepreneurial spirit that builds reality out of dreams, and the self-serving ambition that threatens to destroy the very fabric of our society.

The authors are insiders. They founded The Company, nurtured it, helped it grow, gave it wings—and then watched it die a very painful, very public death. Power and Winn chronicle the brash self-confidence and remarkable coincidences that shaped their firm. They also examine the methods, motivations, and moral decay of those who brought The Company and so many others to their knees.

Flashes of inspiration capping months of grueling work, games of "chicken" won and lost, blackmail schemes, white knights, dire corporate poverty, and billion-dollar IPOs are all part of the drama. Prepare to meet some of the most powerful people in America, in technology and politics, in business and labor, in finance and faith. They all left their fingerprints on The Company.

In the Company of Good and Evil follows the fortunes of The Company's founders: Craig, the visionary entrepreneur; Rex Scatena, the attorney/mentor; Bill Hunt, the merchandiser; Ken, the designer/writer; and Joe Page, the technologist. These five formed the core of a team that changed the world, if only for one brief moment.

The events in this story actually happened. If it reads like a novel, perhaps it is because truth is sometimes more exciting than fiction.

Excerpt from Chapter 1: IPO FEVER

Just because this was the big day, it didn't mean there wasn't work to be done. Linda Harmon picked up her note pad and walked to Rex Scatena's office, hesitating at the open door. The vice chairman finished his phone conversation and waved her in.

"Hi, Linda," he said, smiling. As he rummaged through the papers on his desk, he grabbed his mouse and clicked the refresh button, as he'd done a dozen times this morning. Rex glanced at his screen. Linda's eyes followed.

This time, his Yahoo! Personal Finance page came alive. This was it— the very first public trade of Value America's stock. Linda had no idea what to expect as she squinted against the morning glare. Then, there it was. "Four and a half million." she said, genuinely pleased for her favorite boss. She smiled at Rex and then looked back at the monitor. "No, wait a minute. That's not right." Linda peered at the screen. "It's forty-five million!" she screamed. "Rex, you're worth forty-five million dollars!"

Rex, just north of fifty, was having a little trouble focusing on the screen without his glasses, which he'd misplaced again. But that *still* didn't look like it said $45 million. He squinted, and then remembered that they were pushed back into his hair. Linda leaned in for a closer look. There were an awful lot of zeros there. As they started counting them, the truth hit them both at the same instant.

Rex Scatena's shares were worth four hundred and fifty million dollars.

He sat back in his chair, his eyes glazed over, partially from fatigue and partially from the seductive mathematics of the morning. Rex was no stranger to money; in his former life he had been a prosperous environmental lawyer. But now, it appeared, he had attained wealth beyond the dreams of avarice. Rex was finding it surprisingly hard to comprehend.

From Chapter 7: LIFE IN THE ATTIC

Looking back, two things immediately come to mind. One, those were great times, exciting, heady, inventive, live-life-to-the-fullest times. Two, let's not do that again.

There's something to be said for living your life with your back against the wall, as long as you believe what you're doing is right. That's how we lived during those first months. The adrenaline flowed. The tension was palpable. It seemed like every person we met was either a skunk or a saint. Everything was black or white, do or die, feast or famine, now or never. It was the best of times. It was terrifying.

Craig and Rex concealed a lot of the nasty stuff—no sense in all of us having ulcers. They shielded us from the blood-curdling details, figuring that if the problem brought the company down, we would find out about it soon enough, and if it didn't, we didn't need the distraction. Imminent corporate death was placed on a need-to-know basis.

On the other hand, if they were dancing on the ceiling, it was pretty hard to hide, and the reasons were explained with grins and congratulations. The atmosphere in the Attic was "casual hysteria." The dress code was loose—no, non-existent; anything that covered the crucial body parts was acceptable. Crowded into two big rooms, dialog flowed freely. It was impossible not to be creative in an atmosphere like that.

The building itself lent us its personality. When it rained, water poured in through cracks around the double-hung windows, causing havoc and threatening to short out the power. At the first sign of showers, those of us along the outside walls would cover our computers with plastic trash bags—and go back to work. The furniture added to the ambience. It was worth every penny we had paid for it—nothing. We jammed our desks so close together, one held the other up. It was like living in an anthill.

We were in constant danger of outrunning our resources. It was as if we were in a big wooden roller coaster, and our train was struggling to reach the top of the first hill. We knew we were dangerously overloaded, but we felt sure that if we could just reach that first peak, we'd be in for quite a ride.

From Chapter 10: A CAPITAL VENTURE

When you're strapped for cash, as we were, the only thing that counts is how much of it you actually have. Thus, you'd use cost-based accounting, which told you, "This amount came in, and that amount went out, leaving you this much." It's accounting based upon one's present reality—not unlike a checkbook.

Accrual-based accounting is more Dickensian in nature. Its reality takes into account the Ghosts of Christmas Past, Present, and Yet-to-Come, which is a poetic way of stating that it allocates costs and profits over the entire period in which auditors claim they should be recognized. This method is required of companies engaged in raising or borrowing money. So every publicly traded firm, and those planning to go public, find themselves using this somewhat less straightforward form of arithmetic.

From Chapter 11: ANGELS AND DEVILS

The dazed partners found a park bench facing one of the many museums that comprised the Smithsonian Institution. They sat down, emotionally exhausted from the morning's excursion into the twilight zone.

"Don't you just hate it when I'm right all the time?" Rex asked. "This is scary. These guys clearly don't have any conception of what they'd be buying. I mean, we may have the recipe for the best cake in the world, but at the moment, we're just ingredients in the bowl. There are still a thousand ways to screw this up."

"You've got that right, pardner," Craig said thoughtfully. "You know what picture keeps popping into my head? Don't laugh. I keep seeing the smiling face of Jimmy Hoffa." Rex looked quizzically at Craig.

"Say the unions buy us outright for three hundred large. I don't care how much money they have, that's a considerable chunk of change. So now it's their company, and they'll try to manage it professionally, right?"

"Right so far," Rex said.

"So what would you do if you were in their shoes? You'd hire the best managers money could buy, wouldn't you?"

"Umm, yeah."

"Okay. Now picture yourself as one of these managers. You're in control. You're going to manage things your way, 'cause that's all you know. It's worked before, or at least it's what you were taught in some MBA class. Only this time it doesn't work, because what we do isn't like anything that's been done before. You aren't going to have a clue about what brands want or what retail's all about. All you'll be able to do is look at the numbers and move people around—confuse process with progress."

Rex cleared his throat. His mouth suddenly felt dry.

"And then what do you think happens?" Craig went on. "Their managers will fail. They'll look for an alibi. That'll be us, the loose cannons, the entrepreneurs. So they'll get rid of us, which ought to be okay, because we'd be rich. But they'll fail even faster with us gone. So what do you think they'll do then—accept responsibility? Not a chance in hell. They'll tell our union friends that we stiffed them, sold them smoke and mirrors, a house of cards. Our friends won't be pleased, not happy at all."

"No, not happy at all," Rex repeated glumly.

"Yeah, but they won't be angry at *their* managers. These types don't accept responsibility. Oh no. They'll blame us. *Us,* my friend. So what do these guys do when they're really unhappy?"

"I suppose three hundred million takes the situation a little beyond broken windows and slashed tires."

"Cement shoes?" he joked.

"Oh, man, I hope not."

From Chapter 12: FUZZY MATH

"Your ideas," Mark said dourly, "are counter to Wall Street's view."

"Yes, I know," Craig said. "Hopefully, they'll discover the truth before somebody gets hurt."

Andrea couldn't take it anymore. She slammed her palm down on the table. "Mark! Would you please just...*shush up!* This is the only model in this space that makes any sense. This guy understands what e-commerce ought to be. Every one of his core concepts is right on the money, including the one you haven't trashed yet, the one about being comprehensive. His idea about building the infrastructure to bring brands and consumers together is exactly how online retailing should work. I don't know what *your* problem is, but *he's* right."

Mark rocked back in his chair. He had a big grin on his face. "I know that. But the Street's got a lot invested in the Amazon model, and his plan is radical—a whole new paradigm. You know as well as I do, Andrea, when other analysts hear this stuff, they're gonna come down hard on Mr. Winn. He's going to gore every one of their sacred cows, and they aren't going to take it lying down. People have made too much money to let somebody waltz in and prick this dot-com balloon. I just wanted to make sure Craig here could handle the pressure, that's all."

Andrea tried her best to give Mark a dirty look.

"Sorry about hammering you like that," Mark said. "Normally my advice would be to keep low, not rock the boat—you know, don't point out the flaws in their reasoning. But I can't see that you have much choice. Everything you stand for flies in the face of what Wall Street believes."

Craig analyzed what Mark had said. "So if I run the company in accordance with their metrics, I'm dead because they're wrong. If I stand up and present the merits of our model, I'm dead because it's in their interest to say I'm wrong. Do I have this right?

"Yep, that's pretty much it in a nutshell."

"Sounds like a classic Greek tragedy. So where do we go from here?"

"We want to lead your IPO." Mark replied. "Damn the torpedoes."

From Chapter 17: ROWING UP A WATERFALL

Rex broke the spell. "It's over, isn't it?" He wasn't asking. Slowly, he placed both palms on the old table, pushed back his chair, and stood.

"Looks that way, pal," Craig agreed as he rose to his feet. "We gave it our best shot. I'm sorry I dragged you into this. I...I really thought we were going to make a go of it."

Rex had been staring vaguely at the floor, but he suddenly lifted his head and looked Craig in the eyes. "I have only one thing to say." He didn't say anything for a moment. Then, looking back down, he murmured, "Thank you." Forcing himself to establish eye contact, Rex displayed the depth of character that had endeared him to Craig so long ago. "It may be over, but I don't regret a minute of it. This has been the greatest time of my life. I'm proud to have been a part of it." He gave Craig a manly hug. "You know what? Given the chance, I'd do it all again."

Rex started to leave but turned around before reaching the door. "You remember watching cartoons when you were a kid?"

"Sure," Craig smiled.

"Ol' Wile E. Coyote got hammered every time he tried to catch the Roadrunner, didn't he? Well, think about this. No matter how deep he cratered into the canyon floor, he was always back the next Saturday morning."

From Chapter 29: THE WICKED WITCH

You don't just wake up one morning and say, "I think I'll bankrupt my company today." It takes preparation, expensive lawyers, and time. Dorchak must have started planning her get-even-richer-quicker scheme within days of the $30 million heist from the board. She had to. She had a colossal problem. Her Q2 revenues were seventy percent below Wall Street's expectations and about a third of the prior quarter's. If that were announced, she would instantly become the laughingstock of the business world, the poster girl for failure. She'd do anything to avoid that.

The last possible date for making her failed Q2 performance public was fast approaching. As soon as she released her quarterly results, the entire business world would know she was a fraud. She had burned both Winn and her fellow board members to cover her butt *last* quarter. She was fresh out of diversions.

This time the answer to her little credibility problem lay in the arcane language of bankruptcy law. A bankrupt company doesn't have to publish a quarterly report card. And make no mistake, Glenda Dorchak was willing to do *anything,* no matter the cost, to keep from revealing that her tenure as CEO had been a con, an elaborate snatch-and-run.

By filing bankruptcy this soon, she could still claim she had done her best, but that the disaster Winn had left behind was beyond redemption. That was good, but it got better. The $30 mil she'd received could be legally diverted from the shareholders and creditors to—you guessed it— the "capable hands of the experienced and professional" management team.

It looked like Christmas in August. But *surely* she wouldn't bankrupt a company that had tens of millions in cash for her own personal gain! *Surely* she wouldn't do it within months of her glowing "we're growing; we're flourishing; we've just had the best day in Value America's history" diatribe. *Sure* she would, and did. Dorchak was as easy to predict as a bad girl on prom night. She and Value America were going down.

From Chapter 30: THE SUN ALSO RISES

"By telling our story, we'd reveal what really happened, why dot-coms rose, why they fell, and how and why e-tail will rise again. But dot-com was just an accelerant, a catalyst that helped make our characters seem larger than life. And it caused everything to happen so much faster. The real story is that *corporate* America is dying from the same thing that ultimately killed Value America."

Craig quietly agonized for a long moment and then said, "You don't believe in fate, do you, Ken?"

"No. I believe in providence."

"Remember what I always called you?"

"Yeah. It was embarrassing. You called me the company's patron saint."

"What else did I say?"

Like a schoolboy reciting his lesson, I repeated the words Craig had said so often. "You said that as long as I was with the company, God would never let anything bad happen to us."

"Remember the date you resigned? And the time?"

"No, not exactly. Sometime in November."

"I do. It was November 23rd, 1999, 3:45 PM. Fifteen minutes later, the board met to preside over the company's execution."

"I…I had no idea." My head was swimming.

"Still think we shouldn't tell this story?"

"No. You're right. The world needs to hear what happened. But think about it. The heat's off you for the first time in ages. You don't have to relive the pain—and it will be painful, you know. You could just let the whole thing drop, enjoy your life. Living well is the best revenge, right?"

Craig smiled, walked over to his desk, and picked up his Bible. "Think so?" It fell open to the book of Ecclesiastes, the wisdom of Solomon again. Craig didn't even flip the page. This is what he read:

"What does pleasure accomplish? I amassed silver and gold. Yet when I surveyed all that my hands had done and what I had toiled to achieve, everything was meaningless, chasing after the wind…. There is a time for everything, and a season for every activity under heaven. A time to tear down and a time to build, a time to weep and a time to laugh, a time to be silent and a time to speak…."